A DANCE WITH DRAGONS
I: DREAMS AND DUST

George R.R. Martin is the author of fourteen novels, including five volumes of *A Song of Ice and Fire*, several collections of short stories and numerous screen plays for television dramas and feature films. He lives in Santa Fe, New Mexico.

D0369246

By George R.R. Martin

A DANCE WITH DRAGONS

I: DREAMS AND DUST

BOOK FIVE OF
A Song of Ice and Fire

GEORGE R.R. MARTIN

HARPER
Voyager

HarperVoyager
An imprint of HarperCollins*Publishers* Ltd
77–85 Fulham Palace Road,
Hammersmith, London W6 8JB

www.harpercollins.co.uk

This paperback edition 2014
1

Previously published in paperback by Voyager in 2012

First published in Great Britain by Voyager in 2011

A catalogue record for this book is
available from the British Library

ISBN: 9780007548286

Set in Minion by Palimpsest Book Production Limited,
Falkirk, Stirlingshire

Printed and bound in Great Britain by
Clays Ltd, St Ives plc

MIX
Paper from
responsible sources
FSC **FSC™ C007454**
www.fsc.org

FSC™ is a non-profit international organisation established to promote
the responsible management of the world's forests. Products carrying the
FSC label are independently certified to assure consumers that they come
from forests that are managed to meet the social, economic and
ecological needs of present and future generations,
and other controlled sources.

Find out more about HarperCollins and the environment at
www.harpercollins.co.uk/green

this one is for my fans

for Lodey, Trebla, Stego, Pod,
Caress, Yags, X-Ray and Mr. X,
Kate, Chataya, Mormont, Mich,
Jamie, Vanessa, Ro,
for Stubby, Louise, Agravaine,
Wert, Malt, Jo,
Mouse, Telisiane, Blackfyre,
Bronn Stone, Coyote's Daughter,
and the rest of the madmen and wild women of
the Brotherhood Without Banners

for my website wizards
Elio and Linda, lords of Westeros,
Winter and Fabio of WIC,
and Gibbs of Dragonstone, who started it all

for men and women of Asshai in Spain
who sang to us of a bear and a maiden fair
and the fabulous fans of Italy
who gave me so much wine
for my readers in Finland, Germany,
Brazil, Portugal, France, and the Netherlands
and all the other distant lands
where you've been waiting for this dance

and for all the friends and fans
I have yet to meet

thanks for your patience

A CAVIL ON CHRONOLOGY

It has been a while between books, I know. So a reminder may be in order.

The book you hold in your hands is the fifth volume of *A Song of Ice and Fire*. The fourth volume was *A Feast for Crows*. However, this volume does not follow that one in the traditional sense, so much as run in tandem with it.

Both *Dance* and *Feast* take up the story immediately after the events of the third volume in the series, *A Storm of Swords*. Whereas *Feast* focused on events in and around King's Landing, on the Iron Islands, and down in Dorne, *Dance* takes us north to Castle Black and the Wall (and beyond), and across the narrow sea to Pentos and Slaver's Bay, to pick up the tales of Tyrion Lannister, Jon Snow, Daenerys Targaryen, and all the other characters you did not see in the preceding volume. Rather than being sequential, the two books are parallel . . . divided geographically, rather than chronologically.

But only up to a point.

A Dance with Dragons is a longer book than *A Feast for Crows*, and covers a longer time period. In the latter half of this volume, you will notice certain of the viewpoint characters from *A Feast for Crows* popping up again. And that means just what you think it means: the narrative has moved past the time frame of *Feast*, and the two streams have once again rejoined each other.

Next up, *The Winds of Winter*. Wherein, I hope, everybody will be shivering together once again . . .

—George R.R. Martin
April 2011

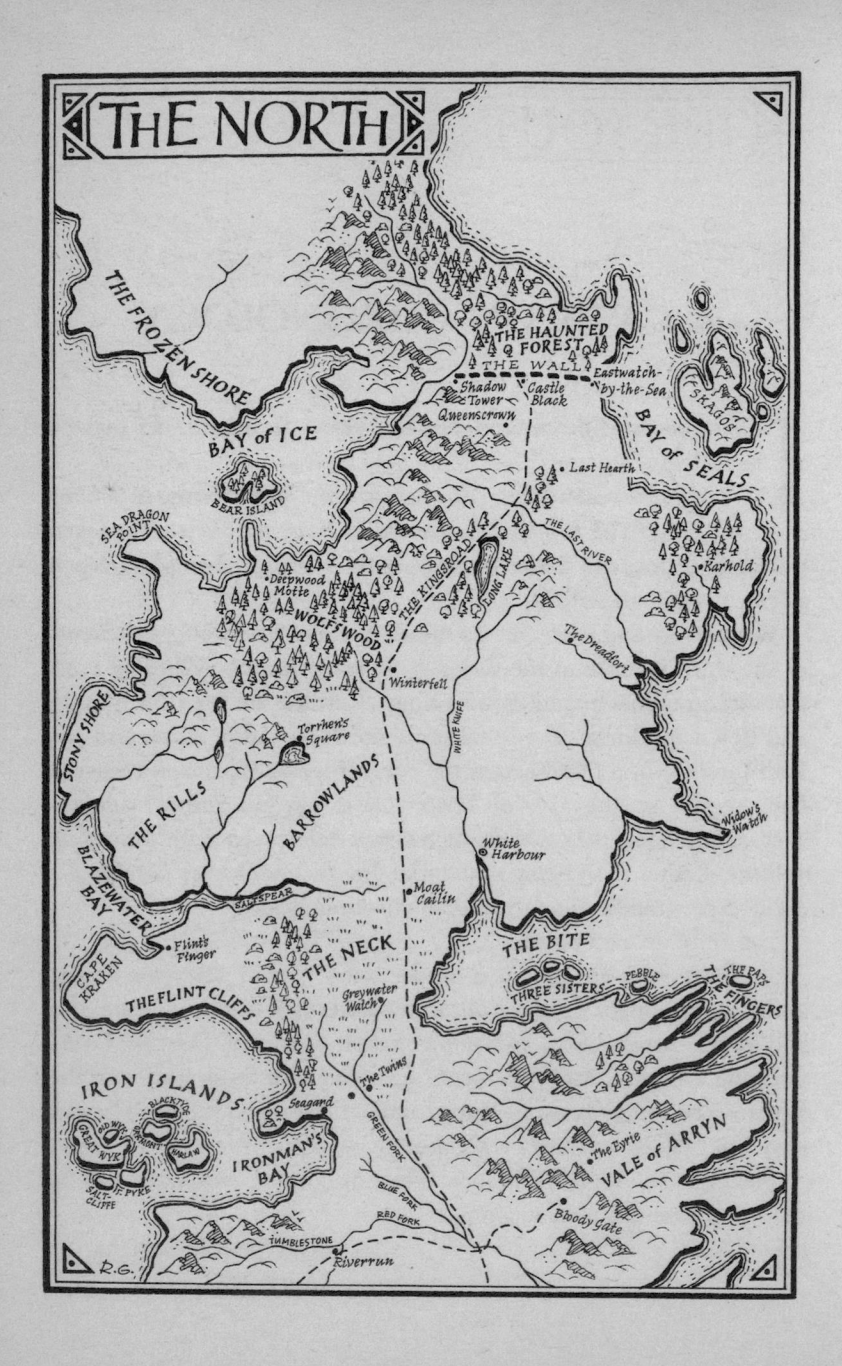

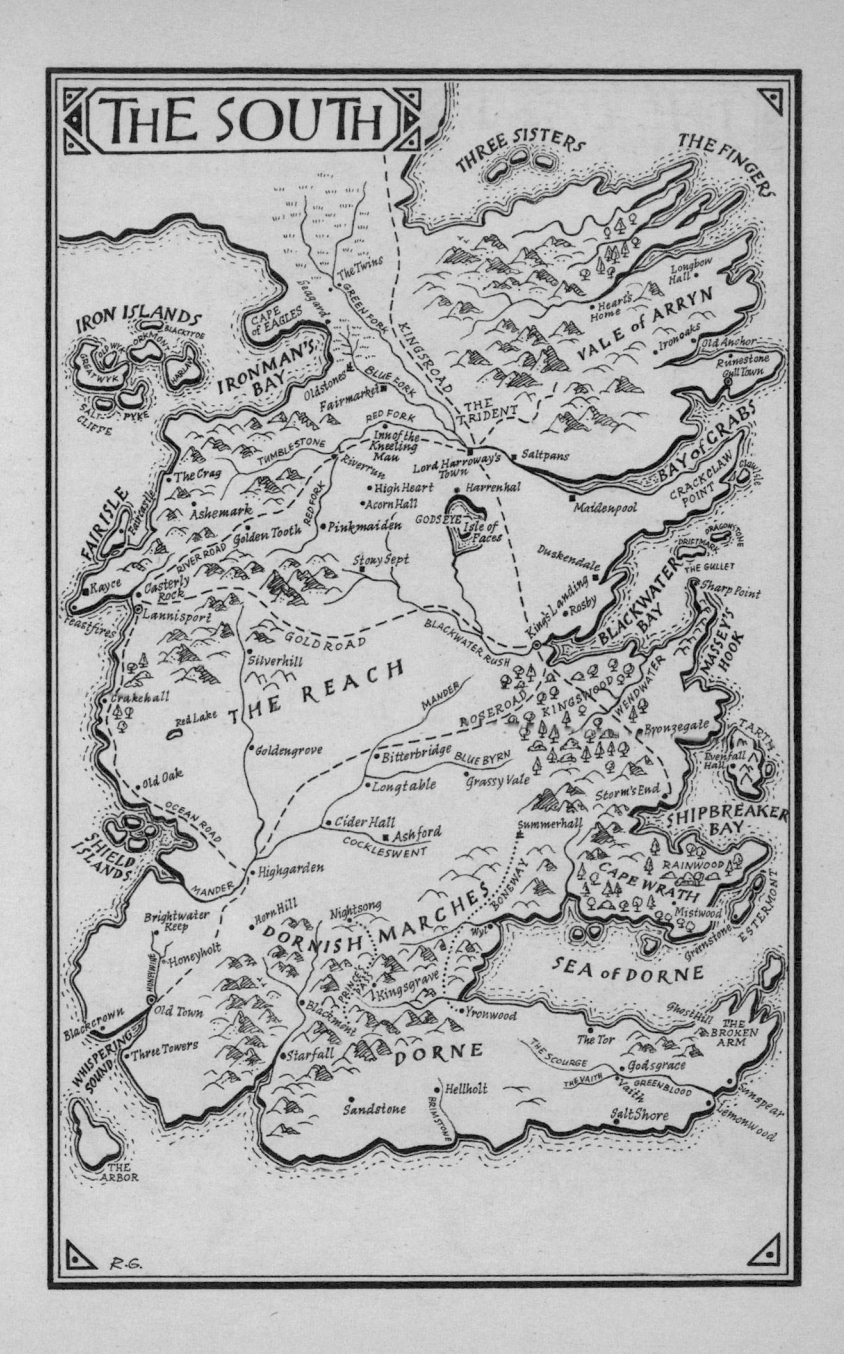

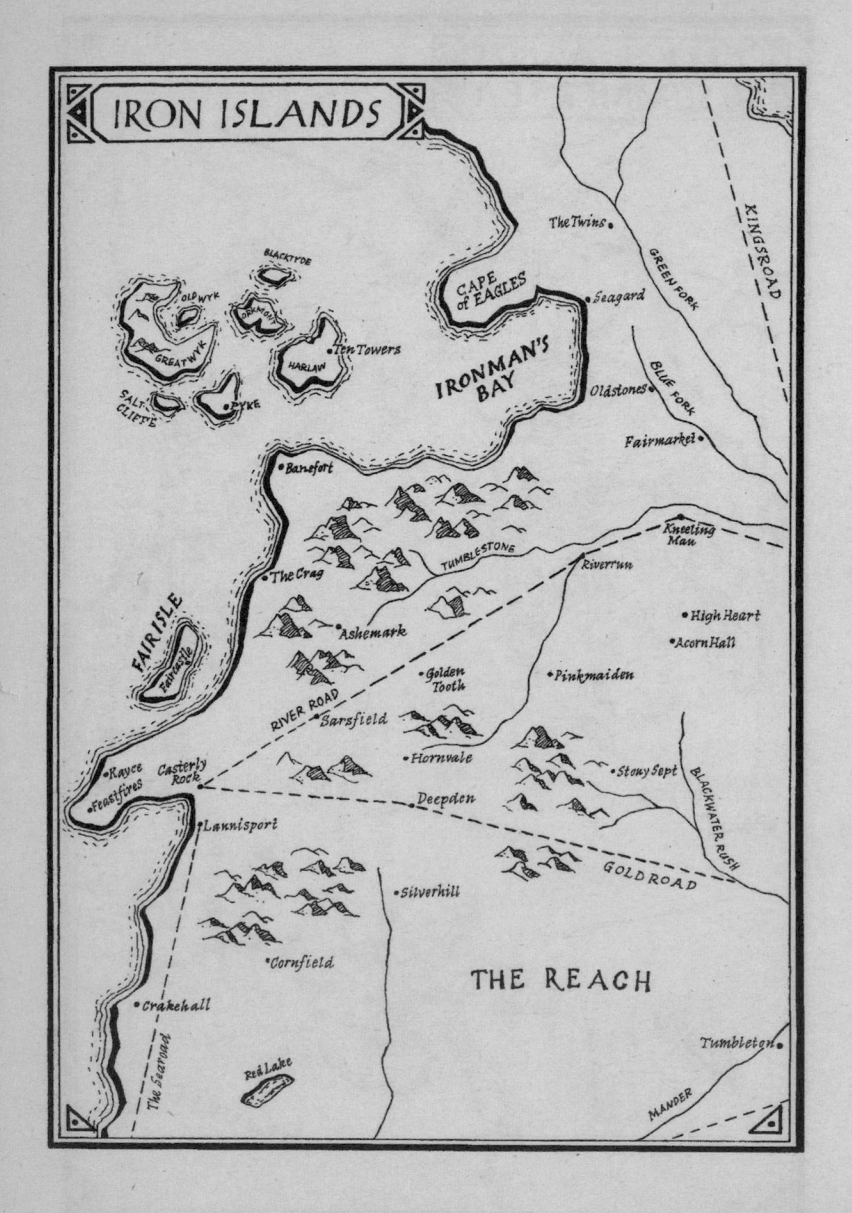

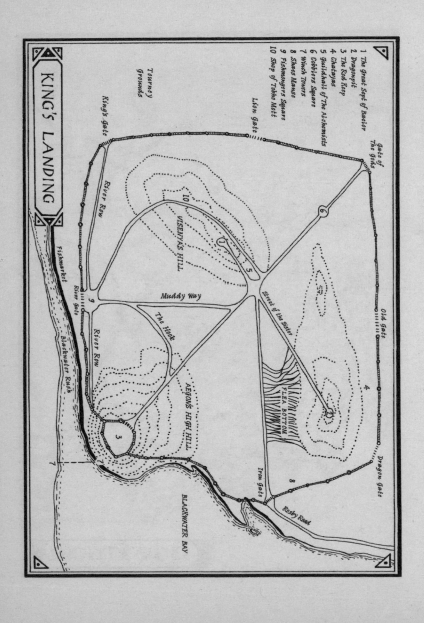

KING'S LANDING

1 The Great Sept of Baelor
2 Dragonpit
3 The Red Keep
4 Chataya's
5 Guildhall of The Alchemists
6 Cobbler's Square
7 Winch Towers
8 Shaes Manse
9 Fishmongers Square
10 Shop of Tobho Mott

Gate of The Gods
Old Gate
Dragon Gate
Lion Gate
King's Gate
Tourney grounds
River Row
VISENYA'S HILL
Muddy Way
Fishmarket
River Gate
The Hook
River Row
AEGON'S HIGH HILL
Blackwater Rush
Street of the Sisters
FLEA BOTTOM
Iron Gate
Rosby Road
BLACKWATER BAY

PROLOGUE

The night was rank with the smell of man.

The warg stopped beneath a tree and sniffed, his grey-brown fur dappled by shadow. A sigh of piney wind brought the man-scent to him, over fainter smells that spoke of fox and hare, seal and stag, even wolf. Those were man-smells too, the warg knew; the stink of old skins, dead and sour, near drowned beneath the stronger scents of smoke and blood and rot. Only man stripped the skins from other beasts and wore their hides and hair.

Wargs have no fear of man, as wolves do. Hate and hunger coiled in his belly, and he gave a low growl, calling to his one-eyed brother, to his small sly sister. As he raced through the trees, his packmates followed hard on his heels. They had caught the scent as well. As he ran, he saw through their eyes too and glimpsed himself ahead. The breath of the pack puffed warm and white from long grey jaws. Ice had frozen between their paws, hard as stone, but the hunt was on now, the prey ahead. *Flesh,* the warg thought, *meat.*

A man alone was a feeble thing. Big and strong, with good sharp eyes, but dull of ear and deaf to smells. Deer and elk and even hares were faster, bears and boars fiercer in a fight. But men in packs were dangerous. As the wolves closed on the prey, the warg heard the wailing of a pup, the crust of last night's snow breaking under clumsy man-paws, the rattle of hardskins and the long grey claws men carried.

Swords, a voice inside him whispered, *spears.*

The trees had grown icy teeth, snarling down from the bare brown branches. One Eye ripped through the undergrowth, spraying snow. His packmates followed. Up a hill and down the slope beyond, until the wood opened before them and the men were there. One was female. The fur-wrapped bundle she clutched was her pup. *Leave her for last,* the voice whispered, *the males are the danger.* They were roaring at each other as men did, but the warg could smell their terror. One had a wooden tooth as tall as he was. He flung it, but his hand was shaking and the tooth sailed high.

Then the pack was on them.

His one-eyed brother knocked the tooth-thrower back into a snowdrift and tore his throat out as he struggled. His sister slipped behind the other male and took him from the rear. That left the female and her pup for him.

She had a tooth too, a little one made of bone, but she dropped it when the warg's jaws closed around her leg. As she fell, she wrapped both arms around her noisy pup. Underneath her furs the female was just skin and bones, but her dugs were full of milk. The sweetest meat was on the pup. The wolf saved the choicest parts for his brother. All around the carcasses, the frozen snow turned pink and red as the pack filled its bellies.

Leagues away, in a one-room hut of mud and straw with a thatched roof and a smoke hole and a floor of hard-packed earth, Varamyr shivered and coughed and licked his lips. His eyes were red, his lips cracked, his throat dry and parched, but the taste of blood and fat filled his mouth, even as his swollen belly cried for nourishment. *A child's flesh,* he thought, remembering Bump. *Human meat.* Had he sunk so low as to hunger after human meat? He could almost hear Haggon growling at him. "Men may eat the flesh of beasts and beasts the flesh of men, but the man who eats the flesh of man is an abomination."

Abomination. That had always been Haggon's favorite word. *Abomination, abomination, abomination.* To eat of human meat was abomination, to mate as wolf with wolf was abomination, and to seize the body of another man was the worst abomination of all.

Haggon was weak, afraid of his own power. He died weeping and alone when I ripped his second life from him. Varamyr had devoured his heart himself. *He taught me much and more, and the last thing I learned from him was the taste of human flesh.*

That was as a wolf, though. He had never eaten the meat of men with human teeth. He would not grudge his pack their feast, however. The wolves were as famished as he was, gaunt and cold and hungry, and the prey . . . *two men and a woman, a babe in arms, fleeing from defeat to death. They would have perished soon in any case, from exposure or starvation. This way was better, quicker. A mercy.*

"A mercy," he said aloud. His throat was raw, but it felt good to hear a human voice, even his own. The air smelled of mold and damp, the ground was cold and hard, and his fire was giving off more smoke than heat. He moved as close to the flames as he dared, coughing and shivering by turns, his side throbbing where his wound had opened. Blood had soaked his breeches to the knee and dried into a hard brown crust.

Thistle had warned him that might happen. "I sewed it up the best I could," she'd said, "but you need to rest and let it mend, or the flesh will tear open again."

Thistle had been the last of his companions, a spearwife tough as an old root, warty, windburnt, and wrinkled. The others had deserted them along the way. One by one they fell behind or forged ahead, making for their old villages, or the Milkwater, or Hardhome, or a lonely death in the woods. Varamyr did not know, and could not care. *I should have taken one of them when I had the chance. One of the twins, or the big man with the scarred face, or the youth with the red hair.* He had been afraid, though. One of the others might have realized what was happening. Then they would have turned on him and killed him. And Haggon's words had haunted him, and so the chance had passed.

After the battle there had been thousands of them struggling through the forest, hungry, frightened, fleeing the carnage that had descended on them at the Wall. Some had talked of returning to the homes that they'd abandoned, others of mounting a second assault upon the gate, but most were lost, with no notion of where to go or what to do. They had escaped the black-cloaked crows and the knights in their grey steel, but more relentless enemies stalked them now. Every day left more corpses by the trails. Some died of hunger, some of cold, some of sickness. Others were slain by those who had been their brothers-in-arms when they marched south with Mance Rayder, the King-Beyond-the-Wall.

Mance is fallen, the survivors told each other in despairing voices, *Mance is taken, Mance is dead*. "Harma's dead and Mance is captured, the rest run off and left us," Thistle had claimed, as she was sewing up his wound. "Tormund, the Weeper, Sixskins, all them brave raiders. Where are they now?"

She does not know me, Varamyr realized then, *and why should she?* Without his beasts he did not look like a great man. *I was Varamyr Sixskins, who broke bread with Mance Rayder*. He had named himself Varamyr when he was ten. *A name fit for a lord, a name for songs, a mighty name, and fearsome*. Yet he had run from the crows like a frightened rabbit. The terrible Lord Varamyr had gone craven, but he could not bear that she should know that, so he told the spearwife that his name was Haggon. Afterward he wondered why *that* name had come to his lips, of all those he might have chosen. *I ate his heart and drank his blood, and still he haunts me*.

One day, as they fled, a rider came galloping through the woods on a gaunt white horse, shouting that they all should make for the Milkwater, that the Weeper was gathering warriors to cross the Bridge of Skulls and take the Shadow Tower. Many followed him; more did not. Later, a dour warrior in fur and amber went from cookfire to cookfire, urging all the survivors to head north and take refuge in the valley of the Thenns. Why he thought they would be safe there when the Thenns themselves had fled the place Varamyr never learned, but hundreds followed him. Hundreds more went off with the woods witch who'd had a vision of a fleet of ships coming to carry the free folk south. "We must seek the sea," cried Mother Mole, and her followers turned east.

Varamyr might have been amongst them if only he'd been stronger. The sea was grey and cold and far away, though, and he knew that he would never live to see it. He was nine times dead and dying, and this would be his true death. *A squirrel-skin cloak,* he remembered, *he knifed me for a squirrel-skin cloak.*

Its owner had been dead, the back of her head smashed into red pulp flecked with bits of bone, but her cloak looked warm and thick. It was snowing, and Varamyr had lost his own cloaks at the Wall. His sleeping pelts and woolen smallclothes, his sheepskin boots and fur-lined gloves, his store of mead and hoarded food, the hanks of hair he took from the women he bedded, even the golden arm rings Mance had given him, all lost and left behind. *I burned and I died and then I ran, half-mad with pain and terror.* The memory still shamed him, but he had not been alone. Others had run as well, hundreds of them, thousands. *The battle was lost. The knights had come, invincible in their steel, killing everyone who stayed to fight. It was run or die.*

Death was not so easily outrun, however. So when Varamyr came upon the dead woman in the wood, he knelt to strip the cloak from her, and never saw the boy until he burst from hiding to drive the long bone knife into his side and rip the cloak out of his clutching fingers. "His mother," Thistle told him later, after the boy had run off. "It were his mother's cloak, and when he saw you robbing her . . ."

"She was dead," Varamyr said, wincing as her bone needle pierced his flesh. "Someone smashed her head. Some crow."

"No crow. Hornfoot men. I saw it." Her needle pulled the gash in his side closed. "Savages, and who's left to tame them?" *No one. If Mance is dead, the free folk are doomed.* The Thenns, giants, and the Hornfoot men, the cave-dwellers with their filed teeth, and the men of the western shore with their chariots of bone . . . all of them were doomed as well. Even the crows. They might not know it yet, but those black-cloaked bastards would perish with the rest. The enemy was coming.

Haggon's rough voice echoed in his head. "You will die a dozen deaths, boy, and every one will hurt . . . but when your true death comes, you will live again. The second life is simpler and sweeter, they say."

Varamyr Sixskins would know the truth of that soon enough. He could taste his true death in the smoke that hung acrid in the air, feel it in the heat beneath his fingers when he slipped a hand under his clothes to touch his wound. The chill was in him too, though, deep down in his bones. This time it would be cold that killed him.

His last death had been by fire. *I burned.* At first, in his confusion, he thought some archer on the Wall had pierced him with a flaming arrow . . . but the fire had been *inside* him, consuming him. And the pain . . .

Varamyr had died nine times before. He had died once from a spear thrust, once with a bear's teeth in his throat, and once in a wash of blood as he brought forth a stillborn cub. He died his first death when he was only six, as his father's axe crashed through his skull. Even that had not been so agonizing as the fire in his guts, crackling along his wings, *devouring* him. When he tried to fly from it, his terror fanned the flames and made them burn hotter. One moment he had been soaring above the Wall, his eagle's eyes marking the movements of the men below. Then the flames had turned his heart into a blackened cinder and sent his spirit screaming back into his own skin, and for a little while he'd gone mad. Even the memory was enough to make him shudder.

That was when he noticed that his fire had gone out.

Only a grey-and-black tangle of charred wood remained, with a few embers glowing in the ashes. *There's still smoke, it just needs wood.* Gritting his teeth against the pain, Varamyr crept to the pile of broken branches Thistle had gathered before she went off hunting, and tossed a few sticks onto the ashes. "Catch," he croaked. "*Burn.*" He blew upon the embers and said a wordless prayer to the nameless gods of wood and hill and field.

The gods gave no answer. After a while, the smoke ceased to rise as well. Already the little hut was growing colder. Varamyr had no flint, no tinder, no dry kindling. He would never get the fire burning again, not by himself. "Thistle," he called out, his voice hoarse and edged with pain. "*Thistle!*"

Her chin was pointed and her nose flat, and she had a mole on one cheek with four dark hairs growing from it. An ugly face, and hard, yet he would have given much to glimpse it in the door of the hut. *I should have taken her before she left.* How long had she been gone? Two days? Three? Varamyr was uncertain. It was dark inside the hut, and he had been drifting in and out of sleep, never quite sure if it was day or night outside. "Wait," she'd said. "I will be back with food." So like a fool he'd waited, dreaming of Haggon and Bump and all the wrongs he had done in his long life, but days and nights had passed and Thistle had not returned. *She won't be coming back.* Varamyr wondered if he had given himself away. Could she tell what he was thinking just from looking at him, or had he muttered in his fever dream?

Abomination, he heard Haggon saying. It was almost as if he were here, in this very room. "She is just some ugly spearwife," Varamyr told him. "I am a great man. I am Varamyr, the warg, the skinchanger, it is not right that she should live and I should die." No one answered. There was no one there. Thistle was gone. She had abandoned him, the same as all the rest.

His own mother had abandoned him as well. *She cried for Bump, but she never cried for me.* The morning his father pulled him out of bed to deliver him to Haggon, she would not even look at him. He had shrieked and kicked as he was dragged into the woods, until his father slapped him and told him to be quiet. "You belong with your own kind," was all he said when he flung him down at Haggon's feet.

He was not wrong, Varamyr thought, shivering. *Haggon taught me much and more. He taught me how to hunt and fish, how to butcher a carcass and bone a fish, how to find my way through the woods. And he taught me the way of the warg and the secrets of the skinchanger, though my gift was stronger than his own.*

Years later he had tried to find his parents, to tell them that their Lump had become the great Varamyr Sixskins, but both of them were dead and burned. *Gone into the trees and streams, gone into the rocks and earth. Gone to dirt and ashes.* That was what the woods witch told his mother, the day Bump died. Lump did not want to be a clod of earth. The boy had dreamed of a day when bards would sing of his deeds and pretty girls would kiss him. *When I am grown I will be the King-Beyond-the-Wall,* Lump had promised himself. He never had, but he had come close. Varamyr Sixskins was a name men feared. He rode to battle on the back of a snow bear thirteen feet tall, kept three wolves and a shadowcat in thrall, and sat at the right hand of Mance

Rayder. *It was Mance who brought me to this place. I should not have listened. I should have slipped inside my bear and torn him to pieces.*

Before Mance, Varamyr Sixskins had been a lord of sorts. He lived alone in a hall of moss and mud and hewn logs that had once been Haggon's, attended by his beasts. A dozen villages did him homage in bread and salt and cider, offering him fruit from their orchards and vegetables from their gardens. His meat he got himself. Whenever he desired a woman he sent his shadowcat to stalk her, and whatever girl he'd cast his eye upon would follow meekly to his bed. Some came weeping, aye, but still they came. Varamyr gave them his seed, took a hank of their hair to remember them by, and sent them back. From time to time, some village hero would come with spear in hand to slay the beastling and save a sister or a lover or a daughter. Those he killed, but he never harmed the women. Some he even blessed with children. *Runts. Small, puny things, like Lump, and not one with the gift.*

Fear drove him to his feet, reeling. Holding his side to staunch the seep of blood from his wound, Varamyr lurched to the door and swept aside the ragged skin that covered it to face a wall of white. *Snow.* No wonder it had grown so dark and smoky inside. The falling snow had buried the hut.

When Varamyr pushed at it, the snow crumbled and gave way, still soft and wet. Outside, the night was white as death; pale thin clouds danced attendance on a silver moon, while a thousand stars watched coldly. He could see the humped shapes of other huts buried beneath drifts of snow, and beyond them the pale shadow of a weirwood armored in ice. To the south and west the hills were a vast white wilderness where nothing moved except the blowing snow. "Thistle," Varamyr called feebly, wondering how far she could have gone. *"Thistle. Woman. Where are you?"*

Far away, a wolf gave howl.

A shiver went through Varamyr. He knew that howl as well as Lump had once known his mother's voice. *One Eye.* He was the oldest of his three, the biggest, the fiercest. Stalker was leaner, quicker, younger, Sly more cunning, but both went in fear of One Eye. The old wolf was fearless, relentless, savage.

Varamyr had lost control of his other beasts in the agony of the eagle's death. His shadowcat had raced into the woods, whilst his snow bear turned her claws on those around her, ripping apart four men before falling to a spear. She would have slain Varamyr had he come within her reach. The bear hated him, had raged each time he wore her skin or climbed upon her back.

His wolves, though . . .

My brothers. My pack. Many a cold night he had slept with his wolves, their shaggy bodies piled up around him to help keep him warm. *When I die they will feast upon my flesh and leave only bones to greet the thaw come spring.* The thought was queerly comforting. His wolves had often foraged for him as they roamed; it seemed only fitting that he should feed them in the end. He might well begin his second life tearing at the warm dead flesh of his own corpse.

Dogs were the easiest beasts to bond with; they lived so close to men that they were almost human. Slipping into a dog's skin was like putting on an old boot, its leather softened by wear. As a boot was shaped to accept a foot, a dog was shaped to accept a collar, even a collar no human eye could see. Wolves were harder. A man might befriend a wolf, even break a wolf, but no man could truly *tame* a wolf. "Wolves and women wed for life," Haggon often said. "You take one, that's a marriage. The wolf is part of you from that day on, and you're part of him. Both of you will change."

Other beasts were best left alone, the hunter had declared. Cats were vain and cruel, always ready to turn on you. Elk and deer were prey; wear their skins too long, and even the bravest man became a coward. Bears, boars, badgers, weasels . . . Haggon did not hold with such. "Some skins you never want to wear, boy. You won't like what you'd become." Birds were the worst, to hear him tell it. "Men were not meant to leave the earth. Spend too much time in the clouds and you never want to come back down again. I know skinchangers who've tried hawks, owls, ravens. Even in their own skins, they sit moony, staring up at the bloody blue."

Not all skinchangers felt the same, however. Once, when Lump was ten, Haggon had taken him to a gathering of such. The wargs were the most numerous in that company, the wolf-brothers, but the boy had found the others stranger and more fascinating. Borroq looked so much like his boar that all he lacked was tusks, Orell had his eagle, Briar her shadowcat (the moment he saw them, Lump wanted a shadowcat of his own), the goat woman Grisella . . .

None of them had been as strong as Varamyr Sixskins, though, not even Haggon, tall and grim with his hands as hard as stone. The hunter died weeping after Varamyr took Greyskin from him, driving him out to claim the beast for his own. *No second life for you, old man.* Varamyr Threeskins, he'd called himself back then. Greyskin made four, though the old wolf was frail and almost toothless and soon followed Haggon into death.

Varamyr could take any beast he wanted, bend them to his will, make their flesh his own. Dog or wolf, bear or badger . . .

Thistle, he thought.

Haggon would call it an abomination, the blackest sin of all, but Haggon was dead, devoured, and burned. Mance would have cursed him as well, but Mance was slain or captured. *No one will ever know. I will be Thistle the spearwife, and Varamyr Sixskins will be dead.* His gift would perish with his body, he expected. He would lose his wolves, and live out the rest of his days as some scrawny, warty woman . . . but he would live. *If she comes back. If I am still strong enough to take her.*

A wave of dizziness washed over Varamyr. He found himself upon his knees, his hands buried in a snowdrift. He scooped up a fistful of snow and filled his mouth with it, rubbing it through his beard and against his cracked lips, sucking down the moisture. The water was so cold that he could barely bring himself to swallow, and he realized once again how hot he was.

The snowmelt only made him hungrier. It was food his belly craved, not water. The snow had stopped falling, but the wind was rising, filling the air with crystal, slashing at his face as he struggled through the drifts, the wound in his side opening and closing again. His breath made a ragged white cloud. When he reached the weirwood tree, he found a fallen branch just long enough to use as a crutch. Leaning heavily upon it, he staggered toward the nearest hut. Perhaps the villagers had forgotten something when they fled . . . a sack of apples, some dried meat, anything to keep him alive until Thistle returned.

He was almost there when his crutch snapped beneath his weight, and his legs went out from under him.

How long he sprawled there with his blood reddening the snow Varamyr could not have said. *The snow will bury me.* It would be a peaceful death. *They say you feel warm near the end, warm and sleepy.* It would be good to feel warm again, though it made him sad to think that he would never see the green lands, the warm lands beyond the Wall that Mance used to sing about. "The world beyond the Wall is not for our kind," Haggon used to say. "The free folk fear skin-changers, but they honor us as well. South of the Wall, the kneelers hunt us down and butcher us like pigs."

You warned me, Varamyr thought, *but it was you who showed me Eastwatch too.* He could not have been more than ten. Haggon traded a dozen strings of amber and a sled piled high with pelts for six skins of wine, a block of salt, and a copper kettle. Eastwatch was a better place to trade than Castle Black; that was where the ships came, laden with goods from the fabled lands beyond the sea. The crows knew Haggon as a hunter and a friend to the Night's Watch, and welcomed the news he brought of life beyond their Wall. Some knew him for a skinchanger too, but no one spoke of that. It was there at Eastwatch-by-the-Sea that the boy he'd been first began to dream of the warm south.

Varamyr could feel the snowflakes melting on his brow. *This is not so bad as burning. Let me sleep and never wake, let me begin my second life.* His wolves were close now. He could feel them. He would leave this feeble flesh behind, become one with them, hunting the night and howling at the moon. The warg would become a true wolf. *Which, though?*

Not Sly. Haggon would have called it abomination, but Varamyr had often slipped inside her skin as she was being mounted by One Eye. He did not want to spend his new life as a bitch, though, not unless he had no other choice. Stalker might suit him better, the younger male . . . though One Eye was larger and fiercer, and it was One Eye who took Sly whenever she went into heat.

"They say you forget," Haggon had told him, a few weeks before his own death. "When the man's flesh dies, his spirit lives on inside the beast, but every day his memory fades, and the beast becomes a little less a warg, a little more a wolf, until nothing of the man is left and only the beast remains."

Varamyr knew the truth of that. When he claimed the eagle that had been Orell's, he could feel the other skinchanger raging at his presence. Orell had been slain by the turncloak crow Jon Snow, and his hate for his killer had been so strong that Varamyr found himself hating the beastling boy as well. He had known what Snow was the moment he saw that great white direwolf stalking silent at his side. One skinchanger can always sense another. *Mance should have let me take the direwolf. There would be a second life worthy of a king.* He could have done it, he did not doubt. The gift was strong in Snow, but the youth was untaught, still fighting his nature when he should have gloried in it.

Varamyr could see the weirwood's red eyes staring down at him from the white trunk. *The gods are weighing me.* A shiver went through him. He had done bad things, terrible things. He had stolen, killed, raped. He had gorged on human flesh and lapped the blood of dying men as it gushed red and hot from their torn throats. He had stalked foes through the woods, fallen on them as they slept, clawed their entrails from their bellies and scattered them across the muddy earth. *How sweet their meat had tasted.* "That was the beast, not me," he said in a hoarse whisper. "That was the gift you gave me."

The gods made no reply. His breath hung pale and misty in the air. He could feel ice forming in his beard. Varamyr Sixskins closed his eyes.

He dreamt an old dream of a hovel by the sea, three dogs whimpering, a woman's tears.

Bump. She weeps for Bump, but she never wept for me.

Lump had been born a month before his proper time, and he was sick so often that no one expected him to live. His mother waited until he was almost four to give him a proper name, and by then it was too late. The whole village had taken to calling him Lump, the name his sister Meha had given him when he was still in their mother's belly. Meha had given Bump his name as well, but Lump's little brother had been born in his proper time, big and red and robust, sucking greedily at Mother's teats. She was going to name him after Father. *Bump died, though. He died when he was two and I was six, three days before his nameday.*

"Your little one is with the gods now," the woods witch told his mother, as she wept. "He'll never hurt again, never hunger, never cry. The gods have taken him down into the earth, into the trees. The gods are all around us, in the rocks and streams, in the birds and beasts. Your Bump has gone to join them. He'll be the world and all that's in it."

The old woman's words had gone through Lump like a knife. *Bump sees. He is watching me. He knows.* Lump could not hide from him, could not slip behind his mother's skirts or run off with the dogs to escape his father's fury. *The dogs.* Loptail, Sniff, the Growler. *They were good dogs. They were my friends.*

When his father found the dogs sniffing round Bump's body, he had no way of knowing which had done it, so he took his axe to all three. His hands shook so badly that it took two blows to silence Sniff and four to put the Growler down. The smell of blood hung heavy in the air, and the sounds the dying dogs had made were terrible to hear, yet Loptail still came when father called him. He was the oldest dog, and his training overcame his terror. By the time Lump slipped inside his skin it was too late.

No, Father, please, he tried to say, but dogs cannot speak the tongues of men, so all that emerged was a piteous whine. The axe crashed into the middle of the old dog's skull, and inside the hovel the boy let out a scream. *That was how they knew.* Two days later, his father dragged him into the woods. He brought his axe, so Lump thought he meant to put him down the same way he had done the dogs. Instead he'd given him to Haggon.

Varamyr woke suddenly, violently, his whole body shaking. "Get up," a voice was screaming, "get up, we have to go. There are hundreds of them." The snow had covered him with a stiff white blanket. *So cold.* When he tried to move, he found that his hand was frozen to the ground. He left some skin behind when he tore it loose. "Get up," she screamed again, "they're *coming.*"

Thistle had returned to him. She had him by the shoulders and was shaking him, shouting in his face. Varamyr could smell her breath and feel the warmth of it upon cheeks gone numb with cold. *Now,* he thought, *do it now, or die.*

He summoned all the strength still in him, leapt out of his own skin, and forced himself inside her.

Thistle arched her back and screamed.

Abomination. Was that her, or him, or Haggon? He never knew. His old flesh fell back into the snowdrift as her fingers loosened. The spearwife twisted violently, shrieking. His shadowcat used to fight him wildly, and the snow bear had gone half-mad for a time, snapping at trees and rocks and empty air, but this was worse. "Get out, *get out!*" he heard her own mouth shouting. Her body staggered, fell, and rose again, her hands flailed, her legs jerked this way and that in some grotesque dance as his spirit and her own fought for the flesh. She sucked down a mouthful of the frigid air, and Varamyr had half a heartbeat to glory in the taste of it and the strength of this young body before her teeth snapped together and filled his mouth with blood. She raised her hands to his face. He tried to push them down again, but the hands would not obey, and she was clawing at his eyes. *Abomination,* he remembered, drowning in blood and pain and madness. When he tried to scream, she spat their tongue out.

The white world turned and fell away. For a moment it was as if he were inside the weirwood, gazing out through carved red eyes as a dying man twitched feebly on the ground and a madwoman danced blind and bloody underneath the moon, weeping red tears and ripping at her clothes. Then both were gone and he was rising, melting, his spirit borne on some cold wind. He was in the snow and in the clouds, he was a sparrow, a squirrel, an oak. A horned owl flew silently between his trees, hunting a hare; Varamyr was inside the owl, inside the hare, inside the trees. Deep below the frozen ground, earthworms burrowed blindly in the dark, and he was them as well. *I am the wood, and everything that's in it,* he thought, exulting. A hundred ravens took to the air, cawing as they felt him pass. A great elk trumpeted, unsettling the children clinging to his back. A sleeping direwolf raised his head to snarl at empty air. Before their hearts could beat again he had passed on, searching for his own, for One Eye, Sly, and Stalker, for his pack. His wolves would save him, he told himself.

That was his last thought as a man.

True death came suddenly; he felt a shock of cold, as if he had been plunged into the icy waters of a frozen lake. Then he found himself rushing over moonlit snows with his packmates close behind him. Half the world was dark. *One Eye,* he knew. He bayed, and Sly and Stalker gave echo.

When they reached the crest the wolves paused. *Thistle,* he remembered, and a part of him grieved for what he had lost and another part for what he'd done. Below, the world had turned to ice. Fingers of frost crept slowly up the weirwood, reaching out for each other. The empty village was no longer empty. Blue-eyed shadows walked amongst the mounds of snow. Some wore brown and some wore black and some were naked, their flesh gone white as snow. A wind was sighing through the hills, heavy with their scents: dead flesh, dry blood, skins that stank of mold and rot and urine. Sly gave a growl and bared her teeth, her ruff bristling. *Not men. Not prey. Not these.*

The things below moved, but did not live. One by one, they raised their heads toward the three wolves on the hill. The last to look was the thing that had been Thistle. She wore wool and fur and leather, and over that she wore a coat of hoarfrost that crackled when she moved and glistened in the moonlight. Pale pink icicles hung from her fingertips, ten long knives of frozen blood. And in the pits where her eyes had been, a pale blue light was flickering, lending her coarse features an eerie beauty they had never known in life.

She sees me.

TYRION

He drank his way across the narrow sea.

The ship was small, his cabin smaller, but the captain would not allow him abovedecks. The rocking of the deck beneath his feet made his stomach heave, and the wretched food tasted even worse when retched back up. But why did he need salt beef, hard cheese, and bread crawling with worms when he had wine to nourish him? It was red and sour, very strong. Sometimes he heaved the wine up too, but there was always more.

"The world is full of wine," he muttered in the dankness of his cabin. His father never had any use for drunkards, but what did that matter? His father was dead. He'd killed him. *A bolt in the belly, my lord, and all for you. If only I was better with a crossbow, I would have put it through that cock you made me with, you bloody bastard.*

Belowdecks, there was neither night nor day. Tyrion marked time by the comings and goings of the cabin boy who brought the meals he did not eat. The boy always brought a brush and bucket too, to clean up. "Is this Dornish wine?" Tyrion asked him once, as he pulled a stopper from a skin. "It reminds me of a certain snake I knew. A droll fellow, till a mountain fell on him."

The cabin boy did not answer. He was an ugly boy, though admittedly more comely than a certain dwarf with half a nose and a scar from eye to chin. "Have I offended you?" Tyrion asked, as the boy was scrubbing. "Were you commanded not to talk to me? Or did some dwarf diddle your mother?" That went unanswered too. "Where are we sailing? Tell me that." Jaime had made mention of the Free Cities, but had never said which one. "Is it Braavos? Tyrosh? Myr?" Tyrion would sooner have gone to Dorne. *Myrcella is older than Tommen, by Dornish law the Iron Throne is hers. I will help her claim her rights, as Prince Oberyn suggested.*

Oberyn was dead, though, his head smashed to bloody ruin by the armored fist of Ser Gregor Clegane. And without the Red Viper to urge him on, would Doran Martell even consider such a chancy scheme? *He might clap me in chains instead and hand me back to my sweet sister.* The Wall might be safer. Old Bear Mormont said the Night's Watch had need of men like Tyrion. *Mormont might be dead, though. By now Slynt may be the lord commander.* That butcher's son was not like to have forgotten who sent him to the Wall. *Do I really want to spend the rest of my life eating salt beef and porridge with murderers and thieves?* Not that the rest of his life would last very long, Janos Slynt would see to that.

The cabin boy wet his brush and scrubbed on manfully. "Have you ever visited the pleasure houses of Lys?" the dwarf inquired. "Might that be where whores go?" Tyrion could not seem to recall the Valyrian word for whore, and in any case it was too late. The boy tossed his brush back in his bucket and took his leave.

The wine has blurred my wits. He had learned to read High Valyrian at his maester's knee, though what they spoke in the Nine Free Cities . . . well, it was not so much a dialect as nine dialects on the way to becoming separate tongues. Tyrion had some Braavosi and a smattering of Myrish. In Tyrosh he should be able to curse the gods, call a man a cheat, and order up an ale, thanks to a sellsword he had once known at the Rock. *At least in Dorne they speak the Common Tongue.* Like Dornish food and Dornish law, Dornish speech was spiced with the flavors of the Rhoyne, but a man could comprehend it. *Dorne, yes, Dorne for me.* He crawled into his bunk, clutching that thought like a child with a doll.

Sleep had never come easily to Tyrion Lannister. Aboard that ship it seldom came at all, though from time to time he managed to drink sufficient wine to pass out for a while. At least he did not dream. He had dreamed enough for one small life. *And of such follies: love, justice, friendship, glory. As well the dream of being tall.* It was all beyond his reach, Tyrion knew now. But he did not know where whores go.

"Wherever whores go," his father had said. *His last words, and what words they were.* The crossbow *thrumm*ed, Lord Tywin sat back down, and Tyrion Lannister found himself waddling through the darkness with Varys at his side. He must have clambered back down the shaft, two hundred and thirty rungs to where orange embers glowed in the mouth of an iron dragon. He remembered none of it. Only the sound the crossbow made, and the stink of his father's bowels opening. *Even in his dying, he found a way to shit on me.*

Varys had escorted him through the tunnels, but they never spoke until they emerged beside the Blackwater, where Tyrion had won a famous victory and lost a nose. That was when the dwarf turned to the eunuch and said, "I've killed my father," in the same tone a man might use to say, "I've stubbed my toe."

The master of whisperers had been dressed as a begging brother, in a moth-eaten robe of brown roughspun with a cowl that shadowed his smooth fat cheeks and bald round head. "You should not have climbed that ladder," he said reproachfully.

"Wherever whores go." Tyrion had warned his father not to say that word. *If I had not loosed, he would have seen my threats were empty. He would have taken the crossbow from my hands, as once he took Tysha from my arms. He was rising when I killed him.*

"I killed Shae too," he confessed to Varys.

"You knew what she was."

"I did. But I never knew what he was."

Varys tittered. "And now you do."

I should have killed the eunuch as well. A little more blood on his hands, what would it matter? He could not say what had stayed his dagger. Not gratitude. Varys had saved him from a headsman's sword, but only because Jaime had compelled him. *Jaime . . . no, better not to think of Jaime.*

He found a fresh skin of wine instead and sucked at it as if it were a woman's breast. The sour red ran down his chin and soaked through his soiled tunic, the same one he had been wearing in his cell. The deck was swaying beneath his feet, and when he tried to rise it lifted sideways and smashed him hard against a bulkhead. *A storm,* he realized, *or else I am even drunker than I knew.* He retched the wine up and lay in it a while, wondering if the ship would sink. *Is this your vengeance, Father? Has the Father Above made you his Hand?* "Such are the wages of the kinslayer," he said as the wind howled outside. It did not seem fair to drown the cabin boy and the captain and all the rest for something he had done, but when had the gods ever been fair? And around about then, the darkness gulped him down.

When he stirred again, his head felt like to burst and the ship was spinning round in dizzy circles, though the captain was insisting that they'd come to port. Tyrion told him to be quiet and kicked feebly as a huge bald sailor tucked him under one arm and carried him squirming to the hold, where an empty wine cask awaited him. It was a squat little cask, and a tight fit even for a dwarf. Tyrion pissed himself in his struggles, for all the good it did. He was crammed face-first into the cask with his knees pushed up against his ears. The stub of his nose itched horribly, but his arms were pinned so tightly that he could not reach to scratch it. *A palanquin fit for a man of my stature,* he thought as they hammered shut the lid. He could hear voices shouting as he was hoisted up. Every bounce cracked his head against the bottom of the cask. The world went round and round as the cask rolled downward, then stopped with a crash that made him want to scream. Another cask slammed into his, and Tyrion bit his tongue.

That was the longest journey he had ever taken, though it could not have lasted more than half an hour. He was lifted and lowered, rolled and stacked, upended and righted and rolled again. Through the wooden staves he heard men shouting, and once a horse whickered nearby. His stunted legs began to cramp, and soon hurt so badly that he forgot the hammering in his head.

It ended as it had begun, with another roll that left him dizzy and more jouncing. Outside, strange voices were speaking in a tongue he did not know. Someone started pounding on the top of the cask and the lid cracked open suddenly. Light came flooding in, and cool air as well. Tyrion gasped greedily and tried to stand, but only managed to knock the cask over sideways and spill himself out onto a hard-packed earthen floor.

Above him loomed a grotesque fat man with a forked yellow beard, holding a wooden mallet and an iron chisel. His bedrobe was large enough to serve as a tourney pavilion, but its loosely knotted belt had come undone, exposing a huge white belly and a pair of heavy breasts that sagged like sacks of suet covered with coarse yellow hair. He reminded Tyrion of a dead sea cow that had once washed up in the caverns under Casterly Rock.

The fat man looked down and smiled. "A drunken dwarf," he said, in the Common Tongue of Westeros.

"A rotting sea cow." Tyrion's mouth was full of blood. He spat it at the fat man's feet. They were in a long, dim cellar with barrel-vaulted ceilings, its stone walls spotted with nitre. Casks of wine and ale surrounded them, more than enough drink to see a thirsty dwarf safely through the night. *Or through a life.*

"You are insolent. I like that in a dwarf." When the fat man laughed, his flesh bounced so vigorously that Tyrion was afraid he might fall and crush him. "Are you hungry, my little friend? Weary?"

"Thirsty." Tyrion struggled to his knees. "And filthy."

The fat man sniffed. "A bath first, just so. Then food and a soft bed, yes? My servants shall see to it." His host put the mallet and chisel aside. "My house is yours. Any friend of my friend across the water is a friend to Illyrio Mopatis, yes."

And any friend of Varys the Spider is someone I will trust just as far as I can throw him.

The fat man made good on the promised bath, though. No sooner did Tyrion lower himself into the hot water and close his eyes than he was fast asleep. He woke naked on a goose-down feather bed so soft it felt as if he had been swallowed by a cloud. His tongue was growing hair and his throat was raw, but his cock was as hard as an iron bar. He rolled from the bed, found a chamber pot, and commenced to filling it, with a groan of pleasure.

The room was dim, but there were bars of yellow sunlight showing between the slats of the shutters. Tyrion shook the last drops off and waddled over patterned Myrish carpets as soft as new spring grass. Awkwardly he climbed the window seat and flung the shutters open to see where Varys and the gods had sent him.

Beneath his window six cherry trees stood sentinel around a marble pool, their slender branches bare and brown. A naked boy stood on the water, poised to duel with a bravo's blade in hand. He was lithe and handsome, no older than sixteen, with straight blond hair that brushed his shoulders. So lifelike did he seem that it took the dwarf a long moment to realize he was made of painted marble, though his sword shimmered like true steel.

Across the pool stood a brick wall twelve feet high, with iron spikes along its top. Beyond that was the city. A sea of tiled rooftops crowded close around a bay. He saw square brick towers, a great red temple, a distant manse upon a hill. In the far distance, sunlight shimmered off deep water. Fishing boats were moving across the bay, their sails rippling in the wind, and he could see the masts of larger ships poking up along the shore. *Surely one is bound for Dorne, or for Eastwatch-by-the-Sea.* He had no means to pay for passage, though, nor was he made to pull an oar. *I suppose I could sign on as a cabin boy and earn my way by letting the crew bugger me up and down the narrow sea.*

He wondered where he was. *Even the air smells different here.* Strange spices scented the chilly autumn wind, and he could hear faint cries drifting over the wall from the streets beyond. It sounded something like Valyrian, but he did not recognize more than one word in five. *Not Braavos,* he concluded, *nor Tyrosh.* Those bare branches and the chill in the air argued against Lys and Myr and Volantis as well.

When he heard the door opening behind him, Tyrion turned to confront his fat host. "This is Pentos, yes?"

"Just so. Where else?"

Pentos. Well, it was not King's Landing, that much could be said for it. "Where do whores go?" he heard himself ask.

"Whores are found in brothels here, as in Westeros. You will have no need of such, my little friend. Choose from amongst my serving-women. None will dare refuse you."

"Slaves?" the dwarf asked pointedly.

The fat man stroked one of the prongs of his oiled yellow beard, a gesture Tyrion found remarkably obscene. "Slavery is forbidden in Pentos, by the terms of the treaty the Braavosi imposed on us a hundred years ago. Still, they will not refuse you." Illyrio gave a ponderous half bow. "But now my little friend must excuse me. I have the honor to be a magister of this great city, and the prince has summoned us to session." He smiled, showing a mouth full of crooked yellow teeth. "Explore the manse and grounds as you like, but on no account stray beyond the walls. It is best that no man knows that you were here."

"*Were?* Have I gone somewhere?"

"Time enough to speak of that this evening. My little friend and I shall eat and drink and make great plans, yes?"

"Yes, my fat friend," Tyrion replied. *He thinks to use me for his profit.* It was all profit with the merchant princes of the Free Cities. "Spice soldiers and cheese lords," his lord father called them, with contempt. Should a day ever dawn when Illyrio Mopatis saw more profit in a dead dwarf than a live one, Tyrion would find himself packed into another wine cask by dusk. *It would be well if I was gone before that day arrives.* That it would arrive he did not doubt; Cersei was not like to forget him, and even Jaime might be vexed to find a quarrel in Father's belly.

A light wind was riffling the waters of the pool below, all around the naked swordsman. It reminded him of how Tysha would riffle his hair during the false spring of their marriage, before he helped his father's guardsmen rape her. He had been thinking of those guardsmen during his flight, trying to recall how many there had been. You would think he might remember that, but no. A dozen? A score? A hundred? He could not say. They had all been grown men, tall and strong . . . though all men were tall to a dwarf of thirteen years. *Tysha knew their number.* Each of them had given her a silver stag, so she would only need to count the coins. *A silver for each and a gold for me.* His father had insisted that he pay her too. *A Lannister always pays his debts.*

"Wherever whores go," he heard Lord Tywin say once more, and once more the bowstring *thrummed*.

The magister had invited him to explore the manse. He found clean clothes in a cedar chest inlaid with lapis and mother-of-pearl. The clothes had been made for a small boy, he realized as he struggled into them. The fabrics were rich enough, if a little musty, but the cut was too long in the legs and too short in the arms, with a collar that would have turned his face as black as Joffrey's had he somehow contrived to get it fastened. Moths had been at them too. *At least they do not stink of vomit.*

Tyrion began his explorations with the kitchen, where two fat women and a potboy watched him warily as he helped himself to cheese, bread, and figs. "Good morrow to you, fair ladies," he said with a bow. "Do you know where whores go?" When they did not respond, he repeated the question in High Valyrian, though he had to say *courtesan* in place of *whore*. The younger, fatter cook gave him a shrug that time.

He wondered what they would do if he took them by the hand and dragged them to his bedchamber. *None will dare refuse you,* Illyrio claimed, but somehow Tyrion did not think he meant these two. The younger woman was old enough to be his mother, and the older was likely *her* mother. Both were near as fat as Illyrio, with teats that were larger than his head. *I could smother myself in flesh.* There were worse ways to die. The way his lord father had died, for one. *I should have made him shit a little gold before expiring.* Lord Tywin might have been niggardly with his approval and affection, but he had always been open-handed when it came to coin. *The only thing more pitiful than a dwarf without a nose is a dwarf without a nose who has no gold.*

Tyrion left the fat women to their loaves and kettles and went in search of the cellar where Illyrio had decanted him the night before. It was not hard to find. There was enough wine there to keep him drunk for a hundred years; sweet reds from the Reach and sour reds from Dorne, pale Pentoshi ambers, the green nectar of Myr, three score casks of Arbor gold, even wines from the fabled east, from Qarth and Yi Ti and Asshai by the Shadow. In the end, Tyrion chose a cask of strongwine marked as the private stock of Lord Runceford Redwyne, the grandfather of the present Lord of the Arbor. The taste of it was languorous and heady on the tongue, the color a purple so dark that it looked almost black in the dim-lit cellar. Tyrion filled a cup, and a flagon for good measure, and carried them up to the gardens to drink beneath those cherry trees he'd seen.

As it happened, he left by the wrong door and never found the pool he had spied from his window, but it made no matter. The gardens behind the manse were just as pleasant, and far more extensive. He wandered through them for a time, drinking. The walls would have shamed any proper castle, and the ornamental iron spikes along the top looked strangely naked without heads to adorn them. Tyrion pictured how his sister's head might look up there, with tar in her golden hair and flies buzzing in and out of her mouth. *Yes, and Jaime must have the spike beside her,* he decided. *No one must ever come between my brother and my sister.*

With a rope and a grapnel he might be able to get over that wall. He had strong arms and he did not weigh much. He should be able to clamber over, if he did not impale himself on a spike. *I will search for a rope on the morrow,* he resolved.

He saw three gates during his wanderings—the main entrance with its gatehouse, a postern by the kennels, and a garden gate hidden behind a tangle of pale ivy. The last was chained, the others guarded. The guards were plump, their faces as smooth as babies' bottoms, and every man of them wore a spiked bronze cap. Tyrion knew eunuchs when he saw them. He knew their sort by reputation. They feared nothing and felt no pain, it was said, and were loyal to their masters unto death. *I could make good use of a few hundred of mine own,* he reflected. *A pity I did not think of that before I became a beggar.*

He walked along a pillared gallery and through a pointed arch, and found himself in a tiled courtyard where a woman was washing clothes at a well. She looked to be his own age, with dull red hair and a broad face dotted by freckles. "Would you like some wine?" he asked her. She looked at him uncertainly. "I have no cup for you, we'll have to share." The washerwoman went back to wringing out tunics and hanging them to dry. Tyrion settled on a stone bench with his flagon. "Tell me, how far should I trust Magister Illyrio?" The name made her look up. "That far?" Chuckling, he crossed his stunted legs and took a drink. "I am loath to play whatever part the cheesemonger has in mind for me, yet how can I refuse him? The gates are guarded. Perhaps you might smuggle me out under your skirts? I'd be so grateful; why, I'll even wed you. I have two wives already, why not three? Ah, but where would we live?" He gave her as pleasant a smile as a man with half a nose could manage. "I have a niece in Sunspear, did I tell you? I could make rather a lot of mischief in Dorne with Myrcella. I could set my niece and nephew at war, wouldn't that be droll?" The washer-woman pinned up one of Illyrio's tunics, large enough to double as a sail. "I should be ashamed to think such evil thoughts, you're quite right. Better if I sought the Wall instead. All crimes are wiped clean when a man joins the Night's Watch, they say. Though I fear they would not let me keep you, sweetling. No women in the Watch, no sweet freckly wives to warm your bed at night, only cold winds, salted cod, and small beer. Do you think I might stand taller in black, my lady?" He filled his cup again. "What do you say? North or south? Shall I atone for old sins or make some new ones?"

The washerwoman gave him one last glance, picked up her basket, and walked away. *I cannot seem to hold a wife for very long,* Tyrion reflected. Somehow his flagon had gone dry. *Perhaps I should stumble back down to the cellars.* The strongwine was making his head spin, though, and the cellar steps were very steep. "Where do whores go?" he asked the wash flapping on the line. Perhaps he should have asked the washerwoman. *Not to imply that you're a whore, my dear, but perhaps you know where they go.* Or better yet, he should have asked his father. "Wherever whores go," Lord Tywin said. *She loved me. She was a crofter's daughter, she loved me and she wed me, she put her trust in me.*

The empty flagon slipped from his hand and rolled across the yard. Tyrion pushed himself off the bench and went to fetch it. As he did, he saw some mushrooms growing up from a cracked paving tile. Pale white they were, with speckles, and red-ribbed undersides dark as blood. The dwarf snapped one off and sniffed it. *Delicious,* he thought, *and deadly.*

There were seven of the mushrooms. Perhaps the Seven were trying to tell him something. He picked them all, snatched a glove down from the line, wrapped them carefully, and stuffed them down his pocket. The effort made him dizzy, so afterward he crawled back onto the bench, curled up, and shut his eyes.

When he woke again, he was back in his bedchamber, drowning in the goose-down feather bed once more while a blond girl shook his shoulder. "My lord," she said, "your bath awaits. Magister Illyrio expects you at table within the hour."

Tyrion propped himself against the pillows, his head in his hands. "Do I dream, or do you speak the Common Tongue?"

"Yes, my lord. I was bought to please the king." She was blue-eyed and fair, young and willowy.

"I am sure you did. I need a cup of wine."

She poured for him. "Magister Illyrio said that I am to scrub your back and warm your bed. My name—"

"—is of no interest to me. Do you know where whores go?"

She flushed. "Whores sell themselves for coin."

"Or jewels, or gowns, or castles. But where do they go?"

The girl could not grasp the question. "Is it a riddle, m'lord? I'm no good at riddles. Will you tell me the answer?"

No, he thought. *I despise riddles, myself.* "I will tell you nothing. Do me the same favor." *The only part of you that interests me is the part between your legs,* he almost said. The words were on his tongue, but somehow never passed his lips. *She is not Shae,* the dwarf told himself, *only some little fool who thinks I play at riddles.* If truth be told, even her cunt did not interest him much. *I must be sick, or dead.* "You mentioned a bath? We must not keep the great cheesemonger waiting."

As he bathed, the girl washed his feet, scrubbed his back, and brushed his hair. Afterward she rubbed sweet-smelling ointment into his calves to ease the aches, and dressed him once again in boy's clothing, a musty pair of burgundy breeches and a blue velvet doublet lined with cloth-of-gold. "Will my lord want me after he has eaten?" she asked as she was lacing up his boots.

"No. I am done with women." *Whores.*

The girl took that disappointment too well for his liking. "If m'lord would prefer a boy, I can have one waiting in his bed."

M'lord would prefer his wife. M'lord would prefer a girl named Tysha. "Only if he knows where whores go."

The girl's mouth tightened. *She despises me,* he realized, *but no more than I despise myself.* That he had fucked many a woman who loathed the very sight of him, Tyrion Lannister had no doubt, but the others had at least the grace to feign affection. *A little honest loathing might be refreshing, like a tart wine after too much sweet.*

"I believe I have changed my mind," he told her. "Wait for me abed. Naked, if you please, I'll be a deal too drunk to fumble at your clothing. Keep your mouth shut and your thighs open and the two of us should get on splendidly." He gave her a leer, hoping for a taste of fear, but all she gave him was revulsion. *No one fears a dwarf.* Even Lord Tywin had not been afraid, though Tyrion had held a crossbow in his hands. "Do you moan when you are being fucked?" he asked the bedwarmer.

"If it please m'lord."

"It might please m'lord to strangle you. That's how I served my last whore. Do you think your master would object? Surely not. He has a hundred more like you, but no one else like me." This time, when he grinned, he got the fear he wanted.

Illyrio was reclining on a padded couch, gobbling hot peppers and pearl onions from a wooden bowl. His brow was dotted with beads of sweat, his pig's eyes shining above his fat cheeks. Jewels danced when he moved his hands; onyx and opal, tiger's eye and tourmaline, ruby, amethyst, sapphire, emerald, jet and jade, a black diamond, and a green pearl. *I could live for years on his rings,* Tyrion mused, *though I'd need a cleaver to claim them.*

"Come sit, my little friend." Illyrio waved him closer.

The dwarf clambered up onto a chair. It was much too big for him, a cushioned throne intended to accommodate the magister's massive buttocks, with thick sturdy legs to bear his weight. Tyrion Lannister had lived all his life in a world that was too big for him, but in the manse of Illyrio Mopatis the sense of disproportion assumed grotesque dimensions. *I am a mouse in a mammoth's lair,* he mused, *though at least the mammoth keeps a good cellar.* The thought made him thirsty. He called for wine.

"Did you enjoy the girl I sent you?" Illyrio asked.

"If I had wanted a girl I would have asked for one."

"If she failed to please . . ."

"She did all that was required of her."

"I would hope so. She was trained in Lys, where they make an art of love. The king enjoyed her greatly."

"I kill kings, hadn't you heard?" Tyrion smiled evilly over his wine cup. "I want no royal leavings."

"As you wish. Let us eat." Illyrio clapped his hands together, and serving men came running.

They began with a broth of crab and monkfish, and cold egg lime soup as well. Then came quails in honey, a saddle of lamb, goose livers drowned in wine, buttered parsnips, and suckling pig. The sight of it all made Tyrion feel queasy, but he forced himself to try a spoon of soup for the sake of politeness, and once he had tasted it he was lost. The cooks might be old and fat, but they knew their business. He had never eaten so well, even at court.

As he was sucking the meat off the bones of his quail, he asked Illyrio about the morning's summons. The fat man shrugged. "There are troubles in the east. Astapor has fallen, and Meereen. Ghiscari slave cities that were old when the world was young." The suckling pig was carved. Illyrio reached for a piece of the crackling, dipped it in a plum sauce, and ate it with his fingers.

"Slaver's Bay is a long way from Pentos." Tyrion speared a goose liver on the point of his knife. *No man is as cursed as the kinslayer,* he mused, *but I could learn to like this hell.*

"This is so," Illyrio agreed, "but the world is one great web, and a man dare not touch a single strand lest all the others tremble. More wine?" Illyrio popped a pepper into his mouth. "No, something better." He clapped his hands together.

At the sound a serving man entered with a covered dish. He placed it in front of Tyrion, and Illyrio leaned across the table to remove the lid. "Mushrooms," the magister announced, as the smell wafted up. "Kissed with garlic and bathed in butter. I am told the taste is exquisite. Have one, my friend. Have two."

Tyrion had a fat black mushroom halfway to his mouth, but something in Illyrio's voice made him stop abruptly. "After you, my lord." He pushed the dish toward his host.

"No, no." Magister Illyrio pushed the mushrooms back. For a heartbeat it seemed as if a mischievous boy was peering out from inside the cheesemonger's bloated flesh. "After you. I insist. Cook made them specially for you."

"Did she indeed?" He remembered the cook, the flour on her hands, heavy breasts shot through with dark blue veins. "That was kind of her, but . . . no." Tyrion eased the mushroom back into the lake of butter from which it had emerged.

"You are too suspicious." Illyrio smiled through his forked yellow beard. Oiled every morning to make it gleam like gold, Tyrion suspected. "Are you craven? I had not heard that of you."

"In the Seven Kingdoms it is considered a grave breach of hospitality to poison your guest at supper."

"Here as well." Illyrio Mopatis reached for his wine cup. "Yet when a guest plainly wishes to end his own life, why, his host must oblige him, no?" He took a gulp. "Magister Ordello was poisoned by a mushroom not half a year ago. The pain is not so much, I am told. Some cramping in the gut, a sudden ache behind the eyes, and it is done. Better a mushroom than a sword through your neck, is it not so? Why die with the taste of blood in your mouth when it could be butter and garlic?"

The dwarf studied the dish before him. The smell of garlic and butter had his mouth watering. Some part of him wanted those mushrooms, even knowing what they were. He was not brave enough to take cold steel to his own belly, but a bite of mushroom would not be so hard. That frightened him more than he could say. "You mistake me," he heard himself say.

"Is it so? I wonder. If you would sooner drown in wine, say the word and it shall be done, and quickly. Drowning cup by cup wastes time and wine both."

"You mistake me," Tyrion said again, more loudly. The buttered mushrooms glistened in the lamplight, dark and inviting. "I have no wish to die, I promise you. I have . . ." His voice trailed off into uncertainty. *What do I have? A life to live? Work to do? Children to raise, lands to rule, a woman to love?*

"You have nothing," finished Magister Illyrio, "but we can change that." He plucked a mushroom from the butter, and chewed it lustily. "Delicious."

"The mushrooms are not poisoned." Tyrion was irritated.

"No. Why should I wish you ill?" Magister Illyrio ate another. "We must show a little trust, you and I. Come, eat." He clapped his hands again. "We have work to do. My little friend must keep his strength up."

The serving men brought out a heron stuffed with figs, veal cutlets blanched with almond milk, creamed herring, candied onions, foul-smelling cheeses, plates of snails and sweetbreads, and a black swan in her plumage. Tyrion refused the swan, which reminded him of a supper with his sister. He helped himself to heron and herring, though, and a few of the sweet onions. And the serving men filled his wine cup anew each time he emptied it.

"You drink a deal of wine for such a little man."

"Kinslaying is dry work. It gives a man a thirst."

The fat man's eyes glittered like the gemstones on his fingers. "There are those in Westeros who would say that killing Lord Lannister was merely a good beginning."

"They had best not say it in my sister's hearing, or they will find themselves short a tongue." The dwarf tore a loaf of bread in half. "And you had best be careful what you say of my family, magister. Kinslayer or no, I am a lion still."

That seemed to amuse the lord of cheese no end. He slapped a meaty thigh and said, "You Westerosi are all the same. You sew some beast upon a scrap of silk, and suddenly you are all lions or dragons or eagles. I can take you to a real lion, my little friend. The prince keeps a pride in his menagerie. Would you like to share a cage with them?"

The lords of the Seven Kingdoms did make rather much of their sigils, Tyrion had to admit. "Very well," he conceded. "A Lannister is not a lion. Yet I am still my father's son, and Jaime and Cersei are mine to kill."

"How odd that you should mention your fair sister," said Illyrio, between snails. "The queen has offered a lordship to the man who brings her your head, no matter how humble his birth."

It was no more than Tyrion had expected. "If you mean to take her up on it, make her spread her legs for you as well. The best part of me for the best part of her, that's a fair trade."

"I would sooner have mine own weight in gold." The cheesemonger laughed so hard that Tyrion feared he was about to rupture. "All the gold in Casterly Rock, why not?"

"The gold I grant you," the dwarf said, relieved that he was not about to drown in a gout of half-digested eels and sweetmeats, "but the Rock is mine."

"Just so." The magister covered his mouth and belched a mighty belch. "Do you think King Stannis will give it to you? I am told he is a great one for the law. Your brother wears the white cloak, so you are heir by all the laws of Westeros."

"Stannis might well grant me Casterly Rock," said Tyrion, "but for the small matter of regicide and kinslaying. For those he would shorten me by a head, and I am short enough as I stand. But why would you think I mean to join Lord Stannis?"

"Why else would you go the Wall?"

"Stannis is at the Wall?" Tyrion rubbed at his nose. "What in seven bloody hells is Stannis doing at the Wall?"

"Shivering, I would think. It is warmer down in Dorne. Perhaps he should have sailed that way."

Tyrion was beginning to suspect that a certain freckled washerwoman knew more of the Common Speech than she pretended. "My niece Myrcella is in Dorne, as it happens. And I have half a mind to make her a queen."

Illyrio smiled as his serving men spooned out bowls of black cherries in sweet cream for them both. "What has this poor child done to you that you would wish her dead?"

"Even a kinslayer is not required to slay *all* his kin," said Tyrion, wounded. "Queen her, I said. Not kill her."

The cheesemonger spooned up cherries. "In Volantis they use a coin with a crown on one face and a death's-head on the other. Yet it is the same coin. To queen her is to kill her. Dorne might rise for Myrcella, but Dorne alone is not enough. If you are as clever as our friend insists, you know this."

Tyrion looked at the fat man with new interest. *He is right on both counts. To queen her is to kill her. And I knew that.* "Futile gestures are all that remain to me. This one would make my sister weep bitter tears, at least."

Magister Illyrio wiped sweet cream from his mouth with the back of a fat hand. "The road to Casterly Rock does not go through Dorne, my little friend. Nor does it run beneath the Wall. Yet there is such a road, I tell you."

"I am an attainted traitor, a regicide, and kinslayer." This talk of roads annoyed him. *Does he think this is a game?*

"What one king does, another may undo. In Pentos we have a prince, my friend. He presides at ball and feast and rides about the city in a palanquin of ivory and gold. Three heralds go before him with the golden scales of trade, the iron sword of war, and the silver scourge of justice. On the first day of each new year he must deflower the maid of the fields and the maid of the seas." Illyrio leaned forward, elbows on the table. "Yet should a crop fail or a war be lost, we cut his throat to appease the gods and choose a new prince from amongst the forty families."

"Remind me never to become the Prince of Pentos."

"Are your Seven Kingdoms so different? There is no peace in Westeros, no justice, no faith . . . and soon enough, no food. When men are starving and sick of fear, they look for a savior."

"They may look, but if all they find is Stannis—"

"Not Stannis. Nor Myrcella." The yellow smile widened. "*Another.* Stronger than Tommen, gentler than Stannis, with a better claim than the girl Myrcella. A savior come from across the sea to bind up the wounds of bleeding Westeros."

"Fine words." Tyrion was unimpressed. "Words are wind. Who is this bloody savior?"

"A dragon." The cheesemonger saw the look on his face at that, and laughed. "A dragon with three heads."

DAENERYS

She could hear the dead man coming up the steps. The slow, measured sound of footsteps went before him, echoing amongst the purple pillars of her hall. Daenerys Targaryen awaited him upon the ebon bench that she had made her throne. Her eyes were soft with sleep, her silver-gold hair all tousled.

"Your Grace," said Ser Barristan Selmy, the lord commander of her Queensguard, "there is no need for you to see this."

"He died for me." Dany clutched her lion pelt to her chest. Underneath, a sheer white linen tunic covered her to midthigh. She had been dreaming of a house with a red door when Missandei woke her. There had been no time to dress.

"*Khaleesi*," whispered Irri, "you must not touch the dead man. It is bad luck to touch the dead."

"Unless you killed them yourself." Jhiqui was bigger-boned than Irri, with wide hips and heavy breasts. "That is known."

"It is known," Irri agreed.

Dothraki were wise where horses were concerned, but could be utter fools about much else. *They are only girls, besides.* Her handmaids were of an age with her—women grown to look at them, with their black hair, copper skin, and almond-shaped eyes, but girls all the same. They had been given to her when she wed Khal Drogo. It was Drogo who had given her the pelt she wore, the head and hide of a *hrakkar,* the white lion of the Dothraki sea. It was too big for her and had a musty smell, but it made her feel as if her sun-and-stars was still near her.

Grey Worm appeared atop the steps first, a torch in hand. His bronze cap was crested with three spikes. Behind him followed four of his Unsullied, bearing the dead man on their shoulders. Their caps had only one spike each, and their faces showed so little they might have been cast of bronze as well. They laid the corpse down at her feet. Ser Barristan pulled back the bloodstained shroud. Grey Worm lowered the torch, so she might see.

The dead man's face was smooth and hairless, though his cheeks had been slashed open ear to ear. He had been a tall man, blue-eyed and fair of face. *Some child of Lys or Old Volantis, snatched off a ship by corsairs and sold into bondage in red Astapor.* Though his eyes were open, it was his wounds that wept. There were more wounds than she could count.

"Your Grace," Ser Barristan said, "there was a harpy drawn on the bricks in the alley where he was found . . ."

" . . . drawn in blood." Daenerys knew the way of it by now. The Sons of the Harpy did their butchery by night, and over each kill they left their mark. "Grey Worm, why was this man alone? Had he no partner?" By her command, when the Unsullied walked the streets of Meereen by night they always walked in pairs.

"My queen," replied the captain, "your servant Stalwart Shield had no duty last night. He had gone to a . . . a certain place . . . to drink, and have companionship."

"A certain place? What do you mean?"

"A house of pleasure, Your Grace."

A brothel. Half of her freedmen were from Yunkai, where the Wise Masters had been famed for training bedslaves. *The way of the seven sighs.* Brothels had sprouted up like mushrooms all over Meereen. *It is all they know. They need to survive.* Food was more costly every day, whilst the price of flesh grew cheaper. In the poorer districts between the stepped pyramids of Meereen's slaver nobility, there were brothels catering to every conceivable erotic taste, she knew. *Even so . . .* "What could a eunuch hope to find in a brothel?"

"Even those who lack a man's parts may still have a man's heart, Your Grace," said Grey Worm. "This one has been told that your servant Stalwart Shield sometimes gave coin to the women of the brothels to lie with him and hold him."

The blood of the dragon does not weep. "Stalwart Shield," she said, dry-eyed. "That was his name?"

"If it please Your Grace."

"It is a fine name." The Good Masters of Astapor had not allowed their slave soldiers even names. Some of her Unsullied reclaimed their birth names after she had freed them; others chose new names for themselves. "Is it known how many attackers fell upon Stalwart Shield?"

"This one does not know. Many."

"Six or more," said Ser Barristan. "From the look of his wounds, they swarmed him from all sides. He was found with an empty scabbard. It may be that he wounded some of his attackers."

Dany said a silent prayer that somewhere one of the Harpy's Sons was dying even now, clutching at his belly and writhing in pain. "Why did they cut open his cheeks like that?"

"Gracious queen," said Grey Worm, "his killers had forced the genitals of a goat down the throat of your servant Stalwart Shield. This one removed them before bringing him here."

They could not feed him his own genitals. The Astapori left him neither root nor stem. "The Sons grow bolder," Dany observed. Until now, they had limited their attacks to unarmed freedmen, cutting them down in the streets or breaking into their homes under the cover of darkness to murder them in their beds. "This is the first of my soldiers they have slain."

"The first," Ser Barristan warned, "but not the last."

I am still at war, Dany realized, *only now I am fighting shadows.* She had hoped for a respite from the killing, for some time to build and heal.

Shrugging off the lion pelt, she knelt beside the corpse and closed the dead man's eyes, ignoring Jhiqui's gasp. "Stalwart Shield shall not be forgotten. Have him washed and dressed for battle and bury him with cap and shield and spears."

"It shall be as Your Grace commands," said Grey Worm.

"Send men to the Temple of the Graces and ask if any man has come to the Blue Graces with a sword wound. And spread the word that we will pay good gold for the short sword of Stalwart Shield. Inquire of the butchers and the herdsmen, and learn who has been gelding goats of late." Perhaps some goatherd would confess. "Henceforth, no man of mine walks alone after dark."

"These ones shall obey."

Daenerys pushed her hair back. "Find these cowards for me. Find them, so that I might teach the Harpy's Sons what it means to wake the dragon."

Grey Worm saluted her. His Unsullied closed the shroud once more, lifted the dead man onto their shoulders, and bore him from the hall. Ser Barristan Selmy remained behind. His hair was white, and there were crow's-feet at the corners of his pale blue eyes. Yet his back was still unbent, and the years had not yet robbed him of his skill at arms. "Your Grace," he said, "I fear your eunuchs are ill suited for the tasks you set them."

Dany settled on her bench and wrapped her pelt about her shoulders once again. "The Unsullied are my finest warriors."

"Soldiers, not warriors, if it please Your Grace. They were made for the battlefield, to stand shoulder to shoulder behind their shields with their spears thrust out before them. Their training teaches them to obey, fearlessly, perfectly, without thought or hesitation . . . not to unravel secrets or ask questions."

"Would knights serve me any better?" Selmy was training knights for her, teaching the sons of slaves to fight with lance and longsword in the Westerosi fashion . . . but what good would lances do against cowards who killed from the shadows?

"Not in this," the old man admitted. "And Your Grace has no knights, save me. It will be years before the boys are ready."

"Then who, if not Unsullied? Dothraki would be even worse." Dothraki fought from horseback. Mounted men were of more use in open fields and hills than in the narrow streets and alleys of the city. Beyond Meereen's walls of many-colored brick, Dany's rule was tenuous at best. Thousands of slaves still toiled on vast estates in the hills, growing wheat and olives, herding sheep and goats, and mining salt and copper. Meereen's storehouses held ample supplies of grain, oil, olives, dried fruit, and salted meat, but the stores were dwindling. So Dany had dispatched her tiny *khalasar* to subdue the hinterlands, under the command of her three bloodriders, whilst Brown Ben Plumm took his Second Sons south to guard against Yunkish incursions.

The most crucial task of all she had entrusted to Daario Naharis, glib-tongued Daario with his gold tooth and trident beard, smiling his wicked smile through purple whiskers. Beyond the eastern hills was a range of rounded sandstone mountains, the Khyzai Pass, and Lhazar. If Daario could convince the Lhazarene to reopen the overland trade routes, grains could be brought down the river or over the hills at need . . . but the Lamb Men had no reason to love Meereen. "When the Stormcrows return from Lhazar, perhaps I can use them in the streets," she told Ser Barristan, "but until then I have only the Unsullied." Dany rose. "You must excuse me, ser. The petitioners will soon be at my gates. I must don my floppy ears and become their queen again. Summon Reznak and the Shavepate, I'll see them when I'm dressed."

"As Your Grace commands." Selmy bowed.

The Great Pyramid shouldered eight hundred feet into the sky, from its huge square base to the lofty apex where the queen kept her private chambers, surrounded by greenery and fragrant pools. As a cool blue dawn broke over the city, Dany walked out onto the terrace. To the west sunlight blazed off the golden domes of the Temple of the Graces, and etched deep shadows behind the stepped pyramids of the mighty. *In some of those pyramids, the Sons of the Harpy are plotting new murders even now, and I am powerless to stop them.*

Viserion sensed her disquiet. The white dragon lay coiled around a pear tree, his head resting on his tail. When Dany passed his eyes came open, two pools of molten gold. His horns were gold as well, and the scales that ran down his back from head to tail. "You're lazy," she told him, scratching under his jaw. His scales were hot to the touch, like armor left too long in the sun. *Dragons are fire made flesh.* She had read that in one of the books Ser Jorah had given her as a wedding gift. "You should be hunting with your brothers. Have you and Drogon been fighting again?" Her dragons were growing wild of late. Rhaegal had snapped at Irri, and Viserion had set Reznak's *tokar* ablaze the last time the seneschal had called. *I have left them too much to themselves, but where am I to find the time for them?*

Viserion's tail lashed sideways, thumping the trunk of the tree so hard that a pear came tumbling down to land at Dany's feet. His wings unfolded, and he half flew, half hopped onto the parapet. *He grows,* she thought as he launched himself into the sky. *They are all three growing. Soon they will be large enough to bear my weight.* Then she would fly as Aegon the Conqueror had flown, up and up, until Meereen was so small that she could blot it out with her thumb.

She watched Viserion climb in widening circles until he was lost to sight beyond the muddy waters of the Skahazadhan. Only then did Dany go back inside the pyramid, where Irri and Jhiqui were waiting to brush the tangles from her hair and garb her as befit the Queen of Meereen, in a Ghiscari *tokar.*

The garment was a clumsy thing, a long loose shapeless sheet that had to be wound around her hips and under an arm and over a shoulder, its dangling fringes carefully layered and displayed. Wound too loose, it was like to fall off; wound too tight, it would tangle, trip, and bind. Even wound properly, the *tokar* required its wearer to hold it in place with the left hand. Walking in a *tokar* demanded small, mincing steps and exquisite balance, lest one tread upon those heavy trailing fringes. It was not a garment meant for any man who had to work. The *tokar* was a *master's* garment, a sign of wealth and power.

Dany had wanted to ban the *tokar* when she took Meereen, but her advisors had convinced her otherwise. "The Mother of Dragons must don the *tokar* or be forever hated," warned the Green Grace, Galazza Galare. "In the wools of Westeros or a gown of Myrish lace, Your Radiance shall forever remain a stranger amongst us, a grotesque outlander, a barbarian conqueror. Meereen's queen must be a lady of

Old Ghis." Brown Ben Plumm, the captain of the Second Sons, had put it more succinctly. "Man wants to be the king o' the rabbits, he best wear a pair o' floppy ears."

The floppy ears she chose today were made of sheer white linen, with a fringe of golden tassels. With Jhiqui's help, she wound the *tokar* about herself correctly on her third attempt. Irri fetched her crown, wrought in the shape of the three-headed dragon of her House. Its coils were gold, its wings silver, its three heads ivory, onyx, and jade. Dany's neck and shoulders would be stiff and sore from the weight of it before the day was done. *A crown should not sit easy on the head.* One of her royal forebears had said that, once. *Some Aegon, but which one?* Five Aegons had ruled the Seven Kingdoms of Westeros. There would have been a sixth, but the Usurper's dogs had murdered her brother's son when he was still a babe at the breast. *If he had lived, I might have married him. Aegon would have been closer to my age than Viserys.* Dany had only been conceived when Aegon and his sister were murdered. Their father, her brother Rhaegar, perished even earlier, slain by the Usurper on the Trident. Her brother Viserys had died screaming in Vaes Dothrak with a crown of molten gold upon his head. *They will kill me too if I allow it. The knives that slew my Stalwart Shield were meant for me.*

She had not forgotten the slave children the Great Masters had nailed up along the road from Yunkai. They had numbered one hundred sixty-three, a child every mile, nailed to mileposts with one arm outstretched to point her way. After Meereen had fallen, Dany had nailed up a like number of Great Masters. Swarms of flies had attended their slow dying, and the stench had lingered long in the plaza. Yet some days she feared that she had not gone far enough. These Meereenese were a sly and stubborn people who resisted her at every turn. They had freed their slaves, yes . . . only to hire them back as servants at wages so meagre that most could scarce afford to eat. Those too old or young to be of use had been cast into the streets, along with the infirm and the crippled. And still the Great Masters gathered atop their lofty pyramids to complain of how the dragon queen had filled their noble city with hordes of unwashed beggars, thieves, and whores.

To rule Meereen I must win the Meereenese, however much I may despise them. "I am ready," she told Irri.

Reznak and Skahaz waited atop the marble steps. "Great queen," declared Reznak mo Reznak, "you are so radiant today I fear to look on you." The seneschal wore a *tokar* of maroon silk with a golden fringe. A small, damp man, he smelled as if he had bathed in perfume and spoke a bastard form of High Valyrian, much corrupted and flavored with a thick Ghiscari growl.

"You are kind to say so," Dany answered, in the same tongue.

"My queen," growled Skahaz mo Kandaq, of the shaven head. Ghiscari hair was dense and wiry; it had long been the fashion for the men of the Slaver Cities to tease it into horns and spikes and wings. By shaving, Skahaz had put old Meereen behind him to accept the new, and his kin had done the same after his example. Others followed, though whether from fear, fashion, or ambition, Dany could not say; shavepates, they were called. Skahaz was *the* Shavepate . . . and the vilest of traitors to the Sons of the Harpy and their ilk. "We were told about the eunuch."

"His name was Stalwart Shield."

"More will die unless the murderers are punished." Even with his shaven scalp, Skahaz had an odious face—a beetled brow, small eyes with heavy bags beneath them, a big nose dark with blackheads, oily skin that looked more yellow than the usual amber of Ghiscari. It was a blunt, brutal, angry face. She could only pray it was an honest one as well.

"How can I punish them when I do not know who they are?" Dany demanded of him. "Tell me that, bold Skahaz."

"You have no lack of enemies, Your Grace. You can see their pyramids from your terrace. Zhak, Hazkar, Ghazeen, Merreq, Loraq, all the old slaving families. Pahl. Pahl, most of all. A house of women now. Bitter old women with a taste for blood. Women do not forget. Women do not forgive."

No, Dany thought, *and the Usurper's dogs will learn that, when I return to Westeros.* It was true that there was blood between her and the House of Pahl. Oznak zo Pahl had been cut down by Strong Belwas in single combat. His father, commander of Meereen's city watch, had died defending the gates when Joso's Cock smashed them into splinters. Three uncles had been among the hundred sixty-three on the plaza. "How much gold have we offered for information concerning the Sons of the Harpy?" Dany asked.

"One hundred honors, if it please Your Radiance."

"One thousand honors would please us more. Make it so."

"Your Grace has not asked for my counsel," said Skahaz Shavepate, "but I say that blood must pay for blood. Take one man from each of the families I have named and kill him. The next time one of yours is slain, take two from each great House and kill them both. There will not be a third murder."

Reznak squealed in distress. "Noooo . . . gentle queen, such savagery would bring down the ire of the gods. We will find the murderers, I promise you, and when we do they will prove to be baseborn filth, you shall see."

The seneschal was as bald as Skahaz, though in his case the gods were responsible. "Should any hair be so insolent as to appear, my barber stands with razor ready," he had assured her when she raised him up. There were times when Dany wondered if that razor might not be better saved for Reznak's throat. He was a useful man, but she liked him little and trusted him less. The Undying of Qarth had told her she would be thrice betrayed. Mirri Maz Duur had been the first, Ser Jorah the second. Would Reznak be the third? The Shavepate? Daario? *Or will it be someone I would never suspect, Ser Barristan or Grey Worm or Missandei?*

"Skahaz," she told the Shavepate, "I thank you for your counsel. Reznak, see what one thousand honors may accomplish." Clutching her *tokar*, Daenerys swept past them down the broad marble stair. She took one step at a time, lest she trip over her fringe and go tumbling headfirst into court.

Missandei announced her. The little scribe had a sweet, strong voice. "*All kneel for Daenerys Stormborn, the Unburnt, Queen of Meereen, Queen of the Andals and the Rhoynar and the First Men, Khaleesi of Great Grass Sea, Breaker of Shackles, and Mother of Dragons.*"

The hall had filled. Unsullied stood with their backs to the pillars, holding shields and spears, the spikes on their caps jutting upward like a row of knives. The Meereenese had gathered beneath the eastern windows. Her freedmen stood well apart from their former masters. *Until they stand together, Meereen will know no peace.* "Arise." Dany settled onto her bench. The hall rose. *That at least they do as one.*

Reznak mo Reznak had a list. Custom demanded that the queen begin with the Astapori envoy, a former slave who called himself Lord Ghael, though no one seemed to know what he was lord of.

Lord Ghael had a mouth of brown and rotten teeth and the pointed yellow face of a weasel. He also had a gift. "Cleon the Great sends these slippers as a token of his love for Daenerys Stormborn, the Mother of Dragons."

Irri slid the slippers onto Dany's feet. They were gilded leather, decorated with green freshwater pearls. *Does the butcher king believe a pair of pretty slippers will win my hand?* "King Cleon is most generous. You may thank him for his lovely gift." *Lovely, but made for a child.* Dany had small feet, yet the pointed slippers mashed her toes together.

"Great Cleon will be pleased to know they pleased you," said Lord Ghael. "His Magnificence bids me say that he stands ready to defend the Mother of Dragons from all her foes."

If he proposes again that I wed King Cleon, I'll throw a slipper at his head, Dany thought, but for once the Astapori envoy made no mention of a royal marriage. Instead he said, "The time has come for Astapor and Meereen to end the savage reign of the Wise Masters of Yunkai, who are sworn foes to all those who live in freedom. Great Cleon bids me tell you that he and his new Unsullied will soon march."

His new Unsullied are an obscene jape. "King Cleon would be wise to tend his own gardens and let the Yunkai'i tend theirs." It was not that Dany harbored any love for Yunkai. She was coming to regret leaving the Yellow City untaken after defeating its army in the field. The Wise Masters had returned to slaving as soon as she moved on, and were busy raising levies, hiring sellswords, and making alliances against her.

Cleon the self-styled Great was no better, however. The Butcher

King had restored slavery to Astapor, the only change being that the former slaves were now the masters and the former masters were now the slaves.

"I am only a young girl and know little of the ways of war," she told Lord Ghael, "but we have heard that Astapor is starving. Let King Cleon feed his people before he leads them out to battle." She made a gesture of dismissal. Ghael withdrew.

"Magnificence," prompted Reznak mo Reznak, "will you hear the noble Hizdahr zo Loraq?"

Again? Dany nodded, and Hizdahr strode forth; a tall man, very slender, with flawless amber skin. He bowed on the same spot where Stalwart Shield had lain in death not long before. *I need this man,* Dany reminded herself. Hizdahr was a wealthy merchant with many friends in Meereen, and more across the seas. He had visited Volantis, Lys, and Qarth, had kin in Tolos and Elyria, and was even said to wield some influence in New Ghis, where the Yunkai'i were trying to stir up enmity against Dany and her rule.

And he was rich. Famously and fabulously rich . . .

And like to grow richer, if I grant his petition. When Dany had closed the city's fighting pits, the value of pit shares had plummeted. Hizdahr zo Loraq had grabbed them up with both hands, and now owned most of the fighting pits in Meereen.

The nobleman had wings of wiry red-black hair sprouting from his temples. They made him look as if his head were about to take flight. His long face was made even longer by a beard bound with rings of gold. His purple *tokar* was fringed with amethysts and pearls. "Your Radiance will know the reason I am here."

"Why, it must be because you have no other purpose but to plague me. How many times have I refused you?"

"Five times, Your Magnificence."

"Six now. I will not have the fighting pits reopened."

"If Your Majesty will hear my arguments . . ."

"I have. Five times. Have you brought new arguments?"

"Old arguments," Hizdahr admitted, "new words. Lovely words, and courteous, more apt to move a queen."

"It is your cause I find wanting, not your courtesies. I have heard your arguments so often I could plead your case myself. Shall I?" Dany leaned forward. "The fighting pits have been a part of Meereen since the city was founded. The combats are profoundly religious in nature, a blood sacrifice to the gods of Ghis. The *mortal art* of Ghis is not mere butchery but a display of courage, skill, and strength most pleasing to your gods. Victorious fighters are pampered and acclaimed, and the slain are honored and remembered. By reopening the pits I would show the people of Meereen that I respect their ways and customs. The pits are far-famed across the world. They draw trade to Meereen, and fill the city's coffers with coin from the ends of the earth. All men share a taste for blood, a taste the pits help slake. In that way they make Meereen more tranquil. For criminals condemned to die upon the sands, the pits represent a judgment by battle, a last chance for a man to prove his innocence." She leaned back again, with a toss of her head. "There. How have I done?"

"Your Radiance has stated the case much better than I could have hoped to do myself. I see that you are eloquent as well as beautiful. I am quite persuaded."

She had to laugh. "Ah, but I am not."

"Your Magnificence," whispered Reznak mo Reznak in her ear, "it is customary for the city to claim one-tenth of all the profits from the fighting pits, after expenses, as a tax. That coin might be put to many noble uses."

"It might . . . though if we *were* to reopen the pits, we should take our tenth *before* expenses. I am only a young girl and know little of such matters, but I dwelt with Xaro Xhoan Daxos long enough to learn that much. Hizdahr, if you could marshal armies as you marshal arguments, you could conquer the world . . . but my answer is still *no*. For the sixth time."

"The queen has spoken." He bowed again, as deeply as before. His pearls and amethysts clattered softly against the marble floor. A very limber man was Hizdahr zo Loraq.

He might be handsome, but for that silly hair. Reznak and the Green Grace had been urging Dany to take a Meereenese noble for her husband, to reconcile the city to her rule. Hizdahr zo Loraq might be worth a careful look. *Sooner him than Skahaz.* The Shavepate had offered to set aside his wife for her, but the notion made her shudder. Hizdahr at least knew how to smile.

"Magnificence," said Reznak, consulting his list, "the noble Grazdan zo Galare would address you. Will you hear him?"

"It would be my pleasure," said Dany, admiring the glimmer of the gold and the sheen of the green pearls on Cleon's slippers while doing her best to ignore the pinching in her toes. Grazdan, she had been forewarned, was a cousin of the Green Grace, whose support she had found invaluable. The priestess was a voice for peace, acceptance, and obedience to lawful authority. *I can give her cousin a respectful hearing, whatever he desires.*

What he desired turned out to be gold. Dany had refused to compensate any of the Great Masters for the value of their slaves, but the Meereenese kept devising other ways to squeeze coin from her. The noble Grazdan had once owned a slave woman who was a very fine weaver, it seemed; the fruits of her loom were greatly valued, not only in Meereen, but in New Ghis and Astapor and Qarth. When this woman had grown old, Grazdan had purchased half a dozen young girls and commanded the crone to instruct them in the secrets of her craft. The old woman was dead now. The young ones, freed, had opened a shop by the harbor wall to sell their weavings. Grazdan zo Galare asked that he be granted a portion of their earnings. "They owe their skill to me," he insisted. "I plucked them from the auction bloc and gave them to the loom."

Dany listened quietly, her face still. When he was done, she said, "What was the name of the old weaver?"

"The slave?" Grazdan shifted his weight, frowning. "She was . . . Elza, it might have been. Or Ella. It was six years ago she died. I have owned so many slaves, Your Grace."

"Let us say Elza. Here is our ruling. From the girls, you shall have nothing. It was Elza who taught them weaving, not you. From you, the girls shall have a new loom, the finest coin can buy. That is for forgetting the name of the old woman."

Reznak would have summoned another *tokar* next, but Dany insisted that he call upon a freedman. Thereafter she alternated between the former masters and the former slaves. Many and more of the matters brought before her involved redress. Meereen had been sacked savagely after its fall. The stepped pyramids of the mighty had been spared the worst of the ravages, but the humbler parts of the city had been given over to an orgy of looting and killing as the city's slaves rose up and the starving hordes who had followed her from Yunkai and Astapor poured through the broken gates. Her Unsullied had finally restored order, but the sack left a plague of problems in its wake. And so they came to see the queen.

A rich woman came, whose husband and sons had died defending the city walls. During the sack she had fled to her brother in fear. When she returned, she found her house had been turned into a brothel. The whores had bedecked themselves in her jewels and clothes. She wanted her house back, and her jewels. "They can keep the clothes," she allowed. Dany granted her the jewels but ruled the house was lost when she abandoned it.

A former slave came, to accuse a certain noble of the Zhak. The man had recently taken to wife a freedwoman who had been the noble's bedwarmer before the city fell. The noble had taken her maidenhood, used her for his pleasure, and gotten her with child. Her new husband wanted the noble gelded for the crime of rape, and he wanted a purse of gold as well, to pay him for raising the noble's bastard as his own. Dany granted him the gold, but not the gelding. "When he lay with her, your wife was his property, to do with as he would. By law, there was no rape." Her decision did not please him, she could see, but if she gelded every man who ever forced a bedslave, she would soon rule a city of eunuchs.

A boy came, younger than Dany, slight and scarred, dressed up in a frayed grey *tokar* trailing silver fringe. His voice broke when he told of how two of his father's household slaves had risen up the night the gate broke. One had slain his father, the other his elder brother. Both had raped his mother before killing her as well. The boy had escaped with no more than the scar upon his face, but one of the murderers was still living in his father's house, and the other had joined the queen's soldiers as one of the Mother's Men. He wanted them both hanged.

I am queen over a city built on dust and death. Dany had no choice but to deny him. She had declared a blanket pardon for all crimes committed during the sack. Nor would she punish slaves for rising up against their masters.

When she told him, the boy rushed at her, but his feet tangled in his *tokar* and he went sprawling headlong on the purple marble. Strong Belwas was on him at once. The huge brown eunuch yanked him up one-handed and shook him like a mastiff with a rat. "Enough, Belwas," Dany called. "Release him." To the boy she said, "Treasure that *tokar,* for it saved your life. You are only a boy, so we will forget what happened here. You should do the same." But as he left the boy looked back over his shoulder, and when she saw his eyes Dany thought, *The Harpy has another Son.*

By midday Daenerys was feeling the weight of the crown upon her head, and the hardness of the bench beneath her. With so many still waiting on her pleasure, she did not stop to eat. Instead she dispatched Jhiqui to the kitchens for a platter of flatbread, olives, figs, and cheese. She nibbled whilst she listened, and sipped from a cup of watered wine. The figs were fine, the olives even finer, but the wine left a tart metallic aftertaste in her mouth. The small pale yellow grapes native to these regions produced a notably inferior vintage. *We shall have no trade in wine.* Besides, the Great Masters had burned the best arbors along with the olive trees.

In the afternoon a sculptor came, proposing to replace the head of the great bronze harpy in the Plaza of Purification with one cast in Dany's image. She denied him with as much courtesy as she could muster. A pike of unprecedented size had been caught in the Skahazadhan, and the fisherman wished to give it to the queen. She admired the fish extravagantly, rewarded the fisherman with a purse of silver, and sent the pike to her kitchens. A coppersmith had fashioned her a suit of burnished rings to wear to war. She accepted it with fulsome thanks; it was lovely to behold, and all that burnished copper would flash prettily in the sun, though if actual battle threatened, she would sooner be clad in steel. Even a young girl who knew nothing of the ways of war knew *that.*

The slippers the Butcher King had sent her had grown too

uncomfortable. Dany kicked them off and sat with one foot tucked beneath her and the other swinging back and forth. It was not a very regal pose, but she was tired of being regal. The crown had given her a headache, and her buttocks had gone to sleep. "Ser Barristan," she called, "I know what quality a king needs most."

"Courage, Your Grace?"

"Cheeks like iron," she teased. "All I do is sit."

"Your Grace takes too much on herself. You should allow your councillors to shoulder more of your burdens."

"I have too many councillors and too few cushions." Dany turned to Reznak. "How many more?"

"Three-and-twenty, if it please Your Magnificence. With as many claims." The seneschal consulted some papers. "One calf and three goats. The rest will be sheep or lambs, no doubt."

"Three-and-twenty." Dany sighed. "My dragons have developed a prodigious taste for mutton since we began to pay the shepherds for their kills. Have these claims been proven?"

"Some men have brought burnt bones."

"Men make fires. Men cook mutton. Burnt bones prove nothing. Brown Ben says there are red wolves in the hills outside the city, and jackals and wild dogs. Must we pay good silver for every lamb that goes astray between Yunkai and the Skahazadhan?"

"No, Magnificence." Reznak bowed. "Shall I send these rascals away, or will you want them scourged?"

Daenerys shifted on the bench. "No man should ever fear to come to me." Some claims were false, she did not doubt, but more were genuine. Her dragons had grown too large to be content with rats and cats and dogs. *The more they eat, the larger they will grow,* Ser Barristan had warned her, *and the larger they grow, the more they'll eat.* Drogon especially ranged far afield and could easily devour a sheep a day. "Pay them for the value of their animals," she told Reznak, "but henceforth claimants must present themselves at the Temple of the Graces and swear a holy oath before the gods of Ghis."

"It shall be done." Reznak turned to the petitioners. "Her Magnificence the Queen has consented to compensate each of you for the animals you have lost," he told them in the Ghiscari tongue. "Present yourselves to my factors on the morrow, and you shall be paid in coin or kind, as you prefer."

The pronouncement was received in sullen silence. *You would think they might be happier,* Dany thought. *They have what they came for. Is there no way to please these people?*

One man lingered behind as the rest were filing out—a squat man with a windburnt face, shabbily dressed. His hair was a cap of coarse red-black wire cropped about his ears, and in one hand he held a sad cloth sack. He stood with his head down, gazing at the marble floor as if he had quite forgotten where he was. *And what does this one want?* Dany wondered.

"*All kneel for Daenerys Stormborn, the Unburnt, Queen of Meereen, Queen of the Andals and the Rhoynar and the First Men,* Khaleesi *of Great Grass Sea, Breaker of Shackles, and Mother of Dragons,*" cried Missandei in her high, sweet voice.

As Dany stood, her *tokar* began to slip. She caught it and tugged it back in place. "You with the sack," she called, "did you wish to speak with us? You may approach."

When he raised his head, his eyes were red and raw as open sores. Dany glimpsed Ser Barristan sliding closer, a white shadow at her side. The man approached in a stumbling shuffle, one step and then another, clutching his sack. *Is he drunk, or ill?* she wondered. There was dirt beneath his cracked yellow fingernails.

"What is it?" Dany asked. "Do you have some grievance to lay before us, some petition? What would you have of us?"

His tongue flicked nervously over chapped, cracked lips. "I . . . I brought . . ."

"Bones?" she said, impatiently. "Burnt bones?"

He lifted the sack, and spilled its contents on the marble.

Bones they were, broken bones and blackened. The longer ones had been cracked open for their marrow.

"It were the black one," the man said, in a Ghiscari growl, "the winged shadow. He come down from the sky and . . . and . . ."

No. Dany shivered. *No, no, oh no.*

"Are you deaf, fool?" Reznak mo Reznak demanded of the man.

"Did you not hear my pronouncement? See my factors on the morrow, and you shall be paid for your sheep."

"Reznak," Ser Barristan said quietly, "hold your tongue and open your eyes. Those are no sheep bones."

No, Dany thought, *those are the bones of a child.*

JON

The white wolf raced through a black wood, beneath a pale cliff as tall as the sky. The moon ran with him, slipping through a tangle of bare branches overhead, across the starry sky.

"Snow," the moon murmured. The wolf made no answer. Snow crunched beneath his paws. The wind sighed through the trees.

Far off, he could hear his packmates calling to him, like to like. They were hunting too. A wild rain lashed down upon his black brother as he tore at the flesh of an enormous goat, washing the blood from his side where the goat's long horn had raked him. In another place, his little sister lifted her head to sing to the moon, and a hundred small grey cousins broke off their hunt to sing with her. The hills were warmer where they were, and full of food. Many a night his sister's pack gorged on the flesh of sheep and cows and horses, the prey of men, and sometimes even on the flesh of man himself.

"Snow," the moon called down again, cackling. The white wolf padded along the man trail beneath the icy cliff. The taste of blood was on his tongue, and his ears rang to the song of the hundred cousins. Once they had been six, five whimpering blind in the snow beside their dead mother, sucking cool milk from her hard dead nipples whilst he crawled off alone. Four remained . . . and one the white wolf could no longer sense.

"Snow," the moon insisted.

The white wolf ran from it, racing toward the cave of night where the sun had hidden, his breath frosting in the air. On starless nights the great cliff was as black as stone, a darkness towering high above the wide world, but when the moon came out it shimmered pale and icy as a frozen stream. The wolf's pelt was thick and shaggy, but when the wind blew along the ice no fur could keep the chill out. On the other side the wind was colder still, the wolf sensed. That was where his brother was, the grey brother who smelled of summer.

"Snow." An icicle tumbled from a branch. The white wolf turned and bared his teeth. "*Snow!*" His fur rose bristling, as the woods dissolved around him. "*Snow, snow, snow!*" He heard the beat of wings. Through the gloom a raven flew.

It landed on Jon Snow's chest with a *thump* and a scrabbling of claws. "*SNOW!*" it screamed into his face.

"I hear you." The room was dim, his pallet hard. Grey light leaked through the shutters, promising another bleak cold day. "Is this how you woke Mormont? Get your feathers out of my face." Jon wriggled an arm out from under his blankets to shoo the raven off. It was a big bird, old and bold and scruffy, utterly without fear. "*Snow,*" it cried, flapping to his bedpost. "*Snow, snow.*" Jon filled his fist with a pillow and let fly, but the bird took to the air. The pillow struck the wall and burst, scattering stuffing everywhere just as Dolorous Edd Tollett poked his head through the door. "Beg pardon," he said, ignoring the flurry of feathers, "shall I fetch m'lord some breakfast?"

"*Corn,*" cried the raven. "*Corn, corn.*"

"Roast raven," Jon suggested. "And half a pint of ale." Having a steward fetch and serve for him still felt strange; not long ago, it would have been him fetching breakfast for Lord Commander Mormont.

"Three corns and one roast raven," said Dolorous Edd. "Very good, m'lord, only Hobb's made boiled eggs, black sausage, and apples stewed with prunes. The apples stewed with prunes are excellent, except for the prunes. I won't eat prunes myself. Well, there was one time when Hobb chopped them up with chestnuts and carrots and hid them in a hen. Never trust a cook, my lord. They'll prune you when you least expect it."

"Later." Breakfast could wait; Stannis could not. "Any trouble from the stockades last night?"

"Not since you put guards on the guards, m'lord."

"Good." A thousand wildlings had been penned up beyond the Wall, the captives Stannis Baratheon had taken when his knights had smashed Mance Rayder's patchwork host. Many of the prisoners were women, and some of the guards had been sneaking them out to warm their beds. King's men, queen's men, it did not seem to matter; a few black brothers had tried the same thing. Men were men, and these were the only women for a thousand leagues.

"Two more wildlings turned up to surrender," Edd went on. "A mother with a girl clinging to her skirts. She had a boy babe too, all swaddled up in fur, but he was dead."

"*Dead*," said the raven. It was one of the bird's favorite words. "*Dead, dead, dead.*"

They had free folk drifting in most every night, starved half-frozen creatures who had run from the battle beneath the Wall only to crawl back when they realized there was no safe place to run to. "Was the mother questioned?" Jon asked. Stannis Baratheon had smashed Mance Rayder's host and made the King-Beyond-the-Wall his captive . . . but the wildlings were still out there, the Weeper and Tormund Giantsbane and thousands more.

"Aye, m'lord," said Edd, "but all she knows is that she ran off during the battle and hid in the woods after. We filled her full of porridge, sent her to the pens, and burned the babe."

Burning dead children had ceased to trouble Jon Snow; live ones were another matter. *Two kings to wake the dragon. The father first and then the son, so both die kings.* The words had been murmured by one of the queen's men as Maester Aemon had cleaned his wounds. Jon had tried to dismiss them as his fever talking. Aemon had demurred. "There is power in a king's blood," the old maester had warned, "and better men than Stannis have done worse things than this." *The king can be harsh and unforgiving, aye, but a babe still on the breast? Only a monster would give a living child to the flames.*

Jon pissed in darkness, filling his chamber pot as the Old Bear's raven muttered complaints. The wolf dreams had been growing stronger, and he found himself remembering them even when awake. *Ghost knows that Grey Wind is dead.* Robb had died at the Twins, betrayed by men he'd believed his friends, and his wolf had perished with him. Bran and Rickon had been murdered too, beheaded at the behest of Theon Greyjoy, who had once been their lord father's ward . . . but if dreams did not lie, their direwolves had escaped. At Queenscrown, one had come out of the darkness to save Jon's life. *Summer, it had to be. His fur was grey, and Shaggydog is black.* He wondered if some part of his dead brothers lived on inside their wolves.

He filled his basin from the flagon of water beside his bed, washed his face and hands, donned a clean set of black woolens, laced up a black leather jerkin, and pulled on a pair of well-worn boots. Mormont's raven watched with shrewd black eyes, then fluttered to the window. "Do you take me for your thrall?" When Jon folded back the window with its thick diamond-shaped panes of yellow glass, the chill of the morning hit him in the face. He took a breath to clear away the cobwebs of the night as the raven flapped away. *That bird is too clever by half.* It had been the Old Bear's companion for long years, but that had not stopped it from eating Mormont's face once he died.

Outside his bedchamber a flight of steps descended to a larger room furnished with a scarred pinewood table and a dozen oak-and-leather chairs. With Stannis in the King's Tower and the Lord Commander's Tower burned to a shell, Jon had established himself in Donal Noye's modest rooms behind the armory. In time, no doubt, he would need larger quarters, but for the moment these would serve whilst he accustomed himself to command.

The grant that the king had presented him for signature was on the table beneath a silver drinking cup that had once been Donal Noye's. The one-armed smith had left few personal effects: the cup, six pennies and a copper star, a niello brooch with a broken clasp, a musty brocade doublet that bore the stag of Storm's End. *His treasures were his tools, and the swords and knives he made. His life was at the forge.* Jon moved the cup aside and read the parchment once again.

If I put my seal to this, I will forever be remembered as the lord commander who gave away the Wall, he thought, *but if I should refuse . . .*

Stannis Baratheon was proving to be a prickly guest, and a restless one. He had ridden down the kingsroad almost as far as Queenscrown, prowled through the empty hovels of Mole's Town, inspected the ruined forts at Queensgate and Oakenshield. Each night he walked atop the Wall with Lady Melisandre, and during the days he visited the stockades, picking captives out for the red woman to question. *He does not like to be balked.* This would not be a pleasant morning, Jon feared.

From the armory came a clatter of shields and swords, as the latest lot of boys and raw recruits armed themselves. He could hear the voice of Iron Emmett telling them to be quick about it. Cotter Pyke had not been pleased to lose him, but the young ranger had a gift for training men. *He loves to fight, and he'll teach his boys to love it too.* Or so he hoped.

Jon's cloak hung on a peg by the door, his sword belt on another. He donned them both and made his way to the armory. The rug where Ghost slept was empty, he saw. Two guardsmen stood inside the doors, clad in black cloaks and iron halfhelms, spears in their hands. "Will m'lord be wanting a tail?" asked Garse.

"I think I can find the King's Tower by myself." Jon hated having guards trailing after him everywhere he went. It made him feel like a mother duck leading a procession of ducklings.

Iron Emmett's lads were well at it in the yard, blunted swords slamming into shields and ringing against one another. Jon stopped to watch a moment as Horse pressed Hop-Robin back toward the well. Horse had the makings of a good fighter, he decided. He was strong and getting stronger, and his instincts were sound. Hop-Robin was another tale. His clubfoot was bad enough, but he was afraid of getting hit as well. *Perhaps we can make a steward of him.* The fight ended abruptly, with Hop-Robin on the ground.

"Well fought," Jon said to Horse, "but you drop your shield too low when pressing an attack. You will want to correct that, or it is like to get you killed."

"Yes, m'lord. I'll keep it higher next time." Horse pulled Hop-Robin to his feet, and the smaller boy made a clumsy bow.

A few of Stannis's knights were sparring on the far side of the yard. *King's men in one corner and queen's men in another,* Jon did not fail to note, *but only a few. It's too cold for most of them.* As he strode past them, a booming voice called after him. "BOY! YOU THERE! *BOY!*"

Boy was not the worst of the things that Jon Snow had been called since being chosen lord commander. He ignored it.

"*Snow,*" the voice insisted, "*Lord Commander.*"

This time he stopped. "Ser?"

The knight overtopped him by six inches. "A man who bears Valyrian steel should use it for more than scratching his arse."

Jon had seen this one about the castle—a knight of great renown, to hear him tell it. During the battle beneath the Wall, Ser Godry Farring had slain a fleeing giant, pounding after him on horseback and driving a lance through his back, then dismounting to hack off the creature's pitiful small head. The queen's men had taken to calling him Godry the Giantslayer.

Jon remembered Ygritte, crying. *I am the last of the giants.* "I use Longclaw when I must, ser."

"How well, though?" Ser Godry drew his own blade. "Show us. I promise not to hurt you, lad."

How kind of you. "Some other time, ser. I fear that I have other duties just now."

"You fear. I see that." Ser Godry grinned at his friends. "He fears," he repeated, for the slow ones.

"You will excuse me." Jon showed them his back.

Castle Black seemed a bleak and forlorn place in the pale dawn light. *My command,* Jon Snow reflected ruefully, *as much a ruin as it is a stronghold.* The Lord Commander's Tower was a shell, the Common Hall a pile of blackened timbers, and Hardin's Tower looked as if the next gust of wind would knock it over . . . though it had looked that way for years. Behind them rose the Wall: immense, forbidding, frigid, acrawl with builders pushing up a new switchback stair to join the remnants of the old. They worked from dawn to dusk. Without the stair, there was no way to reach the top of the Wall save by winch. That would not serve if the wildlings should attack again.

Above the King's Tower the great golden battle standard of House Baratheon cracked like a whip from the roof where Jon Snow had prowled with bow in hand not long ago, slaying Thenns and free folk beside Satin and Deaf Dick Follard. Two queen's men stood shivering on the steps, their hands tucked up into their armpits and their spears leaning against the door. "Those cloth gloves will never serve," Jon told them. "See Bowen Marsh on the morrow, and he'll give you each a pair of leather gloves lined with fur."

"We will, m'lord, and thank you," said the older guard.

"That's if our bloody hands aren't froze off," the younger added, his breath a pale mist. "I used to think that it got cold up in the Dornish Marches. What did I know?"

Nothing, thought Jon Snow, *the same as me.*

Halfway up the winding steps, he came upon Samwell Tarly, headed down. "Are you coming from the king?" Jon asked him.

"Maester Aemon sent me with a letter."

"I see." Some lords trusted their maesters to read their letters and convey the contents, but Stannis insisted on breaking the seals himself. "How did Stannis take it?"

"Not happily, by his face." Sam dropped his voice to a whisper. "I am not supposed to speak of it."

"Then don't." Jon wondered which of his father's bannermen had refused King Stannis homage this time. *He was quick enough to spread the word when Karhold declared for him.* "How are you and your longbow getting on?"

"I found a good book about archery." Sam frowned. "Doing it is harder than reading about it, though. I get blisters."

"Keep at it. We may need your bow on the Wall if the Others turn up some dark night."

"Oh, I hope not."

More guards stood outside the king's solar. "No arms are allowed in His Grace's presence, my lord," their serjeant said. "I'll need that sword. Your knives as well." It would do no good to protest, Jon knew. He handed them his weaponry.

Within the solar the air was warm. Lady Melisandre was seated near the fire, her ruby glimmering against the pale skin of her throat. Ygritte had been kissed by fire; the red priestess *was* fire, and her hair was blood and flame. Stannis stood behind the rough-hewn table where the Old Bear had once been wont to sit and take his meals. Covering the table was a large map of the north, painted on a ragged piece of hide. A tallow candle weighed down one end of it, a steel gauntlet the other.

The king wore lambswool breeches and a quilted doublet, yet somehow he looked as stiff and uncomfortable as if he had been clad in plate and mail. His skin was pale leather, his beard cropped so short that it might have been painted on. A fringe about his temples was all that remained of his black hair. In his hand was a parchment with a broken seal of dark green wax.

Jon took a knee. The king frowned at him, and rattled the parchment angrily. "Rise. Tell me, who is *Lyanna Mormont*?"

"One of Lady Maege's daughters, Sire. The youngest. She was named for my lord father's sister."

"To curry your lord father's favor, I don't doubt. I know how that game is played. How old is this wretched girl child?"

Jon had to think a moment. "Ten. Or near enough to make no matter. Might I know how she has offended Your Grace?"

Stannis read from the letter. "*Bear Island knows no king but the King in the North, whose name is STARK.* A girl of ten, you say, and she presumes to scold her lawful king." His close-cropped beard lay like a shadow over his hollow cheeks. "See that you keep these tidings to yourself, Lord Snow. Karhold is with me, that is all the men need know. I will not have your brothers trading tales of how this child spat on me."

"As you command, Sire." Maege Mormont had ridden south with Robb, Jon knew. Her eldest daughter had joined the Young Wolf's host as well. Even if both of them had died, however, Lady Maege had other daughters, some with children of their own. Had they gone with Robb as well? Surely Lady Maege would have left at least one of the older girls behind as castellan. He did not understand why Lyanna should be writing Stannis, and could not help but wonder if the girl's answer might have been different if the letter had been sealed with a direwolf instead of a crowned stag, and signed by Jon Stark, Lord of Winterfell. *It is too late for such misgivings. You made your choice.*

"Two score ravens were sent out," the king complained, "yet we get no response but silence and defiance. Homage is the duty every leal subject owes his king. Yet your father's bannermen all turn their back on me, save the Karstarks. Is Arnolf Karstark the only man of honor in the north?"

Arnolf Karstark was the late Lord Rickard's uncle. He had been made the castellan of Karhold when his nephew and his sons went south with Robb, and he had been the first to respond to King Stannis's call for homage, with a raven declaring his allegiance. *The Karstarks have no other choice,* Jon might have said. Rickard Karstark had betrayed the direwolf and spilled the blood of lions. The stag was Karhold's only hope. "In times as confused as these, even men of honor must wonder where their duty lies. Your Grace is not the only king in the realm demanding homage."

Lady Melisandre stirred. "Tell me, Lord Snow . . . where were these other kings when the wild people stormed your Wall?"

"A thousand leagues away and deaf to our need," Jon replied. "I have not forgotten that, my lady. Nor will I. But my father's bannermen have wives and children to protect, and smallfolk who will die should they choose wrongly. His Grace asks much of them. Give them time, and you will have your answers."

"Answers such as this?" Stannis crushed Lyanna's letter in his fist.

"Even in the north men fear the wroth of Tywin Lannister. Boltons make bad enemies as well. It is not happenstance that put a flayed man on their banners. They north rode with Robb, bled with him, died for him. They have supped on grief and death, and now you come to offer them another serving. Do you blame them if they hang back? Forgive me, Your Grace, but some will look at you and see only another doomed pretender."

"If His Grace is doomed, your realm is doomed as well," said Lady Melisandre. "Remember that, Lord Snow. It is the one true king of Westeros who stands before you."

Jon kept his face a mask. "As you say, my lady."

Stannis snorted. "You spend your words as if every one were a golden dragon. I wonder, how much gold do you have laid by?"

"Gold?" *Are those the dragons the red woman means to wake? Dragons made of gold?* "Such taxes as we collect are paid in kind, Your Grace. The Watch is rich in turnips but poor in coin."

"Turnips are not like to appease Salladhor Saan. I require gold or silver."

"For that, you need White Harbor. The city cannot compare to Oldtown or King's Landing, but it is still a thriving port. Lord Manderly is the richest of my lord father's bannermen."

"Lord Too-Fat-to-Sit-a-Horse." The letter that Lord Wyman Manderly had sent back from White Harbor had spoken of his age and infirmity, and little more. Stannis had commanded Jon not to speak of that one either.

"Perhaps his lordship would fancy a wildling wife," said Lady Melisandre. "Is this fat man married, Lord Snow?"

"His lady wife is long dead. Lord Wyman has two grown sons, and grandchildren by the elder. And he *is* too fat to sit a horse, thirty stone at least. Val would never have him."

"Just once you might try to give me an answer that would please me, Lord Snow," the king grumbled.

"I would hope the truth would please you, Sire. Your men call Val a princess, but to the free folk she is only the sister of their king's dead wife. If you force her to marry a man she does not want, she is like to slit his throat on their wedding night. Even if she accepts her husband, that does not mean the wildlings will follow him, or you. The only man who can bind them to your cause is Mance Rayder."

"I know that," Stannis said, unhappily. "I have spent hours speaking with the man. He knows much and more of our true enemy, and there is cunning in him, I'll grant you. Even if he were to renounce his kingship, though, the man remains an oathbreaker. Suffer one deserter to live, and you encourage others to desert. No. Laws should be made of iron, not of pudding. Mance Rayder's life is forfeit by every law of the Seven Kingdoms."

"The law ends at the Wall, Your Grace. You could make good use of Mance."

"I mean to. I'll *burn* him, and the north will see how I deal with turncloaks and traitors. I have other men to lead the wildlings. And I have Rayder's son, do not forget. Once the father dies, his whelp will be the King-Beyond-the-Wall."

"Your Grace is mistaken." *You know nothing, Jon Snow,* Ygritte used to say, but he had learned. "The babe is no more a prince than Val is a princess. You do not become King-Beyond-the-Wall because your father was."

"Good," said Stannis, "for I will suffer no other kings in Westeros. Have you signed the grant?"

"No, Your Grace." *And now it comes.* Jon closed his burned fingers and opened them again. "You ask too much."

"*Ask?* I *asked* you to be Lord of Winterfell and Warden of the North. I *require* these castles."

"We have ceded you the Nightfort."

"Rats and ruins. It is a niggard's gift that costs the giver nothing. Your own man Yarwyck says it will be half a year before the castle can be made fit for habitation."

"The other forts are no better."

"I know that. It makes no matter. They are all we have. There are nineteen forts along the Wall, and you have men in only three of them. I mean to have every one of them garrisoned again before the year is out."

"I have no quarrel with that, Sire, but it is being said that you also mean to grant these castles to your knights and lords, to hold as their own seats as vassals to Your Grace."

"Kings are expected to be open-handed to their followers. Did Lord Eddard teach his bastard nothing? Many of my knights and lords abandoned rich lands and stout castles in the south. Should their loyalty go unrewarded?"

"If Your Grace wishes to lose all of my lord father's bannermen, there is no more certain way than by giving northern halls to southron lords."

"How can I lose men I do not have? I had hoped to bestow Winterfell on a northman, you may recall. A son of Eddard Stark. He threw my offer in my face." Stannis Baratheon with a grievance was like a mastiff with a bone; he gnawed it down to splinters.

"By right Winterfell should go to my sister Sansa."

"Lady Lannister, you mean? Are you so eager to see the Imp perched on your father's seat? I promise you, that will not happen whilst I live, Lord Snow."

Jon knew better than to press the point. "Sire, some claim that you mean to grant lands and castles to Rattleshirt and the Magnar of Thenn."

"Who told you that?"

The talk was all over Castle Black. "If you must know, I had the tale from Gilly."

"Who is *Gilly*?"

"The wet nurse," said Lady Melisandre. "Your Grace gave her freedom of the castle."

"Not for running tales. She's wanted for her teats, not for her tongue. I'll have more milk from her, and fewer *messages.*"

"Castle Black needs no useless mouths," Jon agreed. "I am sending Gilly south on the next ship out of Eastwatch."

Melisandre touched the ruby at her neck. "Gilly is giving suck to Dalla's son as well as her own. It seems cruel of you to part our little prince from his milk brother, my lord."

Careful now, careful. "Mother's milk is all they share. Gilly's son is larger and more robust. He kicks the prince and pinches him, and shoves him from the breast. Craster was his father, a cruel man and greedy, and blood tells."

The king was confused. "I thought the wet nurse was this man Craster's *daughter*?"

"Wife and daughter both, Your Grace. Craster married all his daughters. Gilly's boy was the fruit of their union."

"Her own *father* got this child on her?" Stannis sounded shocked. "We are well rid of her, then. I will not suffer such abominations here. This is not King's Landing."

"I can find another wet nurse. If there's none amongst the wildlings, I will send to the mountain clans. Until such time, goat's milk should suffice for the boy, if it please Your Grace."

"Poor fare for a prince . . . but better than whore's milk, aye." Stannis drummed his fingers on the map. "If we may return to the matter of these forts . . ."

"Your Grace," said Jon, with chilly courtesy, "I have housed your men and fed them, at dire cost to our winter stores. I have clothed them so they would not freeze."

Stannis was not appeased. "Aye, you've shared your salt pork and porridge, and you've thrown us some black rags to keep us warm. Rags the wildlings would have taken off your corpses if I had not come north."

Jon ignored that. "I have given you fodder for your horses, and once the stair is done I will lend you builders to restore the Nightfort. I have even agreed to allow you to settle wildlings on the Gift, which was given to the Night's Watch in perpetuity."

"You offer me empty lands and desolations, yet deny me the castles I require to reward my lords and bannermen."

"The Night's Watch built those castles . . ."

"And the Night's Watch abandoned them."

" . . . to defend the Wall," Jon finished stubbornly, "not as seats for southron lords. The stones of those forts are mortared with the blood and bones of my brothers, long dead. I cannot give them to you."

"Cannot or will not?" The cords in the king's neck stood out sharp as swords. "I offered you a name."

"I have a name, Your Grace."

"Snow. Was ever a name more ill-omened?" Stannis touched his sword hilt. "Just who do you imagine that you are?"

"The watcher on the walls. The sword in the darkness."

"Don't prate your words at me." Stannis drew the blade he called Lightbringer. "*Here* is your sword in the darkness." Light rippled up and down the blade, now red, now yellow, now orange, painting the king's face in harsh, bright hues. "Even a green boy should be able to see that. Are you blind?"

"No, Sire. I agree these castles must be garrisoned—"

"The boy commander agrees. How fortunate."

"—by the Night's Watch."

"You do not have the men."

"Then give me men, Sire. I will provide officers for each of the abandoned forts, seasoned commanders who know the Wall and the lands beyond, and how best to survive the coming winter. In return for all we've given you, grant me the men to fill out the garrisons. Men-at-arms, crossbowmen, raw boys. I will even take your wounded and infirm."

Stannis stared at him incredulously, then gave a bark of laughter. "You are bold enough, Snow, I grant you that, but you're mad if you think my men will take the black."

"They can wear any color cloak they choose, so long as they obey my officers as they would your own."

The king was unmoved. "I have knights and lords in my service, scions of noble Houses old in honor. They cannot be expected to serve under poachers, peasants, and murderers."

Or bastards, Sire? "Your own Hand is a smuggler."

"*Was* a smuggler. I shortened his fingers for that. They tell me that you are the nine-hundred-ninety-eighth man to command the Night's Watch, Lord Snow. What do you think the nine-hundred-ninety-ninth might say about these castles? The sight of your head on a spike might inspire him to be more helpful." The king laid his bright blade down on the map, along the Wall, its steel shimmering like sunlight on water. "You are only lord commander by my sufferance. You would do well to remember that."

"I am lord commander because my brothers chose me." There were mornings when Jon Snow did not quite believe it himself, when he woke up thinking surely this was some mad dream. *It's like putting on new clothes,* Sam had told him. *The fit feels strange at first, but once you've worn them for a while you get to feeling comfortable.*

"Alliser Thorne complains about the manner of your choosing, and I cannot say he does not have a grievance." The map lay between them like a battleground, drenched by the colors of the glowing sword. "The count was done by a *blind man* with your fat friend by his elbow. And Slynt names you a turncloak."

And who would know one better than Slynt? "A turncloak would tell you what you wished to hear and betray you later. Your Grace knows that I was fairly chosen. My father always said you were a just man." *Just but harsh* had been Lord Eddard's exact words, but Jon did not think it would be wise to share that.

"Lord Eddard was no friend to me, but he was not without some sense. He would have given me these castles."

Never. "I cannot speak to what my father might have done. I took an oath, Your Grace. The Wall is mine."

"For now. We will see how well you hold it." Stannis pointed at him. "Keep your ruins, as they mean so much to you. I promise you, though, if any remain empty when the year is out, I will take them with your leave or without it. And if even one should fall to the foe, your head will soon follow. Now get out."

Lady Melisandre rose from her place near the hearth. "With your leave, Sire, I will show Lord Snow back to his chambers."

"Why? He knows the way." Stannis waved them both away. "Do what you will. Devan, food. Boiled eggs and lemon water."

After the warmth of the king's solar, the turnpike stair felt bone-chillingly cold. "Wind's rising, m'lady," the serjeant warned Melisandre as he handed Jon back his weapons. "You might want a warmer cloak."

"I have my faith to warm me." The red woman walked beside Jon down the steps. "His Grace is growing fond of you."

"I can tell. He only threatened to behead me twice."

Melisandre laughed. "It is his silences you should fear, not his words." As they stepped out into the yard, the wind filled Jon's cloak and sent it flapping against her. The red priestess brushed the black wool aside and slipped her arm through his. "It may be that you are not wrong about the wildling king. I shall pray for the Lord of Light to send me guidance. When I gaze into the flames, I can see through stone and earth, and find the truth within men's souls. I can speak to kings long dead and children not yet born, and watch the years and seasons flicker past, until the end of days."

"Are your fires never wrong?"

"Never . . . though we priests are mortal and sometimes err, mistaking *this must come* for *this may come.*"

Jon could feel her heat, even through his wool and boiled leather. The sight of them arm in arm was drawing curious looks. *They will be whispering in the barracks tonight.* "If you can truly see the morrow in your flames, tell me when and where the next wildling attack will come." He slipped his arm free.

"R'hllor sends us what visions he will, but I shall seek for this man Tormund in the flames." Melisandre's red lips curled into a smile. "I have seen you in my fires, Jon Snow."

"Is that a threat, my lady? Do you mean to burn me too?"

"You mistake my meaning." She gave him a searching look. "I fear that I make you uneasy, Lord Snow."

Jon did not deny it. "The Wall is no place for a woman."

"You are wrong. I have dreamed of your Wall, Jon Snow. Great was the lore that raised it, and great the spells locked beneath its ice. We walk beneath one of the hinges of the world." Melisandre gazed up at it, her breath a warm moist cloud in the air. "This is my place as it is yours, and soon enough you may have grave need of me. Do not refuse my friendship, Jon. I have seen you in the storm, hard-pressed, with enemies on every side. You have so many enemies. Shall I tell you their names?"

"I know their names."

"Do not be so certain." The ruby at Melisandre's throat gleamed red. "It is not the foes who curse you to your face that you must fear, but those who smile when you are looking and sharpen their knives when you turn your back. You would do well to keep your wolf close beside you. Ice, I see, and daggers in the dark. Blood frozen red and hard, and naked steel. It was very cold."

"It is always cold on the Wall."

"You think so?"

"I *know* so, my lady."

"Then you know nothing, Jon Snow," she whispered.

BRAN

*A*re we there yet?

Bran never said the words aloud, but they were often on his lips as their ragged company trudged through groves of ancient oaks and towering grey-green sentinels, past gloomy soldier pines and bare brown chestnut trees. *Are we near?* the boy would wonder, as Hodor clambered up a stony slope, or descended into some dark crevice where drifts of dirty snow cracked beneath his feet. *How much farther?* he would think, as the great elk splashed across a half-frozen stream. *How much longer? It's so cold. Where is the three-eyed crow?*

Swaying in his wicker basket on Hodor's back, the boy hunched down, ducking his head as the big stableboy passed beneath the limb of an oak. The snow was falling again, wet and heavy. Hodor walked with one eye frozen shut, his thick brown beard a tangle of hoarfrost, icicles drooping from the ends of his bushy mustache. One gloved hand still clutched the rusty iron longsword he had taken from the crypts below Winterfell, and from time to time he would lash out at a branch, knocking loose a spray of snow. "Hod-d-d-dor," he would mutter, his teeth chattering.

The sound was strangely reassuring. On their journey from Winterfell to the Wall, Bran and his companions had made the miles shorter by talking and telling tales, but it was different here. Even

Hodor felt it. His *hodor*s came less often than they had south of the Wall. There was a stillness to this wood like nothing Bran had ever known before. Before the snows began, the north wind would swirl around them and clouds of dead brown leaves would kick up from the ground with a faint small rustling sound that reminded him of roaches scurrying in a cupboard, but now all the leaves were buried under a blanket of white. From time to time a raven would fly overhead, big black wings slapping against the cold air. Elsewise the world was silent.

Just ahead, the elk wove between the snowdrifts with his head down, his huge rack of antlers crusted with ice. The ranger sat astride his broad back, grim and silent. *Coldhands* was the name that the fat boy Sam had given him, for though the ranger's face was pale, his hands were black and hard as iron, and cold as iron too. The rest of him was wrapped in layers of wool and boiled leather and ringmail, his features shadowed by his hooded cloak and a black woolen scarf about the lower half of his face.

Behind the ranger, Meera Reed wrapped her arms around her brother, to shelter him from the wind and cold with the warmth of her own body. A crust of frozen snot had formed below Jojen's nose, and from time to time he shivered violently. *He looks so small,* Bran thought, as he watched him sway. *He looks smaller than me now, and weaker too, and I'm the cripple.*

Summer brought up the rear of their little band. The direwolf's breath frosted the forest air as he padded after them, still limping on the hind leg that had taken the arrow back at Queenscrown. Bran felt the pain of the old wound whenever he slipped inside the big wolf's skin. Of late Bran wore Summer's body more often than his own; the wolf felt the bite of the cold, despite the thickness of his fur, but he could see farther and hear better and smell more than the boy in the basket, bundled up like a babe in swaddling clothes.

Other times, when he was tired of being a wolf, Bran slipped into Hodor's skin instead. The gentle giant would whimper when he felt him, and thrash his shaggy head from side to side, but not as violently as he had the first time, back at Queenscrown. *He knows it's me,* the boy liked to tell himself. *He's used to me by now.* Even so, he never felt comfortable inside Hodor's skin. The big stableboy never understood what was happening, and Bran could taste the fear at the back of his mouth. It was better inside Summer. *I am him, and he is me. He feels what I feel.*

Sometimes Bran could sense the direwolf sniffing after the elk, wondering if he could bring the great beast down. Summer had grown accustomed to horses at Winterfell, but this was an elk and elk were prey. The direwolf could sense the warm blood coursing beneath the elk's shaggy hide. Just the smell was enough to make the slaver run from between his jaws, and when it did Bran's mouth would water at the thought of rich, dark meat.

From a nearby oak a raven *quork*ed, and Bran heard the sound of wings as another of the big black birds flapped down to land beside it. By day only half a dozen ravens stayed with them, flitting from tree to tree or riding on the antlers of the elk. The rest of the murder flew ahead or lingered behind. But when the sun sank low they would return, descending from the sky on night-black wings until every branch of every tree was thick with them for yards around. Some would fly to the ranger and mutter at him, and it seemed to Bran that he understood their *quork*s and *squawk*s. *They are his eyes and ears. They scout for him, and whisper to him of dangers ahead and behind.*

As now. The elk stopped suddenly, and the ranger vaulted lightly from his back to land in knee-deep snow. Summer growled at him, his fur bristling. The direwolf did not like the way that Coldhands smelled. *Dead meat, dry blood, a faint whiff of rot. And cold. Cold over all.*

"What is it?" Meera wanted to know.

"Behind us," Coldhands announced, his voice muffled by the black wool scarf across his nose and mouth.

"Wolves?" Bran asked. They had known for days that they were being followed. Every night they heard the mournful howling of the pack, and every night the wolves seemed a little closer. *Hunters, and hungry. They can smell how weak we are.* Often Bran woke shivering hours before the dawn, listening to the sound of them calling to one another in the distance as he waited for the sun to rise. *If there are wolves, there must be prey,* he used to think, until it came to him that *they* were the prey.

The ranger shook his head. "Men. The wolves still keep their distance. These men are not so shy."

Meera Reed pushed back her hood. The wet snow that had covered it tumbled to the ground with a soft *thump.* "How many men? Who are they?"

"Foes. I'll deal with them."

"I'll come with you."

"You'll stay. The boy must be protected. There is a lake ahead, hard frozen. When you come on it, turn north and follow the shoreline. You'll come to a fishing village. Take refuge there until I can catch up with you."

Bran thought that Meera meant to argue until her brother said, "Do as he says. He knows this land." Jojen's eyes were a dark green, the color of moss, but heavy with a weariness that Bran had never seen in them before. *The little grandfather.* South of the Wall, the boy from the crannogs had seemed to be wise beyond his years, but up here he was as lost and frightened as the rest of them. Even so, Meera always listened to him.

That was still true. Coldhands slipped between the trees, back the way they'd come, with four ravens flapping after him. Meera watched him go, her cheeks red with cold, breath puffing from her nostrils. She pulled her hood back up and gave the elk a nudge, and their trek resumed. Before they had gone twenty yards, though, she turned to glance behind them and said, "*Men,* he says. What men? Does he mean wildlings? Why won't he say?"

"He said he'd go and deal with them," said Bran.

"He *said,* aye. He said he would take us to this three-eyed crow too. That river we crossed this morning is the same one we crossed four days ago, I swear. We're going in circles."

"Rivers turn and twist," Bran said uncertainly, "and where there's lakes and hills, you need to go around."

"There's been too much *going around,*" Meera insisted, "and too many secrets. I don't like it. I don't like *him.* And I don't trust him. Those hands of his are bad enough. He hides his face, and will not speak a name. Who is he? *What* is he? Anyone can put on a black cloak. Anyone, or any *thing*. He does not eat, he never drinks, he does not seem to feel the cold."

It's true. Bran had been afraid to speak of it, but he had noticed. Whenever they took shelter for the night, while he and Hodor and the Reeds huddled together for warmth, the ranger kept apart. Sometimes Coldhands closed his eyes, but Bran did not think he slept. And there was something else . . .

"The scarf." Bran glanced about uneasily, but there was not a raven to be seen. All the big black birds had left them when the ranger did. No one was listening. Even so, he kept his voice low. "The scarf over his mouth, it never gets all hard with ice, like Hodor's beard. Not even when he talks."

Meera gave him a sharp look. "You're right. We've never seen his breath, have we?"

"No." A puff of white heralded each of Hodor's *hodor*s. When Jojen or his sister spoke, their words could be seen too. Even the elk left a warm fog upon the air when he exhaled.

"If he does not breathe . . ."

Bran found himself remembering the tales Old Nan had told him when he was a babe. *Beyond the Wall the monsters live, the giants and the ghouls, the stalking shadows and the dead that walk,* she would say, tucking him in beneath his scratchy woolen blanket, *but they cannot pass so long as the Wall stands strong and the men of the Night's Watch are true. So go to sleep, my little Brandon, my baby boy, and dream sweet dreams. There are no monsters here.* The ranger wore the black of the Night's Watch, but what if he was not a man at all? What if he was some monster, taking them to the other monsters to be devoured?

"The ranger saved Sam and the girl from the wights," Bran said, hesitantly, "and he's taking me to the three-eyed crow."

"Why won't this three-eyed crow come to us? Why couldn't *he* meet us at the Wall? Crows have wings. My brother grows weaker every day. How long can we go on?"

Jojen coughed. "Until we get there."

They came upon the promised lake not long after, and turned north as the ranger had bid them. That was the easy part.

The water was frozen, and the snow had been falling for so long that Bran had lost count of the days, turning the lake into a vast white wilderness. Where the ice was flat and the ground was bumpy, the going was easy, but where the wind had pushed the snow up into ridges, sometimes it was hard to tell where the lake ended and the shore began. Even the trees were not as infallible a guide as they might have hoped, for there were wooded islands in the lake, and wide areas ashore where no trees grew.

The elk went where he would, regardless of the wishes of Meera and Jojen on his back. Mostly he stayed beneath the trees, but where the shore curved away westward he would take the more direct path across the frozen lake, shouldering through snowdrifts taller than Bran as the ice crackled underneath his hooves. Out there the wind was stronger, a cold north wind that howled across the lake, knifed through their layers of wool and leather, and set them all to shivering. When it blew into their faces, it would drive the snow into their eyes and leave them as good as blind.

Hours passed in silence. Ahead, shadows began to steal between the trees, the long fingers of the dusk. Dark came early this far north. Bran had come to dread that. Each day seemed shorter than the last, and where the days were cold, the nights were bitter cruel.

Meera halted them again. "We should have come on the village by now." Her voice sounded hushed and strange.

"Could we have passed it?" Bran asked.

"I hope not. We need to find shelter before nightfall."

She was not wrong. Jojen's lips were blue, Meera's cheeks dark red. Bran's own face had gone numb. Hodor's beard was solid ice. Snow caked his legs almost to the knee, and Bran had felt him stagger more than once. No one was as strong as Hodor, no one. If even his great strength was failing . . .

"Summer can find the village," Bran said suddenly, his words misting in the air. He did not wait to hear what Meera might say, but closed his eyes and let himself flow from his broken body.

As he slipped inside Summer's skin, the dead woods came to sudden life. Where before there had been silence, now he heard: wind in the trees, Hodor's breathing, the elk pawing at the ground in search of fodder. Familiar scents filled his nostrils: wet leaves and dead grass, the rotted carcass of a squirrel decaying in the brush, the sour stink of man-sweat, the musky odor of the elk. *Food. Meat.* The elk sensed his interest. He turned his head toward the direwolf, wary, and lowered his great antlers.

He is not prey, the boy whispered to the beast who shared his skin. *Leave him. Run.*

Summer ran. Across the lake he raced, his paws kicking up sprays of snow behind him. The trees stood shoulder to shoulder, like men in a battle line, all cloaked in white. Over roots and rocks the direwolf sped, through a drift of old snow, the crust crackling beneath his weight. His paws grew wet and cold. The next hill was covered with pines, and the sharp scent of their needles filled the air. When he reached the top, he turned in a circle, sniffing at the air, then raised his head and howled.

The smells were there. Mansmells.

Ashes, Bran thought, *old and faint, but ashes.* It was the smell of burnt wood, soot, and charcoal. A dead fire.

He shook the snow off his muzzle. The wind was gusting, so the smells were hard to follow. The wolf turned this way and that, sniffing. All around were heaps of snow and tall trees garbed in white. The wolf let his tongue loll out between his teeth, tasting the frigid air, his breath misting as snowflakes melted on his tongue. When he trotted toward the scent, Hodor lumbered after him at once. The elk took longer to decide, so Bran returned reluctantly to his own body and said, "That way. Follow Summer. I smelled it."

As the first sliver of a crescent moon came peeking through the clouds, they finally stumbled into the village by the lake. They had almost walked straight through it. From the ice, the village looked no different than a dozen other spots along the lakeshore. Buried under drifts of snow, the round stone houses could just as easily have been boulders or hillocks or fallen logs, like the deadfall that Jojen had mistaken for a building the day before, until they dug down into it and found only broken branches and rotting logs.

The village was empty, abandoned by the wildlings who had once lived there, like all the other villages they had passed. Some had been burned, as if the inhabitants had wanted to make certain they could not come creeping back, but this one had been spared the torch. Beneath the snow they found a dozen huts and a longhall, with its sod roof and thick walls of rough-hewn logs.

"At least we will be out of the wind," Bran said.

"Ho*dor*," said Hodor.

Meera slid down from the elk's back. She and her brother helped lift Bran out of the wicker basket. "Might be the wildlings left some food behind," she said.

That proved a forlorn hope. Inside the longhall they found the ashes of a fire, floors of hard-packed dirt, a chill that went bone deep. But at least they had a roof above their heads and log walls to keep the wind off. A stream ran nearby, covered with a film of ice. The elk had to crack it with his hoof to drink. Once Bran and Jojen and Hodor were safely settled, Meera fetched back some chunks of broken ice for them to suck on. The melting water was so cold it made Bran shudder.

Summer did not follow them into the longhall. Bran could feel the big wolf's hunger, a shadow of his own. "Go hunt," he told him, "but you leave the elk alone." Part of him was wishing he could go hunting too. Perhaps he would, later.

Supper was a fistful of acorns, crushed and pounded into paste, so bitter that Bran gagged as he tried to keep it down. Jojen Reed did not even make the attempt. Younger and frailer than his sister, he was growing weaker by the day.

"Jojen, you have to eat," Meera told him.

"Later. I just want to rest." Jojen smiled a wan smile. "This is not the day I die, sister. I promise you."

"You almost fell off the elk."

"Almost. I am cold and hungry, that's all."

"Then eat."

"Crushed acorns? My belly hurts, but that will only make it worse. Leave me be, sister. I'm dreaming of roast chicken."

"Dreams will not sustain you. Not even greendreams."

"Dreams are what we have."

All we have. The last of the food that they had brought from the south was ten days gone. Since then hunger walked beside them day and night. Even Summer could find no game in these woods. They lived on crushed acorns and raw fish. The woods were full of frozen streams and cold black lakes, and Meera was as good a fisher with her three-pronged frog spear as most men were with hook and line. Some days her lips were blue with cold by the time she waded back to them with her catch wriggling on her tines. It had been three days since Meera caught a fish, however. Bran's belly felt so hollow it might have been three years.

After they choked down their meagre supper, Meera sat with her back against a wall, sharpening her dagger on a whetstone. Hodor squatted down beside the door, rocking back and forth on his haunches and muttering, "Hodor, hodor, hodor."

Bran closed his eyes. It was too cold to talk, and they dare not light a fire. Coldhands had warned them against that. *These woods are not as empty as you think,* he had said. *You cannot know what the light might summon from the darkness.* The memory made him shiver, despite the warmth of Hodor beside him.

Sleep would not come, could not come. Instead there was wind, the biting cold, moonlight on snow, and fire. He was back inside Summer, long leagues away, and the night was rank with the smell of blood. The scent was strong. *A kill, not far.* The flesh would still be warm. Slaver ran between his teeth as the hunger woke inside him. *Not elk. Not deer. Not this.*

The direwolf moved toward the meat, a gaunt grey shadow sliding from tree to tree, through pools of moonlight and over mounds of snow. The wind gusted around him, shifting. He lost the scent, found it, then lost it again. As he searched for it once more, a distant sound made his ears prick up.

Wolf, he knew at once. Summer stalked toward the sound, wary now. Soon enough the scent of blood was back, but now there were other smells: piss and dead skins, bird shit, feathers, and wolf, wolf, wolf. *A pack.* He would need to fight for his meat.

They smelled him too. As he moved out from amongst the darkness of the trees into the bloody glade, they were watching him. The female was chewing on a leather boot that still had half a leg in it, but she let it fall at his approach. The leader of the pack, an old male with a grizzled white muzzle and a blind eye, moved out to meet him, snarling, his teeth bared. Behind him, a younger male showed his fangs as well.

The direwolf's pale yellow eyes drank in the sights around them. A nest of entrails coiled through a bush, entangled with the branches. Steam rising from an open belly, rich with the smells of blood and meat. A head staring sightlessly up at a horned moon, cheeks ripped and torn down to bloody bone, pits for eyes, neck ending in a ragged stump. A pool of frozen blood, glistening red and black.

Men. The stink of them filled the world. Alive, they had been as many as the fingers on a man's paw, but now they were none. *Dead. Done. Meat.* Cloaked and hooded, once, but the wolves had torn their clothing into pieces in their frenzy to get at the flesh. Those who still had faces wore thick beards crusted with ice and frozen snot. The falling snow had begun to bury what remained of them, so pale against the black of ragged cloaks and breeches. *Black.*

Long leagues away, the boy stirred uneasily.

Black. Night's Watch. They were Night's Watch.

The direwolf did not care. They were meat. He was hungry.

The eyes of the three wolves glowed yellow. The direwolf swung his head from side to side, nostrils flaring, then bared his fangs in a snarl. The younger male backed away. The direwolf could smell the fear in him. *Tail,* he knew. But the one-eyed wolf answered with a growl and moved to block his advance. *Head. And he does not fear me though I am twice his size.*

Their eyes met.

Warg!

Then the two rushed together, wolf and direwolf, and there was no more time for thought. The world shrank down to tooth and claw, snow flying as they rolled and spun and tore at one another, the other wolves snarling and snapping around them. His jaws closed on matted fur slick with hoarfrost, on a limb thin as a dry stick, but the one-eyed wolf clawed at his belly and tore himself free, rolled, lunged for him. Yellow fangs snapped closed on his throat, but he shook off his old grey cousin as he would a rat, then charged after him, knocked him down. Rolling, ripping, kicking, they fought until the both of them were ragged and fresh blood dappled the snows around them. But finally the old one-eyed wolf lay down and showed his belly. The direwolf snapped at him twice more, sniffed at his butt, then lifted a leg over him.

A few snaps and a warning growl, and the female and the tail submitted too. The pack was his.

The prey as well. He went from man to man, sniffing, before settling on the biggest, a faceless thing who clutched black iron in one hand. His other hand was missing, severed at the wrist, the stump bound up in leather. Blood flowed thick and sluggish from the slash across his throat. The wolf lapped at it with his tongue, licked the ragged eyeless ruin of his nose and cheeks, then buried his muzzle in his neck and tore it open, gulping down a gobbet of sweet meat. No flesh had ever tasted half as good.

When he was done with that one, he moved to the next, and devoured the choicest bits of that man too. Ravens watched him from the trees, squatting dark-eyed and silent on the branches as snow drifted down around them. The other wolves made do with his leavings; the old male fed first, then the female, then the tail. They were his now. They were pack.

No, the boy whispered, *we have another pack. Lady's dead and maybe Grey Wind too, but somewhere there's still Shaggydog and Nymeria and Ghost. Remember Ghost?*

Falling snow and feasting wolves began to dim. Warmth beat against his face, comforting as a mother's kisses. *Fire,* he thought, *smoke.* His nose twitched to the smell of roasting meat. And then the forest fell away, and he was back in the longhall again, back in his broken body, staring at a fire. Meera Reed was turning a chunk of raw red flesh above the flames, letting it char and spit. "Just in time," she said. Bran rubbed his eyes with the heel of his hand and wriggled backwards against the wall to sit. "You almost slept through supper. The ranger found a sow."

Behind her, Hodor was tearing eagerly at a chunk of hot charred flesh as blood and grease ran down into his beard. Wisps of smoke rose from between his fingers. "Hodor," he muttered between bites, "hodor, hodor." His sword lay on the earthen floor beside him. Jojen Reed nipped at his own joint with small bites, chewing each chunk of meat a dozen times before swallowing.

The ranger killed a pig. Coldhands stood beside the door, a raven on his arm, both staring at the fire. Reflections from the flames glittered off four black eyes. *He does not eat,* Bran remembered, *and he fears the flames.*

"You said no fire," he reminded the ranger.

"The walls around us hide the light, and dawn is close. We will be on our way soon."

"What happened to the men? The foes behind us?"

"They will not trouble you."

"Who were they? Wildlings?"

Meera turned the meat to cook the other side. Hodor was chewing and swallowing, muttering happily under his breath. Only Jojen seemed aware of what was happening as Coldhands turned his head to stare at Bran. "They were foes."

Men of the Night's Watch. "You killed them. You and the ravens. Their faces were all torn, and their eyes were gone." Coldhands did not deny it. "They were your *brothers.* I saw. The wolves had ripped their clothes up, but I could still tell. Their cloaks were black. Like your hands." Coldhands said nothing. "Who are you? *Why are your hands black?*"

The ranger studied his hands as if he had never noticed them before. "Once the heart has ceased to beat, a man's blood runs down into his extremities, where it thickens and congeals." His voice rattled in his throat, as thin and gaunt as he was. "His hands and feet swell up and turn as black as pudding. The rest of him becomes as white as milk."

Meera Reed rose, her frog spear in her hand, a chunk of smoking meat still impaled upon its tines. "Show us your face."

The ranger made no move to obey.

"He's dead." Bran could taste the bile in his throat. "Meera, he's some dead thing. The monsters cannot pass so long as the Wall stands and the men of the Night's Watch stay true, that's what Old Nan used to say. He came to meet us at the Wall, but he could not pass. He sent Sam instead, with that wildling girl."

Meera's gloved hand tightened around the shaft of her frog spear. "Who sent you? Who is this three-eyed crow?"

"A friend. Dreamer, wizard, call him what you will. The last green-seer." The longhall's wooden door banged open. Outside, the night wind howled, bleak and black. The trees were full of ravens, screaming. Coldhands did not move.

"A monster," Bran said.

The ranger looked at Bran as if the rest of them did not exist. "Your monster, Brandon Stark."

"*Yours,*" the raven echoed, from his shoulder. Outside the door, the ravens in the trees took up the cry, until the night wood echoed to the murderer's song of "*Yours, yours, yours.*"

"Jojen, did you dream this?" Meera asked her brother. "Who is he? What is he? What do we do now?"

"We go with the ranger," said Jojen. "We have come too far to turn back now, Meera. We would never make it back to the Wall alive. We go with Bran's monster, or we die."

TYRION

They departed Pentos by the Sunrise Gate, though Tyrion Lannister never glimpsed the sunrise. "It will be as if you had never come to Pentos, my little friend," promised Magister Illyrio, as he drew shut the litter's purple velvet drapes. "No man must see you leave the city, as no man saw you enter."

"No man except the sailors who stuffed me in that barrel, the cabin boy who cleaned up after me, the girl you sent to warm my bed, and that treacherous freckled washerwoman. Oh, and your guards. Unless you removed their wits along with their balls, they know you're not alone in here." The litter was suspended between eight mammoth draft horses on heavy leather straps. Four eunuchs paced beside the horses, two to either side, and more were trudging along behind to guard the baggage train.

"Unsullied tell no tales," Illyrio assured him. "And the galley that delivered you is on her way to Asshai even now. It will be two years before she returns, if the seas are kind. As for my household, they love me well. None would betray me."

Cherish that thought, my fat friend. One day we will carve those words upon your crypt. "We should be aboard that galley," the dwarf said. "The fastest way to Volantis is by sea."

"The sea is hazardous," replied Illyrio. "Autumn is a season rife with storms, and pirates still make their dens upon the Stepstones and venture forth to prey on honest men. It would never do for my little friend to fall into such hands."

"There are pirates on the Rhoyne as well."

"River pirates." The cheesemonger gave a yawn, covering his mouth with the back of his hand. "Cockroach captains scurrying after crumbs."

"One hears talk of stone men as well."

"They are real enough, poor damned things. But why speak of such things? The day is too fine for such talk. We shall see the Rhoyne soon, and there you shall be rid of Illyrio and his big belly. Till then, let us drink and dream. We have sweet wine and savories to enjoy. Why dwell upon disease and death?"

Why indeed? Tyrion heard the *thrum* of a crossbow once again, and wondered. The litter swayed side to side, a soothing movement that made him feel as if he were a child being rocked to sleep in his mother's arms. *Not that I would know what that was like.* Silk pillows stuffed with goose down cushioned his cheeks. The purple velvet walls curved overhead to form a roof, making it pleasantly warm within despite the autumn chill outside.

A train of mules trailed behind them, carrying chests and casks and barrels, and hampers of delectables to keep the lord of cheese from growing peckish. They nibbled on spiced sausage that morning, washed down with a dark smokeberry brown. Jellied eels and Dornish reds filled their afternoon. Come evening there were sliced hams, boiled eggs, and roasted larks stuffed with garlic and onions, with pale ales and Myrish fire wines to help in their digestion. The litter was as slow as it was comfortable, however, and the dwarf soon found himself itching with impatience.

"How many days until we reach the river?" he asked Illyrio that evening. "At this pace, your queen's dragons will be larger than Aegon's three before I can lay eyes upon them."

"Would it were so. A large dragon is more fearsome than a small one." The magister shrugged. "Much as it would please me to welcome Queen Daenerys to Volantis, I must rely on you and Griff for that. I can serve her best in Pentos, smoothing the way for her return. So long as I am with you, though . . . well, an old fat man must have his comforts, yes? Come, drink a cup of wine."

"Tell me," Tyrion said as he drank, "why should a magister of Pentos give three figs who wears the crown in Westeros? Where is the gain for you in this venture, my lord?"

The fat man dabbed grease from his lips. "I am an old man, grown weary of this world and its treacheries. Is it so strange that I should wish to do some good before my days are done, to help a sweet young girl regain her birthright?"

Next you will be offering me a suit of magic armor and a palace in Valyria. "If Daenerys is no more than a sweet young girl, the Iron Throne will cut her into sweet young pieces."

"Fear not, my little friend. The blood of Aegon the Dragon flows in her veins."

Along with the blood of Aegon the Unworthy, Maegor the Cruel, and Baelor the Befuddled. "Tell me more of her."

The fat man grew pensive. "Daenerys was half a child when she came to me, yet fairer even than my second wife, so lovely I was tempted to claim her for myself. Such a fearful, furtive thing, however, I knew I should get no joy from coupling with her. Instead I summoned a bedwarmer and fucked her vigorously until the madness passed. If truth be told, I did not think Daenerys would survive for long amongst the horselords."

"That did not stop you selling her to Khal Drogo . . ."

"Dothraki neither buy nor sell. Say rather that her brother Viserys gave her to Drogo to win the khal's friendship. A vain young man, and greedy. Viserys lusted for his father's throne, but he lusted for Daenerys too, and was loath to give her up. The night before the princess wed he tried to steal into her bed, insisting that if he could not have her hand, he would claim her maidenhead. Had I not taken the precaution of posting guards upon her door, Viserys might have undone years of planning."

"He sounds an utter fool."

"Viserys was Mad Aerys's son, just so. Daenerys . . . Daenerys is quite different." He popped a roasted lark into his mouth and crunched it noisily, bones and all. "The frightened child who sheltered in my manse died on the Dothraki sea, and was reborn in blood and fire. This dragon queen who wears her name is a true Targaryen. When I sent ships to bring her home, she turned toward Slaver's Bay. In a short span of days she conquered Astapor, made Yunkai bend the knee, and sacked Meereen. Mantarys will be next, if she marches west along the old Valyrian roads. If she comes by sea, well . . . her fleet must take on food and water at Volantis."

"By land or by sea, there are long leagues between Meereen and Volantis," Tyrion observed.

"Five hundred fifty, as the dragon flies, through deserts, mountains, swamps, and demon-haunted ruins. Many and more will perish, but those who survive will be stronger by the time they reach Volantis . . . where they shall find you and Griff awaiting them, with fresh forces and sufficient ships to carry them all across the sea to Westeros."

Tyrion pondered all he knew of Volantis, oldest and proudest of the Nine Free Cities. Something was awry here. Even with half a nose, he could smell it. "It's said there are five slaves for every free man in Volantis. Why would the triarchs assist a queen who smashed the slave trade?" He pointed at Illyrio. "For that matter, why would you? Slavery may be forbidden by the laws of Pentos, yet you have a finger in that trade as well, and maybe a whole hand. And yet you conspire for the dragon queen, and not against her. Why? What do you hope to gain from Queen Daenerys?"

"Are we back to that again? You are a persistent little man." Illyrio gave a laugh and slapped his belly. "As you will. The Beggar King swore that I should be his master of coin, and a lordly lord as well. Once he wore his golden crown, I should have my choice of castles . . . even Casterly Rock, if I desired."

Tyrion snorted wine back up the scarred stump that had been his nose. "My father would have loved to hear that." ·

"Your lord father had no cause for concern. Why would I want a rock? My manse is large enough for any man, and more comfortable than your drafty Westerosi castles. Master of coin, though . . ." The fat man peeled another egg. "I am fond of coins. Is there any sound as sweet as the clink of gold on gold?"

A sister's screams. "Are you quite certain that Daenerys will make good her brother's promises?"

"She will, or she will not." Illyrio bit the egg in half. "I told you, my little friend, not all that a man does is done for gain. Believe as you wish, but even fat old fools like me have friends, and debts of affection to repay."

Liar, thought Tyrion. *There is something in this venture worth more to you than coin or castles.* "You meet so few men who value friendship over gold these days."

"Too true," the fat man said, deaf to the irony.

"How is it that the Spider became so dear to you?"

"We were young together, two green boys in Pentos."

"Varys came from Myr."

"So he did. I met him not long after he arrived, one step ahead of the slavers. By day he slept in the sewers, by night he prowled the rooftops like a cat. I was near as poor, a bravo in soiled silks, living by my blade. Perhaps you chanced to glimpse the statue by my pool? Pytho Malanon carved that when I was six-and-ten. A lovely thing, though now I weep to see it."

"Age makes ruins of us all. I am still in mourning for my nose. But Varys . . ."

"In Myr he was a prince of thieves, until a rival thief informed on him. In Pentos his accent marked him, and once he was known for a eunuch he was despised and beaten. Why he chose me to protect him I may never know, but we came to an arrangement. Varys spied on lesser thieves and took their takings. I offered my help to their victims, promising to recover their valuables for a fee. Soon every man who had suffered a loss knew to come to me, whilst city's footpads and cutpurses sought out Varys . . . half to slit his throat, the other half to sell him what they'd stolen. We both grew rich, and richer still when Varys trained his mice."

"In King's Landing he kept little birds."

"Mice, we called them then. The older thieves were fools who thought no further than turning a night's plunder into wine. Varys preferred orphan boys and young girls. He chose the smallest, the ones who were quick and quiet, and taught them to climb walls and slip down chimneys. He taught them to read as well. We left the gold and gems for common thieves. Instead our mice stole letters, ledgers, charts . . . later, they would read them and leave them where they lay.

Secrets are worth more than silver or sapphires, Varys claimed. Just so. I grew so respectable that a cousin of the Prince of Pentos let me wed his maiden daughter, whilst whispers of a certain eunuch's talents crossed the narrow sea and reached the ears of a certain king. A very *anxious* king, who did not wholly trust his son, nor his wife, nor his Hand, a friend of his youth who had grown arrogant and overproud. I do believe that you know the rest of this tale, is that not so?"

"Much of it," Tyrion admitted. "I see that you are somewhat more than a cheesemonger after all."

Illyrio inclined his head. "You are kind to say so, my little friend. And for my part, I see that you are just as quick as Lord Varys claimed." He smiled, showing all his crooked yellow teeth, and shouted for another jar of Myrish fire wine.

When the magister drifted off to sleep with the wine jar at his elbow, Tyrion crept across the pillows to work it loose from its fleshy prison and pour himself a cup. He drained it down, and yawned, and filled it once again. *If I drink enough fire wine,* he told himself, *perhaps I'll dream of dragons.*

When he was still a lonely child in the depths of Casterly Rock, he oft rode dragons through the nights, pretending he was some lost Targaryen princeling, or a Valyrian dragonlord soaring high o'er fields and mountains. Once, when his uncles asked him what gift he wanted for his nameday, he begged them for a dragon. "It wouldn't need to be a big one. It could be little, like I am." His uncle Gerion thought that was the funniest thing he had ever heard, but his uncle Tygett said, "The last dragon died a century ago, lad." That had seemed so monstrously unfair that the boy had cried himself to sleep that night.

Yet if the lord of cheese could be believed, the Mad King's daughter had hatched three living dragons. *Two more than even a Targaryen should require.* Tyrion was almost sorry that he had killed his father. He would have enjoyed seeing Lord Tywin's face when he learned that there was a Targaryen queen on her way to Westeros with three dragons, backed by a scheming eunuch and a cheesemonger half the size of Casterly Rock.

The dwarf was so stuffed that he had to undo his belt and the topmost laces on his breeches. The boy's clothes his host had dressed him in made him feel like ten pounds of sausage in a five-pound skin. *If we eat this way every day I will be the size of Illyrio before I meet this dragon queen.* Outside the litter night had fallen. Inside all was dark. Tyrion listened to Illyrio's snores, the creak of the leather straps, the slow *clop clop* of the team's ironshod hooves on the hard Valyrian road, but his heart was listening for the beat of leathern wings.

When he woke, dawn had come. The horses plodded on, the litter creaking and swaying between them. Tyrion pulled the curtain back an inch to peer outside, but there was little to see but ochre fields, bare brown elms, and the road itself, a broad stone highway that ran straight as a spear to the horizon. He had read about Valyrian roads, but this was the first he had seen. The Freehold's grasp had reached as far as Dragonstone, but never to the mainland of Westeros itself. *Odd, that. Dragonstone is no more than a rock. The wealth was farther west, but they had dragons. Surely they knew that it was there.*

He had drunk too much last night. His head was pounding, and even the gentle swaying of the litter was enough to make his gorge rise in his throat. Though he said no word of complaint, his distress must have been plain to Illyrio Mopatis. "Come, drink with me," the fat man said. "A scale from the dragon that burned you, as they say." He poured for them from a flagon of blackberry wine so sweet that it drew more flies than honey. Tyrion shooed them off with the back of his hand and drank deep. The taste was so cloying that it was all he could do to keep it down. The second cup went down easier, however. Even so, he had no appetite, and when Illyrio offered him a bowl of blackberries in cream he waved it off. "I dreamed about the queen," he said. "I was on my knees before her, swearing my allegiance, but she mistook me for my brother, Jaime, and fed me to her dragons."

"Let us hope this dream was not prophetic. You are a clever imp, just as Varys said, and Daenerys will have need of clever men about her. Ser Barristan is a valiant knight and true; but none, I think, has ever called him cunning."

"Knights know only one way to solve a problem. They couch their lances and charge. A dwarf has a different way of looking at the world. What of you, though? You are a clever man yourself."

"You flatter me." Illyrio waggled his hand. "Alas, I am not made for travel, so I will send you to Daenerys in my stead. You did Her Grace a great service when you slew your father, and it is my hope that you will do her many more. Daenerys is not the fool her brother was. She will make good use of you."

As kindling? Tyrion thought, smiling pleasantly.

They changed out teams only thrice that day but seemed to halt twice an hour at the least so Illyrio could climb down from the litter and have himself a piss. *Our lord of cheese is the size of an elephant, but he has a bladder like a peanut,* the dwarf mused. During one stop, he used the time to have a closer look at the road. Tyrion knew what he would find: not packed earth, nor bricks, nor cobbles, but a ribbon of fused stone raised a half foot above the ground to allow rainfall and snowmelt to run off its shoulders. Unlike the muddy tracks that passed for roads in the Seven Kingdoms, the Valyrian roads were wide enough for three wagons to pass abreast, and neither time nor traffic marred them. They still endured, unchanging, four centuries after Valyria itself had met its Doom. He looked for ruts and cracks but found only a pile of warm dung deposited by one of the horses.

The dung made him think of his lord father. *Are you down in some hell, Father? A nice cold hell where you can look up and see me help restore Mad Aerys's daughter to the Iron Throne?*

As they resumed their journey, Illyrio produced a bag of roasted chestnuts and began to speak once more of the dragon queen. "Our last news of Queen Daenerys is old and stale, I fear. By now she will have left Meereen, we must assume. She has her host at last, a ragged host of sellswords, Dothraki horselords, and Unsullied infantry, and she will no doubt lead them west, to take back her father's throne." Magister Illyrio twisted open a pot of garlic snails, sniffed at them, and smiled. "At Volantis, you will have fresh tidings of Daenerys, we must hope," he said, as he sucked one from its shell. "Dragons and young girls are both capricious, and it may be that you will need to adjust your plans. Griff will know what to do. Will you have a snail? The garlic is from my own gardens."

I could ride a snail and make a better pace than this litter of yours. Tyrion waved the dish away. "You place a deal of trust in this man Griff. Another friend of your childhood?"

"No. A sellsword, you would call him, but Westerosi born. Daenerys needs men worthy of her cause." Illyrio raised a hand. "I know! *'Sellswords put gold before honor,'* you are thinking. *'This man Griff will sell me to my sister.'* Not so. I trust Griff as I would trust a brother."

Another mortal error. "Then I shall do likewise."

"The Golden Company marches toward Volantis as we speak, there to await the coming of our queen out of the east."

Beneath the gold, the bitter steel. "I had heard the Golden Company was under contract with one of the Free Cities."

"Myr." Illyrio smirked. "Contracts can be broken."

"There is more coin in cheese than I knew," said Tyrion. "How did you accomplish that?"

The magister waggled his fat fingers. "Some contracts are writ in ink, and some in blood. I say no more."

The dwarf pondered that. The Golden Company was reputedly the finest of the free companies, founded a century ago by Bittersteel, a bastard son of Aegon the Unworthy. When another of Aegon's Great Bastards tried to seize the Iron Throne from his trueborn half-brother, Bittersteel joined the revolt. Daemon Blackfyre had perished on the Redgrass Field, however, and his rebellion with him. Those followers of the Black Dragon who survived the battle yet refused to bend the knee fled across the narrow sea, among them Daemon's younger sons, Bittersteel, and hundreds of landless lords and knights who soon found themselves forced to sell their swords to eat. Some joined the Ragged Standard, some the Second Sons or Maiden's Men. Bittersteel saw the strength of House Blackfyre scattering to the four winds, so he formed the Golden Company to bind the exiles together.

From that day to this, the men of the Golden Company had lived and died in the Disputed Lands, fighting for Myr or Lys or Tyrosh in their pointless little wars, and dreaming of the land their fathers had lost. They were exiles and sons of exiles, dispossessed and unforgiven . . . yet formidable fighters still.

"I admire your powers of persuasion," Tyrion told Illyrio. "How did you convince the Golden Company to take up the cause of our sweet queen when they have spent so much of their history fighting *against* the Targaryens?"

Illyrio brushed away the objection as if it were a fly. "Black or red, a dragon is still a dragon. When Maelys the Monstrous died upon the Stepstones, it was the end of the male line of House Blackfyre." The cheesemonger smiled through his forked beard. "And Daenerys will give the exiles what Bittersteel and the Blackfyres never could. She will take them home."

With fire and sword. It was the kind of homecoming that Tyrion wished for as well. "Ten thousand swords makes for a princely gift, I grant you. Her Grace should be most pleased."

The magister gave a modest bob of his head, chins jiggling. "I would never presume to say what might please Her Grace."

Prudent of you. Tyrion knew much and more about the gratitude of kings. Why should queens be any different?

Soon enough the magister was fast asleep, leaving Tyrion to brood alone. He wondered what Barristan Selmy would think of riding into battle with the Golden Company. During the War of the Ninepenny Kings, Selmy had cut a bloody path through their ranks to slay the last of the Blackfyre Pretenders. *Rebellion makes for queer bedfellows. And none more queer than this fat man and me.*

The cheesemonger woke when they stopped to change the horses and sent for a fresh hamper. "How far have we come?" the dwarf asked him as they stuffed themselves with cold capon and a relish made of carrots, raisins, and bits of lime and orange.

"This is Andalos, my friend. The land your Andals came from. They took it from the hairy men who were here before them, cousins to the hairy men of Ib. The heart of Hugor's ancient realm lies north of us, but we are passing through its southern marches. In Pentos, these are called the Flatlands. Farther east stand the Velvet Hills, whence we are bound."

Andalos. The Faith taught that the Seven themselves had once walked the hills of Andalos in human form. "The Father reached his hand into the heavens and pulled down seven stars," Tyrion recited from memory, "and one by one he set them on the brow of Hugor of the Hill to make a glowing crown."

Magister Illyrio gave him a curious look. "I did not dream my little friend was so devout."

The dwarf shrugged. "A relic of my boyhood. I knew I would not make a knight, so I decided to be High Septon. That crystal crown adds a foot to a man's height. I studied the holy books and prayed until I had scabs on both my knees, but my quest came to a tragic end. I reached that certain age and fell in love."

"A maiden? I know the way of that." Illyrio thrust his right hand up his left sleeve and drew out a silver locket. Inside was a painted likeness of a woman with big blue eyes and pale golden hair streaked by silver. "Serra. I found her in a Lysene pillow house and brought her home to warm my bed, but in the end I wed her. Me, whose first wife had been a cousin of the Prince of Pentos. The palace gates were closed to me thereafter, but I did not care. The price was small enough, for Serra."

"How did she die?" Tyrion knew that she was dead; no man spoke so fondly of a woman who had abandoned him.

"A Braavosi trading galley called at Pentos on her way back from the Jade Sea. The *Treasure* carried cloves and saffron, jet and jade, scarlet samite, green silk . . . and the grey death. We slew her oarsmen as they came ashore and burned the ship at anchor, but the rats crept down the oars and paddled to the quay on cold stone feet. The plague took two thousand before it ran its course." Magister Illyrio closed the locket. "I keep her hands in my bedchamber. Her hands that were so soft . . ."

Tyrion thought of Tysha. He glanced out at the fields where once the gods had walked. "What sort of gods make rats and plagues and dwarfs?" Another passage from *The Seven-Pointed Star* came back to him. "The Maid brought him forth a girl as supple as a willow with eyes like deep blue pools, and Hugor declared that he would have her for his bride. So the Mother made her fertile, and the Crone foretold that she would bear the king four-and-forty mighty sons. The Warrior gave strength to their arms, whilst the Smith wrought for each a suit of iron plates."

"Your Smith must have been Rhoynish," Illyrio quipped. "The Andals learned the art of working iron from the Rhoynar who dwelt along the river. This is known."

"Not by our septons." Tyrion gestured at the fields. "Who dwells in these Flatlands of yours?"

"Tillers and toilers, bound to the land. There are orchards, farms, mines . . . I own some such myself, though I seldom visit them. Why should I spend my days out here, with the myriad delights of Pentos close at hand?"

"Myriad delights." *And huge thick walls.* Tyrion swirled his wine in his cup. "We have seen no towns since Pentos."

"There are ruins." Illyrio waved a chicken leg toward the curtains. "The horselords come this way, whenever some khal takes it into his head to gaze upon the sea. The Dothraki are not fond of towns, you will know this even in Westeros."

"Fall upon one of these *khalasar*s and destroy it, and you may find that the Dothraki are not so quick to cross the Rhoyne."

"It is cheaper to buy off foes with food and gifts."

If only I had thought to bring a nice cheese to the battle on the Blackwater, I might still have all my nose. Lord Tywin had always held the Free Cities in contempt. *They fight with coins instead of swords,* he used to say. *Gold has its uses, but wars are won with iron.* "Give gold to a foe and he will just come back for more, my father always said."

"Is this the selfsame father that you murdered?" Illyrio tossed his chicken bone from the litter. "Sellswords will not stand against Dothraki screamers. That was proved at Qohor."

"Not even your brave Griff?" mocked Tyrion.

"Griff is different. He has a son he dotes on. Young Griff, the boy is called. There never was a nobler lad."

The wine, the food, the sun, the sway of the litter, the buzzing of the flies, all conspired to make Tyrion sleepy. So he slept, woke, drank. Illyrio matched him cup for cup. And as the sky turned a dusky purple, the fat man began to snore.

That night Tyrion Lannister dreamed of a battle that turned the hills of Westeros as red as blood. He was in the midst of it, dealing death with an axe as big as he was, fighting side by side with Barristan the Bold and Bittersteel as dragons wheeled across the sky above them. In the dream he had two heads, both noseless. His father led the enemy, so he slew him once again. Then he killed his brother, Jaime, hacking at his face until it was a red ruin, laughing every time he struck a blow. Only when the fight was finished did he realize that his second head was weeping.

When he woke his stunted legs were stiff as iron. Illyrio was eating olives. "Where are we?" Tyrion asked him.

"We have not yet left the Flatlands, my hasty friend. Soon our road shall pass into the Velvet Hills. There we begin our climb toward Ghoyan Drohe, upon the Little Rhoyne."

Ghoyan Drohe had been a Rhoynar city, until the dragons of Valyria had reduced it to a smoldering desolation. *I am traveling through years as well as leagues,* Tyrion reflected, *back through history to the days when dragons ruled the earth.*

Tyrion slept and woke and slept again, and day and night seemed not to matter. The Velvet Hills proved a disappointment. "Half the whores in Lannisport have breasts bigger than these hills," he told Illyrio. "You ought to call them the Velvet Teats." They saw a circle of standing stones that Illyrio claimed had been raised by giants, and later a deep lake. "Here lived a den of robbers who preyed on all who passed this way," Illyrio said. "It is said they still dwell beneath the water. Those who fish the lake are pulled under and devoured." The next evening they came upon a huge Valyrian sphinx crouched beside the road. It had a dragon's body and a woman's face.

"A dragon queen," said Tyrion. "A pleasant omen."

"Her king is missing." Illyrio pointed out the smooth stone plinth on which the second sphinx once stood, now grown over with moss and flowering vines. "The horselords built wooden wheels beneath him and dragged him back to Vaes Dothrak."

That is an omen too, thought Tyrion, *but not as hopeful.*

That night, drunker than usual, he broke into sudden song.

> *He rode through the streets of the city,*
> *down from his hill on high,*
> *O'er the wynds and the steps and the cobbles,*
> *he rode to a woman's sigh.*
> *For she was his secret treasure,*
> *she was his shame and his bliss.*
> *And a chain and a keep are nothing,*
> *compared to a woman's kiss.*

Those were all the words he knew, aside from the refrain. *Hands of gold are always cold, but a woman's hands are warm.* Shae's hands had beat at him as the golden hands dug into her throat. He did not remember if they'd been warm or not. As the strength went out of her, her blows became moths fluttering about his face. Each time he gave the chain another twist the golden hands dug deeper. *A chain and a keep are nothing, compared to a woman's kiss.* Had he kissed her one last time, after she was dead? He could not remember . . . though he still recalled the first time they had kissed, in his tent beside the Green Fork. How sweet her mouth had tasted.

He remembered the first time with Tysha as well. *She did not know how, no more than I did. We kept bumping our noses, but when I touched her tongue with mine she trembled.* Tyrion closed his eyes to bring her face to mind, but instead he saw his father, squatting on a privy with his bedrobe hiked up about his waist. "Wherever whores go," Lord Tywin said, and the crossbow *thrum*med.

The dwarf rolled over, pressing half a nose deep into the silken pillows. Sleep opened beneath him like a well, and he threw himself into it with a will and let the darkness eat him up.

THE MERCHANT'S MAN

A dventure stank.

She boasted sixty oars, a single sail, and a long lean hull that promised speed. *Small, but she might serve,* Quentyn thought when he saw her, but that was before he went aboard and got a good whiff of her. *Pigs,* was his first thought, but after a second sniff he changed his mind. Pigs had a cleaner smell. This stink was piss and rotting meat and nightsoil, this was the reek of corpse flesh and weeping sores and wounds gone bad, so strong that it overwhelmed the salt air and fish smell of the harbor.

"I want to retch," he said to Gerris Drinkwater. They were waiting for the ship's master to appear, sweltering in the heat as the stench wafted up from the deck beneath them.

"If the captain smells anything like his ship, he may mistake your vomit for perfume," Gerris replied.

Quentyn was about to suggest that they try another ship when the master finally made his appearance, with two vile-looking crewmen at his side. Gerris greeted him with a smile. Though he did not speak the Volantene tongue as well as Quentyn, their ruse required that he speak for them. Back in the Planky Town Quentyn had played the wineseller, but the mummery had chafed at him, so when the Dornishmen changed ships at Lys they had changed roles as well. Aboard the *Meadowlark,* Cletus Yronwood became the merchant,

Quentyn the servant; in Volantis, with Cletus slain, Gerris had assumed the master's role.

Tall and fair, with blue-green eyes, sandy hair streaked by the sun, and a lean and comely body, Gerris Drinkwater had a swagger to him, a confidence bordering on arrogance. He never seemed ill at ease, and even when he did not speak the language, he had ways of making himself understood. Quentyn cut a poor figure by comparison— short-legged and stocky, thickly built, with hair the brown of new-turned earth. His forehead was too high, his jaw too square, his nose too broad. *A good honest face,* a girl had called it once, *but you should smile more.*

Smiles had never come easily for Quentyn Martell, any more than they did for his lord father.

"How swift is your *Adventure*?" Gerris said, in a halting approximation of High Valyrian.

The *Adventure*'s master recognized the accent and responded in the Common Tongue of Westeros. "There is none swifter, honored lord. *Adventure* can run down the wind itself. Tell me where you wish to sail, and swiftly I shall bring you there."

"I seek passage to Meereen for myself and two servants."

That gave the captain pause. "I am no stranger to Meereen. I could find the city again, aye . . . but why? There are no slaves to be had in Meereen, no profit to be found there. The silver queen has put an end to that. She has even closed the fighting pits, so a poor sailor cannot even amuse himself as he waits to fill his holds. Tell me, my Westerosi friend, what is there in Meereen that you should want to go there?"

The most beautiful woman in the world, thought Quentyn. *My bride-to-be, if the gods are good.* Sometimes at night he lay awake imagining her face and form, and wondering why such a woman would ever want to marry him, of all the princes in the world. *I am Dorne,* he told himself. *She will want Dorne.*

Gerris answered with the tale they had concocted. "Wine is our family trade. My father owns extensive vineyards back in Dorne, and wishes me to find new markets. It is hoped that the good folk of Meereen will welcome what I sell."

"Wine? *Dornish* wine?" The captain was not convinced. "The slave cities are at war. Can it be you do not know this?"

"The fighting is between Yunkai and Astapor, we had heard. Meereen is not involved."

"Not as yet. But soon. An envoy from the Yellow City is in Volantis even now, hiring swords. The Long Lances have already taken ship for Yunkai, and the Windblown and the Company of the Cat will follow once they have finished filling out their ranks. The Golden Company marches east as well. All this is known."

"If you say so. I deal in wine, not wars. Ghiscari wine is poor stuff, all agree. The Meereenese will pay a good price for my fine Dornish vintages."

"Dead men do not care what kind of wine they drink." The master of *Adventure* fingered his beard. "I am not the first captain you have approached, I think. Nor the tenth."

"No," Gerris admitted.

"How many, then? A hundred?"

Close enough, thought Quentyn. The Volantenes were fond of boasting that the hundred isles of Braavos could be dropped into their deep harbor and drowned. Quentyn had never seen Braavos, but he could believe it. Rich and ripe and rotted, Volantis covered the mouth of the Rhoyne like a warm wet kiss, stretching across hill and marsh on both sides of the river. Ships were everywhere, coming down the river or headed out to sea, crowding the wharves and piers, taking on cargo or off-loading it: warships and whalers and trading galleys, carracks and skiffs, cogs, great cogs, longships, swan ships, ships from Lys and Tyrosh and Pentos, Qartheen spicers big as palaces, ships from Tolos and Yunkai and the Basilisks. So many that Quentyn, seeing the port for the first time from the deck of the *Meadowlark,* had told his friends that they would only linger here three days.

Yet twenty days had passed, and here they remained, still shipless. The captains of the *Melantine,* the *Triarch's Daughter,* and the *Mermaid's Kiss* had all refused them. A mate on the *Bold Voyager* had laughed in their faces. The master of the *Dolphin* berated them for wasting his time, and the owner of the *Seventh Son* accused them of being pirates. All on the first day.

Only the captain of the *Fawn* had given them reasons for his refusal. "It is true that I am sailing east," he told them, over watered wine. "South around Valyria and thence into the sunrise. We will take on water and provisions at New Ghis, then bend all oars toward Qarth and the Jade Gates. Every voyage has perils, long ones more than most. Why should I seek out more danger by turning into Slaver's Bay? The *Fawn* is my livelihood. I will not risk her to take three mad Dornishmen into the middle of a war."

Quentyn had begun to think that they might have done better to buy their own ship in the Planky Town. That would have drawn unwanted attention, however. The Spider had informers everywhere, even in the halls of Sunspear. "Dorne will bleed if your purpose is discovered," his father had warned him, as they watched the children frolic in the pools and fountains of the Water Gardens. "What we do is treason, make no mistake. Trust only your companions, and do your best to avoid attracting notice."

So Gerris Drinkwater gave the captain of *Adventure* his most disarming smile. "Truth be told, I have not kept count of all the cowards who refused us, but at the Merchant's House I heard it said that you were a bolder sort of man, the sort who might risk anything for sufficient gold."

A smuggler, Quentyn thought. That was how the other traders styled *Adventure*'s master, back at the Merchant's House. "He is a smuggler and a slaver, half pirate and half pander, but it may be that he is your best hope," the innkeep had told them.

The captain rubbed thumb and forefinger together. "And how much gold would you deem sufficient for such a voyage?"

"Thrice your usual fee for passage to Slaver's Bay."

"For each of you?" The captain showed his teeth in something that might have been intended as a smile though it gave his narrow face a feral look. "Perhaps. It is true, I am a bolder man than most. How soon will you wish to leave?"

"The morrow would not be too soon."

"Done. Return an hour before first light, with your friends and your wines. Best to be under way whilst Volantis sleeps, so no one will ask us inconvenient questions about our destination."

"As you say. An hour before first light."

The captain's smile widened. "I am pleased that I can help you. We will have a happy voyage, yes?"

"I am certain of it," said Gerris. The captain called for ale then, and the two of them drank a toast to their venture.

"A sweet man," Gerris said afterward, as he and Quentyn made their way down to the foot of the pier where their hired *hathay* waited. The air hung hot and heavy, and the sun was so bright that both of them were squinting.

"This is a sweet city," Quentyn agreed. *Sweet enough to rot your teeth.* Sweet beets were grown in profusion hereabouts, and were served with almost every meal. The Volantenes made a cold soup of them, as thick and rich as purple honey. Their wines were sweet as well. "I fear our happy voyage will be short, however. That sweet man does not mean to take us to Meereen. He was too quick to accept your offer. He'll take thrice the usual fee, no doubt, and once he has us aboard and out of sight of land, he'll slit our throats and take the rest of our gold as well."

"Or chain us to an oar, beside those wretches we were smelling. We need to find a better class of smuggler, I think."

Their driver awaited them beside his *hathay.* In Westeros, it might have been called an oxcart, though it was a deal more ornate than any cart that Quentyn had ever seen in Dorne, and lacked an ox. The *hathay* was pulled by a dwarf elephant, her hide the color of dirty snow. The streets of Old Volantis were full of such.

Quentyn would have preferred to walk, but they were miles from their inn. Besides, the innkeep at the Merchant's House had warned him that traveling afoot would taint them in the eyes of foreign captains and the native-born Volantenes alike. Persons of quality traveled by palanquin, or in the back of a *hathay* . . . and as it happened the innkeep had a cousin who owned several such contrivances and would be pleased to serve them in this matter.

Their driver was one of the cousin's slaves, a small man with a wheel tattooed upon one cheek, naked but for a breechclout and a pair of sandals. His skin was the color of teak, his eyes chips of flint. After he had helped them up onto the cushioned bench between the cart's two huge wooden wheels, he clambered onto the elephant's back. "The Merchant's House," Quentyn told him, "but go along the wharves." Beyond the waterfront and its breezes, the streets and alleys of Volantis were hot enough to drown a man in his own sweat, at least on this side of the river.

The driver shouted something at his elephant in the local tongue. The beast began to move, trunk swaying from side to side. The cart lurched along behind her, the driver hooting at sailors and slaves alike to clear the way. It was easy enough to tell one from the other. The slaves were all tattooed: a mask of blue feathers, a lightning bolt that ran from jaw to brow, a coin upon the cheek, a leopard's spots, a skull, a jug. Maester Kedry said there were five slaves for every free man in Volantis though he had not lived long enough to verify his estimate. He had perished on the morning the corsairs swarmed aboard the *Meadowlark*.

Quentyn lost two other friends that same day—Willam Wells with his freckles and his crooked teeth, fearless with a lance, and Cletus Yronwood, handsome despite his lazy eye, always randy, always laughing. Cletus had been Quentyn's dearest friend for half his life, a brother in all but blood. "Give your bride a kiss for me," Cletus had whispered to him, just before he died.

The corsairs had come aboard in the darkness before the dawn, as the *Meadowlark* was anchored off the coast of the Disputed Lands. The crew had beaten them off, at the cost of twelve lives. Afterward the sailors stripped the dead corsairs of boots and belts and weapons, divvied up their purses, and yanked gemstones from their ears and rings from their fingers. One of the corpses was so fat that the ship's cook had to cut his fingers off with a meat cleaver to claim his rings. It took three Meadowlarks to roll the body into the sea. The other pirates were chucked in after him, without a word of prayer or ceremony.

Their own dead received more tender treatment. The sailors sewed their bodies up in canvas, weighed down with ballast stones so they might sink more quickly. The captain of the *Meadowlark* led his crew in a prayer for the souls of their slain shipmates. Then he turned to his Dornish passengers, the three who still remained of the six who had come aboard at the Planky Town. Even the big man had emerged, pale and greensick and unsteady on his feet, struggling up from the depths of the ship's hold to pay his last respects. "One of you should say some words for your dead, before we give them to the sea," the captain said. Gerris had obliged, lying with every other word, since he dare not tell the truth of who they'd been or why they'd come.

It was not supposed to end like that for them. "This will be a tale to tell our grandchildren," Cletus had declared the day they set out from his father's castle. Will made a face at that, and said, "A tale to tell tavern wenches, you mean, in hopes they'll lift their skirts." Cletus had slapped him on the back. "For grandchildren, you need children. For children, you need to lift some skirts." Later, in the Planky Town, the Dornishmen had toasted Quentyn's future bride, made ribald japes about his wedding night to come, and talked about the things they'd see, the deeds they'd do, the glory they would win. *All they won was a sailcloth sack filled with ballast stones.*

As much as he mourned Will and Cletus, it was the maester's loss that Quentyn felt most keenly. Kedry had been fluent in the tongues of all of the Free Cities, and even the mongrel Ghiscari that men spoke along the shores of Slaver's Bay. "Maester Kedry will accompany you," his father said the night they parted. "Heed his counsel. He has devoted half his life to the study of the Nine Free Cities." Quentyn wondered if things might not have gone a deal easier if only he were here to guide them.

"I would sell my mother for a bit of breeze," said Gerris, as they rolled through the dockside throngs. "It's moist as the Maiden's cunt, and still shy of noon. I hate this city."

Quentyn shared the feeling. The sullen wet heat of Volantis sapped his strength and left him feeling dirty. The worst part was knowing that nightfall would bring no relief. Up in the high meadows north of Lord Yronwood's estates, the air was always crisp and cool after dark, no matter how hot the day had been. Not here. In Volantis, the nights were almost as hot as the days.

"The *Goddess* sails for New Ghis on the morrow," Gerris reminded him. "That at least would bring us closer."

"New Ghis is an island, and a much smaller port than this. We would be closer, yes, but we could find ourselves stranded. And New Ghis has allied with the Yunkai'i." That news had not come as a surprise to Quentyn. New Ghis and Yunkai were both Ghiscari cities. "If Volantis should ally with them as well—"

"We need to find a ship from Westeros," suggested Gerris, "some trader out of Lannisport or Oldtown."

"Few come this far, and those who do fill their holds with silk and spice from the Jade Sea, then bend their oars for home."

"Perhaps a Braavosi ship? One hears of purple sails as far away as Asshai and the islands of the Jade Sea."

"The Braavosi are descended from escaped slaves. They do not trade in Slaver's Bay."

"Do we have enough gold to *buy* a ship?"

"And who will sail her? You? Me?" Dornishmen had never been seafarers, not since Nymeria burned her ten thousand ships. "The seas around Valyria are perilous, and thick with corsairs."

"I have had enough of corsairs. Let's not buy a ship."

This is still just a game to him, Quentyn realized, *no different than the time he led six of us up into the mountains to find the old lair of the Vulture King.* It was not in Gerris Drinkwater's nature to imagine they might fail, let alone that they might die. Even the deaths of three friends had not served to chasten him, it would seem. *He leaves that to me. He knows my nature is as cautious as his is bold.*

"Perhaps the big man is right," Ser Gerris said. "Piss on the sea, we can finish the journey overland."

"You know why he says that," Quentyn said. "He'd rather die than set foot on another ship." The big man had been greensick every day of their voyage. In Lys, it had taken him four days to recover his strength. They'd had to take rooms in an inn so Maester Kedry could tuck him into a feather bed and feed him broths and potions until some pink returned to his cheeks.

It was possible to go overland to Meereen, that much was true. The old Valyrian roads would take them there. *Dragon roads,* men called the great stone roadways of the Freehold, but the one that ran eastward from Volantis to Meereen had earned a more sinister name: *the demon road.*

"The demon road is dangerous, and too *slow*," Quentyn said. "Tywin Lannister will send his own men after the queen once word of her reaches King's Landing." His father had been certain of that. "His will come with knives. If they reach her first—"

"Let's hope her dragons will sniff them out and eat them," said Gerris. "Well, if we cannot find a ship, and you will not let us ride, we had as well book passage back to Dorne."

Crawl back to Sunspear defeated, with my tail between my legs? His father's disappointment would be more than Quentyn could bear, and the scorn of the Sand Snakes would be withering. Doran Martell had put the fate of Dorne into his hands, he could not fail him, not whilst life remained.

Heat shimmers rose off the street as the *hathay* rattled and jounced along on its iron-rimmed wheels, giving a dreamlike quality to their surroundings. In amongst the warehouses and the wharves, shops and stalls of many sorts crowded the waterfront. Here fresh oysters could be bought, here iron chains and manacles, here *cyvasse* pieces carved of ivory and jade. Here were temples too, where sailors came to sacrifice to foreign gods, cheek by jowl with pillow houses where women called down from balconies to men below. "Have a look at that one," Gerris urged, as they passed one pillow house. "I think she's in love with you."

And how much does a whore's love cost? Truth be told, girls made Quentyn anxious, especially the pretty ones.

When first he'd come to Yronwood, he had been smitten with Ynys, the eldest of Lord Yronwood's daughters. Though he never said a word about his feelings, he nursed his dreams for years . . . until the day she was dispatched to wed Ser Ryon Allyrion, the heir to Godsgrace. The last time he had seen her, she'd had one boy at her breast and another clinging to her skirts.

After Ynys had come the Drinkwater twins, a pair of tawny young maidens who loved hawking, hunting, climbing rocks, and making Quentyn blush. One of them had given him his first kiss, though he never knew which one. As daughters of a landed knight, the twins were too lowborn to marry, but Cletus did not think that was any reason to stop kissing them. "After you're wed you can take one of them for a paramour. Or both, why not?" But Quentyn thought of several reasons why not, so he had done his best to avoid the twins thereafter, and there had been no second kiss.

More recently, the youngest of Lord Yronwood's daughters had taken to following him about the castle. Gwyneth was but twelve, a small, scrawny girl whose dark eyes and brown hair set her apart in that house of blue-eyed blondes. She was clever, though, as quick with words as with her hands, and fond of telling Quentyn that he had to wait for her to flower, so she could marry him.

That was before Prince Doran had summoned him to the Water Gardens. And now the most beautiful woman in the world was waiting in Meereen, and he meant to do his duty and claim her for his bride. *She will not refuse me. She will honor the agreement.* Daenerys Targaryen would need Dorne to win the Seven Kingdoms, and that meant that she would need him. *It does not mean that she will love me, though. She may not even like me.*

The street curved where the river met the sea, and there along the bend a number of animal sellers were clustered together, offering jeweled lizards, giant banded snakes, and agile little monkeys with striped tails and clever pink hands. "Perhaps your silver queen would like a monkey," said Gerris.

Quentyn had no idea what Daenerys Targaryen might like. He had promised his father that he would bring her back to Dorne, but more and more he wondered if he was equal to the task.

I never asked for this, he thought.

Across the wide blue expanse of the Rhoyne, he could see the Black Wall that had been raised by the Valyrians when Volantis was no more than an outpost of their empire: a great oval of fused stone two hundred feet high and so thick that six four-horse chariots could race around its top abreast, as they did each year to celebrate the founding of the city. Outlanders, foreigners, and freedmen were not allowed inside the Black Wall save at the invitation of those who dwelt within, scions of the Old Blood who could trace their ancestry back to Valyria itself.

The traffic was thicker here. They were near the western end of the Long Bridge, which linked the two halves of the city. Wayns and carts and *hathay*s crowded the streets, all of them coming from the bridge or making for it. Slaves were everywhere, as numerous as roaches, scurrying about their masters' business.

Not far from Fishermonger's Square and the Merchant's House, shouts erupted from a cross street, and a dozen Unsullied spearmen in ornate armor and tiger-skin cloaks appeared as if from nowhere, waving everyone aside so the triarch could pass through atop his elephant. The triarch's elephant was a grey-skinned behemoth clad in elaborate enameled armor that clattered softly as he moved, the castle on its back so tall that it scraped the top of the ornamental stone arch he was passing underneath. "The triarchs are considered so elevated that their feet are not allowed to touch the ground during their year of service," Quentyn informed his companion. "They ride everywhere on elephants."

"Blocking up the streets and leaving heaps of dung for the likes of us to contend with," said Gerris. "Why Volantis needs three princes when Dorne makes do with one, I will never know."

"The triarchs are neither kings nor princes. Volantis is a freehold, like Valyria of old. All freeborn landholders share the rule. Even women are allowed to vote, provided they own land. The three triarchs are chosen from amongst those noble families who can prove unbroken descent from old Valyria, to serve until the first day of the new year. And you would know all this if you had troubled to read the book that Maester Kedry gave you."

"It had no pictures."

"There were maps."

"Maps do not count. If he had told me it was about tigers and elephants, I might have given it a try. It looked suspiciously like a history."

When their *hathay* reached the edge of the Fishermonger's Square, their elephant lifted her trunk and made a honking noise like some huge white goose, reluctant to plunge into the tangle of wayns, palanquins, and foot traffic ahead. Their driver prodded her with his heel and kept her moving.

The fishmongers were out in strength, crying the morning catch. Quentyn understood one word in two at best, but he did not need to know the words to know the fish. He saw cod and sailfish and sardines, barrels of mussels and clams. Eels hung along the front of one stall. Another displayed a gigantic turtle, strung up by its legs on iron chains, heavy as a horse. Crabs scrabbled inside casks of brine and seaweed. Several of the vendors were frying chunks of fish with onions and beets, or selling peppery fish stew out of small iron kettles.

In the center of the square, under the cracked and headless statue of a dead triarch, a crowd had begun to gather about some dwarfs putting on a show. The little men were done up in wooden armor, miniature knights preparing for a joust. Quentyn saw one mount a dog, as the other hopped onto a pig . . . only to slide right off again, to a smattering of laughter.

"They look amusing," Gerris said. "Shall we stop and watch them fight? A laugh might serve you well, Quent. You look like an old man who has not moved his bowels in half a year."

I am eight-and-ten, six years younger than you, Quentyn thought. *I am no old man.* Instead he said, "I have no need for comic dwarfs. Unless they have a ship."

"A small one, I would think."

Four stories tall, the Merchant's House dominated the docks and wharves and storehouses that surrounded it. Here traders from Oldtown and King's Landing mingled with their counterparts from Braavos and Pentos and Myr, with hairy Ibbenese, pale-skinned voyagers from Qarth, coal-black Summer Islanders in feathered cloaks, even masked shadowbinders from Asshai by the Shadow.

The paving stones felt warm beneath his feet when Quentyn climbed down from the *hathay*, even through the leather of his boots. Outside the Merchant's House a trestle table had been set up in the shade and decorated with striped blue-and-white pennons that fluttered at every breath of air. Four hard-eyed sellswords lounged around the table, calling out to every passing man and boy. *Windblown,* Quentyn knew. The serjeants were looking for fresh meat to fill their ranks before they sailed for Slaver's Bay. *And every man who signs with them is another sword for Yunkai, another blade meant to drink the blood of my bride-to-be.*

One of the Windblown shouted at them. "I do not speak your

tongue," Quentyn answered. Though he could read and write High Valyrian, he had little practice speaking it. And the Volantene apple had rolled a fair distance from the Valyrian tree.

"Westerosi?" the man answered, in the Common Tongue.

"Dornishmen. My master is a wineseller."

"Master? Fuck that. Are you a slave? Come with us and be your own master. Do you want to die abed? We'll teach you sword and spear. You'll ride to battle with the Tattered Prince and come home richer than a lord. Boys, girls, gold, whatever you want, if you're man enough to take it. We're the Windblown, and we fuck the goddess slaughter up her arse."

Two of the sellswords began to sing, bellowing out the words to some marching song. Quentyn understood enough to get the gist. *We are the Windblown,* they sang. *Blow us east to Slaver's Bay, we'll kill the butcher king and fuck the dragon queen.*

"If Cletus and Will were still with us, we could come back with the big man and kill the lot of them," said Gerris.

Cletus and Will are dead. "Pay them no mind," Quentyn said. The sellswords threw taunts at their backs as they pushed through the doors of the Merchant's House, mocking them as bloodless cravens and frightened girls.

The big man was waiting in their rooms on the second floor. Though the inn had come well recommended by the master of the *Meadowlark,* that did not mean Quentyn was willing to leave their goods and gold unguarded. Every port had thieves, rats, and whores, and Volantis had more than most.

"I was about to go out looking for you," Ser Archibald Yronwood said as he slid the bar back to admit them. It was his cousin Cletus who had started calling him *the big man,* but the name was well deserved. Arch was six-and-a-half-feet tall, broad of shoulder, huge of belly, with legs like tree trunks, hands the size of hams, and no neck to speak of. Some childhood malady had made all his hair fall out. His bald head reminded Quentyn of a smooth pink boulder. "So," he demanded, "what did the smuggler say? Do we have a boat?"

"A ship," corrected Quentyn. "Aye, he'll take us, but only as far as the nearest hell."

Gerris sat upon a sagging bed and pulled off his boots. "Dorne is sounding more attractive every moment."

The big man said, "I still say we would do better to ride the demon road. Might be it's not as perilous as men say. And if it is, that only means more glory for those who dare it. Who would dare molest us? Drink with his sword, me with my hammer, that's more than any demon could digest."

"And if Daenerys is dead before we reach her?" Quentyn said. "We must have a ship. Even if it is *Adventure*."

Gerris laughed. "You must be more desperate for Daenerys than I knew if you'd endure that stench for months on end. After three days, I'd be begging them to murder me. No, my prince, I pray you, not *Adventure*."

"Do you have a better way?" Quentyn asked him.

"I do. It's just now come to me. It has its risks, and it is not what you would call honorable, I grant you . . . but it will get you to your queen quicker than the demon road."

"Tell me," said Quentyn Martell.

JON

Jon Snow read the letter over until the words began to blur and run together. *I cannot sign this. I will not sign this.*

He almost burned the parchment then and there. Instead he took a sip of ale, the dregs of the half cup that remained from his solitary supper the night before. *I have to sign it. They chose me to be their lord commander. The Wall is mine, and the Watch as well. The Night's Watch takes no part.*

It was a relief when Dolorous Edd Tollett opened the door to tell him that Gilly was without. Jon set Maester Aemon's letter aside. "I will see her." He dreaded this. "Find Sam for me. I will want to speak with him next."

"He'll be down with the books. My old septon used to say that books are dead men talking. Dead men should keep quiet, is what I say. No one wants to hear a dead man's yabber." Dolorous Edd went off muttering of worms and spiders.

When Gilly entered, she went at once to her knees. Jon came around the table and drew her to her feet. "You don't need to take a knee for me. That's just for kings." Though a wife and mother, Gilly still seemed half a child to him, a slender little thing wrapped up in one of Sam's old cloaks. The cloak was so big on her that she could have hidden several other girls beneath its folds. "The babes are well?" he asked her.

The wildling girl smiled timidly from under her cowl. "Yes, m'lord.

I was scared I wouldn't have milk enough for both, but the more they suck, the more I have. They're strong."

"I have something hard to tell you." He almost said *ask,* but caught himself at the last instant.

"Is it Mance? Val begged the king to spare him. She said she'd let some kneeler marry her and never slit his throat if only Mance could live. That Lord o'Bones, he's to be spared. Craster always swore he'd kill him if he ever showed his face about the keep. Mance never did half the things he done."

All Mance ever did was lead an army down upon the realm he once swore to protect. "Mance said our words, Gilly. Then he turned his cloak, wed Dalla, and crowned himself King-Beyond-the-Wall. His life is in the king's hands now. It's not him we need to talk about. It's his son. Dalla's boy."

"The babe?" Her voice trembled. "He never broke no oath, m'lord. He sleeps and cries and sucks, is all; he's never done no harm to no one. Don't let her burn him. Save him, please."

"Only you can do that, Gilly." Jon told her how.

Another woman would have shrieked at him, cursed him, damned him down to seven hells. Another woman might have flown at him in rage, slapped him, kicked him, raked at his eyes with her nails. Another woman might have thrown her defiance in his teeth.

Gilly shook her head. "No. Please, no."

The raven picked up the word. "*No,*" it screamed.

"Refuse, and the boy will burn. Not on the morrow, nor the day after . . . but soon, whenever Melisandre needs to wake a dragon or raise a wind or work some other spell requiring king's blood. Mance will be ash and bone by then, so she will claim his son for the fire, and Stannis will not deny her. If you do not take the boy away, *she will burn him.*"

"I'll go," said Gilly. "I'll take him, I'll take the both o' them, Dalla's boy *and* mine." Tears rolled down her cheeks. If not for the way the candle made them glisten, Jon might never have known that she was weeping. *Craster's wives would have taught their daughters to shed their tears into a pillow. Perhaps they went outside to weep, well away from Craster's fists.*

Jon closed the fingers of his sword hand. "Take both boys and the queen's men will ride after you and drag you back. The boy will still burn . . . and you with him." *If I comfort her, she may think that tears can move me. She has to realize that I will not yield.* "You'll take one boy, and that one Dalla's."

"A mother can't leave her son, or else she's cursed forever. Not a *son*. We *saved* him, Sam and me. Please. Please, m'lord. We saved him from the cold."

"Men say that freezing to death is almost peaceful. Fire, though . . . do you see the candle, Gilly?"

She looked at the flame. "Yes."

"Touch it. Put your hand over the flame."

Her big brown eyes grew bigger still. She did not move.

"Do it." *Kill the boy.* "Now."

Trembling, the girl reached out her hand, held it well above the flickering candle flame.

"Down. Let it kiss you."

Gilly lowered her hand. An inch. Another. When the flame licked her flesh, she snatched her hand back and began to sob.

"Fire is a cruel way to die. Dalla died to give this child life, but you have nourished him, cherished him. You saved your own boy from the ice. Now save hers from the fire."

"They'll burn my babe, then. The red woman. If she can't have Dalla's, she'll burn mine."

"Your son has no king's blood. Melisandre gains nothing by giving him to the fire. Stannis wants the free folk to fight for him, he will not burn an innocent without good cause. Your boy will be safe. I will find a wet nurse for him and he'll be raised here at Castle Black under my protection. He'll learn to hunt and ride, to fight with sword and axe and bow. I'll even see that he is taught to read and write." Sam would like that. "And when he is old enough, he will learn the truth of who he is. He'll be free to seek you out if that is what he wants."

"You will make a crow of him." She wiped at her tears with the back of a small pale hand. "I won't. I won't."

Kill the boy, thought Jon. "You will. Else I promise you, the day that they burn Dalla's boy, yours will die as well."

"*Die,*" shrieked the Old Bear's raven. "*Die, die, die.*"

The girl sat hunched and shrunken, staring at the candle flame, tears glistening in her eyes. Finally Jon said, "You have my leave to go. Do not speak of this, but see that you are ready to depart an hour before first light. My men will come for you."

Gilly got to her feet. Pale and wordless, she departed, with never a look back at him. Jon heard her footsteps as she rushed through the armory. She was almost running.

When he went to close the door, Jon saw that Ghost was stretched out beneath the anvil, gnawing on the bone of an ox. The big white direwolf looked up at his approach. "Past time that you were back." He returned to his chair, to read over Maester Aemon's letter once again.

Samwell Tarly turned up a few moments later, clutching a stack of books. No sooner had he entered than Mormont's raven flew at him demanding corn. Sam did his best to oblige, offering some kernels from the sack beside the door. The raven did its best to peck through his palm. Sam yowled, the bird flapped off, corn scattered. "Did that wretch break the skin?" Jon asked.

Sam gingerly removed his glove. "He did. I'm *bleeding.*"

"We all shed our blood for the Watch. Wear thicker gloves." Jon shoved a chair toward him with a foot. "Sit, and have a look at this." He handed Sam the parchment.

"What is it?"

"A paper shield."

Sam read it slowly. "A letter to King Tommen?"

"At Winterfell, Tommen fought my brother Bran with wooden swords," Jon said, remembering. "He wore so much padding he looked like a stuffed goose. Bran knocked him to the ground." He went to the window and threw the shutters open. The air outside was cold and bracing, though the sky was a dull grey. "Yet Bran's dead, and pudgy pink-faced Tommen is sitting on the Iron Throne, with a crown nestled amongst his golden curls."

That got an odd look from Sam, and for a moment he looked as if he wanted to say something. Instead he swallowed and turned back to the parchment. "You haven't signed the letter."

Jon shook his head. "The Old Bear begged the Iron Throne for help a hundred times. They sent him Janos Slynt. No letter will make the Lannisters love us better. Not once they hear that we've been helping Stannis."

"Only to defend the Wall, not in his rebellion. That's what it *says* here."

"The distinction may escape Lord Tywin." Jon snatched the letter back. "Why would he help us now? He never did before."

"Well, he will not want it said that Stannis rode to the defense of the realm whilst King Tommen was playing with his toys. That would bring scorn down upon House Lannister."

"It's death and destruction I want to bring down upon House Lannister, not scorn." Jon read from the letter. "*The Night's Watch takes no part in the wars of the Seven Kingdoms. Our oaths are sworn to the realm, and the realm now stands in dire peril. Stannis Baratheon aids us against our foes from beyond the Wall, though we are not his men . . .*"

Sam squirmed in his seat. "Well, we're *not*. Are we?"

"I gave Stannis food, shelter, and the Nightfort, plus leave to settle some free folk in the Gift. That's all."

"Lord Tywin will say it was too much."

"Stannis says it's not enough. The more you give a king, the more he wants. We are walking on a bridge of ice with an abyss on either side. Pleasing one king is difficult enough. Pleasing two is hardly possible."

"Yes, but . . . if the Lannisters should prevail and Lord Tywin decides that we betrayed the king by aiding Stannis, it could mean the end of the Night's Watch. He has the Tyrells behind him, with all the strength of Highgarden. And he did defeat Lord Stannis on the Blackwater."

"The Blackwater was one battle. Robb won all his battles and still lost his head. If Stannis can raise the north . . ."

Sam hesitated, then said, "The Lannisters have northmen of their own. Lord Bolton and his bastard."

"Stannis has the Karstarks. If he can win White Harbor . . ."

"If," Sam stressed. "If not . . . my lord, even a paper shield is better than none."

"I suppose so." *Him and Aemon both.* Somehow he had hoped that Sam Tarly might see it differently. *It is only ink and parchment.* Resigned, he grabbed the quill and signed. "Get the sealing wax." *Before I change my mind.* Sam hastened to obey. Jon fixed the lord commander's seal and handed him the letter. "Take this to Maester Aemon when you leave, and tell him to dispatch a bird to King's Landing."

"I will." Sam sounded relieved. "My lord, if I might ask . . . I saw Gilly leaving. She was almost crying."

"Val sent her to plead for Mance again," Jon lied, and they talked for a while of Mance and Stannis and Melisandre of Asshai, until the raven ate the last corn kernel and screamed, "*Blood.*"

"I am sending Gilly away," Jon said. "Her and the boy. We will need to find another wet nurse for his milk brother."

"Goat's milk might serve, until you do. It's better for a babe than cow's milk." Talking about breasts plainly made Sam uncomfortable, and suddenly he began to speak of history, and boy commanders who had lived and died hundreds of years ago. Jon cut him off with, "Tell me something useful. Tell me of our enemy."

"The Others." Sam licked his lips. "They are mentioned in the annals, though not as often as I would have thought. The annals I've found and looked at, that is. There's more I haven't found, I know. Some of the older books are falling to pieces. The pages crumble when I try and turn them. And the *really* old books . . . either they have crumbled all away or they are buried somewhere that I haven't looked yet or . . . well, it could be that there are no such books and never were. The oldest histories we have were written after the Andals came to Westeros. The First Men only left us runes on rocks, so everything we think we know about the Age of Heroes and the Dawn Age and the Long Night comes from accounts set down by septons thousands of years later. There are archmaesters at the Citadel who question all of it. Those old histories are full of kings who reigned for hundreds of years, and knights riding around a thousand years before there *were* knights. You know the tales, Brandon the Builder, Symeon Star-Eyes, Night's King . . . we say that you're the nine-hundred-and-ninety-eighth Lord Commander of the Night's Watch, but the oldest list I've found shows six hundred seventy-four commanders, which suggests that it was written during—"

"Long ago," Jon broke in. "What about the Others?"

"I found mention of dragonglass. The children of the forest used to give the Night's Watch a hundred obsidian daggers every year, during the Age of Heroes. The Others come when it is cold, most of the tales agree. Or else it gets cold when they come. Sometimes they appear during snowstorms and melt away when the skies clear. They hide from the light of the sun and emerge by night . . . or else night falls when they emerge. Some stories speak of them riding the corpses of dead animals. Bears, direwolves, mammoths, horses, it makes no matter, so long as the beast is dead. The one that killed Small Paul was riding a dead horse, so that part's plainly true. Some accounts speak of giant ice spiders too. I don't know what those are. Men who fall in battle against the Others must be burned, or else the dead will rise again as their thralls."

"We knew all this. The question is, how do we fight them?"

"The armor of the Others is proof against most ordinary blades, if the tales can be believed, and their own swords are so cold they shatter steel. Fire will dismay them, though, and they are vulnerable to obsidian. I found one account of the Long Night that spoke of the last hero slaying Others with a blade of dragonsteel. Supposedly they could not stand against it."

"Dragonsteel?" The term was new to Jon. "*Valyrian* steel?"

"That was my first thought as well."

"So if I can just convince the lords of the Seven Kingdoms to give us their Valyrian blades, all is saved? That won't be hard." *No harder than asking them to give up their coin and castles.* He gave a bitter laugh. "Did you find who the Others are, where they come from, what they want?"

"Not yet, my lord, but it may be that I've just been reading the wrong books. There are hundreds I have not looked at yet. Give me more time and I will find whatever there is to be found."

"There is no more time. You need to get your things together, Sam. You're going with Gilly."

"Going?" Sam gaped at him openmouthed, as if he did not understand the meaning of the word. "I'm going? To Eastwatch, my lord? Or . . . where am I . . ."

"Oldtown."

"*Oldtown?*" Sam repeated, in a high-pitched squeak.

"Aemon as well."

"Aemon? *Maester* Aemon? But . . . he's one hundred and two years old, my lord, he can't . . . you're sending him *and* me? Who will tend the ravens? If there's sick or wounded, who . . ."

"Clydas. He's been with Aemon for years."

"Clydas is only a steward, and his eyes are going bad. You need a *maester.* Maester Aemon is so frail, a sea voyage . . . it might . . . he's old, and . . ."

"His life will be at risk. I am aware of that, Sam, but the risk is greater here. Stannis knows who Aemon is. If the red woman requires king's blood for her spells . . ."

"Oh." Sam's fat cheeks seemed to drain of color.

"Dareon will join you at Eastwatch. My hope is that his songs will win some men for us in the south. The *Blackbird* will deliver you to Braavos. From there, you'll arrange your own passage to Oldtown. If you still mean to claim Gilly's babe as your bastard, send her and the child on to Horn Hill. Elsewise, Aemon will find a servant's place for her at the Citadel."

"My b-b-bastard. Yes, I . . . my mother and my sisters will help Gilly with the child. Dareon could see her to Oldtown just as well as me. I'm . . . I've been working at my archery every afternoon with Ulmer, as you commanded . . . well, except when I'm in the vaults, but you told me to find out about the Others. The longbow makes my shoulders ache and raises blisters on my fingers." He showed Jon his hand. "I still do it, though. I can hit the target more often than not now, but I'm still the worst archer who ever bent a bow. I like Ulmer's stories, though. Someone needs to write them down and put them in a book."

"You do it. They have parchment and ink at the Citadel, as well as longbows. I will expect you to continue with your practice. Sam, the Night's Watch has hundreds of men who can loose an arrow, but

only a handful who can read or write. I need you to become my new
maester."

"My lord, I . . . my work is here, the books . . ."

". . . will be here when you return to us."

Sam put a hand to his throat. "My lord, the Citadel . . . they make
you cut up corpses there. I cannot wear a chain."

"You can. You will. Maester Aemon is old and blind. His strength
is leaving him. Who will take his place when he dies? Maester Mullin
at the Shadow Tower is more fighter than scholar, and Maester
Harmune of Eastwatch is drunk more than he's sober."

"If you ask the Citadel for more maesters . . ."

"I mean to. We'll have need of every one. Aemon Targaryen is not
so easily replaced, however." *This is not going as I had hoped.* He had
known Gilly would be hard, but he had assumed Sam would be glad
to trade the dangers of the Wall for the warmth of Oldtown. "I was
certain this would please you," he said, puzzled. "There are so many
books at the Citadel that no man can hope to read them all. You
would do well there, Sam. I know you would."

"No. I could read the books, but . . . a m-maester must be a healer
and b-b-blood makes me faint." His hand shook, to prove the truth
of that. "I'm Sam the Scared, not Sam the Slayer."

"Scared? Of what? The chidings of old men? Sam, you saw the
wights come swarming up the Fist, a tide of living dead men with
black hands and bright blue eyes. You slew an Other."

"It was the d-d-d-dragonglass, not me."

"Be quiet," Jon snapped. After Gilly, he had no patience for the fat
boy's fears. "You lied and schemed and plotted to make me lord
commander. You *will* obey me. You'll go to the Citadel and forge a
chain, and if you have to cut up corpses, so be it. At least in Oldtown
the corpses won't object."

"My lord, my f-f-f-father, Lord Randyll, he, he, he, he, he . . . the
life of a maester is a life of *servitude.* No son of House Tarly will ever
wear a chain. The men of Horn Hill do not bow and scrape to petty
lords. Jon, I cannot disobey my *father.*"

Kill the boy, Jon thought. *The boy in you, and the one in him. Kill
the both of them, you bloody bastard.* "You have no father. Only

brothers. Only us. Your life belongs to the Night's Watch, so go and stuff your smallclothes into a sack, along with anything else you care to take to Oldtown. You leave an hour before sunrise. And here's another order. From this day forth, you will *not* call yourself a craven. You've faced more things this past year than most men face in a lifetime. You can face the Citadel, but you'll face it as a Sworn Brother of the Night's Watch. I can't command you to be brave, but I *can* command you to hide your fears. You said the words, Sam. Remember?"

"I . . . I'll try."

"You won't try. You will obey."

"*Obey.*" Mormont's raven flapped its great black wings.

Sam seemed to sag. "As my lord commands. Does . . . does Maester Aemon know?"

"It was as much his idea as mine." Jon opened the door for him. "No farewells. The fewer folk who know of this, the better. An hour before first light, by the lichyard."

Sam fled from him just as Gilly had.

Jon was tired. *I need sleep.* He had been up half the night poring over maps, writing letters, and making plans with Maester Aemon. Even after stumbling into his narrow bed, rest had not come easily. He knew what he would face today, and found himself tossing restlessly as he brooded on Maester Aemon's final words. "Allow me to give my lord one last piece of counsel," the old man had said, "the same counsel that I once gave my brother when we parted for the last time. He was three-and-thirty when the Great Council chose him to mount the Iron Throne. A man grown with sons of his own, yet in some ways still a boy. Egg had an innocence to him, a sweetness we all loved. *Kill the boy within you,* I told him the day I took ship for the Wall. *It takes a man to rule. An Aegon, not an Egg. Kill the boy and let the man be born.*" The old man felt Jon's face. "You are half the age that Egg was, and your own burden is a crueler one, I fear. You will have little joy of your command, but I think you have the strength in you to do the things that must be done. Kill the boy, Jon Snow. Winter is almost upon us. Kill the boy and let the man be born."

Jon donned his cloak and strode outside. He made the rounds of

Castle Black each day, visiting the men on watch and hearing their reports first hand, watching Ulmer and his charges at the archery butts, talking with king's men and queen's men alike, walking the ice atop the Wall to have a look at the forest. Ghost padded after him, a white shadow at his side.

Kedge Whiteye had the Wall when Jon made his ascent. Kedge had seen forty-odd namedays, thirty of them on the Wall. His left eye was blind, his right eye mean. In the wild, alone with axe and garron, he was as good a ranger as any in the Watch, but he had never gotten on well with the other men. "A quiet day," he told Jon. "Nothing to report, except the wrong-way rangers."

"The wrong-way rangers?" Jon asked.

Kedge grinned. "A pair of knights. Went riding off an hour ago, south along the kingsroad. When Dywen saw them buggering off, he said the southron fools were riding the wrong way."

"I see," said Jon.

He found out more from Dywen himself, as the old forester sucked down a bowl of barley broth in the barracks. "Aye, m'lord, I saw them. Horpe and Massey, it were. Claimed Stannis sent 'em out, but never said where or what for or when they would be back."

Ser Richard Horpe and Ser Justin Massey were both queen's men, and high in the king's councils. *A pair of common freeriders would have served if all that Stannis had in mind was scouting,* Jon Snow reflected, *but knights are better suited to act as messengers or envoys.* Cotter Pyke had sent word from Eastwatch that the Onion Lord and Salladhor Saan had set sail for White Harbor to treat with Lord Manderly. It made sense that Stannis would send out other envoys. His Grace was not a patient man.

Whether the wrong-way rangers would return was another question. Knights they might be, but they did not know the north. *There will be eyes along the kingsroad, not all of them friendly.* It was none of Jon's concern, though. *Let Stannis have his secrets. The gods know that I have mine.*

Ghost slept at the foot of the bed that night, and for once Jon did not dream he was a wolf. Even so, he slept fitfully, tossing for hours before sliding down into a nightmare. Gilly was in it, weeping, pleading with him to leave her babes alone, but he ripped the children from her arms and hacked their heads off, then swapped the heads around and told her to sew them back in place.

When he woke, he found Edd Tollett looming over him in the darkness of his bedchamber. "M'lord? It is time. The hour of the wolf. You left orders to be woken."

"Bring me something hot." Jon threw off his blankets.

Edd was back by the time that he had dressed, pressing a steaming cup into his hands. Jon expected hot mulled wine, and was surprised to find that it was soup, a thin broth that smelled of leeks and carrots but seemed to have no leeks or carrots in it. *The smells are stronger in my wolf dreams,* he reflected, *and food tastes richer too. Ghost is more alive than I am.* He left the empty cup upon the forge.

Kegs was on his door this morning. "I will want to speak with Bedwyck and with Janos Slynt," Jon told him. "Have them both here at first light."

Outside the world was black and still. *Cold, but not dangerously cold. Not yet. It will be warmer when the sun comes up. If the gods are good, the Wall may weep.* When they reached the lichyard, the column had already formed up. Jon had given Black Jack Bulwer command of the escort, with a dozen mounted rangers under him, and two wayns. One was piled high with chests and crates and sacks, provisions for the journey. The other had a stiff roof of boiled leather to keep the wind off. Maester Aemon was seated in the back of it, huddled in a bearskin that made him look as small as a child. Sam and Gilly stood nearby. Her eyes were red and puffy, but the boy was in her arms, bundled tight. Whether it was her boy or Dalla's he could not be sure. He had only seen the two together a few times. Gilly's boy was older, Dalla's more robust, but they were close enough in age and size so that no one who did not know them well would be able to easily tell one from the other.

"Lord Snow," Maester Aemon called out, "I left a book for you in my chambers. The *Jade Compendium.* It was written by the Volantene adventurer Colloquo Votar, who traveled to the east and visited all the lands of the Jade Sea. There is a passage you may find of interest. I've told Clydas to mark it for you."

"I'll be sure to read it."

Maester Aemon wiped his nose. "Knowledge is a weapon, Jon. Arm yourself well before you ride forth to battle."

"I will." Jon felt something wet and cold upon his face. When he raised his eyes, he saw that it was snowing. *A bad omen.* He turned to Black Jack Bulwer. "Make as good a time as you can, but take no foolish risks. You have an old man and a suckling babe with you. See that you keep them warm and well fed."

"You do the same, m'lord." Gilly did not seem in any haste to climb into the wayn. "You do the same for t'other. Find another wet nurse, like you said. You promised me you would. The boy . . . Dalla's boy . . . the little prince, I mean . . . you find him some good woman, so he grows up big and strong."

"You have my word."

"Don't you name him. Don't you do that, till he's past two years. It's ill luck to name them when they're still on the breast. You crows may not know that, but it's true."

"As you command, my lady."

"Don't you call me that. I'm a mother, not a lady. I'm Craster's wife and Craster's daughter, and a *mother.*" She gave the babe to Dolorous Edd as she climbed into the wayn and covered herself with furs. When Edd gave her back the child, Gilly put him to her breast. Sam turned away from the sight, red-faced, and heaved himself up onto his mare. "*Let's do this,*" commanded Black Jack Bulwer, snapping his whip. The wayns rolled forward.

Sam lingered a moment. "Well," he said, "farewell."

"And to you, Sam," said Dolorous Edd. "Your boat's not like to sink, I don't think. Boats only sink when I'm aboard."

Jon was remembering. "The first time I saw Gilly she was pressed back against the wall of Craster's Keep, this skinny dark-haired girl with her big belly, cringing away from Ghost. He had gotten in among her rabbits, and I think she was frightened that he would tear her open and devour the babe . . . but it was not the wolf she should have been afraid of, was it?"

"She has more courage than she knows," said Sam.

"So do you, Sam. Have a swift, safe voyage, and take care of her and Aemon and the child." The cold trickles on his face reminded Jon of the day he'd bid farewell to Robb at Winterfell, never knowing that it was for the last time. "And pull your hood up. The snowflakes are melting in your hair."

By the time the little column had dwindled in the distance, the eastern sky had gone from black to grey and the snow was falling heavily. "Giant will be waiting on the lord commander's pleasure," Dolorous Edd reminded him. "Janos Slynt as well."

"Yes." Jon Snow glanced up at the Wall, towering over them like a cliff of ice. *A hundred leagues from end to end, and seven hundred feet high.* The strength of the Wall was its height; the length of the Wall was its weakness. Jon remembered something his father had said once. *A wall is only as strong as the men who stand behind it.* The men of the Night's Watch were brave enough, but they were far too few for the task that confronted them.

Giant was waiting in the armory. His real name was Bedwyck. At a hair and a half over five feet he was the smallest man in the Night's Watch. Jon came directly to the point. "We need more eyes along the Wall. Waycastles where our patrols can get out of the cold and find hot food and a fresh mount. I am putting a garrison in Icemark and giving you command of it."

Giant put the tip of his little finger in his ear to clean out the wax. "Command? Me? M'lord knows I'm just a crofter's get, on the Wall for poaching?"

"You've been a ranger for a dozen years. You survived the Fist of the First Men and Craster's Keep, and came back to tell the tale. The younger men look up to you."

The small man laughed. "Only dwarfs look up to me. I don't read, my lord. On a good day I can write my name."

"I've sent to Oldtown for more maesters. You'll have two ravens for when your need is urgent. When it's not, send riders. Until we have more maesters and more birds, I mean to establish a line of beacon towers along the top of the Wall."

"And how many poor fools will I be commanding?"

"Twenty, from the Watch," said Jon, "and half as many men from Stannis." *Old, green, or wounded.* "They won't be his best men, and none will take the black, but they'll obey. Make what use of them you can. Four of the brothers I'm sending with you will be Kingslanders who came to the Wall with Lord Slynt. Keep one eye on that lot and watch for climbers with the other."

"We can watch, m'lord, but if enough climbers gain the top o' the Wall, thirty men won't be enough to throw them off."

Three hundred might not be enough. Jon kept that doubt to himself. It was true that climbers were desperately vulnerable whilst on the ascent. Stones and spears and pots of burning pitch could be rained down on them from above, and all they could do was cling desperately to the ice. Sometimes the Wall itself seemed to shake them off, as a dog might shake off fleas. Jon had seen that for himself, when a sheet of ice cracked beneath Val's lover Jarl, sending him to his death.

If the climbers reached the top of the Wall undetected, however, everything changed. Given time, they could carve out a toehold for themselves up there, throwing up ramparts of their own and dropping ropes and ladders for thousands more to clamber over after them. That was how Raymun Redbeard had done it, Raymun who had been King-Beyond-the-Wall in the days of his grandfather's grandfather. Jack Musgood had been the lord commander in those days. Jolly Jack, he was called before Redbeard came down upon the north; Sleepy Jack, forever after. Raymun's host had met a bloody end on the shores of Long Lake, caught between Lord Willam of Winterfell and the Drunken Giant, Harmond Umber. Red-beard had been slain by Artos the Implacable, Lord Willam's younger brother. The Watch arrived too late to fight the wildlings, but in time to bury them, the task that Artos Stark assigned them in his wroth as he grieved above the headless corpse of his fallen brother.

Jon did not intend to be remembered as Sleepy Jon Snow. "Thirty men will stand a better chance than none," he told Giant.

"True enough," the small man said. "Is it just to be Icemark, then, or will m'lord be opening t'other forts as well?"

"I mean to garrison all of them, in time," said Jon, "but for the moment, it will just be Icemark and Greyguard."

"And has m'lord decided who's to command at Greyguard?"

"Janos Slynt," said Jon. *Gods save us.* "A man does not rise to command of the gold cloaks without ability. Slynt was born a butcher's son. He was captain of the Iron Gate when Manly Stokeworth died, and Jon Arryn raised him up and put the defense of King's Landing into his hands. Lord Janos cannot be as great a fool as he seems." *And I want him well away from Alliser Thorne.*

"Might be that's so," said Giant, "but I'd still send him to the kitchens to help Three-Finger Hobb cut up the turnips."

If I did, I'd never dare to eat another turnip.

Half the morning passed before Lord Janos reported as commanded. Jon was cleaning Longclaw. Some men would have given that task to a steward or a squire, but Lord Eddard had taught his sons to care for their own weapons. When Kegs and Dolorous Edd arrived with Slynt, Jon thanked them and bid Lord Janos sit.

That he did, albeit with poor grace, crossing his arms, scowling, and ignoring the naked steel in his lord commander's hands. Jon slid the oilcloth down his bastard sword, watching the play of morning light across the ripples, thinking how easily the blade would slide through skin and fat and sinew to part Slynt's ugly head from his body. All of a man's crimes were wiped away when he took the black, and all of his allegiances as well, yet he found it hard to think of Janos Slynt as a brother. *There is blood between us. This man helped slay my father and did his best to have me killed as well.*

"Lord Janos." Jon sheathed his sword. "I am giving you command of Greyguard."

That took Slynt aback. "Greyguard . . . Greyguard was where you climbed the Wall with your wildling friends . . ."

"It was. The fort is in a sorry state, admittedly. You will restore it as best you can. Start by clearing back the forest. Steal stones from the structures that have collapsed to repair those still standing." *The work will be hard and brutal,* he might have added. *You'll sleep on stone, too exhausted to complain or plot, and soon you'll forget what it was like to be warm, but you might remember what it was to be a man.* "You will have thirty men. Ten from here, ten from the Shadow Tower, and ten lent to us by King Stannis."

Slynt's face had turned the color of a prune. His meaty jowls began to quiver. "Do you think I cannot see what you are doing? Janos Slynt is not a man to be gulled so easily. I was charged with the defense of King's Landing when you were soiling your swaddling clothes. Keep your ruin, bastard."

I am giving you a chance, my lord. It is more than you ever gave my father. "You mistake me, my lord," Jon said. "That was a command, not an offer. It is forty leagues to Greyguard. Pack up your arms and armor, say your farewells, and be ready to depart at first light on the morrow."

"No." Lord Janos lurched to his feet, sending his chair crashing over backwards. "I will *not* go meekly off to freeze and die. No traitor's bastard gives commands to Janos Slynt! I am not without friends, I warn you. Here, and in King's Landing too. I was the Lord of Harrenhal! Give your ruin to one of the blind fools who cast a stone for you, I will not have it. Do you hear me, boy? *I will not have it!*"

"You will."

Slynt did not deign to answer that, but he kicked the chair aside as he departed.

He still sees me as a boy, Jon thought, *a green boy, to be cowed by angry words.* He could only hope that a night's sleep would bring Lord Janos to his senses.

The next morning proved that hope was vain.

Jon found Slynt breaking his fast in the common room. Ser Alliser Thorne was with him, and several of their cronies. They were laughing about something when Jon came down the steps with Iron Emmett and Dolorous Edd, and behind them Mully, Horse, Red Jack Crabb, Rusty Flowers, and Owen the Oaf. Three-Finger Hobb was ladling out porridge from his kettle. Queen's men, king's men, and black brothers sat at their separate tables, some bent over bowls of porridge, others filling their bellies with fried bread and bacon. Jon saw Pyp and Grenn at one table, Bowen Marsh at another. The air smelled of smoke and grease, and the clatter of knives and spoons echoed off the vaulted ceiling.

All the voices died at once.

"Lord Janos," Jon said, "I will give you one last chance. Put down that spoon and get to the stables. I have had your horse saddled and bridled. It is a long, hard road to Greyguard."

"Then you had best be on your way, boy." Slynt laughed, dribbling porridge down his chest. "Greyguard's a good place for the likes of you, I'm thinking. Well away from decent godly folk. The mark of the beast is on you, bastard."

"You are refusing to obey my order?"

"You can stick your order up your bastard's arse," said Slynt, his jowls quivering.

Alliser Thorne smiled a thin smile, his black eyes fixed on Jon. At another table, Godry the Giantslayer began to laugh.

"As you will." Jon nodded to Iron Emmett. "Please take Lord Janos to the Wall—"

—and confine him to an ice cell, he might have said. A day or ten cramped up inside the ice would leave him shivering and feverish and begging for release, Jon did not doubt. *And the moment he is out, he and Thorne will begin to plot again.*

—and tie him to his horse, he might have said. If Slynt did not wish to go to Greyguard as its commander, he could go as its cook. *It will only be a matter of time until he deserts, then. And how many others will he take with him?*

"—and hang him," Jon finished.

Janos Slynt's face went as white as milk. The spoon slipped from his fingers. Edd and Emmett crossed the room, their footsteps ringing on the stone floor. Bowen Marsh's mouth opened and closed though no words came out. Ser Alliser Thorne reached for his sword hilt. *Go on,* Jon thought. Longclaw was slung across his back. *Show your steel. Give me cause to do the same.*

Half the men in the hall were on their feet. Southron knights and men-at-arms, loyal to King Stannis or the red woman or both, and Sworn Brothers of the Night's Watch. Some had chosen Jon to be their lord commander. Others had cast their stones for Bowen Marsh, Ser Denys Mallister, Cotter Pyke . . . and some for Janos Slynt. *Hundreds of them, as I recall.* Jon wondered how many of those men were in the cellar right now. For a moment the world balanced on a sword's edge.

Alliser Thorne took his hand from his sword and stepped aside to let Edd Tollett pass.

Dolorous Edd took hold of Slynt by one arm, Iron Emmett by the other. Together they hauled him from the bench. "No," Lord Janos protested, flecks of porridge spraying from his lips. "No, unhand me. He's just a boy, a *bastard.* His father was a traitor. The mark of the beast is on him, that wolf of his . . . *Let go of me!* You will rue the day you laid hands on Janos Slynt. I have friends in King's Landing. I warn you—" He was still protesting as they half-marched, half-dragged him up the steps.

Jon followed them outside. Behind him, the cellar emptied. At the cage, Slynt wrenched loose for a moment and tried to make a fight of it, but Iron Emmett caught him by the throat and slammed him back against the iron bars until he desisted. By then all of Castle Black had come outside to watch. Even Val was at her window, her long golden braid across one shoulder. Stannis stood on the steps of the King's Tower, surrounded by his knights.

"If the boy thinks that he can frighten me, he is mistaken," they heard Lord Janos said. "He would not dare to hang me. Janos Slynt has friends, *important* friends, you'll see . . ." The wind whipped away the rest of his words.

This is wrong, Jon thought. "Stop."

Emmett turned back, frowning. "My lord?"

"I will not hang him," said Jon. "Bring him here."

"Oh, Seven save us," he heard Bowen Marsh cry out.

The smile that Lord Janos Slynt smiled then had all the sweetness of rancid butter. Until Jon said, "Edd, fetch me a block," and unsheathed Longclaw.

By the time a suitable chopping block was found, Lord Janos had retreated into the winch cage, but Iron Emmett went in after him and dragged him out. "No," Slynt cried, as Emmett half-shoved and half-pulled him across the yard. "Unhand me . . . you cannot . . . when Tywin Lannister hears of this, you will all rue—"

Emmett kicked his legs out from under him. Dolorous Edd planted a foot on his back to keep him on his knees as Emmett shoved the block beneath his head. "This will go easier if you stay still," Jon Snow promised him. "Move to avoid the cut, and you will still die, but your dying will be uglier. Stretch out your neck, my lord." The pale morning sunlight ran up and down his blade as Jon clasped the hilt of the bastard sword with both hands and raised it high. "If you have any last words, now is the time to speak them," he said, expecting one last curse.

Janos Slynt twisted his neck around to stare up at him. "Please, my lord. Mercy. I'll . . . I'll go, I will, I . . ."

No, thought Jon. *You closed that door.* Longclaw descended.

"Can I have his boots?" asked Owen the Oaf, as Janos Slynt's head went rolling across the muddy ground. "They're almost new, those boots. Lined with fur."

Jon glanced back at Stannis. For an instant their eyes met. Then the king nodded and went back inside his tower.

TYRION

He woke alone, and found the litter halted.

A pile of crushed cushions remained to show where Illyrio had sprawled. The dwarf's throat felt dry and raspy. He had dreamed . . . what had he dreamed? He did not remember.

Outside, voices were speaking in a tongue he did not know. Tyrion swung his legs through the curtains and hopped to the ground, to find Magister Illyrio standing by the horses with two riders looming over him. Both wore shirts of worn leather beneath cloaks of dark brown wool, but their swords were sheathed and the fat man did not look to be in danger.

"I need a piss," the dwarf announced. He waddled off the road, undid his breeches, and relieved himself into a tangle of thorns. It took quite a long time.

"He pisses well, at least," a voice observed.

Tyrion flicked the last drops off and tucked himself away. "Pissing is the least of my talents. You ought to see me shit." He turned to Magister Illyrio. "Are these two known to you, magister? They look like outlaws. Should I find my axe?"

"Your *axe*?" exclaimed the larger of the riders, a brawny man with a shaggy beard and a shock of orange hair. "Did you hear that, Haldon? The little man wants to fight with us!"

His companion was older, clean-shaved, with a lined ascetic face.

His hair had been pulled back and tied in a knot behind his head. "Small men oft feel a need to prove their courage with unseemly boasts," he declared. "I doubt if he could kill a duck."

Tyrion shrugged. "Fetch the duck."

"If you insist." The rider glanced at his companion.

The brawny man unsheathed a bastard sword. "I'm Duck, you mouthy little pisspot."

Oh, gods be good. "I had a smaller duck in mind."

The big man roared with laughter. "Did you hear, Haldon? He wants a *smaller* Duck!"

"I should gladly settle for a quieter one." The man called Haldon studied Tyrion with cool grey eyes before turning back to Illyrio. "You have some chests for us?"

"And mules to carry them."

"Mules are too slow. We have pack horses, we'll shift the chests to them. Duck, attend to that."

"Why is it always Duck who attends to things?" The big man slipped his sword back in its sheath. "What do *you* attend to, Haldon? Who is the knight here, you or me?" Yet he stomped off toward the baggage mules all the same.

"How fares our lad?" asked Illyrio as the chests were being secured. Tyrion counted six, oaken chests with iron hasps. Duck shifted them easily enough, hoisting them on one shoulder.

"He is as tall as Griff now. Three days ago he knocked Duck into a horse trough."

"I wasn't *knocked*. I fell in just to make him laugh."

"Your ploy was a success," said Haldon. "I laughed myself."

"There is a gift for the boy in one of the chests. Some candied ginger. He was always fond of it." Illyrio sounded oddly sad. "I thought I might continue on to Ghoyan Drohe with you. A farewell feast before you start downriver . . ."

"We have no time for feasts, my lord," said Haldon. "Griff means to strike downriver the instant we are back. News has been coming upriver, none of it good. Dothraki have been seen north of Dagger Lake, outriders from old Motho's *khalasar*, and Khal Zekko is not far behind him, moving through the Forest of Qohor."

The fat man made a rude noise. "Zekko visits Qohor every three or four years. The Qohorik give him a sack of gold and he turns east again. As for Motho, his men are near as old as he is, and there are fewer every year. The threat is—"

"—Khal Pono," Haldon finished. "Motho and Zekko flee from him, if the tales are true. The last reports had Pono near the headwaters of the Selhoru with a *khalasar* of thirty thousand. Griff does not want to risk being caught up in the crossing if Pono should decide to risk the Rhoyne." Haldon glanced at Tyrion. "Does your dwarf ride as well as he pisses?"

"He rides," Tyrion broke in, before the lord of cheese could answer for him, "though he rides best with a special saddle and a horse that he knows well. He talks as well."

"So he does. I am Haldon, the healer in our little band of brothers. Some call me Halfmaester. My companion is Ser Duck."

"Ser *Rolly,*" said the big man. "Rolly Duckfield. Any knight can make a knight, and Griff made me. And you, dwarf?"

Illyrio spoke up quickly. "Yollo, he is called."

Yollo? Yollo sounds like something you might name a monkey. Worse, it was a Pentoshi name, and any fool could see that Tyrion was no Pentoshi. "In Pentos I am Yollo," he said quickly, to make what amends he could, "but my mother named me Hugor Hill."

"Are you a little king or a little bastard?" asked Haldon.

Tyrion realized he would do well to be careful around Haldon Halfmaester. "Every dwarf is a bastard in his father's eyes."

"No doubt. Well, Hugor Hill, answer me this. How did Serwyn of the Mirror Shield slay the dragon Urrax?"

"He approached behind his shield. Urrax saw only his own reflection until Serwyn had plunged his spear through his eye."

Haldon was unimpressed. "Even Duck knows that tale. Can you tell me the name of the knight who tried the same ploy with Vhagar during the Dance of the Dragons?"

Tyrion grinned. "Ser Byron Swann. He was roasted for his trouble . . . only the dragon was Syrax, not Vhagar."

"I fear that you're mistaken. In *The Dance of the Dragons, A True Telling,* Maester Munkun writes—"

"—that it was Vhagar. *Grand* Maester Munkun errs. Ser Byron's squire saw his master die, and wrote his daughter of the manner of it. His account says it was Syrax, Rhaenyra's she-dragon, which makes more sense than Munken's version. Swann was the son of a marcher lord, and Storm's End was for Aegon. Vhagar was ridden by Prince Aemond, Aegon's brother. Why should Swann want to slay her?"

Haldon pursed his lips. "Try not to tumble off the horse. If you do, best waddle back to Pentos. Our shy maid will not wait for man nor dwarf."

"Shy maids are my favorite sort. Aside from wanton ones. Tell me, where do whores go?"

"Do I look like a man who frequents whores?"

Duck laughed derisively. "He don't dare. Lemore would make him pray for pardon, the lad would want to come along, and Griff might cut his cock off and stuff it down his throat."

"Well," said Tyrion, "a maester does not need a cock."

"Haldon's only half a maester, though."

"You seem to find the dwarf amusing, Duck," said Haldon. "He can ride with you." He wheeled his mount about.

It took another few moments for Duck to finish securing Illyrio's chests to the three pack horses. By that time Haldon had vanished. Duck seemed unconcerned. He swung into the saddle, grabbed Tyrion by the collar, and hoisted the little man up in front of him. "Hold tight to the pommel and you'll do fine. The mare's got a nice sweet gait, and the dragon road's smooth as a maiden's arse." Gathering the reins in his right hand and the leads in his left, Ser Rolly set off at a brisk trot.

"Good fortune," Illyrio called after them. "Tell the boy I am sorry that I will not be with him for his wedding. I will rejoin you in Westeros. That I swear, by my sweet Serra's hands."

The last that Tyrion Lannister saw of Illyrio Mopatis, the magister was standing by his litter in his brocade robes, his massive shoulders slumped. As his figure dwindled in their dust, the lord of cheese looked almost small.

Duck caught up with Haldon Halfmaester a quarter mile on. Thereafter the riders continued side by side. Tyrion clung to the high pommel with his short legs splayed out awkwardly, knowing he could look forward to blisters, cramps, and saddle sores.

"I wonder what the pirates of Dagger Lake will make of our dwarf?" Haldon said as they rode on.

"Dwarf stew?" suggested Duck.

"Urho the Unwashed is the worst of them," Haldon confided. "His stench alone is enough to kill a man."

Tyrion shrugged. "Fortunately, I have no nose."

Haldon gave him a thin smile. "If we should encounter the Lady Korra on *Hag's Teeth*, you may soon be lacking other parts as well. Korra the Cruel, they call her. Her ship is crewed by beautiful young maids who geld every male they capture."

"Terrifying. I may well piss my breeches."

"Best not," Duck warned darkly.

"As you say. If we encounter this Lady Korra, I will just slip into a skirt and say that I am Cersei, the famous bearded beauty of King's Landing."

This time Duck laughed, and Haldon said, "What a droll little fellow you are, Yollo. They say that the Shrouded Lord will grant a boon to any man who can make him laugh. Perhaps His Grey Grace will choose you to ornament his stony court."

Duck glanced at his companion uneasily. "It's not good to jape of that one, not when we're so near the Rhoyne. He hears."

"Wisdom from a duck," said Haldon. "I beg your pardon, Yollo. You need not look so pale, I was only playing with you. The Prince of Sorrows does not bestow his grey kiss lightly."

His grey kiss. The thought made his flesh crawl. Death had lost its terror for Tyrion Lannister, but greyscale was another matter. *The Shrouded Lord is just a legend,* he told himself, *no more real than the ghost of Lann the Clever that some claim haunts Casterly Rock.* Even so, he held his tongue.

The dwarf's sudden silence went unnoticed, as Duck had begun to regale him with his own life story. His father had been an armorer at Bitterbridge, he said, so he had been born with the sound of steel ringing in his ears and had taken to swordplay at an early age. Such a large and likely lad drew the eye of old Lord Caswell, who offered him a place in his garrison, but the boy had wanted more. He watched Caswell's weakling son named a page, a squire, and finally a knight. "A weedy pinch-faced sneak, he was, but the old lord had four daughters and only the one son, so no one was allowed to say a word against him. T'other squires hardly dared to lay a finger on him in the yard."

"You were not so timid, though." Tyrion could see where this tale was going easily enough.

"My father made a longsword for me to mark my sixteenth nameday," said Duck, "but Lorent liked the look of it so much he took it for himself, and my bloody father never dared to tell him no. When I complained, Lorent told me to my face that my hand was made to hold a hammer, not a sword. So I went and got a hammer and beat him with it, till both his arms and half his ribs were broken. After that I had to leave the Reach, quick as it were. I made it across the water to the Golden Company. I did some smithing for a few years as a 'prentice, then Ser Harry Strickland took me on as squire. When Griff sent word downriver that he needed someone to help train his son to arms, Harry sent him me."

"And Griff knighted you?"

"A year later."

Haldon Halfmaester smiled a thin smile. "Tell our little friend how you came by your name, why don't you?"

"A knight needs more than just the one name," the big man insisted, "and, well, we were in a field when he dubbed me, and I looked up and saw these ducks, so . . . don't laugh, now."

Just after sunset, they left the road to rest in an overgrown yard beside an old stone well. Tyrion hopped down to work the cramps out of his calves whilst Duck and Haldon were watering the horses. Tough brown grass and weed trees sprouted from the gaps between the cobbles, and the mossy walls of what once might have been a huge stone manse. After the animals had been tended to, the riders shared a simple supper of salt pork and cold white beans, washed down with ale. Tyrion found the plain fare a pleasant change from all the rich food he had eaten with Illyrio. "Those chests we brought you," he said as they were chewing. "Gold for the Golden Company,

I thought at first, until I saw Ser Rolly hoist a chest onto one shoulder. If it were full of coin, he could never have lifted it so easily."

"It's just armor," said Duck, with a shrug.

"Clothing as well," Haldon broke in. "Court clothes, for all our party. Fine woolens, velvets, silken cloaks. One does not come before a queen looking shabby . . . nor empty-handed. The magister has been kind enough to provide us with suitable gifts."

Come moonrise, they were back in their saddles, trotting eastward under a mantle of stars. The old Valyrian road glimmered ahead of them like a long silver ribbon winding through wood and dale. For a little while Tyrion Lannister felt almost at peace. "Lomas Longstrider told it true. The road's a wonder."

"Lomas Longstrider?" asked Duck.

"A scribe, long dead," said Haldon. "He spent his life traveling the world and writing about the lands he visited in two books he called *Wonders* and *Wonders Made by Man*."

"An uncle of mine gave them to me when I was just a boy," said Tyrion. "I read them until they fell to pieces."

"*The gods made seven wonders, and mortal man made nine*," quoted the Halfmaester. "Rather impious of mortal man to do the gods two better, but there you are. The stone roads of Valyria were one of Longstrider's nine. The fifth, I believe."

"The fourth," said Tyrion, who had committed all sixteen of the wonders to memory as a boy. His uncle Gerion liked to set him on the table during feasts and make him recite them. *I liked that well enough, didn't I? Standing there amongst the trenchers with every eye upon me, proving what a clever little imp I was.* For years afterward, he had cherished a dream that one day he would travel the world and see Longstrider's wonders for himself.

Lord Tywin had put an end to that hope ten days before his dwarf son's sixteenth nameday, when Tyrion asked to tour the Nine Free Cities, as his uncles had done at that same age. "My brothers could be relied upon to bring no shame upon House Lannister," his father had replied. "Neither ever wed a whore." And when Tyrion had reminded him that in ten days he would be a man grown, free to travel where he wished, Lord Tywin had said, "No man is free. Only children and fools think elsewise. Go, by all means. Wear motley and stand upon your head to amuse the spice lords and the cheese kings. Just see that you pay your own way and put aside any thoughts of returning." At that the boy's defiance had crumbled. "If it is useful occupation you require, useful occupation you shall have," his father then said. So to mark his manhood, Tyrion was given charge of all the drains and cisterns within Casterly Rock. *Perhaps he hoped I'd fall into one.* But Tywin had been disappointed in that. The drains never drained half so well as when he had charge of them.

I need a cup of wine, to wash the taste of Tywin from my mouth. A skin of wine would serve me even better.

They rode all night, with Tyrion sleeping fitfully, dozing against the pommel and waking suddenly. From time to time he would begin to slip sideways from the saddle, but Ser Rolly would get a hand on him and yank him upright once again. By dawn the dwarf's legs were aching and his cheeks were chafed and raw.

It was the next day before they reached the site of Ghoyan Drohe, hard beside the river. "The fabled Rhoyne," said Tyrion when he glimpsed the slow green waterway from atop a rise.

"The Little Rhoyne," said Duck.

"It is that." *A pleasant enough river, I suppose, but the smallest fork of the Trident is twice as wide, and all three of them run swifter.* The city was no more impressive. Ghoyan Drohe had never been large, Tyrion recalled from his histories, but it had been a fair place, green and flowering, a city of canals and fountains. *Until the war. Until the dragons came.* A thousand years later, the canals were choked with reeds and mud, and pools of stagnant water gave birth to swarms of flies. The broken stones of temples and palaces were sinking back into the earth, and gnarled old willows grew thick along the riverbanks.

A few people still remained amidst the squalor, tending little gardens in amongst the weeds. The sound of iron hooves ringing on the old Valyrian road sent most of them darting back into the holes they'd crawled from, but the bolder ones lingered in the sun long enough to stare at the passing riders with dull, incurious eyes. One naked girl with mud up to her knees could not seem to take her eyes off Tyrion. *She has never seen a dwarf before,* he realized, *much less a dwarf without a nose.* He made a face and stuck his tongue out, and the girl began to cry.

"What did you do to her?" Duck asked.

"I blew her a kiss. All the girls cry when I kiss them."

Beyond the tangled willows the road ended abruptly and they turned north for a short ways and rode beside the water, until the brush gave way and they found themselves beside an old stone quay, half-submerged and surrounded by tall brown weeds. "*Duck!*" came a shout. "*Haldon!*" Tyrion craned his head to one side, and saw a boy standing on the roof of a low wooden building, waving a wide-brimmed straw hat. He was a lithe and well-made youth, with a lanky build and a shock of dark blue hair. The dwarf put his age at fifteen, sixteen, or near enough to make no matter.

The roof the boy was standing on turned out to be the cabin of the *Shy Maid,* an old ramshackle single-masted poleboat. She had a broad beam and a shallow draft, ideal for making her way up the smallest of streams and crabwalking over sandbars. *A homely maid,* thought Tyrion, *but sometimes the ugliest ones are the hungriest once abed.* The poleboats that plied the rivers of Dorne were often brightly painted and exquisitely carved, but not this maid. Her paintwork was a muddy greyish brown, mottled and flaking; her big curved tiller, plain and unadorned. *She looks like dirt,* he thought, *but no doubt that's the point.*

Duck was hallooing back by then. The mare splashed through the shallows, trampling down the reeds. The boy leapt down off the cabin roof to the poleboat's deck, and the rest of the *Shy Maid*'s crew made their appearance. An older couple with a Rhoynish cast to their features stood close beside the tiller, whilst a handsome septa in a soft white robe stepped through the cabin door and pushed a lock of dark brown hair from her eyes.

But there was no mistaking Griff. "That will be enough shouting," he said. A sudden silence fell upon the river.

This one will be trouble, Tyrion knew at once.

Griff's cloak was made from the hide and head of a red wolf of the Rhoyne. Under the pelt he wore brown leather stiffened with iron rings. His clean-shaved face was leathery too, with wrinkles at the corners of his eyes. Though his hair was as blue as his son's, he had red roots and redder eyebrows. At his hip hung a sword and dagger. If he was happy to have Duck and Haldon back again, he hid it well, but he did not trouble to conceal his displeasure at the sight of Tyrion. "A dwarf? What's this?"

"I know, you were hoping for a wheel of cheese." Tyrion turned to Young Griff and gave the lad his most disarming smile. "Blue hair may serve you well in Tyrosh, but in Westeros children will throw stones at you and girls will laugh in your face."

The lad was taken aback. "My mother was a lady of Tyrosh. I dye my hair in memory of her."

"What is this creature?" Griff demanded.

Haldon answered. "Illyrio sent a letter to explain."

"I will have it, then. Take the dwarf to my cabin."

I do not like his eyes, Tyrion reflected, when the sellsword sat down across from him in the dimness of the boat's interior, with a scarred plank table and a tallow candle between them. They were ice blue, pale, cold. The dwarf misliked pale eyes. Lord Tywin's eyes had been pale green and flecked with gold.

He watched the sellsword read. That he *could* read said something all by itself. How many sellswords could boast of that? *He hardly moves his lips at all,* Tyrion reflected.

Finally Griff looked up from the parchment, and those pale eyes narrowed. "Tywin Lannister dead? At *your* hand?"

"At my finger. This one." Tyrion held it up for Griff to admire. "Lord Tywin was sitting on a privy, so I put a crossbow bolt through his bowels to see if he really did shit gold. He didn't. A pity, I could have used some gold. I also slew my mother, somewhat earlier. Oh, and my nephew Joffrey, I poisoned him at his wedding feast and watched him choke to death. Did the cheesemonger leave that part out? I mean to add my brother and sister to the list before I'm done, if it please your queen."

"*Please* her? Has Illyrio taken leave of his senses? Why does he imagine that Her Grace would welcome the service of a self-confessed kingslayer and betrayer?"

A fair question, thought Tyrion, but what he said was, "The king I slew was sitting on her throne, and all those I betrayed were lions, so it seems to me that I have already done the queen good service." He scratched the stump of his nose. "Have no fear, I won't kill you, you are no kin of mine. Might I see what the cheesemonger wrote? I do love to read about myself."

Griff ignored the request. Instead he touched the letter to the candle flame and watched the parchment blacken, curl, and flare up. "There is blood between Targaryen and Lannister. Why would you support the cause of Queen Daenerys?"

"For gold and glory," the dwarf said cheerfully. "Oh, and hate. If you had ever met my sister, you would understand."

"I understand hate well enough." From the way Griff said the word, Tyrion knew that much was true. *He has supped on hate himself, this one. It has warmed him in the night for years.*

"Then we have that in common, ser."

"I am no knight."

Not only a liar, but a bad one. That was clumsy and stupid, my lord. "And yet Ser Duck says you knighted him."

"Duck talks too much."

"Some might wonder that a duck can talk at all. No matter, *Griff*. You are no knight and I am Hugor Hill, a little monster. *Your* little monster, if you like. You have my word, all that I desire is to be leal servant of your dragon queen."

"And how do you propose to serve her?"

"With my tongue." He licked his fingers, one by one. "I can tell Her Grace how my sweet sister thinks, if you call it thinking. I can tell her captains the best way to defeat my brother, Jaime, in battle. I know which lords are brave and which are craven, which are loyal and which are venal. I can deliver allies to her. And I know much and more of dragons, as your halfmaester will tell you. I'm amusing too, and I don't eat much. Consider me your own true imp."

Griff weighed that for a moment. "Understand this, dwarf. You are the last and least of our company. Hold your tongue and do as you are told, or you will soon wish you had."

Yes, Father, Tyrion almost said. "As you say, my lord."

"I am no lord."

Liar. "It was a courtesy, my friend."

"I am not your friend either."

No knight, no lord, no friend. "A pity."

"Spare me your irony. I will take you as far as Volantis. If you show yourself to be obedient and useful, you may remain with us, to serve the queen as best you can. Prove yourself more trouble than you are worth, and you can go your own way."

Aye, and my way will take me to the bottom of the Rhoyne with fish nibbling at what's left of my nose. "Valar dohaeris."

"You may sleep on the deck or in the hold, as you prefer. Ysilla will find bedding for you."

"How kind of her." Tyrion made a waddling bow, but at the cabin door, he turned back. "What if we should find the queen and discover that this talk of dragons was just some sailor's drunken fancy? This wide world is full of such mad tales. Grumkins and snarks, ghosts and ghouls, mermaids, rock goblins, winged horses, winged pigs . . . winged lions."

Griff stared at him, frowning. "I have given you fair warning, Lannister. Guard your tongue or lose it. Kingdoms are at hazard here. Our lives, our names, our honor. This is no game we're playing for your amusement."

Of course it is, thought Tyrion. *The game of thrones.* "As you say, Captain," he murmured, bowing once again.

DAVOS

Lightning split the northern sky, etching the black tower of the Night Lamp against the blue-white sky. Six heartbeats later came the thunder, like a distant drum.

The guards marched Davos Seaworth across a bridge of black basalt and under an iron portcullis showing signs of rust. Beyond lay a deep salt moat and a drawbridge supported by a pair of massive chains. Green waters surged below, sending up plumes of spray to smash against the foundations of the castle. Then came a second gatehouse, larger than the first, its stones bearded with green algae. Davos stumbled across a muddy yard with his hands bound at the wrists. A cold rain stung his eyes. The guards prodded him up the steps, into Breakwater's cavernous stone keep.

Once inside, the captain removed his cloak and hung it from a peg, so as not to leave puddles on the threadbare Myrish carpet. Davos did the same, fumbling at the clasp with his bound hands. He had not forgotten the courtesies he had learned on Dragonstone during his years of service.

They found the lord alone in the gloom of his hall, making a supper of beer and bread and sister's stew. Twenty iron sconces were mounted along his thick stone walls, but only four held torches, and none of them was lit. Two fat tallow candles gave a meagre, flickering light. Davos could hear the rain lashing at the walls, and a steady dripping where the roof had sprung a leak.

"M'lord," said the captain, "we found this man in the Belly o' the Whale, trying to buy his way off island. He had twelve dragons on him, and this thing too." The captain put it on the table by the lord: a wide ribbon of black velvet trimmed with cloth-of-gold, and bearing three seals; a crowned stag stamped in golden beeswax, a flaming heart in red, a hand in white.

Davos waited wet and dripping, his wrists chafing where the wet rope dug into his skin. One word from this lord and he would soon be hanging from the Gallows Gate of Sisterton, but at least he was out of the rain, with solid stone beneath his feet in place of a heaving deck. He was soaked and sore and haggard, worn thin by grief and betrayal, and sick to death of storms.

The lord wiped his mouth with the back of his hand and picked up the ribbon for a closer squint. Lightning flashed outside, making the arrow loops blaze blue and white for half a heartbeat. *One, two, three, four,* Davos counted, before the thunder came. When it quieted, he listened to the dripping, and the duller roar beneath his feet, where the waves were smashing against Breakwater's huge stone arches and swirling through its dungeons. He might well end up down there, fettered to a wet stone floor and left to drown when the tide came rushing in. *No,* he tried to tell himself, *a smuggler might die that way, but not a King's Hand. I'm worth more if he sells me to his queen.*

The lord fingered the ribbon, frowning at the seals. He was an ugly man, big and fleshy, with an oarsman's thick shoulders and no neck. Coarse grey stubble, going white in patches, covered his cheeks and chin. Above a massive shelf of brow he was bald. His nose was lumpy and red with broken veins, his lips thick, and he had a sort of webbing between the three middle fingers of his right hand. Davos had heard that some of the lords of the Three Sisters had webbed hands and feet, but he had always put that down as just another sailor's story.

The lord leaned back. "Cut him free," he said, "and peel those gloves off him. I want to see his hands."

The captain did as he was told. As he jerked up his captive's maimed left hand the lightning flashed again, throwing the shadow of Davos Seaworth's shortened fingers across the blunt and brutal face of Godric Borrell, Lord of Sweetsister. "Any man can steal a ribbon," the lord said, "but those fingers do not lie. You are the onion knight."

"I have been called that, my lord." Davos was a lord himself, and had been a knight for long years now, but deep down he was still what he had always been, a smuggler of common birth who had bought his knighthood with a hold of onions and salt fish. "I have been called worse things too."

"Aye. Traitor. Rebel. Turncloak."

He bristled at the last. "I have never turned my cloak, my lord. I am a king's man."

"Only if Stannis is a king." The lord weighed him with hard black eyes. "Most knights who land upon my shores seek me in my hall, not in the Belly of the Whale. A vile smuggler's den, that place. Are you returning to your old trade, onion knight?"

"No, my lord. I was looking for passage to White Harbor. The king sent me, with a message for its lord."

"Then you are in the wrong place, with the wrong lord." Lord Godric seemed amused. "This is Sisterton, on Sweetsister."

"I know it is." There was nothing sweet about Sisterton, though. It was a vile town, a sty, small and mean and rank with the odors of pig shit and rotting fish. Davos remembered it well from his smuggling days. The Three Sisters had been a favorite haunt of smugglers for hundreds of years, and a pirate's nest before that. Sisterton's streets were mud and planks, its houses daub-and-wattle hovels roofed with straw, and by the Gallows Gate there were always hanged men with their entrails dangling out.

"You have friends here, I do not doubt," said the lord. "Every smuggler has friends on the Sisters. Some of them are my friends as well. The ones who aren't, them I hang. I let them strangle slowly, with their guts slapping up against their knees." The hall grew bright again, as lightning lit the windows. Two heartbeats later came the thunder. "If it is White Harbor that you want, why are you in Sisterton? What brought you here?"

A king's command and a friend's betrayal, Davos might have said. Instead he answered, "Storms."

Nine-and-twenty ships had set sail from the Wall. If half of them were still afloat, Davos would be shocked. Black skies, bitter winds, and lashing rains had hounded them all the way down the coast. The galleys *Oledo* and *Old Mother's Son* had been driven onto the rocks of Skagos, the isle of unicorns and cannibals where even the Blind Bastard had feared to land; the great cog *Saathos Saan* had foundered off the Grey Cliffs. "Stannis will be paying for them," Salladhor Saan had fumed. "He will be paying for them with good gold, every one." It was as if some angry god was exacting payment for their easy voyage north, when they had ridden a steady southerly from Dragonstone to the Wall. Another gale had ripped away the rigging of the *Bountiful Harvest,* forcing Salla to have her taken under tow. Ten leagues north of Widow's Watch the seas rose again, slamming the *Harvest* into one of the galleys towing her and sinking both. The rest of the Lysene fleet had been scattered across the narrow sea. Some would straggle into one port or another. Others would never be seen again.

"Salladhor the Beggar, that's what your king has made me," Salladhor Saan complained to Davos, as the remnants of his fleet limped across the Bite. "Salladhor the Smashed. Where are my ships? And my gold, where is all the gold that I was promised?" When Davos had tried to assure him that he would have his payment, Salla had erupted. "When, *when*? On the morrow, on the new moon, when the red comet comes again? He is promising me gold and gems, always promising, but this gold I have not seen. I have his word, he is saying, oh yes, his royal word, he writes it down. Can Salladhor Saan eat the king's word? Can he quench his thirst with parchments and waxy seals? Can he tumble promises into a feather bed and fuck them till they squeal?"

Davos had tried to persuade him to stay true. If Salla abandoned Stannis and his cause, he pointed out, he abandoned all hope of collecting the gold that was due him. A victorious King Tommen was not like to pay his defeated uncle's debts, after all. Salla's only hope was to remain loyal to Stannis Baratheon until he won the Iron

Throne. Elsewise he would never see a groat of his money. He had to be patient.

Perhaps some lord with honey on his tongue might have swayed the Lysene pirate prince, but Davos was an onion knight, and his words had only provoked Salla to fresh outrage. "On Dragonstone I was patient," he said, "when the red woman burned wooden gods and screaming men. All the long way to the Wall I was patient. At Eastwatch I was patient . . . and cold, so very cold. Bah, I say. Bah to your patience, and bah to your king. My men are hungry. They are wishing to fuck their wives again, to count their sons, to see the Stepstones and the pleasure gardens of Lys. Ice and storms and empty promises, these they are *not* wanting. This north is much too cold, and getting colder."

I knew the day would come, Davos told himself. *I was fond of the old rogue, but never so great a fool as to trust him.*

"Storms." Lord Godric said the word as fondly as another man might say his lover's name. "Storms were sacred on the Sisters before the Andals came. Our gods of old were the Lady of the Waves and the Lord of the Skies. They made storms every time they mated." He leaned forward. "These kings never bother with the Sisters. Why should they? We are small and poor. And yet you're here. Delivered to me by the storms."

Delivered to you by a friend, Davos thought.

Lord Godric turned to his captain. "Leave this man with me. He was never here."

"No, m'lord. Never." The captain took his leave, his wet boots leaving damp footprints across the carpet. Beneath the floor the sea was rumbling and restless, pounding at the castle's feet. The outer door closed with a sound like distant thunder, and again the lightning came, as if in answer.

"My lord," said Davos, "if you would send me on to White Harbor, His Grace would count it as an act of friendship."

"I could send you to White Harbor," the lord allowed. "Or I could send you to some cold wet hell."

Sisterton is hell enough. Davos feared the worst. The Three Sisters were fickle bitches, loyal only to themselves. Supposedly they were sworn to the Arryns of the Vale, but the Eyrie's grasp upon the islands was tenuous at best.

"Sunderland would require me to hand you over if he knew of you." Borrell did fealty for Sweetsister, as Longthorpe did for Longsister and Torrent for Littlesister; all were sworn to Triston Sunderland, the Lord of the Three Sisters. "He'd sell you to the queen for a pot of that Lannister gold. Poor man needs every dragon, with seven sons all determined to be knights." The lord picked up a wooden spoon and attacked his stew again. "I used to curse the gods who gave me only daughters until I heard Triston bemoaning the cost of destriers. You would be surprised to know how many fish it takes to buy a decent suit of plate and mail."

I had seven sons as well, but four are burned and dead. "Lord Sunderland is sworn to the Eyrie," Davos said. "By rights he should deliver me to Lady Arryn." He would stand a better chance with her than with the Lannisters, he judged. Though she had taken no part in the War of the Five Kings, Lysa Arryn was a daughter of Riverrun, and aunt to the Young Wolf.

"Lysa Arryn's dead," Lord Godric said, "murdered by some singer. Lord Littlefinger rules the Vale now. Where are the pirates?" When Davos did not answer, he rapped his spoon against the table. "The Lyseni. Torrent spied their sails from Littlesister, and before him the Flints from Widow's Watch. Orange sails, and green, and pink. Salladhor Saan. Where is he?"

"At sea." Salla would be sailing around the Fingers and down the narrow sea. He was returning to the Stepstones with what few ships remained him. Perhaps he would acquire a few more along the way, if he came upon some likely merchantmen. *A little piracy to help the leagues go by.* "His Grace has sent him south, to trouble the Lannisters and their friends." The lie was one he had rehearsed as he rowed toward Sisterton through the rain. Soon or late the world would learn that Salladhor Saan had abandoned Stannis Baratheon, leaving him without a fleet, but they would not hear it from the lips of Davos Seaworth.

Lord Godric stirred his stew. "Did that old pirate Saan make you swim to shore?"

"I came ashore in an open boat, my lord." Salla had waited until the beacon of the Night Lamp shone off the *Valyrian*'s port bow before he put him off. Their friendship had been worth that much, at least. The Lyseni would gladly have taken him south with him, he avowed, but Davos had refused. Stannis needed Wyman Manderly, and had trusted Davos to win him. He would not betray that trust, he told Salla. "Bah," the pirate prince replied, "he will kill you with these honors, old friend. He will kill you."

"I have never had a King's Hand beneath my roof before," Lord Godric said. "Would Stannis ransom you, I wonder?"

Would he? Stannis had given Davos lands and titles and offices, but would he pay good gold to buy back his life? *He has no gold. Else he'd still have Salla.* "You will find His Grace at Castle Black if my lord would like to ask that of him."

Borrell grunted. "Is the Imp at Castle Black as well?"

"The Imp?" Davos did not understand the question. "He is at King's Landing, condemned to die for the murder of his nephew."

"The Wall is the last to learn, my father used to say. The dwarf's escaped. He twisted through the bars of his cell and tore his own father apart with his bare hands. A guardsman saw him flee, red from head to heel, as if he'd bathed in blood. The queen will make a lord of any man who kills him."

Davos struggled to believe what he was hearing. "You are telling me that Tywin Lannister is dead?"

"At his son's hand, aye." The lord took a drink of beer. "When there were kings on the Sisters, we did not suffer dwarfs to live. We cast them all into the sea, as an offering to the gods. The septons made us stop that. A pack of pious fools. Why would the gods give a man such a shape but to mark him as a monster?"

Lord Tywin dead. This changes all. "My lord, will you grant me leave to send a raven to the Wall? His Grace will want to know of Lord Tywin's death."

"He'll know. But not from me. Nor you, so long as you are here beneath my leaky roof. I'll not have it said that I gave Stannis aid and counsel. The Sunderlands dragged the Sisters into two of the Blackfyre Rebellions, and we all suffered grievously for that." Lord

Godric waved his spoon toward a chair. "Sit. Before you fall, ser. My hall is cold and damp and dark, but not without some courtesy. We'll find dry clothes for you, but first you'll eat." He shouted, and a woman entered the hall. "We have a guest to feed. Bring beer and bread and sister's stew."

The beer was brown, the bread black, the stew a creamy white. She served it in a trencher hollowed out of a stale loaf. It was thick with leeks, carrots, barley, and turnips white and yellow, along with clams and chunks of cod and crabmeat, swimming in a stock of heavy cream and butter. It was the sort of stew that warmed a man right down to his bones, just the thing for a wet, cold night. Davos spooned it up gratefully.

"You have tasted sister's stew before?"

"I have, my lord." The same stew was served all over the Three Sisters, in every inn and tavern.

"This is better than what you've had before. Gella makes it. My daughter's daughter. Are you married, onion knight?"

"I am, my lord."

"A pity. Gella's not. Homely women make the best wives. There's three kinds of crabs in there. Red crabs and spider crabs and conquerors. I won't eat spider crab, except in sister's stew. Makes me feel half a cannibal." His lordship gestured at the banner hanging above the cold black hearth. A spider crab was embroidered there, white on a grey-green field. "We heard tales that Stannis burned his Hand."

The Hand who went before me. Melisandre had given Alester Florent to her god on Dragonstone, to conjure up the wind that bore them north. Lord Florent had been strong and silent as the queen's men bound him to the post, as dignified as any half-naked man could hope to be, but as the flames licked up his legs he had begun to scream, and his screams had blown them all the way to Eastwatch-by-the-Sea, if the red woman could be believed. Davos had misliked that wind. It had seemed to him to smell of burning flesh, and the sound of it was anguished as it played amongst the lines. *It could as easily have been me.* "I did not burn," he assured Lord Godric, "though Eastwatch almost froze me."

"The Wall will do that." The woman brought them a fresh loaf of bread, still hot from the oven. When Davos saw her hand, he stared. Lord Godric did not fail to make note of it. "Aye, she has the mark. Like all Borrells, for five thousand years. My daughter's daughter. Not the one who makes the stew." He tore the bread apart and offered half to Davos. "Eat. It's good."

It was, though any stale crust would have tasted just as fine to Davos; it meant he was a guest here, for this one night at least. The lords of the Three Sisters had a black repute, and none more so than Godric Borrell, Lord of Sweetsister, Shield of Sisterton, Master of Breakwater Castle, and Keeper of the Night Lamp . . . but even robber lords and wreckers were bound by the ancient laws of hospitality. *I will see the dawn, at least,* Davos told himself. *I have eaten of his bread and salt.*

Though there were stranger spices than salt in this sister's stew. "Is it saffron that I'm tasting?" Saffron was worth more than gold. Davos had only tasted it once before, when King Robert had sent a half a fish to him at a feast on Dragonstone.

"Aye. From Qarth. There's pepper too." Lord Godric took a pinch between his thumb and forefinger and sprinkled his own trencher. "Cracked black pepper from Volantis, nothing finer. Take as much as you require if you're feeling peppery. I've got forty chests of it. Not to mention cloves and nutmeg, and a pound of saffron. Took it off a sloe-eyed maid." He laughed. He still had all his teeth, Davos saw, though most of them were yellow and one on the top was black and dead. "She was making for Braavos, but a gale swept her into the Bite and she smashed up against some of my rocks. So you see, you are not the only gift the storms have brought me. The sea's a treacherous cruel thing."

Not as treacherous as men, thought Davos. Lord Godric's forebears had been pirate kings until the Starks came down on them with fire and sword. These days the Sistermen left open piracy to Salladhor Saan and his ilk and confined themselves to wrecking. The beacons that burned along the shores of the Three Sisters were supposed to warn of shoals and reefs and rocks and lead the way to safety, but on stormy nights and foggy ones, some Sistermen would use false lights to draw unwary captains to their doom.

"The storms did you a kindness, blowing you to my door," Lord Godric said. "You'd have found a cold welcome in White Harbor. You come too late, ser. Lord Wyman means to bend his knee, and not to Stannis." He took a swallow of his beer. "The Manderlys are no northmen, not down deep. 'Twas no more than nine hundred years ago when they came north, laden down with all their gold and gods. They'd been great lords on the Mander until they overreached themselves and the green hands slapped them down. The wolf king took their gold, but he gave them land and let them keep their gods." He mopped at his stew with a chunk of bread. "If Stannis thinks the fat man will ride the stag, he's wrong. The *Lionstar* put in at Sisterton twelve days ago to fill her water casks. Do you know her? Crimson sails and a gold lion on her prow. And full of Freys, making for White Harbor."

"Freys?" That was the last thing that Davos would have expected. "The Freys killed Lord Wyman's son, we heard."

"Aye," Lord Godric said, "and the fat man was so wroth that he took a vow to live on bread and wine till he had his vengeance. But before the day was out, he was stuffing clams and cakes into his mouth again. There's ships that go between the Sisters and White Harbor all the time. We sell them crabs and fish and goat cheese, they sell us wood and wool and hides. From all I hear, his lordship's fatter than ever. So much for vows. Words are wind, and the wind from Manderly's mouth means no more than the wind escaping out his bottom." The lord tore off another chunk of bread to swipe out his trencher. "The Freys were bringing the fat fool a bag of bones. Some call that courtesy, to bring a man his dead son's bones. Had it been my son, I would have returned the courtesy and thanked the Freys before I hanged them, but the fat man's too noble for that." He stuffed the bread into his mouth, chewed, swallowed. "I had the Freys to supper. One sat just where you're sitting now. *Rhaegar,* he named himself. I almost laughed right in his face. He'd lost his wife, he said, but he meant to get himself a new one in White Harbor. Ravens have been flying back and forth. Lord Wyman and Lord Walder have made a pact, and mean to seal it with a marriage."

Davos felt as though the lord had punched him in the belly. *If he tells it true, my king is lost.* Stannis Baratheon had desperate need of White Harbor. If Winterfell was the heart of the north, White Harbor was its mouth. Its firth had remained free of ice even in the depths of winter for centuries. With winter coming on, that could mean much and more. So could the city's silver. The Lannisters had all the gold of Casterly Rock, and had wed the wealth of Highgarden. King Stannis's coffers were exhausted. *I must try, at least. There may be some way that I can stop this marriage.* "I have to reach White Harbor," he said. "Your lordship, I beg you, help me."

Lord Godric began to eat his trencher, tearing it apart in his big hands. The stew had softened the stale bread. "I have no love for northmen," he announced. "The maesters say the Rape of the Three Sisters was two thousand years ago, but Sisterton has not forgotten. We were a free people before that, with our kings ruling over us. Afterward, we had to bend our knees to the Eyrie to get the northmen out. The wolf and the falcon fought over us for a thousand years, till between the two of them they had gnawed all the fat and flesh off the bones of these poor islands. As for your King Stannis, when he was Robert's master of ships he sent a fleet into my port without my leave and made me hang a dozen fine friends. Men like you. He went so far as to threaten to hang *me* if it should happen that some ship went aground because the Night Lamp had gone black. I had to eat his arrogance." He ate some of the trencher. "Now he comes north humbled, with his tail between his legs. Why should I give him any aid? Answer me that."

Because he is your rightful king, Davos thought. *Because he is a strong man and a just one, the only man who can restore the realm and defend it against the peril that gathers in the north. Because he has a magic sword that glows with the light of the sun.* The words caught in his throat. None of them would sway the Lord of Sweetsister. None of them would get him a foot closer to White Harbor. *What answer does he want? Must I promise him gold we do not have? A highborn husband for his daughter's daughter? Lands, honors, titles?* Lord Alester Florent had tried to play that game, and the king had burned him for it.

"The Hand has lost his tongue, it seems. He has no taste for sister's stew, or truth." Lord Godric wiped his mouth.

"The lion is dead," said Davos, slowly. "There's your truth, my lord. Tywin Lannister is dead."

"What if he is?"

"Who rules now in King's Landing? Not Tommen, he is just a child. Is it Ser Kevan?"

Candlelight gleamed in Lord Godric's black eyes. "If it were, you'd be in chains. It's the queen who rules."

Davos understood. *He nurses doubts. He does not want to find himself upon the losing side.* "Stannis held Storm's End against the Tyrells and the Redwynes. He took Dragonstone from the last Targaryens. He smashed the Iron Fleet off Fair Isle. This child king will not prevail against him."

"This child king commands the wealth of Casterly Rock and the power of Highgarden. He has the Boltons and the Freys." Lord Godric rubbed his chin. "Still . . . in this world only winter is certain. Ned Stark told my father that, here in this very hall."

"Ned Stark was here?"

"At the dawn of Robert's Rebellion. The Mad King had sent to the Eyrie for Stark's head, but Jon Arryn sent him back defiance. Gulltown stayed loyal to the throne, though. To get home and call his banners, Stark had to cross the mountains to the Fingers and find a fisherman to carry him across the Bite. A storm caught them on the way. The fisherman drowned, but his daughter got Stark to the Sisters before the boat went down. They say he left her with a bag of silver and a bastard in her belly. Jon Snow, she named him, after Arryn.

"Be that as it may. My father sat where I sit now when Lord Eddard came to Sisterton. Our maester urged us to send Stark's head to Aerys, to prove our loyalty. It would have meant a rich reward. The Mad King was open-handed with them as pleased him. By then we knew that Jon Arryn had taken Gulltown, though. Robert was the first man to gain the wall, and slew Marq Grafton with his own hand. 'This Baratheon is fearless,' I said. 'He fights the way a king should fight.' Our maester chuckled at me and told us that Prince Rhaegar was certain to defeat this rebel. That was when Stark said, 'In this world only winter is certain. We may lose our heads, it's true . . . but what if we prevail?' My father sent him on his way with his head still on his shoulders. 'If you lose,' he told Lord Eddard, 'you were never here.' "

"No more than I was," said Davos Seaworth.

JON

They brought forth the King-Beyond-the-Wall with his hands bound by hempen rope and a noose around his neck.

The other end of the rope was looped about the saddle horn of Ser Godry Farring's courser. The Giantslayer and his mount were armored in silvered steel inlaid with niello. Mance Rayder wore only a thin tunic that left his limbs naked to the cold. *They could have let him keep his cloak,* Jon Snow thought, *the one the wildling woman patched with strips of crimson silk.*

Small wonder that the Wall was weeping.

"Mance knows the haunted forest better than any ranger," Jon had told King Stannis, in his final effort to convince His Grace that the King-Beyond-the-Wall would be of more use to them alive than dead. "He knows Tormund Giantsbane. He has fought the Others. And he had the Horn of Joramun and did not blow it. He did not bring down the Wall when he could have."

His words fell on deaf ears. Stannis had remained unmoved. The law was plain; a deserter's life was forfeit.

Beneath the weeping Wall, Lady Melisandre raised her pale white hands. "*We all must choose,*" she proclaimed. "Man or woman, young or old, lord or peasant, our choices are the same." Her voice made Jon Snow think of anise and nutmeg and cloves. She stood at the king's side on a wooden scaffold raised above the pit. "We choose light or we choose darkness. We choose good or we choose evil. We choose the true god or the false."

Mance Rayder's thick grey-brown hair blew about his face as he walked. He pushed it from his eyes with bound hands, smiling. But when he saw the cage, his courage failed him. The queen's men had made it from the trees of the haunted forest, from saplings and supple branches, pine boughs sticky with sap, and the bone-white fingers of the weirwoods. They'd bent them and twisted them around and through each other to weave a wooden lattice, then hung it high above a deep pit filled with logs, leaves, and kindling.

The wildling king recoiled from the sight. "No," he cried, "*mercy*. This is not right, I'm not the king, they—"

Ser Godry gave a pull on the rope. The King-Beyond-the-Wall had no choice but to stumble after him, the rope choking off his words. When he lost his feet, Godry dragged him the rest of the way. Mance was bloody when the queen's men half-shoved, half-carried him to the cage. A dozen men-at-arms heaved together to hoist him into the air.

Lady Melisandre watched him rise. "*FREE FOLK!* Here stands your king of lies. And here is the horn he promised would bring down the Wall." Two queen's men brought forth the Horn of Joramun, black and banded with old gold, eight feet long from end to end. Runes were carved into the golden bands, the writing of the First Men. Joramun had died thousands of years ago, but Mance had found his grave beneath a glacier, high up in the Frostfangs. *And Joramun blew the Horn of Winter, and woke giants from the earth.* Ygritte had told Jon that Mance never found the horn. *She lied, or else Mance kept it secret even from his own.*

A thousand captives watched through the wooden bars of their stockade as the horn was lifted high. All were ragged and half-starved. *Wildlings,* the Seven Kingdoms called them; they named themselves *the free folk.* They looked neither wild nor free—only hungry, frightened, numb.

"The Horn of Joramun?" Melisandre said. "No. Call it the Horn of Darkness. If the Wall falls, night falls as well, the long night that never ends. It must not happen, *will* not happen! The Lord of Light has seen his children in their peril and sent a champion to them, Azor Ahai reborn." She swept a hand toward Stannis, and the great ruby at her throat pulsed with light.

He is stone and she is flame. The king's eyes were blue bruises, sunk deep in a hollow face. He wore grey plate, a fur-trimmed cloak of cloth-of-gold flowing from his broad shoulders. His breastplate had a flaming heart inlaid above his own. Girding his brows was a red-gold crown with points like twisting flames. Val stood beside him, tall and fair. They had crowned her with a simple circlet of dark bronze, yet she looked more regal in bronze than Stannis did in gold. Her eyes were grey and fearless, unflinching. Beneath an ermine cloak, she wore white and gold. Her honey-blond hair had been done up in a thick braid that hung over her right shoulder to her waist. The chill in the air had put color in her cheeks.

Lady Melisandre wore no crown, but every man there knew that she was Stannis Baratheon's real queen, not the homely woman he had left to shiver at Eastwatch-by-the-Sea. Talk was, the king did not mean to send for Queen Selyse and their daughter until the Nightfort was ready for habitation. Jon felt sorry for them. The Wall offered few of the comforts that southron ladies and little highborn girls were used to, and the Nightfort offered none. That was a grim place, even at the best of times.

"*FREE FOLK!*" cried Melisandre. "Behold the fate of those who choose the darkness!"

The Horn of Joramun burst into flame.

It went up with a *whoosh* as swirling tongues of green and yellow fire leapt up crackling all along its length. Jon's garron shied nervously, and up and down the ranks others fought to still their mounts as well. A moan came from the stockade as the free folk saw their hope afire. A few began to shout and curse, but most lapsed into silence. For half a heartbeat the runes graven on the gold bands seemed to shimmer in the air. The queen's men gave a heave and sent the horn tumbling down into the fire pit.

Inside his cage, Mance Rayder clawed at the noose about his neck with bound hands and screamed incoherently of treachery and witchery, denying his kingship, denying his people, denying his name, denying all that he had ever been. He shrieked for mercy and cursed the red woman and began to laugh hysterically.

Jon watched unblinking. He dare not appear squeamish before his brothers. He had ordered out two hundred men, more than half the garrison of Castle Black. Mounted in solemn sable ranks with tall spears in hand, they had drawn up their hoods to shadow their faces . . . and hide the fact that so many were greybeards and green boys. The free folk feared the Watch. Jon wanted them to take that fear with them to their new homes south of the Wall.

The horn crashed amongst the logs and leaves and kindling. Within three heartbeats the whole pit was aflame. Clutching the bars of his cage with bound hands, Mance sobbed and begged. When the fire reached him he did a little dance. His screams became one long, wordless shriek of fear and pain. Within his cage, he fluttered like a burning leaf, a moth caught in a candle flame.

Jon found himself remembering a song.

> *Brothers, oh brothers, my days here are done,*
> *the Dornishman's taken my life,*
> *But what does it matter, for all men must die,*
> *and I've tasted the Dornishman's wife!*

Val stood on the platform as still as if she had been carved of salt. *She will not weep nor look away.* Jon wondered what Ygritte would have done in her place. *The women are the strong ones.* He found himself thinking about Sam and Maester Aemon, about Gilly and the babe. *She will curse me with her dying breath, but I saw no other way.* Eastwatch reported savage storms upon the narrow sea. *I meant to keep them safe. Did I feed them to the crabs instead?* Last night he had dreamed of Sam drowning, of Ygritte dying with his arrow in her (it had not been his arrow, but in his dreams it always was), of Gilly weeping tears of blood.

Jon Snow had seen enough. "Now," he said.

Ulmer of the Kingswood jammed his spear into the ground, unslung his bow, and slipped a black arrow from his quiver. Sweet

Donnel Hill threw back his hood to do the same. Garth Greyfeather and Bearded Ben nocked shafts, bent their bows, loosed.

One arrow took Mance Rayder in the chest, one in the gut, one in the throat. The fourth struck one of the cage's wooden bars, and quivered for an instant before catching fire. A woman's sobs echoed off the Wall as the wildling king slid bonelessly to the floor of his cage, wreathed in fire. "And now his Watch is done," Jon murmured softly. Mance Rayder had been a man of the Night's Watch once, before he changed his black cloak for one slashed with bright red silk.

Up on the platform, Stannis was scowling. Jon refused to meet his eyes. The bottom had fallen out of the wooden cage, and its bars were crumbling. Every time the fire licked upward, more branches tumbled free, cherry red and black. "The Lord of Light made the sun and moon and stars to light our way, and gave us fire to keep the night at bay," Melisandre told the wildlings. "None can withstand his flames."

"*None can withstand his flames,*" the queen's men echoed.

The red woman's robes of deep-dyed scarlet swirled about her, and her coppery hair made a halo round her face. Tall yellow flames danced from her fingertips like claws. "*FREE FOLK!* Your false gods cannot help you. Your false horn did not save you. Your false king brought you only death, despair, defeat . . . but here stands the true king. *BEHOLD HIS GLORY!*"

Stannis Baratheon drew Lightbringer.

The sword glowed red and yellow and orange, alive with light. Jon had seen the show before . . . but not like *this,* never before like this. Lightbringer was the sun made steel. When Stannis raised the blade above his head, men had to turn their heads or cover their eyes. Horses shied, and one threw his rider. The blaze in the fire pit seemed to shrink before this storm of light, like a small dog cowering before a larger one. The Wall itself turned red and pink and orange, as waves of color danced across the ice. *Is this the power of king's blood?*

"Westeros has but one king," said Stannis. His voice rang harsh, with none of Melisandre's music. "With this sword I defend my subjects and destroy those who menace them. Bend the knee, and I promise you food, land, and justice. Kneel and live. Or go and die. The choice is yours." He slipped Lightbringer into its scabbard, and the world darkened once again, as if the sun had gone behind a cloud. "Open the gates."

"*OPEN THE GATES,*" bellowed Ser Clayton Suggs, in a voice as deep as a warhorn. "*OPEN THE GATES,*" echoed Ser Corliss Penny, commanding the guards. "*OPEN THE GATES,*" cried the serjeants. Men scrambled to obey. Sharpened stakes were wrenched from the ground, planks were dropped across deep ditches, and the stockade gates were thrown wide. Jon Snow raised his hand and lowered it, and his black ranks parted right and left, clearing a path to the Wall, where Dolorous Edd Tollett pushed open the iron gate.

"Come," urged Melisandre. "Come to the light . . . or run back to the darkness." In the pit below her, the fire was crackling. "If you choose life, come to me."

And they came. Slowly at first, some limping or leaning on their fellows, the captives began to emerge from their rough-hewn pen. *If you would eat, come to me,* Jon thought. *If you would not freeze or starve, submit.* Hesitant, wary of some trap, the first few prisoners edged across the planks and through the ring of the stakes, toward Melisandre and the Wall. More followed, when they saw that no harm had come to those who went before. Then more, until it was a steady stream. Queen's men in studded jacks and halfhelms handed each passing man, woman, or child a piece of white weirwood: a stick, a splintered branch as pale as broken bone, a spray of blood-red leaves. *A piece of the old gods to feed the new.* Jon flexed the fingers of his sword hand.

The heat from the fire pit was palpable even at a distance; for the wildlings, it had to be blistering. He saw men cringing as they neared the flames, heard children cry. A few turned for the forest. He watched a young woman stumble away with a child on either hand. Every few steps she looked back to make certain no one was coming after them, and when she neared the trees she broke into a run. One greybeard took the weirwood branch they handed him and used it as a weapon, laying about with it until the queen's men converged on him with spears. The others had to step around his body, until Ser Corliss had it thrown in the fire. More of the free folk chose the woods after that—one in ten, perhaps.

But most came on. Behind them was only cold and death. Ahead was hope. They came on, clutching their scraps of wood until the time came to feed them to the flames. R'hllor was a jealous deity, ever hungry. So the new god devoured the corpse of the old, and cast gigantic shadows of Stannis and Melisandre upon the Wall, black against the ruddy red reflections on the ice.

Sigorn was the first to kneel before the king. The new Magnar of Thenn was a younger, shorter version of his father—lean, balding, clad in bronze greaves and a leather shirt sewn with bronze scales. Next came Rattleshirt in clattering armor made of bones and boiled leather, his helm a giant's skull. Under the bones lurked a ruined and wretched creature with cracked brown teeth and a yellow tinge to the whites of his eyes. *A small, malicious, treacherous man, as stupid as he is cruel.* Jon did not believe for a moment that he would keep faith. He wondered what Val was feeling as she watched him kneel, forgiven.

Lesser leaders followed. Two clan chiefs of the Hornfoot men, whose feet were black and hard. An old wisewoman revered by the peoples of the Milkwater. A scrawny dark-eyed boy of two-and-ten, the son of Alfyn Crowkiller. Halleck, brother to Harma Dogshead, with her pigs. Each took a knee before the king.

It is too cold for this mummer's show, thought Jon. "The free folk despise kneelers," he had warned Stannis. "Let them keep their pride, and they will love you better." His Grace would not listen. He said, "It is swords I need from them, not kisses."

Having knelt, the wildlings shuffled past the ranks of the black brothers to the gate. Jon had detailed Horse and Satin and half a dozen others to lead them through the Wall with torches. On the far side, bowls of hot onion soup awaited them, and chunks of black bread and sausage. Clothes as well: cloaks, breeches, boots, tunics, good leather gloves. They would sleep on piles of clean straw, with fires blazing to keep the chill of night at bay. This king was nothing if not methodical. Soon or late, however, Tormund Giantsbane would assault the Wall again, and when that hour came Jon wondered whose side Stannis's new-made subjects would choose. *You can give them land and mercy, but the free folk choose their own kings, and it was Mance they chose, not you.*

Bowen Marsh edged his mount up next to Jon's. "This is a day I never thought to see." The Lord Steward had thinned notably since suffering a head wound at the Bridge of Skulls. Part of one ear was gone. *He no longer looks much like a pomegranate,* Jon thought. Marsh said, "We bled to stop the wildlings at the Gorge. Good men were slain there, friends and brothers. For what?"

"The realm will curse us all for this," declared Ser Alliser Thorne in a venomous tone. "Every honest man in Westeros will turn his head and spit at the mention of the Night's Watch."

What would you know of honest men? "Quiet in the ranks." Ser Alliser had grown more circumspect since Lord Janos had lost his head, but the malice was still there. Jon had toyed with the idea of giving him the command Slynt had refused, but he wanted the man close. *He was always the more dangerous of the two.* Instead he had dispatched a grizzled steward from the Shadow Tower to take command at Greyguard.

He hoped the two new garrisons would make a difference. *The Watch can make the free folk bleed, but in the end we cannot hope to stop them.* Giving Mance Rayder to the fire did not change the truth of that. *We are still too few and they are still too many, and without rangers, we're good as blind. I have to send men out. But if I do, will they come back again?*

The tunnel through the Wall was narrow and twisting, and many of the wildlings were old or ill or wounded, so the going was painfully slow. By the time the last of them had bent the knee, night had fallen. The pit fire was burning low, and the king's shadow on the Wall had shrunk to a quarter of its former height. Jon Snow could see his breath in the air. *Cold,* he thought, *and getting colder. This mummer's show has gone on long enough.*

Two score captives lingered by the stockade. Four giants were among them, massive hairy creatures with sloped shoulders, legs as large as tree trunks, and huge splayed feet. Big as they were, they might still have passed through the Wall, but one would not leave his mammoth, and the others would not leave him. The rest of those who remained were all of human stature. Some were dead and some were dying; more were their kin or close companions, unwilling to abandon them even for a bowl of onion soup.

Some shivering, some too numb to shiver, they listened as the king's voice rumbled off the Wall. "You are free to go," Stannis told them. "Tell your people what you witnessed. Tell them that you saw the true king, and that they are welcome in his realm, so long as they keep his peace. Elsewise, they had best flee or hide. I will brook no further attacks upon my Wall."

"*One realm, one god, one king!*" cried Lady Melisandre.

The queen's men took up the cry, beating the butts of their spears against their shields. "*One realm, one god, one king! STANNIS! STANNIS! ONE REALM, ONE GOD, ONE KING!*"

Val did not join the chant, he saw. Nor did the brothers of the Night's Watch. During the tumult the few remaining wildlings melted into the trees. The giants were the last to go, two riding on the back of a mammoth, the other two afoot. Only the dead were left behind. Jon watched Stannis descend from the platform, with Melisandre by his side. *His red shadow. She never leaves his side for long.* The king's honor guard fell in around them—Ser Godry, Ser Clayton, and a dozen other knights, queen's men all. Moonlight shimmered on their armor and the wind whipped at their cloaks. "Lord Steward," Jon told Marsh, "break up that stockade for firewood and throw the corpses in the flames."

"As my lord commands." Marsh barked out orders, and a swarm of his stewards broke from ranks to attack the wooden walls. The Lord Steward watched them, frowning. "These wildlings . . . do you think they will keep faith, my lord?"

"Some will. Not all. We have our cowards and our knaves, our weaklings and our fools, as do they."

"Our vows . . . we are sworn to protect the realm . . ."

"Once the free folk are settled in the Gift, they will become part of the realm," Jon pointed out. "These are desperate days, and like to grow more desperate. We have seen the face of our real foe, a dead white face with bright blue eyes. The free folk have seen that face as well. Stannis is not wrong in this. We must make common cause with the wildlings."

"Common cause against a common foe, I could agree with that," said Bowen Marsh, "but that does not mean we should allow tens of thousands of half-starved savages through the Wall. Let them return to their villages and fight the Others there, whilst we seal the gates. It will not be difficult, Othell tells me. We need only fill the tunnels with chunks of stone and pour water through the murder holes. The Wall does the rest. The cold, the weight . . . in a moon's turn, it will be as if no gate had ever been. Any foe would need to hack his way through."

"Or climb."

"Unlikely," said Bowen Marsh. "These are not raiders, out to steal a wife and some plunder. Tormund will have old women with him, children, herds of sheep and goats, even *mammoths*. He needs a *gate*, and only three of those remain. And if he should send climbers up, well, defending against climbers is as simple as spearing fish in a kettle."

Fish never climb out of the kettle and shove a spear through your belly. Jon had climbed the Wall himself.

Marsh went on. "Mance Rayder's bowmen must have loosed ten thousand arrows at us, judging from the number of spent shafts we've gathered up. Fewer than a hundred reached our men atop the Wall, most of those lifted by some errant gust of wind. Red Alyn of the Rosewood was the only man to die up there, and it was his fall that killed him, not the arrow that pricked his leg. Donal Noye died to hold the gate. A gallant act, yes . . . but if the gate had been sealed, our brave armorer might still be with us. Whether we face a hundred foes or a hundred thousand, so long as we're atop the Wall and they're below, they cannot do us harm."

He's not wrong. Mance Rayder's host had broken against the Wall like a wave upon a stony shore, though the defenders were no more than a handful of old men, green boys, and cripples. Yet what Bowen was suggesting went against all of Jon's instincts. "If we seal the gates, we cannot send out rangers," he pointed out. "We will be as good as blind."

"Lord Mormont's last ranging cost the Watch a quarter of its men, my lord. We need to conserve what strength remains us. Every death diminishes us, and we are stretched so thin . . . Take the high ground and win the battle, my uncle used to say. No ground is higher than the Wall, Lord Commander."

"Stannis promises land, food, and justice to any wildlings who bend the knee. He will never permit us to seal the gates."

Marsh hesitated. "Lord Snow, I am not one to bear tales, but there has been talk that you are becoming too . . . too friendly with Lord Stannis. Some even suggest that you are . . . a . . ."

A rebel and a turncloak, aye, and a bastard and a warg as well. Janos Slynt might be gone, but his lies lingered. "I know what they say." Jon had heard the whispers, had seen men turn away when he crossed the yard. "What would they have me do, take up swords against Stannis and the wildlings both? His Grace has thrice the fighting men we do, and is our guest besides. The laws of hospitality protect him. And we owe him and his a debt."

"Lord Stannis helped us when we needed help," Marsh said doggedly, "but he is still a rebel, and his cause is doomed. As doomed as we'll be if the Iron Throne marks us down as traitors. We must be certain that we do not choose the losing side."

"It is not my intent to choose any side," said Jon, "but I am not as certain of the outcome of this war as you seem to be, my lord. Not with Lord Tywin dead." If the tales coming up the kingsroad could be believed, the King's Hand had been murdered by his dwarf son whilst sitting on a privy. Jon had known Tyrion Lannister, briefly. *He took my hand and named me friend.* It was hard to believe the little man had it in him to murder his own sire, but the fact of Lord Tywin's demise seemed to be beyond doubt. "The lion in King's Landing is a cub, and the Iron Throne has been known to cut grown men to ribbons."

"A boy he may be, my lord, but . . . King Robert was well loved, and most men still accept that Tommen is his son. The more they see of Lord Stannis the less they love him, and fewer still are fond of Lady Melisandre with her fires and this grim red god of hers. They complain."

"They complained about Lord Commander Mormont too. Men love to complain about their wives and lords, he told me once. Those without wives complain twice as much about their lords." Jon Snow glanced toward the stockade. Two walls were down, a third falling fast. "I will leave you to finish here, Bowen. Make certain every corpse is burned. Thank you for your counsel. I promise you, I will think on all you've said."

Smoke and drifting ash still lingered in the air about the pit as Jon trotted back to the gate. There he dismounted, to walk his garron through the ice to the south side. Dolorous Edd went before him with a torch. Its flames licked the ceiling, so cold tears trickled down upon them with every step.

"It was a relief to see that horn burn, my lord," Edd said. "Just last night I dreamt I was pissing off the Wall when someone decided to give the horn a toot. Not that I'm complaining. It was better than my old dream, where Harma Dogshead was feeding me to her pigs."

"Harma's dead," Jon said.

"But not the pigs. They look at me the way Slayer used to look at ham. Not to say that the wildlings mean us harm. Aye, we hacked their gods apart and made them burn the pieces, but we gave them onion soup. What's a god compared to a nice bowl of onion soup? I could do with one myself."

The odors of smoke and burned flesh still clung to Jon's blacks. He knew he had to eat, but it was company he craved, not food. *A cup of wine with Maester Aemon, some quiet words with Sam, a few laughs with Pyp and Grenn and Toad.* Aemon and Sam were gone, though, and his other friends . . . "I will take supper with the men this evening."

"Boiled beef and beets." Dolorous Edd always seemed to know what was cooking. "Hobb says he's out of horseradish, though. What good is boiled beef without horseradish?"

Since the wildlings had burned the old common hall, the men of the Night's Watch took their meals in the stone cellar below the armory, a cavernous space divided by two rows of square stone pillars, with barrel-vaulted ceilings and great casks of wine and ale along the walls. When Jon entered, four builders were playing at tiles at the table nearest the steps. Closer to the fire sat a group of rangers and a few king's men, talking quietly.

The younger men were gathered at another table, where Pyp had stabbed a turnip with his knife. "The night is dark and full of turnips," he announced in a solemn voice. "Let us all pray for venison, my children, with some onions and a bit of tasty gravy." His friends laughed—Grenn, Toad, Satin, the whole lot of them.

Jon Snow did not join the laughter. "Making mock of another man's prayer is fool's work, Pyp. And dangerous."

"If the red god's offended, let him strike me down."

All the smiles had died. "It was the priestess we were laughing at," said Satin, a lithe and pretty youth who had once been a whore in Oldtown. "We were only having a jape, my lord."

"You have your gods and she has hers. Leave her be."

"She won't let our gods be," argued Toad. "She calls the Seven false gods, m'lord. The old gods too. She made the wildlings burn weirwood branches. You saw."

"Lady Melisandre is not part of my command. You are. I won't have bad blood between the king's men and my own."

Pyp laid a hand on Toad's arm. "Croak no more, brave Toad, for our Great Lord Snow has spoken." Pyp hopped to his feet and gave Jon a mocking bow. "I beg pardon. Henceforth, I shall not even waggle my ears save by your lordship's lordly leave."

He thinks this is all some game. Jon wanted to shake some sense into him. "Waggle your ears all you like. It's your tongue waggling that makes the trouble."

"I'll see that he's more careful," Grenn promised, "and I'll clout him if he's not." He hesitated. "My lord, will you sup with us? Owen, shove over and make room for Jon."

Jon wanted nothing more. *No,* he had to tell himself, *those days are gone.* The realization twisted in his belly like a knife. They had chosen him to rule. The Wall was his, and their lives were his as well. *A lord may love the men that he commands,* he could hear his lord father saying, *but he cannot be a friend to them. One day he may need to sit in judgment on them, or send them forth to die.* "Another day," the lord commander lied. "Edd, best see to your own supper. I have work to finish."

The outside air seemed even colder than before. Across the castle, he could see candlelight shining from the windows of the King's Tower. Val stood on the tower roof, gazing up at the Wall. Stannis kept her closely penned in rooms above his own, but he did allow her to walk the battlements for exercise. *She looks lonely,* Jon thought. *Lonely, and lovely.* Ygritte had been pretty in her own way, with her red hair kissed by fire, but it was her smile that made her face come alive. Val did not need to smile; she would have turned men's heads in any court in the wide world.

All the same, the wildling princess was not beloved of her gaolers. She scorned them all as "kneelers," and had thrice attempted to escape. When one man-at-arms grew careless in her presence she had snatched his dagger from its sheath and stabbed him in the neck. Another inch to the left and he might have died.

Lonely and lovely and lethal, Jon Snow reflected, *and I might have had her. Her, and Winterfell, and my lord father's name.* Instead he had chosen a black cloak and a wall of ice. Instead he had chosen honor. *A bastard's sort of honor.*

The Wall loomed on his right as he crossed the yard. Its high ice glimmered palely, but down below all was shadow. At the gate a dim orange glow shone through the bars where the guards had taken refuge from the wind. Jon could hear the creak of chains as the winch cage swung and scraped against the ice. Up top, the sentries would be huddling in the warming shed around a brazier, shouting to be heard above the wind. Or else they would have given up the effort, and each man would be sunk in his own pool of silence. *I should be walking the ice. The Wall is mine.*

He was walking beneath the shell of the Lord Commander's Tower, past the spot where Ygritte had died in his arms, when Ghost appeared beside him, his warm breath steaming in the cold. In the moonlight, his red eyes glowed like pools of fire. The taste of hot blood filled Jon's mouth, and he knew that Ghost had killed that night. *No,* he thought. *I am a man, not a wolf.* He rubbed his mouth with the back of a gloved hand and spat.

Clydas still occupied the rooms beneath the rookery. At Jon's knock, he came shuffling, a taper in his hand, to open the door a crack. "Do I intrude?" asked Jon.

"Not at all." Clydas opened the door wider. "I was mulling wine. Will my lord take a cup?"

"With pleasure." His hands were stiff from cold. He pulled off his gloves and flexed his fingers.

Clydas returned to the hearth to stir the wine. *He's sixty if he's a day. An old man. He only seemed young compared with Aemon.* Short and round, he had the dim pink eyes of some nocturnal creature. A few white hairs clung to his scalp. When Clydas poured, Jon held the cup with both hands, sniffed the spices, swallowed. The warmth spread through his chest. He drank again, long and deep, to wash the taste of blood from his mouth.

"The queen's men are saying that the King-Beyond-the-Wall died craven. That he cried for mercy and denied he was a king."

"He did. Lightbringer was brighter than I'd ever seen it. As bright as the sun." Jon raised his cup. "To Stannis Baratheon and his magic sword." The wine was bitter in his mouth.

"His Grace is not an easy man. Few are, who wear a crown. Many good men have been bad kings, Maester Aemon used to say, and some bad men have been good kings."

"He would know." Aemon Targaryen had seen nine kings upon the Iron Throne. He had been a king's son, a king's brother, a king's uncle. "I looked at that book Maester Aemon left me. The *Jade Compendium.* The pages that told of Azor Ahai. Lightbringer was his sword. Tempered with his wife's blood if Votar can be believed. Thereafter Lightbringer was never cold to the touch, but warm as Nissa Nissa had been warm. In battle the blade burned fiery hot. Once Azor Ahai fought a monster. When he thrust the sword through the belly of the beast, its blood began to boil. Smoke and steam poured from its mouth, its eyes melted and dribbled down its cheeks, and its body burst into flame."

Clydas blinked. "A sword that makes its own heat . . ."

". . . would be a fine thing on the Wall." Jon put aside his wine cup and drew on his black moleskin gloves. "A pity that the sword that Stannis wields is cold. I'll be curious to see how *his* Lightbringer behaves in battle. Thank you for the wine. Ghost, with me." Jon Snow raised the hood of his cloak and pulled at the door. The white wolf followed him back into the night.

The armory was dark and silent. Jon nodded to the guards before making his way past the silent racks of spears to his rooms. He hung his sword belt from a peg beside the door and his cloak from another. When he peeled off his gloves, his hands were stiff and cold. It took him a long while to get the candles lit. Ghost curled up on his rug and went to sleep, but Jon could not rest yet. The scarred pinewood table was covered with maps of the Wall and the lands beyond, a roster of rangers, and a letter from the Shadow Tower written in Ser Denys Mallister's flowing hand.

He read the letter from the Shadow Tower again, sharpened a quill, and unstoppered a pot of thick black ink. He wrote two letters, the first to Ser Denys, the second to Cotter Pyke. Both of them had been hounding him for more men. Halder and Toad he dispatched west to the Shadow Tower, Grenn and Pyp to Eastwatch-by-the-Sea. The ink would not flow properly, and all his words seemed curt and crude and clumsy, yet he persisted.

When he finally put the quill down, the room was dim and chilly, and he could feel its walls closing in. Perched above the window, the Old Bear's raven peered down at him with shrewd black eyes. *My last friend,* Jon thought ruefully. *And I had best outlive you, or you'll eat my face as well.* Ghost did not count. Ghost was closer than a friend. Ghost was part of him.

Jon rose and climbed the steps to the narrow bed that had once been Donal Noye's. *This is my lot,* he realized as he undressed, *from now until the end of my days.*

DAENERYS

"What is it?" she cried, as Irri shook her gently by the shoulder. It was the black of night outside. *Something is wrong,* she knew at once. "Is it Daario? What's happened?" In her dream they had been man and wife, simple folk who lived a simple life in a tall stone house with a red door. In her dream he had been kissing her all over—her mouth, her neck, her breasts.

"No, *Khaleesi,*" Irri murmured, "it is your eunuch Grey Worm and the bald men. Will you see them?"

"Yes." Her hair was disheveled and her bedclothes all atangle, Dany realized. "Help me dress. I'll have a cup of wine as well. To clear my head." *To drown my dream.* She could hear the soft sounds of sobs. "Who is that weeping?"

"Your slave Missandei." Jhiqui had a taper in her hand.

"My servant. I have no slaves." Dany did not understand. "Why does she weep?"

"For him who was her brother," Irri told her.

The rest she had from Skahaz, Reznak, and Grey Worm, when they were ushered into her presence. Dany knew their tidings were bad before a word was spoken. One glance at the Shavepate's ugly face sufficed to tell her that. "The Sons of the Harpy?"

Skahaz nodded. His mouth was grim.

"How many dead?"

Reznak wrung his hands. "N-nine, Magnificence. Foul work it was, and wicked. A dreadful night, dreadful."

Nine. The word was a dagger in her heart. Every night the shadow war was waged anew beneath the stepped pyramids of Meereen. Every morn the sun rose upon fresh corpses, with harpies drawn in blood on the bricks beside them. Any freedman who became too prosperous or too outspoken was marked for death. *Nine in one night, though . . .* That frightened her. "Tell me."

Grey Worm answered. "Your servants were set upon as they walked the bricks of Meereen to keep Your Grace's peace. All were well armed, with spears and shields and short swords. Two by two they walked, and two by two they died. Your servants Black Fist and Cetherys were slain by crossbow bolts in Mazdhan's Maze. Your servants Mossador and Duran were crushed by falling stones beneath the river wall. Your servants Eladon Goldenhair and Loyal Spear were poisoned at a wineshop where they were accustomed to stop each night upon their rounds."

Mossador. Dany made a fist. Missandei and her brothers had been taken from their home on Naath by raiders from the Basilisk Isles and sold into slavery in Astapor. Young as she was, Missandei had shown such a gift for tongues that the Good Masters had made a scribe of her. Mossador and Marselen had not been so fortunate. They had been gelded and made into Unsullied. "Have any of the murderers been captured?"

"Your servants have arrested the owner of the wineshop and his daughters. They plead their ignorance and beg for mercy."

They all plead ignorance and beg for mercy. "Give them to the Shavepate. Skahaz, keep each apart from the others and put them to the question."

"It will be done, Your Worship. Would you have me question them sweetly, or sharply?"

"Sweetly, to begin. Hear what tales they tell and what names they give you. It may be they had no part in this." She hesitated. "Nine, the noble Reznak said. Who else?"

"Three freedmen, murdered in their homes," the Shavepate said.

"A moneylender, a cobbler, and the harpist Rylona Rhee. They cut her fingers off before they killed her."

The queen flinched. Rylona Rhee had played the harp as sweetly as the Maiden. When she had been a slave in Yunkai, she had played for every highborn family in the city. In Meereen she had become a leader amongst the Yunkish freedmen, their voice in Dany's councils. "We have no captives but this wineseller?"

"None, this one grieves to confess. We beg your pardon."

Mercy, thought Dany. *They will have the dragon's mercy.* "Skahaz, I have changed my mind. Question the man sharply."

"I could. Or I could question the daughters sharply whilst the father looks on. That will wring some names from him."

"Do as you think best, but bring me names." Her fury was a fire in her belly. "I will have no more Unsullied slaughtered. Grey Worm, pull your men back to their barracks. Henceforth let them guard my walls and gates and person. From this day, it shall be for Meereenese to keep the peace in Meereen. Skahaz, make me a new watch, made up in equal parts of shavepates and freedmen."

"As you command. How many men?"

"As many as you require."

Reznak mo Reznak gasped. "Magnificence, where is the coin to come from to pay wages for so many men?"

"From the pyramids. Call it a blood tax. I will have a hundred pieces of gold from every pyramid for each freedman that the Harpy's Sons have slain."

That brought a smile to the Shavepate's face. "It will be done," he said, "but Your Radiance should know that the Great Masters of Zhak and Merreq are making preparations to quit their pyramids and leave the city."

Daenerys was sick unto death of Zhak and Merreq; she was sick of all the Mereenese, great and small alike. "Let them go, but see that they take no more than the clothes upon their backs. Make certain that all their gold remains here with us. Their stores of food as well."

"Magnificence," murmured Reznak mo Reznak, "we cannot know that these great nobles mean to join your enemies. More like they are simply making for their estates in the hills."

"They will not mind us keeping their gold safe, then. There is nothing to buy in the hills."

"They are afraid for their children," Reznak said.

Yes, Daenerys thought, *and so am I.* "We must keep them safe as well. I will have two children from each of them. From the other pyramids as well. A boy and a girl."

"Hostages," said Skahaz, happily.

"Pages and cupbearers. If the Great Masters make objection, explain to them that in Westeros it is a great honor for a child to be chosen to serve at court." She left the rest unspoken. "Go and do as I've commanded. I have my dead to mourn."

When she returned to her rooms atop the pyramid, she found Missandei crying softly on her pallet, trying as best she could to muffle the sound of her sobs. "Come sleep with me," she told the little scribe. "Dawn will not come for hours yet."

"Your Grace is kind to this one." Missandei slipped under the sheets. "He was a good brother."

Dany wrapped her arms about the girl. "Tell me of him."

"He taught me how to climb a tree when we were little. He could catch fish with his hands. Once I found him sleeping in our garden with a hundred butterflies crawling over him. He looked so beautiful that morning, this one . . . I mean, I loved him."

"As he loved you." Dany stroked the girl's hair. "Say the word, my sweet, and I will send you from this awful place. I will find a ship somehow and send you home. To Naath."

"I would sooner stay with you. On Naath I'd be afraid. What if the slavers came again? I feel safe when I'm with you."

Safe. The word made Dany's eyes fill up with tears. "I want to keep you safe." Missandei was only a child. With her, she felt as if she could be a child too. "No one ever kept me safe when I was little. Well, Ser Willem did, but then he died, and Viserys . . . I want to protect you but . . . it is so hard. To be strong. I don't always know what I should do. I *must* know, though. I am all they have. I am the queen . . . the . . . the . . ."

" . . . mother," whispered Missandei.

"Mother to dragons." Dany shivered.

"No. Mother to us all." Missandei hugged her tighter. "Your Grace should sleep. Dawn will be here soon, and court."

"We'll both sleep, and dream of sweeter days. Close your eyes." When she did, Dany kissed her eyelids and made her giggle.

Kisses came easier than sleep, however. Dany shut her eyes and tried to think of home, of Dragonstone and King's Landing and all the other places that Viserys had told her of, in a kinder land than this . . . but her thoughts kept turning back to Slaver's Bay, like ships caught in some bitter wind. When Missandei was sound asleep, Dany slipped from her arms and stepped out into the predawn air to lean upon the cool brick parapet and gaze out across the city. A thousand roofs stretched out below her, painted in shades of ivory and silver by the moon.

Somewhere beneath those roofs, the Sons of the Harpy were gathered, plotting ways to kill her and all those who loved her and put her children back in chains. Somewhere down there a hungry child was crying for milk. Somewhere an old woman lay dying. Somewhere a man and a maid embraced, and fumbled at each other's clothes with eager hands. But up here there was only the sheen of moonlight on pyramids and pits, with no hint what lay beneath. Up here there was only her, alone.

She was the blood of the dragon. She could kill the Sons of the Harpy, and the sons of the sons, and the sons of the sons of the sons. But a dragon could not feed a hungry child nor help a dying woman's pain. *And who would ever dare to love a dragon?*

She found herself thinking of Daario Naharis once again, Daario with his gold tooth and trident beard, his strong hands resting on the hilts of his matched *arakh* and stiletto, hilts wrought of gold in the shape of naked women. The day he took his leave of her, as she was bidding him farewell, he had brushed the balls of his thumbs lightly across them, back and forth. *I am jealous of a sword hilt,* she had realized, *of women made of gold.* Sending him to the Lamb Men had been wise. She was a queen, and Daario Naharis was not the stuff of kings.

"It has been so long," she had said to Ser Barristan, just yesterday. "What if Daario has betrayed me and gone over to my enemies?"

Three treasons will you know. "What if he met another woman, some princess of the Lhazarene?"

The old knight neither liked nor trusted Daario, she knew. Even so, he had answered gallantly. "There is no woman more lovely than Your Grace. Only a blind man could believe otherwise, and Daario Naharis was not blind."

No, she thought. *His eyes are a deep blue, almost purple, and his gold tooth gleams when he smiles for me.*

Ser Barristan was sure he would return, though. Dany could only pray that he was right.

A bath will help soothe me. She padded barefoot through the grass to her terrace pool. The water felt cool on her skin, raising goosebumps. Little fish nibbled at her arms and legs. She closed her eyes and floated.

A soft rustle made her open them again. She sat up with a soft splash. "Missandei?" she called. "Irri? Jhiqui?"

"They sleep," came the answer.

A woman stood under the persimmon tree, clad in a hooded robe that brushed the grass. Beneath the hood, her face seemed hard and shiny. *She is wearing a mask,* Dany knew, *a wooden mask finished in dark red lacquer.* "Quaithe? Am I dreaming?" She pinched her ear and winced at the pain. "I dreamt of you on *Balerion,* when first we came to Astapor."

"You did not dream. Then or now."

"What are you doing here? How did you get past my guards?"

"I came another way. Your guards never saw me."

"If I call out, they will kill you."

"They will swear to you that I am not here."

"*Are* you here?"

"No. Hear me, Daenerys Targaryen. The glass candles are burning. Soon comes the pale mare, and after her the others. Kraken and dark flame, lion and griffin, the sun's son and the mummer's dragon. Trust none of them. Remember the Undying. Beware the perfumed seneschal."

"Reznak? Why should I fear him?" Dany rose from the pool. Water trickled down her legs, and gooseflesh covered her arms in the cool night air. "If you have some warning for me, speak plainly. What do you want of me, Quaithe?"

Moonlight shone in the woman's eyes. "To show you the way."

"I remember the way. I go north to go south, east to go west, back to go forward. And to touch the light I have to pass beneath the shadow." She squeezed the water from her silvery hair. "I am half-sick of riddling. In Qarth I was a beggar, but here I am a queen. I command you—"

"*Daenerys.* Remember the Undying. Remember who you are."

"The blood of the dragon." *But my dragons are roaring in the darkness.* "I remember the Undying. *Child of three,* they called me. Three mounts they promised me, three fires, and three treasons. One for blood and one for gold and one for . . ."

"Your Grace?" Missandei stood in the door of the queen's bedchamber, a lantern in her hand. "Who are you talking to?"

Dany glanced back toward the persimmon tree. There was no woman there. No hooded robe, no lacquer mask, no Quaithe.

A shadow. A memory. No one. She was the blood of the dragon, but Ser Barristan had warned her that in that blood there was a taint. *Could I be going mad?* They had called her father mad, once. "I was praying," she told the Naathi girl. "It will be light soon. I had best eat something, before court."

"I will bring you food to break your fast."

Alone again, Dany went all the way around the pyramid in hopes of finding Quaithe, past the burned trees and scorched earth where her men had tried to capture Drogon. But the only sound was the wind in the fruit trees, and the only creatures in the gardens were a few pale moths.

Missandei returned with a melon and a bowl of hard-cooked eggs, but Dany found she had no appetite. As the sky lightened and the stars faded one by one, Irri and Jhiqui helped her don a *tokar* of violet silk fringed in gold.

When Reznak and Skahaz appeared, she found herself looking at them askance, mindful of the three treasons. *Beware the perfumed seneschal.* She sniffed suspiciously at Reznak mo Reznak. *I could command the Shavepate to arrest him and put him to the question.*

Would that forestall the prophecy? Or would some other betrayer take his place? *Prophecies are treacherous,* she reminded herself, *and Reznak may be no more than he appears.*

In the purple hall, Dany found her ebon bench piled high about with satin pillows. The sight brought a wan smile to her lips. *Ser Barristan's work,* she knew. The old knight was a good man, but sometimes very literal. *It was only a jape, ser,* she thought, but she sat on one of the pillows just the same.

Her sleepless night soon made itself felt. Before long she was fighting off a yawn as Reznak prattled about the craftsmen's guilds. The stonemasons were wroth with her, it seemed. The bricklayers as well. Certain former slaves were carving stone and laying bricks, stealing work from guild journeymen and masters alike. "The freedmen work too cheaply, Magnificence," Reznak said. "Some call themselves journeymen, or even masters, titles that belong by rights only to the craftsmen of the guilds. The masons and the bricklayers do respectfully petition Your Worship to uphold their ancient rights and customs."

"The freedmen work cheaply because they are hungry," Dany pointed out. "If I forbid them to carve stone or lay bricks, the chandlers, the weavers, and the goldsmiths will soon be at my gates asking that they be excluded from those trades as well." She considered a moment. "Let it be written that henceforth only guild members shall be permitted to name themselves journeymen or masters . . . provided the guilds open their rolls to any freedman who can demonstrate the requisite skills."

"So shall it be proclaimed," said Reznak. "Will it please Your Worship to hear the noble Hizdahr zo Loraq?"

Will he never admit defeat? "Let him step forth."

Hizdahr was not in a *tokar* today. Instead he wore a simple robe of grey and blue. He was shorn as well. *He has shaved off his beard and cut his hair,* she realized. The man had not gone shavepate, not quite, but at least those absurd wings of his were gone. "Your barber has served you well, Hizdahr. I hope you have come to show me his work and not to plague me further about the fighting pits."

He made a deep obeisance. "Your Grace, I fear I must."

Dany grimaced. Even her own people would give no rest about the matter. Reznak mo Reznak stressed the coin to be made through taxes. The Green Grace said that reopening the pits would please the gods. The Shavepate felt it would win her support against the Sons of the Harpy. "Let them fight," grunted Strong Belwas, who had once been a champion in the pits. Ser Barristan suggested a tourney instead; his orphans could ride at rings and fight a mêlée with blunted weapons, he said, a suggestion Dany knew was as hopeless as it was well-intentioned. It was blood the Meereenese yearned to see, not skill. Elsewise the fighting slaves would have worn armor. Only the little scribe Missandei seemed to share the queen's misgivings.

"I have refused you six times," Dany reminded Hizdahr.

"Your Radiance has seven gods, so perhaps she will look upon my seventh plea with favor. Today I do not come alone. Will you hear my friends? There are seven of them as well." He brought them forth one by one. "Here is Khrazz. Here Barsena Blackhair, ever valiant. Here Camarron of the Count and Goghor the Giant. This is the Spotted Cat, this Fearless Ithoke. Last, Belaquo Bonebreaker. They have come to add their voices to mine own, and ask Your Grace to let our fighting pits reopen."

Dany knew his seven, by name if not by sight. All had been amongst the most famed of Meereen's fighting slaves ... and it had been the fighting slaves, freed from their shackles by her sewer rats, who led the uprising that won the city for her. She owed them a blood debt. "I will hear you," she allowed.

One by one, each of them asked her to let the fighting pits reopen. "Why?" she demanded, when Ithoke had finished. "You are no longer slaves, doomed to die at a master's whim. I freed you. Why should you wish to end your lives upon the scarlet sands?"

"I train since three," said Goghor the Giant. "I kill since six. Mother of Dragons says I am free. Why not free to fight?"

"If it is fighting you want, fight for me. Swear your sword to the Mother's Men or the Free Brothers or the Stalwart Shields. Teach my other freedmen how to fight."

Goghor shook his head. "Before, I fight for master. You say, fight for you. I say, fight for me." The huge man thumped his chest with a fist as big as a ham. "For gold. For glory."

"Goghor speaks for us all." The Spotted Cat wore a leopard skin across one shoulder. "The last time I was sold, the price was three hundred thousand honors. When I was a slave, I slept on furs and ate red meat off the bone. Now that I'm free, I sleep on straw and eat salt fish, when I can get it."

"Hizdahr swears that the winners shall share half of all the coin collected at the gates," said Khrazz. "*Half,* he swears it, and Hizdahr is an honorable man."

No, a cunning man. Daenerys felt trapped. "And the losers? What shall they receive?"

"Their names shall be graven on the Gates of Fate amongst the other valiant fallen," declared Barsena. For eight years she had slain every other woman sent against her, it was said. "All men must die, and women too . . . but not all will be remembered."

Dany had no answer for that. *If this is truly what my people wish, do I have the right to deny it to them? It was their city before it was mine, and it is their own lives they wish to squander.* "I will consider all you've said. Thank you for your counsel." She rose. "We will resume on the morrow."

"*All kneel for Daenerys Stormborn, the Unburnt, Queen of Meereen, Queen of the Andals and the Rhoynar and the First Men,* Khaleesi *of Great Grass Sea, Breaker of Shackles, and Mother of Dragons,*" Missandei called.

Ser Barristan escorted her back up to her chambers. "Tell me a tale, ser," Dany said as they climbed. "Some tale of valor with a happy ending." She felt in need of happy endings. "Tell me how you escaped from the Usurper."

"Your Grace. There is no valor in running for your life."

Dany seated herself on a cushion, crossed her legs, and gazed up at him. "Please. It was the Young Usurper who dismissed you from the Kingsguard . . ."

"Joffrey, aye. They gave my age for a reason, though the truth was elsewise. The boy wanted a white cloak for his dog Sandor Clegane and his mother wanted the Kingslayer to be her lord commander.

When they told me, I . . . I took off my cloak as they commanded, threw my sword at Joffrey's feet, and spoke unwisely."

"What did you say?"

"The truth . . . but truth was never welcome at that court. I walked from the throne room with my head high, though I did not know where I was going. I had no home but White Sword Tower. My cousins would find a place for me at Harvest Hall, I knew, but I had no wish to bring Joffrey's displeasure down upon them. I was gathering my things when it came to me that I had brought this on myself by taking Robert's pardon. He was a good knight but a bad king, for he had no right to the throne he sat. That was when I knew that to redeem myself I must find the true king, and serve him loyally with all the strength that still remained me."

"My brother Viserys."

"Such was my intent. When I reached the stables the gold cloaks tried to seize me. Joffrey had offered me a tower to die in, but I had spurned his gift, so now he meant to offer me a dungeon. The commander of the City Watch himself confronted me, emboldened by my empty scabbard, but he had only three men with him and I still had my knife. I slashed one man's face open when he laid his hands upon me, and rode through the others. As I spurred for the gates I heard Janos Slynt shouting for them to go after me. Once outside the Red Keep, the streets were congested, else I might have gotten away clean. Instead they caught me at the River Gate. The gold cloaks who had pursued me from the castle shouted for those at the gate to stop me, so they crossed their spears to bar my way."

"And you without your sword? How did you get past them?"

"A true knight is worth ten guardsmen. The men at the gate were taken by surprise. I rode one down, wrenched away his spear, and drove it through the throat of my closest pursuer. The other broke off once I was through the gate, so I spurred my horse to a gallop and rode hellbent along the river until the city was lost to sight behind me. That night I traded my horse for a handful of pennies and some rags, and the next morning I joined the stream of smallfolk making their way to King's Landing. I'd gone out the Mud Gate, so I returned through the Gate of the Gods, with dirt on my face, stubble on my cheeks, and no weapon but a wooden staff. In roughspun clothes and mud-caked boots, I was just one more old man fleeing the war. The gold cloaks took a stag from me and waved me through. King's Landing was crowded with smallfolk who'd come seeking refuge from the fighting. I lost myself amongst them. I had a little silver, but I needed that to pay my passage across the narrow sea, so I slept in septs and alleys and took my meals in pot shops. I let my beard grow out and cloaked myself in age. The day Lord Stark lost his head, I was there, watching. Afterward I went into the Great Sept and thanked the seven gods that Joffrey had stripped me of my cloak."

"Stark was a traitor who met a traitor's end."

"Your Grace," said Selmy, "Eddard Stark played a part in your father's fall, but he bore you no ill will. When the eunuch Varys told us that you were with child, Robert wanted you killed, but Lord Stark spoke against it. Rather than countenance the murder of children, he told Robert to find himself another Hand."

"Have you forgotten Princess Rhaenys and Prince Aegon?"

"Never. That was Lannister work, Your Grace."

"Lannister or Stark, what difference? Viserys used to call them *the Usurper's dogs*. If a child is set upon by a pack of hounds, does it matter which one tears out his throat? All the dogs are just as guilty. The guilt . . ." The word caught in her throat. *Hazzea,* she thought, and suddenly she heard herself say, "I have to see the pit," in a voice as small as a child's whisper. "Take me down, ser, if you would."

A flicker of disapproval crossed the old man's face, but it was not his way to question his queen. "As you command."

The servants' steps were the quickest way down—not grand, but steep and straight and narrow, hidden in the walls. Ser Barristan brought a lantern, lest she fall. Bricks of twenty different colors pressed close around them, fading to grey and black beyond the lantern light. Thrice they passed Unsullied guards, standing as if they had been carved from stone. The only sound was the soft scruff of their feet upon the steps.

At ground level the Great Pyramid of Meereen was a hushed place, full of dust and shadows. Its outer walls were thirty feet thick. Within them, sounds echoed off arches of many-colored bricks, and amongst the stables, stalls, and storerooms. They passed beneath three massive arches, down a torchlit ramp into the vaults beneath the pyramid, past cisterns, dungeons, and torture chambers where slaves had been scourged and skinned and burned with red-hot irons. Finally they came to a pair of huge iron doors with rusted hinges, guarded by Unsullied.

At her command, one produced an iron key. The door opened, hinges shrieking. Daenerys Targaryen stepped into the hot heart of darkness and stopped at the lip of a deep pit. Forty feet below, her dragons raised their heads. Four eyes burned through the shadows—two of molten gold and two of bronze.

Ser Barristan took her by the arm. "No closer."

"You think they would harm *me*?"

"I do not know, Your Grace, but I would sooner not risk your person to learn the answer."

When Rhaegal roared, a gout of yellow flame turned darkness into day for half a heartbeat. The fire licked along the walls, and Dany felt the heat upon her face, like the blast from an oven. Across the pit, Viserion's wings unfolded, stirring the stale air. He tried to fly to her, but the chains snapped taut as he rose and slammed him down onto his belly. Links as big as a man's fist bound his feet to the floor. The iron collar about his neck was fastened to the wall behind him. Rhaegal wore matching chains. In the light of Selmy's lantern, his scales gleamed like jade. Smoke rose from between his teeth. Bones were scattered on the floor at his feet, cracked and scorched and splintered. The air was uncomfortably hot and smelled of sulfur and charred meat.

"They are larger." Dany's voice echoed off the scorched stone walls. A drop of sweat trickled down her brow and fell onto her breast. "Is it true that dragons never stop growing?"

"If they have food enough, and space to grow. Chained up in here, though . . ."

The Great Masters had used the pit as a prison. It was large enough to hold five hundred men . . . and more than ample for two dragons. *For how long, though? What will happen when they grow too large for the pit? Will they turn on one another with flame and claw? Will they grow wan and weak, with withered flanks and shrunken wings? Will their fires go out before the end?*

What sort of mother lets her children rot in darkness?

If I look back, I am doomed, Dany told herself . . . but how could she not look back? *I should have seen it coming. Was I so blind, or did I close my eyes willfully, so I would not have to see the price of power?*

Viserys had told her all the tales when she was little. He loved to talk of dragons. She knew how Harrenhal had fallen. She knew about the Field of Fire and the Dance of the Dragons. One of her forebears, the third Aegon, had seen his own mother devoured by his uncle's dragon. And there were songs beyond count of villages and kingdoms that lived in dread of dragons till some brave dragonslayer rescued them. At Astapor the slaver's eyes had melted. On the road to Yunkai, when Daario tossed the heads of Sallor the Bald and Prendahl na Ghezn at her feet, her children made a feast of them. Dragons had no fear of men. And a dragon large enough to gorge on sheep could take a child just as easily.

Her name had been Hazzea. She was four years old. *Unless her father lied. He might have lied.* No one had seen the dragon but him. His proof was burned bones, but burned bones proved nothing. He might have killed the little girl himself, and burned her afterward. He would not have been the first father to dispose of an unwanted girl child, the Shavepate claimed. *The Sons of the Harpy might have done it, and made it look like dragon's work to make the city hate me.* Dany wanted to believe that . . . but if that was so, why had Hazzea's father waited until the audience hall was almost empty to come forward? If his purpose had been to inflame the Meereenese against her, he would have told his tale when the hall was full of ears to hear.

The Shavepate had urged her to put the man to death. "At least rip out his tongue. This man's lie could destroy us all, Magnificence." Instead Dany chose to pay the blood price. No one could tell her the worth of a daughter, so she set it at one hundred times the worth of a lamb. "I would give Hazzea back to you if I could," she told the father, "but some things are beyond the power of even a queen. Her bones shall be laid to rest in the Temple of the Graces, and a hundred candles shall burn day and night in her memory. Come back to me each year upon her nameday, and your other children shall not want . . . but this tale must never pass your lips again."

"Men will ask," the grieving father had said. "They will ask me where Hazzea is and how she died."

"She died of a snakebite," Reznak mo Reznak insisted. "A ravening wolf carried her off. A sudden sickness took her. Tell them what you will, but never speak of dragons."

Viserion's claws scrabbled against the stones, and the huge chains rattled as he tried to make his way to her again. When he could not, he gave a roar, twisted his head back as far as he was able, and spat golden flame at the wall behind him. *How soon till his fire burns hot enough to crack stone and melt iron?*

Once, not long ago, he had ridden on her shoulder, his tail coiled round her arm. Once she had fed him morsels of charred meat from her own hand. He had been the first chained up. Daenerys had led him to the pit herself and shut him up inside with several oxen. Once he had gorged himself he grew drowsy. They had chained him whilst he slept.

Rhaegal had been harder. Perhaps he could hear his brother raging in the pit, despite the walls of brick and stone between them. In the end, they had to cover him with a net of heavy iron chain as he basked on her terrace, and he fought so fiercely that it had taken three days to carry him down the servants' steps, twisting and snapping. Six men had been burned in the struggle.

And Drogon . . .

The winged shadow, the grieving father called him. He was the largest of her three, the fiercest, the wildest, with scales as black as night and eyes like pits of fire.

Drogon hunted far afield, but when he was sated he liked to bask in the sun at the apex of the Great Pyramid, where once the harpy of Meereen had stood. Thrice they had tried to take him there, and thrice they had failed. Two score of her bravest had risked themselves trying to capture him. Almost all had suffered burns, and four of them had died. The last she had seen of Drogon had been at sunset on the night of the third attempt. The black dragon had been flying north across the Skahazadhan toward the tall grasses of the Dothraki sea. He had not returned.

Mother of dragons, Daenerys thought. *Mother of monsters. What have I unleashed upon the world? A queen I am, but my throne is made of burned bones, and it rests on quicksand.* Without dragons, how could she hope to hold Meereen, much less win back Westeros? *I am the blood of the dragon,* she thought. *If they are monsters, so am I.*

REEK

The rat squealed as he bit into it, squirming wildly in his hands, frantic to escape. The belly was the softest part. He tore at the sweet meat, the warm blood running over his lips. It was so good that it brought tears to his eyes. His belly rumbled and he swallowed. By the third bite the rat had ceased to struggle, and he was feeling almost content.

Then he heard the sounds of voices outside the dungeon door.

At once he stilled, fearing even to chew. His mouth was full of blood and flesh and hair, but he dare not spit or swallow. He listened in terror, stiff as stone, to the scuff of boots and the clanking of iron keys. *No,* he thought, *no, please gods, not now, not now.* It had taken him so long to catch the rat. *If they catch me with it, they will take it away, and then they'll tell, and Lord Ramsay will hurt me.*

He knew he ought to hide the rat, but he was so *hungry.* It had been two days since he had eaten, or maybe three. Down here in the dark it was hard to tell. Though his arms and legs were thin as reeds, his belly was swollen and hollow, and ached so much that he found he could not sleep. Whenever he closed his eyes, he found himself remembering Lady Hornwood. After their wedding, Lord Ramsay had locked her away in a tower and starved her to death. In the end she had eaten her own fingers.

He crouched down in a corner of his cell, clutching his prize under his chin. Blood ran from the corners of his mouth as he nibbled at the rat with what remained of his teeth, trying to bolt down as much of the warm flesh as he could before the cell was opened. The meat was stringy, but so rich he thought he might be sick. He chewed and swallowed, picking small bones from the holes in his gums where teeth had been yanked out. It hurt to chew, but he was so hungry he could not stop.

The sounds were growing louder. *Please gods, he isn't coming for me,* he prayed, tearing off one of the rat's legs. It had been a long time since anyone had come for him. There were other cells, other prisoners. Sometimes he heard them screaming, even through the thick stone walls. *The women always scream the loudest.* He sucked at the raw meat and tried to spit out the leg bone, but it only dribbled over his lower lip and tangled in his beard. *Go away,* he prayed, *go away, pass me by, please, please.*

But the footsteps stopped just when they were loudest, and the keys clattered right outside the door. The rat fell from his fingers. He wiped his bloody fingers on his breeches. "No," he mumbled, "*noooo.*" His heels scrabbled at the straw as he tried to push himself into the corner, into the cold damp stone walls.

The sound of the lock turning was the most terrible of all. When the light hit him full in the face, he let out a shriek. He had to cover his eyes with his hands. He would have clawed them out if he'd dared, his head was pounding so. "Take it away, do it in the dark, please, oh please."

"That's not him," said a boy's voice. "Look at him. We've got the wrong cell."

"Last cell on the left," another boy replied. "This is the last cell on the left, isn't it?"

"Aye." A pause. "What's he saying?"

"I don't think he likes the light."

"Would you, if you looked like *that*?" The boy hawked and spat. "And the stench of him. I'm like to choke."

"He's been eating rats," said the second boy. "Look."

The first boy laughed. "He has. That's funny."

I had to. The rats bit him when he slept, gnawing at his fingers and his toes, even at his face, so when he got his hands on one he did not hesitate. Eat or be eaten, those were the only choices. "I did it," he mumbled, "I did, I did, I ate him, they do the same to me, please . . ."

The boys moved closer, the straw crunching softly under their feet. "Talk to me," said one of them. He was the smaller of the two, a thin boy, but clever. "Do you remember who you are?"

The fear came bubbling up inside him, and he moaned.

"Talk to me. Tell me your name."

My name. A scream caught in his throat. They had taught him his name, they had, they *had,* but it had been so long that he'd forgotten. *If I say it wrong, he'll take another finger, or worse, he'll . . . he'll . . .* He would not think about that, he could not think about that. There were needles in his jaw, in his eyes. His head was pounding. "Please," he squeaked, his voice thin and weak. He sounded a hundred years old. Perhaps he was. *How long have I been in here?* "Go," he mumbled, through broken teeth and broken fingers, his eyes closed tight against the terrible bright light. "Please, you can have the rat, don't hurt me . . ."

"*Reek,*" said the larger of the boys. "Your name is Reek. Remember?" He was the one with the torch. The smaller boy had the ring of iron keys.

Reek? Tears ran down his cheeks. "I remember. I do." His mouth opened and closed. "My name is Reek. It rhymes with leek." In the dark he did not need a name, so it was easy to forget. *Reek, Reek, my name is Reek.* He had not been born with that name. In another life he had been someone else, but here and now, his name was Reek. He remembered.

He remembered the boys as well. They were clad in matching lambs-wool doublets, silver-grey with dark blue trim. Both were squires, both were eight, and both were Walder Frey. *Big Walder and Little Walder, yes.* Only the big one was Little and the little one was Big, which amused the boys and confused the rest of the world. "I know you," he whispered, through cracked lips. "I know your names."

"You're to come with us," said Little Walder.

"His lordship has need of you," said Big Walder.

Fear went through him like a knife. *They are only children,* he thought. *Two boys of eight.* He could overcome two boys of eight, surely. Even as weak as he was, he could take the torch, take the keys, take the dagger sheathed on Little Walder's hip, escape. *No. No, it is too easy. It is a trap. If I run, he will take another finger from me, he will take more of my teeth.*

He had run before. Years ago, it seemed, when he still had some strength in him, when he had still been defiant. That time it had been Kyra with the keys. She told him she had stolen them, that she knew a postern gate that was never guarded. "Take me back to Winterfell, m'lord," she begged, pale-faced and trembling. "I don't know the way. I can't escape alone. Come with me, please." And so he had. The gaoler was dead drunk in a puddle of wine, with his breeches down around his ankles. The dungeon door was open and the postern gate had been unguarded, just as she had said. They waited for the moon to go behind a cloud, then slipped from the castle and splashed across the Weeping Water, stumbling over stones, half-frozen by the icy stream. On the far side, he had kissed her. "You've saved us," he said. *Fool. Fool.*

It had all been a trap, a game, a jape. Lord Ramsay loved the chase and preferred to hunt two-legged prey. All night they ran through the darkling wood, but as the sun came up the sound of a distant horn came faintly through the trees, and they heard the baying of a pack of hounds. "We should split up," he told Kyra as the dogs drew closer. "They cannot track us both." The girl was crazed with fear, though, and refused to leave his side, even when he swore that he would raise a host of ironborn and come back for her if she should be the one they followed.

Within the hour, they were taken. One dog knocked him to the ground, and a second bit Kyra on the leg as she scrambled up a hillside. The rest surrounded them, baying and snarling, snapping at them every time they moved, holding them there until Ramsay Snow rode up with his huntsmen. He was still a bastard then, not yet a Bolton. "There you are," he said, smiling down at them from the saddle. "You wound me, wandering off like this. Have you grown tired of my hospitality so soon?" That was when Kyra seized a stone and threw it at his head. It missed by a good foot, and Ramsay smiled. "You must be punished."

Reek remembered the desperate, frightened look in Kyra's eyes. She had never looked so young as she did in that moment, still half a girl, but there was nothing he could do. *She brought them down on us,* he thought. *If we had separated as I wanted, one of us might have gotten away.*

The memory made it hard to breathe. Reek turned away from the torch with tears glimmering in his eyes. *What does he want of me this time?* he thought, despairing. *Why won't he just leave me be? I did no wrong, not this time, why won't they just leave me in the dark?* He'd had a rat, a fat one, warm and wriggling . . .

"Should we wash him?" asked Little Walder.

"His lordship likes him stinky," said Big Walder. "That's why he named him Reek."

Reek. My name is Reek, it rhymes with bleak. He had to remember that. *Serve and obey and remember who you are, and no more harm will come to you. He promised, his lordship promised.* Even if he had wanted to resist, he did not have the strength. It had been scourged from him, starved from him, flayed from him. When Little Walder pulled him up and Big Walder waved the torch at him to herd him from the cell, he went along as docile as a dog. If he'd had a tail, he would have tucked it down between his legs.

If I had a tail, the Bastard would have cut it off. The thought came unbidden, a vile thought, dangerous. His lordship was not a bastard anymore. *Bolton, not Snow.* The boy king on the Iron Throne had made Lord Ramsay legitimate, giving him the right to use his lord father's name. Calling him *Snow* reminded him of his bastardy and sent him into a black rage. Reek must remember that. And his name, he must remember his name. For half a heartbeat it eluded him, and that frightened him so badly that he tripped on the steep dungeon steps and tore his breeches open on the stone, drawing blood. Little Walder had to shove the torch at him to get him back on his feet and moving again.

Out in the yard, night was settling over the Dreadfort and a full moon was rising over the castle's eastern walls. Its pale light cast the shadows of the tall triangular merlons across the frozen ground, a line of sharp black teeth. The air was cold and damp and full of half-forgotten smells. *The world,* Reek told himself, *this is what the world smells like.* He did not know how long he had been down there in the dungeons, but it had to have been half a year at least. *That long, or longer. What if it has been five years, or ten, or twenty? Would I even know? What if I went mad down there, and half my life is gone?* But no, that was folly. It could not have been so long. The boys were still boys. If it had been ten years, they would have grown into men. He had to remember that. *I must not let him drive me mad. He can take my fingers and my toes, he can put out my eyes and slice my ears off, but he cannot take my wits unless I let him.*

Little Walder led the way with torch in hand. Reek followed meekly, with Big Walder just behind him. The dogs in the kennels barked as they went by. Wind swirled through the yard, cutting through the thin cloth of the filthy rags he wore and raising gooseprickles on his skin. The night air was cold and damp, but he saw no sign of snow though surely winter was close at hand. Reek wondered if he would be alive to see the snows come. *How many fingers will I have? How many toes?* When he raised a hand, he was shocked to see how white it was, how fleshless. *Skin and bones,* he thought. *I have an old man's hands.* Could he have been wrong about the boys? What if they were not Little Walder and Big Walder after all, but the *sons* of the boys he'd known?

The great hall was dim and smoky. Rows of torches burned to left and right, grasped by skeletal human hands jutting from the walls. High overhead were wooden rafters black from smoke, and a vaulted ceiling lost in shadow. The air was heavy with the smells of wine and ale and roasted meat. Reek's stomach rumbled noisily at the scents, and his mouth began to water.

Little Walder pushed him stumbling past the long tables where the men of the garrison were eating. He could feel their eyes upon him. The best places, up near the dais, were occupied by Ramsay's favorites, the Bastard's Boys. Ben Bones, the old man who kept his lordship's beloved hunting hounds. Damon, called Damon Dance-for-Me, fair-haired and boyish. Grunt, who had lost his tongue for speaking carelessly in Lord Roose's hearing. Sour Alyn. Skinner. Yellow Dick. Farther down, below the salt, were others that Reek knew by sight if not by name: sworn swords and serjeants, soldiers and gaolers and torturers. But there were strangers too, faces he did not know. Some wrinkled their noses as he passed, whilst others laughed at the sight of him. *Guests,* Reek thought, *his lordship's friends, and I am brought up to amuse them.* A shiver of fear went through him.

At the high table the Bastard of Bolton sat in his lord father's seat, drinking from his father's cup. Two old men shared the high table with him, and Reek knew at a glance that both were lords. One was gaunt, with flinty eyes, a long white beard, and a face as hard as a winter frost. His jerkin was a ragged bearskin, worn and greasy. Underneath he wore a ringmail byrnie, even at table. The second lord was thin as well, but twisted where the first was straight. One of his shoulders was much higher than the other, and he stooped over his trencher like a vulture over carrion. His eyes were grey and greedy, his teeth yellow, his forked beard a tangle of snow and silver. Only a few wisps of white hair still clung to his spotted skull, but the cloak he wore was soft and fine, grey wool trimmed with black sable and fastened at the shoulder with a starburst wrought in beaten silver.

Ramsay was clad in black and pink—black boots, black belt and scabbard, black leather jerkin over a pink velvet doublet slashed with dark red satin. In his right ear gleamed a garnet cut in the shape of a drop of blood. Yet for all the splendor of his garb, he remained an ugly man, big-boned and slope-shouldered, with a fleshiness to him that suggested that in later life he would run to fat. His skin was pink and blotchy, his nose broad, his mouth small, his hair long and dark and dry. His lips were wide and meaty, but the thing men noticed first about him were his eyes. He had his lord father's eyes—small, close-set, queerly pale. *Ghost grey,* some men called the shade, but in truth his eyes were all but colorless, like two chips of dirty ice.

At the sight of Reek, he smiled a wet-lipped smile. "There he is. My sour old friend." To the men beside him he said, "Reek has been with me since I was a boy. My lord father gave him to me as a token of his love."

The two lords exchanged a look. "I had heard your serving man was dead," said the one with the stooped shoulder. "Slain by the Starks, they said."

Lord Ramsay chuckled. "The ironmen will tell you that what is dead may never die, but rises again, harder and stronger. Like Reek. He smells of the grave, though, I grant you that."

"He smells of nightsoil and stale vomit." The stoop-shouldered old lord tossed aside the bone that he'd been gnawing on and wiped his fingers on the tablecloth. "Is there some reason you must needs inflict him upon us whilst we're eating?"

The second lord, the straight-backed old man in the mail byrnie, studied Reek with flinty eyes. "Look again," he urged the other lord. "His hair's gone white and he is three stone thinner, aye, but this is no serving man. Have you forgotten?"

The crookback lord looked again and gave a sudden snort. "*Him?* Can it be? Stark's ward. Smiling, always smiling."

"He smiles less often now," Lord Ramsay confessed. "I may have broken some of his pretty white teeth."

"You would have done better to slit his throat," said the lord in mail. "A dog who turns against his master is fit for naught but skinning."

"Oh, he's been skinned, here and there," said Ramsay.

"Yes, my lord. I was bad, my lord. Insolent and . . ." He licked his lip, trying to think of what else he had done. *Serve and obey,* he told himself, *and he'll let you live, and keep the parts that you still have. Serve and obey and remember your name. Reek, Reek, it rhymes with meek.* ". . . bad and . . ."

"There's blood on your mouth," Ramsay observed. "Have you been chewing on your fingers again, Reek?"

"No. No, my lord, I swear." Reek had tried to bite his own ring finger off once, to stop it hurting after they had stripped the skin from it. Lord Ramsay would never simply cut off a man's finger. He preferred to flay it and let the exposed flesh dry and crack and fester. Reek had been whipped and racked and cut, but there was no pain half so excruciating as the pain that followed flaying. It was the sort of pain that drove men mad, and it could not be endured for long. Soon or late the victim would scream, "Please, no more, no more, stop it hurting, *cut it off*," and Lord Ramsay would oblige. It was a game they played. Reek had learned the rules, as his hands and feet could testify, but that one time he had forgotten and tried to end the pain himself, with his teeth. Ramsay had not been pleased, and the offense had cost Reek another toe. "I ate a rat," he mumbled.

"A rat?" Ramsay's pale eyes glittered in the torchlight. "All the rats in the Dreadfort belong to my lord father. How dare you make a meal of one without my leave."

Reek did not know what to say, so he said nothing. One wrong word could cost him another toe, even a finger. Thus far he had lost two fingers off his left hand and the pinky off his right, but only the little toe off his right foot against three from his left. Sometimes Ramsay would make japes about balancing him out. *My lord was only japing,* he tried to tell himself. *He does not want to hurt me, he told me so, he only does it when I give him cause.* His lord was merciful and kind. He might have flayed his face off for some of the things Reek had said, before he'd learned his true name and proper place.

"This grows tedious," said the lord in the mail byrnie. "Kill him and be done with it."

Lord Ramsay filled his cup with ale. "That would spoil our celebration, my lord. Reek, I have glad tidings for you. I am to be wed. My lord father is bringing me a Stark girl. Lord Eddard's daughter, Arya. You remember little Arya, don't you?"

Arya Underfoot, he almost said. *Arya Horseface.* Robb's younger sister, brown-haired, long-faced, skinny as a stick, always dirty. *Sansa was the pretty one.* He remembered a time when he had thought that Lord Eddard Stark might marry him to Sansa and claim him for a son, but that had only been a child's fancy. Arya, though . . . "I remember her. Arya."

"She shall be the Lady of Winterfell, and me her lord."

She is only a girl. "Yes, my lord. Congratulations."

"Will you attend me at my wedding, Reek?"

He hesitated. "If you wish it, my lord."

"Oh, I do."

He hesitated again, wondering if this was some cruel trap. "Yes, my lord. If it please you. I would be honored."

"We must take you out of that vile dungeon, then. Scrub you pink again, get you some clean clothes, some food to eat. Some nice soft porridge, would you like that? Perhaps a pease pie laced with bacon. I have a little task for you, and you'll need your strength back if you are to serve me. You do want to serve me, I know."

"Yes, my lord. More than anything." A shiver went through him. "I'm your Reek. Please let me serve you. Please."

"Since you ask so nicely, how can I deny you?" Ramsay Bolton smiled. "I ride to war, Reek. And you will be coming with me, to help me fetch home my virgin bride."

BRAN

Something about the way the raven screamed sent a shiver running up Bran's spine. *I am almost a man grown,* he had to remind himself. *I have to be brave now.*

But the air was sharp and cold and full of fear. Even Summer was afraid. The fur on his neck was bristling. Shadows stretched against the hillside, black and hungry. All the trees were bowed and twisted by the weight of ice they carried. Some hardly looked like trees at all. Buried from root to crown in frozen snow, they huddled on the hill like giants, monstrous and misshapen creatures hunched against the icy wind.

"They are here." The ranger drew his longsword.

"Where?" Meera's voice was hushed.

"Close. I don't know. Somewhere."

The raven shrieked again. "Hodor," whispered Hodor. He had his hands tucked up beneath his armpits. Icicles hung from the brown briar of his beard, and his mustache was a lump of frozen snot, glittering redly in the light of sunset.

"Those wolves are close as well," Bran warned them. "The ones that have been following us. Summer can smell them whenever we're downwind."

"Wolves are the least of our woes," said Coldhands. "We have to climb. It will be dark soon. You would do well to be inside before night comes. Your warmth will draw them." He glanced to the west, where the light of the setting sun could be seen dimly through the trees, like the glow of a distant fire.

"Is this the only way in?" asked Meera.

"The back door is three leagues north, down a sinkhole."

That was all he had to say. Not even Hodor could climb down into a sinkhole with Bran heavy on his back, and Jojen could no more walk three leagues than run a thousand.

Meera eyed the hill above. "The way looks clear."

"*Looks,*" the ranger muttered darkly. "Can you feel the cold? There's something here. *Where are they?*"

"Inside the cave?" suggested Meera.

"The cave is warded. They cannot pass." The ranger used his sword to point. "You can see the entrance there. Halfway up, between the weirwoods, that cleft in the rock."

"I see it," said Bran. Ravens were flying in and out.

Hodor shifted his weight. "Hodor."

"A fold in the rock, that's all I see," said Meera.

"There's a passage there. Steep and twisty at first, a runnel through the rock. If you can reach it, you'll be safe."

"What about you?"

"The cave is warded."

Meera studied the cleft in the hillside. "It can't be more than a thousand yards from here to there."

No, thought Bran, *but all those yards are upward.* The hill was steep and thickly wooded. The snow had stopped three days ago, but none of it had melted. Beneath the trees, the ground was blanketed in white, still pristine and unbroken. "No one's here," said Bran, bravely. "Look at the snow. There are no footprints."

"The white walkers go lightly on the snow," the ranger said. "You'll find no prints to mark their passage." A raven descended from above to settle on his shoulder. Only a dozen of the big black birds remained with them. The rest had vanished along the way; every dawn when they arose, there had been fewer of them. "*Come,*" the bird squawked. "*Come, come.*"

The three-eyed crow, thought Bran. *The greenseer.* "It's not so far,"

he said. "A little climb, and we'll be safe. Maybe we can have a fire."
All of them were cold and wet and hungry, except the ranger, and
Jojen Reed was too weak to walk unaided.

"You go." Meera Reed bent down beside her brother. He was settled
in the bole of an oak, eyes closed, shivering violently. What little of
his face could be seen beneath his hood and scarf was as colorless as
the surrounding snow, but breath still puffed faintly from his nostrils
whenever he exhaled. Meera had been carrying him all day. *Food and
fire will set him right again,* Bran tried to tell himself, though he wasn't
sure it would. "I can't fight and carry Jojen both, the climb's too steep,"
Meera was saying. "Hodor, you take Bran up to that cave."

"Hodor." Hodor clapped his hands together.

"Jojen just needs to eat," Bran said, miserably. It had been twelve
days since the elk had collapsed for the third and final time, since
Coldhands had knelt beside it in the snowbank and murmured a
blessing in some strange tongue as he slit its throat. Bran wept like
a little girl when the bright blood came rushing out. He had never
felt more like a cripple than he did then, watching helplessly as Meera
Reed and Coldhands butchered the brave beast who had carried them
so far. He told himself he would not eat, that it was better to go
hungry than to feast upon a friend, but in the end he'd eaten twice,
once in his own skin and once in Summer's. As gaunt and starved as
the elk had been, the steaks the ranger carved from him had sustained
them for seven days, until they finished the last of them huddled over
a fire in the ruins of an old hillfort.

"He needs to eat," Meera agreed, smoothing her brother's brow.
"We all do, but there's no food here. *Go.*"

Bran blinked back a tear and felt it freeze upon his cheek. Coldhands
took Hodor by the arm. "The light is fading. If they're not here now,
they will be soon. Come."

Wordless for once, Hodor slapped the snow off his legs, and plowed
upward through the snowdrifts with Bran upon his back. Coldhands
stalked beside them, his blade in a black hand. Summer came after.
In some places the snow was higher than he was, and the big direwolf
had to stop and shake it off after plunging through the thin crust. As
they climbed, Bran turned awkwardly in his basket to watch as Meera

slid an arm beneath her brother to lift him to his feet. *He's too heavy for her. She's half-starved, she's not as strong as she was.* She clutched her frog spear in her other hand, jabbing the tines into the snow for a little more support. Meera had just begun to struggle up the hill, half-dragging and half-carrying her little brother, when Hodor passed between two trees, and Bran lost sight of them.

The hill grew steeper. Drifts of snow cracked under Hodor's boots. Once a rock moved beneath his foot and he slid backwards, and almost went tumbling back down the hill. The ranger caught him by the arm and saved him. "Hodor," said Hodor. Every gust of wind filled the air with fine white powder that shone like glass in the last light of day. Ravens flapped around them. One flew ahead and vanished inside the cave. *Only eighty yards now,* Bran thought, *that's not far at all.*

Summer stopped suddenly, at the bottom of a steep stretch of unbroken white snow. The direwolf turned his head, sniffed the air, then snarled. Fur bristling, he began to back away.

"Hodor, stop," said Bran. "Hodor. *Wait.*" Something was wrong. Summer smelled it, and so did he. *Something bad. Something close.* "Hodor, no, go back."

Coldhands was still climbing, and Hodor wanted to keep up. "Hodor, hodor, hodor," he grumbled loudly, to drown out Bran's complaints. His breathing had grown labored. Pale mist filled the air. He took a step, then another. The snow was almost waist deep and the slope was very steep. Hodor was leaning forward, grasping at rocks and trees with his hands as he climbed. Another step. Another. The snow Hodor disturbed slid downhill, starting a small avalanche behind them.

Sixty yards. Bran craned himself sideways to better see the cave. Then he saw something else. "A fire!" In the little cleft between the weirwood trees was a flickering glow, a ruddy light calling through the gathering gloom. "Look, someone—"

Hodor screamed. He twisted, stumbled, fell.

Bran felt the world slide sideways as the big stableboy spun violently around. A jarring impact drove the breath from him. His mouth was full of blood and Hodor was thrashing and rolling, crushing the crippled boy beneath him.

Something has hold of his leg. For half a heartbeat Bran thought maybe a root had gotten tangled round his ankle . . . until the root moved. *A hand,* he saw, as the rest of the wight came bursting from beneath the snow.

Hodor kicked at it, slamming a snow-covered heel full into the thing's face, but the dead man did not even seem to feel it. Then the two of them were grappling, punching and clawing at each other, sliding down the hill. Snow filled Bran's mouth and nose as they rolled over, but in a half a heartbeat he was rolling up again. Something slammed against his head, a rock or a chunk of ice or a dead man's fist, he could not tell, and he found himself out of his basket, sprawled across the hillside, spitting snow, his gloved hand full of hair that he'd torn from Hodor's head.

All around him, wights were rising from beneath the snow.

Two, three, four. Bran lost count. They surged up violently amidst sudden clouds of snow. Some wore black cloaks, some ragged skins, some nothing. All of them had pale flesh and black hands. Their eyes glowed like pale blue stars.

Three of them descended on the ranger. Bran saw Coldhands slash one across the face. The thing kept right on coming, driving him back into the arms of another. Two more were going after Hodor, lumbering clumsily down the slope. Meera was going to climb right into this, Bran realized, with a sick sense of helpless terror. He smashed the snow and shouted out a warning.

Something grabbed hold of him.

That was when his shout became a scream. Bran filled a fist with snow and threw it, but the wight did not so much as blink. A black hand fumbled at his face, another at his belly. Its fingers felt like iron. *He's going to pull my guts out.*

But suddenly Summer was between them. Bran glimpsed skin tear like cheap cloth, heard the splintering of bone. He saw a hand and wrist rip loose, pale fingers wriggling, the sleeve faded black roughspun. *Black,* he thought, *he's wearing black, he was one of the Watch.* Summer flung the arm aside, twisted, and sank his teeth into the dead man's neck under the chin. When the big grey wolf wrenched free, he took most of the creature's throat out in an explosion of pale rotten meat.

The severed hand was still moving. Bran rolled away from it. On his belly, clawing at the snow, he glimpsed the trees above, pale and snow-cloaked, the orange glow between.

Fifty yards. If he could drag himself fifty yards, they could not get him. Damp seeped through his gloves as he clutched at roots and rocks, crawling toward the light. *A little farther, just a little farther. Then you can rest beside the fire.*

The last light had vanished from amongst the trees by then. Night had fallen. Coldhands was hacking and cutting at the circle of dead men that surrounded him. Summer was tearing at the one that he'd brought down, its face between his teeth. No one was paying any mind to Bran. He crawled a little higher, dragging his useless legs behind him. *If I can reach that cave . . .*

"Hooooodor" came a whimper, from somewhere down below.

And suddenly he was not Bran, the broken boy crawling through the snow, suddenly he was Hodor halfway down the hill, with the wight raking at his eyes. Roaring, he came lurching to his feet, throwing the thing violently aside. It went to one knee, began to rise again. Bran ripped Hodor's longsword from his belt. Deep inside he could hear poor Hodor whimpering still, but outside he was seven feet of fury with old iron in his hand. He raised the sword and brought it down upon the dead man, grunting as the blade sheared through wet wool and rusted mail and rotted leather, biting deep into the bones and flesh beneath. "*HODOR!*" he bellowed, and slashed again. This time he took the wight's head off at the neck, and for half a moment he exulted . . . until a pair of dead hands came groping blindly for his throat.

Bran backed away, bleeding, and Meera Reed was there, driving her frog spear deep into the wight's back. "Hodor," Bran roared again, waving her uphill. "*Hodor, hodor.*" Jojen was twisting feebly where she'd laid him down. Bran went to him, dropped the longsword, gathered the boy into Hodor's arm, and lurched back to his feet. "*HODOR!*" he bellowed.

Meera led the way back up the hill, jabbing at the wights when they came near. The things could not be hurt, but they were slow and clumsy. "Hodor," Hodor said with every step. "Hodor, hodor." He wondered what Meera would think if he should suddenly tell her that he loved her.

Up above them, flaming figures were dancing in the snow.

The wights, Bran realized. *Someone set the wights on fire.*

Summer was snarling and snapping as he danced around the closest, a great ruin of a man wreathed in swirling flame. *He shouldn't get so close, what is he doing?* Then he saw himself, sprawled facedown in the snow. Summer was trying to drive the thing away from him. *What will happen if it kills me?* the boy wondered. *Will I be Hodor for good or all? Will I go back into Summer's skin? Or will I just be dead?*

The world moved dizzily around him. White trees, black sky, red flames, everything was whirling, shifting, spinning. He felt himself stumbling. He could hear Hodor screaming, "Hodor hodor hodor hodor. Hodor hodor hodor hodor. Hodor hodor hodor hodor hodor." A cloud of ravens was pouring from the cave, and he saw a little girl with a torch in hand, darting this way and that. For a moment Bran thought it was his sister Arya . . . madly, for he knew his little sister was a thousand leagues away, or dead. And yet there she was, whirling, a scrawny thing, ragged, wild, her hair atangle. Tears filled Hodor's eyes and froze there.

Everything turned inside out and upside down, and Bran found himself back inside his own skin, half-buried in the snow. The burning wight loomed over him, etched tall against the trees in their snowy shrouds. It was one of the naked ones, Bran saw, in the instant before the nearest tree shook off the snow that covered it and dropped it all down upon his head.

The next he knew, he was lying on a bed of pine needles beneath a dark stone roof. *The cave. I'm in the cave.* His mouth still tasted of blood where he'd bitten his tongue, but a fire was burning to his right, the heat washing over his face, and he had never felt anything so good. Summer was there, sniffing round him, and Hodor, soaking wet. Meera cradled Jojen's head in her lap. And the Arya thing stood over them, clutching her torch.

"The snow," Bran said. "It fell on me. Buried me."

"Hid you. I pulled you out." Meera nodded at the girl. "It was her who saved us, though. The torch . . . fire kills them."

"Fire *burns* them. Fire is always hungry."

That was not Arya's voice, nor any child's. It was a woman's voice, high and sweet, with a strange music in it like none that he had ever heard and a sadness that he thought might break his heart. Bran squinted, to see her better. It *was* a girl, but smaller than Arya, her skin dappled like a doe's beneath a cloak of leaves. Her eyes were queer—large and liquid, gold and green, slitted like a cat's eyes. *No one has eyes like that.* Her hair was a tangle of brown and red and gold, autumn colors, with vines and twigs and withered flowers woven through it.

"Who are you?" Meera Reed was asking.

Bran knew. "She's a child. A child of the forest." He shivered, as much from wonderment as cold. They had fallen into one of Old Nan's tales.

"The First Men named us children," the little woman said. "The giants called us *woh dak nag gran,* the squirrel people, because we were small and quick and fond of trees, but we are no squirrels, no children. Our name in the True Tongue means *those who sing the song of earth.* Before your Old Tongue was ever spoken, we had sung our songs ten thousand years."

Meera said, "You speak the Common Tongue now."

"For him. The Bran boy. I was born in the time of the dragon, and for two hundred years I walked the world of men, to watch and listen and learn. I might be walking still, but my legs were sore and my heart was weary, so I turned my feet for home."

"Two hundred years?" said Meera.

The child smiled. "Men, they are the children."

"Do you have a name?" asked Bran.

"When I am needing one." She waved her torch toward the black crack in the back wall of the cave. "Our way is down. You must come with me now."

Bran shivered again. "The ranger . . ."

"He cannot come."

"They'll kill him."

"No. They killed him long ago. Come now. It is warmer down deep, and no one will hurt you there. He is waiting for you."

"The three-eyed crow?" asked Meera.

"The greenseer." And with that she was off, and they had no choice but to follow. Meera helped Bran back up onto Hodor's back, though his basket was half-crushed and wet from melting snow. Then she slipped an arm around her brother and shouldered him back onto his feet once more. His eyes opened. "What?" he said. "Meera? Where are we?" When he saw the fire, he smiled. "I had the strangest dream."

The way was cramped and twisty, and so low that Hodor soon was crouching. Bran hunched down as best he could, but even so, the top of his head was soon scraping and bumping against the ceiling. Loose dirt crumbled at each touch and dribbled down into his eyes and hair, and once he smacked his brow on a thick white root growing from the tunnel wall, with tendrils hanging from it and spiderwebs between its fingers.

The child went in front with the torch in hand, her cloak of leaves whispering behind her, but the passage turned so much that Bran soon lost sight of her. Then the only light was what was reflected off the passage walls. After they had gone down a little, the cave divided, but the left branch was dark as pitch, so even Hodor knew to follow the moving torch to the right.

The way the shadows shifted made it seem as if the walls were moving too. Bran saw great white snakes slithering in and out of the earth around him, and his heart thumped in fear. He wondered if they had blundered into a nest of milk snakes or giant grave worms, soft and pale and squishy. *Grave worms have teeth.*

Hodor saw them too. "Hodor," he whimpered, reluctant to go on. But when the girl child stopped to let them catch her, the torchlight steadied, and Bran realized that the snakes were only white roots like the one he'd hit his head on. "It's weirwood roots," he said. "Remember the heart tree in the godswood, Hodor? The white tree with the red leaves? A tree can't hurt you."

"Hodor." Hodor plunged ahead, hurrying after the child and her torch, deeper into the earth. They passed another branching, and another, then came into an echoing cavern as large as the great hall of Winterfell, with stone teeth hanging from its ceiling and more poking up through its floor. The child in the leafy cloak wove a path through them. From time to time she stopped and waved her torch at them impatiently. *This way,* it seemed to say, *this way, this way, faster.*

There were more side passages after that, more chambers, and Bran heard dripping water somewhere to his right. When he looked off that way, he saw eyes looking back at them, slitted eyes that glowed bright, reflecting back the torchlight. *More children,* he told himself, *the girl is not the only one,* but Old Nan's tale of Gendel's children came back to him as well.

The roots were everywhere, twisting through earth and stone, closing off some passages and holding up the roofs of others. *All the color is gone,* Bran realized suddenly. The world was black soil and white wood. The heart tree at Winterfell had roots as thick around as a giant's legs, but these were even thicker. And Bran had never seen so many of them. *There must be a whole grove of weirwoods growing up above us.*

The light dwindled again. Small as she was, the child-who-was-not-a-child moved quickly when she wanted. As Hodor thumped after her, something crunched beneath his feet. His halt was so sudden that Meera and Jojen almost slammed into his back.

"Bones," said Bran. "It's bones." The floor of the passage was littered with the bones of birds and beasts. But there were other bones as well, big ones that must have come from giants and small ones that could have been from children. On either side of them, in niches carved from the stone, skulls looked down on them. Bran saw a bear skull and a wolf skull, half a dozen human skulls and near as many giants. All the rest were small, queerly formed. *Children of the forest.* The roots had grown in and around and through them, every one. A few had ravens perched atop them, watching them pass with bright black eyes.

The last part of their dark journey was the steepest. Hodor made the final descent on his arse, bumping and sliding downward in a clatter of broken bones, loose dirt, and pebbles. The girl child was waiting for them, standing on one end of a natural bridge above a yawning chasm. Down below in the darkness, Bran heard the sound of rushing water. *An underground river.*

"Do we have to cross?" Bran asked, as the Reeds came sliding down behind him. The prospect frightened him. If Hodor slipped on that narrow bridge, they would fall and fall.

"No, boy," the child said. "Behind you." She lifted her torch higher, and the light seemed to shift and change. One moment the flames burned orange and yellow, filling the cavern with a ruddy glow; then all the colors faded, leaving only black and white. Behind them Meera gasped. Hodor turned.

Before them a pale lord in ebon finery sat dreaming in a tangled nest of roots, a woven weirwood throne that embraced his withered limbs as a mother does a child.

His body was so skeletal and his clothes so rotted that at first Bran took him for another corpse, a dead man propped up so long that the roots had grown over him, under him, and through him. What skin the corpse lord showed was white, save for a bloody blotch that crept up his neck onto his cheek. His white hair was fine and thin as root hair and long enough to brush against the earthen floor. Roots coiled around his legs like wooden serpents. One burrowed through his breeches into the desiccated flesh of his thigh, to emerge again from his shoulder. A spray of dark red leaves sprouted from his skull, and grey mushrooms spotted his brow. A little skin remained, stretched across his face, tight and hard as white leather, but even that was fraying, and here and there the brown and yellow bone beneath was poking through.

"Are you the three-eyed crow?" Bran heard himself say. *A three-eyed crow should have three eyes. He has only one, and that one red.* Bran could feel the eye staring at him, shining like a pool of blood in the torchlight. Where his other eye should have been, a thin white root grew from an empty socket, down his cheek, and into his neck.

"A . . . crow?" The pale lord's voice was dry. His lips moved slowly, as if they had forgotten how to form words. "Once, aye. Black of garb and black of blood." The clothes he wore were rotten and faded, spotted with moss and eaten through with worms, but once they had been black. "I have been many things, Bran. Now I am as you see me, and now you will understand why I could not come to you . . . except in dreams. I have watched you for a long time, watched you with a thousand eyes and one. I saw your birth, and that of your lord father before you. I saw your first step, heard your first word, was part of your first dream. I was watching when you fell. And now you are come to me at last, Brandon Stark, though the hour is late."

"I'm here," Bran said, "only I'm broken. Will you . . . will you fix me . . . my legs, I mean?"

"No," said the pale lord. "That is beyond my powers."

Bran's eyes filled with tears. *We came such a long way.* The chamber echoed to the sound of the black river.

"You will never walk again, Bran," the pale lips promised, "but you will fly."

TYRION

For a long while he did not stir, but lay unmoving upon the heap of old sacks that served him for a bed, listening to the wind in the lines, to the lapping of the river at the hull. A full moon floated above the mast. *It is following me downriver, watching me like some great eye.* Despite the warmth of the musty skins that covered him, a shiver went through the little man. *I need a cup of wine. A dozen cups of wine.* But the moon would blink before that whoreson Griff let him quench his thirst. Instead he drank water, and was condemned to sleepless nights and days of sweats and shakes.

The dwarf sat up, cradling his head in his hands. *Did I dream?* All memory of it had fled. The nights had never been kind to Tyrion Lannister. He slept badly even on soft feather beds. On the *Shy Maid*, he made his bed atop the roof of the cabin, with a coil of hempen rope for a pillow. He liked it better up here than in the boat's cramped hold. The air was fresher, and the river sounds were sweeter than Duck's snoring. There was a price to be paid for such joys, though; the deck was hard, and he woke stiff and sore, his legs cramped and aching.

They were throbbing now, his calves gone hard as wood. He kneaded them with his fingers, trying to rub the ache away, but when he stood the pain was still enough to make him grimace. *I need to bathe.* His boy's clothes stank, and so did he. The others bathed in the river, but thus far he had not joined them. Some of the turtles he'd seen in the shallows looked big enough to bite him in half. *Bonesnappers,* Duck called them. Besides, he did not want Lemore to see him naked.

A wooden ladder led down from the cabin roof. Tyrion pulled on his boots and descended to the afterdeck, where Griff sat wrapped in a wolfskin cloak beside an iron brazier. The sellsword kept the night watch by himself, rising as the rest of his band sought their beds and retiring when the sun came up.

Tyrion squatted across from him and warmed his hands over the coals. Across the water nightingales were singing. "Day soon," he said to Griff.

"Not soon enough. We need to be under way." If it had been up to Griff, the *Shy Maid* would continue downstream by night as well as day, but Yandry and Ysilla refused to risk their poleboat in the dark. The Upper Rhoyne was full of snags and sawyers, any one of which could rip out the *Shy Maid*'s hull. Griff did not want to hear it. What he wanted was Volantis.

The sellsword's eyes were always moving, searching the night for . . . what? *Pirates? Stone men? Slave-catchers?* The river had perils, the dwarf knew, but Griff himself struck Tyrion as more dangerous than any of them. He reminded Tyrion of Bronn, though Bronn had a sellsword's black humor and Griff had no humor at all.

"I would kill for a cup of wine," muttered Tyrion.

Griff made no reply. *You will die before you drink,* his pale eyes seemed to say. Tyrion had drunk himself blind his first night on the *Shy Maid*. The next day he awoke with dragons fighting in his skull. Griff took one look at him retching over the side of the poleboat, and said, "You are done with drink."

"Wine helps me sleep," Tyrion had protested. *Wine drowns my dreams,* he might have said.

"Then stay awake," Griff had replied, implacable.

To the east, the first pale light of day suffused the sky above the river. The waters of the Rhoyne slowly went from black to blue, to match the sellsword's hair and beard. Griff got to his feet. "The others should wake soon. The deck is yours." As the nightingales fell silent, the river larks took up their song. Egrets splashed amongst the reeds and left their tracks across the sandbars. The clouds in the sky were aglow: pink and purple, maroon and gold, pearl and saffron. One looked like a dragon. *Once a man has seen a dragon in flight, let him stay at home and tend his garden in content,* someone had written once, *for this wide world has no greater wonder.* Tyrion scratched at his scar and tried to recall the author's name. Dragons had been much in his thoughts of late.

"Good morrow, Hugor." Septa Lemore had emerged in her white robes, cinched at the waist with a woven belt of seven colors. Her hair flowed loose about her shoulders. "How did you sleep?"

"Fitfully, good lady. I dreamed of you again." *A waking dream.* He could not sleep, so he had eased a hand between his legs and imagined the septa atop him, breasts bouncing.

"A wicked dream, no doubt. You are a wicked man. Will you pray with me and ask forgiveness for your sins?"

Only if we pray in the fashion of the Summer Isles. "No, but do give the Maiden a long, sweet kiss for me."

Laughing, the septa walked to the prow of the boat. It was her custom to bathe in the river every morning. "Plainly, this boat was not named for you," Tyrion called as she disrobed.

"The Mother and the Father made us in their image, Hugor. We should glory in our bodies, for they are the work of gods."

The gods must have been drunk when they got to me. The dwarf watched Lemore slip into the water. The sight always made him hard. There was something wonderfully wicked about the thought of peeling the septa out of those chaste white robes and spreading her legs. *Innocence despoiled,* he thought . . . though Lemore was not near as innocent as she appeared. She had stretch marks on her belly that could only have come from childbirth.

Yandry and Ysilla had risen with the sun and were going about their business. Yandry stole a glance at Septa Lemore from time to time as he was checking the lines. His small dark wife, Ysilla, took no notice. She fed some wood chips to the brazier on the afterdeck, stirred the coals with a blackened blade, and began to knead the dough for the morning biscuits.

When Lemore climbed back onto the deck, Tyrion savored the sight of water trickling between her breasts, her smooth skin glowing golden in the morning light. She was past forty, more handsome than pretty, but still easy on the eye. *Being randy is the next best thing to being drunk,* he decided. It made him feel as if he was still alive. "Did you see the turtle, Hugor?" the septa asked him, wringing water from her hair. "The big ridgeback?"

The early morning was the best time for seeing turtles. During the day they would swim down deep, or hide in cuts along the banks, but when the sun was newly risen they came to the surface. Some liked to swim beside the boat. Tyrion had glimpsed a dozen different sorts: large turtles and small ones, flatbacks and red-ears, softshells and bonesnappers, brown turtles, green turtles, black turtles, clawed turtles and horned turtles, turtles whose ridged and patterned shells were covered with whorls of gold and jade and cream. Some were so large they could have borne a man upon their backs. Yandry swore the Rhoynar princes used to ride them across the river. He and his wife were Greenblood born, a pair of Dornish orphans come home to Mother Rhoyne.

"I missed the ridgeback." *I was watching the naked woman.*

"I am sad for you." Lemore slipped her robe over her head. "I know you only rise so early in hopes of seeing turtles."

"I like to watch the sun come up as well." It was like watching a maiden rising naked from her bath. Some might be prettier than others, but every one was full of promise. "The turtles have their charms, I will allow. Nothing delights me so much as the sight of a nice pair of shapely . . . shells."

Septa Lemore laughed. Like everyone else aboard the *Shy Maid,* she had her secrets. She was welcome to them. *I do not want to know her, I only want to fuck her.* She knew it too. As she hung her septa's crystal about her neck, to nestle in the cleft between her breasts, she teased him with a smile.

Yandry pulled up the anchor, slid one of the long poles off the cabin roof, and pushed them off. Two of the herons raised their heads to watch as the *Shy Maid* drifted away from the bank, out into the current. Slowly the boat began to move downstream. Yandry went to the tiller. Ysilla was turning the biscuits. She laid an iron pan atop the brazier and put the bacon in. Some days she cooked biscuits and bacon; some days bacon and biscuits. Once every fortnight there might be a fish, but not today.

When Ysilla turned her back, Tyrion snatched a biscuit off the brazier, darting away just in time to avoid a smack from her fearsome wooden spoon. They were best when eaten hot, dripping with honey and butter. The smell of the bacon cooking soon fetched Duck up from the hold. He sniffed over the brazier, received a swack from Ysilla's spoon, and went back to have his morning piss off the stern.

Tyrion waddled over to join him. "Now here's a sight to see," he quipped as they were emptying their bladders, "a dwarf and a duck, making the mighty Rhoyne that much mightier."

Yandry snorted in derision. "Mother Rhoyne has no need of your water, Yollo. She is the greatest river in the world."

Tyrion shook off the last few drops. "Big enough to drown a dwarf, I grant you. The Mander is as broad, though. So is the Trident, near its mouth. The Blackwater runs deeper."

"You do not know the river. Wait, and you will see."

The bacon turned crisp, the biscuits golden brown. Young Griff stumbled up onto deck yawning. "Good morrow, all." The lad was shorter than Duck, but his lanky build suggested that he had not yet come into his full growth. *This beardless boy could have any maiden in the Seven Kingdoms, blue hair or no. Those eyes of his would melt them.* Like his sire, Young Griff had blue eyes, but where the father's eyes were pale, the son's were dark. By lamplight they turned black, and in the light of dusk they seemed purple. His eyelashes were as long as any woman's.

"I smell bacon," the lad said, pulling on his boots.

"Good bacon," said Ysilla. "Sit."

She fed them on the afterdeck, pressing honeyed biscuits on Young Griff and hitting Duck's hand with her spoon whenever he made a grab for more bacon. Tyrion pulled apart two biscuits, filled them with bacon, and carried one to Yandry at the tiller. Afterward he helped Duck to raise the *Shy Maid*'s big lateen sail. Yandry took them out into the center of the river, where the current was strongest. The *Shy Maid* was a sweet boat. Her draft was so shallow she could work her way up even the smallest of the river's vassal streams, negotiating sandbars that would have stranded larger vessels, yet with her sail raised and a current under her, she could make good speed. That could mean life and death on the upper reaches of the Rhoyne, Yandry claimed. "There is no law above the Sorrows, not for a thousand years."

"And no *people*, so far as I can see." He'd glimpsed some ruins along the banks, piles of masonry overgrown by vines and moss and flowers, but no other signs of human habitation.

"You do not know the river, Yollo. A pirate boat may lurk up any stream, and escaped slaves oft hide amongst the ruins. The slave-catchers seldom come so far north."

"Slave-catchers would be a welcome change from turtles." Not being an escaped slave, Tyrion need not fear being caught. And no pirate was like to bother a poleboat moving downstream. The valuable goods came up the river from Volantis.

When the bacon was gone, Duck punched Young Griff in the shoulder. "Time to raise some bruises. Swords today, I think."

"Swords?" Young Griff grinned. "Swords will be sweet."

Tyrion helped him dress for the bout, in heavy breeches, padded doublet, and a dinted suit of old steel plate. Ser Rolly shrugged into his mail and boiled leather. Both set helms upon their heads and chose blunted longswords from the bundle in the weapons chest. They set to on the afterdeck, having at each other lustily whilst the rest of the morning company looked on.

When they fought with mace or blunted longaxe, Ser Rolly's greater size and strength would quickly overwhelm his charge; with swords the contests were more even. Neither man had taken up a shield this morning, so it was a game of slash and parry, back and forth across the deck. The river rang to the sounds of their combat. Young Griff landed more blows, though Duck's were harder. After a while, the bigger man began to tire. His cuts came a little slower, a little lower. Young Griff turned them all and launched a furious attack that forced Ser Rolly back. When they reached the stern, the lad tied up their blades and slammed a shoulder into Duck, and the big man went into the river.

He came up sputtering and cursing, bellowing for someone to fish him out before a 'snapper ate his privates. Tyrion tossed a line to him. "Ducks should swim better than that," he said as he and Yandry were hauling the knight back aboard the *Shy Maid*.

Ser Rolly grabbed Tyrion by the collar. "Let us see how dwarfs swim," he said, chucking him headlong into the Rhoyne.

The dwarf laughed last; he could paddle passably well, and did . . . until his legs began to cramp. Young Griff extended him a pole. "You are not the first to try and drown me," he told Duck, as he was pouring river water from his boot. "My father threw me down a well the day I was born, but I was so ugly that the water witch who lived down there spat me back." He pulled off the other boot, then did a cartwheel along the deck, spraying all of them.

Young Griff laughed. "Where did you learn that?"

"The mummers taught me," he lied. "My mother loved me best of all her children because I was so small. She nursed me at her breast till I was seven. That made my brothers jealous, so they stuffed me in a sack and sold me to a mummer's troupe. When I tried to run off the master mummer cut off half my nose, so I had no choice but to go with them and learn to be amusing."

The truth was rather different. His uncle had taught him a bit of tumbling when he was six or seven. Tyrion had taken to it eagerly. For half a year he cartwheeled his merry way about Casterly Rock, bringing smiles to the faces of septons, squires, and servants alike. Even Cersei laughed to see him once or twice.

All that ended abruptly the day his father returned from a sojourn in King's Landing. That night at supper Tyrion surprised his sire by walking the length of the high table on his hands. Lord Tywin was not pleased. "The gods made you a dwarf. Must you be a fool as well? You were born a lion, not a monkey."

And you're a corpse, Father, so I'll caper as I please.

"You have a gift for making men smile," Septa Lemore told Tyrion as he was drying off his toes. "You should thank the Father Above. He gives gifts to all his children."

"He does," he agreed pleasantly. *And when I die, please let them bury with me a crossbow, so I can thank the Father Above for his gifts the same way I thanked the father below.*

His clothing was still soaked from his involuntary swim, clinging to his arms and legs uncomfortably. Whilst Young Griff went off with Septa Lemore to be instructed in the mysteries of the Faith, Tyrion stripped off the wet clothes and donned dry ones. Duck had a good guffaw when he emerged on deck again. He could not blame him. Dressed as he was, he made a comic sight. His doublet was divided down the middle; the left side was purple velvet with bronze studs; the right, yellow wool embroidered in green floral patterns. His breeches were similarly split; the right leg was solid green, the left leg striped in red and white. One of Illyrio's chests had been packed with a child's clothing, musty but well made. Septa Lemore had slit each garment apart, then sewn them back together, joining half of this to half of that to fashion a crude motley. Griff had even insisted that Tyrion help with the cutting and sewing. No doubt he meant for it to be humbling, but Tyrion enjoyed the needlework. Lemore was always pleasant company, despite her penchant for scolding him whenever he said something rude about the gods. *If Griff wants to cast me as the fool, I'll play the game.* Somewhere, he knew, Lord Tywin Lannister was horrified, and that took the sting from it.

His other duty was anything but foolish. *Duck has his sword, I my quill and parchment.* Griff had commanded him to set down all he knew of dragonlore. The task was a formidable one, but the dwarf labored at it every day, scratching away as best he could as he sat cross-legged on the cabin roof.

Tyrion had read much and more of dragons through the years. The greater part of those accounts were idle tales and could not be relied on, and the books that Illyrio had provided them were not the ones he might have wished for. What he really wanted was the complete text of *The Fires of the Freehold,* Galendro's history of Valyria. No complete copy was known to Westeros, however; even the Citadel's lacked twenty-seven scrolls. *They must have a library in Old Volantis, surely. I may find a better copy there, if I can find a way inside the Black Walls to the city's heart.*

He was less hopeful concerning Septon Barth's *Dragons, Wyrms, and Wyverns: Their Unnatural History.* Barth had been a blacksmith's son who rose to be King's Hand during the reign of Jaehaerys the Conciliator. His enemies always claimed he was more sorcerer than septon. Baelor the Blessed had ordered all Barth's writings destroyed when he came to the Iron Throne. Ten years ago, Tyrion had read a fragment of *Unnatural History* that had eluded the Blessed Baelor, but he doubted that any of Barth's work had found its way across the narrow sea. And of course there was even less chance of his coming on the fragmentary, anonymous, blood-soaked tome sometimes called *Blood and Fire* and sometimes *The Death of Dragons,* the only surviving copy of which was supposedly hidden away in a locked vault beneath the Citadel.

When the Halfmaester appeared on deck, yawning, the dwarf was writing down what he recalled concerning the mating habits of dragons, on which subject Barth, Munkun, and Thomax held markedly divergent views. Haldon stalked to the stern to piss down at the sun where it shimmered on the water, breaking apart with every puff of wind. "We should reach the junction with the Noyne by evening, Yollo," the Halfmaester called out.

Tyrion glanced up from his writing. "My name is Hugor. Yollo is hiding in my breeches. Shall I let him out to play?"

"Best not. You might frighten the turtles." Haldon's smile was as sharp as the blade of a dagger. "What did you tell me was the name of that street in Lannisport where you were born, Yollo?"

"It was an alley. It had no name." Tyrion took a mordant pleasure in inventing the details of the colorful life of Hugor Hill, also known as Yollo, a bastard out of Lannisport. *The best lies are seasoned with a bit of truth.* The dwarf knew he sounded like a westerman, and a highborn westerman at that, so Hugor must needs be some lordling's by-blow. Born in Lannisport because he knew that city better than Oldtown or King's Landing, and cities were where most dwarfs ended up, even those whelped by Goodwife Bumpkin in the turnip patch. The countryside had no grotesqueries or mummer shows . . . though it did have wells aplenty, to swallow up unwanted kittens, three-headed calves, and babes like him.

"I see you have been defacing more good parchment, Yollo." Haldon laced up his breeches.

"Not all of us can be half a maester." Tyrion's hand was cramping. He put his quill aside and flexed his stubby fingers. "Fancy another game of *cyvasse*?" The Halfmaester always defeated him, but it was a way to pass the time.

"This evening. Will you join us for Young Griff's lesson?"

"Why not? Someone needs to correct your errors."

There were four cabins on the *Shy Maid*. Yandry and Ysilla shared one, Griff and Young Griff another. Septa Lemore had a cabin to herself, as did Haldon. The Halfmaester's cabin was the largest of the four. One wall was lined with bookshelves and bins stacked with old scrolls and parchments; another held racks of ointments, herbs, and potions. Golden light slanted through the wavy yellow glass of the round window. The furnishings included a bunk, a writing desk, a chair, a stool, and the Halfmaester's *cyvasse* table, strewn with carved wooden pieces.

The lesson began with languages. Young Griff spoke the Common Tongue as if he had been born to it, and was fluent in High Valyrian, the low dialects of Pentos, Tyrosh, Myr, and Lys, and the trade talk of sailors. The Volantene dialect was as new to him as it was to Tyrion, so every day they learned a few more words whilst Haldon corrected their mistakes. Meereenese was harder; its roots were Valyrian as well, but the tree had been grafted onto the harsh, ugly tongue of Old Ghis. "You need a bee up your nose to speak Ghiscari properly," Tyrion complained. Young Griff laughed, but the Halfmaester only said, "Again." The boy obeyed, though he rolled his eyes along with his zzzs this time. *He has a better ear than me,* Tyrion was forced to admit, *though I'll wager my tongue is still more nimble.*

Geometry followed languages. There the boy was less adroit, but Haldon was a patient teacher, and Tyrion was able to make himself of use as well. He had learned the mysteries of squares and circles and triangles from his father's maesters at Casterly Rock, and they came back more quickly than he would have thought.

By the time they turned to history, Young Griff was growing restive. "We were discussing the history of Volantis," Haldon said to him. "Can you tell Yollo the difference between a tiger and an elephant?"

"Volantis is the oldest of the Nine Free Cities, first daughter of Valyria," the lad replied, in a bored tone. "After the Doom it pleased the Volantenes to consider themselves the heirs of the Freehold and rightful rulers of the world, but they were divided as to how dominion might best be achieved. The Old Blood favored the sword, while the merchants and moneylenders advocated trade. As they contended for rule of the city, the factions became known as the tigers and elephants, respectively.

"The tigers held sway for almost a century after the Doom of Valyria. For a time they were successful. A Volantene fleet took Lys and a Volantene army captured Myr, and for two generations all three cities were ruled from within the Black Walls. That ended when the tigers tried to swallow Tyrosh. Pentos came into the war on the Tyroshi side, along with the Westerosi Storm King. Braavos provided a Lyseni exile with a hundred warships, Aegon Targaryen flew forth from Dragonstone on the Black Dread, and Myr and Lys rose up in rebellion. The war left the Disputed Lands a waste, and freed Lys and Myr from the yoke. The tigers suffered other defeats as well. The fleet they sent to reclaim Valyria vanished in the Smoking Sea. Qohor and Norvos broke their power on the Rhoyne when the fire galleys fought on Dagger Lake. Out of the east came the Dothraki, driving smallfolk from their hovels and nobles from their estates, until only grass and ruins remained from the forest of Qohor to the headwaters of the Selhoru. After a century of war, Volantis found herself broken, bankrupt, and depopulated. It was then that the elephants rose up. They have held sway ever since. Some years the tigers elect a triarch, and some years they do not, but never more than one, so the elephants have ruled the city for three hundred years."

"Just so," said Haldon. "And the present triarchs?"

"Malaquo is a tiger, Nyessos and Doniphos are elephants."

"And what lesson can we draw from Volantene history?"

"If you want to conquer the world, you best have dragons."

Tyrion could not help but laugh.

Later, when Young Griff went up on deck to help Yandry with the sails and poles, Haldon set up his *cyvasse* table for their game. Tyrion watched with mismatched eyes, and said, "The boy is bright. You have done well by him. Half the lords in Westeros are not so learned, sad to say. Languages, history, songs, sums . . . a heady stew for some sellsword's son."

"A book can be as dangerous as a sword in the right hands," said Haldon. "Try to give me a better battle this time, Yollo. You play *cyvasse* as badly as you tumble."

"I am trying to lull you into a false sense of confidence," said Tyrion, as they arranged their tiles on either side of a carved wooden screen. "You *think* you taught me how to play, but things are not always as they seem. Perhaps I learned the game from the cheesemonger, have you considered that?"

"Illyrio does not play *cyvasse*."

No, thought the dwarf, *he plays the game of thrones, and you and Griff and Duck are only pieces, to be moved where he will and sacrificed at need, just as he sacrificed Viserys*. "The blame must fall on you, then. If I play badly, it is your doing."

The Halfmaester chuckled. "Yollo, I shall miss you when the pirates cut your throat."

"Where are these famous pirates? I am beginning to think that you and Illyrio made them all up."

"They are thickest on the stretch of river between Ar Noy and the Sorrows. Above the ruins of Ar Noy, the Qohorik rule the river, and below the Sorrows the galleys of Volantis hold sway, but neither city claims the waters in between, so the pirates have made it their own. Dagger Lake is full of islands where they lurk in hidden caves and secret strongholds. Are you ready?"

"For you? Beyond a doubt. For the pirates? Less so."

Haldon removed the screen. Each of them contemplated the other's opening array. "You are learning," the Halfmaester said.

Tyrion almost grabbed his dragon but thought better of it. Last game he had brought her out too soon and lost her to a trebuchet. "If we do meet these fabled pirates, I may join up with them. I'll tell them that my name is Hugor Halfmaester." He moved his light horse toward Haldon's mountains.

Haldon answered with an elephant. "Hugor Halfwit would suit you better."

"I only need half my wits to be a match for you." Tyrion moved up his heavy horse to support the light. "Perhaps you would care to wager on the outcome?"

The Halfmaester arched an eyebrow. "How much?"

"I have no coin. We'll play for secrets."

"Griff would cut my tongue out."

"Afraid, are you? I would be if I were you."

"The day you defeat me at *cyvasse* will be the day turtles crawl out my arse." The Halfmaester moved his spears. "You have your wager, little man."

Tyrion stretched a hand out for his dragon.

It was three hours later when the little man finally crept back up on deck to empty his bladder. Duck was helping Yandry wrestle down the sail, while Ysilla took the tiller. The sun hung low above the reed-beds along the western bank, as the wind began to gust and rip. *I need that skin of wine,* the dwarf thought. His legs were cramped from squatting on that stool, and he felt so light-headed that he was lucky not to fall into the river.

"Yollo," Duck called. "Where's Haldon?"

"He's taken to his bed, in some discomfort. There are turtles crawling out his arse." He left the knight to sort that out and crawled up the ladder to the cabin roof. Off to the east, there was darkness gathering behind a rocky island.

Septa Lemore found him there. "Can you feel the storms in the air, Hugor Hill? Dagger Lake is ahead of us, where pirates prowl. And beyond that lie the Sorrows."

Not mine. I carry mine own sorrows with me, everywhere I go. He thought of Tysha and wondered where whores go. *Why not Volantis? Perhaps I'll find her there. A man should cling to hope.* He wondered what he would say to her. *I am sorry that I let them rape you, love. I thought you were a whore. Can you find it in your heart to forgive me? I want to go back to our cottage, to the way it was when we were man and wife.*

The island fell away behind them. Tyrion saw ruins rising along the eastern bank: crooked walls and fallen towers, broken domes and rows of rotted wooden pillars, streets choked by mud and overgrown with purple moss. *Another dead city, ten times as large as Ghoyan Drohe.* Turtles lived there now, big bonesnappers. The dwarf could see them basking in the sun, brown and black hummocks with jagged ridges down the center of their shells. A few saw the *Shy Maid* and slid down into the water, leaving ripples in their wake. This would not be a good place for a swim.

Then, through the twisted half-drowned trees and wide wet streets, he glimpsed the silvery sheen of sunlight upon water. *Another river,* he knew at once, *rushing toward the Rhoyne.* The ruins grew taller as the land grew narrower, until the city ended on a point of land where stood the remains of a colossal palace of pink and green marble, its collapsed domes and broken spires looming large above a row of covered archways. Tyrion saw more 'snappers sleeping in the slips where half a hundred ships might once have docked. He knew where he was then. *That was Nymeria's palace, and this is all that remains of Ny Sar, her city.*

"Yollo," shouted Yandry as the *Shy Maid* passed the point, "tell me again of those Westerosi rivers as big as Mother Rhoyne."

"I did not know," he called back. "No river in the Seven Kingdoms is half so wide as this." The new river that had joined them was a close twin to the one they had been sailing down, and that one alone had almost matched the Mander or the Trident.

"This is Ny Sar, where the Mother gathers in her Wild Daughter, Noyne," said Yandry, "but she will not reach her widest point until she meets her other daughters. At Dagger Lake the Qhoyne comes rushing in, the Darkling Daughter, full of gold and amber from the Axe and pinecones from the Forest of Qohor. South of there the Mother meets Lhorulu, the Smiling Daughter from the Golden Fields. Where they join once stood Chroyane, the festival city, where the streets were made of water and the houses made of gold. Then south and east again for long leagues, until at last comes creeping in Selhoru, the Shy Daughter who hides her course in reeds and writhes. There Mother Rhoyne waxes so wide that a man upon a boat in the center of the stream cannot see a shore to either side. You shall see, my little friend."

I shall, the dwarf was thinking, when he spied a rippling ahead not six yards from the boat. He was about to point it out to Lemore when it came to the surface with a wash of water that rocked the *Shy Maid* sideways.

It was another turtle, a horned turtle of enormous size, its dark green shell mottled with brown and overgrown with water moss and crusty black river molluscs. It raised its head and bellowed, a deep-throated thrumming roar louder than any warhorn that Tyrion had ever heard. "We are blessed," Ysilla was crying loudly, as tears streamed down her face. "We are blessed, we are blessed."

Duck was hooting, and Young Griff too. Haldon came out on deck to learn the cause of the commotion . . . but too late. The giant turtle had vanished below the water once again. "What was the cause of all that noise?" the Halfmaester asked.

"A turtle," said Tyrion. "A turtle bigger than this boat."

"It was *him*," cried Yandry. "The Old Man of the River."

And why not? Tyrion grinned. *Gods and wonders always appear, to attend the birth of kings.*

DAVOS

The *Merry Midwife* stole into White Harbor on the evening tide, her patched sail rippling with every gust of wind.

She was an old cog, and even in her youth no one had ever called her pretty. Her figurehead showed a laughing woman holding an infant by one foot, but the woman's cheeks and the babe's bottom were both pocked by wormholes. Uncounted layers of drab brown paint covered her hull; her sails were grey and tattered. She was not a ship to draw a second glance, unless it was to wonder how she stayed afloat. The *Merry Midwife* was known in White Harbor too. For years she had plied a humble trade between there and Sisterton.

It was not the sort of arrival that Davos Seaworth had anticipated when he'd set sail with Salla and his fleet. All this had seemed simpler then. The ravens had not brought King Stannis the allegiance of White Harbor, so His Grace would send an envoy to treat with Lord Manderly in person. As a show of strength, Davos would arrive aboard Salla's galleas *Valyrian*, with the rest of the Lysene fleet behind her. Every hull was striped: black and yellow, pink and blue, green and white, purple and gold. The Lyseni loved bright hues, and Salladhor Saan was the most colorful of all. *Salladhor the Splendid,* Davos thought, *but the storms wrote an end to all of that.*

Instead he would smuggle himself into the city, as he might have done twenty years before. Until he knew how matters stood here, it was more prudent to play the common sailor, not the lord.

White Harbor's walls of whitewashed stone rose before them, on the eastern shore where the White Knife plunged into the firth. Some of the city's defenses had been strengthened since the last time Davos had been here, half a dozen years before. The jetty that divided the inner and outer harbors had been fortified with a long stone wall, thirty feet tall and almost a mile long, with towers every hundred yards. There was smoke rising from Seal Rock as well, where once there had been only ruins. *That could be good or bad, depending on what side Lord Wyman chooses.*

Davos had always been fond of this city, since first he'd come here as a cabin boy on *Cobblecat.* Though small compared to Oldtown and King's Landing, it was clean and well-ordered, with wide straight cobbled streets that made it easy for a man to find his way. The houses were built of whitewashed stone, with steeply pitched roofs of dark grey slate. Roro Uhoris, the *Cobblecat*'s cranky old master, used to claim that he could tell one port from another just by the way they smelled. Cities were like women, he insisted; each one had its own unique scent. Oldtown was as flowery as a perfumed dowager. Lannisport was a milkmaid, fresh and earthy, with woodsmoke in her hair. King's Landing reeked like some unwashed whore. But White Harbor's scent was sharp and salty, and a little fishy too. "She smells the way a mermaid ought to smell," Roro said. "She smells of the sea."

She still does, thought Davos, but he could smell the peat smoke drifting off Seal Rock too. The sea stone dominated the approaches to the outer harbor, a massive grey-green upthrust looming fifty feet above the waters. Its top was crowned with a circle of weathered stones, a ringfort of the First Men that had stood desolate and abandoned for hundreds of years. It was not abandoned now. Davos could see scorpions and spitfires behind the standing stones, and crossbowmen peering between them. *It must be cold up there, and wet.* On all his previous visits, seals could be seen basking on the broken rocks below. The Blind Bastard always made him count them whenever the *Cobblecat* set sail from White Harbor; the more seals there were, Roro said, the more luck they would have on their voyage. There were no seals now. The smoke and the soldiers had frightened them away. *A wiser man would see a caution in that. If I had a thimble full of sense, I would have gone with Salla.* He could have made his way back south, to Marya and their sons. *I have lost four sons in the king's service, and my fifth serves as his squire. I should have the right to cherish the two boys who still remain. It has been too long since I saw them.*

At Eastwatch, the black brothers told him there was no love between the Manderlys of White Harbor and the Boltons of the Dreadfort. The Iron Throne had raised Roose Bolton up to Warden of the North, so it stood to reason that Wyman Manderly should declare for Stannis. *White Harbor cannot stand alone. The city needs an ally, a protector. Lord Wyman needs King Stannis as much as Stannis needs him.* Or so it seemed at Eastwatch.

Sisterton had undermined those hopes. If Lord Borrell told it true, if the Manderlys meant to join their strength to the Boltons and the Freys . . . no, he would not dwell on that. He would know the truth soon enough. He prayed he had not come too late.

That jetty wall conceals the inner harbor, he realized, as the *Merry Midwife* was pulling down her sail. The outer harbor was larger, but the inner harbor offered better anchorage, sheltered by the city wall on one side and the looming mass of the Wolf's Den on another, and now by the jetty wall as well. At Eastwatch-by-the-Sea, Cotter Pyke told Davos that Lord Wyman was building war galleys. There could have been a score of ships concealed behind those walls, waiting only a command to put to sea.

Behind the city's thick white walls, the New Castle rose proud and pale upon its hill. Davos could see the domed roof of the Sept of the Snows as well, surmounted by tall statues of the Seven. The Manderlys had brought the Faith north with them when they were driven from the Reach. White Harbor had its godswood too, a brooding tangle of root and branch and stone locked away behind the crumbling black walls of the Wolf's Den, an ancient fortress that served only as a prison now. But for the most part the septons ruled here.

The merman of House Manderly was everywhere in evidence, flying from the towers of the New Castle, above the Seal Gate, and along the city walls. At Eastwatch, the northmen insisted that White Harbor would never abandon its allegiance to Winterfell, but Davos saw no sign of the direwolf of Stark. *There are no lions either. Lord Wyman cannot have declared for Tommen yet, or he would have raised his standard.*

The dockside wharves were swarming. A clutter of small boats were tied up along the fish market, off-loading their catches. He saw three river runners too, long lean boats built tough to brave the swift currents and rocky shoots of the White Knife. It was the seagoing vessels that interested him most, however; a pair of carracks as drab and tattered as the *Merry Midwife*, the trading galley *Storm Dancer*, the cogs *Brave Magister* and *Horn of Plenty*, a galleas from Braavos marked by her purple hull and sails . . .

. . . and there beyond, the warship.

The sight of her sent a knife through his hopes. Her hull was black and gold, her figurehead a lion with an upraised paw. *Lionstar,* read the letters on her stern, beneath a fluttering banner that bore the arms of the boy king on the Iron Throne. A year ago, he would not have been able to read them, but Maester Pylos had taught him some of the letters back on Dragonstone. For once, the reading gave him little pleasure. Davos had been praying that the galley had been lost in the same storms that had ravaged Salla's fleet, but the gods had not been so kind. The Freys were here, and he would need to face them.

The *Merry Midwife* tied up to the end of a weathered wooden pier in the outer harbor, well away from *Lionstar*. As her crew made her fast to the pilings and lowered a gangplank, her captain sauntered up to Davos. Casso Mogat was a mongrel of the narrow sea, fathered on a Sisterton whore by an Ibbenese whaler. Only five feet tall and very hirsute, he dyed his hair and whiskers a mossy green. It made him look like a tree stump in yellow boots. Despite his appearance, he seemed a good sailor, though a hard master to his crew. "How long will you be gone?"

"A day at least. It may be longer." Davos had found that lords liked to keep you waiting. They did it to make you anxious, he suspected, and to demonstrate their power.

"The *Midwife* will linger here three days. No longer. They will look for me back in Sisterton."

"If things go well, I could be back by the morrow."

"And if these things go badly?"

I may not be back at all. "You need not wait for me."

A pair of customs men were clambering aboard as he went down the gangplank, but neither gave him so much as a glance. They were there to see the captain and inspect the hold; common seamen did not concern them, and few men looked as common as Davos. He was of middling height, his shrewd peasant's face weathered by wind and sun, his grizzled beard and brown hair well salted with grey. His garb was plain as well: old boots, brown breeches and blue tunic, a woolen mantle of undyed wool, fastened with a wooden clasp. He wore a pair of salt-stained leather gloves to hide the stubby fingers of the hand that Stannis had shortened, so many years ago. Davos hardly looked a lord, much less a King's Hand. That was all to the good until he knew how matters stood here.

He made his way along the wharf and through the fish market. The *Brave Magister* was taking on some mead. The casks stood four high along the pier. Behind one stack he glimpsed three sailors throwing dice. Farther on the fishwives were crying the day's catch, and a boy was beating time on a drum as a shabby old bear danced in a circle for a ring of river runners. Two spearmen had been posted at the Seal Gate, with the badge of House Manderly upon their breasts, but they were too intent on flirting with a dockside whore to pay Davos any mind. The gate was open, the portcullis raised. He joined the traffic passing through.

Inside was a cobbled square with a fountain at its center. A stone merman rose from its waters, twenty feet tall from tail to crown. His curly beard was green and white with lichen, and one of the prongs of his trident had broken off before Davos had been born, yet somehow he still managed to impress. *Old Fishfoot* was what the locals called him. The square was named for some dead lord, but no one ever called it anything but Fishfoot Yard.

The Yard was teeming this afternoon. A woman was washing her smallclothes in Fishfoot's fountain and hanging them off his trident to dry. Beneath the arches of the peddler's colonnade the scribes and money changers had set up for business, along with a hedge wizard, a herb woman, and a very bad juggler. A man was selling apples from a barrow, and a woman was offering herring with chopped onions. Chickens and children were everywhere underfoot. The huge oak-and-iron doors of the Old Mint had always been closed when Davos had been in Fishfoot Yard before, but today they stood open. Inside he glimpsed hundreds of women, children, and old men, huddled on the floor on piles of furs. Some had little cookfires going.

Davos stopped beneath the colonnade and traded a halfpenny for an apple. "Are people living in the Old Mint?" he asked the apple seller.

"Them as have no other place to live. Smallfolk from up the White Knife, most o' them. Hornwood's people too. With that Bastard o' Bolton running loose, they all want to be inside the walls. I don't know what his lordship means to do with all o' them. Most turned up with no more'n the rags on their backs."

Davos felt a pang of guilt. *They came here for refuge, to a city untouched by the fighting, and here I turn up to drag them back into the war.* He took a bite of the apple and felt guilty about that as well. "How do they eat?"

The apple seller shrugged. "Some beg. Some steal. Lots o' young girls taking up the trade, the way girls always do when it's all they got to sell. Any boy stands five feet tall can find a place in his lordship's barracks, long as he can hold a spear."

He's raising men, then. That might be good . . . or bad, depending. The apple was dry and mealy, but Davos made himself take another bite. "Does Lord Wyman mean to join the Bastard?"

"Well," said the apple seller, "the next time his lordship comes down here hunkering for an apple, I'll be sure and ask him."

"I heard his daughter was to wed some Frey."

"His granddaughter. I heard that too, but his lordship forgot t' invite me to the wedding. Here, you going to finish that? I'll take the rest back. Them seeds is good."

Davos tossed him back the core. *A bad apple, but it was worth half a penny to learn that Manderly is raising men.* He made his way around Old Fishfoot, past where a young girl was selling cups of fresh milk from her nanny goat. He was remembering more of the city now that he was here. Down past where Old Fishfoot's trident pointed was an alley where they sold fried cod, crisp and golden brown outside and flaky white within. Over there was a brothel, cleaner than most, where a sailor could enjoy a woman without fear of being robbed or killed. Off the other way, in one of those houses that clung to the walls of the Wolf's Den like barnacles to an old hull, there used to be a brewhouse where they made a black beer so thick and tasty that a cask of it could fetch as much as Arbor gold in Braavos and the Port of Ibben, provided the locals left the brewer any to sell.

It was wine he wanted, though—sour, dark, and dismal. He strolled across the yard and down a flight of steps, to a winesink called the Lazy Eel, underneath a warehouse full of sheepskins. Back in his smuggling days, the Eel had been renowned for offering the oldest whores and vilest wine in White Harbor, along with meat pies full of lard and gristle that were inedible on their best days and poisonous on their worst. With fare like that, most locals shunned the place, leaving it for sailors who did not know any better. You never saw a city guardsman down in the Lazy Eel, or a customs officer.

Some things never change. Inside the Eel, time stood still. The barrel-vaulted ceiling was stained black with soot, the floor was hard-packed earth, the air smelled of smoke and spoiled meat and stale vomit. The fat tallow candles on the tables gave off more smoke than light, and the wine that Davos ordered looked more brown than red in the gloom. Four whores were seated near the door, drinking. One gave him a hopeful smile as he entered. When Davos shook his head, the woman said something that made her companions laugh. After that none of them paid him any mind.

Aside from the whores and the proprietor, Davos had the Eel to himself. The cellar was large, full of nooks and shadowed alcoves where a man could be alone. He took his wine to one of them and sat with his back to a wall to wait.

Before long, he found himself staring at the hearth. The red woman could see the future in the fire, but all that Davos Seaworth ever saw were the shadows of the past: the burning ships, the fiery chain, the green shadows flashing across the belly of the clouds, the Red Keep brooding over all. Davos was a simple man, raised up by chance and war and Stannis. He did not understand why the gods would take four lads as young and strong as his sons, yet spare their weary father.

Some nights he thought he had been left to rescue Edric Storm . . . but by now King Robert's bastard boy was safe in the Stepstones, yet Davos still remained. *Do the gods have some other task for me?* he wondered. *If so, White Harbor may be some part of it.* He tried the wine, then poured half his cup onto the floor beside his foot.

As dusk fell outside, the benches at the Eel began to fill with sailors. Davos called to the proprietor for another cup. When he brought it, he brought him a candle too. "You want food?" the man asked. "We got meat pies."

"What kind of meat is in them?"

"The usual kind. It's good."

The whores laughed. "It's grey, he means," one said.

"Shut your bloody yap. You eat them."

"I eat all kinds o' shit. Don't mean I like it."

Davos blew the candle out as soon as the proprietor moved off, and sat back in the shadows. Seamen were the worst gossips in the world when the wine was flowing, even wine as cheap as this. All he need do was listen.

Most of what he heard he'd learned in Sisterton, from Lord Godric or the denizens of the Belly of the Whale. Tywin Lannister was dead, butchered by his dwarf son; his corpse had stunk so badly that no one had been able to enter the Great Sept of Baelor for days afterward; the Lady of the Eyrie had been murdered by a singer; Littlefinger ruled the Vale now, but Bronze Yohn Royce had sworn to bring him down; Balon Greyjoy had died as well, and his brothers were fighting for the Seastone Chair; Sandor Clegane had turned outlaw and was plundering and killing in the lands along the Trident; Myr and Lys and Tyrosh were embroiled in another war; a slave revolt was raging in the east.

Other tidings were of greater interest. Robett Glover was in the city and had been trying to raise men, with little success. Lord Manderly had turned a deaf ear to his pleas. White Harbor was weary of war, he was reported to have said. That was bad. The Ryswells and the Dustins had surprised the ironmen on the Fever River and put their longships to the torch. That was worse. And now the Bastard of Bolton was riding south with Hother Umber to join them for an attack on Moat Cailin. "The Whoresbane his own self," claimed a riverman who'd just brought a load of hides and timber down the White Knife, "with three hundred spearmen and a hundred archers. Some Hornwood men have joined them, and Cerwyns too." That was worst of all.

"Lord Wyman best send some men to fight if he knows what's good for him," said the old fellow at the end of the table. "Lord Roose, he's the Warden now. White Harbor's honor bound to answer his summons."

"What did any Bolton ever know o' honor?" said the Eel's proprietor as he filled their cups with more brown wine.

"Lord Wyman won't go no place. He's too bloody fat."

"I heard how he was ailing. All he does is sleep and weep, they say. He's too sick to get out o' his bed most days."

"Too *fat,* you mean."

"Fat or thin's got naught to do with it," said the Eel's proprietor. "The lions got his son."

No one spoke of King Stannis. No one even seemed to know that His Grace had come north to help defend the Wall. Wildlings and wights and giants had been all the talk at Eastwatch, but here no one seemed to be giving them so much as a thought.

Davos leaned into the firelight. "I thought the Freys killed his son. That's what we heard in Sisterton."

"They killed Ser Wendel," said the proprietor. "His bones are resting in the Snowy Sept with candles all around them, if you want to have a look. Ser Wylis, though, he's still a captive."

Worse and worse. He had known that Lord Wyman had two sons, but he'd thought that both of them were dead. *If the Iron Throne has a hostage . . .* Davos had fathered seven sons himself, and lost four on the Blackwater. He knew he would do whatever gods or men required of him to protect the other three. Steffon and Stannis were thousands of leagues from the fighting and safe from harm, but Devan was at Castle Black, a squire to the king. *The king whose cause may rise or fall with White Harbor.*

His fellow drinkers were talking about dragons now. "You're bloody mad," said an oarsman off *Storm Dancer.* "The Beggar King's been dead for years. Some Dothraki horselord cut his head off."

"So they tell us," said the old fellow. "Might be they're lying, though. He died half a world away, if he died at all. Who's to say? If a king wanted me dead, might be I'd oblige him and pretend to be a corpse. None of us has ever seen his body."

"I never saw Joffrey's corpse, nor Robert's," growled the Eel's proprietor. "Maybe they're all alive as well. Maybe Baelor the Blessed's just been having him a little nap all these years."

The old fellow made a face. "Prince Viserys weren't the only dragon, were he? Are we sure they killed Prince Rhaegar's son? A babe, he was."

"Wasn't there some princess too?" asked a whore. She was the same one who'd said the meat was grey.

"Two," said the old fellow. "One was Rhaegar's daughter, t'other was his sister."

"Daena," said the riverman. "That was the sister. Daena of Dragonstone. Or was it Daera?"

"Daena was old King Baelor's wife," said the oarsman. "I rowed on a ship named for her once. The *Princess Daena*."

"If she was a king's wife, she'd be a queen."

"Baelor never had a queen. He was holy."

"Don't mean he never wed his sister," said the whore. "He just never bedded her, is all. When they made him king, he locked her up in a tower. His other sisters too. There was three."

"Daenela," the proprietor said loudly. "That was her name. The Mad King's daughter, I mean, not Baelor's bloody wife."

"*Daenerys,*" Davos said. "She was named for the Daenerys who wed the Prince of Dorne during the reign of Daeron the Second. I don't know what became of her."

"I do," said the man who'd started all the talk of dragons, a Braavosi oarsman in a somber woolen jack. "When we were down to Pentos we moored beside a trader called the *Sloe-Eyed Maid,* and I got to drinking with her captain's steward. He told me a pretty tale about some slip of a girl who come aboard in Qarth, to try and book passage back to Westeros for her and three dragons. Silver hair she had, and purple eyes. 'I took her to the captain my own self,' this steward swore to me, 'but he wasn't having none of that. There's more profit in cloves and saffron, he tells me, and spices won't set fire to your sails.'"

Laughter swept the cellar. Davos did not join in. He knew what had befallen the *Sloe-Eyed Maid*. The gods were cruel to let a man sail across half the world, then send him chasing a false light when he was almost home. *That captain was a bolder man than me,* he thought, as he made his way to the door. One voyage to the east, and a man could live as rich as a lord until the end of his days. When he'd been younger, Davos had dreamed of making such voyages himself, but the years went dancing by like moths around a flame, and somehow the time had never been quite right. *One day,* he told himself. *One day when the war is done and King Stannis sits the Iron Throne and has no more need of onion knights. I'll take Devan with me. Steff and Stanny too if they're old enough. We'll see these dragons and all the wonders of the world.*

Outside the wind was gusting, making the flames shiver in the oil lamps that lit the yard. It had grown colder since the sun went down, but Davos remembered Eastwatch, and how the wind would come screaming off the Wall at night, knifing through even the warmest cloak to freeze a man's blood right in his veins. White Harbor was a warm bath by comparison.

There were other places he might get his ears filled: an inn famous for its lamprey pies, the alehouse where the wool factors and the customs men did their drinking, a mummer's hall where bawdy entertainments could be had for a few pennies. But Davos felt that he had heard enough. *I've come too late.* Old instinct made him reach for his chest, where once he'd kept his fingerbones in a little sack on a leather thong. There was nothing there. He had lost his luck in the fires of the Blackwater, when he'd lost his ship and sons.

What must I do now? He pulled his mantle tighter. *Do I climb the hill and present myself at the gates of the New Castle, to make a futile plea? Return to Sisterton? Make my way back to Marya and my boys? Buy a horse and ride the kingsroad, to tell Stannis that he has no friends in White Harbor, and no hope?*

Queen Selyse had feasted Salla and his captains, the night before the fleet had set sail. Cotter Pyke had joined them, and four other high officers of the Night's Watch. Princess Shireen had been allowed to attend as well. As the salmon was being served, Ser Axell Florent had entertained the table with the tale of a Targaryen princeling who kept an ape as a pet. This prince liked to dress the creature in his dead son's clothes and pretend he was a child, Ser Axell claimed, and from time to time he would propose marriages for him. The lords so honored always declined politely, but of course they did decline. "Even dressed in silk and velvet, an ape remains an ape," Ser Axell said. "A wiser prince would have known that you cannot send an ape to do a man's work." The queen's men laughed, and several grinned at Davos. *I am no ape,* he'd thought. *I am as much a lord as you, and a better man.* But the memory still stung.

The Seal Gate had been closed for the night. Davos would not be able to return to the *Merry Midwife* till dawn. He was here for the night. He gazed up at Old Fishfoot with his broken trident. *I have come through rain and wrack and storm. I will not go back without doing what I came for, no matter how hopeless it may seem.* He might have lost his fingers and his luck, but he was no ape in velvet. He was a King's Hand.

Castle Stair was a street with steps, a broad white stone way that led up from the Wolf's Den by the water to the New Castle on its hill. Marble mermaids lit the way as Davos climbed, bowls of burning whale oil cradled in their arms. When he reached the top, he turned to look behind him. From here he could see down into the harbors. Both of them. Behind the jetty wall, the inner harbor was crowded with war galleys. Davos counted twenty-three. Lord Wyman was a fat man, but not an idle one, it seemed.

The gates of the New Castle had been closed, but a postern opened when he shouted, and a guard emerged to ask his business. Davos showed him the black and gold ribbon that bore the royal seals. "I need to see Lord Manderly at once," he said. "My business is with him, and him alone."

DAENERYS

T he dancers shimmered, their sleek shaved bodies covered
with a fine sheen of oil. Blazing torches whirled from hand
to hand to the beat of drums and the trilling of a flute.
Whenever two torches crossed in the air, a naked girl leapt between
them, spinning. The torchlight shone off oiled limbs and breasts
and buttocks.

The three men were erect. The sight of their arousal was arousing,
though Daenerys Targaryen found it comical as well. The men were
all of a height, with long legs and flat bellies, every muscle as sharply
etched as if it had been chiseled out of stone. Even their faces looked
the same, somehow . . . which was passing strange, since one had skin
as dark as ebony, while the second was as pale as milk, and the third
gleamed like burnished copper.

Are they meant to inflame me? Dany stirred amongst her silken
cushions. Against the pillars her Unsullied stood like statues in
their spiked caps, their smooth faces expressionless. Not so the
whole men. Reznak mo Reznak's mouth was open, and his lips
glistened wetly as he watched. Hizdahr zo Loraq was saying something to the man beside him, yet all the time his eyes were on the
dancing girls. The Shavepate's ugly, oily face was as stern as ever,
but he missed nothing.

It was harder to know what her honored guest was dreaming. The pale, lean, hawk-faced man who shared her high table was resplendent in robes of maroon silk and cloth-of-gold, his bald head shining in the torchlight as he devoured a fig with small, precise, elegant bites. Opals winked along the nose of Xaro Xhoan Daxos as his head turned to follow the dancers.

In his honor Daenerys had donned a Qartheen gown, a sheer confection of violet samite cut so as to leave her left breast bare. Her silver-gold hair brushed lightly over her shoulder, falling almost to her nipple. Half the men in the hall had stolen glances at her, but not Xaro. *It was the same in Qarth.* She could not sway the merchant prince that way. *Sway him I must, however.* He had come from Qarth upon the galleas *Silken Cloud* with thirteen galleys sailing attendance, his fleet an answered prayer. Meereen's trade had dwindled away to nothing since she had ended slavery, but Xaro had the power to restore it.

As the drums reached a crescendo, three of the girls leapt above the flames, spinning in the air. The male dancers caught them about the waists and slid them down onto their members. Dany watched as the women arched their backs and coiled their legs around their partners while the flutes wept and the men thrust in time to the music. She had seen the act of love before; the Dothraki mated as openly as their mares and stallions. This was the first time she had seen lust put to music, though.

Her face was warm. *The wine,* she told herself. Yet somehow she found herself thinking of Daario Naharis. His messenger had come that morning. The Stormcrows were returning from Lhazar. Her captain was riding back to her, bringing her the friendship of the Lamb Men. *Food and trade,* she reminded herself. *He did not fail me, nor will he. Daario will help me save my city.* The queen longed to see his face, to stroke his three-pronged beard, to tell him her troubles . . . but the Stormcrows were still many days away, beyond the Khyzai Pass, and she had a realm to rule.

Smoke hung between the purple pillars. The dancers knelt, heads bowed. "You were splendid," Dany told them. "Seldom have I seen such grace, such beauty." She beckoned to Reznak mo Reznak, and the seneschal scurried to her side. Beads of sweat dotted his bald, wrinkled head. "Escort our guests to the baths, that they may refresh themselves, and bring them food and drink."

"It shall be my great honor, Magnificence."

Daenerys held out her cup for Irri to refill. The wine was sweet and strong, redolent with the smell of eastern spices, much superior to the thin Ghiscari wines that had filled her cup of late. Xaro perused the fruits on the platter Jhiqui offered him and chose a persimmon. Its orange skin matched the color of the coral in his nose. He took a bite and pursed his lips. "Tart."

"Would my lord prefer something sweeter?"

"Sweetness cloys. Tart fruit and tart women give life its savor." Xaro took another bite, chewed, swallowed. "Daenerys, sweet queen, I cannot tell you what pleasure it gives me to bask once more in your presence. A child departed Qarth, as lost as she was lovely. I feared she was sailing to her doom, yet now I find her here enthroned, mistress of an ancient city, surrounded by a mighty host that she raised up out of dreams."

No, she thought, *out of blood and fire.* "I am glad you came to me. It is good to see your face again, my friend." *I will not trust you, but I need you. I need your Thirteen, I need your ships, I need your trade.*

For centuries Meereen and her sister cities Yunkai and Astapor had been the linchpins of the slave trade, the place where Dothraki khals and the corsairs of the Basilisk Isles sold their captives and the rest of the world came to buy. Without slaves, Meereen had little to offer traders. Copper was plentiful in the Ghiscari hills, but the metal was not as valuable as it had been when bronze ruled the world. The cedars that had once grown tall along the coast grew no more, felled by the axes of the Old Empire or consumed by dragonfire when Ghis made war against Valyria. Once the trees had gone, the soil baked beneath the hot sun and blew away in thick red clouds. "It was these calamities that transformed my people into slavers," Galazza Galare had told her, at the Temple of the Graces. *And I am the calamity that will change these slavers back into people,* Dany had sworn to herself.

"I had to come," said Xaro in a languid tone. "Even far away in

Qarth, fearful tales had reached my ears. I wept to hear them. It is said that your enemies have promised wealth and glory and a hundred virgin slave girls to any man who slays you."

"The Sons of the Harpy." *How does he know that?* "They scrawl on walls by night and cut the throats of honest freedmen as they sleep. When the sun comes up they hide like roaches. They fear my Brazen Beasts." Skahaz mo Kandaq had given her the new watch she had asked for, made up in equal numbers of freedmen and shavepate Meereenese. They walked the streets both day and night, in dark hoods and brazen masks. The Sons of the Harpy had promised grisly death to any traitor who dared serve the dragon queen, and to their kith and kin as well, so the Shavepate's men went about as jackals, owls, and other beasts, keeping their true faces hidden. "I might have cause to fear the Sons if they saw me wandering alone through the streets, but only if it was night and I was naked and unarmed. They are craven creatures."

"A craven's knife can slay a queen as easily as a hero's. I would sleep more soundly if I knew my heart's delight had kept her fierce horselords close around her. In Qarth, you had three bloodriders who never left your side. Wherever have they gone?"

"Aggo, Jhoqo, and Rakharo still serve me." *He is playing games with me.* Dany could play as well. "I am only a young girl and know little of such things, but older, wiser men tell me that to hold Meereen I must control its hinterlands, all the land west of Lhazar as far south as the Yunkish hills."

"Your hinterlands are not precious to me. Your person is. Should any ill befall you, this world would lose its savor."

"My lord is good to care so much, but I am well protected." Dany gestured toward where Barristan Selmy stood with one hand resting on his sword hilt. "Barristan the Bold, they call him. Twice he has saved me from assassins."

Xaro gave Selmy a cursory inspection. "Barristan the Old, did you say? Your bear knight was younger, and devoted to you."

"I do not wish to speak of Jorah Mormont."

"To be sure. The man was coarse and hairy." The merchant prince leaned across the table. "Let us speak instead of love, of dreams and desire and Daenerys, the fairest woman in this world. I am drunk with the sight of you."

She was no stranger to the overblown courtesies of Qarth. "If you are drunk, blame the wine."

"No wine is half so intoxicating as your beauty. My manse has seemed as empty as a tomb since Daenerys departed, and all the pleasures of the Queen of Cities have been as ashes in my mouth. Why did you abandon me?"

I was hounded from your city in fear for my life. "It was time. Qarth wished me gone."

"Who? The Pureborn? They have water in their veins. The Spicers? There are curds between their ears. And the Undying are all dead. You should have taken me to husband. I am almost certain that I asked you for your hand. Begged you, even."

"Only half a hundred times," Dany teased. "You gave up too easily, my lord. For I *must* marry, all agree."

"A *khaleesi* must have a khal," said Irri, as she filled the queen's cup once again. "This is known."

"Shall I ask again?" wondered Xaro. "No, I know that smile. It is a cruel queen who dices with men's hearts. Humble merchants like myself are no more than stones beneath your jeweled sandals." A single tear ran slowly down his pale white cheek.

Dany knew him too well to be moved. Qartheen men could weep at will. "Oh, stop that." She took a cherry from the bowl on the table and threw it at his nose. "I may be a young girl, but I am not so foolish as to wed a man who finds a fruit platter more enticing than my breast. I saw which dancers you were watching."

Xaro wiped away his tear. "The same ones Your Grace was following, I believe. You see, we are alike. If you will not take me for your husband, I am content to be your slave."

"I want no slave. I free you." His jeweled nose made a tempting target. This time Dany threw an apricot at him.

Xaro caught it in the air and took a bite. "Whence came this madness? Should I count myself fortunate that you did not free my own slaves when you were my guest in Qarth?"

I was a beggar queen and you were Xaro of the Thirteen, Dany thought, *and all you wanted were my dragons.* "Your slaves seemed well treated and content. It was not till Astapor that my eyes were opened. Do you know how Unsullied are made and trained?"

"Cruelly, I have no doubt. When a smith makes a sword, he thrusts the blade into the fire, beats on it with a hammer, then plunges it into iced water to temper the steel. If you would savor the sweet taste of the fruit, you must water the tree."

"This tree has been watered with blood."

"How else, to grow a soldier? Your Radiance enjoyed my dancers. Would it surprise you to know that they are slaves, bred and trained in Yunkai? They have been dancing since they were old enough to walk. How else to achieve such *perfection*?" He took a swallow of his wine. "They are expert in all the erotic arts as well. I had thought to make Your Grace a gift of them."

"By all means." Dany was unsurprised. "I shall free them."

That made him wince. "And what would they do with freedom? As well give a fish a suit of mail. They were made to dance."

"Made by who? Their masters? Perhaps your dancers would sooner build or bake or farm. Have you asked them?"

"Perhaps your elephants would sooner be nightingales. Instead of sweet song, Meereen's nights would be filled with thunderous trumpetings, and your trees would shatter beneath the weight of great grey birds." Xaro sighed. "Daenerys, my delight, beneath that sweet young breast beats a tender heart . . . but take counsel from an older, wiser head. Things are not always as they seem. Much that may seem evil can be good. Consider rain."

"Rain?" *Does he take me for a fool, or just a child?*

"We curse the rain when it falls upon our heads, yet without it we should starve. The world *needs* rain . . . and slaves. You make a face, but it is true. Consider Qarth. In art, music, magic, trade, all that makes us more than beasts, Qarth sits above the rest of mankind as you sit at the summit of this pyramid . . . but below, in place of bricks, the magnificence that is the Queen of Cities rests upon the backs of *slaves.* Ask yourself, if all men must grub in the dirt for food, how shall any man lift his eyes to contemplate the stars? If each of us must break his back to build a hovel, who shall raise the temples to glorify the gods? For some men to be great, others must be enslaved."

He was too eloquent for her. Dany had no answer for him, only the raw feeling in her belly. "Slavery is not the same as rain," she insisted. "I have been rained on and I have been sold. It is *not the same*. No man wants to be *owned*."

Xaro gave a languid shrug. "As it happens, when I came ashore in your sweet city, I chanced to see upon the riverbank a man who had once been a guest in my manse, a merchant who dealt in rare spices and choice wines. He was naked from the waist up, red and peeling, and seemed to be digging a hole."

"Not a hole. A ditch, to bring water from the river to the fields. We mean to plant beans. The beanfields must have water."

"How kind of my old friend to help with the digging. And how very unlike him. Is it possible he was given no choice in the matter? No, surely not. You have no slaves in Meereen."

Dany flushed. "Your friend is being paid with food and shelter. I cannot give him back his wealth. Meereen needs beans more than it needs rare spices, and beans require water."

"Would you set my dancers to digging ditches as well? Sweet queen, when he saw me, my old friend fell to his knees and begged me to buy him as a slave and take him back to Qarth."

She felt as if he'd slapped her. "Buy him, then."

"If it please you. I know it will please *him*." He put his hand upon her arm. "There are truths only a friend may tell you. I helped you when you came to Qarth a beggar, and I have crossed long leagues and stormy seas to help you once again. Is there some place where we might speak frankly?"

Dany could feel the warmth of his fingers. *He was warm in Qarth as well,* she recalled, *until the day he had no more use for me.* She rose to her feet. "Come," she said, and Xaro followed her through the pillars, to the wide marble steps that led up to her private chambers at the apex of the pyramid.

"Oh most beautiful of women," Xaro said, as they began to climb, "there are footsteps behind us. We are followed."

"My old knight does not frighten you, surely? Ser Barristan is sworn to keep my secrets."

She took him out onto the terrace that overlooked the city. A full moon swam in the black sky above Meereen. "Shall we walk?" Dany slipped her arm through his. The air was heavy with the scent of night-blooming flowers. "You spoke of help. Trade with me, then. Meereen has salt to sell, and wine . . ."

"Ghiscari wine?" Xaro made a sour face. "The sea provides all the salt that Qarth requires, but I would gladly take as many olives as you cared to sell me. Olive oil as well."

"I have none to offer. The slavers burned the trees." Olives had been grown along the shores of Slaver's Bay for centuries; but the Meereenese had put their ancient groves to the torch as Dany's host advanced on them, leaving her to cross a blackened wasteland. "We are replanting, but it takes seven years before an olive tree begins to bear, and thirty years before it can truly be called productive. What of copper?"

"A pretty metal, but fickle as a woman. Gold, now . . . gold is *sincere*. Qarth will gladly give you gold . . . for slaves."

"Meereen is a free city of free men."

"A poor city that once was rich. A hungry city that once was fat. A bloody city that once was peaceful."

His accusations stung. There was too much truth in them. "Meereen will be rich and fat and peaceful once again, and free as well. Go to the Dothraki if you must have slaves."

"Dothraki make slaves, Ghiscari train them. And to reach Qarth, the horselords must needs drive their captives across the red waste. Hundreds would die, if not thousands . . . and many horses too, which is why no khal will risk it. And there is this: Qarth wants no *khalasars* seething round our walls. The stench of all those horses . . . meaning no offense, *Khaleesi*."

"A horse has an honest smell. That is more than can be said of some great lords and merchant princes."

Xaro took no notice of the sally. "Daenerys, let me be honest with you, as befits a friend. You will *not* make Meereen rich and fat and peaceful. You will only bring it to destruction, as you did Astapor. You are aware that there was battle joined at the Horns of Hazzat? The Butcher King has fled back to his palace, his new Unsullied running at his heels."

"This is known." Brown Ben Plumm had sent back word of the battle from the field. "The Yunkai'i have bought themselves new sellswords, and two legions from New Ghis fought beside them."

"Two will soon become four, then ten. And Yunkish envoys have been sent to Myr and Volantis to hire more blades. The Company of the Cat, the Long Lances, the Windblown. Some say that the Wise Masters have bought the Golden Company as well."

Her brother Viserys had once feasted the captains of the Golden Company, in hopes they might take up his cause. *They ate his food and heard his pleas and laughed at him.* Dany had only been a little girl, but she remembered. "I have sellswords too."

"Two companies. The Yunkai'i will send twenty against you if they must. And when they march, they will not march alone. Tolos and Mantarys have agreed to an alliance."

That was ill news, if true. Daenerys had sent missions to Tolos and Mantarys, hoping to find new friends to the west to balance the enmity of Yunkai to the south. Her envoys had not returned. "Meereen has made alliance with Lhazar."

That only made him chuckle. "The Dothraki horselords call the Lhazarene the *Lamb Men.* When you shear them, all they do is bleat. They are not a martial people."

Even a sheepish friend is better than none. "The Wise Masters should follow their example. I spared Yunkai before, but I will not make that mistake again. If they should dare attack me, this time I shall raze their Yellow City to the ground."

"And whilst you are razing Yunkai, my sweet, Meereen shall rise behind you. Do not close your eyes to your peril, Daenerys. Your eunuchs are fine soldiers, but they are too few to match the hosts that Yunkai will send against you, once Astapor has fallen."

"My freedman—" Dany started.

"Bedslaves, barbers, and brickmakers win no battles."

He was wrong in that, she hoped. The freedmen had been a rabble once, but she had organized the men of fighting age into companies and commanded Grey Worm to make them into soldiers. *Let him think what he will.* "Have you forgotten? I have *dragons.*"

"Do you? In Qarth, you were seldom seen without a dragon on your shoulder . . . yet now that shapely shoulder is as fair and bare as your sweet breast, I observe."

"My dragons have grown, my shoulders have not. They range far afield, hunting." *Hazzea, forgive me.* She wondered how much Xaro knew, what whispers he had heard. "Ask the Good Masters of Astapor about my dragons if you doubt them." *I saw a slaver's eyes melt and go running down his cheeks.* "Tell me true, old friend, why did you seek me out if not to trade?"

"To bring a gift, for the queen of my heart."

"Say on." *What trap is this, now?*

"The gift you begged of me in Qarth. Ships. There are thirteen galleys in the bay. Yours, if you will have them. I have brought you a fleet, to carry you home to Westeros."

A fleet. It was more than she could hope for, so of course it made her wary. In Qarth, Xaro had offered her thirty ships . . . for a dragon. "And what price do you ask for these ships?"

"None. I no longer lust for dragons. I saw their work at Astapor on my way here, when my *Silken Cloud* put in for water. The ships are yours, sweet queen. Thirteen galleys, and men to pull the oars."

Thirteen. To be sure. Xaro was one of the Thirteen. No doubt he had convinced each of his fellow members to give up one ship. She knew the merchant prince too well to think that he would sacrifice thirteen of his *own* ships. "I must consider this. May I inspect these ships?"

"You have grown suspicious, Daenerys."

Always. "I have grown wise, Xaro."

"Inspect all you wish. When you are satisfied, swear to me that you shall return to Westeros forthwith, and the ships are yours. Swear by your dragons and your seven-faced god and the ashes of your fathers, and *go.*"

"And if I should decide to wait a year, or three?"

A mournful look crossed Xaro's face. "That would make me very sad, my sweet delight . . . for young and strong as you now seem, you shall not live so long. Not here."

He offers the honeycomb with one hand and shows the whip with the other. "The Yunkai'i are not so fearsome as all that."

"Not all your enemies are in the Yellow City. Beware men with cold hearts and blue lips. You had not been gone from Qarth a fortnight when Pyat Pree set out with three of his fellow warlocks, to seek for you in Pentos."

Dany was more amused than afraid. "It is good I turned aside, then. Pentos is half a world from Meereen."

"This is so," he allowed, "yet soon or late word must reach them of the dragon queen of Slaver's Bay."

"Is that meant to frighten me? I lived in fear for fourteen years, my lord. I woke afraid each morning and went to sleep afraid each night . . . but my fears were burned away the day I came forth from the fire. Only one thing frightens me now."

"And what is it that you fear, sweet queen?"

"I am only a foolish young girl." Dany rose on her toes and kissed his cheek. "But not so foolish as to tell you that. My men shall look at these ships. Then you shall have my answer."

"As you say." He touched her bare breast lightly, and whispered, "Let me stay and help persuade you."

For a moment she was tempted. Perhaps the dancers had stirred her after all. *I could close my eyes and pretend that he was Daario.* A dream Daario would be safer than the real one. But she pushed the thought aside. "No, my lord. I thank you, but no." Dany slipped from his arms. "Some other night, perhaps."

"Some other night." His mouth was sad, but his eyes seemed more relieved than disappointed.

If I were a dragon, I could fly to Westeros, she thought when he was gone. *I would have no need of Xaro or his ships.* Dany wondered how many men thirteen galleys could hold. It had taken three to carry her and her *khalasar* from Qarth to Astapor, but that was before she had acquired eight thousand Unsullied, a thousand sellswords, and a vast horde of freedmen. *And the dragons, what am I to do with them?* "Drogon," she whispered softly, "where are you?" For a moment she could almost see him sweeping across the sky, his black wings swallowing the stars.

She turned her back upon the night, to where Barristan Selmy stood silent in the shadows. "My brother once told me a Westerosi riddle. Who listens to everything yet hears nothing?"

"A knight of the Kingsguard." Selmy's voice was solemn.

"You heard Xaro make his offer?"

"I did, Your Grace." The old knight took pains not to look at her bare breast as he spoke to her.

Ser Jorah would not turn his eyes away. He loved me as a woman, where Ser Barristan loves me only as his queen. Mormont had been an informer, reporting to her enemies in Westeros, yet he had given her good counsel too. "What do you think of it? Of him?"

"Of him, little and less. These ships, though . . . Your Grace, with these ships we might be home before year's end."

Dany had never known a home. In Braavos, there had been a house with a red door, but that was all. "Beware of Qartheen bearing gifts, especially merchants of the Thirteen. There is some trap here. Perhaps these ships are rotten, or . . ."

"If they were so unseaworthy, they could not have crossed the sea from Qarth," Ser Barristan pointed out, "but Your Grace was wise to insist upon inspection. I will take Admiral Groleo to the galleys at first light with his captains and two score of his sailors. We can crawl over every inch of those ships."

It was good counsel. "Yes, make it so." *Westeros. Home.* But if she left, what would happen to her city? *Meereen was never your city,* her brother's voice seemed to whisper. *Your cities are across the sea. Your Seven Kingdoms, where your enemies await you. You were born to serve them blood and fire.*

Ser Barristan cleared his throat and said, "This warlock that the merchant spoke of . . ."

"Pyat Pree." She tried to recall his face, but all she could see were his lips. The wine of the warlocks had turned them blue. *Shade-of-the-evening,* it was called. "If a warlock's spell could kill me, I would be dead by now. I left their palace all in ashes." *Drogon saved me when they would have drained my life from me. Drogon burned them all.*

"As you say, Your Grace. Still. I will be watchful."

She kissed him on the cheek. "I know you will. Come, walk me back down to the feast."

The next morning Dany woke as full of hope as she had been since first she came to Slaver's Bay. Daario would soon be at her side once more, and together they would sail for Westeros. *For home.* One of her young hostages brought her morning meal, a plump shy girl named Mezzara, whose father ruled the pyramid of Merreq, and Dany gave her a happy hug and thanked her with a kiss.

"Xaro Xhoan Daxos has offered me thirteen galleys," she told Irri and Jhiqui as they were dressing her for court.

"Thirteen is a bad number, *Khaleesi,*" murmured Jhiqui, in the Dothraki tongue. "It is known."

"It is known," Irri agreed.

"Thirty would be better," Daenerys agreed. "Three hundred better still. But thirteen may suffice to carry us to Westeros."

The two Dothraki girls exchanged a look. "The poison water is accursed, *Khaleesi,*" said Irri. "Horses cannot drink it."

"I do not intend to drink it," Dany promised them.

Only four petitioners awaited her that morning. As ever, Lord Ghael was the first to present himself, looking even more wretched than usual. "Your Radiance," he moaned, as he fell to the marble at her feet, "the armies of the Yunkai'i descend on Astapor. I beg you, come south with all your strength!"

"I warned your king that this war of his was folly," Dany reminded him. "He would not listen."

"Great Cleon sought only to strike down the vile slavers of Yunkai."

"Great Cleon is a slaver himself."

"I know that the Mother of Dragons will not abandon us in our hour of peril. Lend us your Unsullied to defend our walls."

And if I do, who will defend my walls? "Many of my freedmen were slaves in Astapor. Perhaps some will wish to help defend your king. That is their choice, as free men. I gave Astapor its freedom. It is up to you to defend it."

"We are all dead, then. You gave us death, not freedom." Ghael leapt to his feet and spat into her face.

Strong Belwas seized him by the shoulder and slammed him down onto the marble so hard that Dany heard Ghael's teeth crack. The Shavepate would have done worse, but she stopped him.

"Enough," she said, dabbing at her cheek with the end of her *tokar*. "No one has ever died from spittle. Take him away."

They dragged him out feet first, leaving several broken teeth and a trail of blood behind. Dany would gladly have sent the rest of the petitioners away . . . but she was still their queen, so she heard them out and did her best to give them justice.

Late that afternoon Admiral Groleo and Ser Barristan returned from their inspection of the galleys. Dany assembled her council to hear them. Grey Worm was there for the Unsullied, Skahaz mo Kandaq for the Brazen Beasts. In the absence of her bloodriders, a wizened *jaqqa rhan* called Rommo, squint-eyed and bowlegged, came to speak for her Dothraki. Her freedmen were represented by the captains of the three companies she had formed—Mollono Yos Dob of the Stalwart Shields, Symon Stripeback of the Free Brothers, Marselen of the Mother's Men. Reznak mo Reznak hovered at the queen's elbow, and Strong Belwas stood behind her with his huge arms crossed. Dany would not lack for counsel.

Groleo had been a most unhappy man since they had broken up his ship to build the siege engines that won Meereen for her. Dany had tried to console him by naming him her lord admiral, but it was a hollow honor; the Meereenese fleet had sailed for Yunkai when Dany's host approached the city, so the old Pentoshi was an admiral without ships. Yet now he was smiling through his ragged salt-streaked beard in a way that the queen could scarce remember.

"The ships are sound, then?" she said, hoping.

"Sound enough, Your Grace. They are old ships, aye, but most are well maintained. The hull of the *Pureborn Princess* is worm-eaten. I'd not want to take her beyond the sight of land. The *Narraqqa* could stand a new rudder and lines, and the *Banded Lizard* has some cracked oars, but they will serve. The rowers are slaves, but if we offer them an honest oarsman's wage, most will stay with us. Rowing's all they know. Those who leave can be replaced from my own crews. It is a long hard voyage to Westeros, but these ships are sound enough to get us there, I'd judge."

Reznak mo Reznak gave a piteous moan. "Then it is true. Your Worship means to abandon us." He wrung his hands. "The Yunkai'i will restore the Great Masters the instant you are gone, and we who have so faithfully served your cause will be put to the sword, our sweet wives and maiden daughters raped and enslaved."

"Not mine," grumbled Skahaz Shavepate. "I will kill them first, with mine own hand." He slapped his sword hilt.

Dany felt as if he had slapped her face instead. "If you fear what may follow when I leave, come with me to Westeros."

"Wherever the Mother of Dragons goes, the Mother's Men will go as well," announced Marselen, Missandei's remaining brother.

"How?" asked Symon Stripeback, named for the tangle of scars that ridged his back and shoulders, a reminder of the whippings he had suffered as a slave in Astapor. "Thirteen ships . . . that's not enough. A hundred ships might not be enough."

"Wooden horses are no good," objected Rommo, the old *jaqqa rhan.* "Dothraki will ride."

"These ones could march overland along the shore," suggested Grey Worm. "The ships could keep pace and resupply the column."

"That might serve until you reached the ruins of Bhorash," said the Shavepate. "Beyond that, your ships would need to turn south past Tolos and the Isle of Cedars and sail around Valyria, whilst the foot continued on to Mantarys by the old dragon road."

"The *demon road,* they call it now," said Mollono Yos Dob. The plump commander of the Stalwart Shields looked more like a scribe than a soldier, with his inky hands and heavy paunch, but he was as clever as they came. "Many and more of us would die."

"Those left behind in Meereen would envy them their easy deaths," moaned Reznak. "They will make *slaves* of us, or throw us in the pits. All will be as it was, or worse."

"Where is your courage?" Ser Barristan lashed out. "Her Grace freed you from your chains. It is for you to sharpen your swords and defend your own freedom when she leaves."

"Brave words, from one who means to sail into the sunset,"

Symon Stripeback snarled back. "Will you look back at our dying?"

"Your Grace—"

"Magnificence—"

"Your Worship—"

"*Enough.*" Dany slapped the table. "No one will be left to die. You are all my people." Her dreams of home and love had blinded her. "I will not abandon Meereen to the fate of Astapor. It grieves me to say so, but Westeros must wait."

Groleo was aghast. "We *must* accept these ships. If we refuse this gift . . ."

Ser Barristan went to one knee before her. "My queen, your realm has need of you. You are not wanted here, but in Westeros men will flock to your banners by the thousands, great lords and noble knights. '*She is come,*' they will shout to one another, in glad voices. '*Prince Rhaegar's sister has come home at last.*'"

"If they love me so much, they will wait for me." Dany stood. "Reznak, summon Xaro Xhoan Daxos."

She received the merchant prince alone, seated on her bench of polished ebony, on the cushions Ser Barristan had brought her. Four Qartheen sailors accompanied him, bearing a rolled tapestry upon their shoulders. "I have brought another gift for the queen of my heart," Xaro announced. "It has been in my family vaults since before the Doom that took Valyria."

The sailors unrolled the tapestry across the floor. It was old, dusty, faded . . . and huge. Dany had to move to Xaro's side before the patterns became plain. "A map? It is beautiful." It covered half the floor. The seas were blue, the lands were green, the mountains black and brown. Cities were shown as stars in gold or silver thread. *There is no Smoking Sea,* she realized. *Valyria is not yet an island.*

"There you see Astapor, and Yunkai, and Meereen." Xaro pointed at three silver stars beside the blue of Slaver's Bay. "Westeros is . . . somewhere down there." His hand waved vaguely toward the far end of the hall. "You turned north when you should have continued south and west, across the Summer Sea, but with my gift you shall soon be back where you belong. Accept my galleys with a joyful heart, and bend your oars westward."

Would that I could. "My lord, I will gladly have those ships, but I cannot give you the promise that you ask." She took his hand. "Give me the galleys, and I swear that Qarth will have the friendship of Meereen until the stars go out. Let me trade with them, and you will have a good part of the profits."

Xaro's glad smile died upon his lips. "What are you saying? Are you telling me you will not go?"

"I *cannot* go."

Tears welled from his eyes, creeping down his nose, past emeralds, amethysts, and black diamonds. "I told the Thirteen that you would heed my wisdom. It grieves me to learn that I was wrong. Take these ships and sail away, or you will surely die screaming. You cannot know how many enemies you have made."

I know one stands before me now, weeping mummer's tears. The realization made her sad.

"When I went to the Hall of a Thousand Thrones to beg the Pureborn for your life, I said that you were no more than a child," Xaro went on, "but Egon Emeros the Exquisite rose and said, 'She is a *foolish* child, mad and heedless and too dangerous to live.' When your dragons were small they were a wonder. Grown, they are death and devastation, a flaming sword above the world." He wiped away the tears. "I should have slain you in Qarth."

"I was a guest beneath your roof and ate of your meat and mead," she said. "In memory of all you did for me, I will forgive those words . . . *once* . . . but never presume to threaten me again."

"Xaro Xhoan Daxos does not threaten. He promises."

Her sadness turned to fury. "And I promise you that if you are not gone before the sun comes up, we will learn how well a liar's tears can quench dragonfire. Leave me, Xaro. *Quickly.*"

He went but left his world behind. Dany seated herself upon her bench again to gaze across the blue silk sea, toward distant Westeros. *One day,* she promised herself.

The next morning Xaro's galleas was gone, but the "gift" that he had brought her remained behind in Slaver's Bay. Long red streamers flew from the masts of the thirteen Qartheen galleys, writhing in the wind. And when Daenerys descended to hold court, a messenger from the ships awaited her. He spoke no word but laid at her feet a black satin pillow, upon which rested a single bloodstained glove.

"What is this?" Skahaz demanded. "A bloody glove . . ."

". . . means war," said the queen.

JON

"Careful of the rats, my lord." Dolorous Edd led Jon down the steps, a lantern in one hand. "They make an awful squeal if you step on them. My mother used to make a similar sound when I was a boy. She must have had some rat in her, now that I think of it. Brown hair, beady little eyes, liked cheese. Might be she had a tail too, I never looked to see."

All of Castle Black was connected underground by a maze of tunnels that the brothers called *the wormways*. It was dark and gloomy underneath the earth, so the wormways were little used in summer, but when the winter winds began to blow and the snows began to fall, the tunnels became the quickest way to move about the castle. The stewards were making use of them already. Jon saw candles burning in several wall niches as they made their way along the tunnel, their footsteps echoing ahead of them.

Bowen Marsh was waiting at a junction where four wormways met. With him he had Wick Whittlestick, tall and skinny as a spear. "These are the counts from three turns ago," Marsh told Jon, offering him a thick sheaf of papers, "for comparison with our present stores. Shall we start with the granaries?"

They moved through the grey gloom beneath the earth. Each storeroom had a solid oaken door closed with an iron padlock as big as a supper plate. "Is pilferage a problem?" Jon asked.

"Not as yet," said Bowen Marsh. "Once winter comes, though, your lordship might be wise to post guards down here."

Wick Whittlestick wore the keys on a ring about his neck. They all looked alike to Jon, yet somehow Wick found the right one for every door. Once inside, he would take a fist-sized chunk of chalk from his pouch and mark each cask and sack and barrel as he counted them while Marsh compared the new count to the old.

In the granaries were oats and wheat and barley, and barrels of coarse ground flour. In the root cellars strings of onions and garlic dangled from the rafters, and bags of carrots, parsnips, radishes, and white and yellow turnips filled the shelves. One storeroom held wheels of cheese so large it took two men to move them. In the next, casks of salt beef, salt pork, salt mutton, and salt cod were stacked ten feet high. Three hundred hams and three thousand long black sausages hung from ceiling beams below the smokehouse. In the spice locker they found peppercorns, cloves, and cinnamon, mustard seeds, coriander, sage and clary sage and parsley, blocks of salt. Elsewhere were casks of apples and pears, dried peas, dried figs, bags of walnuts, bags of chestnuts, bags of almonds, planks of dry smoked salmon, clay jars packed with olives in oil and sealed with wax. One storeroom offered potted hare, haunch of deer in honey, pickled cabbage, pickled beets, pickled onions, pickled eggs, and pickled herring.

As they moved from one vault to another, the wormways seemed to grow colder. Before long Jon could see their breath frosting in the lantern light. "We're beneath the Wall."

"And soon inside it," said Marsh. "The meat won't spoil in the cold. For long storage, it's better than salting."

The next door was made of rusty iron. Behind it was a flight of wooden steps. Dolorous Edd led the way with his lantern. Up top they found a tunnel as long as Winterfell's great hall though no wider than the wormways. The walls were ice, bristling with iron hooks. From each hook hung a carcass: skinned deer and elk, sides of beef, huge sows swinging from the ceiling, headless sheep and goats, even horse and bear. Hoarfrost covered everything.

As they did their count, Jon peeled the glove off his left hand and touched the nearest haunch of venison. He could feel his fingers sticking, and when he pulled them back he lost a bit of skin. His fingertips were numb. *What did you expect? There's a mountain of ice above your head, more tons than even Bowen Marsh could count.* Even so, the room felt colder than it should.

"It is worse than I feared, my lord," Marsh announced when he was done. He sounded gloomier than Dolorous Edd.

Jon had just been thinking that all the meat in the world surrounded them. *You know nothing, Jon Snow.* "How so? This seems a deal of food to me."

"It was a long summer. The harvests were bountiful, the lords generous. We had enough laid by to see us through three years of winter. Four, with a bit of scrimping. Now, though, if we must go on feeding all these king's men and queen's men and wildlings . . . Mole's Town alone has a thousand useless mouths, and still they come. Three more turned up yesterday at the gates, a dozen the day before. It cannot go on. Settling them on the Gift, that's well and good, but it is too late to plant crops. We'll be down to turnips and pease porridge before the year is out. After that we'll be drinking the blood of our own horses."

"Yum," declared Dolorous Edd. "Nothing beats a hot cup of horse blood on a cold night. I like mine with a pinch of cinnamon sprinkled on top."

The Lord Steward paid him no mind. "There will be sickness too," he went on, "bleeding gums and loose teeth. Maester Aemon used to say that lime juice and fresh meat would remedy that, but our limes were gone a year ago and we do not have enough fodder to keep herds afoot for fresh meat. We should butcher all but a few breeding pairs. It's past time. In winters past, food could be brought up the kingsroad from the south, but with the war . . . it is still autumn, I know, but I would advise we go on winter rations nonetheless, if it please my lord."

The men will love that. "If we must. We'll cut each man's portion by a quarter." *If my brothers are complaining of me now, what will they say when they're eating snow and acorn paste?*

"That will help, my lord." The Lord Steward's tone made it plain that he did not think that it would help *enough.*

Dolorous Edd said, "Now I understand why King Stannis let the wildlings through the Wall. He means for us to eat them."

Jon had to smile. "It will not come to that."

"Oh, good," said Edd. "They look a stringy lot, and my teeth are not as sharp as when I was younger."

"If we had sufficient coin, we could buy food from the south and bring it in by ship," the Lord Steward said.

We could, thought Jon, *if we had the gold, and someone willing to sell us food.* Both of those were lacking. *Our best hope may be the Eyrie.* The Vale of Arryn was famously fertile and had gone untouched during the fighting. Jon wondered how Lady Catelyn's sister would feel about feeding Ned Stark's bastard. As a boy, he often felt as if the lady grudged him every bite.

"We can always hunt if need be," Wick Whittlestick put in. "There's still game in the woods."

"And wildlings, and darker things," said Marsh. "I would not send out hunters, my lord. I would not."

No. You would close our gates forever and seal them up with stone and ice. Half of Castle Black agreed with the Lord Steward's views, he knew. The other half heaped scorn on them. "Seal our gates and plant your fat black arses on the Wall, aye, and the free folk'll come swarming o'er the Bridge o' Skulls or through some gate you thought you'd sealed five hundred years ago," the old forester Dywen had declared loudly over supper, two nights past. "We don't have the men to watch a hundred leagues o' Wall. Tormund Giantsbutt and the bloody Weeper knows it too. Ever see a duck frozen in a pond, with his feet in the ice? It works the same for crows." Most rangers echoed Dywen, whilst the stewards and builders inclined toward Bowen Marsh.

But that was a quandary for another day. Here and now, the problem was food. "We cannot leave King Stannis and his men to starve, even if we wished to," Jon said. "If need be, he could simply take all this at swordpoint. We do not have the men to stop them. The wildlings must be fed as well."

"How, my lord?" asked Bowen Marsh.

Would that I knew. "We will find a way."

By the time they returned to the surface, the shadows of the afternoon were growing long. Clouds streaked the sky like tattered banners, grey and white and torn. The yard outside the armory was empty, but inside Jon found the king's squire awaiting him. Devan was a skinny lad of some twelve years, brown of hair and eye. They found him frozen by the forge, hardly daring to move as Ghost sniffed him up and down. "He won't hurt you," Jon said, but the boy flinched at the sound of his voice, and that sudden motion made the direwolf bare his teeth. "*No!*" Jon said. "Ghost, leave him be. *Away.*" The wolf slunk back to his ox bone, silence on four feet.

Devan looked as pale as Ghost, his face damp with perspiration. "M-my lord. His Grace c-commands your presence." The boy was clad in Baratheon gold and black, with the flaming heart of a queen's man sewn above his own.

"You mean *requests,*" said Dolorous Edd. "His Grace *requests* the presence of the lord commander. That's how I'd say it."

"Leave it be, Edd." Jon was in no mood for such squabbles.

"Sir Richard and Ser Justin have returned," said Devan. "Will you come, my lord?"

The wrong-way rangers. Massey and Horpe had ridden south, not north. Whatever they had learned did not concern the Night's Watch, but Jon was curious all the same. "If it would please His Grace." He followed the young squire back across the yard. Ghost padded after them until Jon said, "No. *Stay!*" Instead the direwolf ran off.

In the King's Tower, Jon was stripped of his weapons and admitted to the royal presence. The solar was hot and crowded. Stannis and his captains were gathered over the map of the north. The wrong-way rangers were amongst them. Sigorn was there as well, the young Magnar of Thenn, clad in a leather hauberk sewn with bronze scales. Rattleshirt sat scratching at the manacle on his wrist with a cracked yellow fingernail. Brown stubble covered his sunken cheeks and receding chin, and strands of dirty hair hung across his eyes. "Here he comes," he said when he saw Jon, "the brave boy who slew Mance Rayder when he was caged and bound." The big square-cut gem that adorned his iron cuff glimmered redly. "Do you like my ruby, Snow? A token o' love from Lady Red."

Jon ignored him and took a knee. "Your Grace," announced the squire Devan, "I've brought Lord Snow."

"I can see that. Lord Commander. You know my knights and captains, I believe."

"I have that honor." He had made it a point to learn all he could of the men around the king. *Queen's men, all.* It struck Jon as odd that there were no king's men about the king, but that seemed to be the way of it. The king's men had incurred Stannis's ire on Dragonstone if the talk Jon heard was true.

"There is wine. Or water boiled with lemons."

"Thank you, but no."

"As you wish. I have a gift for you, Lord Snow." The king waved a hand at Rattleshirt. "Him."

Lady Melisandre smiled. "You did say you wanted men, Lord Snow. I believe our Lord of Bones still qualifies."

Jon was aghast. "Your Grace, this man cannot be trusted. If I keep him here, someone will slit his throat for him. If I send him ranging, he'll just go back over to the wildlings."

"Not me. I'm done with those bloody fools." Rattleshirt tapped the ruby on his wrist. "Ask your red witch, bastard."

Melisandre spoke softly in a strange tongue. The ruby at her throat throbbed slowly, and Jon saw that the smaller stone on Rattleshirt's wrist was brightening and darkening as well. "So long as he wears the gem he is bound to me, blood and soul," the red priestess said. "This man will serve you faithfully. The flames do not lie, Lord Snow."

Perhaps not, Jon thought, *but you do.*

"I'll range for you, bastard," Rattleshirt declared. "I'll give you sage counsel or sing you pretty songs, as you prefer. I'll even fight for you. Just don't ask me to wear your cloak."

You are not worthy of one, Jon thought, but he held his tongue. No good would come of squabbling before the king.

King Stannis said, "Lord Snow, tell me of Mors Umber."

The Night's Watch takes no part, Jon thought, but another voice within him said, *Words are not swords.* "The elder of the Greatjon's uncles. Crowfood, they call him. A crow once took him for dead and pecked out his eye. He caught the bird in his fist and bit its head off.

When Mors was young he was a fearsome fighter. His sons died on the Trident, his wife in childbed. His only daughter was carried off by wildlings thirty years ago."

"*That's* why he wants the head," said Harwood Fell.

"Can this man Mors be trusted?" asked Stannis.

Has Mors Umber bent the knee? "Your Grace should have him swear an oath before his heart tree."

Godry the Giantslayer guffawed. "I had forgotten that you northmen worship trees."

"What sort of god lets himself be pissed upon by dogs?" asked Farring's crony Clayton Suggs.

Jon chose to ignore them. "Your Grace, might I know if the Umbers have declared for you?"

"Half of them, and only if I meet this Crowfood's price," said Stannis, in an irritated tone. "He wants Mance Rayder's skull for a drinking cup, and he wants a pardon for his brother, who has ridden south to join Bolton. Whoresbane, he's called."

Ser Godry was amused by that as well. "What names these northmen have! Did this one bite the head off some whore?"

Jon regarded him coolly. "You might say so. A whore who tried to rob him, fifty years ago in Oldtown." Odd as it might seem, old Hoarfrost Umber had once believed his youngest son had the makings of a maester. Mors loved to boast about the crow who took his eye, but Hother's tale was only told in whispers . . . most like because the whore he'd disemboweled had been a man. "Have other lords declared for Bolton too?"

The red priestess slid closer to the king. "I saw a town with wooden walls and wooden streets, filled with men. Banners flew above its walls: a moose, a battle-axe, three pine trees, longaxes crossed beneath a crown, a horse's head with fiery eyes."

"Hornwood, Cerwyn, Tallhart, Ryswell, and Dustin," supplied Ser Clayton Suggs. "Traitors, all. Lapdogs of the Lannisters."

"The Ryswells and Dustins are tied to House Bolton by marriage," Jon informed him. "These others have lost their lords in the fighting. I do not know who leads them now. Crowfood is no lapdog, though. Your Grace would do well to accept his terms."

Stannis ground his teeth. "He informs me that Umber will not fight Umber, for any cause."

Jon was not surprised. "If it comes to swords, see where Hother's banner flies and put Mors on the other end of the line."

The Giantslayer disagreed. "You would make His Grace look weak. I say, show our strength. Burn Last Hearth to the ground and ride to war with Crowfood's head mounted on a spear, as a lesson to the next lord who presumes to offer half his homage."

"A fine plan if what you want is every hand in the north raised against you. Half is more than none. The Umbers have no love for the Boltons. If Whoresbane has joined the Bastard, it can only be because the Lannisters hold the Greatjon captive."

"That is his pretext, not his reason," declared Ser Godry. "If the nephew dies in chains, these uncles can claim his lands and lordship for themselves."

"The Greatjon has sons and daughters both. In the north the children of a man's body still come before his uncles, ser."

"Unless they die. Dead children come last everywhere."

"Suggest that in the hearing of Mors Umber, Ser Godry, and you will learn more of death than you might wish."

"I have slain a giant, boy. Why should I fear some flea-ridden northman who paints one on his shield?"

"The giant was running away. Mors won't be."

The big knight flushed. "You have a bold tongue in the king's solar, boy. In the yard you sang a different song."

"Oh, leave off, Godry," said Ser Justin Massey, a loose-limbed, fleshy knight with a ready smile and a mop of flaxen hair. Massey had been one of the wrong-way rangers. "We all know what a big giant sword you have, I'm sure. No need for you to wave it in our faces yet again."

"The only thing waving here is your tongue, Massey."

"*Be quiet,*" Stannis snapped. "Lord Snow, attend me. I have lingered here in the hopes that the wildlings would be fool enough to mount another attack upon the Wall. As they will not oblige me, it is time I dealt with my other foes."

"I see." Jon's tone was wary. *What does he want of me?* "I have no love for Lord Bolton or his son, but the Night's Watch cannot take up arms against them. Our vows prohibit—"

"I know all about your vows. Spare me your rectitude, Lord Snow, I have strength enough without you. I have a mind to march against the Dreadfort." When he saw the shock on Jon's face, he smiled. "Does that surprise you? Good. What surprises one Snow may yet surprise another. The Bastard of Bolton has gone south, taking Hother Umber with him. On that Mors Umber and Arnolf Karstark are agreed. That can only mean a strike at Moat Cailin, to open the way for his lord father to return to the north. The bastard must think I am too busy with the wildlings to trouble him. Well and good. The boy has shown me his throat. I mean to rip it out. Roose Bolton may regain the north, but when he does he will find that his castle, herds, and harvest all belong to me. If I take the Dreadfort unawares—"

"You won't," Jon blurted.

It was as if he whacked a wasps' nest with a stick. One of the queen's men laughed, one spat, one muttered a curse, and the rest all tried to talk at once. "The boy has milkwater in his veins," said Ser Godry the Giantslayer. And Lord Sweet huffed, "The craven sees an outlaw behind every blade of grass."

Stannis raised a hand for silence. "Explain your meaning."

Where to begin? Jon moved to the map. Candles had been placed at its corners to keep the hide from rolling up. A finger of warm wax was puddling out across the Bay of Seals, slow as a glacier. "To reach the Dreadfort, Your Grace must travel down the kingsroad past the Last River, turn south by east and cross the Lonely Hills." He pointed. "Those are Umber lands, where they know every tree and every rock. The kingsroad runs along their western marches for a hundred leagues. Mors will cut your host to pieces unless you meet his terms and win him to your cause."

"Very well. Let us say I do that."

"That will bring you to the Dreadfort," said Jon, "but unless your host can outmarch a raven or a line of beacon fires, the castle will know of your approach. It will be an easy thing for Ramsay Bolton to cut off your retreat and leave you far from the Wall, without food or refuge, surrounded by your foes."

"Only if he abandons his siege of Moat Cailin."

"Moat Cailin will fall before you ever reach the Dreadfort. Once Lord Roose has joined his strength to Ramsay's, they will have you outnumbered five to one."

"My brother won battles at worse odds."

"You assume Moat Cailin will fall quickly, Snow," objected Justin Massey, "but the ironmen are doughty fighters, and I've heard it said that the Moat has never been taken."

"*From the south.* A small garrison in Moat Cailin can play havoc with any army coming up the causeway, but the ruins are vulnerable from the north and east." Jon turned back to Stannis. "Sire, this is a bold stroke, but the risk—" *The Night's Watch takes no part. Baratheon or Bolton should be the same to me.* "If Roose Bolton should catch you beneath his walls with his main strength, it will be the end for all of you."

"Risk is part of war," declared Ser Richard Horpe, a lean knight with a ravaged face whose quilted doublet showed three death's-head moths on a field of ash and bone. "Every battle is a gamble, Snow. The man who does nothing also takes a risk."

"There are risks and risks, Ser Richard. This one . . . it is too much, too soon, too far away. I know the Dreadfort. It is a strong castle, all of stone, with thick walls and massive towers. With winter coming you will find it well provisioned. Centuries ago, House Bolton rose up against the King in the North, and Harlon Stark laid siege to the Dreadfort. It took him two years to starve them out. To have any hope of taking the castle, Your Grace would need siege engines, towers, battering rams . . ."

"Siege towers can be raised if need be," Stannis said. "Trees can be felled for rams if rams are required. Arnolf Karstark writes that fewer than fifty men remain at the Dreadfort, half of them servants. A strong castle weakly held is weak."

"Fifty men inside a castle are worth five hundred outside."

"That depends upon the men," said Richard Horpe. "These will be greybeards and green boys, the men this bastard did not deem fit for battle. Our own men were blooded and tested on the Blackwater, and they are led by knights."

"You saw how we went through the wildlings." Ser Justin pushed back a lock of flaxen hair. "The Karstarks have sworn to join us at the Dreadfort, and we will have our wildlings as well. Three hundred men of fighting age. Lord Harwood made a count as they were passing through the gate. Their women fight as well."

Stannis gave him a sour look. "Not for me, ser. I want no widows wailing in my wake. The women will remain here, with the old, the wounded, and the children. They will serve as hostages for the loyalty of their husbands and fathers. The wildling men will form my van. The Magnar will command them, with their own chiefs as serjeants. First, though, we must needs arm them."

He means to plunder our armory, Jon realized. *Food and clothing, land and castles, now weapons. He draws me in deeper every day.* Words might not be swords, but *swords* were swords. "I could find three hundred spears," he said, reluctantly. "Helms as well, if you'll take them old and dinted and red with rust."

"Armor?" asked the Magnar. "Plate? Mail?"

"When Donal Noye died we lost our armorer." The rest Jon left unspoken. *Give the wildlings mail and they'll be twice as great a danger to the realm.*

"Boiled leather will suffice," said Ser Godry. "Once we've tasted battle, the survivors can loot the dead."

The few who live that long. If Stannis placed the free folk in the van, most would perish quickly. "Drinking from Mance Rayder's skull may give Mors Umber pleasure, but seeing wildlings cross his lands will not. The free folk have been raiding the Umbers since the Dawn of Days, crossing the Bay of Seals for gold and sheep and women. One of those carried off was Crowfood's *daughter*. Your Grace, leave the wildlings here. Taking them will only serve to turn my lord father's bannermen against you."

"Your father's bannermen seem to have no liking for my cause in any case. I must assume they see me as . . . what was it that you called me, Lord Snow? *Another doomed pretender?*" Stannis stared at the map. For a long moment the only sound was the king grinding his teeth. "Leave me. All of you. Lord Snow, remain."

The brusque dismissal did not sit well with Justin Massey, but he had no choice but to smile and withdraw. Horpe followed him out, after giving Jon a measured look. Clayton Suggs drained his cup dry and muttered something to Harwood Fell that made the younger man laugh. *Boy* was part of it. Suggs was an upjumped hedge knight, as crude as he was strong. The last man to take his leave was Rattleshirt. At the door, he gave Jon a mocking bow, grinning through a mouthful of brown and broken teeth.

All of you did not seem to include Lady Melisandre. *The king's red shadow.* Stannis called to Devan for more lemon water. When his cup was filled the king drank, and said, "Horpe and Massey aspire to your father's seat. Massey wants the wildling princess too. He once served my brother Robert as squire and acquired his appetite for female flesh. Horpe will take Val to wife if I command it, but it is battle he lusts for. As a squire he dreamed of a white cloak, but Cersei Lannister spoke against him and Robert passed him over. Perhaps rightly. Ser Richard is too fond of killing. Which would you have as Lord of Winterfell, Snow? The smiler or the slayer?"

Jon said, "Winterfell belongs to my sister Sansa."

"I have heard all I need to hear of Lady Lannister and her claim." The king set the cup aside. "*You* could bring the north to me. Your father's bannermen would rally to the son of Eddard Stark. Even Lord Too-Fat-to-Sit-a-Horse. White Harbor would give me a ready source of supply and a secure base to which I could retreat at need. It is not too late to amend your folly, Snow. Take a knee and swear that bastard sword to me, and rise as Jon Stark, Lord of Winterfell and Warden of the North."

How many times will he make me say it? "My sword is sworn to the Night's Watch."

Stannis looked disgusted. "Your father was a stubborn man as well. *Honor,* he called it. Well, honor has its costs, as Lord Eddard learned to his sorrow. If it gives you any solace, Horpe and Massey are doomed to disappointment. I am more inclined to bestow Winterfell upon Arnolf Karstark. A good northman."

"A northman." *Better a Karstark than a Bolton or a Greyjoy,* Jon told himself, but the thought gave him little solace. "The Karstarks abandoned my brother amongst his enemies."

"After your brother took off Lord Rickard's head. Arnolf was a thousand leagues away. He has Stark blood in him. The blood of Winterfell."

"No more than half the other Houses of the north."

"Those other Houses have not declared for me."

"Arnolf Karstark is an old man with a crooked back, and even in his youth he was never the fighter Lord Rickard was. The rigors of the campaign may well kill him."

"He has heirs," Stannis snapped. "Two sons, six grandsons, some daughters. If Robert had fathered trueborn sons, many who are dead might still be living."

"Your Grace would do better with Mors Crowfood."

"The Dreadfort will be the proof of that."

"Then you mean to go ahead with this attack?"

"Despite the counsel of the great Lord Snow? Aye. Horpe and Massey may be ambitious, but they are not wrong. I dare not sit idle whilst Roose Bolton's star waxes and mine wanes. I must strike and show the north that I am still a man to fear."

"The merman of Manderly was not amongst those banners Lady Melisandre saw in her fires," Jon said. "If you had White Harbor and Lord Wyman's knights . . ."

"*If* is a word for fools. We have had no word from Davos. It may be he never reached White Harbor. Arnolf Karstark writes that the storms have been fierce upon the narrow sea. Be that as it may. I have no time to grieve, nor wait upon the whims of Lord Too-Fat. I must consider White Harbor lost to me. Without a son of Winterfell to stand beside me, I can only hope to win the north by battle. That requires stealing a leaf from my brother's book. Not that Robert ever read one. I must deal my foes a mortal blow before they know that I am on them."

Jon realized that his words were wasted. Stannis would take the Dreadfort or die in the attempt. *The Night's Watch takes no part*, a voice said, but another replied, *Stannis fights for the realm, the ironmen for thralls and plunder.* "Your Grace, I know where you might find more men. Give me the wildlings, and I will gladly tell you where and how."

"I gave you Rattleshirt. Be content with him."

"I want them all."

"Some of your own Sworn Brothers would have me believe that you are half a wildling yourself. Is it true?"

"To you they are only arrow fodder. I can make better use of them upon the Wall. Give them to me to do with as I will, and I'll show you where to find your victory . . . and men as well."

Stannis rubbed the back of his neck. "You haggle like a crone with a codfish, Lord Snow. Did Ned Stark father you on some fishwife? How many men?"

"Two thousand. Perhaps three."

"Three *thousand*? What manner of men are these?"

"Proud. Poor. Prickly where their honor is concerned but fierce fighters."

"This had best not be some bastard's trick. Will I trade three hundred fighters for three thousand? Aye, I will. I am not an utter fool. If I leave the girl with you as well, do I have your word that you will keep our princess closely?"

She is not a princess. "As you wish, Your Grace."

"Do I need to make you swear an oath before a tree?"

"No." *Was that a jape?* With Stannis, it was hard to tell.

"Done, then. Now, where are these men?"

"You'll find them here." Jon spread his burned hand across the map, west of the kingsroad and south of the Gift.

"Those mountains?" Stannis grew suspicious. "I see no castles marked there. No roads, no towns, no villages."

"The map is not the land, my father often said. Men have lived in the high valleys and mountain meadows for thousands of years, ruled by their clan chiefs. Petty lords, you would call them, though they do not use such titles amongst themselves. Clan champions fight with huge two-handed greatswords, while the common men sling stones and batter one another with staffs of mountain ash. A quarrelsome folk, it must be said. When they are not fighting one another, they tend their herds, fish the Bay of Ice, and breed the hardiest mounts you'll ever ride."

"And they will fight for me, you believe?"

"If you ask them."

"Why should I beg for what is owed me?"

"*Ask,* I said, not *beg.*" Jon pulled back his hand. "It is no good sending messages. Your Grace will need to go to them yourself. Eat their bread and salt, drink their ale, listen to their pipers, praise the beauty of their daughters and the courage of their sons, and you'll have their swords. The clans have not seen a king since Torrhen Stark bent his knee. Your coming does them honor. *Command* them to fight for you, and they will look at one another and say, 'Who is this man? He is no king of mine.'"

"How many clans are you speaking of?"

"Two score, small and large. Flint, Wull, Norrey, Liddle . . . win Old Flint and Big Bucket, the rest will follow."

"Big *Bucket?*"

"The Wull. He has the biggest belly in the mountains, and the most men. The Wulls fish the Bay of Ice and warn their little ones that ironmen will carry them off if they don't behave. To reach them Your Grace must pass through the Norrey's lands, however. They live the nearest to the Gift and have always been good friends to the Watch. I could give you guides."

"Could?" Stannis missed little. "Or will?"

"Will. You'll need them. And some sure-footed garrons too. The paths up there are little more than goat tracks."

"Goat tracks?" The king's eyes narrowed. "I speak of moving swiftly, and you waste my time with *goat tracks?*"

"When the Young Dragon conquered Dorne, he used a goat track to bypass the Dornish watchtowers on the Boneway."

"I know that tale as well, but Daeron made too much of it in that vainglorious book of his. Ships won that war, not goat tracks. Oakenfist broke the Planky Town and swept halfway up the Greenblood whilst the main Dornish strength was engaged in the Prince's Pass." Stannis drummed his fingers on the map. "These mountain lords will not hinder my passage?"

"Only with feasts. Each will try to outdo the others with his hospitality. My lord father said he never ate half so well as when visiting the clans."

"For three thousand men, I suppose I can endure some pipes and porridge," the king said, though his tone begrudged even that.

Jon turned to Melisandre. "My lady, fair warning. The old gods are strong in those mountains. The clansmen will not suffer insults to their heart trees."

That seemed to amuse her. "Have no fear, Jon Snow, I will not trouble your mountain savages and their dark gods. My place is here with you and your brave brothers."

That was the last thing Jon Snow would have wanted, but before he could object, the king said, "Where would you have me lead these stalwarts if not against the Dreadfort?"

Jon glanced down at the map. "Deepwood Motte." He tapped it with a finger. "If Bolton means to fight the ironmen, so must you. Deepwood is a motte-and-bailey castle in the midst of thick forest, easy to creep up on unawares. A *wooden* castle, defended by an earthen dike and a palisade of logs. The going will be slower through the mountains, admittedly, but up there your host can move unseen, to emerge almost at the gates of Deepwood."

Stannis rubbed his jaw. "When Balon Greyjoy rose the first time, I beat the ironmen at sea, where they are fiercest. On land, taken unawares . . . aye. I have won a victory over the wildlings and their King-Beyond-the-Wall. If I can smash the ironmen as well, the north will know it has a king again."

And I will have a thousand wildlings, thought Jon, *and no way to feed even half that number.*

TYRION

The *Shy Maid* moved through the fog like a blind man groping his way down an unfamiliar hall.

Septa Lemore was praying. The mists muffled the sound of her voice, making it seem small and hushed. Griff paced the deck, mail clinking softly beneath his wolfskin cloak. From time to time he touched his sword, as if to make certain that it still hung at his side. Rolly Duckfield was pushing at the starboard pole, Yandry at the larboard. Ysilla had the tiller.

"I do not like this place," Haldon Halfmaester muttered.

"Frightened of a little fog?" mocked Tyrion, though in truth there was quite a lot of fog. At the prow of the *Shy Maid*, Young Griff stood with the third pole, to push them away from hazards as they loomed up through the mists. The lanterns had been lit fore and aft, but the fog was so thick that all the dwarf could see from amidships was a light floating out ahead of him and another following behind. His own task was to tend the brazier and make certain that the fire did not go out.

"This is no common fog, Hugor Hill," Ysilla insisted. "It stinks of sorcery, as you would know if you had a nose to smell it. Many a voyager has been lost here, poleboats and pirates and great river galleys too. They wander forlorn through the mists, searching for a sun they cannot find until madness or hunger claim their lives.

There are restless spirits in the air here and tormented souls below the water."

"There's one now," said Tyrion. Off to starboard a hand large enough to crush the boat was reaching up from the murky depths. Only the tops of two fingers broke the river's surface, but as the *Shy Maid* eased on past he could see the rest of the hand rippling below the water and a pale face looking up. Though his tone was light, he was uneasy. This was a bad place, rank with despair and death. *Ysilla is not wrong. This fog is not natural.* Something foul grew in the waters here, and festered in the air. *Small wonder the stone men go mad.*

"You should not make mock," warned Ysilla. "The whispering dead hate the warm and quick and ever seek for more damned souls to join them."

"I doubt they have a shroud my size." The dwarf stirred the coals with a poker.

"Hatred does not stir the stone men half so much as hunger." Haldon Halfmaester had wrapped a yellow scarf around his mouth and nose, muffling his voice. "Nothing any sane man would want to eat grows in these fogs. Thrice each year the triarchs of Volantis send a galley upriver with provisions, but the mercy ships are oft late and sometimes bring more mouths than food."

Young Griff said, "There must be fish in the river."

"I would not eat any fish taken from these waters," said Ysilla. "I would not."

"We'd do well not to breathe the fog either," said Haldon. "Garin's Curse is all about us."

The only way not to breathe the fog is not to breathe. "Garin's Curse is only greyscale," said Tyrion. The curse was oft seen in children, especially in damp, cold climes. The afflicted flesh stiffened, calcified, and cracked, though the dwarf had read that greyscale's progress could be stayed by limes, mustard poultices, and scalding-hot baths (the maesters said) or by prayer, sacrifice, and fasting (the septons insisted). Then the disease passed, leaving its young victims disfigured but alive. Maesters and septons alike agreed that children marked by greyscale could never be touched by the rarer mortal form of the affliction, nor by its terrible swift cousin, the grey plague. "Damp is said to be the culprit," he said. "Foul humors in the air. Not curses."

"The conquerors did not believe either, Hugor Hill," said Ysilla. "The men of Volantis and Valyria hung Garin in a golden cage and made mock as he called upon his Mother to destroy them. But in the night the waters rose and drowned them, and from that day to this they have not rested. They are down there still beneath the water, they who were once the lords of fire. Their cold breath rises from the murk to make these fogs, and their flesh has turned as stony as their hearts."

The stump of Tyrion's nose was itching fiercely. He gave it a scratch. *The old woman may be right. This place is no good. I feel as if I am back in the privy again, watching my father die.* He would go mad as well if he had to spend his days in this grey soup whilst his flesh and bones turned to stone.

Young Griff did not seem to share his misgivings. "Let them try and trouble us, we'll show them what we're made of."

"We are made of blood and bone, in the image of the Father and the Mother," said Septa Lemore. "Make no vainglorious boasts, I beg you. Pride is a grievous sin. The stone men were proud as well, and the Shrouded Lord was proudest of them all."

The heat from the glowing coals brought a flush to Tyrion's face. "Is there a Shrouded Lord? Or is he just some tale?"

"The Shrouded Lord has ruled these mists since Garin's day," said Yandry. "Some say that he himself is Garin, risen from his watery grave."

"The dead do not rise," insisted Haldon Halfmaester, "and no man lives a thousand years. Yes, there is a Shrouded Lord. There have been a score of them. When one dies another takes his place. This one is a corsair from the Basilisk Islands who believed the Rhoyne would offer richer pickings than the Summer Sea."

"Aye, I've heard that too," said Duck, "but there's another tale I like better. The one that says he's not like t'other stone men, that he started as a statue till a grey woman came out of the fog and kissed him with lips as cold as ice."

"*Enough,*" said Griff. "Be quiet, all of you."

Septa Lemore sucked in her breath. "*What was that?*"

"Where?" Tyrion saw nothing but the fog.

"Something moved. I saw the water rippling."

"A turtle," the prince announced cheerfully. "A big 'snapper, that's all it was." He thrust his pole out ahead of them and pushed them away from a towering green obelisk.

The fog clung to them, damp and chilly. A sunken temple loomed up out of the greyness as Yandry and Duck leaned upon their poles and paced slowly from prow to stern, pushing. They passed a marble stair that spiraled up from the mud and ended jaggedly in air. Beyond, half-seen, were other shapes: shattered spires, headless statues, trees with roots bigger than their boat.

"This was the most beautiful city on the river, and the richest," said Yandry. "Chroyane, the festival city."

Too rich, thought Tyrion, *too beautiful. It is never wise to tempt the dragons.* The drowned city was all around them. A half-seen shape flapped by overhead, pale leathery wings beating at the fog. The dwarf craned his head around to get a better look, but the thing was gone as suddenly as it had appeared.

Not long after, another light floated into view. "Boat," a voice called across the water, faintly. "Who are you?"

"*Shy Maid,*" Yandry shouted back.

"*Kingfisher.* Up or down?"

"Down. Hides and honey, ale and tallow."

"Up. Knives and needles, lace and linen, spice wine."

"What word from old Volantis?" Yandry called.

"War," the word came back.

"Where?" Griff shouted. "When?"

"When the year turns," came the answer, "Nyessos and Malaquo go hand in hand, and the elephants show stripes." The voice faded as the other boat moved away from them. They watched its light dwindle and disappear.

"Is it wise to shout through the fog at boats we cannot see?" asked Tyrion. "What if they were pirates?" They had been fortunate where the pirates were concerned, slipping down Dagger Lake by night, unseen and unmolested. Once Duck had caught a glimpse of a hull that he insisted belonged to Urho the Unwashed. The *Shy Maid* had been upwind, however, and Urho—if Urho it had been—had shown no interest in them.

"The pirates will not sail into the Sorrows," said Yandry.

"Elephants with stripes?" Griff muttered. "What is that about? Nyessos and Malaquo? Illyrio has paid Triarch Nyessos enough to own him eight times over."

"In gold or cheese?" quipped Tyrion.

Griff rounded on him. "Unless you can cut this fog with your next witticism, keep it to yourself."

Yes, Father, the dwarf almost said. *I'll be quiet. Thank you.* He did not know these Volantenes, yet it seemed to him that elephants and tigers might have good reason to make common cause when faced with dragons. *Might be the cheesemonger has misjudged the situation. You can buy a man with gold, but only blood and steel will keep him true.*

The little man stirred the coals again and blew on them to make them burn brighter. *I hate this. I hate this fog, I hate this place, and I am less than fond of Griff.* Tyrion still had the poison mushrooms he had plucked from the grounds of Illyrio's manse, and there were days when he was sore tempted to slip them into Griff's supper. The trouble was, Griff scarce seemed to eat.

Duck and Yandry pushed against the poles. Ysilla turned the tiller. Young Griff pushed the *Shy Maid* away from a broken tower whose windows stared down like blind black eyes. Overhead her sail hung limp and heavy. The water deepened under her hull, until their poles could not touch bottom, but still the current pushed them downstream, until . . .

All Tyrion could see was something massive rising from the river, humped and ominous. He took it for a hill looming above a wooded island, or some colossal rock overgrown with moss and ferns and hidden by the fog. As the *Shy Maid* drew nearer, though, the shape of it came clearer. A wooden keep could be seen beside the water, rotted and overgrown. Slender spires took form above it, some of them snapped off like broken spears. Roofless towers appeared and disappeared, thrusting blindly upward. Halls and galleries drifted past:

graceful buttresses, delicate arches, fluted columns, terraces and bowers.

All ruined, all desolate, all fallen.

The grey moss grew thickly here, covering the fallen stones in great mounds and bearding all the towers. Black vines crept in and out of windows, through doors and over archways, up the sides of high stone walls. The fog concealed three-quarters of the palace, but what they glimpsed was more than enough for Tyrion to know that this island fastness had been ten times the size of the Red Keep once and a hundred times more beautiful. He knew where he was. "The Palace of Love," he said softly.

"That was the Rhoynar name," said Haldon Halfmaester, "but for a thousand years this has been the Palace of Sorrow."

The ruin was sad enough, but knowing what it had been made it even sadder. *There was laughter here once,* Tyrion thought. *There were gardens bright with flowers and fountains sparkling golden in the sun. These steps once rang to the sound of lovers' footsteps, and beneath that broken dome marriages beyond count were sealed with a kiss.* His thoughts turned to Tysha, who had so briefly been his lady wife. *It was Jaime,* he thought, despairing. *He was my own blood, my big strong brother. When I was small he brought me toys, barrel hoops and blocks and a carved wooden lion. He gave me my first pony and taught me how to ride him. When he said that he had bought you for me, I never doubted him. Why would I? He was Jaime, and you were just some girl who'd played a part. I had feared it from the start, from the moment you first smiled at me and let me touch your hand. My own father could not love me. Why would you if not for gold?*

Through the long grey fingers of the fog, he heard again the deep shuddering *thrum* of a bowstring snapping taut, the grunt Lord Tywin made as the quarrel took him beneath the belly, the slap of cheeks on stone as he sat back down to die. "Wherever whores go," he said. *And where is that?* Tyrion wanted to ask him. *Where did Tysha go, Father?* "How much more of this fog must we endure?"

"Another hour should see us clear of the Sorrows," said Haldon Halfmaester. "From there on, this should be a pleasure cruise. There's a village around every bend along the lower Rhoyne. Orchards and vineyards and fields of grain ripening in the sun, fisherfolk on the water, hot baths and sweet wines. Selhorys, Valysar, and Volon Therys are walled towns so large they would be cities in the Seven Kingdoms. I believe I'll—"

"Light ahead," warned Young Griff.

Tyrion saw it too. Kingfisher, *or another poleboat,* he told himself, but somehow he knew that was not right. His nose itched. He scratched at it savagely. The light grew brighter as the *Shy Maid* approached it. A soft star in the distance, it glimmered faintly through the fog, beckoning them on. Shortly it became two lights, then three: a ragged row of beacons rising from the water.

"The Bridge of Dream," Griff named it. "There will be stone men on the span. Some may start to wail at our approach, but they are not like to molest us. Most stone men are feeble creatures, clumsy, lumbering, witless. Near the end they all go mad, but that is when they are most dangerous. If need be, fend them off with the torches. On no account let them touch you."

"They may not even see us," said Haldon Halfmaester. "The fog will hide us from them until we are almost at the bridge, and then we will be past before they know that we are here."

Stone eyes are blind eyes, thought Tyrion. The mortal form of greyscale began in the extremities, he knew: a tingling in a fingertip, a toenail turning black, a loss of feeling. As the numbness crept into the hand, or stole past the foot and up leg, the flesh stiffened and grew cold and the victim's skin took on a greyish hue, resembling stone. He had heard it said that there were three good cures for greyscale: axe and sword and cleaver. Hacking off afflicted parts did sometimes stop the spread of the disease, Tyrion knew, but not always. Many a man had sacrificed one arm or foot, only to find the other going grey. Once that happened, hope was gone. Blindness was common when the stone reached the face. In the final stages the curse turned inward, to muscles, bones, and inner organs.

Ahead of them, the bridge grew larger. *The Bridge of Dream,* Griff called it, but this dream was smashed and broken. Pale stone arches marched off into the fog, reaching from the Palace of Sorrow to the river's western bank. Half of them had collapsed, pulled down by the weight of the grey moss that draped them and the thick black vines that snaked upward from the water. The broad wooden span of the bridge had rotted through, but some of the lamps that lined the way were still aglow. As the *Shy Maid* drew closer, Tyrion could see the shapes of stone men moving in the light, shuffling aimlessly around the lamps like slow grey moths. Some were naked, others clad in shrouds.

Griff drew his longsword. "Yollo, light the torches. Lad, take Lemore back to her cabin and stay with her."

Young Griff gave his father a stubborn look. "Lemore knows where her cabin is. I want to stay."

"We are sworn to protect you," Lemore said softly.

"I don't need to be protected. I can use a sword as well as Duck. I'm half a knight."

"And half a boy," said Griff. "Do as you are told. Now."

The youth cursed under his breath and flung his pole down onto the deck. The sound echoed queerly in the fog, and for a moment it was as if poles were falling around them. "Why should I run and hide? Haldon is staying, and Ysilla. Even Hugor."

"Aye," said Tyrion, "but I'm small enough to hide behind a duck." He thrust half a dozen torches into the brazier's glowing coals and watched the oiled rags flare up. *Don't stare at the fire,* he told himself. The flames would leave him night blind.

"You're a *dwarf,*" Young Griff said scornfully.

"My secret is revealed," Tyrion agreed. "Aye, I'm less than half of Haldon, and no one gives a mummer's fart whether I live or die." *Least of all me.* "You, though . . . you are everything."

"Dwarf," said Griff, "I warned you—"

A wail came shivering through the fog, faint and high.

Lemore whirled, trembling. "Seven save us all."

The broken bridge was a bare five yards ahead. Around its piers, the water rippled white as the foam from a madman's mouth. Forty feet above, the stone men moaned and muttered beneath a flickering lamp. Most took no more notice of the *Shy Maid* than of a drifting log. Tyrion clutched his torch tighter and found that he was holding his breath. And then they were beneath the bridge, white walls heavy with curtains of grey fungus looming to either side, water foaming angrily around them. For a moment it looked as though they might crash into the right-hand pier, but Duck raised his pole and shoved off, back into the center of the channel, and a few heartbeats later they were clear.

Tyrion had no sooner exhaled than Young Griff grabbed hold of his arm. "What do you mean? I am *everything*? What did you mean by that? Why am I everything?"

"Why," said Tyrion, "if the stone men had taken Yandry or Griff or our lovely Lemore, we would have grieved for them and gone on. Lose *you,* and this whole enterprise is undone, and all those years of feverish plotting by the cheesemonger and the eunuch will have been for naught . . . isn't that so?"

The boy looked to Griff. "He knows who I am."

If I did not know before, I would now. By then the *Shy Maid* was well downstream of the Bridge of Dream. All that remained was a dwindling light astern, and soon enough that would be gone as well. "You're Young Griff, son of Griff the sellsword," said Tyrion. "Or perhaps you are the Warrior in mortal guise. Let me take a closer look." He held up his torch, so that the light washed over Young Griff's face.

"Leave off," Griff commanded, "or you will wish you had."

The dwarf ignored him. "The blue hair makes your eyes seem blue, that's good. And the tale of how you color it in honor of your dead Tyroshi mother was so touching it almost made me cry. Still, a curious man might wonder why some sellsword's whelp would need a soiled septa to instruct him in the Faith, or a chainless maester to tutor him in history and tongues. And a clever man might question why your father would engage a hedge knight to train you in arms instead of simply sending you off to apprentice with one of the free companies. It is almost as if someone wanted to keep you hidden whilst still preparing you for . . . what? Now, there's a puzzlement, but I'm sure that in time it will come to me. I must admit, you have noble features for a dead boy."

The boy flushed. "*I am not dead.*"

"How not? My lord father wrapped your corpse in a crimson cloak and laid you down beside your sister at the foot of the Iron Throne, his gift to the new king. Those who had the stomach to lift the cloak said that half your head was gone."

The lad backed off a step, confused. "Your—?"

"—*father,* aye. Tywin of House Lannister. Perhaps you may have heard of him."

Young Griff hesitated. "*Lannister?* Your father—"

"—is dead. At my hand. If it please Your Grace to call me Yollo or Hugor, so be it, but know that I was born Tyrion of House Lannister, trueborn son of Tywin and Joanna, both of whom I slew. Men will tell you that I am a kingslayer, a kinslayer, and a liar, and all of that is true . . . but then, we are a company of liars, are we not? Take your feigned father. *Griff,* is it?" The dwarf sniggered. "You should thank the gods that Varys the Spider is a part of this plot of yours. *Griff* would not have fooled the cockless wonder for an instant, no more than it did me. *No lord,* my lordship says, *no knight.* And I'm no dwarf. Just saying a thing does not make it true. Who better to raise Prince Rhaegar's infant son than Prince Rhaegar's dear friend Jon Connington, once Lord of Griffin's Roost and Hand of the King?"

"Be quiet." Griff's voice was uneasy.

On the larboard side of the boat, a huge stone hand was visible just below the water. Two fingers broke the surface. *How many of those are there?* Tyrion wondered. A trickle of moisture ran down his spine and made him shudder. The Sorrows drifted by them. Peering through the mists, he glimpsed a broken spire, a headless hero, an ancient tree torn from the ground and upended, its huge roots twisting through the roof and windows of a broken dome. *Why does all of this seem so familiar?*

Straight on, a tilted stairway of pale marble rose up out of the dark water in a graceful spiral, ending abruptly ten feet above their heads. *No,* thought Tyrion, *that is not possible.*

"Ahead." Lemore's voice was shivery. "A light."

All of them looked. All of them saw it.

"*Kingfisher,*" said Griff. "Her, or some other like her." But he drew his sword again.

No one said a word. The *Shy Maid* moved with the current. Her sail had not been raised since she first entered the Sorrows. She had no way to move but with the river. Duck stood squinting, clutching his pole with both hands. After a time even Yandry stopped pushing. Every eye was on the distant light. As they grew closer, it turned into two lights. Then three.

"The Bridge of Dream," said Tyrion.

"Inconceivable," said Haldon Halfmaester. "We've left the bridge behind. Rivers only run one way."

"Mother Rhoyne runs how she will," murmured Yandry.

"Seven save us," said Lemore.

Up ahead, the stone men on the span began to wail. A few were pointing down at them. "Haldon, get the prince below," commanded Griff.

It was too late. The current had them in its teeth. They drifted inexorably toward the bridge. Yandry stabbed out with his pole to keep them from smashing into a pier. The thrust shoved them sideways, through a curtain of pale grey moss. Tyrion felt tendrils brush against his face, soft as a whore's fingers. Then there was a crash behind him, and the deck tilted so suddenly that he almost lost his feet and went pitching over the side.

A stone man crashed down into the boat.

He landed on the cabin roof, so heavily that the *Shy Maid* seemed to rock, and roared a word down at them in a tongue that Tyrion did not know. A second stone man followed, landing back beside the tiller. The weathered planks splintered beneath the impact, and Ysilla let out a shriek.

Duck was closest to her. The big man did not waste time reaching for his sword. Instead he swung his pole, slamming it into the stone man's chest and knocking him off the boat into the river, where he sank at once without a sound.

Griff was on the second man the instant he shambled down off the cabin roof. With a sword in his right hand and a torch in his left, he drove the creature backwards. As the current swept the *Shy Maid* beneath the bridge, their shifting shadows danced upon the mossy walls. When the stone man moved aft, Duck blocked his way, pole in hand. When he went forward, Haldon Halfmaester waved a second torch at him and drove him back. He had no choice but to come straight at Griff. The captain slid aside, his blade flashing. A spark flew where the steel bit into the stone man's calcified grey flesh, but his arm tumbled to the deck all the same. Griff kicked the limb aside. Yandry and Duck had come up with their poles. Together they forced the creature over the side and into the black waters of the Rhoyne.

By then the *Shy Maid* had drifted out from under the broken bridge. "Did we get them all?" asked Duck. "How many jumped?"

"Two," said Tyrion, shivering.

"Three," said Haldon. "Behind you."

The dwarf turned, and there he stood.

The leap had shattered one of his legs, and a jagged piece of pale bone jutted out through the rotted cloth of his breeches and the grey meat beneath. The broken bone was speckled with brown blood, but still he lurched forward, reaching for Young Griff. His hand was grey and stiff, but blood oozed between his knuckles as he tried to close his fingers to grasp. The boy stood staring, as still as if he too were made of stone. His hand was on his sword hilt, but he seemed to have forgotten why.

Tyrion kicked the lad's leg out from under him and leapt over him when he fell, thrusting his torch into the stone man's face to send him stumbling backwards on his shattered leg, flailing at the flames with stiff grey hands. The dwarf waddled after him, slashing with the torch, jabbing it at the stone man's eyes. *A little farther. Back, one more step, another.* They were at the edge of the deck when the creature rushed him, grabbed the torch, and ripped it from his hands. *Bugger me,* thought Tyrion.

The stone man flung the torch away. There was a soft *hiss* as the black waters quenched the flames. The stone man howled. He had been a Summer Islander, before; his jaw and half his cheek had turned to stone, but his skin was black as midnight where it was not grey. Where he had grasped the torch, his skin had cracked and split. Blood was seeping from his knuckles though he did not seem to feel it. That was some small mercy, Tyrion supposed. Though mortal, greyscale was supposedly not painful.

"*Stand aside!*" someone shouted, far away, and another voice said,

"The prince! Protect the boy!" The stone man staggered forward, his hands outstretched and grasping.

Tyrion drove a shoulder into him.

It felt like slamming into a castle wall, but this castle stood upon a shattered leg. The stone man went over backwards, grabbing hold of Tyrion as he fell. They hit the river with a towering splash, and Mother Rhoyne swallowed up the two of them.

The sudden cold hit Tyrion like a hammer. As he sank he felt a stone hand fumbling at his face. Another closed around his arm, dragging him down into darkness. Blind, his nose full of river, choking, sinking, he kicked and twisted and fought to pry the clutching fingers off his arm, but the stone fingers were unyielding. Air bubbled from his lips. The world was black and growing blacker. He could not breathe.

There are worse ways to die than drowning. And if truth be told, he had perished long ago, back in King's Landing. It was only his revenant who remained, the small vengeful ghost who throttled Shae and put a crossbow bolt through the great Lord Tywin's bowels. No man would mourn the thing that he'd become. *I'll haunt the Seven Kingdoms,* he thought, sinking deeper. *They would not love me living, so let them dread me dead.*

When he opened his mouth to curse them all, black water filled his lungs, and the dark closed in around him.

DAVOS

"His lordship will hear you now, smuggler."

The knight wore silver armor, his greaves and gauntlet inlaid with niello to suggest flowing fronds of seaweed. The helm beneath his arm was the head of the merling king, with a crown of mother-of-pearl and a jutting beard of jet and jade. His own beard was as grey as the winter sea.

Davos rose. "May I know your name, ser?"

"Ser Marlon Manderly." He was a head taller than Davos and three stones heavier, with slate-grey eyes and a haughty way of speaking. "I have the honor to be Lord Wyman's cousin and commander of his garrison. Follow me."

Davos had come to White Harbor as an envoy, but they had made him a captive. His chambers were large, airy, and handsomely furnished, but there were guards outside his doors. From his window he could see the streets of White Harbor beyond the castle walls, but he was not allowed to walk them. He could see the harbor too, and had watched *Merry Midwife* make her way down the firth. Casso Mogat had waited four days instead of three before departing. Another fortnight had passed since then.

Lord Manderly's household guard wore cloaks of blue-green wool and carried silver tridents in place of common spears. One went before him, one behind, and one to either side. They walked past the faded banners, broken shields, and rusted swords of a hundred ancient victories, and a score of wooden figures, cracked and worm-riddled, that could only have adorned the prows of ships.

Two marble mermen flanked his lordship's court, Fishfoot's smaller cousins. As the guards threw open the doors, a herald slammed the butt of his staff against an old plank floor. "*Ser Davos of House Seaworth*," he called in a ringing voice.

As many times as he had visited White Harbor, Davos had never set foot inside the New Castle, much less the Merman's Court. Its walls and floor and ceiling were made of wooden planks notched cunningly together and decorated with all the creatures of the sea. As they approached the dais, Davos trod on painted crabs and clams and starfish, half-hidden amongst twisting black fronds of seaweed and the bones of drowned sailors. On the walls to either side, pale sharks prowled painted blue-green depths, whilst eels and octopods slithered amongst rocks and sunken ships. Shoals of herring and great codfish swam between the tall arched windows. Higher up, near where the old fishing nets drooped down from the rafters, the surface of the sea had been depicted. To his right a war galley stroked serene against the rising sun; to his left, a battered old cog raced before a storm, her sails in rags. Behind the dais a kraken and grey leviathan were locked in battle beneath the painted waves.

Davos had hoped to speak with Wyman Manderly alone, but he found a crowded court. Along the walls, the women outnumbered the men by five to one; what few males he did see had long grey beards or looked too young to shave. There were septons as well, and holy sisters in white robes and grey. Near the top of the hall stood a dozen men in the blue and silver-grey of House Frey. Their faces had a likeness a blind man could have seen; several wore the badge of the Twins, two towers connected by a bridge.

Davos had learned to read men's faces long before Maester Pylos had taught him to read words on paper. *These Freys would gladly see me dead,* he realized at a glance.

Nor did he find any welcome in the pale blue eyes of Wyman Manderly. His lordship's cushioned throne was wide enough to accommodate three men of common girth, yet Manderly threatened to overflow it. His lordship *sagged* into his seat, his shoulders slumped, his legs splayed, his hands resting on the arms of his throne as if the weight of them were too much to bear. *Gods be good,* thought Davos, when he saw Lord Wyman's face, *this man looks half a corpse.* His skin was pallid, with an undertone of grey.

Kings and corpses always draw attendants, the old saying went. So it was with Manderly. Left of the high seat stood a maester nigh as fat as the lord he served, a rosy-cheeked man with thick lips and a head of golden curls. Ser Marlon claimed the place of honor at his lordship's right hand. On a cushioned stool at his feet perched a plump pink lady. Behind Lord Wyman stood two younger women, sisters by the look of them. The elder wore her brown hair bound in a long braid. The younger, no more than fifteen, had an even longer braid, dyed a garish green.

None chose to honor Davos with a name. The maester was the first to speak. "You stand before Wyman Manderly, Lord of White Harbor and Warden of the White Knife, Shield of the Faith, Defender of the Dispossessed, Lord Marshal of the Mander, a Knight of the Order of the Green Hand," he said. "In the Merman's Court, it is customary for vassals and petitioners to kneel."

The onion knight would have bent his knee, but a King's Hand could not; to do so would suggest that the king he served was less than this fat lord. "I have not come as a petitioner," Davos replied. "I have a string of titles too. Lord of the Rainwood, Admiral of the Narrow Sea, Hand of the King."

The plump woman on the stool rolled her eyes. "An admiral without ships, a hand without fingers, in service to a king without a throne. Is this a knight who comes before us, or the answer to a child's riddle?"

"He is a messenger, good-daughter," Lord Wyman said, "an onion of ill omen. Stannis did not like the answer his ravens brought him, so he has sent this ... this *smuggler.*" He squinted at Davos through eyes half-buried in rolls of fat. "You have visited our city before, I think, taking coin from our pockets and food off our table. How much did you steal from me, I wonder?"

Not enough that you ever missed a meal. "I paid for my smuggling at Storm's End, my lord." Davos pulled off his glove and held up his left hand, with its four shortened fingers.

"Four fingertips, for a lifetime's worth of theft?" said the woman on the stool. Her hair was yellow, her face round and pink and fleshy. "You got off cheaply, Onion Knight."

Davos did not deny it. "If it please my lord, I would request a privy audience."

It did not please the lord. "I keep no secrets from my kin, nor from my leal lords and knights, good friends all."

"My lord," said Davos, "I would not want my words to be heard by His Grace's enemies . . . or by your lordship's."

"Stannis may have enemies in this hall. I do not."

"Not even the men who slew your son?" Davos pointed. "These Freys were amongst his hosts at the Red Wedding."

One of the Freys stepped forward, a knight long and lean of limb, clean-shaved but for a grey mustache as thin as a Myrish stiletto. "The Red Wedding was the Young Wolf's work. He changed into a beast before our eyes and tore out the throat of my cousin Jinglebell, a harmless simpleton. He would have slain my lord father too, if Ser Wendel had not put himself in the way."

Lord Wyman blinked back tears. "Wendel was always a brave boy. I was not surprised to learn he died a hero."

The enormity of the lie made Davos gasp. "Is it your claim that *Robb Stark* killed Wendel Manderly?" he asked the Frey.

"And many more. Mine own son Tytos was amongst them, and my daughter's husband. When Stark changed into a wolf, his northmen did the same. The mark of the beast was on them all. Wargs birth other wargs with a bite, it is well-known. It was all my brothers and I could do to put them down before they slew us all."

The man was *smirking* as he told the tale. Davos wanted to peel his lips off with a knife. "Ser, may I have your name?"

"Ser Jared, of House Frey."

"Jared of House Frey, I name you liar."

Ser Jared seemed amused. "Some men cry when slicing onions, but I have never had that weakness." Steel whispered against leather as he drew his sword. "If you are indeed a knight, ser, defend that slander with your body."

Lord Wyman's eyes fluttered open. "I'll have no bloodshed in the Merman's Court. Put up your steel, Ser Jared, else I must ask you to leave my presence."

Ser Jared sheathed his sword. "Beneath your lordship's roof, your lordship's word is law . . . but I shall want a reckoning with this onion lord before he leaves this city."

"*Blood!*" howled the woman on the stool. "That's what this ill onion wants of us, my lord. See how he stirs up trouble? Send him away, I beg you. He wants the blood of your people, the blood of your brave sons. Send him *away*. Should the queen hear that you gave audience to this traitor, she may question our own loyalty. She might . . . she could . . . she . . ."

"It will not come to that, good-daughter," Lord Wyman said. "The Iron Throne shall have no cause to doubt us."

Davos misliked the sound of that, but he had not come all this way to hold his tongue. "The boy on the Iron Throne is a usurper," he said, "and I am no traitor, but the Hand of Stannis Baratheon, the First of His Name, the trueborn King of Westeros."

The fat maester cleared his throat. "Stannis Baratheon was brother to our late King Robert, may the Father judge him justly. Tommen is the issue of Robert's body. The laws of succession are clear in such a case. A son must come before a brother."

"Maester Theomore speaks truly," said Lord Wyman. "He is wise in all such matters, and has always given me good counsel."

"A *trueborn* son comes before a brother," Davos agreed, "but Tommen-called-Baratheon is bastard-born, as his brother Joffrey was before him. They were sired by the Kingslayer, in defiance of all the laws of gods and men."

Another of the Freys spoke up. "He speaks treason with his own lips, my lord. Stannis took his thieving fingers. You should take his lying tongue."

"Take his head, rather," suggested Ser Jared. "Or let him meet me on the field of honor."

"What would a Frey know of honor?" Davos threw back.

Four of the Freys started forward until Lord Wyman halted them with an upraised hand. "Step back, my friends. I will hear him out before I . . . before I deal with him."

"Can you offer any proof of this incest, ser?" Maester Theomore asked, folding his soft hands atop his belly.

Edric Storm, thought Davos, *but I sent him far away across the narrow sea, to keep him safe from Melisandre's fires.* "You have the word of Stannis Baratheon that all I've said is true."

"Words are wind," said the young woman behind Lord Wyman's high seat, the handsome one with the long brown braid. "And men will lie to get their way, as any maid could tell you."

"Proof requires more than some lord's unsupported word," declared Maester Theomore. "Stannis Baratheon would not be the first man who ever lied to win a throne."

The pink woman pointed a plump finger down at Davos. "We want no part of any treason, you. We are good people in White Harbor, lawful, loyal people. Pour no more poison in our ears, or my good-father will send you to the Wolf's Den."

How have I offended this one? "Might I have the honor of my lady's name?"

The pink woman gave an angry sniff and let the maester answer. "The Lady Leona is wife to Lord Wyman's son Ser Wylis, presently a captive of the Lannisters."

She speaks from fear. If White Harbor should declare for Stannis, her husband would answer with his life. *How can I ask Lord Wyman to condemn his son to death? What would I do in his place if Devan were a hostage?* "My lord," said Davos, "I pray no harm will come to your son, or to any man of White Harbor."

"Another lie," said Lady Leona from her stool.

Davos thought it best to ignore her. "When Robb Stark took up arms against the bastard Joffrey-called-Baratheon, White Harbor marched with him. Lord Stark has fallen, but his war goes on."

"Robb Stark was my liege lord," said Lord Wyman. "Who is this man Stannis? Why does he trouble us? He never felt the need to journey north before, as best I can recall. Yet he turns up now, a beaten cur with his helm in his hand, begging for alms."

"He came to save the realm, my lord," Davos insisted. "To defend your lands against the ironborn and the wildlings."

Next to the high seat, Ser Marlon Manderly gave a snort of disdain. "It has been centuries since White Harbor has seen any wildlings, and the ironmen have never troubled this coast. Does Lord Stannis propose to defend us from snarks and dragons too?"

Laughter swept the Merman's Court, but at Lord Wyman's feet, Lady Leona began to sob. "Ironmen from the isles, wildlings from beyond the Wall . . . and now this traitor lord with his outlaws, rebels, and sorcerers." She pointed a finger at Davos. "We have heard of your red witch, oh yes. She would turn us against the Seven to bow before a fire demon!"

Davos had no love for the red priestess, but he dare not let Lady Leona go unanswered. "Lady Melisandre is a priestess of the red god. Queen Selyse has adopted her faith, along with many others, but more of His Grace's followers still worship the Seven. Myself among them." He prayed no one would ask him to explain about the sept at Dragonstone or the godswood at Storm's End. *If they ask, I must needs tell them. Stannis would not have me lie.*

"The Seven defend White Harbor," Lady Leona declared. "We do not fear your red queen or her god. Let her send what spells she will. The prayers of godly men will shield us against evil."

"Indeed." Lord Wyman gave Lady Leona a pat on the shoulder. "Lord Davos, if you *are* a lord, I know what your so-called king would have of me. Steel and silver and a bended knee." He shifted his weight to lean upon an elbow. "Before he was slain, Lord Tywin offered White Harbor full pardon for our support of the Young Wolf. He promised that my son would be returned to me once I paid a ransom of three thousand dragons and proved my loyalty beyond a doubt. Roose Bolton, who is named our Warden of the North, requires that I give up my claim to Lord Hornwood's lands and castles but swears my other holdings shall remain untouched. Walder Frey, his good-father, offers one of his daughters to be my wife, and husbands for my son's daughters here behind me. These terms seem generous to me, a good basis for a fair and lasting peace. You would have me spurn them. So I ask you, Onion Knight— what does Lord Stannis offer me in return for my allegiance?"

War and woe and the screams of burning men, Davos might have said. "The chance to do your duty," he replied instead. That was the answer Stannis would have given Wyman Manderly. *The Hand should speak with the king's voice.*

Lord Wyman sagged back in his chair. "Duty. I see."

"White Harbor is not strong enough to stand alone. You need His Grace as much as he needs you. Together you can defeat your common enemies."

"My lord," said Ser Marlon, in his ornate silver armor, "will you permit me to ask a few questions of Lord Davos?"

"As you wish, cousin." Lord Wyman closed his eyes.

Ser Marlon turned to Davos. "How many northern lords have declared for Stannis? Tell us that."

"Arnolf Karstark has vowed to join His Grace."

"Arnolf is no true lord, only a castellan. What castles does Lord Stannis hold at present, pray?"

"His Grace has taken the Nightfort for his seat. In the south, he holds Storm's End and Dragonstone."

Maester Theomore cleared his throat. "Only for the nonce. Storm's End and Dragonstone are lightly held and must soon fall. And the Nightfort is a haunted ruin, a drear and dreadful place."

Ser Marlon went on. "How many men can Stannis put into the field, can you tell us that? How many knights ride with him? How many bowmen, how many freeriders, how many men-at-arms?"

Too few, Davos knew. Stannis had come north with no more than fifteen hundred men . . . but if he told them that, his mission here was doomed. He fumbled for words and found none.

"Your silence is all the answer I require, ser. Your king brings us only enemies." Ser Marlon turned to his lord cousin. "Your lordship asked the onion knight what Stannis offers us. Let me answer. He offers us defeat and death. He would have you mount a horse of air and give battle with a sword of wind."

The fat lord opened his eyes slowly, as if the effort were almost too much for him. "My cousin cuts to the bone, as ever. Do you have any more to say to me, Onion Knight, or can we put an end to this mummer's farce? I grow weary of your face."

Davos felt a stab of despair. *His Grace should have sent another man, a lord or knight or maester, someone who could speak for him without tripping on his own tongue.* "Death," he heard himself say, "there will be death, aye. Your lordship lost a son at the Red Wedding. I lost four upon the Blackwater. And why? Because the Lannisters stole the throne. Go to King's Landing and look on Tommen with your own eyes, if you doubt me. A blind man could see it. What does Stannis offer you? Vengeance. Vengeance for my sons and yours, for your husbands and your fathers and your brothers. Vengeance for your murdered lord, your murdered king, your butchered princes. *Vengeance!*"

"Yes," piped a girl's voice, thin and high.

It belonged to the half-grown child with the blonde eyebrows and the long green braid. "They killed Lord Eddard and Lady Catelyn and King Robb," she said. "He was our *king*! He was brave and good, and the Freys *murdered* him. If Lord Stannis will avenge him, we should join Lord Stannis."

Manderly pulled her close. "Wylla, every time you open your mouth you make me want to send you to the silent sisters."

"I only said—"

"We heard what you said," said the older girl, her sister. "A child's foolishness. Speak no ill of our friends of Frey. One of them will be your lord and husband soon."

"No," the girl declared, shaking her head. "I won't. I won't *ever*. They killed *the king*."

Lord Wyman flushed. "You will. When the appointed day arrives, you will speak your wedding vows, else you will join the silent sisters and never speak again."

The poor girl looked stricken. "Grandfather, *please . . .*"

"Hush, child," said Lady Leona. "You heard your lord grandfather. *Hush!* You know nothing."

"I know about the promise," insisted the girl. "Maester Theomore, tell them! A thousand years before the Conquest, a promise was made, and oaths were sworn in the Wolf's Den before the old gods and the new. When we were sore beset and friendless, hounded from our homes and in peril of our lives, the wolves took us in and nourished us and protected us against our enemies. The city is built upon the land they gave us. In return we swore that we should always be their men. *Stark* men!"

The maester fingered the chain about his neck. "Solemn oaths were sworn to the Starks of Winterfell, aye. But Winterfell has fallen and House Stark has been extinguished."

"That's because they *killed them all*!"

Another Frey spoke up. "Lord Wyman, if I may?"

Wyman Manderly gave him a nod. "Rhaegar. We are always pleased to hear your noble counsel."

Rhaegar Frey acknowledged the compliment with a bow. He was thirty, or nigh unto, round-shouldered and kettle-bellied, but richly dressed in a doublet of soft grey lambswool trimmed in cloth-of-silver. His cloak was cloth-of-silver too, lined with vair and clasped at the collar with a brooch in the shape of the twin towers. "Lady Wylla," he said to the girl with the green braid, "loyalty is a virtue. I hope you will be as loyal to Little Walder when you are joined in wedlock. As to the Starks, that House is extinguished only in the male line. Lord Eddard's sons are dead, but his daughters live, and the younger girl is coming north to wed brave Ramsay Bolton."

"Ramsay *Snow*," Wylla Manderly threw back.

"Have it as you will. By any name, he shall soon be wed to Arya Stark. If you would keep faith with your promise, give *him* your allegiance, for he shall be your Lord of Winterfell."

"He won't ever be *my* lord! He made Lady Hornwood marry him, then shut her in a dungeon and made her eat her *fingers*."

A murmur of assent swept the Merman's Court. "The maid tells it true," declared a stocky man in white and purple, whose cloak was fastened with a pair of crossed bronze keys. "Roose Bolton's cold and cunning, aye, but a man can deal with Roose. We've all known worse. But this bastard son of his . . . they say he's mad and cruel, a monster."

"*They* say?" Rhaegar Frey sported a silky beard and a sardonic smile. "His *enemies* say, aye . . . but it was the Young Wolf who was the monster. More beast than boy, that one, puffed up with pride and bloodlust. And he was faithless, as my lord grandfather learned to his sorrow." He spread his hands. "I do not fault White Harbor for supporting him. My grandsire made the same grievous mistake. In all the Young Wolf's battles, White Harbor and the Twins fought side by side beneath his banners. Robb Stark betrayed us all. He abandoned the north to the cruel mercies of the ironmen to carve out a fairer kingdom for himself along the Trident. Then he abandoned the river-lords who had risked much and more for him, breaking his marriage pact with my grandfather to wed the first western wench who caught his eye. The Young Wolf? He was a vile dog and died like one."

The Merman's Court had grown still. Davos could feel the chill in the air. Lord Wyman was looking down at Rhaegar as if he were a roach in need of a hard heel . . . yet then, abruptly, he gave a ponderous nod that set his chins to wobbling. "A dog, aye. He brought us only grief and death. A vile dog indeed. Say on."

Rhaegar Frey went on. "Grief and death, aye . . . and this onion lord will bring you more with his talk of vengeance. Open your eyes, as my lord grandsire did. The War of the Five Kings is all but done. Tommen is our king, our *only* king. We must help him bind up the wounds of this sad war. As Robert's trueborn son, the heir of stag and lion, the Iron Throne is his by rights."

"Wise words, and true," said Lord Wyman Manderly.

"They *weren't*." Wylla Manderly stamped her foot.

"Be quiet, wretched child," scolded Lady Leona. "Young girls should be an ornament to the eye, not an ache in the ear." She seized the girl by her braid and pulled her squealing from the hall. *There went my only friend in this hall,* thought Davos.

"Wylla has always been a willful child," her sister said, by way of apology. "I fear that she will make a willful wife."

Rhaegar shrugged. "Marriage will soften her, I have no doubt. A firm hand and a quiet word."

"If not, there are the silent sisters." Lord Wyman shifted in his seat. "As for you, Onion Knight, I have heard sufficient treason for one day. You would have me risk my city for a false king and a false god. You would have me sacrifice my only living son so Stannis Baratheon can plant his puckered arse upon a throne to which he has no right. I will not do it. Not for you. Not for your lord. Not for any man." The Lord of White Harbor pushed himself to his feet. The effort brought a red flush to his neck. "You *are* still a smuggler, ser, come to steal my gold and blood. You would take my son's head. I think I shall take yours instead. *Guards!* Seize this man!"

Before Davos could even think to move, he was surrounded by silver tridents. "My lord," he said, "I am an envoy."

"Are you? You came sneaking into my city like a smuggler. I say you are no lord, no knight, no envoy, only a thief and a spy, a peddler of lies and treasons. I should tear your tongue out with hot pincers and deliver you to the Dreadfort to be flayed. But the Mother is merciful, and so am I." He beckoned to Ser Marlon. "Cousin, take this creature to the Wolf's Den and cut off his head and hands. I want them brought to me before I sup. I shall not be able to eat a bite until I see this smuggler's head upon a spike, with an onion shoved between his lying teeth."

REEK

They gave him a horse and a banner, a soft woolen doublet and a warm fur cloak, and set him loose. For once, he did not stink. "Come back with that castle," said Damon Dance-for-Me as he helped Reek climb shaking into the saddle, "or keep going and see how far you get before we catch you. He'd like that, he would." Grinning, Damon gave the horse a lick across the rump with his whip, and the old stot whinnied and lurched into motion.

Reek did not dare to look back, for fear that Damon and Yellow Dick and Grunt and the rest were coming after him, that all of this was just another of Lord Ramsay's japes, some cruel test to see what he would do if they gave him a horse and set him free. *Do they think that I will run?* The stot they had given him was a wretched thing, knock-kneed and half-starved; he could never hope to outdistance the fine horses Lord Ramsay and his hunters would be riding. And Ramsay loved nothing more than to set his girls baying on the trail of some fresh prey.

Besides, where would he run to? Behind him were the camps, crowded with Dreadfort men and those the Ryswells had brought from the Rills, with the Barrowton host between them. South of Moat Cailin, another army was coming up the causeway, an army of Boltons and Freys marching beneath the banners of the Dreadfort. East of the road lay a bleak and barren shore and a cold salt sea, to the west the swamps and bogs of the Neck, infested with serpents, lizard lions, and bog devils with their poisoned arrows.

He would not run. He could not run.

I will deliver him the castle. I will. I must.

It was a grey day, damp and misty. The wind was from the south, moist as a kiss. The ruins of Moat Cailin were visible in the distance, threaded through with wisps of morning mist. His horse moved toward them at a walk, her hooves making faint wet squelching sounds as they pulled free of the grey-green muck.

I have come this way before. It was a dangerous thought, and he regretted it at once. "No," he said, "no, that was some other man, that was before you knew your name." His name was Reek. He had to remember that. *Reek, Reek, it rhymes with leek.*

When that other man had come this way, an army had followed close behind him, the great host of the north riding to war beneath the grey-and-white banners of House Stark. Reek rode alone, clutching a peace banner on a pinewood staff. When that other man had come this way, he had been mounted on a courser, swift and spirited. Reek rode a broken-down stot, all skin and bone and ribs, and he rode her slowly for fear he might fall off. The other man had been a good rider, but Reek was uneasy on horseback. It had been so long. He was no rider. He was not even a man. He was Lord Ramsay's creature, lower than a dog, a worm in human skin. "You will pretend to be a prince," Lord Ramsay told him last night, as Reek was soaking in a tub of scalding water, "but we know the truth. You're Reek. You'll always be Reek, no matter how sweet you smell. Your nose may lie to you. Remember your name. Remember who you are."

"Reek," he said. "Your Reek."

"Do this little thing for me, and you can be my dog and eat meat every day," Lord Ramsay promised. "You will be tempted to betray me. To run or fight or join our foes. No, quiet, I'll not hear you deny it. Lie to me, and I'll take your tongue. A man *would* turn against me in your place, but we know what you are, don't we? Betray me if you want, it makes no matter . . . but count your fingers first and know the cost."

Reek knew the cost. *Seven,* he thought, *seven fingers. A man can make do with seven fingers. Seven is a sacred number.* He remembered how much it had hurt when Lord Ramsay had commanded Skinner to lay his ring finger bare.

The air was wet and heavy, and shallow pools of water dotted the ground. Reek picked his way between them carefully, following the remnants of the log-and-plank road that Robb Stark's vanguard had laid down across the soft ground to speed the passage of his host. Where once a mighty curtain wall had stood, only scattered stones remained, blocks of black basalt so large it must once have taken a hundred men to hoist them into place. Some had sunk so deep into the bog that only a corner showed; others lay strewn about like some god's abandoned toys, cracked and crumbling, spotted with lichen. Last night's rain had left the huge stones wet and glistening, and the morning sunlight made them look as if they were coated in some fine black oil.

Beyond stood the towers.

The Drunkard's Tower leaned as if it were about to collapse, just as it had for half a thousand years. The Children's Tower thrust into the sky as straight as a spear, but its shattered top was open to the wind and rain. The Gatehouse Tower, squat and wide, was the largest of the three, slimy with moss, a gnarled tree growing sideways from the stones of its north side, fragments of broken wall still standing to the east and west. *The Karstarks took the Drunkard's Tower and the Umbers the Children's Tower,* he recalled. *Robb claimed the Gatehouse Tower for his own.*

If he closed his eyes, he could see the banners in his mind's eye, snapping bravely in a brisk north wind. *All gone now, all fallen.* The wind on his cheeks was blowing from the south, and the only banners flying above the remains of Moat Cailin displayed a golden kraken on a field of black.

He was being watched. He could feel the eyes. When he looked up, he caught a glimpse of pale faces peering from behind the battlements of the Gatehouse Tower and through the broken masonry that crowned the Children's Tower, where legend said the children of the forest had once called down the hammer of the waters to break the lands of Westeros in two.

The only dry road through the Neck was the causeway, and the towers of Moat Cailin plugged its northern end like a cork in a bottle. The road was narrow, the ruins so positioned that any enemy coming up from the south must pass beneath and between them. To assault any of the three towers, an attacker must expose his back to arrows from the other two, whilst climbing damp stone walls festooned with streamers of slimy white ghostskin. The swampy ground beyond the causeway was impassable, an endless morass of suckholes, quicksands, and glistening green swards that looked solid to the unwary eye but turned to water the instant you trod upon them, the whole of it infested with venomous serpents and poisonous flowers and monstrous lizard lions with teeth like daggers. Just as dangerous were its people, seldom seen but always lurking, the swamp-dwellers, the frog-eaters, the mud-men. Fenn and Reed, Peat and Boggs, Cray and Quagg, Greengood and Blackmyre, those were the sorts of names they gave themselves. The ironborn called them all *bog devils.*

Reek passed the rotted carcass of a horse, an arrow jutting from its neck. A long white snake slithered into its empty eye socket at his approach. Behind the horse he spied the rider, or what remained of him. The crows had stripped the flesh from the man's face, and a feral dog had burrowed beneath his mail to get at his entrails. Farther on, another corpse had sunk so deep into the muck that only his face and fingers showed.

Closer to the towers, corpses littered the ground on every side. Bloodblooms had sprouted from their gaping wounds, pale flowers with petals plump and moist as a woman's lips.

The garrison will never know me. Some might recall the boy he'd been before he learned his name, but Reek would be a stranger to them. It had been a long while since he last looked into a glass, but he knew how old he must appear. His hair had turned white; much of it had fallen out, and what was left was stiff and dry as straw. The dungeons had left him weak as an old woman and so thin a strong wind could knock him down.

And his hands . . . Ramsay had given him gloves, fine gloves of black leather, soft and supple, stuffed with wool to conceal his missing fingers, but if anyone looked closely, he would see that three of his fingers did not bend.

"*No closer!*" a voice rang out. "What do you want?"

"Words." He spurred the stot onward, waving the peace banner so they could not fail to see it. "I come unarmed."

There was no reply. Inside the walls, he knew, the ironmen were discussing whether to admit him or fill his chest with arrows. *It makes no matter.* A quick death here would be a hundred times better than returning to Lord Ramsay as a failure.

Then the gatehouse doors flung open. "*Quickly.*" Reek was turning toward the sound when the arrow struck. It came from somewhere to his right, where broken chunks of the curtain wall lay half-submerged beneath the bog. The shaft tore through the folds of his banner and hung spent, the point a bare foot from his face. It startled him so badly that he dropped the peace banner and tumbled from his saddle.

"Inside," the voice shouted, "hurry, fool, *hurry!*"

Reek scrambled up the steps on hands and knees as another arrow fluttered over his head. Someone seized him and dragged him inside, and he heard the door crash shut behind him. He was pulled to his feet and shoved against a wall. Then a knife was at his throat, a bearded face so close to his that he could count the man's nose hairs. "Who are you? What's your purpose here? Quick now, or I'll do you the same as him." The guard jerked his head toward a body rotting on the floor beside the door, its flesh green and crawling with maggots.

"I am ironborn," Reek answered, lying. The boy he'd been before had been ironborn, true enough, but Reek had come into this world in the dungeons of the Dreadfort. "Look at my face. I am Lord Balon's son. Your prince." He would have said the name, but somehow the words caught in his throat. *Reek, I'm Reek, it rhymes with squeak.* He had to forget that for a little while, though. No man would ever yield to a creature such as Reek, no matter how desperate his situation. He must pretend to be a prince again.

His captor stared at his face, squinting, his mouth twisted in suspicion. His teeth were brown, and his breath stank of ale and onion. "Lord Balon's sons were killed."

"My brothers. Not me. Lord Ramsay took me captive after

Winterfell. He's sent me here to treat with you. Do you command here?"

"Me?" The man lowered his knife and took a step backwards, almost stumbling over the corpse. "Not me, m'lord." His mail was rusted, his leathers rotting. On the back of one hand an open sore wept blood. "Ralf Kenning has the command. The captain said. I'm on the door, is all."

"And who is this?" Reek gave the corpse a kick.

The guard stared at the dead man as if seeing him for the first time. "Him . . . he drank the water. I had to cut his throat for him, to stop his screaming. Bad belly. You can't drink the water. That's why we got the ale." The guard rubbed his face, his eyes red and inflamed. "We used to drag the dead down into the cellars. All the vaults are flooded down there. No one wants to take the trouble now, so we just leave them where they fall."

"The cellar is a better place for them. Give them to the water. To the Drowned God."

The man laughed. "No gods down there, m'lord. Only rats and water snakes. White things, thick as your leg. Sometimes they slither up the steps and bite you in your sleep."

Reek remembered the dungeons underneath the Dreadfort, the rat squirming between his teeth, the taste of warm blood on his lips. *If I fail, Ramsay will send me back to that, but first he'll flay the skin from another finger.* "How many of the garrison are left?"

"Some," said the ironman. "I don't know. Fewer than we was before. Some in the Drunkard's Tower too, I think. Not the Children's Tower. Dagon Codd went over there a few days back. Only two men left alive, he said, and they was eating on the dead ones. He killed them both, if you can believe that."

Moat Cailin has fallen, Reek realized then, *only no one has seen fit to tell them.* He rubbed his mouth to hide his broken teeth, and said, "I need to speak with your commander."

"Kenning?" The guard seemed confused. "He don't have much to say these days. He's dying. Might be he's dead. I haven't seen him since . . . I don't remember when . . ."

"Where is he? Take me to him."

"Who will keep the door, then?"

"Him." Reek gave the corpse a kick.

That made the man laugh. "Aye. Why not? Come with me, then." He pulled a torch down from a wall sconce and waved it till it blazed up bright and hot. "This way." The guard led him through a door and up a spiral stair, the torchlight glimmering off black stone walls as they climbed.

The chamber at the top of the steps was dark, smoky, and oppressively hot. A ragged skin had been hung across the narrow window to keep the damp out, and a slab of peat smoldered in a brazier. The smell in the room was foul, a miasma of mold and piss and nightsoil, of smoke and sickness. Soiled rushes covered the floor, whilst a heap of straw in the corner passed for a bed.

Ralf Kenning lay shivering beneath a mountain of furs. His arms were stacked beside him—sword and axe, mail hauberk, iron warhelm. His shield bore the storm god's cloudy hand, lightning crackling from his fingers down to a raging sea, but the paint was discolored and peeling, the wood beneath starting to rot.

Ralf was rotting too. Beneath the furs he was naked and feverish, his pale puffy flesh covered with weeping sores and scabs. His head was misshapen, one cheek grotesquely swollen, his neck so engorged with blood that it threatened to swallow his face. The arm on that same side was big as a log and crawling with white worms. No one had bathed him or shaved him for many days, from the look of him. One eye wept pus, and his beard was crusty with dried vomit. "What happened to him?" asked Reek.

"He was on the parapets and some bog devil loosed an arrow at him. It was only a graze, but ... they poison their shafts, smear the points with shit and worse things. We poured boiling wine into the wound, but it made no difference."

I cannot treat with this thing. "Kill him," Reek told the guard. "His wits are gone. He's full of blood and worms."

The man gaped at him. "The captain put him in command."

"You'd put a dying horse down."

"What horse? I never had no horse."

I did. The memory came back in a rush. Smiler's screams had sounded almost human. His mane afire, he had reared up on his hind legs, blind with pain, lashing out with his hooves. *No, no. Not mine, he was not mine, Reek never had a horse.* "I will kill him for you." Reek snatched up Ralf Kenning's sword where it leaned against his shield. He still had fingers enough to clasp the hilt. When he laid the edge of the blade against the swollen throat of the creature on the straw, the skin split open in a gout of black blood and yellow pus. Kenning jerked violently, then lay still. An awful stench filled the room. Reek bolted for the steps. The air was damp and cold there, but much cleaner by comparison. The ironman stumbled out after him, white-faced and struggling not to retch. Reek grasped him by the arm. "Who was second-in-command? Where are the rest of the men?"

"Up on the battlements, or in the hall. Sleeping, drinking. I'll take you if you like."

"Do it now." Ramsay had only given him a day.

The hall was dark stone, high ceilinged and drafty, full of drifting smoke, its stone walls spotted by huge patches of pale lichen. A peat fire burned low in a hearth blackened by the hotter blazes of years past. A massive table of carved stone filled the chamber, as it had for centuries. *There was where I sat, the last time I was here,* he remembered. *Robb was at the head of the table, with the Greatjon to his right and Roose Bolton on his left. The Glovers sat next to Helman Tallhart. Karstark and his sons were across from them.*

Two dozen ironborn sat drinking at the table. A few looked at him with dull, flat eyes when he entered. The rest ignored him. All the men were strangers to him. Several wore cloaks fastened by brooches in the shape of silver codfish. The Codds were not well regarded in the Iron Islands; the men were said to be thieves and cowards, the women wantons who bedded with their own fathers and brothers. It did not surprise him that his uncle had chosen to leave these men behind when the Iron Fleet went home. *This will make my task that much easier.* "Ralf Kenning is dead," he said. "Who commands here?"

The drinkers stared at him blankly. One laughed. Another spat. Finally one of the Codds said, "Who asks?"

"Lord Balon's son." *Reek, my name is Reek, it rhymes with cheek.* "I am here at the command of Ramsay Bolton, Lord of the Hornwood and heir to the Dreadfort, who captured me at Winterfell. His host is north of you, his father's to the south, but Lord Ramsay is prepared to be merciful if you yield Moat Cailin to him before the sun goes down." He drew out the letter that they'd given him and tossed it on the table before the drinkers.

One of them picked it up and turned it over in his hands, picking at the pink wax that sealed it. After a moment he said, "Parchment. What good is that? It's cheese we need, and meat."

"Steel, you mean," said the man beside him, a greybeard whose left arm ended in a stump. "Swords. Axes. Aye, and bows, a hundred more bows, and men to loose the arrows."

"Ironborn do not surrender," said a third voice.

"Tell that to my father. Lord Balon bent the knee when Robert broke his wall. Elsewise he would have died. As you will if you do not yield." He gestured at the parchment. "Break the seal. Read the words. That is a safe conduct, written in Lord Ramsay's own hand. Give up your swords and come with me, and his lordship will feed you and give you leave to march unmolested to the Stony Shore and find a ship for home. Elsewise you die."

"Is that a threat?" One of the Codds pushed to his feet. A big man, but pop-eyed and wide of mouth, with dead white flesh. He looked as if his father had sired him on a fish, but he still wore a longsword. "Dagon Codd yields to no man."

No, please, you have to listen. The thought of what Ramsay would do to him if he crept back to camp without the garrison's surrender was almost enough to make him piss his breeches. *Reek, Reek, it rhymes with leak.* "Is that your answer?" The words rang feebly in his ears. "Does this codfish speak for all of you?"

The guard who had met him at the door seemed less certain. "Victarion commanded us to hold, he did. I heard him with my own ears. *Hold here till I return,* he told Kenning."

"Aye," said the one-armed man. "That's what he said. The kingsmoot called, but he swore that he'd be back, with a driftwood crown upon his head and a thousand men behind him."

"My uncle is never coming back," Reek told them. "The kingswood crowned his brother Euron, and the Crow's Eye has other wars to fight. You think my uncle values you? He doesn't. You are the ones he left behind to die. He scraped you off the same way he scrapes mud off his boots when he wades ashore."

Those words struck home. He could see it in their eyes, in the way they looked at one another or frowned above their cups. *They all feared they'd been abandoned, but it took me to turn fear into certainty.* These were not the kin of famous captains nor the blood of the great Houses of the Iron Islands. These were the sons of thralls and salt wives.

"If we yield, we walk away?" said the one-armed man. "Is that what it says on this here writing?" He nudged the roll of parchment, its wax seal still unbroken.

"Read it for yourself," he answered, though he was almost certain that none of them could read. "Lord Ramsay treats his captives honorably so long as they keep faith with him." *He has only taken toes and fingers and that other thing, when he might have had my tongue, or peeled the skin off my legs from heel to thigh.* "Yield up your swords to him, and you will live."

"Liar." Dagon Codd drew his longsword. "You're the one they call Turncloak. Why should we believe your promises?"

He is drunk, Reek realized. *The ale is speaking.* "Believe what you want. I have brought Lord Ramsay's message. Now I must return to him. We'll sup on wild boar and neeps, washed down with strong red wine. Those who come with me will be welcome at the feast. The rest of you will die within a day. The Lord of the Dreadfort will bring his knights up the causeway, whilst his son leads his own men down on you from the north. No quarter will be granted. The ones that die fighting will be the lucky ones. Those who live will be given to the bog devils."

"*Enough,*" snarled Dagon Codd. "You think you can frighten ironborn with *words*? Begone. Run back to your master before I open your belly, pull your entrails out, and make you eat them."

He might have said more, but suddenly his eyes gaped wide. A throwing axe sprouted from the center of his forehead with a solid *thunk*. Codd's sword fell from his fingers. He jerked like a fish on a hook, then crashed face-first onto the table.

It was the one-armed man who'd flung the axe. As he rose to his feet he had another in his hand. "Who else wants to die?" he asked the other drinkers. "Speak up, I'll see you do." Thin red streams were spreading out across the stone from the pool of blood where Dagon Codd's head had come to rest. "Me, I mean to live, and that don't mean staying here to rot."

One man took a swallow of ale. Another turned his cup over to wash away a finger of blood before it reached the place where he was seated. No one spoke. When the one-armed man slid the throwing axe back through his belt, Reek knew he had won. He almost felt a man again. *Lord Ramsay will be pleased with me.*

He pulled down the kraken banner with his own two hands, fumbling some because of his missing fingers but thankful for the fingers that Lord Ramsay had allowed him to keep. It took the better part of the afternoon before the ironborn were ready to depart. There were more of them than he would have guessed—forty-seven in the Gatehouse Tower and another eighteen in the Drunkard's Tower. Two of those were so close to dead there was no hope for them, another five too weak to walk. That still left fifty-eight who were fit enough to fight. Weak as they were, they would have taken three times their own number with them if Lord Ramsay had stormed the ruins. *He did well to send me,* Reek told himself as he climbed back onto his stot to lead his ragged column back across the boggy ground to where the northmen were encamped. "Leave your weapons here," he told the prisoners. "Swords, bows, daggers. Armed men will be slain on sight."

It took them thrice as long to cover the distance as it had taken Reek alone. Crude litters had been patched together for four of the men who could not walk; the fifth was carried by his son, upon his back. It made for slow going, and all the ironborn were well aware of how exposed they were, well within bowshot of the bog devils and their poisoned arrows. *If I die, I die.* Reek only prayed the archer knew his business, so death would be quick and clean. *A man's death, not the end Ralf Kenning suffered.*

The one-armed man walked at the head of the procession, limping heavily. His name, he said, was Adrack Humble, and he had a rock wife and three salt wives back on Great Wyk. "Three of the four had big bellies when we sailed," he boasted, "and Humbles run to twins. First thing I'll need to do when I get back is count up my new sons. Might be I'll even name one after you, m'lord."

Aye, name him Reek, he thought, *and when he's bad you can cut his toes off and give him rats to eat.* He turned his head and spat, and wondered if Ralf Kenning hadn't been the lucky one.

A light rain had begun to piss down out of the slate-grey sky by the time Lord Ramsay's camp appeared in front of them. A sentry watched them pass in silence. The air was full of drifting smoke from the cookfires drowning in the rain. A column of riders came wheeling up behind them, led by a lordling with a horsehead on his shield. *One of Lord Ryswell's sons,* Reek knew. *Roger, or maybe Rickard.* He could not tell the two of them apart. "Is this all of them?" the rider asked from atop a chestnut stallion.

"All who weren't dead, my lord."

"I thought there would be more. We came at them three times, and three times they threw us back."

We are ironborn, he thought, with a sudden flash of pride, and for half a heartbeat he was a prince again, Lord Balon's son, the blood of Pyke. Even thinking was dangerous, though. He had to remember his name. *Reek, my name is Reek, it rhymes with weak.*

They were just outside the camp when the baying of a pack of hounds told of Lord Ramsay's approach. Whoresbane was with him, along with half a dozen of his favorites, Skinner and Sour Alyn and Damon Dance-for-Me, and the Walders Big and Little too. The dogs swarmed around them, snapping and snarling at the strangers. *The Bastard's girls,* Reek thought, before he remembered that one must never, never, *never* use that word in Ramsay's presence.

Reek swung down from his saddle and took a knee. "My lord, Moat Cailin is yours. Here are its last defenders."

"So few. I had hoped for more. They were such stubborn foes." Lord Ramsay's pale eyes shone. "You must be starved. Damon, Alyn, see to them. Wine and ale, and all the food that they can eat. Skinner, show their wounded to our maesters."

"Aye, my lord."

A few of the ironborn muttered thanks before they shambled off toward the cookfires in the center of the camp. One of the Codds even tried to kiss Lord Ramsay's ring, but the hounds drove him back before he could get close, and Alison took a chunk of his ear. Even as the blood streamed down his neck, the man bobbed and bowed and praised his lordship's mercy.

When the last of them were gone, Ramsay Bolton turned his smile on Reek. He clasped him by the back of the head, pulled his face close, kissed him on his cheek, and whispered, "My old friend Reek. Did they really take you for their prince? What bloody fools, these ironmen. The gods are laughing."

"All they want is to go home, my lord."

"And what do *you* want, my sweet Reek?" Ramsay murmured, as softly as a lover. His breath smelled of mulled wine and cloves, so sweet. "Such valiant service deserves a reward. I cannot give you back your fingers or your toes, but surely there is something you would have of me. Shall I free you instead? Release you from my service? Do you want to go with them, return to your bleak isles in the cold grey sea, be a prince again? Or would you sooner stay my leal serving man?"

A cold knife scraped along his spine. *Be careful,* he told himself, *be very, very careful.* He did not like his lordship's smile, the way his eyes were shining, the spittle glistening at the corner of his mouth. He had seen such signs before. *You are no prince. You're Reek, just Reek, it rhymes with freak. Give him the answer that he wants.*

"My lord," he said, "my place is here, with you. I'm your Reek. I only want to serve you. All I ask . . . a skin of wine, that would be reward enough for me . . . red wine, the strongest that you have, all the wine a man can drink . . ."

Lord Ramsay laughed. "You're not a man, Reek. You're just my creature. You'll have your wine, though. Walder, see to it. And fear not, I won't return you to the dungeons, you have my word as a Bolton. We'll make a dog of you instead. Meat every day, and I'll even leave you teeth enough to eat it. You can sleep beside my girls. Ben, do you have a collar for him?"

"I'll have one made, m'lord," said old Ben Bones.

The old man did better than that. That night, besides the collar, there was a ragged blanket too, and half a chicken. Reek had to fight the dogs for the meat, but it was the best meal he'd had since Winterfell.

And the wine . . . the wine was dark and sour, but *strong*. Squatting amongst the hounds, Reek drank until his head swam, retched, wiped his mouth, and drank some more. Afterward he lay back and closed his eyes. When he woke a dog was licking vomit from his beard, and dark clouds were scuttling across the face of a sickle moon. Somewhere in the night, men were screaming. He shoved the dog aside, rolled over, and went back to sleep.

The next morning Lord Ramsay dispatched three riders down the causeway to take word to his lord father that the way was clear. The flayed man of House Bolton was hoisted above the Gatehouse Tower, where Reek had hauled down the golden kraken of Pyke. Along the rotting-plank road, wooden stakes were driven deep into the boggy ground; there the corpses festered, red and dripping. *Sixty-three,* he knew, *there are sixty-three of them.* One was short half an arm. Another had a parchment shoved between its teeth, its wax seal still unbroken.

Three days later, the vanguard of Roose Bolton's host threaded its way through the ruins and past the row of grisly sentinels—four hundred mounted Freys clad in blue and grey, their spearpoints glittering whenever the sun broke through the clouds. Two of old Lord Walder's sons led the van. One was brawny, with a massive jut of jaw and arms thick with muscle. The other had hungry eyes close-set above a pointed nose, a thin brown beard that did not quite conceal the weak chin beneath it, a bald head. *Hosteen and Aenys.* He remembered them from before he knew his name. Hosteen was a bull, slow to anger but implacable once roused, and by repute the fiercest fighter of Lord Walder's get. Aenys was older, crueler, and more clever—a commander, not a swordsman. Both were seasoned soldiers.

The northmen followed hard behind the van, their tattered banners streaming in the wind. Reek watched them pass. Most were afoot, and there were so few of them. He remembered the great host that marched south with Young Wolf, beneath the direwolf of Winterfell. Twenty thousand swords and spears had gone off to war with Robb, or near enough to make no matter, but only two in ten were coming back, and most of those were Dreadfort men.

Back where the press was thickest at the center of the column rode a man armored in dark grey plate over a quilted tunic of blood-red leather. His rondels were wrought in the shape of human heads, with open mouths that shrieked in agony. From his shoulders streamed a pink woolen cloak embroidered with droplets of blood. Long streamers of red silk fluttered from the top of his closed helm. *No crannogman will slay Roose Bolton with a poisoned arrow,* Reek thought when he first saw him. An enclosed wagon groaned along behind him, drawn by six heavy draft horses and defended by crossbowmen, front and rear. Curtains of dark blue velvet concealed the wagon's occupants from watching eyes.

Farther back came the baggage train—lumbering wayns laden with provisions and loot taken in the war, and carts crowded with wounded men and cripples. And at the rear, more Freys. At least a thousand, maybe more: bowmen, spearmen, peasants armed with scythes and sharpened sticks, freeriders and mounted archers, and another hundred knights to stiffen them.

Collared and chained and back in rags again, Reek followed with the other dogs at Lord Ramsay's heels when his lordship strode forth to greet his father. When the rider in the dark armor removed his helm, however, the face beneath was not one that Reek knew. Ramsay's smile curdled at the sight, and anger flashed across his face. "What is this, some mockery?"

"Just caution," whispered Roose Bolton, as he emerged from behind the curtains of the enclosed wagon.

The Lord of the Dreadfort did not have a strong likeness to his bastard son. His face was clean-shaved, smooth-skinned, ordinary, not handsome but not quite plain. Though Roose had been in battles, he bore no scars. Though well past forty, he was as yet unwrinkled, with scarce a line to tell of the passage of time. His lips were so thin that when he pressed them together they seemed to vanish altogether. There was an agelessness about him, a stillness; on Roose Bolton's face, rage and joy looked much the same. All he and Ramsay had in common were their eyes. *His eyes are ice.* Reek wondered if Roose Bolton ever cried. *If so, do the tears feel cold upon his cheeks?*

Once, a boy called Theon Greyjoy had enjoyed tweaking Bolton as they sat at council with Robb Stark, mocking his soft voice and making japes about leeches. *He must have been mad. This is no man to jape with.* You had only to look at Bolton to know that he had more cruelty in his pinky toe than all the Freys combined.

"Father." Lord Ramsay knelt before his sire.

Lord Roose studied him for a moment. "You may rise." He turned to help two young women down from inside the wagon.

The first was short and very fat, with a round red face and three chins wobbling beneath a sable hood. "My new wife," Roose Bolton said. "Lady Walda, this is my natural son. Kiss your stepmother's hand, Ramsay." He did. "And I am sure you will recall the Lady Arya. Your betrothed."

The girl was slim, and taller than he remembered, but that was only to be expected. *Girls grow fast at that age.* Her dress was grey wool bordered with white satin; over it she wore an ermine cloak clasped with a silver wolf's head. Dark brown hair fell halfway down her back. And her eyes . . .

That is not Lord Eddard's daughter.

Arya had her father's eyes, the grey eyes of the Starks. A girl her age might let her hair grow long, add inches to her height, see her chest fill out, but she could not change the color of her eyes. *That's Sansa's little friend, the steward's girl. Jeyne, that was her name. Jeyne Poole.*

"Lord Ramsay." The girl dipped down before him. That was wrong as well. *The real Arya Stark would have spat into his face.* "I pray that I will make you a good wife and give you strong sons to follow after you."

"That you will," promised Ramsay, "and soon."

JON

His candle had guttered out in a pool of wax, but morning light was shining through the shutters of his window. Jon had fallen asleep over his work again. Books covered his table, tall stacks of them. He'd fetched them up himself, after spending half the night searching through dusty vaults by lantern light. Sam was right, the books desperately needed to be sorted, listed, and put in order, but that was no task for stewards who could neither read nor write. It would need to wait for Sam's return.

If he does return. Jon feared for Sam and Maester Aemon. Cotter Pyke had written from Eastwatch to report that the *Storm Crow* had sighted the wreckage of a galley along the coast of Skagos. Whether the broken ship was *Blackbird*, one of Stannis Baratheon's sellsails, or some passing trader, the crew of the *Storm Crow* had not been able to discern. *I meant to send Gilly and the babe to safety. Did I send them to their graves instead?*

Last night's supper had congealed beside his elbow, scarce touched. Dolorous Edd had filled his trencher almost to overflowing to allow Three-Finger Hobb's infamous three-meat stew to soften the stale bread. The jest among the brothers was that the three meats were mutton, mutton, and mutton, but carrot, onion, and turnip would have been closer to the mark. A film of cold grease glistened atop the remains of the stew.

Bowen Marsh had urged him to move into the Old Bear's former chambers in the King's Tower after Stannis vacated them, but Jon had declined. Moving into the king's chambers could too easily be taken to mean he did not expect the king to return.

A strange listlessness had settled over Castle Black since Stannis had marched south, as if the free folk and the black brothers alike were holding their breath, waiting to see what would come. The yards and dining hall were empty more oft than not, the Lord Commander's Tower was a shell, the old common hall a pile of blackened timbers, and Hardin's Tower looked as if the next gust of wind would knock it over. The only sound of life that Jon could hear was the faint clash of swords coming from the yard outside the armory. Iron Emmett was shouting at Hop-Robin to keep his shield up. *We had all best keep our shields up.*

Jon washed and dressed and left the armory, stopping in the yard outside just long enough to say a few words of encouragement to Hop-Robin and Emmett's other charges. He declined Ty's offer of a tail, as usual. He would have men enough about him; if it came to blood, two more would hardly matter. He did take Longclaw, though, and Ghost followed at his heels.

By the time he reached the stable, Dolorous Edd had the lord commander's palfrey saddled and bridled and waiting for him. The wayns were forming up beneath Bowen Marsh's watchful eye. The Lord Steward was trotting down the column, pointing and fussing, his cheeks red from the cold. When he spied Jon, they reddened even more. "Lord Commander. Are you still intent on this . . ."

". . . folly?" finished Jon. "Please tell me you were not about to say *folly,* my lord. Yes, I am. We have been over this. Eastwatch wants more men. The Shadow Tower wants more men. Greyguard and Icemark as well, I have no doubt, and we have fourteen other castles still sitting empty, long leagues of Wall that remain unwatched and undefended."

Marsh pursed his lips. "Lord Commander Mormont—"

"—is dead. And not at wildling hands, but at the hands of his own Sworn Brothers, men he trusted. Neither you nor I can know what he would or would not have done in my place." Jon wheeled his horse around. "Enough talk. Away."

Dolorous Edd had heard the entire exchange. As Bowen Marsh

trotted off, he nodded toward his back and said, "Pomegranates. All those seeds. A man could choke to death. I'd sooner have a turnip. Never knew a turnip to do a man any harm."

It was at times like this that Jon missed Maester Aemon the most. Clydas tended to the ravens well enough, but he had not a tenth of Aemon Targaryen's knowledge or experience, and even less of his wisdom. Bowen was a good man in his way, but the wound he had taken at the Bridge of Skulls had hardened his attitudes, and the only song he ever sang now was his familiar refrain about sealing the gates. Othell Yarwyck was as stolid and unimaginative as he was taciturn, and the First Rangers seemed to die as quick as they were named. *The Night's Watch has lost too many of its best men,* Jon reflected, as the wagons began to move. *The Old Bear, Qhorin Halfhand, Donal Noye, Jarmen Buckwell, my uncle . . .*

A light snow began to fall as the column made its way south along the kingsroad, the long line of wagons wending past fields and streams and wooded hillsides, with a dozen spearmen and a dozen archers riding escort. The last few trips had seen some ugliness at Mole's Town, a little pushing and shoving, some muttered curses, a lot of sullen looks. Bowen Marsh felt it best not to take chances, and for once he and Jon were agreed.

The Lord Steward led the way. Jon rode a few yards back, Dolorous Edd Tollett at his side. Half a mile south of Castle Black, Edd urged his garron close to Jon's and said, "M'lord? Look up there. The big drunkard on the hill."

The drunkard was an ash tree, twisted sideways by centuries of wind. And now it had a face. A solemn mouth, a broken branch for a nose, two eyes carved deep into the trunk, gazing north up the kingsroad, toward the castle and the Wall.

The wildlings brought their gods with them after all. Jon was not surprised. Men do not give up their gods so easily. The whole pageant that Lady Melisandre had orchestrated beyond the Wall suddenly seemed as empty as a mummer's farce. "Looks a bit like you, Edd," he said, trying to make light of it.

"Aye, m'lord. I don't have leaves growing out my nose, but elsewise . . . Lady Melisandre won't be happy."

"She's not like to see it. See that no one tells her."

"She sees things in those fires, though."

"Smoke and cinders."

"And people burning. Me, most like. With leaves up my nose. I always feared I'd burn, but I was hoping to die first."

Jon glanced back at the face, wondering who had carved it. He had posted guards around Mole's Town, both to keep his crows away from the wildling women and to keep the free folk from slipping off southward to raid. Whoever had carved up the ash had eluded his sentries, plainly. And if one man could slip through the cordon, others could as well. *I could double the guard again,* he thought sourly. *Waste twice as many men, men who might otherwise be walking the Wall.*

The wagons continued on their slow way south through frozen mud and blowing snow. A mile farther on, they came upon a second face, carved into a chestnut tree that grew beside an icy stream, where its eyes could watch the old plank bridge that spanned its flow. "Twice as much trouble," announced Dolorous Edd.

The chestnut was leafless and skeletal, but its bare brown limbs were not empty. On a low branch overhanging the stream a raven sat hunched, its feathers ruffled up against the cold. When it spied Jon it spread its wings and gave a scream. When he raised his fist and whistled, the big black bird came flapping down, crying, "*Corn, corn, corn.*"

"Corn for the free folk," Jon told him. "None for you." He wondered if they would all be reduced to eating ravens before the coming winter had run its course.

The brothers on the wagons had seen this face as well, Jon did not doubt. No one spoke of it, but the message was plain to read for any man with eyes. Jon had once heard Mance Rayder say that most kneelers were sheep. "Now, a dog can herd a flock of sheep," the King-Beyond-the-Wall had said, "but free folk, well, some are shadowcats and some are stones. One kind prowls where they please and will tear your dogs to pieces. The other will not move at all unless you kick them." Neither shadowcats nor stones were like to give up the gods they had worshiped all their lives to bow down before one they hardly knew.

Just north of Mole's Town they came upon the third watcher, carved into the huge oak that marked the village perimeter, its deep eyes fixed upon the kingsroad. *That is not a friendly face,* Jon Snow reflected. The faces that the First Men and the children of the forest had carved into the weirwoods in eons past had stern or savage visages more oft than not, but the great oak looked especially angry, as if it were about to tear its roots from the earth and come roaring after them. *Its wounds are as fresh as the wounds of the men who carved it.*

Mole's Town had always been larger than it seemed; most of it was underground, sheltered from the cold and snow. That was more true than ever now. The Magnar of Thenn had put the empty village to the torch when he passed through on his way to attack Castle Black, and only heaps of blackened beams and old scorched stones remained above-ground . . . but down beneath the frozen earth, the vaults and tunnels and deep cellars still endured, and that was where the free folk had taken refuge, huddled together in the dark like the moles from which the village took its name.

The wagons drew up in a crescent in front of what had once been the village smithy. Nearby a swarm of red-faced children were building a snow fort, but they scattered at the sight of the black-cloaked brothers, vanishing down one hole or another. A few moments later the adults began to emerge from the earth. A stench came with them, the smell of unwashed bodies and soiled clothing, of nightsoil and urine. Jon saw one of his men wrinkle his nose and say something to the man beside him. *Some jape about the smell of freedom,* he guessed. Too many of his brothers were making japes about the stench of the savages in Mole's Town.

Pig ignorance, Jon thought. The free folk were no different than the men of the Night's Watch; some were clean, some dirty, but most were clean at times and dirty at other times. This stink was just the smell of a thousand people jammed into cellars and tunnels that had been dug to shelter no more than a hundred.

The wildlings had done this dance before. Wordless, they formed up in lines behind the wagons. There were three women for every man, many with children—pale skinny things clutching at their skirts.

Jon saw very few babes in arms. *The babes in arms died during the march,* he realized, *and those who survived the battle died in the king's stockade.*

The fighters had fared better. Three hundred men of fighting age, Justin Massey had claimed in council. Lord Harwood Fell had counted them. *There will be spearwives too. Fifty, sixty, maybe as many as a hundred.* Fell's count had included men who had suffered wounds, Jon knew. He saw a score of those—men on crude crutches, men with empty sleeves and missing hands, men with one eye or half a face, a legless man carried between two friends. And every one grey-faced and gaunt. *Broken men,* he thought. *The wights are not the only sort of living dead.*

Not all the fighting men were broken, though. Half a dozen Thenns in bronze scale armor stood clustered round one cellar stair, watching sullenly and making no attempt to join the others. In the ruins of the old village smithy Jon spied a big bald slab of a man he recognized as Halleck, the brother of Harma Dogshead. Harma's pigs were gone, though. *Eaten, no doubt.* Those two in furs were Hornfoot men, as savage as they were scrawny, barefoot even in the snow. *There are wolves amongst these sheep, still.*

Val had reminded him of that, on his last visit with her. "Free folk and kneelers are more alike than not, Jon Snow. Men are men and women women, no matter which side of the Wall we were born on. Good men and bad, heroes and villains, men of honor, liars, cravens, brutes . . . we have plenty, as do you."

She was not wrong. The trick was telling one from the other, parting the sheep from the goats.

The black brothers began to pass out food. They'd brought slabs of hard salt beef, dried cod, dried beans, turnips, carrots, sacks of barley meal and wheaten flour, pickled eggs, barrels of onions and apples. "You can have an onion or an apple," Jon heard Hairy Hal tell one woman, "but not both. You got to pick."

The woman did not seem to understand. "I need two of each. One o' each for me, t'others for my boy. He's sick, but an apple will set him right."

Hal shook his head. "He has to come get his own apple. Or his onion. Not both. Same as you. Now, is it an apple or an onion? Be quick about it, now, there's more behind you."

"An apple," she said, and he gave her one, an old dried thing, small and withered.

"Move along, woman," shouted a man three places back. "It's cold out here."

The woman paid the shout no mind. "Another apple," she said to Hairy Hal. "For my son. Please. This one is so little."

Hal looked to Jon. Jon shook his head. They would be out of apples soon enough. If they started giving two to everyone who wanted two, the latecomers would get none.

"Out of the way," a girl behind the woman said. Then she shoved her in the back. The woman staggered, lost her apple, and fell. The other food-stuffs in her arms went flying. Beans scattered, a turnip rolled into a mud puddle, a sack of flour split and spilled its precious contents in the snow.

Angry voices rose, in the Old Tongue and the Common. More shoving broke out at another wagon. "It's not *enough,*" an old man snarled. "You bloody crows are starving us to death." The woman who'd been knocked down was scrabbling on her knees after her food. Jon saw the flash of naked steel a few yards away. His own bowmen nocked arrows to their strings.

He turned in his saddle. "Rory. Quiet them."

Rory lifted his great horn to his lips and blew.

AAAAhoooooooooooooooooooooooooooooooooooooooooooooooo.

The tumult and the shoving died. Heads turned. A child began to cry. Mormont's raven walked from Jon's left shoulder to his right, bobbing its head and muttering, "*Snow, snow, snow.*"

Jon waited until the last echoes had faded, then spurred his palfrey forward where everyone could see him. "We're feeding you as best we can, as much as we can spare. Apples, onions, neeps, carrots . . . there's a long winter ahead for all of us, and our stores are not inexhaustible."

"You crows eat good enough." Halleck shoved forward.

For now. "We hold the Wall. The Wall protects the realm . . . and you now. You know the foe we face. You know what's coming down on us. Some of you have faced them before. Wights and white walkers, dead things with blue eyes and black hands. I've seen them too, fought them, sent one to hell. They kill, then they send your dead against you. The giants were not able to stand against them, nor you Thenns, the ice-river clans, the Hornfoots, the free folk . . . and as the days grow shorter and the nights colder, they are growing stronger. You left your homes and came south in your hundreds and your thousands . . . why, but to escape them? To be safe. Well, it's the Wall that keeps you safe. It's *us* that keeps you safe, the black crows you despise."

"Safe and starved," said a squat woman with a windburned face, a spearwife by the look of her.

"You want more food?" asked Jon. "The food's for fighters. Help us hold the Wall, and you'll eat as well as any crow." *Or as poorly, when the food runs short.*

A silence fell. The wildlings exchanged wary looks. "*Eat,*" the raven muttered. "*Corn, corn.*"

"Fight for you?" This voice was thickly accented. Sigorn, the young Magnar of Thenn, spoke the Common Tongue haltingly at best. "Not fight for you. Kill you better. Kill all you."

The raven flapped its wings. "*Kill, kill.*"

Sigorn's father, the old Magnar, had been crushed beneath the falling stair during his attack on Castle Black. *I would feel the same if someone asked me to make common cause with the Lannisters,* Jon told himself. "Your father tried to kill us all," he reminded Sigorn. "The Magnar was a brave man, yet he failed. And if he had succeeded . . . who would hold the Wall?" He turned away from the Thenns. "Winterfell's walls were strong as well, but Winterfell stands in ruins today, burned and broken. A wall is only as good as the men defending it."

An old man with a turnip cradled against his chest said, "You kill us, you starve us, now you want t' make us slaves."

A chunky red-faced man shouted assent. "I'd sooner go naked than wear one o' them black rags on my back."

One of the spearwives laughed. "Even your wife don't want to see *you* naked, Butts."

A dozen voices all began to speak at once. The Thenns were

shouting in the Old Tongue. A little boy began to cry. Jon Snow waited until all of it had died down, then turned to Hairy Hal and said, "Hal, what was it that you told this woman?"

Hal looked confused. "About the food, you mean? An apple or an onion? That's all I said. They got to pick."

"*You have to pick*," Jon Snow repeated. "All of you. No one is asking you to take our vows, and I do not care what gods you worship. My own gods are the old gods, the gods of the North, but you can keep the red god, or the Seven, or any other god who hears your prayers. It's spears we need. Bows. Eyes along the Wall.

"I will take any boy above the age of twelve who knows how to hold a spear or string a bow. I will take your old men, your wounded, and your cripples, even those who can no longer fight. There are other tasks they may be able to perform. Fletching arrows, milking goats, gathering firewood, mucking out our stables . . . the work is endless. And yes, I will take your women too. I have no need of blushing maidens looking to be protected, but I will take as many spearwives as will come."

"And girls?" a girl asked. She looked as young as Arya had, the last time Jon had seen her.

"Sixteen and older."

"You're taking boys as young as twelve."

Down in the Seven Kingdoms boys of twelve were often pages or squires; many had been training at arms for years. Girls of twelve were children. *These are wildlings, though.* "As you will. Boys *and* girls as young as twelve. But only those who know how to obey an order. That goes for all of you. I will never ask you to kneel to me, but I will set captains over you, and serjeants who will tell you when to rise and when to sleep, where to eat, when to drink, what to wear, when to draw your swords and loose your arrows. The men of the Night's Watch serve for life. I will not ask that of you, but so long as you are on the Wall you will be under my command. Disobey an order, and I'll have your head off. Ask my brothers if I won't. They've seen me do it."

"*Off*," screamed the Old Bear's raven. "*Off, off, off.*"

"The choice is yours," Jon Snow told them. "Those who want to help us hold the Wall, return to Castle Black with me and I'll see you armed and fed. The rest of you, get your turnips and your onions and crawl back inside your holes."

The girl was the first to come forward. "I can fight. My mother was a spearwife." Jon nodded. *She may not even be twelve,* he thought, as she squirmed between a pair of old men, but he was not about to turn away his only recruit.

A pair of striplings followed her, boys no older than fourteen. Next a scarred man with a missing eye. "I seen them too, the dead ones. Even crows are better'n that." A tall spearwife, an old man on crutches, a moonfaced boy with a withered arm, a young man whose red hair reminded Jon of Ygritte.

And then Halleck. "I don't like you, crow," he growled, "but I never liked the Mance neither, no more'n my sister did. Still, we fought for him. Why not fight for you?"

The dam broke then. Halleck was a man of note. *Mance was not wrong.* "Free folk don't follow names, or little cloth animals sewn on a tunic," the King-Beyond-the-Wall had told him. "They won't dance for coins, they don't care how you style yourself or what that chain of office means or who your grandsire was. They follow strength. They follow the man."

Halleck's cousins followed Halleck, then one of Harma's banner-bearers, then men who'd fought with her, then others who had heard tales of their prowess. Greybeards and green boys, fighting men in their prime, wounded men and cripples, a good score of spearwives, even three Hornfoot men.

But no Thenns. The Magnar turned and vanished back into the tunnels, and his bronze-clad minions followed hard at his heels.

By the time the last withered apple had been handed out, the wagons were crowded with wildlings, and they were sixty-three stronger than when the column had set out from Castle Black that morning. "What will you do with them?" Bowen Marsh asked Jon on the ride back up the kingsroad.

"Train them, arm them, and split them up. Send them where they're needed. Eastwatch, the Shadow Tower, Icemark, Greyguard. I mean to open three more forts as well."

The Lord Steward glanced back. "Women too? Our brothers are not accustomed to having women amongst them, my lord. Their vows . . . there will be fights, rapes . . ."

"These women have knives and know how to use them."

"And the first time one of these spearwives slits the throat of one of our brothers, what then?"

"We will have lost a man," said Jon, "but we have just gained sixty-three. You're good at counting, my lord. Correct me if I'm wrong, but my reckoning leaves us sixty-two ahead."

Marsh was unconvinced. "You've added sixty-three more mouths, my lord . . . but how many are fighters, and whose side will they fight on? If it's the Others at the gates, most like they'll stand with us, I grant you . . . but if it's Tormund Giantsbane or the Weeping Man come calling with ten thousand howling killers, what then?"

"Then we'll know. So let us hope it never comes to that."

TYRION

He dreamt of his lord father and the Shrouded Lord. He dreamt that they were one and the same, and when his father wrapped stone arms around him and bent to give him his grey kiss, he woke with his mouth dry and rusty with the taste of blood and his heart hammering in his chest.

"Our dead dwarf has returned to us," Haldon said.

Tyrion shook his head to clear away the webs of dream. *The Sorrows. I was lost in the Sorrows.* "I am not dead."

"That remains to be seen." The Halfmaester stood over him. "Duck, be a fine fowl and boil some broth for our little friend here. He must be famished."

He was on the *Shy Maid,* Tyrion saw, under a scratchy blanket that smelled of vinegar. *The Sorrows are behind us. It was just a dream I dreamed as I was drowning.* "Why do I stink of vinegar?"

"Lemore has been washing you with it. Some say it helps prevent the greyscale. I am inclined to doubt that, but there was no harm in trying. It was Lemore who forced the water from your lungs after Griff had pulled you up. You were as cold as ice, and your lips were blue. Yandry said we ought to throw you back, but the lad forbade it."

The prince. Memory came rushing back: the stone man reaching out with cracked grey hands, the blood seeping from his knuckles.

He was heavy as a boulder, pulling me under. "Griff brought me up?" *He must hate me, or he would have let me die.* "How long have I been sleeping? What place is this?"

"Selhorys." Haldon produced a small knife from his sleeve. "Here," he said, tossing it underhand at Tyrion.

The dwarf flinched. The knife landed between his feet and stood quivering in the deck. He plucked it out. "What's this?"

"Take off your boots. Prick each of your toes and fingers."

"That sounds . . . painful."

"I hope so. Do it."

Tyrion yanked off one boot and then the other, peeled down his hose, squinted at his toes. It seemed to him they looked no better or worse than usual. He poked gingerly at one big toe.

"Harder," urged Haldon Halfmaester.

"Do you want me to draw blood?"

"If need be."

"I'll have a scab on every toe."

"The purpose of the exercise is not to count your toes. I want to see you wince. So long as the pricks hurt, you are safe. It is only when you cannot feel the blade that you will have cause to fear."

Greyscale. Tyrion grimaced. He stabbed another toe, cursed as a bead of blood welled up around the knife's point. "That hurt. Are you happy?"

"Dancing with joy."

"Your feet smell worse than mine, Yollo." Duck had a cup of broth. "Griff warned you not to lay hands upon the stone men."

"Aye, but he forgot to warn the stone men not to lay their hands upon me."

"As you prick, look for patches of dead grey skin, for nails beginning to turn black," said Haldon. "If you see such signs, do not hesitate. Better to lose a toe than a foot. Better to lose an arm than spend your days wailing on the Bridge of Dream. Now the other foot, if you please. Then your fingers."

The dwarf recrossed his stunted legs and began to prick the other set of toes. "Shall I prick my prick as well?"

"It would not hurt."

"It would not hurt *you* is what you mean. Though I had as well slice it off for all the use I make of it."

"Feel free. We will have it tanned and stuffed and sell it for a fortune. A dwarf's cock has magical powers."

"I have been telling all the women that for years." Tyrion drove the dagger's point into the ball of his thumb, watched the blood bead up, sucked it away. "How long must I continue to torture myself? When will we be certain that I'm clean?"

"Truly?" said the Halfmaester. "Never. You swallowed half the river. You may be going grey even now, turning to stone from inside out, starting with your heart and lungs. If so, pricking your toes and bathing in vinegar will not save you. When you're done, come have some broth."

The broth was good, though Tyrion noted that the Halfmaester kept the table between them as he ate. The *Shy Maid* was moored to a weathered pier on the east bank of the Rhoyne. Two piers down, a Volantene river galley was discharging soldiers. Shops and stalls and storehouses huddled beneath a sandstone wall. The towers and domes of the city were visible beyond it, reddened by the light of the setting sun.

No, not a city. Selhorys was still accounted a mere town, and was ruled from Old Volantis. This was not Westeros.

Lemore emerged on deck with the prince in tow. When she saw Tyrion, she rushed across the deck to hug him. "The Mother is merciful. We have prayed for you, Hugor."

You did, at least. "I won't hold that against you."

Young Griff's greeting was less effusive. The princeling was in a sullen mood, angry that he had been forced to remain on the *Shy Maid* instead of going ashore with Yandry and Ysilla. "We only want to keep you safe," Lemore told him. "These are unsettled times."

Haldon Halfmaester explained. "On the way down from the Sorrows to Selhorys, we thrice glimpsed riders moving south along the river's eastern shore. Dothraki. Once they were so close we could hear the bells tinkling in their braids, and sometimes at night their fires could be seen beyond the eastern hills. We passed warships as well, Volantene river galleys crammed with slave soldiers. The triarchs fear an attack upon Selhorys, plainly."

Tyrion understood that quick enough. Alone amongst the major river towns, Selhorys stood upon the eastern bank of the Rhoyne, making it much more vulnerable to the horselords than its sister towns across the river. *Even so, it is a small prize. If I were khal, I would feint at Selhorys, let the Volantenes rush to defend it, then swing south and ride hard for Volantis itself.*

"I know how to use a sword," Young Griff was insisting.

"Even the bravest of your forebears kept his Kingsguard close about him in times of peril." Lemore had changed out of her septa's robes into garb more befitting the wife or daughter of a prosperous merchant. Tyrion watched her closely. He had sniffed out the truth beneath the dyed blue hair of Griff and Young Griff easily enough, and Yandry and Ysilla seemed to be no more than they claimed to be, whilst Duck was somewhat less. Lemore, though . . . *Who is she, really? Why is she here? Not for gold, I'd judge. What is this prince to her? Was she ever a true septa?*

Haldon took note of her change of garb as well. "What are we to make of this sudden loss of faith? I preferred you in your septa's robes, Lemore."

"I preferred her naked," said Tyrion.

Lemore gave him a reproachful look. "That is because you have a wicked soul. Septa's robes scream of Westeros and might draw unwelcome eyes onto us." She turned back to Prince Aegon. "You are not the only one who must needs hide."

The lad did not seem appeased. *The perfect prince but still half a boy for all that, with little and less experience of the world and all its woes.* "Prince Aegon," said Tyrion, "since we're both stuck aboard this boat, perhaps you will honor me with a game of *cyvasse* to while away the hours?"

The prince gave him a wary look. "I am sick of *cyvasse.*"

"Sick of losing to a dwarf, you mean?"

That pricked the lad's pride, just as Tyrion had known it would. "Go fetch the board and pieces. This time I mean to smash you."

They played on deck, sitting cross-legged behind the cabin. Young Griff arrayed his army for attack, with dragon, elephants, and heavy horse up front. *A young man's formation, as bold as it is foolish. He risks all for the quick kill.* He let the prince have first move. Haldon stood behind them, watching the play.

When the prince reached for his dragon, Tyrion cleared his throat. "I would not do that if I were you. It is a mistake to bring your dragon out too soon." He smiled innocently. "Your father knew the dangers of being overbold."

"Did you know my true father?"

"Well, I saw him twice or thrice, but I was only ten when Robert killed him, and mine own sire had me hidden underneath a rock. No, I cannot claim I knew Prince Rhaegar. Not as your false father did. Lord Connington was the prince's dearest friend, was he not?"

Young Griff pushed a lock of blue hair out of his eyes. "They were squires together at King's Landing."

"A true friend, our Lord Connington. He must be, to remain so fiercely loyal to the grandson of the king who took his lands and titles and sent him into exile. A pity about that. Elsewise Prince Rhaegar's friend might have been on hand when my father sacked King's Landing, to save Prince Rhaegar's precious little son from getting his royal brains dashed out against a wall."

The lad flushed. "That was not me. I told you. That was some tanner's son from Pisswater Bend whose mother died birthing him. His father sold him to Lord Varys for a jug of Arbor gold. He had other sons but had never tasted Arbor gold. Varys gave the Pisswater boy to my lady mother and carried me away."

"Aye." Tyrion moved his elephants. "And when the pisswater prince was safely dead, the eunuch smuggled you across the narrow sea to his fat friend the cheesemonger, who hid you on a poleboat and found an exile lord willing to call himself your father. It does make for a splendid story, and the singers will make much of your escape once you take the Iron Throne . . . assuming that our fair Daenerys takes you for her consort."

"She will. She must."

"*Must?*" Tyrion made a *tsk*ing sound. "That is not a word queens like to hear. You are her perfect prince, agreed, bright and bold and comely as any maid could wish. Daenerys Targaryen is no maid, however. She is the widow of a Dothraki khal, a mother of dragons and sacker of cities, Aegon the Conqueror with teats. She may not prove as willing as you wish."

"She'll be willing." Prince Aegon sounded shocked. It was plain that he had never before considered the possibility that his bride-to-be might refuse him. "You don't know her." He picked up his heavy horse and put it down with a *thump.*

The dwarf shrugged. "I know that she spent her childhood in exile, impoverished, living on dreams and schemes, running from one city to the next, always fearful, never safe, friendless but for a brother who was by all accounts half-mad . . . a brother who sold her maidenhood to the Dothraki for the promise of an army. I know that somewhere out upon the grass her dragons hatched, and so did she. I know she is proud. How not? What else was left her but pride? I know she is strong. How not? The Dothraki despise weakness. If Daenerys had been weak, she would have perished with Viserys. I know she is fierce. Astapor, Yunkai, and Meereen are proof enough of that. She has crossed the grasslands and the red waste, survived assassins and conspiracies and fell sorceries, grieved for a brother and a husband and a son, trod the cities of the slavers to dust beneath her dainty sandaled feet. Now, how do you suppose this queen will react when you turn up with your begging bowl in hand and say, 'Good morrow to you, Auntie. I am your nephew, Aegon, returned from the dead. I've been hiding on a poleboat all my life, but now I've washed the blue dye from my hair and I'd like a dragon, please . . . and oh, did I mention, my claim to the Iron Throne is stronger than your own?'"

Aegon's mouth twisted in fury. "I will *not* come to my aunt a beggar. I will come to her a kinsman, with an army."

"A small army." *There, that's made him good and angry.* The dwarf could not help but think of Joffrey. *I have a gift for angering princes.* "Queen Daenerys has a large one, and no thanks to you." Tyrion moved his crossbows.

"Say what you want. She will be my bride, Lord Connington will see to it. I trust him as much as if he were my own blood."

"Perhaps you should be the fool instead of me. *Trust no one,* my prince. Not your chainless maester, not your false father, not the gallant Duck nor the lovely Lemore nor these other fine friends who grew you from a bean. Above all, trust not the cheesemonger, nor the Spider, nor this little dragon queen you mean to marry. All that mistrust will sour your stomach and keep you awake by night, 'tis true, but better that than the long sleep that does not end." The dwarf pushed his black dragon across a range of mountains. "But what do I know? Your false father is a great lord, and I am just some twisted little monkey man. Still, I'd do things differently."

That got the boy's attention. "How differently?"

"If I were you? I would go west instead of east. Land in Dorne and raise my banners. The Seven Kingdoms will never be more ripe for conquest than they are right now. A boy king sits the Iron Throne. The north is in chaos, the riverlands a devastation, a rebel holds Storm's End and Dragonstone. When winter comes, the realm will starve. And who remains to deal with all of this, who rules the little king who rules the Seven Kingdoms? Why, my own sweet sister. There is no one else. My brother, Jaime, thirsts for battle, not for power. He's run from every chance he's had to rule. My uncle Kevan would make a passably good regent if someone pressed the duty on him, but he will never reach for it. The gods shaped him to be a follower, not a leader." *Well, the gods and my lord father.* "Mace Tyrell would grasp the sceptre gladly, but mine own kin are not like to step aside and give it to him. And everyone hates Stannis. Who does that leave? Why, only Cersei.

"Westeros is torn and bleeding, and I do not doubt that even now my sweet sister is binding up the wounds . . . with salt. Cersei is as gentle as King Maegor, as selfless as Aegon the Unworthy, as wise as Mad Aerys. She never forgets a slight, real or imagined. She takes caution for cowardice and dissent for defiance. And she is greedy. Greedy for power, for honor, for love. Tommen's rule is bolstered by all of the alliances that my lord father built so carefully, but soon enough she will destroy them, every one. Land and raise your banners, and men will flock to your cause. Lords great and small, and smallfolk too. But do not wait too long, my prince. The moment will not last. The tide that lifts you now will soon recede. Be certain you reach Westeros before my sister falls and someone more competent takes her place."

"But," Prince Aegon said, "without Daenerys and her dragons, how could we hope to win?"

"You do not *need* to win," Tyrion told him. "All you need to do is raise your banners, rally your supporters, and hold, until Daenerys arrives to join her strength to yours."

"You said she might not have me."

"Perhaps I overstated. She may take pity on you when you come begging for her hand." The dwarf shrugged. "Do you want to wager your throne upon a woman's whim? Go to Westeros, though . . . ah, then you are a rebel, not a beggar. Bold, reckless, a true scion of House Targaryen, walking in the footsteps of Aegon the Conqueror. A *dragon*.

"I told you, I know our little queen. Let her hear that her brother Rhaegar's murdered son is still alive, that this brave boy has raised the dragon standard of her forebears in Westeros once more, that he is fighting a desperate war to avenge his father and reclaim the Iron Throne for House Targaryen, hard-pressed on every side . . . and she will fly to your side as fast as wind and water can carry her. You are the last of her line, and this Mother of Dragons, this Breaker of Chains, is above all a *rescuer*. The girl who drowned the slaver cities in blood rather than leave strangers to their chains can scarcely abandon her own brother's son in his hour of peril. And when she reaches Westeros, and meets you for the first time, you will meet as equals, man and woman, not queen and supplicant. How can she help but love you then, I ask you?" Smiling, he seized his dragon, flew it across the board. "I hope Your Grace will pardon me. Your king is trapped. Death in four."

The prince stared at the playing board. "My dragon—"

"—is too far away to save you. You should have moved her to the center of the battle."

"But you said—"

"I lied. *Trust no one.* And keep your dragon close."

Young Griff jerked to his feet and kicked over the board. *Cyvasse* pieces flew in all directions, bouncing and rolling across the deck of the *Shy Maid*. "Pick those up," the boy commanded.

He may well be a Targaryen after all. "If it please Your Grace." Tyrion got down on his hands and knees and began to crawl about the deck, gathering up pieces.

It was close to dusk when Yandry and Ysilla returned to the *Shy Maid*. A porter trotted at their heels, pushing a wheelbarrow heaped high with provisions: salt and flour, fresh-churned butter, slabs of bacon wrapped in linen, sacks of oranges, apples, and pears. Yandry had a wine cask on one shoulder, while Ysilla had slung a pike over hers. The fish was as large as Tyrion.

When she saw the dwarf standing at the end of the gangplank, Ysilla stopped so suddenly that Yandry blundered into her, and the pike almost slid off her back into the river. Duck helped her rescue it. Ysilla glared at Tyrion and made a peculiar stabbing gesture with three of her fingers. *A sign to ward off evil.* "Let me help you with that fish," he said to Duck.

"No," Ysilla snapped. "Stay away. Touch no food besides the food you eat yourself."

The dwarf raised both hands. "As you command."

Yandry thumped the wine cask down onto the desk. "Where's Griff?" he demanded of Haldon.

"Asleep."

"Then rouse him. We have tidings he'd best hear. The queen's name is on every tongue in Selhorys. They say she still sits in Meereen, sore beset. If the talk in the markets can be believed, Old Volantis will soon join the war against her."

Haldon pursed his lips. "The gossip of fishmongers is not to be relied on. Still, I suppose Griff will want to hear. You know how he is." The Halfmaester went below.

The girl never started for the west. No doubt she had good reasons. Between Meereen and Volantis lay five hundred leagues of deserts, mountains, swamps, and ruins, plus Mantarys with its sinister repute. *A city of monsters, they say, but if she marches overland, where else is she to turn for food and water? The sea would be swifter, but if she does not have the ships . . .*

By the time Griff appeared on deck, the pike was spitting and sizzling over the brazier whilst Ysilla hovered over it with a lemon, squeezing. The sellsword wore his mail and wolfskin cloak, soft leather gloves, dark woolen breeches. If he was surprised to see Tyrion awake, he gave no sign beyond his customary scowl. He took Yandry back to the tiller, where they spoke in low voices, too quietly for the dwarf to hear.

Finally Griff beckoned to Haldon. "We need to know the truth of these rumors. Go ashore and learn what you can. Qavo will know, if you can find him. Try the Riverman and the Painted Turtle. You know his other places."

"Aye. I'll take the dwarf as well. Four ears hear more than two. And you know how Qavo is about his *cyvasse*."

"As you wish. Be back before the sun comes up. If for any reason you're delayed, make your way to the Golden Company."

Spoken like a lord. Tyrion kept the thought to himself.

Haldon donned a hooded cloak, and Tyrion shed his homemade motley for something drab and grey. Griff allowed them each a purse of silver from Illyrio's chests. "To loosen tongues."

Dusk was giving way to darkness as they made their way along the riverfront. Some of the ships they passed appeared deserted, their gangplanks drawn up. Others crawled with armed men who eyed them with suspicion. Under the town walls, parchment lanterns had been lit above the stalls, throwing pools of colored light upon the cobbled path. Tyrion watched as Haldon's face turned green, then red, then purple. Under the cacophony of foreign tongues, he heard queer music playing from somewhere up ahead, a thin high fluting accompanied by drums. A dog was barking too, behind them.

And the whores were out. River or sea, a port was a port, and wherever you found sailors, you'd find whores. *Is that what my father meant? Is that where whores go, to the sea?*

The whores of Lannisport and King's Landing were free women. Their sisters of Selhorys were slaves, their bondage indicated by the tears tattooed beneath their right eyes. *Old as sin and twice as ugly, the lot of them.* It was almost enough to put a man off whoring. Tyrion felt their eyes upon them as he waddled by, and heard them whispering to one another and giggling behind their hands. *You would think they had never seen a dwarf before.*

A squad of Volantene spearmen stood guard at the river gate. Torchlight gleamed off the steel claws that jutted from their gauntlets. Their helms were tiger's masks, the faces beneath marked by green stripes tattooed across both cheeks. The slave soldiers of Volantis were fiercely proud of their tiger stripes, Tyrion knew. *Do they yearn for freedom?* he wondered. *What would they do if this child queen bestowed it on them? What are they, if not tigers? What am I, if not a lion?*

One of the tigers spied the dwarf and said something that made the others laugh. As they reached the gate, he pulled off his clawed gauntlet and the sweaty glove beneath, locked one arm around the dwarf's neck, and roughly rubbed his head. Tyrion was too startled to resist. It was all over in a heartbeat. "Was there some reason for that?" he demanded of the Halfmaester.

"He says that it is good luck to rub the head of a dwarf," Haldon said after an exchange with the guard in his own tongue.

Tyrion forced himself to smile at the man. "Tell him that it is even better luck to suck on a dwarf's cock."

"Best not. Tigers have been known to have sharp teeth."

A different guard motioned them through the gate, waving a torch at them impatiently. Haldon Halfmaester led the way into Selhorys proper, with Tyrion waddling warily at his heels.

A great square opened up before them. Even at this hour, it was crowded and noisy and ablaze with light. Lanterns swung from iron chains above the doors of inns and pleasure houses, but within the gates, they were made of colored glass, not parchment. To their right a nightfire burned outside a temple of red stone. A priest in scarlet robes stood on the temple balcony, haranguing the small crowd that had gathered around the flames. Elsewhere, travelers sat playing *cyvasse* in front of an inn, drunken soldiers wandered in and out of what was obviously a brothel, a woman beat a mule outside a stable. A two-wheeled cart went rumbling past them, pulled by a white dwarf elephant. *This is another world,* thought Tyrion, *but not so different from the world I know.*

The square was dominated by a white marble statue of a headless man in impossibly ornate armor, astride a warhorse similarly arrayed. "Who might that be?" wondered Tyrion.

"Triarch Horonno. A Volantene hero from the Century of Blood. He was returned as triarch every year for forty years, until he wearied of elections and declared himself triarch for life. The Volantenes were not amused. He was put to death soon after. Tied between two elephants and torn in half."

"His statue seems to lack a head."

"He was a tiger. When the elephants came to power, their followers went on a rampage, knocking the heads from the statues of those they blamed for all the wars and deaths." He shrugged. "That was another age. Come, we'd best hear what that priest is going on about. I swear I heard the name Daenerys."

Across the square they joined the growing throng outside the red temple. With the locals towering above him on every hand, the little man found it hard to see much beyond their arses. He could hear most every word the priest was saying, but that was not to say he understood them. "Do you understand what he is saying?" he asked Haldon in the Common Tongue.

"I would if I did not have a dwarf piping in my ear."

"I do not *pipe*." Tyrion crossed his arms and looked behind him, studying the faces of the men and women who had stopped to listen. Everywhere he turned, he saw tattoos. *Slaves. Four of every five of them are slaves.*

"The priest is calling on the Volantenes to go to war," the Halfmaester told him, "but on the side of right, as soldiers of the Lord of Light, R'hllor who made the sun and stars and fights eternally against the darkness. Nyessos and Malaquo have turned away from the light, he says, their hearts darkened by the yellow harpies from the east. He says . . ."

"*Dragons.* I understood that word. He said *dragons.*"

"Aye. The dragons have come to carry her to glory."

"Her. Daenerys?"

Haldon nodded. "Benerro has sent forth the word from Volantis. Her coming is the fulfillment of an ancient prophecy. From smoke and salt was she born to make the world anew. She is Azor Ahai returned . . . and her triumph over darkness will bring a summer that will never end . . . death itself will bend its knee, and all those who die fighting in her cause shall be reborn . . ."

"Do I have to be reborn in this same body?" asked Tyrion. The crowd was growing thicker. He could feel them pressing in around them. "Who is Benerro?"

Haldon raised an eyebrow. "High Priest of the red temple in Volantis. Flame of Truth, Light of Wisdom, First Servant of the Lord of Light, Slave of R'hllor."

The only red priest Tyrion had ever known was Thoros of Myr, the portly, genial, wine-stained roisterer who had loitered about Robert's court swilling the king's finest vintages and setting his sword on fire for mêlées. "Give me priests who are fat and corrupt and cynical," he told Haldon, "the sort who like to sit on soft satin cushions, nibble sweetmeats, and diddle little boys. It's the ones who believe in gods who make the trouble."

"It may be that we can use this trouble to our advantage. I know where we may find answers." Haldon led them past the headless hero to where a big stone inn fronted on the square. The ridged shell of some immense turtle hung above its door, painted in garish colors. Inside a hundred dim red candles burned like distant stars. The air was fragrant with the smell of roasted meat and spices, and a slave girl with a turtle on one cheek was pouring pale green wine.

Haldon paused in the doorway. "There. Those two."

In the alcove two men sat over a carved stone *cyvasse* table, squinting at their pieces by the light of a red candle. One was gaunt and sallow, with thinning black hair and a blade of a nose. The other was wide of shoulder and round of belly, with corkscrew ringlets tumbling past his collar. Neither deigned to look up from their game until Haldon drew up a chair between them and said, "My dwarf plays better *cyvasse* than both of you combined."

The bigger man raised his eyes to gaze at the intruders in distaste and said something in the tongue of Old Volantis, too fast for Tyrion to hope to follow. The thinner one leaned back in his chair. "Is he for sale?" he asked in the Common Tongue of Westeros. "The triarch's grotesquerie is in need of a *cyvasse*-playing dwarf."

"Yollo is no slave."

"What a pity." The thin man shifted an onyx elephant.

Across the *cyvasse* table, the man behind the alabaster army pursed his lips in disapproval. He moved his heavy horse.

"A blunder," said Tyrion. He had as well play his part.

"Just so," the thin man said. He answered with his own heavy horse. A flurry of quick moves followed, until finally the thin man smiled and said, "Death, my friend."

The big man glowered at the board, then rose and growled something in his own tongue. His opponent laughed. "Come now. The dwarf does not stink as bad as that." He beckoned Tyrion toward the empty chair. "Up with you, little man. Put your silver on the table, and we will see how well you play the game."

Which game? Tyrion might have asked. He climbed onto the chair. "I play better with a full belly and a cup of wine to hand." The thin man turned obligingly and called for the slave girl to fetch them food and drink.

Haldon said, "The noble Qavo Nogarys is the customs officer here in Selhorys. I have never once defeated him at *cyvasse*."

Tyrion understood. "Perhaps I will be more fortunate." He opened his purse and stacked silver coins beside the board, one atop another until finally Qavo smiled.

As each of them was setting up his pieces behind the *cyvasse* screen, Haldon said, "What news from downriver? Will it be war?"

Qavo shrugged. "The Yunkai'i would have it so. They style themselves the Wise Masters. Of their wisdom I cannot speak, but they do not lack for cunning. Their envoy came to us with chests of gold and gems and two hundred slaves, nubile girls and smooth-skinned boys trained in the way of the seven sighs. I am told his feasts are memorable and his bribes lavish."

"The Yunkishmen have bought your triarchs?"

"Only Nyessos." Qavo removed the screen and studied the placement of Tyrion's army. "Malaquo may be old and toothless, but he is a tiger still, and Doniphos will not be returned as triarch. The city thirsts for war."

"Why?" wondered Tyrion. "Meereen is long leagues across the sea. How has this sweet child queen offended Old Volantis?"

"Sweet?" Qavo laughed. "If even half the stories coming back from Slaver's Bay are true, this *child* is a monster. They say that she is bloodthirsty, that those who speak against her are impaled on spikes to die lingering deaths. They say she is a sorceress who feeds her dragons on the flesh of newborn babes, an oathbreaker who mocks the gods, breaks truces, threatens envoys, and turns on those who have served her loyally. They say her lust cannot be sated, that she mates with men, women, eunuchs, even dogs and children, and woe betide the lover who fails to satisfy her. She gives her body to men to take their souls in thrall."

Oh, good, thought Tyrion. *If she gives her body to me, she is welcome to my soul, small and stunted though it is.*

"They say," said Haldon. "By *they,* you mean the slavers, the exiles she drove from Astapor and Meereen. Mere calumnies."

"The best calumnies are spiced with truth," suggested Qavo, "but the girl's true sin cannot be denied. This arrogant child has taken it upon herself to smash the slave trade, but that traffic was never confined to Slaver's Bay. It was part of the sea of trade that spanned the world, and the dragon queen has clouded the water. Behind the Black Wall, lords of ancient blood sleep poorly, listening as their kitchen slaves sharpen their long knives. Slaves grow our food, clean our streets, teach our young. They guard our walls, row our galleys, fight our battles. And now when they look east, they see this young queen shining from afar, this *breaker of chains.* The Old Blood cannot suffer that. Poor men hate her too. Even the vilest beggar stands higher than a slave. This dragon queen would rob him of that consolation."

Tyrion advanced his spearmen. Qavo replied with his light horse. Tyrion moved his crossbowmen up a square and said, "The red priest outside seemed to think Volantis should fight for this silver queen, not against her."

"The red priests would be wise to hold their tongues," said Qavo Nogarys. "Already there has been fighting between their followers and those who worship other gods. Benerro's rantings will only serve to bring a savage wrath down upon his head."

"What rantings?" the dwarf asked, toying with his rabble.

The Volantene waved a hand. "In Volantis, thousands of slaves and freedmen crowd the temple plaza every night to hear Benerro shriek of bleeding stars and a sword of fire that will cleanse the world. He has been preaching that Volantis will surely burn if the triarchs take up arms against the silver queen."

"That's a prophecy even I could make. Ah, supper."

Supper was a plate of roasted goat served on a bed of sliced onions. The meat was spiced and fragrant, charred outside and red and juicy within. Tyrion plucked at a piece. It was so hot it burned his fingers, but so good he could not help but reach for another chunk. He washed it down with the pale green Volantene liquor, the closest thing he'd had to wine for ages. "Very good," he said, plucking up his dragon. "The most powerful piece in the game," he announced, as he removed one of Qavo's elephants. "And Daenerys Targaryen has three, it's said."

"Three," Qavo allowed, "against thrice three thousand enemies. Grazdan mo Eraz was not the only envoy sent out from the Yellow City. When the Wise Masters move against Meereen, the legions of New Ghis will fight beside them. Tolosi. Elyrians. Even the Dothraki."

"You have Dothraki outside your own gates," Haldon said.

"Khal Pono." Qavo waved a pale hand in dismissal. "The horselords come, we give them gifts, the horselords go." He moved his catapult again, closed his hand around Tyrion's alabaster dragon, removed it from the board.

The rest was slaughter, though the dwarf held on another dozen moves. "The time has come for bitter tears," Qavo said at last, scooping up the pile of silver. "Another game?"

"No need," said Haldon. "My dwarf has had his lesson in humility. I think it is best we get back to our boat."

Outside in the square, the nightfire was still burning, but the priest was gone and the crowd was long dispersed. The glow of candles glimmered from the windows of the brothel. From inside came the sound of women's laughter. "The night is still young," said Tyrion. "Qavo may not have told us everything. And whores hear much and more from the men they service."

"Do you need a woman so badly, Yollo?"

"A man grows weary of having no lovers but his fingers." *Selhorys may be where whores go. Tysha might be in there even now, with tears tattooed upon her cheek.* "I almost drowned. A man needs a woman after that. Besides, I need to make sure my prick hasn't turned to stone."

The Halfmaester laughed. "I will wait for you in the tavern by the gate. Do not be too long about your business."

"Oh, have no fear on that count. Most women prefer to be done with me as quickly as they can."

The brothel was a modest one compared to those the dwarf had been wont to frequent in Lannisport and King's Landing. The proprietor did not seem to speak any tongue but that of Volantis, but he understood the *clank* of silver well enough and led Tyrion through an archway into a long room that smelled of incense, where four bored slave girls were lounging about in various states of undress. Two had seen at least forty namedays come and go, he guessed; the youngest was perhaps fifteen or sixteen. None was as hideous as the whores he'd seen working the docks, though they fell well short of beauty. One was plainly pregnant. Another was just fat, and sported iron rings in both her nipples. All four had tears tattooed beneath one eye.

"Do you have a girl who speaks the tongue of Westeros?" asked Tyrion. The proprietor squinted, uncomprehending, so he repeated the question in High Valyrian. This time the man seemed to grasp a word or three and replied in Volantene. "Sunset girl" was all the dwarf could get out of his answer. He took that to mean a girl from the Sunset Kingdoms.

There was only one such in the house, and she was not Tysha. She had freckled cheeks and tight red curls upon her head, which gave promise of freckled breasts and red hair between her legs. "She'll do," said Tyrion, "and I'll have a flagon too. Red wine with red flesh." The whore was looking at his noseless face with revulsion in her eyes. "Do I offend you, sweetling? I am an offensive creature, as my father would be glad to tell you if he were not dead and rotting."

Though she did look Westerosi, the girl spoke not a word of the Common Tongue. *Perhaps she was captured by some slaver as a child.* Her bedchamber was small, but there was a Myrish carpet on the floor and a mattress stuffed with feathers in place of straw. *I have seen worse.* "Will you give me your name?" he asked, as he took a cup of wine from her. "No?" The wine was strong and sour and required no translation. "I suppose I shall settle for your cunt." He wiped his mouth with the back of his hand. "Have you ever bedded a monster before? Now's as good a time as any. Out of your clothes and onto your back, if it please you. Or not."

She looked at him uncomprehending, until he took the flagon from her hands and lifted her skirts up over her head. After that she understood what was required of her, though she did not prove the liveliest of partners. Tyrion had been so long without a woman that he spent himself inside her on the third thrust.

He rolled off feeling more ashamed than sated. *This was a mistake. What a wretched creature I've become.* "Do you know a woman by the name of Tysha?" he asked, as he watched his seed dribble out of her onto the bed. The whore did not respond. "Do you know where whores go?" She did not answer that one either. Her back was criss-crossed by ridges of scar tissue. *This girl is as good as dead. I have just fucked a corpse.* Even her eyes looked dead. *She does not even have the strength to loathe me.*

He needed wine. A lot of wine. He seized the flagon with both hands and raised it to his lips. The wine ran red. Down his throat, down his chin. It dripped from his beard and soaked the feather bed. In the candlelight it looked as dark as the wine that had poisoned Joffrey. When he was done he tossed the empty flagon aside and half-rolled and half-staggered to the floor, groping for a chamber pot. There was none to be found. His stomach heaved, and he found himself on his knees, retching on the carpet, that wonderful thick Myrish carpet, as comforting as lies.

The whore cried out in distress. *They will blame her for this,* he realized, ashamed. "Cut off my head and take it to King's Landing," Tyrion urged her. "My sister will make a lady of you, and no one will ever whip you again." She did not understand that either, so he shoved her legs apart, crawled between them, and took her once more. That much she could comprehend, at least.

Afterward the wine was done and so was he, so he wadded up the girl's clothing and tossed it at the door. She took the hint and fled, leaving him alone in the darkness, sinking deeper into his feather bed. *I am stinking drunk.* He dare not close his eyes, for fear of sleep. Beyond the veil of dream, the Sorrows were waiting for him. Stone steps ascending endlessly, steep and slick and treacherous, and somewhere at the top, the Shrouded Lord. *I do not want to meet the Shrouded Lord.* Tyrion fumbled back into his clothes again and groped his way to the stair. *Griff will flay me. Well, why not? If ever a dwarf deserved a skinning, I'm him.*

Halfway down the steps, he lost his footing. Somehow he managed to break his tumble with his hands and turn it into a clumsy thumping cartwheel. The whores in the room below looked up in astonishment when he landed at the foot of the steps. Tyrion rolled onto his feet and gave them a bow. "I am more agile when I'm drunk." He turned to the proprietor. "I fear I ruined your carpet. The girl's not to blame. Let me pay." He pulled out a fistful of coins and tossed them at the man.

"*Imp,*" a deep voice said, behind him.

In the corner of the room, a man sat in a pool of shadow, with a whore squirming on his lap. *I never saw that girl. If I had, I would have taken her upstairs instead of freckles.* She was younger than the others, slim and pretty, with long silvery hair. Lyseni, at a guess . . . but the man whose lap she filled was from the Seven Kingdoms. Burly and broad-shouldered, forty if he was a day, and maybe older. Half his head was bald, but coarse stubble covered his cheeks and chin, and hair grew thickly down his arms, sprouting even from his knuckles.

Tyrion did not like the look of him. He liked the big black bear on his surcoat even less. *Wool. He's wearing wool, in this heat. Who else but a knight would be so fucking mad?* "How pleasant to hear the Common Tongue so far from home," he made himself say, "but I fear you have mistaken me. My name is Hugor Hill. May I buy you a cup of wine, my friend?"

"I've drunk enough." The knight shoved his whore aside and got to his feet. His sword belt hung on a peg beside him. He took it down and drew his blade. Steel whispered against leather. The whores were watching avidly, candlelight shining in their eyes. The proprietor had vanished. "You're mine, *Hugor.*"

Tyrion could no more outrun him than outfight him. Drunk as he was, he could not even hope to outwit him. He spread his hands. "And what do you mean to do with me?"

"Deliver you," the knight said, "to the queen."

DAENERYS

Galazza Galare arrived at the Great Pyramid attended by a dozen White Graces, girls of noble birth who were still too young to have served their year in the temple's pleasure gardens. They made for a pretty portrait, the proud old woman all in green surrounded by the little girls robed and veiled in white, armored in their innocence.

The queen welcomed them warmly, then summoned Missandei to see that the girls were fed and entertained whilst she shared a private supper with the Green Grace.

Her cooks had prepared them a magnificent meal of honeyed lamb, fragrant with crushed mint and served with the small green figs she liked so much. Two of Dany's favorite hostages served the food and kept the cups filled—a doe-eyed little girl called Qezza and a skinny boy named Grazhar. They were brother and sister, and cousins of the Green Grace, who greeted them with kisses when she swept in, and asked them if they had been good.

"They are very sweet, the both of them," Dany assured her. "Qezza sings for me sometimes. She has a lovely voice. And Ser Barristan has been instructing Grazhar and the other boys in the ways of western chivalry."

"They are of my blood," the Green Grace said, as Qezza filled her cup with a dark red wine. "It is good to know they have pleased Your

Radiance. I hope I may do likewise." The old woman's hair was white and her skin was parchment thin, but the years had not dimmed her eyes. They were as green as her robes; sad eyes, full of wisdom. "If you will forgive my saying so, Your Radiance looks . . . weary. Are you sleeping?"

It was all Dany could do not to laugh. "Not well. Last night three Qartheen galleys sailed up the Skahazadhan under the cover of darkness. The Mother's Men loosed flights of fire arrows at their sails and flung pots of burning pitch onto their decks, but the galleys slipped by quickly and suffered no lasting harm. The Qartheen mean to close the river to us, as they have closed the bay. And they are no longer alone. Three galleys from New Ghis have joined them, and a carrack out of Tolos." The Tolosi had replied to her request for an alliance by proclaiming her a whore and demanding that she return Meereen to its Great Masters. Even that was preferable to the answer of Mantarys, which came by way of caravan in a cedar chest. Inside she had found the heads of her three envoys, pickled. "Perhaps your gods can help us. Ask them to send a gale and sweep the galleys from the bay."

"I shall pray and make sacrifice. Mayhaps the gods of Ghis will hear me." Galazza Galare sipped her wine, but her eyes did not leave Dany. "Storms rage within the walls as well as without. More freedmen died last night, or so I have been told."

"Three." Saying it left a bitter taste in her mouth. "The cowards broke in on some weavers, freedwomen who had done no harm to anyone. All they did was make beautiful things. I have a tapestry they gave me hanging over my bed. The Sons of the Harpy broke their loom and raped them before slitting their throats."

"This we have heard. And yet Your Radiance has found the courage to answer butchery with mercy. You have not harmed any of the noble children you hold as hostage."

"Not as yet, no." Dany had grown fond of her young charges. Some were shy and some were bold, some sweet and some sullen, but all were innocent. "If I kill my cupbearers, who will pour my wine and serve my supper?" she said, trying to make light of it.

The priestess did not smile. "The Shavepate would feed them to your dragons, it is said. A life for a life. For every Brazen Beast cut down, he would have a child die."

Dany pushed her food about her plate. She dare not glance over to where Grazhar and Qezza stood, for fear that she might cry. *The Shavepate has a harder heart than mine.* They had fought about the hostages half a dozen times. "The Sons of the Harpy are laughing in their pyramids," Skahaz said, just this morning. "What good are hostages if you will not take their heads?" In his eyes, she was only a weak woman. *Hazzea was enough. What good is peace if it must be purchased with the blood of little children?* "These murders are not their doing," Dany told the Green Grace, feebly. "I am no butcher queen."

"And for that Meereen gives thanks," said Galazza Galare. "We have heard that the Butcher King of Astapor is dead."

"Slain by his own soldiers when he commanded them to march out and attack the Yunkai'i." The words were bitter in her mouth. "He was hardly cold before another took his place, calling himself Cleon the Second. That one lasted eight days before his throat was opened. Then his killer claimed the crown. So did the first Cleon's concubine. King Cutthroat and Queen Whore, the Astapori call them. Their followers are fighting battles in the streets, while the Yunkai'i and their sellswords wait outside the walls."

"These are grievous times. Your Radiance, might I presume to offer you my counsel?"

"You know how much I value your wisdom."

"Then heed me now and marry."

"Ah." Dany had been expecting this.

"Oftimes I have heard you say that you are only a young girl. To look at you, you still seem half a child, too young and frail to face such trials by yourself. You need a king beside you to help you bear these burdens."

Dany speared a chunk of lamb, took a bite from it, chewed slowly. "Tell me, can this king puff his cheeks up and blow Xaro's galleys back to Qarth? Can he clap his hands and break the siege of Astapor? Can he put food in the bellies of my children and bring peace back to my streets?"

"Can you?" the Green Grace asked. "A king is not a god, but there is still much that a strong man might do. When my people look at you, they see a conqueror from across the seas, come to murder us and make slaves of our children. A king could change that. A highborn king of pure Ghiscari blood could reconcile the city to your rule. Elsewise, I fear, your reign must end as it began, in blood and fire."

Dany pushed her food about her plate. "And who would the gods of Ghis have me take as my king and consort?"

"Hizdahr zo Loraq," Galazza Galare said firmly.

Dany did not trouble to feign surprise. "Why Hizdahr? Skahaz is noble born as well."

"Skahaz is Kandaq, Hizdahr Loraq. Your Radiance will forgive me, but only one who is not herself Ghiscari would not understand the difference. Oft have I heard that yours is the blood of Aegon the Conqueror, Jaehaerys the Wise, and Daeron the Dragon. The noble Hizdahr is of the blood of Mazdhan the Magnificent, Hazrak the Handsome, and Zharaq the Liberator."

"His forebears are as dead as mine. Will Hizdahr raise their shades to defend Meereen against its enemies? I need a man with ships and swords. You offer me ancestors."

"We are an old people. Ancestors are important to us. Wed Hizdahr zo Loraq and make a son with him, a son whose father is the harpy, whose mother is the dragon. In him the prophecies shall be fulfilled, and your enemies will melt away like snow."

He shall be the stallion that mounts the world. Dany knew how it went with prophecies. They were made of words, and words were wind. There would be no son for Loraq, no heir to unite dragon and harpy. *When the sun rises in the west and sets in the east, when the seas go dry and mountains blow in the wind like leaves.* Only then would her womb quicken once again . . .

. . . but Daenerys Targaryen had other children, tens of thousands who had hailed her as their mother when she broke their chains. She thought of Stalwart Shield, of Missandei's brother, of the woman Rylona Rhee, who had played the harp so beautifully. No marriage would ever bring them back to life, but if a husband could help end the slaughter, then she owed it to her dead to marry.

If I wed Hizdahr, will that turn Skahaz against me? She trusted Skahaz more than she trusted Hizdahr, but the Shavepate would be a disaster as a king. He was too quick to anger, too slow to forgive. She saw no gain in wedding a man as hated as herself. Hizdahr was well respected, so far as she could see. "What does my prospective husband think of this?" she asked the Green Grace. *What does he think of me?*

"Your Grace need only ask him. The noble Hizdahr awaits below. Send down to him if that is your pleasure."

You presume too much, priestess, the queen thought, but she swallowed her anger and made herself smile. "Why not?" She sent for Ser Barristan and told the old knight to bring Hizdahr to her. "It is a long climb. Have the Unsullied help him up."

By the time the nobleman had made the ascent, the Green Grace had finished eating. "If it please Your Magnificence, I will take my leave. You and the noble Hizdahr will have many things to discuss, I do not doubt." The old woman dabbed a smear of honey off her lips, gave Qezza and Grazhar each a parting kiss upon the brow, and fastened her silken veil across her face. "I shall return to the Temple of the Graces and pray for the gods to show my queen the course of wisdom."

When she was gone, Dany let Qezza fill her cup again, dismissed the children, and commanded that Hizdahr zo Loraq be admitted to her presence. *And if he dares say one word about his precious fighting pits, I may have him thrown off the terrace.*

Hizdahr wore a plain green robe beneath a quilted vest. He bowed low when he entered, his face solemn. "Have you no smile for me?" Dany asked him. "Am I as fearful as all that?"

"I always grow solemn in the presence of such beauty."

It was a good start. "Drink with me." Dany filled his cup herself. "You know why you are here. The Green Grace seems to feel that if I take you for my husband, all my woes will vanish."

"I would never make so bold a claim. Men are born to strive and suffer. Our woes only vanish when we die. I can be of help to you, however. I have gold and friends and influence, and the blood of Old Ghis flows in my veins. Though I have never wed, I have two natural children, a boy and a girl, so I can give you heirs. I can reconcile the city to your rule and put an end to this nightly slaughter in the streets."

"Can you?" Dany studied his eyes. "Why should the Sons of the Harpy lay down their knives for you? Are you one of them?"

"No."

"Would you tell me if you were?"

He laughed. "No."

"The Shavepate has ways of finding the truth."

"I do not doubt that Skahaz would soon have me confessing. A day with him, and I will be one of the Harpy's Sons. Two days, and I will be the Harpy. Three, and it will turn out I slew your father too, back in the Sunset Kingdoms when I was yet a boy. Then he will impale me on a stake and you can watch me die . . . but afterward the killings will go on." Hizdahr leaned closer. "Or you can marry me and let me try to stop them."

"Why would you *want* to help me? For the crown?"

"A crown would suit me well, I will not deny that. It is more than that, however. Is it so strange that I would want to protect my own people, as you protect your freedmen? Meereen cannot endure another war, Your Radiance."

That was a good answer, and an honest one. "I have never wanted war. I defeated the Yunkai'i once and spared their city when I might have sacked it. I refused to join King Cleon when he marched against them. Even now, with Astapor besieged, I stay my hand. And Qarth . . . I have never done the Qartheen any harm . . ."

"Not by intent, no, but Qarth is a city of merchants, and they love the clink of silver coins, the gleam of yellow gold. When you smashed the slave trade, the blow was felt from Westeros to Asshai. Qarth depends upon its slaves. So too Tolos, New Ghis, Lys, Tyrosh, Volantis . . . the list is long, my queen."

"Let them come. In me they shall find a sterner foe than Cleon. I would sooner perish fighting than return my children to bondage."

"There may be another choice. The Yunkai'i can be persuaded to allow all your freedmen to remain free, I believe, if Your Worship will agree that the Yellow City may trade and train slaves unmolested from this day forth. No more blood need flow."

"Save for the blood of those slaves that the Yunkai'i will *trade* and *train*," Dany said, but she recognized the truth in his words even so. *It may be that is the best end we can hope for.* "You have not said you love me."

"I will, if it would please Your Radiance."

"That is not the answer of a man in love."

"What is love? Desire? No man with all his parts could ever look on you and not desire you, Daenerys. That is not why I would marry you, however. Before you came Meereen was dying. Our rulers were old men with withered cocks and crones whose puckered cunts were dry as dust. They sat atop their pyramids sipping apricot wine and talking of the glories of the Old Empire whilst the centuries slipped by and the very bricks of the city crumbled all around them. Custom and caution had an iron grip upon us till you awakened us with fire and blood. A new time has come, and new things are possible. Marry me."

He is not hard to look at, Dany told herself, *and he has a king's tongue.* "Kiss me," she commanded.

He took her hand again, and kissed her fingers.

"Not that way. Kiss me as if I were your wife."

Hizdahr took her by the shoulders as tenderly as if she were a baby bird. Leaning forward, he pressed his lips to hers. His kiss was light and dry and quick. Dany felt no stirrings.

"Shall I . . . kiss you again?" he asked when it was over.

"No." On her terrace, in her bathing pool, the little fish would nibble at her legs as she soaked. Even they kissed with more fervor than Hizdahr zo Loraq. "I do not love you."

Hizdahr shrugged. "That may come, in time. It has been known to happen that way."

Not with us, she thought. *Not whilst Daario is so close. It's him I want, not you.* "One day I will want to return to Westeros, to claim the Seven Kingdoms that were my father's."

"One day all men must die, but it serves no good to dwell on death. I prefer to take each day as it comes."

Dany folded her hands together. "Words are wind, even words like *love* and *peace.* I put more trust in deeds. In my Seven Kingdoms, knights go on quests to prove themselves worthy of the maiden that they love. They seek for magic swords, for chests of gold, for crowns stolen from a dragon's hoard."

Hizdahr arched an eyebrow. "The only dragons that I know are yours, and magic swords are even scarcer. I will gladly bring you rings and crowns and chests of gold if that is your desire."

"Peace is my desire. You say that you can help me end the nightly slaughter in my streets. I say *do it.* Put an end to this shadow war, my lord. That is your quest. Give me ninety days and ninety nights without a murder, and I will know that you are worthy of a throne. Can you do that?"

Hizdahr looked thoughtful. "Ninety days and ninety nights without a corpse, and on the ninety-first we wed?"

"Perhaps," said Dany, with a coy look. "Though young girls have been known to be fickle. I may still want a magic sword."

Hizdahr laughed. "Then you shall have that too, Radiance. Your wish is my command. Best tell your seneschal to begin making preparations for our wedding."

"Nothing would please the noble Reznak more." If Meereen knew that a wedding was in the offing, that alone might buy her a few nights' respite, even if Hizdahr's efforts came to naught. *The Shavepate will not be happy with me, but Reznak mo Reznak will dance for joy.* Dany did not know which of those concerned her more. She needed Skahaz and the Brazen Beasts, and she had come to mistrust all of Reznak's counsel. *Beware the perfumed seneschal. Has Reznak made common cause with Hizdahr and the Green Grace and set some trap to snare me?*

No sooner had Hizdahr zo Loraq taken his leave of her than Ser Barristan appeared behind her in his long white cloak. Years of service in the Kingsguard had taught the white knight how to remain unobtrusive when she was entertaining, but he was never far. *He knows,* she saw at once, *and he disapproves.* The lines around his mouth had deepened. "So," she said to him, "it seems that I may wed again. Are you happy for me, ser?"

"If that is your command, Your Grace."

"Hizdahr is not the husband you would have chosen for me."

"It is not my place to choose your husband."

"It is not," she agreed, "but it is important to me that you should understand. My people are bleeding. Dying. A queen belongs not to herself, but to the realm. Marriage or carnage, those are my choices. A wedding or a war."

"Your Grace, may I speak frankly?"

"Always."

"There is a third choice."

"Westeros?"

He nodded. "I am sworn to serve Your Grace, and to keep you safe from harm wherever you may go. My place is by your side, whether here or in King's Landing . . . but your place is back in Westeros, upon the Iron Throne that was your father's. The Seven Kingdoms will never accept Hizdahr zo Loraq as king."

"No more than Meereen will accept Daenerys Targaryen as queen. The Green Grace has the right of that. I need a king beside me, a king of old Ghiscari blood. Elsewise they will always see me as the uncouth barbarian who smashed through their gates, impaled their kin on spikes, and stole their wealth."

"In Westeros you will be the lost child who returns to gladden her father's heart. Your people will cheer when you ride by, and all good men will love you."

"Westeros is far away."

"Lingering here will never bring it any closer. The sooner we take our leave of this place—"

"I know. I *do*." Dany did not know how to make him see. She wanted Westeros as much as he did, but first she must heal Meereen. "Ninety days is a long time. Hizdahr may fail. And if he does, the trying buys me time. Time to make alliances, to strengthen my defenses, to—"

"And if he does not fail? What will Your Grace do then?"

"Her duty." The word felt cold upon her tongue. "You saw my brother Rhaegar wed. Tell me, did he wed for love or duty?"

The old knight hesitated. "Princess Elia was a good woman, Your Grace. She was kind and clever, with a gentle heart and a sweet wit. I know the prince was very fond of her."

Fond, thought Dany. The word spoke volumes. *I could become fond of Hizdahr zo Loraq, in time. Perhaps.*

Ser Barristan went on. "I saw your father and your mother wed as well. Forgive me, but there was no fondness there, and the realm paid dearly for that, my queen."

"Why did they wed if they did not love each other?"

"Your grandsire commanded it. A woods witch had told him that the prince who was promised would be born of their line."

"A woods witch?" Dany was astonished.

"She came to court with Jenny of Oldstones. A stunted thing, grotesque to look upon. A dwarf, most people said, though dear to Lady Jenny, who always claimed that she was one of the children of the forest."

"What became of her?"

"Summerhall." The word was fraught with doom.

Dany sighed. "Leave me now. I am very weary."

"As you command." Ser Barristan bowed and turned to go. But at the door, he stopped. "Forgive me. Your Grace has a visitor. Shall I tell him to return upon the morrow?"

"Who is it?"

"Naharis. The Stormcrows have returned to the city."

Daario. Her heart gave a flutter in her chest. "How long has . . . when did he . . . ?" She could not seem to get the words out.

Ser Barristan seemed to understand. "Your Grace was with the priestess when he arrived. I knew you would not want to be disturbed. The captain's news can wait until the morrow."

"No." *How could I ever hope to sleep, knowing that my captain is so close?* "Send him up at once. And . . . I will have no more need of you this evening. I shall be safe with Daario. Oh, and send Irri and Jhiqui, if you would be so good. And Missandei." *I need to change, to make myself beautiful.*

She said as much to her handmaids when they came. "What does Your Grace wish to wear?" asked Missandei.

Starlight and seafoam, Dany thought, *a wisp of silk that leaves my left breast bare for Daario's delight. Oh, and flowers for my hair.* When first they met, the captain brought her flowers every day, all the way from Yunkai to Meereen. "Bring the grey linen gown with the pearls on the bodice. Oh, and my white lion's pelt." She always felt safer wrapped in Drogo's lionskin.

Daenerys received the captain on her terrace, seated on a carved stone bench beneath a pear tree. A half-moon floated in the sky above the city, attended by a thousand stars. Daario Naharis entered swaggering. *He swaggers even when he is standing still.* The captain wore striped pantaloons tucked into high boots of purple leather, a white silk shirt, a vest of golden rings. His trident beard was purple, his flamboyant mustachios gold, his long curls equal parts of both. On one hip he wore a stiletto, on the other a Dothraki *arakh.* "Bright queen," he said, "you have grown more beautiful in my absence. How is this thing possible?"

The queen was accustomed to such praise, yet somehow the compliment meant more coming from Daario than from the likes of Reznak, Xaro, or Hizdahr. "Captain. They tell us you did us good service in Lhazar." *I have missed you so much.*

"Your captain lives to serve his cruel queen."

"Cruel?"

Moonlight glimmered in his eyes. "He raced ahead of all his men to see her face the sooner, only to be left languishing whilst she ate lamb and figs with some dried-up old woman."

They never told me you were here, Dany thought, *or I might have played the fool and sent for you at once.* "I was supping with the Green Grace." It seemed best not to mention Hizdahr. "I had urgent need of her wise counsel."

"I have only one urgent need: Daenerys."

"Shall I send for food? You must be hungry."

"I have not eaten in two days, but now that I am here, it is enough for me to feast upon your beauty."

"My beauty will not fill up your belly." She plucked down a pear and tossed it at him. "Eat this."

"If my queen commands it." He took a bite of the pear, his gold tooth gleaming. Juice ran down into his purple beard.

The girl in her wanted to kiss him so much it hurt. *His kisses would be hard and cruel,* she told herself, *and he would not care if I cried out or commanded him to stop.* But the queen in her knew that would be folly. "Tell me of your journey."

He gave a careless shrug. "The Yunkai'i sent some hired swords to close the Khyzai Pass. The Long Lances, they name themselves. We descended on them in the night and sent a few to hell. In Lhazar I slew two of my own serjeants for plotting to steal the gems and gold plate my queen had entrusted to me as gifts for the Lamb Men. Elsewise, all went as I had promised."

"How many men did you lose in the fighting?"

"Nine," said Daario, "but a dozen of the Long Lances decided they would sooner be Stormcrows than corpses, so we came out three ahead. I told them they would live longer fighting with your dragons than against them, and they saw the wisdom in my words."

That made her wary. "They might be spying for Yunkai."

"They are too stupid to be spies. You do not know them."

"Neither do you. Do you trust them?"

"I trust all my men. Just as far as I can spit." He spat out a seed and smiled at her suspicions. "Shall I bring their heads to you? I will, if you command it. One is bald and two have braids and one dyes his beard four different colors. What spy would wear such a beard, I ask you? The slinger can put a stone through a gnat's eye at forty paces, and the ugly one has a way with horses, but if my queen says that they must die . . ."

"I did not say that. I only . . . see that you keep your eye on them, that's all." She felt foolish saying it. She always felt a little foolish when she was with Daario. *Gawky and girlish and slow-witted. What must he think of me?* She changed the subject. "Will the Lamb Men send us food?"

"Grain will come down the Skahazadhan by barge, my queen, and other goods by caravan over the Khyzai."

"Not the Skahazadhan. The river has been closed to us. The seas as well. You will have seen the ships out in the bay. The Qartheen have driven off a third of our fishing fleet and seized another third. The others are too frightened to leave port. What little trade we still had has been cut off."

Daario tossed away the pear stem. "Qartheen have milk in their veins. Let them see your dragons, and they'll run."

Dany did not want to talk about the dragons. Farmers still came to her court with burned bones, complaining of missing sheep, though Drogon had not returned to the city. Some reported seeing him north of the river, above the grass of the Dothraki sea. Down in the pit, Viserion had snapped one of his chains; he and Rhaegal grew more savage every day. Once the iron doors had glowed red-hot, her Unsullied told her, and no one dared to touch them for a day. "Astapor is under siege as well."

"This I knew. One of the Long Lances lived long enough to tell us that men were eating one another in the Red City. He said Meereen's turn would come soon, so I cut his tongue out and fed it to a yellow dog. No dog will eat a liar's tongue. When the yellow dog ate his, I knew he spoke the truth."

"I have war inside the city too." She told him of the Harpy's Sons and the Brazen Beasts, of blood upon the bricks. "My enemies are all around me, within the city and without."

"Attack," he said at once. "A man surrounded by foes cannot defend himself. Try, and the axe will take you in the back whilst you are parrying the sword. No. When faced with many enemies, choose the weakest, kill him, ride over him, and escape."

"Where should I escape to?"

"Into my bed. Into my arms. Into my heart." The hilts of Daario's *arakh* and stiletto were wrought in the shape of golden women, naked and wanton. He brushed his thumbs across them in a way that was remarkably obscene and smiled a wicked smile.

Dany felt blood rushing to her face. It was almost as if he were caressing her. *Would he think me wanton too if I pulled him into bed?* He made her want to be his wanton. *I should never see him alone. He is too dangerous to have near me.* "The Green Grace says that I must take a Ghiscari king," she said, flustered. "She urges me to wed the noble Hizdahr zo Loraq."

"That one?" Daario chuckled. "Why not Grey Worm, if you want a eunuch in your bed? Do you *want* a king?"

I want you. "I want peace. I gave Hizdahr ninety days to end the killings. If he does, I will take him for a husband."

"Take me for your husband. I will do it in nine."

You know I cannot do that, she almost said.

"You are fighting shadows when you should be fighting the men who cast them," Daario went on. "Kill them all and take their treasures, I say. Whisper the command, and your Daario will make you a pile of their heads taller than this pyramid."

"If I knew who they were—"

"Zhak and Pahl and Merreq. Them, and all the rest. The Great Masters. Who else would it be?"

He is as bold as he is bloody. "We have no proof this is their work. Would you have me slaughter my own subjects?"

"Your own subjects would gladly slaughter you."

He had been so long away, Dany had almost forgotten what he was. Sellswords were treacherous by nature, she reminded herself. *Fickle, faithless, brutal. He will never be more than he is. He will never be the stuff of kings.* "The pyramids are strong," she explained to him. "We could take them only at great cost. The moment we attack one the others will rise against us."

"Then winkle them out of their pyramids on some pretext. A wedding might serve. Why not? Promise your hand to Hizdahr and all the Great Masters will come to see you married. When they gather in the Temple of the Graces, turn us loose upon them."

Dany was appalled. *He is a monster. A gallant monster, but a monster still.* "Do you take me for the Butcher King?"

"Better the butcher than the meat. All kings are butchers. Are queens so different?"

"This queen is."

Daario shrugged. "Most queens have no purpose but to warm some king's bed and pop out sons for him. If that's the sort of queen you mean to be, best marry Hizdahr."

Her anger flashed. "Have you forgotten who I am?"

"No. Have you?"

Viserys would have his head off for that insolence. "I am the blood of the dragon. Do not presume to teach me lessons." When Dany stood, the lion pelt slipped from her shoulders and tumbled to the ground. "Leave me."

Daario gave her a sweeping bow. "I live to obey."

When he was gone, Daenerys called Ser Barristan back. "I want the Stormcrows back in the field."

"Your Grace? They have only now returned . . ."

"I want them *gone*. Let them scout the Yunkish hinterlands and give protection to any caravans coming over the Khyzai Pass. Henceforth Daario shall make his reports to you. Give him every honor that is due him and see that his men are well paid, but on no account admit him to my presence."

"As you say, Your Grace."

That night she could not sleep but turned and twisted restlessly in her bed. She even went so far as to summon Irri, hoping her caresses might help ease her way to rest, but after a short while she pushed the Dothraki girl away. Irri was sweet and soft and willing, but she was not Daario.

What have I done? she thought, huddled in her empty bed. *I have waited so long for him to come back, and I send him away.* "He would make a monster of me," she whispered, "a butcher queen." But then she thought of Drogon far away, and the dragons in the pit. *There is blood on my hands too, and on my heart. We are not so different, Daario and I. We are both monsters.*

THE LOST LORD

*I*t should not have taken this long, Griff told himself as he paced the deck of the *Shy Maid*. Had they lost Haldon as they had Tyrion Lannister? Could the Volantenes have taken him? *I should have sent Duckfield with him*. Haldon alone could not be trusted; he had proved that in Selhorys when he let the dwarf escape.

The *Shy Maid* was tied up in one of the meaner sections of the long, chaotic riverfront, between a listing poleboat that had not left the pier in years and the gaily painted mummers' barge. The mummers were a loud and lively lot, always quoting speeches at each other and drunk more oft than not.

The day was hot and sticky, as all the days had been since they left the Sorrows. A ferocious southern sun beat down upon the crowded riverfront of Volon Therys, but heat was the last and least of Griff's concerns. The Golden Company was encamped three miles south of town, well north of where he had expected them, and Triarch Malaquo had come north with five thousand foot and a thousand horse to cut them off from the delta road. Daenerys Targaryen remained a world away, and Tyrion Lannister . . . well, he could be most anywhere. If the gods were good, Lannister's severed head was halfway back to King's Landing by now, but more like the dwarf was hale and whole and somewhere close, stinking drunk and plotting some new infamy.

"Where in the seven hells is Haldon?" Griff complained to Lady Lemore. "How long should it take to buy three horses?"

She shrugged. "My lord, wouldn't it be safer to leave the boy here aboard the boat?"

"Safer, yes. Wiser, no. He is a man grown now, and this is the road that he was born to walk." Griff had no patience for this quibbling. He was sick of hiding, sick of waiting, sick of caution. *I do not have time enough for caution.*

"We have gone to great lengths to keep Prince Aegon hidden all these years," Lemore reminded him. "The time will come for him to wash his hair and declare himself, I know, but that time is not now. Not to a camp of sellswords."

"If Harry Strickland means him ill, hiding him on the *Shy Maid* will not protect him. Strickland has ten thousand swords at his command. We have Duck. Aegon is all that could be wanted in a prince. They need to see that, Strickland and the rest. These are his own men."

"His because they're bought and paid for. Ten thousand armed strangers, plus hangers-on and camp followers. All it takes is one to bring us all to ruin. If Hugor's head was worth a lord's honors, how much will Cersei Lannister pay for the rightful heir to the Iron Throne? You do not know these men, my lord. It has been a dozen years since you last rode with the Golden Company, and your old friend is dead."

Blackheart. Myles Toyne had been so full of life the last time Griff had left him, it was hard to accept that he was gone. *A golden skull atop a pole, and Homeless Harry Strickland in his place.* Lemore was not wrong, he knew. Whatever their sires or their grandsires might have been back in Westeros before their exile, the men of the Golden Company were sell-swords now, and no sellsword could be trusted. Even so . . .

Last night he'd dreamt of Stoney Sept again. Alone, with sword in hand, he ran from house to house, smashing down doors, racing up stairs, leaping from roof to roof, as his ears rang to the sound of distant bells. Deep bronze booms and silver chiming pounded through his skull, a maddening cacophony of noise that grew ever louder until it seemed as if his head would explode.

Seventeen years had come and gone since the Battle of the Bells, yet the sound of bells ringing still tied a knot in his guts. Others might claim that the realm was lost when Prince Rhaegar fell to Robert's warhammer on the Trident, but the Battle of the Trident would never have been fought if the griffin had only slain the stag there in Stoney Sept. *The bells tolled for all of us that day. For Aerys and his queen, for Elia of Dorne and her little daughter, for every true man and honest woman in the Seven Kingdoms. And for my silver prince.*

"The plan was to reveal Prince Aegon only when we reached Queen Daenerys," Lemore was saying.

"That was when we believed the girl was coming west. Our dragon queen has burned that plan to ash, and thanks to that fat fool in Pentos, we have grasped the she-dragon by the tail and burned our fingers to the bone."

"Illyrio could not have been expected to know that the girl would choose to remain at Slaver's Bay."

"No more than he knew that the Beggar King would die young, or that Khal Drogo would follow him into the grave. Very little of what the fat man has anticipated has come to pass." Griff slapped the hilt of his longsword with a gloved hand. "I have danced to the fat man's pipes for years, Lemore. What has it availed us? The prince is a man grown. His time is—"

"*Griff,*" Yandry called loudly, above the clanging of the mummers' bell. "It's Haldon."

So it was. The Halfmaester looked hot and bedraggled as he made his way along the waterfront to the foot of the pier. Sweat had left dark rings beneath the arms of his light linen robes, and he had the same sour look on his long face as at Selhorys, when he returned to the *Shy Maid* to confess that the dwarf was gone. He was leading three horses, however, and that was all that mattered.

"Bring the boy," Griff told Lemore. "See that he's ready."

"As you say," she answered, unhappily.

So be it. He had grown fond of Lemore, but that did not mean he required her approval. Her task had been to instruct the prince in the doctrines of the Faith, and she had done that. No amount of prayer would put him on the Iron Throne, however. That was Griff's task. He had failed Prince Rhaegar once. He would not fail his son, not whilst life remained in his body.

Haldon's horses did not please him. "Were these the best that you could find?" he complained to the Halfmaester.

"They were," said Haldon, in an irritated tone, "and you had best not ask what they cost us. With Dothraki across the river, half the populace of Volon Therys has decided they would sooner be elsewhere, so horseflesh grows more expensive every day."

I should have gone myself. After Selhorys, he had found it difficult to put the same trust in Haldon as previously. *He let the dwarf beguile him with that glib tongue of his. Let him wander off into a whorehouse alone while he lingered like a mooncalf in the square.* The brothel keeper had insisted that the little man had been carried off at swordpoint, but Griff was still not sure he believed that. The Imp was clever enough to have conspired in his own escape. This drunken captor that the whores spoke of could have been some henchman in his hire. *I share the blame. After the dwarf put himself between Aegon and the stone man, I let down my guard. I should have slit his throat the first time I laid eyes on him.*

"They will do well enough, I suppose," he told Haldon. "The camp is only three miles south." The *Shy Maid* would have gotten them there more quickly, but he preferred to keep Harry Strickland ignorant of where he and the prince had been. Nor did he relish the prospect of splashing through the shallows to climb some muddy riverbank. That sort of entrance might serve for a sellsword and his son, but not for a great lord and his prince.

When the lad emerged from the cabin with Lemore by his side, Griff looked him over carefully from head to heel. The prince wore sword and dagger, black boots polished to a high sheen, a black cloak lined with blood-red silk. With his hair washed and cut and freshly dyed a deep, dark blue, his eyes looked blue as well. At his throat he wore three huge square-cut rubies on a chain of black iron, a gift from Magister Illyrio. *Red and black. Dragon colors.* That was good. "You look a proper prince," he told the boy. "Your father would be proud if he could see you."

Young Griff ran his fingers through his hair. "I am sick of this blue dye. We should have washed it out."

"Soon enough." Griff would be glad to go back to his own true colors too, though his once red hair had gone to grey. He clapped the lad on the shoulder. "Shall we go? Your army awaits your coming."

"I like the sound of that. My army." A smile flashed across his face, then vanished. "Are they, though? They're sellswords. Yollo warned me to trust no one."

"There is wisdom in that," Griff admitted. It might have been different if Blackheart still commanded, but Myles Toyne was four years dead, and Homeless Harry Strickland was a different sort of man. He would not say that to the boy, however. That dwarf had already planted enough doubts in his young head. "Not every man is what he seems, and a prince especially has good cause to be wary . . . but go too far down that road, and the mistrust can poison you, make you sour and fearful." *King Aerys was one such. By the end, even Rhaegar saw that plain enough.* "You would do best to walk a middle course. Let men earn your trust with leal service . . . but when they do, be generous and openhearted."

The boy nodded. "I will remember."

They gave the prince the best of the three horses, a big grey gelding so pale that he was almost white. Griff and Haldon rode beside him on lesser mounts. The road ran south beneath the high white walls of Volon Therys for a good half mile. Then they left the town behind, following the winding course of the Rhoyne through willow groves and poppy fields and past a tall wooden windmill whose blades creaked like old bones as they turned.

They found the Golden Company beside the river as the sun was lowering in the west. It was a camp that even Arthur Dayne might have approved of—compact, orderly, defensible. A deep ditch had been dug around it, with sharpened stakes inside. The tents stood in rows, with broad avenues between them. The latrines had been placed beside the river, so the current would wash away the wastes. The horse lines were to the north, and beyond them, two dozen elephants grazed beside the water, pulling up reeds with their trunks. Griff glanced at the great grey beasts with approval. *There is not a warhorse in all of Westeros that will stand against them.*

Tall battle standards of cloth-of-gold flapped atop lofty poles along the perimeters of the camp. Beneath them, armed and armored sentries walked their rounds with spears and crossbows, watching every approach. Griff had feared that the company might have grown lax under Harry Strickland, who had always seemed more concerned with making friends than enforcing discipline; but it would seem his worries had been misplaced.

At the gate, Haldon said something to the serjeant of guards, and a runner was sent off to find a captain. When he turned up, he was just as ugly as the last time Griff laid eyes on him. A big-bellied, shambling hulk of a man, the sellsword had a seamed face crisscrossed with old scars. His right ear looked as if a dog had chewed on it and his left was missing. "Have they made *you* a captain, Flowers?" Griff said. "I thought the Golden Company had standards."

"It's worse than that, you bugger," said Franklyn Flowers. "They knighted me as well." He clasped Griff by the forearm, pulled him into a bone-crushing hug. "You look awful, even for a man's been dead a dozen years. Blue hair, is it? When Harry said you'd be turning up, I almost shit myself. And Haldon, you icy cunt, good to see you too. Still have that stick up your arse?" He turned to Young Griff. "And this would be . . ."

"My squire. Lad, this is Franklyn Flowers."

The prince acknowledged him with a nod. "Flowers is a bastard name. You're from the Reach."

"Aye. My mother was a washerwoman at Cider Hall till one of milord's sons raped her. Makes me a sort o' brown apple Fossoway, the way I see it." Flowers waved them through the gate. "Come with me. Strickland's called all the officers to his tent. War council. The bloody Volantenes are rattling their spears and demanding to know our intentions."

The men of the Golden Company were outside their tents, dicing, drinking, and swatting away flies. Griff wondered how many of them knew who he was. *Few enough. Twelve years is a long time.* Even the men who'd ridden with him might not recognize the exile lord Jon

Connington of the fiery red beard in the lined, clean-shaved face and dyed blue hair of the sellsword Griff. So far as most of them were concerned, Connington had drunk himself to death in Lys after being driven from the company in disgrace for stealing from the war chest. The shame of the lie still stuck in his craw, but Varys had insisted it was necessary. "We want no songs about the gallant exile," the eunuch had tittered, in that mincing voice of his. "Those who die heroic deaths are long remembered, thieves and drunks and cravens soon forgotten."

What does a eunuch know of a man's honor? Griff had gone along with the Spider's scheme for the boy's sake, but that did not mean he liked it any better. *Let me live long enough to see the boy sit the Iron Throne, and Varys will pay for that slight and so much more. Then we'll see who's soon forgotten.*

The captain-general's tent was made of cloth-of-gold and surrounded by a ring of pikes topped with gilded skulls. One skull was larger than the rest, grotesquely malformed. Below it was a second, no larger than a child's fist. *Maelys the Monstrous and his nameless brother.* The other skulls had a sameness to them, though several had been cracked and splintered by the blows that had slain them, and one had filed, pointed teeth. "Which one is Myles?" Griff found himself asking.

"There. On the end." Flowers pointed. "Wait. I'll go announce you." He slipped inside the tent, leaving Griff to contemplate the gilded skull of his old friend. In life, Ser Myles Toyne had been ugly as sin. His famous forebear, the dark and dashing Terrence Toyne of whom the singers sang, had been so fair of face that even the king's mistress could not resist him; but Myles had been possessed of jug ears, a crooked jaw, and the biggest nose that Jon Connington had ever seen. When he smiled at you, though, none of that mattered. Blackheart, his men had named him, for the sigil on his shield. Myles had loved the name and all it hinted at. "A captain-general should be feared, by friend and foe alike," he had once confessed. "If men think me cruel, so much the better." The truth was otherwise. Soldier to the bone, Toyne was fierce but always fair, a father to his men and always generous to the exile lord Jon Connington.

Death had robbed him of his ears, his nose, and all his warmth. The smile remained, transformed into a glittering golden grin. All the skulls were grinning, even Bittersteel's on the tall pike in the center. *What does he have to grin about? He died defeated and alone, a broken man in an alien land.* On his deathbed, Ser Aegor Rivers had famously commanded his men to boil the flesh from his skull, dip it in gold, and carry it before them when they crossed the sea to retake Westeros. His successors had followed his example.

Jon Connington might have been one of those successors if his exile had gone otherwise. He had spent five years with the company, rising from the ranks to a place of honor at Toyne's right hand. Had he stayed, it might well have been him the men turned to after Myles died, instead of Harry Strickland. But Griff did not regret the path he'd chosen. *When I return to Westeros, it will not be as a skull atop a pole.*

Flowers stepped out of the tent. "Go on in."

The high officers of the Golden Company rose from stools and camp chairs as they entered. Old friends greeted Griff with smiles and embraces, the new men more formally. *Not all of them are as glad to see us as they would have me believe.* He sensed knives behind some of the smiles. Until quite recently, most of them had believed that Lord Jon Connington was safely in his grave, and no doubt many felt that was a fine place for him, a man who would steal from his brothers-in-arms. Griff might have felt the same way in their place.

Ser Franklyn did the introductions. Some of the sellsword captains bore bastard names, as Flowers did: Rivers, Hill, Stone. Others claimed names that had once loomed large in the histories of the Seven Kingdoms; Griff counted two Strongs, three Peakes, a Mudd, a Mandrake, a Lothston, a pair of Coles. Not all were genuine, he knew. In the free companies, a man could call himself whatever he chose. By any name, the sellswords displayed a rude splendor. Like many in their trade, they kept their worldly wealth upon their persons: jeweled swords, inlaid armor, heavy torcs, and fine silks were much in evidence, and every man there wore a lord's ransom in golden arm rings. Each ring signified one year's service with the Golden Company. Marq Mandrake, whose pox-scarred face had a hole in one cheek where a slave's mark had been burned away, wore a chain of golden skulls as well.

Not every captain was of Westerosi blood. Black Balaq, a white-haired Summer Islander with skin dark as soot, commanded the company's archers, as in Blackheart's day. He wore a feathered cloak of green and orange, magnificent to behold. The cadaverous Volantene, Gorys Edoryen, had replaced Strickland as paymaster. A leopard skin was draped across one shoulder, and hair as red as blood tumbled to his shoulders in oiled ringlets though his pointed beard was black. The spymaster was new to Griff, a Lyseni named Lysono Maar, with lilac eyes and white-gold hair and lips that would have been the envy of a whore. At first glance, Griff had almost taken him for a woman. His fingernails were painted purple, and his earlobes dripped with pearls and amethysts.

Ghosts and liars, Griff thought, as he surveyed their faces. *Revenants from forgotten wars, lost causes, failed rebellions, a brotherhood of the failed and the fallen, the disgraced and the disinherited. This is my army. This is our best hope.*

He turned to Harry Strickland.

Homeless Harry looked little like a warrior. Portly, with a big round head, mild grey eyes, and thinning hair that he brushed sideways to conceal a bald spot, Strickland sat in a camp chair soaking his feet in a tub of salt water. "You will pardon me if I do not rise," he said by way of greeting. "Our march was wearisome, and my toes are prone to blisters. It is a curse."

It is a mark of weakness. You sound like an old woman. The Stricklands had been part of the Golden Company since its founding, Harry's great-grandsire having lost his lands when he rose with the Black Dragon during the first Blackfyre Rebellion. "Gold for four generations," Harry would boast, as if four generations of exile and defeat were something to take pride in.

"I can make you an ointment for that," said Haldon, "and there are certain mineral salts that will toughen your skin."

"That is kind of you." Strickland beckoned to his squire. "Watkyn, wine for our friends."

"Thank you, but no," said Griff. "We will drink water."

"As you prefer." The captain-general smiled up at the prince. "And this must be your son."

Does he know? Griff wondered. *How much did Myles tell him?* Varys had been adamant about the need for secrecy. The plans that he and Illyrio had made with Blackheart had been known to them alone. The rest of the company had been left ignorant. What they did not know they could not let slip.

That time was done, though. "No man could have asked for a worthier son," Griff said, "but the lad is not of my blood, and his name is not Griff. My lords, I give you Aegon Targaryen, firstborn son of Rhaegar, Prince of Dragonstone, by Princess Elia of Dorne . . . soon, with your help, to be Aegon, the Sixth of His Name, King of Andals, the Rhoynar, and the First Men, and Lord of the Seven Kingdoms."

Silence greeted his announcement. Someone cleared his throat. One of the Coles refilled his wine cup from the flagon. Gorys Edoryen played with one of his corkscrew ringlets and murmured something in a tongue Griff did not know. Laswell Peake coughed, Mandrake and Lothston exchanged a glance. *They know,* Griff realized then. *They have known all along.* He turned to look at Harry Strickland. "When did you tell them?"

The captain-general wriggled his blistered toes in his footbath. "When we reached the river. The company was restless, with good reason. We walked away from an easy campaign in the Disputed Lands, and for what? So we could swelter in this god-awful heat watching our coins melt away and our blades go to rust whilst I turn away rich contracts?"

That news made Griff's skin crawl. "Who?"

"The Yunkishmen. The envoy that they sent to woo Volantis has already dispatched three free companies to Slaver's Bay. He wishes us to be the fourth and offers twice what Myr was paying us, plus a slave for every man in the company, ten for every officer, and a hundred choice maidens all for me."

Bloody hell. "That would require thousands of slaves. Where do the Yunkishmen expect to find so many?"

"In Meereen." Strickland beckoned to his squire. "Watkyn, a towel.

This water's growing cool, and my toes have wrinkled up like raisins. No, not that towel, the soft one."

"You refused him," said Griff.

"I told him I would think on his proposal." Harry winced as his squire toweled his feet. "Gentle with the toes. Think of them as thin-skinned grapes, lad. You want to dry them without crushing them. *Pat,* do not scrub. Yes, like that." He turned back to Griff. "A blunt refusal would have been unwise. The men might rightly ask if I had taken leave of my wits."

"You will have work for your blades soon enough."

"Will we?" asked Lysono Maar. "I assume you know that the Targaryen girl has not started for the west?"

"We heard that tale in Selhorys."

"No tale. Simple truth. The why of it is harder to grasp. Sack Meereen, aye, why not? I would have done the same in her place. The slaver cities reek of gold, and conquest requires coin. But why linger? Fear? Madness? Sloth?"

"The why of it does not matter." Harry Strickland unrolled a pair of striped woolen stockings. "She is in Meereen and we are here, where the Volantenes grow daily more unhappy with our presence. We came to raise up a king and queen who would lead us home to Westeros, but this Targaryen girl seems more intent on planting olive trees than in reclaiming her father's throne. Meanwhile, her foes gather. Yunkai, New Ghis, Tolos. Bloodbeard and the Tattered Prince will both be in the field against her . . . and soon enough the fleets of Old Volantis will descend on her as well. What does she have? Bedslaves with sticks?"

"Unsullied," said Griff. "And dragons."

"Dragons, aye," the captain-general said, "but young ones, hardly more than hatchlings." Strickland eased his sock over his blisters and up his ankle. "How much will they avail her when all these armies close about her city like a fist?"

Tristan Rivers drummed his fingers on his knee. "All the more reason that we must reach her quickly, I say. If Daenerys will not come to us, we must go to Daenerys."

"Can we walk across the waves, ser?" asked Lysono Maar. "I tell you again, we cannot reach the silver queen by sea. I slipped into Volantis myself, posing as a trader, to learn how many ships might be available to us. The harbor teems with galleys, cogs, and carracks of every sort and size, yet even so I soon found myself consorting with smugglers and pirates. We have ten thousand men in the company, as I am sure Lord Connington remembers from his years of service with us. Five hundred knights, each with three horses. Five hundred squires, with one mount apiece. And elephants, we must not forget the elephants. A pirate ship will not suffice. We would need a pirate *fleet* . . . and even if we found one, the word has come back from Slaver's Bay that Meereen has been closed off by blockade."

"We could feign acceptance of the Yunkish offer," urged Gorys Edoryen. "Allow the Yunkai'i to transport us to the east, then return their gold beneath the walls of Meereen."

"One broken contract is stain enough upon the honor of the company." Homeless Harry Strickland paused with his blistered foot in hand. "Let me remind you, it was Myles Toyne who put his seal to this secret pact, not me. I would honor his agreement if I could, but how? It seems plain to me that the Targaryen girl is never coming west. Westeros was her father's kingdom. Meereen is hers. If she can break the Yunkai'i, she'll be Queen of Slaver's Bay. If not, she'll die long before we could hope to reach her."

His words came as no surprise to Griff. Harry Strickland had always been a genial man, better at hammering out contracts than at hammering on foes. He had a nose for gold, but whether he had the belly for battle was another question.

"There is the land route," suggested Franklyn Flowers.

"The demon road is death. We will lose half the company to desertion if we attempt that march, and bury half of those who remain beside the road. It grieves me to say it, but Magister Illyrio and his friends may have been unwise to put so much hope on this child queen."

No, thought Griff, *but they were most unwise to put their hopes on you.*

And then Prince Aegon spoke. "Then put your hopes on me," he said. "Daenerys is Prince Rhaegar's sister, but I am Rhaegar's son. I am the only dragon that you need."

Griff put a black-gloved hand upon Prince Aegon's shoulder. "Spoken boldly," he said, "but think what you are saying."

"I have," the lad insisted. "Why should I go running to my aunt as if I were a beggar? My claim is better than her own. Let her come to me . . . in Westeros."

Franklyn Flowers laughed. "I like it. Sail west, not east. Leave the little queen to her olives and seat Prince Aegon upon the Iron Throne. The boy has stones, give him that."

The captain-general looked as if someone had slapped his face. "Has the sun curdled your brains, Flowers? We need the girl. We need the marriage. If Daenerys accepts our princeling and takes him for her consort, the Seven Kingdoms will do the same. Without her, the lords will only mock his claim and brand him a fraud and a pretender. And how do you propose to get to Westeros? You heard Lysono. There are no ships to be had."

This man is afraid to fight, Griff realized. *How could they have chosen him to take the Blackheart's place?* "No ships for Slaver's Bay. Westeros is another matter. The east is closed to us, not the sea. The triarchs would be glad to see the back of us, I do not doubt. They might even help us arrange passage back to the Seven Kingdoms. No city wants an army on its doorstep."

"He's not wrong," said Lysono Maar.

"By now the lion surely has the dragon's scent," said one of the Coles, "but Cersei's attentions will be fixed upon Meereen and this other queen. She knows nothing of our prince. Once we land and raise our banners, many and more will flock to join us."

"Some," allowed Homeless Harry, "not *many.* Rhaegar's sister has *dragons.* Rhaegar's son does not. We do not have the strength to take the realm without Daenerys and her army. Her Unsullied."

"The first Aegon took Westeros without eunuchs," said Lysono Maar. "Why shouldn't the sixth Aegon do the same?"

"The plan—"

"Which plan?" said Tristan Rivers. "The fat man's plan? The one that changes every time the moon turns? First *Viserys* Targaryen was to join us with fifty thousand Dothraki screamers at his back. Then the Beggar King was dead, and it was to be the sister, a pliable young child queen who was on her way to Pentos with three new-hatched dragons. Instead the girl turns up on Slaver's Bay and leaves a string of burning cities in her wake, and the fat man decides we should meet her by Volantis. Now that plan is in ruins as well.

"I have had enough of Illyrio's plans. Robert Baratheon won the Iron Throne without the benefit of dragons. We can do the same. And if I am wrong and the realm does not rise for us, we can always retreat back across the narrow sea, as Bittersteel once did, and others after him."

Strickland shook his head stubbornly. "The risk—"

"—is not what it was, now that Tywin Lannister is dead. The Seven Kingdoms will never be more ripe for conquest. Another boy king sits the Iron Throne, this one even younger than the last, and rebels are thick upon the ground as autumn leaves."

"Even so," said Strickland, "alone, we cannot hope to—"

Griff had heard enough of the captain-general's cowardice. "We will not be alone. Dorne will join us, *must* join us. Prince Aegon is Elia's son as well as Rhaegar's."

"That's so," the boy said, "and who is there left in Westeros to oppose us? A woman."

"A *Lannister* woman," insisted the captain-general. "The bitch will have the Kingslayer at her side, count on that, and they will have all the wealth of Casterly Rock behind them. And Illyrio says this boy king is betrothed to the Tyrell girl, which means we must face the power of Highgarden as well."

Laswell Peake rapped his knuckles on the table. "Even after a century, some of us still have friends in the Reach. The power of Highgarden may not be what Mace Tyrell imagines."

"Prince Aegon," said Tristan Rivers, "we are your men. Is this your wish, that we sail west instead of east?"

"It is," Aegon replied eagerly. "If my aunt wants Meereen, she's welcome to it. I will claim the Iron Throne by myself, with your swords and your allegiance. Move fast and strike hard, and we can win some easy victories before the Lannisters even know that we have landed. That will bring others to our cause."

Rivers was smiling in approval. Others traded thoughtful looks.

Then Peake said, "I would sooner die in Westeros than on the demon road," and Marq Mandrake chuckled and responded, "Me, I'd sooner live, win lands and some great castle," and Franklyn Flowers slapped his sword hilt and said, "So long as I can kill some Fossoways, I'm for it."

When all of them began to speak at once, Griff knew the tide had turned. *This is a side of Aegon I never saw before.* It was not the prudent course, but he was tired of prudence, sick of secrets, weary of waiting. Win or lose, he would see Griffin's Roost again before he died, and be buried in the tomb beside his father's.

One by one, the men of the Golden Company rose, knelt, and laid their swords at the feet of his young prince. The last to do so was Homeless Harry Strickland, blistered feet and all.

The sun was reddening the western sky and painting scarlet shadows on the golden skulls atop their spears when they took their leave of the captain-general's tent. Franklyn Flowers offered to take the prince around the camp and introduce him to some of what he called *the lads.* Griff gave his consent. "But remember, so far as the company is concerned, he must remain Young Griff until we cross the narrow sea. In Westeros we'll wash his hair and let him don his armor."

"Aye, understood." Flowers clapped a hand on Young Griff's back. "With me. We'll start with the cooks. Good men to know."

When they were gone, Griff turned to the Halfmaester. "Ride back to the *Shy Maid* and return with Lady Lemore and Ser Rolly. We'll need Illyrio's chests as well. All the coin, and the armor. Give Yandry and Ysilla our thanks. Their part in this is done. They will not be forgotten when His Grace comes into his kingdom."

"As you command, my lord."

Griff left him there, and slipped inside the tent that Homeless Harry had assigned him.

The road ahead was full of perils, he knew, but what of it? All men must die. All he asked was time. He had waited so long, surely the gods would grant him a few more years, enough time to see the boy he'd called a son seated on the Iron Throne. To reclaim his lands, his name, his honor. To still the bells that rang so loudly in his dreams whenever he closed his eyes to sleep.

Alone in the tent, as the gold and scarlet rays of the setting sun shone through the open flap, Jon Connington shrugged off his wolf-skin cloak, slipped his mail shirt off over his head, settled on a camp stool, and peeled the glove from his right hand. The nail on his middle finger had turned as black as jet, he saw, and the grey had crept up almost to the first knuckle. The tip of his ring finger had begun to darken too, and when he touched it with the point of his dagger, he felt nothing.

Death, he knew, *but slow. I still have time. A year. Two years. Five. Some stone men live for ten. Time enough to cross the sea, to see Griffin's Roost again. To end the Usurper's line for good and all, and put Rhaegar's son upon the Iron Throne.*

Then Lord Jon Connington could die content.

THE WINDBLOWN

The word passed through the camp like a hot wind. *She is coming. Her host is on the march. She is racing south to Yunkai, to put the city to the torch and its people to the sword, and we are going north to meet her.*

Frog had it from Dick Straw who had it from Old Bill Bone who had it from a Pentoshi named Myrio Myrakis, who had a cousin who served as cupbearer to the Tattered Prince. "Coz heard it in the command tent, from Caggo's own lips," Dick Straw insisted. "We'll march before the day is out, see if we don't."

That much proved true. The command came down from the Tattered Prince through his captains and his serjeants: strike the tents, load the mules, saddle the horses, we march for Yunkai at the break of day. "Not that them Yunkish bastards will be wanting us inside their Yellow City, sniffing round their daughters," predicted Baqq, the squint-eyed Myrish crossbowman whose name meant *Beans.* "We'll get provisions in Yunkai, maybe fresh horses, then it will be on to Meereen to dance with the dragon queen. So hop quick, Frog, and put a nice edge on your master's sword. Might be he'll need it soon."

In Dorne Quentyn Martell had been a prince, in Volantis a merchant's man, but on the shores of Slaver's Bay he was only Frog, squire to the big bald Dornish knight the sellswords called Greenguts.

The men of the Windblown used what names they would, and changed them at a whim. They'd fastened *Frog* on him because he hopped so fast when the big man shouted a command.

Even the commander of the Windblown kept his true name to himself. Some free companies had been born during the century of blood and chaos that had followed the Doom of Valyria. Others had been formed yesterday and would be gone upon the morrow. The Windblown went back thirty years, and had known but one commander, the soft-spoken, sad-eyed Pentoshi nobleman called the Tattered Prince. His hair and mail were silver-grey, but his ragged cloak was made of twists of cloth of many colors, blue and grey and purple, red and gold and green, magenta and vermilion and cerulean, all faded by the sun. When the Tattered Prince was three-and-twenty, as Dick Straw told the story, the magisters of Pentos had chosen him to be their new prince, hours after beheading their old prince. Instead he'd buckled on a sword, mounted his favorite horse, and fled to the Disputed Lands, never to return. He had ridden with the Second Sons, the Iron Shields, and the Maiden's Men, then joined with five brothers-in-arms to form the Windblown. Of those six founders, only he survived.

Frog had no notion whether any of that was true. Since signing into the Windblown in Volantis, he had seen the Tattered Prince only at a distance. The Dornishmen were new hands, raw recruits, arrow fodder, three amongst two thousand. Their commander kept more elevated company. "I am not a squire," Quentyn had protested when Gerris Drinkwater—known here as Dornish Gerrold, to distinguish him from Gerrold Redback and Black Gerrold, and sometimes as Drink, since the big man had slipped and called him that—suggested the ruse. "I earned my spurs in Dorne. I am as much a knight as you are."

But Gerris had the right of it; he and Arch were here to protect Quentyn, and that meant keeping him by the big man's side. "Arch is the best fighter of the three of us," Drinkwater had pointed out, "but only you can hope to wed the dragon queen."

Wed her or fight her; either way, I will face her soon. The more Quentyn heard of Daenerys Targaryen, the more he feared that meeting. The Yunkai'i claimed that she fed her dragons on human flesh and bathed in the blood of virgins to keep her skin smooth and supple. Beans laughed at that but relished the tales of the silver queen's promiscuity. "One of her captains comes of a line where the men have foot-long members," he told them, "but even he's not big enough for her. She rode with the Dothraki and grew accustomed to being fucked by stallions, so now no man can fill her." And Books, the clever Volantene swordsman who always seemed to have his nose poked in some crumbly scroll, thought the dragon queen both murderous and mad. "Her khal killed her brother to make her queen. Then she killed her khal to make herself *khaleesi*. She practices blood sacrifice, lies as easily as she breathes, turns against her own on a whim. She's broken truces, tortured envoys ... her father was mad too. It runs in the blood."

It runs in the blood. King Aerys II *had* been mad, all of Westeros knew that. He had exiled two of his Hands and burned a third. *If Daenerys is as murdeous as her father, must I still marry her?* Prince Doran had never spoken of that possibility.

Frog would be glad to put Astapor behind him. The Red City was the closest thing to hell he ever hoped to know. The Yunkai'i had sealed the broken gates to keep the dead and dying inside the city, but the sights that he had seen riding down those red brick streets would haunt Quentyn Martell forever. A river choked with corpses. The priestess in her torn robes, impaled upon a stake and attended by a cloud of glistening green flies. Dying men staggering through the streets, bloody and befouled. Children fighting over half-cooked puppies. The last free king of Astapor, screaming naked in the pit as he was set on by a score of starving dogs. And fires, fires everywhere. He could close his eyes and see them still: flames whirling from brick pyramids larger than any castle he had ever seen, plumes of greasy smoke coiling upward like great black snakes.

When the wind blew from the south, the air smelled of smoke even here, three miles from the city. Behind its crumbling red brick walls, Astapor was still asmolder, though by now most of the great fires had burned out. Ashes floated lazy on the breeze like fat grey snowflakes. It would be good to go.

The big man agreed. "Past time," he said, when Frog found him dicing with Beans and Books and Old Bill Bone, and losing yet again. The sell-swords loved Greenguts, who bet as fearlessly as he fought, but with far less success. "I'll want my armor, Frog. Did you scrub that blood off my mail?"

"Aye, ser." Greenguts's mail was old and heavy, patched and patched again, much worn. The same was true of his helm, his gorget, greaves, and gauntlets, and the rest of his mismatched plate. Frog's kit was only slightly better, and Ser Gerris's was notably worse. *Company steel,* the armorer had called it. Quentyn had not asked how many other men had worn it before him, how many men had died in it. They had abandoned their own fine armor in Volantis, along with their gold and their true names. Wealthy knights from Houses old in honor did not cross the narrow sea to sell their swords, unless exiled for some infamy. "I'd sooner pose as poor than evil," Quentyn had declared, when Gerris had explained his ruse to them.

It took the Windblown less than an hour to strike their camp. "And now we ride," the Tattered Prince proclaimed from his huge grey warhorse, in a classic High Valyrian that was the closest thing they had to a company tongue. His stallion's spotted hindquarters were covered with ragged strips of cloth torn from the surcoats of men his master had slain. The prince's cloak was sewn together from more of the same. An old man he was, past sixty, yet he still sat straight and tall in the high saddle, and his voice was strong enough to carry to every corner of the field. "Astapor was but a taste," he said, "Meereen will be the feast," and the sellswords sent up a wild cheer. Streamers of pale blue silk fluttered from their lances, whilst fork-tailed blue-and-white banners flew overhead, the standards of the Windblown.

The three Dornishmen cheered with all the rest. Silence would have drawn notice. But as the Windblown rode north along the coast road, close behind Bloodbeard and the Company of the Cat, Frog fell in beside Dornish Gerrold. "Soon," he said, in the Common Tongue of Westeros. There were other Westerosi in the company, but not many, and not near. "We need to do it soon."

"Not here," warned Gerris, with a mummer's empty smile. "We'll speak of this tonight, when we make camp."

It was a hundred leagues from Astapor to Yunkai by the old Ghiscari coast road, and another fifty from Yunkai to Meereen. The free companies, well mounted, could reach Yunkai in six days of hard riding, or eight at a more leisurely pace. The legions from Old Ghis would take half again as long, marching afoot, and the Yunkai'i and their slave soldiers . . . "With their generals, it's a wonder they don't march into the sea," Beans said.

The Yunkai'i did not lack for commanders. An old hero named Yurkhaz zo Yunzak had the supreme command, though the men of the Windblown glimpsed him only at a distance, coming and going in a palanquin so huge it required forty slaves to carry it.

They could not help but see his underlings, however. The Yunkish lordlings scuttled everywhere, like roaches. Half of them seemed to be named Ghazdan, Grazdan, Mazdhan, or Ghaznak; telling one Ghiscari name from another was an art few of the Windblown had mastered, so they gave them mocking styles of their own devising.

Foremost amongst them was the Yellow Whale, an obscenely fat man who always wore yellow silk *tokar*s with golden fringes. Too heavy even to stand unassisted, he could not hold his water, so he always smelled of piss, a stench so sharp that even heavy perfumes could not conceal it. But he was said to be the richest man in Yunkai, and he had a passion for grotesques; his slaves included a boy with the legs and hooves of a goat, a bearded woman, a two-headed monster from Mantarys, and a hermaphrodite who warmed his bed at night. "Cock and cunny both," Dick Straw told them. "The Whale used to own a giant too, liked to watch him fuck his slave girls. Then he died. I hear the Whale'd give a sack o' gold for a new one."

Then there was the Girl General, who rode about on a white horse with a red mane and commanded a hundred strapping slave soldiers that she had bred and trained herself, all of them young, lean, rippling with muscle, and naked but for breechclouts, yellow cloaks, and long bronze shields with erotic inlays. Their mistress could not have been more than sixteen and fancied herself Yunkai's own Daenerys Targaryen.

The Little Pigeon was not quite a dwarf, but he might have passed for one in a bad light. Yet he strutted about as if he were a giant, with his plump little legs spread wide and his plump little chest puffed out. His soldiers were the tallest that any of the Windblown had ever seen; the shortest stood seven feet tall, the tallest close to eight. All were long-faced and long-legged, and the stilts built into the legs of their ornate armor made them longer still. Pink-enameled scales covered their torsos; on their heads were perched elongated helms complete with pointed steel beaks and crests of bobbing pink feathers. Each man wore a long curved sword upon his hip, and each clasped a spear as tall as he was, with a leaf-shaped blade at either end.

"The Little Pigeon breeds them," Dick Straw informed them. "He buys tall slaves from all over the world, mates the men to the women, and keeps their tallest offspring for the Herons. One day he hopes to be able to dispense with the stilts."

"A few sessions on the rack might speed along the process," suggested the big man.

Gerris Drinkwater laughed. "A fearsome lot. Nothing scares me worse than stilt-walkers in pink scales and feathers. If one was after me, I'd laugh so hard my bladder might let go."

"Some say that herons are majestic," said Old Bill Bone.

"If your king eats frogs while standing on one leg."

"Herons are craven," the big man put in. "One time me and Drink and Cletus were hunting, and we came on these herons wading in the shallows, feasting on tadpoles and small fish. They made a pretty sight, aye, but then a hawk passed overhead, and they all took to the wing like they'd seen a dragon. Kicked up so much wind it blew me off my horse, but Cletus nocked an arrow to his string and brought one down. Tasted like duck, but not so greasy."

Even the Little Pigeon and his Herons paled beside the folly of the brothers the sellswords called the Clanker Lords. The last time the slave soldiers of Yunkai'i had faced the dragon queen's Unsullied, they broke and ran. The Clanker Lords had devised a stratagem to prevent that; they chained their troops together in groups of ten, wrist to wrist and ankle to ankle. "None of the poor bastards can run unless they all run," Dick Straw explained, laughing. "And if they do all run, they won't run very fast."

"They don't fucking march very fast either," observed Beans. "You can hear them clanking ten leagues off."

There were more, near as mad or worse: Lord Wobblecheeks, the Drunken Conqueror, the Beastmaster, Pudding Face, the Rabbit, the Charioteer, the Perfumed Hero. Some had twenty soldiers, some two hundred or two thousand, all slaves they had trained and equipped themselves. Every one was wealthy, every one was arrogant, and every one was a captain and commander, answerable to no one but Yurkhaz zo Yunzak, disdainful of mere sellswords, and prone to squabbles over precedence that were as endless as they were incomprehensible.

In the time it took the Windblown to ride three miles, the Yunkai'i had fallen two-and-a-half miles behind. "A pack of stinking yellow fools," Beans complained. "They still ain't managed to puzzle out why the Stormcrows and the Second Sons went over to the dragon queen."

"For gold, they believe," said Books. "Why do you think they're paying us so well?"

"Gold is sweet, but life is sweeter," said Beans. "We were dancing with cripples at Astapor. Do you want to face real Unsullied with that lot on your side?"

"We fought the Unsullied at Astapor," the big man said.

"I said *real* Unsullied. Hacking off some boy's stones with a butcher's cleaver and handing him a pointy hat don't make him Unsullied. That dragon queen's got the real item, the kind that don't break and run when you fart in their general direction."

"Them, and dragons too." Dick Straw glanced up at the sky as if he thought the mere mention of dragons might be enough to bring them down upon the company. "Keep your swords sharp, boys, we'll have us a real fight soon."

A real fight, thought Frog. The words stuck in his craw. The fight beneath the walls of Astapor had seemed real enough to him, though he knew the sellswords felt otherwise. "That was butchery, not battle," the warrior bard Denzo D'han had been heard to declare afterward. Denzo was a captain, and veteran of a hundred battles. Frog's experience was limited to practice yard and tourney ground, so he did not think it was his place to dispute the verdict of such a seasoned warrior.

It seemed like a battle when it first began, though. He remembered how his gut had clenched when he was kicked awake at dawn with the big man looming over him. "Into your armor, slugabed," he'd boomed. "The Butcher's coming out to give us battle. Up, unless you mean to be his meat."

"The Butcher King is dead," Frog had protested sleepily. That was the story all of them had heard as they scrambled from the ships that had brought them from Old Volantis. A second King Cleon had taken the crown and died in turn, supposedly, and now the Astapori were ruled by a whore and a mad barber whose followers were fighting with each other to control the city.

"Maybe they lied," the big man had replied. "Or else this is some other butcher. Might be the first one come back screaming from his tomb to kill some Yunkishmen. Makes no bloody matter, Frog. *Get your armor on.*" The tent slept ten, and all of them had been on their feet by then, wriggling into breeches and boots, sliding long coats of ringmail down onto their shoulders, buckling breastplates, tightening the straps on greaves or vambraces, grabbing for helms and shields and sword belts. Gerris, quick as ever, was the first one fully clad, Arch close behind him. Together they helped Quentyn don his own harness.

Three hundred yards away, Astapor's new Unsullied had been pouring through their gates and forming up in ranks beneath their city's crumbling red brick walls, dawn light glinting off their spiked bronze helmets and the points of their long spears.

The three Dornishmen spilled from the tent together to join the fighters sprinting for the horse lines. *Battle.* Quentyn had trained with spear and sword and shield since he was old enough to walk, but that meant nothing now. *Warrior, make me brave,* Frog had prayed, as drums beat in the distance, *BOOM boom BOOM boom BOOM boom.* The big man pointed out the Butcher King to him, sitting stiff and tall upon an armored horse in a suit of copper scale that flashed brilliantly in the morning sun. He remembered Gerris sidling up just before the fight began. "Stay close to Arch, whatever happens. Remember, you're the only one of us who can get the girl." By then the Astapori were advancing.

Dead or alive, the Butcher King still took the Wise Masters unawares. The Yunkishmen were still running about in fluttering *tokars* trying to get their half-trained slave soldiers into some semblance of order as Unsullied spears came crashing through their siege lines. If not for their allies and their despised hirelings they might well have been overwhelmed, but the Windblown and the Company of the Cat were ahorse in minutes and came thundering down on the Astapori flanks even as a legion from New Ghis pushed through the Yunkish camp from the other side and met the Unsullied spear to spear and shield to shield.

The rest was butchery, but this time it was the Butcher King on the wrong end of the cleaver. Caggo was the one who finally cut him down, fighting through the king's protectors on his monstrous warhorse and opening Cleon the Great from shoulder to hip with one blow of his curved Valyrian *arakh*. Frog did not see it, but those who did claimed Cleon's copper armor rent like silk, and from within came an awful stench and a hundred wriggling grave worms. Cleon had been dead after all. The desperate Astapori had pulled him from his tomb, clapped him into armor, and tied him onto a horse in hopes of giving heart to their Unsullied.

Dead Cleon's fall wrote an end to that. The new Unsullied threw down their spears and shields and ran, only to find the gates of Astapor shut behind them. Frog had done his part in the slaughter that followed, riding down the frightened eunuchs with the other Windblown. Hard by the big man's hip he rode, slashing right and left as their wedge went through the Unsullied like a spearpoint. When they burst through on the other side, the Tattered Prince had wheeled them round and led them through again. It was only coming back that Frog got a good look at the faces beneath the spiked bronze caps and realized that most were no older than he. *Green boys screaming for their mothers,* he'd thought, but he killed them all the same. By the time he'd left the field, his sword was running red with blood and his arm was so tired he could hardly lift it.

Yet that was no real fight, he thought. *The real fight will be on us soon, and we must be away before it comes, or we'll find ourselves fighting on the wrong side.*

That night the Windblown made camp beside the shore of Slaver's Bay. Frog drew the first watch and was sent to guard the horse lines. Gerris met him there just after sundown, as a half-moon shone upon the waters.

"The big man should be here as well," said Quentyn.

"He's gone to look up Old Bill Bone and lose the rest of his silver," Gerris said. "Leave him out of this. He'll do as we say, though he won't like it much."

"No." There was much and more about this Quentyn did not like himself. Sailing on an overcrowded ship tossed by wind and sea, eating hardbread crawling with weevils and drinking black tar rum to sweet oblivion, sleeping on piles of moldy straw with the stench of strangers in his nostrils . . . all that he had expected when he made his mark on that scrap of parchment in Volantis, pledging the Tattered Prince his sword and service for a year. Those were hardships to be endured, the stuff of all adventures.

But what must come next was plain betrayal. The Yunkai'i had brought them from Old Volantis to fight for the Yellow City, but now the Dornishmen meant to turn their cloaks and go over to the other side. That meant abandoning their new brothers-in-arms as well. The Windblown were not the sort of companions Quentyn would have chosen, but he had crossed the sea with them, shared their meat and mead, fought beside them, traded tales with those few whose talk he understood. And if all his tales were lies, well, that was the cost of passage to Meereen.

It is not what you'd call honorable, Gerris had warned them, back at the Merchant's House.

"Daenerys may be halfway to Yunkai by now, with an army at her back," Quentyn said as they walked amongst the horses.

"She may be," Gerris said, "but she's not. We've heard such talk before. The Astapori were convinced Daenerys was coming south with her dragons to break the siege. She didn't come then, and she's not coming now."

"We can't know that, not for certain. We need to steal away before we end up fighting the woman I was sent to woo."

"Wait till Yunkai." Gerris gestured at the hills. "These lands belong to the Yunkai'i. No one is like to want to feed or shelter three deserters. North of Yunkai, that's no-man's-land."

He was not wrong. Even so, Quentyn felt uneasy. "The big man's made too many friends. He knows the plan was always to steal off and make our way to Daenerys, but he's not going to feel good about abandoning men he's fought with. If we wait too long, it's going to feel as if we're deserting them on the eve of battle. He will never do that. You know him as well as I do."

"It's desertion whenever we do it," argued Gerris, "and the Tattered Prince takes a dim view of deserters. He'll send hunters after us, and Seven save us if they catch us. If we're lucky, they'll just chop off a foot to make sure we never run again. If we're unlucky, they'll give us to Pretty Meris."

That last gave Quentyn pause. Pretty Meris frightened him. A Westerosi woman, but taller than he was, just a thumb under six feet. After twenty years amongst the free companies, there was nothing pretty about her, inside or out.

Gerris took him by the arm. "Wait. A few more days, that's all. We have crossed half the world, be patient for a few more leagues. Somewhere north of Yunkai our chance will come."

"If you say," said Frog doubtfully . . .

. . . but for once the gods were listening, and their chance came much sooner than that.

It was two days later. Hugh Hungerford reined up by their cookfire, and said, "Dornish. You're wanted in the command tent."

"Which one of us?" asked Gerris. "We're all Dornish."

"All of you, then." Sour and saturnine, with a maimed hand, Hungerford had been company paymaster for a time, until the Tattered Prince had caught him stealing from the coffers and removed three of his fingers. Now he was just a serjeant.

What could this be? Up to now, Frog had no notion that their commander knew he was alive. Hungerford had already ridden off, however, so there was no time for questions. All they could do was gather up the big man and report as ordered. "Admit to nothing and be prepared to fight," Quentyn told his friends.

"I am always prepared to fight," said the big man.

The great grey sailcloth pavilion that the Tattered Prince liked to call his canvas castle was crowded when the Dornishmen arrived. It took Quentyn only a moment to realize that most of those assembled were from the Seven Kingdoms, or boasted Westerosi blood. *Exiles or the sons of exiles.* Dick Straw claimed there were three score Westerosi in the company; a good third of those were here, including Dick himself, Hugh Hungerford, Pretty Meris, and golden-haired Lewis Lanster, the company's best archer.

Denzo D'han was there as well, with Caggo huge beside him. *Caggo Corpsekiller* the men were calling him now, though not to his face; he was quick to anger, and that curved black sword of his was as nasty as its owner. There were hundreds of Valyrian longswords in the world, but only a handful of Valyrian *arakhs*. Neither Caggo nor D'han was Westerosi, but both were captains and stood high in the Tattered Prince's regard. *His right arm and his left. Something major is afoot.*

It was the Tattered Prince himself who did the speaking. "Orders have come down from Yurkhaz," he said. "What Astapori still survive have come creeping from their hidey-holes, it seems. There's nothing left in Astapor but corpses, so they're pouring out into the country-side, hundreds of them, maybe thousands, all starved and sick. The Yunkai'i don't want them near their Yellow City. We've been commanded to hunt them down and turn them, drive them back to Astapor or north to Meereen. If the dragon queen wants to take them in, she's welcome to them. Half of them have the bloody flux, and even the healthy ones are mouths to feed."

"Yunkai is closer than Meereen," Hugh Hungerford objected. "What if they won't turn, my lord?"

"That's why you have swords and lances, Hugh. Though bows might serve you better. Stay well away from those who show signs of the flux. I'm sending half our strength into the hills. Fifty patrols, twenty riders each. Bloodbeard's got the same orders, so the Cats will be in the field as well."

A look passed between the men, and a few muttered under their breath. Though the Windblown and the Company of the Cat were both under contract to Yunkai, a year ago in the Disputed Lands they had been on opposite sides of the battle lines, and bad blood still lingered. Bloodbeard, the savage commander of the Cats, was a roaring giant with a ferocious appetite for slaughter who made no secret of his disdain for "old greybeards in rags."

Dick Straw cleared his throat. "Begging your pardon, but we're all Seven Kingdoms born here. M'lord never broke up the company by blood or tongue before. Why send us lot together?"

"A fair question. You're to ride east, deep into the hills, then swing wide about Yunkai, making for Meereen. Should you come on any Astapori, drive them north or kill them . . . but know that is not the purpose of your mission. Beyond the Yellow City, you're like to come up against the dragon queen's patrols. Second Sons or Stormcrows. Either will serve. Go over to them."

"Go over to them?" said the bastard knight, Ser Orson Stone. "You'd have us turn our cloaks?"

"I would," said the Tattered Prince.

Quentyn Martell almost laughed aloud. *The gods are mad.*

The Westerosi shifted uneasily. Some stared into their wine cups, as if they hoped to find some wisdom there. Hugh Hungerford frowned. "You think Queen Daenerys will take us in . . ."

"I do."

". . . but if she does, what then? Are we spies? Assassins? *Envoys?* Are you thinking to change sides?"

Caggo scowled. "That is for the prince to decide, Hungerford. Your part is to do as you are told."

"Always." Hungerford raised his two-fingered hand.

"Let us be frank," said Denzo D'han, the warrior bard. "The Yunkai'i do not inspire confidence. Whatever the outcome of this war, the Windblown should share in the spoils of victory. Our prince is wise to keep all roads open."

"Meris will command you," said the Tattered Prince. "She knows my mind in this . . . and Daenerys Targaryen may be more accepting of another woman."

Quentyn glanced back to Pretty Meris. When her cold dead eyes met his, he felt a shiver. *I do not like this.*

Dick Straw still had doubts as well. "The girl would be a fool to trust us. Even with Meris. *Especially* with Meris. Hell, *I* don't trust Meris, and I've fucked her a few times." He grinned, but no one laughed. Least of all Pretty Meris.

"I think you are mistaken, Dick," the Tattered Prince said. "You are all Westerosi. Friends from home. You speak her same tongue, worship her same gods. As for motive, all of you have suffered wrongs at my hands. Dick, I've whipped you more than any man in the company, and you have the back to prove it. Hugh lost three fingers to my discipline. Meris was raped half round the company. Not *this* company, true, but we need not mention that. Will of the Woods, well, you're just filth. Ser Orson blames me for dispatching his brother to the Sorrows and Ser Lucifer is still seething about that slave girl Caggo took from him."

"He could have given her back when he'd had her," Lucifer Long complained. "He had no cause to kill her."

"She was ugly," said Caggo. "That's cause enough."

The Tattered Prince went on as if no one had spoken. "Webber, you nurse claims to lands lost in Westeros. Lanster, I killed that boy you were so fond of. You Dornish three, you think we lied to you. The plunder from Astapor was much less than you were promised in Volantis, and I took the lion's share of it."

"The last part's true," Ser Orson said.

"The best ruses always have some seed of truth," said the Tattered Prince. "Every one of you has ample reason for wanting to abandon me. And Daenerys Targaryen knows that sellswords are a fickle lot. Her own Second Sons and Stormcrows took Yunkish gold but did not hesitate to join her when the tide of battle began to flow her way."

"When should we leave?" asked Lewis Lanster.

"At once. Be wary of the Cats and any Long Lances you may encounter. No one will know your defection is a ruse but those of us in this tent. Turn your tiles too soon, and you will be maimed as deserters or disemboweled as turncloaks."

The three Dornishmen were silent as they left the command tent.

Twenty riders, all speaking the Common Tongue, thought Quentyn. *Whispering has just gotten a deal more dangerous.*

The big man slapped him hard across the back. "So. This is sweet, Frog. A dragon hunt."

THE WAYWARD BRIDE

Asha Greyjoy was seated in Galbart Glover's longhall drinking Galbart Glover's wine when Galbart Glover's maester brought the letter to her.

"My lady." The maester's voice was anxious, as it always was when he spoke to her. "A bird from Barrowton." He thrust the parchment at her as if he could not wait to be rid of it. It was tightly rolled and sealed with a button of hard pink wax.

Barrowton. Asha tried to recall who ruled in Barrowton. *Some northern lord, no friend of mine.* And that seal . . . the Boltons of the Dreadfort went into battle beneath pink banners spattered with little drops of blood. It only stood to reason that they would use pink sealing wax as well.

This is poison that I hold, she thought. *I ought to burn it.* Instead she cracked the seal. A scrap of leather fluttered down into her lap. When she read the dry brown words, her black mood grew blacker still. *Dark wings, dark words.* The ravens never brought glad tidings. The last message sent to Deepwood had been from Stannis Baratheon, demanding homage. This was worse. "The northmen have taken Moat Cailin."

"The Bastard of Bolton?" asked Qarl, beside her.

"*Ramsay Bolton, Lord of Winterfell,* he signs himself. But there are other names as well." Lady Dustin, Lady Cerwyn, and four Ryswells had appended their own signatures beneath his. Beside them was drawn a crude giant, the mark of some Umber.

Those were done in maester's ink, made of soot and coal tar, but the message above was scrawled in brown in a huge, spiky hand. It spoke of the fall of Moat Cailin, of the triumphant return of the Warden of the North to his domains, of a marriage soon to be made. The first words were, "*I write this letter in the blood of ironmen,*" the last, "*I send you each a piece of prince. Linger in my lands, and share his fate.*"

Asha had believed her little brother dead. *Better dead than this.* The scrap of skin had fallen into her lap. She held it to the candle and watched the smoke curl up, until the last of it had been consumed and the flame was licking at her fingers.

Galbart Glover's maester hovered expectantly at her elbow. "There will be no answer," she informed him.

"May I share these tidings with Lady Sybelle?"

"If it please you." Whether Sybelle Glover would find any joy in the fall of Moat Cailin, Asha could not say. Lady Sybelle all but lived in her gods-wood, praying for her children and her husband's safe return. *Another prayer like to go unanswered. Her heart tree is as deaf and blind as our Drowned God.* Robett Glover and his brother Galbart had ridden south with the Young Wolf. If the tales they had heard of the Red Wedding were even half-true, they were not like to ride north again. *Her children are alive, at least, and that is thanks to me.* Asha had left them at Ten Towers in the care of her aunts. Lady Sybelle's infant daughter was still on the breast, and she had judged the girl too delicate to expose to the rigors of another stormy crossing. Asha shoved the letter into the maester's hands. "Here. Let her find some solace here if she can. You have my leave to go."

The maester inclined his head and departed. After he was gone, Tris Botley turned to Asha. "If Moat Cailin has fallen, Torrhen's Square will soon follow. Then it will be our turn."

"Not for a while yet. The Cleftjaw will make them bleed." Torrhen's Square was not a ruin like Moat Cailin, and Dagmer was iron to the bone. He would die before he'd yield.

If my father still lived, Moat Cailin would never have fallen. Balon Greyjoy had known that the Moat was the key to holding the north.

Euron knew that as well; he simply did not care. No more than he cared what happened to Deepwood Motte or Torrhen's Square. "Euron has no interest in Balon's conquests. My nuncle's off chasing dragons." The Crow's Eye had summoned all the strength of the Iron Isles to Old Wyk and sailed out into the deepness of the Sunset Sea, with his brother Victarion following behind like a whipped cur. There was no one left on Pyke to appeal to, save for her own lord husband. "We stand alone."

"Dagmer will smash them," insisted Cromm, who had never met a woman he loved half so much as battle. "They are only wolves."

"The wolves are all slain." Asha picked at the pink wax with her thumbnail. "These are the skinners who slew them."

"We should go to Torrhen's Square and join the fight," urged Quenton Greyjoy, a distant cousin and captain of the *Salty Wench*.

"Aye," said Dagon Greyjoy, a cousin still more distant. Dagon the Drunkard, men called him, but drunk or sober he loved to fight. "Why should the Cleftjaw have all the glory for himself?"

Two of Galbart Glover's serving men brought forth the roast, but that strip of skin had taken Asha's appetite. *My men have given up all hope of victory,* she realized glumly. *All they look for now is a good death.* The wolves would give them that, she had no doubt. *Soon or late, they will come to take this castle back.*

The sun was sinking behind the tall pines of the wolfswood as Asha climbed the wooden steps to the bedchamber that had once been Galbart Glover's. She had drunk too much wine and her head was pounding. Asha Greyjoy loved her men, captains and crew alike, but half of them were fools. *Brave fools, but fools nonetheless. Go to the Cleftjaw, yes, as if we could . . .*

Between Deepwood and Dagmer lay long leagues, rugged hills, thick woods, wild rivers, and more northmen than she cared to contemplate. Asha had four longships and not quite two hundred men . . . including Tristifer Botley, who could not be relied on. For all his talk of love, she could not imagine Tris rushing off to Torrhen's Square to die with Dagmer Cleftjaw.

Qarl followed her up to Galbart Glover's bedchamber. "Get out," she told him. "I want to be alone."

"What you want is me." He tried to kiss her.

Asha pushed him away. "Touch me again and I'll—"

"What?" He drew his dagger. "Undress yourself, girl."

"Fuck yourself, you beardless boy."

"I'd sooner fuck you." One quick slash unlaced her jerkin. Asha reached for her axe, but Qarl dropped his knife and caught her wrist, twisting back her arm until the weapon fell from her fingers. He pushed her back onto Glover's bed, kissed her hard, and tore off her tunic to let her breasts spill out. When she tried to knee him in the groin, he twisted away and forced her legs apart with his knees. "I'll have you now."

"Do it," she spat, "and I'll kill you in your sleep."

She was sopping wet when he entered her. "Damn you," she said. "Damn you damn you damn you." He sucked her nipples till she cried out half in pain and half in pleasure. Her cunt became the world. She forgot Moat Cailin and Ramsay Bolton and his little piece of skin, forgot the kingsmoot, forgot her failure, forgot her exile and her enemies and her husband. Only his hands mattered, only his mouth, only his arms around her, his cock inside her. He fucked her till she screamed, and then again until she wept, before he finally spent his seed inside her womb.

"I am a woman wed," she reminded him, afterward. "You've despoiled me, you beardless boy. My lord husband will cut your balls off and put you in a dress."

Qarl rolled off her. "If he can get out of his chair."

The room was cold. Asha rose from Galbart Glover's bed and took off her torn clothes. The jerkin would need fresh laces, but her tunic was ruined. *I never liked it anyway.* She tossed it on the flames. The rest she left in a puddle by the bed. Her breasts were sore, and Qarl's seed was trickling down her thigh. She would need to brew some moon tea or risk bringing another kraken into the world. *What does it matter? My father's dead, my mother's dying, my brother's being flayed, and there's naught that I can do about any of it. And I'm married. Wedded and bedded . . . though not by the same man.*

When she slipped back beneath the furs, Qarl was asleep. "Now your life is mine. Where did I put my dagger?" Asha pressed herself against his back and slid her arms about him. On the isles he was known as Qarl the Maid, in part to distinguish him from Qarl Shepherd, Queer Qarl Kenning, Qarl Quickaxe, and Qarl the Thrall, but more for his smooth cheeks. When Asha had first met him, Qarl had been trying to raise a beard. "Peach fuzz," she had called it, laughing. Qarl confessed that he had never seen a peach, so she told him he must join her on her next voyage south.

It had still been summer then; Robert sat the Iron Throne, Balon brooded on the Seastone Chair, and the Seven Kingdoms were at peace. Asha sailed the *Black Wind* down the coast, trading. They called at Fair Isle and Lannisport and a score of smaller ports before reaching the Arbor, where the peaches were always huge and sweet. "You see," she'd said, the first time she'd held one up against Qarl's cheek. When she made him try a bite, the juice ran down his chin, and she had to kiss it clean.

That night they'd spent devouring peaches and each other, and by the time daylight returned Asha was sated and sticky and as happy as she'd ever been. *Was that six years ago, or seven?* Summer was a fading memory, and it had been three years since Asha last enjoyed a peach. She still enjoyed Qarl, though. The captains and the kings might not have wanted her, but he did.

Asha had known other lovers; some shared her bed for half a year, some for half a night. Qarl pleased her more than all the rest together. He might shave but once a fortnight, but a shaggy beard does not make a man. She liked the feel of his smooth, soft skin beneath her fingers. She liked the way his long, straight hair brushed against his shoulders. She liked the way he kissed. She liked how he grinned when she brushed her thumbs across his nipples. The hair between his legs was a darker shade of sand than the hair on his head, but fine as down compared to the coarse black bush around her own sex. She liked that too. He had a swimmer's body, long and lean, with not a scar upon him.

A shy smile, strong arms, clever fingers, and two sure swords. What more could any woman want? She would have married Qarl, and gladly, but she was Lord Balon's daughter and he was common-born, the grandson of a thrall. *Too lowborn for me to wed, but not too low for me to suck his cock.* Drunk, smiling, she crawled beneath the furs and took him in her mouth. Qarl stirred in his sleep, and after a moment he began to stiffen. By the time she had him hard again, he was awake and she was wet. Asha draped the furs across her bare shoulders and mounted him, drawing him so deep inside her that she could not tell who had the cock and who the cunt. This time the two of them reached their peak together.

"My sweet lady," he murmured after, in a voice still thick with sleep. "My sweet queen."

No, Asha thought, *I am no queen, nor shall I ever be.* "Go back to sleep." She kissed his cheek, padded across Galbart Glover's bedchamber, and threw the shutters open. The moon was almost full, the night so clear that she could see the mountains, their peaks crowned with snow. *Cold and bleak and inhospitable, but beautiful in the moonlight.* Their summits glimmered pale and jagged as a row of sharpened teeth. The foothills and the smaller peaks were lost in shadow.

The sea was closer, only five leagues north, but Asha could not see it. Too many hills stood in the way. *And trees, so many trees.* The wolfswood, the northmen named the forest. Most nights you could hear the wolves, calling to each other through the dark. *An ocean of leaves. Would it were an ocean of water.*

Deepwood might be closer to the sea than Winterfell, but it was still too far for her taste. The air smelled of pines instead of salt. Northeast of those grim grey mountains stood the Wall, where Stannis Baratheon had raised his standards. *The enemy of my enemy is my friend,* men said, but the other side of that coin was, *the enemy of my friend is my enemy.* The ironborn were the enemies of the northern lords this Baratheon pretender needed desperately. *I could offer him my fair young body,* she thought, pushing a strand of hair from her eyes, but Stannis was wed and so was she, and he and the ironborn were old foes. During her father's first rebellion, Stannis had smashed the Iron Fleet off Fair Isle and subdued Great Wyk in his brother's name.

Deepwood's mossy walls enclosed a wide, rounded hill with a flattened top, crowned by a cavernous longhall with a watchtower at one end, rising fifty feet above the hill. Beneath the hill was the bailey, with its stables, paddock, smithy, well, and sheepfold, defended by a deep ditch, a sloping earthen dike, and a palisade of logs. The outer defenses made an oval, following the contours of the land. There were two gates, each protected by a pair of square wooden towers, and wallwalks around the perimeter. On the south side of the castle, moss grew thick upon the palisade and crept halfway up the towers. To east and west were empty fields. Oats and barley had been growing there when Asha took the castle, only to be crushed underfoot during her attack. A series of hard frosts had killed the crops they'd planted afterward, leaving only mud and ash and wilted, rotting stalks.

It was an old castle, but not a strong one. She had taken it from the Glovers, and the Bastard of Bolton would take it from her. He would not flay her, though. Asha Greyjoy did not intend to be taken alive. She would die as she had lived, with an axe in her hand and a laugh upon her lips.

Her lord father had given her thirty longships to capture Deepwood. Four remained, counting her own *Black Wind,* and one of those belonged to Tris Botley, who had joined her when all her other men were fleeing. *No. That is not just. They sailed home to do homage to their king. If anyone fled, it was me.* The memory still shamed her.

"Go," the Reader had urged, as the captains were bearing her uncle Euron down Nagga's hill to don his driftwood crown.

"Said the raven to the crow. Come with me. I need you to raise the men of Harlaw." Back then, she'd meant to fight.

"The men of Harlaw are here. The ones who count. Some were shouting Euron's name. I will not set Harlaw against Harlaw."

"Euron's mad. And dangerous. That hellhorn . . ."

"I heard it. *Go,* Asha. Once Euron has been crowned, he'll look for you. You dare not let his eye fall upon you."

"If I stand with my other uncles . . ."

". . . you will die outcast, with every hand against you. When you put your name before the captains you submitted yourself to their judgment. You cannot go against that judgment now. Only once has the choice of a kingsmoot been overthrown. Read Haereg."

Only Rodrik the Reader would talk of some old book whilst their lives were balanced on a sword's edge. "If you are staying, so am I," she told him stubbornly.

"Don't be a fool. Euron shows the world his smiling eye tonight, but come the morrow . . . Asha, you are Balon's daughter, and your claim is stronger than his own. So long as you draw breath you remain a danger to him. If you stay, you will be killed or wed to the Red Oarsman. I don't know which would be worse. *Go.* You will not have another chance."

Asha had landed *Black Wind* on the far side of the island for just such an eventuality. Old Wyk was not large. She could be back aboard her ship before the sun came up, on her way to Harlaw before Euron realized she was missing. Yet she hesitated until her uncle said, "Do it for the love you bear me, child. Do not make me watch you die."

So she went. To Ten Towers first, to bid farewell to her mother. "It may be a long while before I come again," Asha warned her. Lady Alannys had not understood. "Where is Theon?" she asked. "Where is my baby boy?" Lady Gwynesse only wanted to know when Lord Rodrik would return. "I am seven years his elder. Ten Towers should be mine."

Asha was still at Ten Towers taking on provisions when the tidings of her marriage reached her. "My wayward niece needs taming," the Crow's Eye was reported to have said, "and I know the man to tame her." He had married her to Erik Ironmaker and named the Anvil-Breaker to rule the Iron Islands whilst he was chasing dragons. Erik had been a great man in his day, a fearless reaver who could boast of having sailed with her grandsire's grandsire, that same Dagon Greyjoy whom Dagon the Drunkard had been named for. Old women on Fair Isle still frightened their grandchildren with tales of Lord Dagon and his men. *I wounded Eric's pride at the kingsmoot,* Asha reflected. *He is not like to forget that.*

She had to pay her nuncle his just due. With one stroke, Euron had turned a rival into a supporter, secured the isles in his absence, and removed Asha as a threat. *And enjoyed a good belly laugh too.* Tris Botley said that the Crow's Eye had used a seal to stand in for her at her wedding. "I hope Erik did not insist on a consummation," she'd said.

I cannot go home, she thought, *but I dare not stay here much longer.* The quiet of the woods unnerved her. Asha had spent her life on islands and on ships. The sea was never silent. The sound of the waves washing against a rocky shore was in her blood, but there were no waves at Deepwood Motte . . . only the trees, the endless trees, soldier pines and sentinels, beech and ash and ancient oaks, chestnut trees and ironwoods and firs. The sound they made was softer than the sea, and she heard it only when the wind was blowing; then the sighing seemed to come from all around her, as if the trees were whispering to one another in some language that she could not understand.

Tonight the whispering seemed louder than before. *A rush of dead brown leaves,* Asha told herself, *bare branches creaking in the wind.* She turned away from the window, away from the woods. *I need a deck beneath my feet again. Or failing that, some food in my belly.* She'd had too much wine tonight, but too little bread and none of that great bloody roast.

The moonlight was bright enough to find her clothes. She donned thick black breeches, a quilted tunic, and a green leather jerkin covered with overlapping plates of steel. Leaving Qarl to his dreams, she padded down the keep's exterior stair, the steps creaking under her bare feet. One of the men walking sentry on the walls spied her making her descent and lifted his spear to her. Asha whistled back at him. As she crossed the inner yard to the kitchens, Galbart Glover's dogs began to bark. *Good,* she thought. *That will drown out the sound of the trees.*

She was cutting a wedge of yellow cheese from a round as big as a cart wheel when Tris Botley stepped into the kitchen, bundled up in a thick fur cloak. "My queen."

"Don't mock me."

"You will always rule my heart. No amount of fools shouting at a kingsmoot can change that."

What am I to do with this boy? Asha could not doubt his devotion. Not only had he stood her champion on Nagga's hill and shouted out her name, but he had even crossed the sea to join her afterward, abandoning his king and kin and home. *Not that he dared defy Euron to his face.* When the Crow's Eye took the fleet to sea Tris had simply lagged behind, changing course only when the other ships were lost to sight. Even that took a certain courage, though; he could never return to the isles. "Cheese?" she asked him. "There's ham as well, and mustard."

"It's not food I want, my lady. You know that." Tris had grown himself a thick brown beard at Deepwood. He claimed it helped to keep his face warm. "I saw you from the watchtower."

"If you have the watch, what are you doing here?"

"Cromm's up there, and Hagen the Horn. How many eyes do we need to watch leaves rustle in the moonlight? We need to talk."

"Again?" She sighed. "You know Hagen's daughter, the one with the red hair. She steers a ship as well as any man and has a pretty face. Seventeen, and I've seen her looking at you."

"I don't want Hagen's daughter." He almost touched her before thinking better of it. "Asha, it is time to go. Moat Cailin was the only thing holding back the tide. If we remain here, the northmen will kill us all, you know that."

"Would you have me run?"

"I would have you live. I love you."

No, she thought, *you love some innocent maiden who lives only in your head, a frightened child in need of your protection.* "I do not love you," she said bluntly, "and I do not run."

"What's here that you should hold so tight to it but pine and mud and foes? We have our ships. Sail away with me, and we'll make new lives upon the sea."

"As pirates?" It was almost tempting. *Let the wolves have back their gloomy woods and retake the open sea.*

"As traders," he insisted. "We'll voyage east as the Crow's Eye did, but we'll come back with silks and spices instead of a dragon's horn. One voyage to the Jade Sea and we'll be as rich as gods. We can have a manse in Oldtown or one of the Free Cities."

"You and me and Qarl?" She saw him flinch at the mention of Qarl's name. "Hagen's girl might like to sail the Jade Sea with you. I am still the kraken's daughter. My place is—"

"—*where*? You cannot return to the isles. Not unless you mean to submit to your lord husband."

Asha tried to picture herself abed with Erik Ironmaker, crushed beneath his bulk, suffering his embraces. *Better him than the Red*

Oarsman or *Left-Hand Lucas Codd*. The Anvil-Breaker had once been a roaring giant, fearsomely strong, fiercely loyal, utterly without fear. *It might not be so bad. He's like to die the first time he tries to do his duty as a husband.* That would make her Erik's widow instead of Erik's wife, which could be better or a good deal worse, depending on his grandsons. *And my nuncle. In the end, all the winds blow me back toward Euron.* "I have hostages, on Harlaw," she reminded him. "And there is still Sea Dragon Point . . . if I cannot have my father's kingdom, why not make one of my own?" Sea Dragon Point had not always been as thinly peopled as it was now. Old ruins could still be found amongst its hills and bogs, the remains of ancient strongholds of the First Men. In the high places, there were weirwood circles left by the children of the forest.

"You are clinging to Sea Dragon Point the way a drowning man clings to a bit of wreckage. What does Sea Dragon have that anyone could ever want? There are no mines, no gold, no silver, not even tin or iron. The land is too wet for wheat or corn."

I do not plan on planting wheat or corn. "What's there? I'll tell you. Two long coastlines, a hundred hidden coves, otters in the lakes, salmon in the rivers, clams along the shore, colonies of seals offshore, tall pines for building ships."

"Who will build these ships, my queen? Where will Your Grace find subjects for her kingdom if the northmen let you have it? Or do you mean to rule over a realm of seals and otters?"

She gave a rueful laugh. "Otters might be easier to rule than men, I grant you. And seals are smarter. No, you may be right. My best course may still be to return to Pyke. There are those on Harlaw who would welcome my return. On Pyke as well. And Euron won no friends on Blacktyde when he slew Lord Baelor. I could find my nuncle Aeron, raise the isles." No one had seen the Damphair since the kingsmoot, but his Drowned Men claimed he was hiding on Great Wyk and would soon come forth to call down the wroth of the Drowned God on the Crow's Eye and his minions.

"The Anvil-Breaker is searching for the Damphair too. He is hunting down the Drowned Men. Blind Beron Blacktyde was taken and put to the question. Even the Old Grey Gull was given shackles. How will you find the priest when all of Euron's men cannot?"

"He is my blood. My father's brother." It was a feeble answer, and Asha knew it.

"Do you know what I think?"

"I am about to, I suspect."

"I think the Damphair's dead. I think the Crow's Eye slit his throat for him. Ironmaker's search is just to make us believe the priest escaped. Euron is afraid to be seen as a kinslayer."

"Never let my nuncle hear you say that. Tell the Crow's Eye he's afraid of kinslaying, and he'll murder one of his own sons just to prove you wrong." Asha was feeling almost sober by then. Tristifer Botley had that effect on her.

"Even if you did find your uncle Damphair, the two of you would fail. You were both *part* of the kingsmoot, so you cannot say it was unlawful called, as Torgon did. You are bound to its decision by all the laws of gods and men. You—"

Asha frowned. "Wait. Torgon? Which Torgon?"

"Torgon the Latecomer."

"He was a king during the Age of Heroes." She recalled that much about him, but little else. "What of him?"

"Torgon Greyiron was the king's eldest son. But the king was old and Torgon restless, so it happened that when his father died he was raiding along the Mander from his stronghold on Greyshield. His brothers sent no word to him but instead quickly called a kingsmoot, thinking that one of them would be chosen to wear the driftwood crown. But the captains and the kings chose Urragon Goodbrother to rule instead. The first thing the new king did was command that all the sons of the old king be put to death, and so they were. After that men called him *Badbrother*, though in truth they'd been no kin of his. He ruled for almost two years."

Asha remembered now. "Torgon came home . . ."

". . . and said the kingsmoot was unlawful since he had not been there to make his claim. Badbrother had proved to be as mean as he was cruel and had few friends left upon the isles. The priests denounced him, the lords rose against him, and his own captains hacked him into pieces. Torgon the Latecomer became the king and ruled for forty years."

Asha took Tris Botley by the ears and kissed him full upon the lips. He was red and breathless by the time she let him go. "What was that?" he said.

"A kiss, it's called. Drown me for a fool, Tris, I should have remembered—" She broke off suddenly. When Tris tried to speak, she shushed him, listening. "That's a warhorn. Hagen." Her first thought was of her husband. Could Erik Ironmaker have come all this way to claim his wayward wife? "The Drowned God loves me after all. Here I was wondering what to do, and he has sent me foes to fight." Asha got to her feet and slammed her knife back into its sheath. "The battle's come to us."

She was trotting by the time she reached the castle bailey, with Tris dogging her heels, but even so she came too late. The fight was done. Asha found two northmen bleeding by the eastern wall not far from the postern gate, with Lorren Longaxe, Six-Toed Harl, and Grimtongue standing over them. "Cromm and Hagen saw them coming over the wall," Grimtongue explained.

"Just these two?" asked Asha.

"Five. We killed two before they could get over, and Harl slew another on the wallwalk. These two made it to the yard."

One man was dead, his blood and brains crusting Lorren's longaxe, but the second was still breathing raggedly, though Grimtongue's spear had pinned him to the ground in a spreading pool of blood. Both were clad in boiled leather and mottled cloaks of brown and green and black, with branches, leaves, and brush sewn about their heads and shoulders.

"Who are you?" Asha asked the wounded man.

"A Flint. Who are you?"

"Asha of House Greyjoy. This is my castle."

"Deepwood be Galbart Glover's seat. No home for squids."

"Are there any more of you?" Asha demanded of him. When he did not answer, she seized Grimtongue's spear and turned it, and the northman cried out in anguish as more blood gushed from his wound. "What was your purpose here?"

"The lady," he said, shuddering. "Gods, stop. We come for the lady. T' rescue her. It was just us five."

Asha looked into his eyes. When she saw the falsehood there, she leaned upon the spear, twisting it. "*How many more?*" she said. "Tell me, or I'll make your dying last until the dawn."

"Many," he finally sobbed, between screams. "*Thousands.* Three thousand, four . . . *aieeee* . . . please . . ."

She ripped the spear out of him and drove it down two-handed through his lying throat. Galbart Glover's maester had claimed the mountain clans were too quarrelsome to ever band together without a Stark to lead them. *He might not have been lying. He might just have been wrong.* She had learned what *that* tasted like at her nuncle's kingsmoot. "These five were sent to open our gates before the main attack," she said. "Lorren, Harl, fetch me Lady Glover and her maester."

"Whole or bloody?" asked Lorren Longaxe.

"Whole and unharmed. Grimtongue, get up that thrice-damned tower and tell Cromm and Hagen to keep a sharp eye out. If they see so much as a hare, I want to know of it."

Deepwood's bailey was soon full of frightened people. Her own men were struggling into armor or climbing up onto the wallwalks. Galbart Glover's folk looked on with fearful faces, whispering to one another. Glover's steward had to be carried up from the cellar, having lost a leg when Asha took the castle. The maester protested noisily until Lorren cracked him hard across the face with a mailed fist. Lady Glover emerged from the godswood on the arm of her bedmaid. "I warned you that this day would come, my lady," she said, when she saw the corpses on the ground.

The maester pushed forward, with blood dripping from a broken nose. "Lady Asha, I beg you, strike your banners and let me bargain for your life. You have used us fairly, and with honor. I will tell them so."

"We will exchange you for the children." Sybelle Glover's eyes were red, from tears and sleepless nights. "Gawen is four now. I missed his nameday. And my sweet girl . . . give me back my children, and no harm need come to you. Nor to your men."

The last part was a lie, Asha knew. *She* might be exchanged, perhaps, shipped back to the Iron Islands to her husband's loving arms. Her cousins would be ransomed too, as would Tris Botley and a few more of her company, those whose kin had coin enough to buy them back. For the rest it would be the axe, the noose, or the Wall. *Still, they have the right to choose.*

Asha climbed on a barrel so all of them could see her. "The wolves are coming down on us with their teeth bared. They will be at our gates before the sun comes up. Shall we throw down our spears and axes and plead with them to spare us?"

"No." Qarl the Maid drew his sword. "No," echoed Lorren Longaxe. "*No*," boomed Rolfe the Dwarf, a bear of a man who stood a head taller than anyone else in her crew. "*Never.*" And Hagen's horn sounded again from on high, ringing out across the bailey.

AHoooooooooooooooooooooooo, the warhorn cried, long and low, a sound to curdle blood. Asha had begun to hate the sound of horns. On Old Wyk her uncle's hellhorn had blown a death knell for her dreams, and now Hagen was sounding what might well be her last hour on earth. *If I must die, I will die with an axe in my hand and a curse upon my lips.*

"To the walls," Asha Greyjoy told her men. She turned her own steps for the watchtower, with Tris Botley right behind her.

The wooden watchtower was the tallest thing this side of the mountains, rising twenty feet above the biggest sentinels and soldier pines in the surrounding woods. "There, Captain," said Cromm, when she made the platform. Asha saw only trees and shadows, the moonlit hills and the snowy peaks beyond. Then she realized that trees were creeping closer. "Oho," she laughed, "these mountain goats have cloaked themselves in pine boughs." The woods were on the move, creeping toward the castle like a slow green tide. She thought back to a tale she had heard as a child, about the children of the forest and their battles with the First Men, when the greenseers turned the trees to warriors.

"We cannot fight so many," Tris Botley said.

"We can fight as many as come, pup," insisted Cromm. "The more there are, the more the glory. Men will sing of us."

Aye, but will they sing of your courage or my folly? The sea was five long leagues away. Would they do better to stand and fight behind Deepwood's deep ditches and wooden walls? *Deepwood's wooden walls did the Glovers small good when I took their castle,* she reminded herself. *Why should they serve me any better?*

"Come the morrow we will feast beneath the sea." Cromm stroked his axe as if he could not wait.

Hagen lowered his horn. "If we die with dry feet, how will we find our way to the Drowned God's watery halls?"

"These woods are full of little streams," Cromm assured him. "All of them lead to rivers, and all the rivers to the sea."

Asha was not ready to die, not here, not yet. "A living man can find the sea more easily than a dead one. Let the wolves keep their gloomy woods. We are making for the ships."

She wondered who was in command of her foes. *If it were me, I would take the strand and put our longships to the torch before attacking Deepwood.* The wolves would not find that easy, though, not without longships of their own. Asha never beached more than half her ships. The other half stood safely off to sea, with orders to raise sail and make for Sea Dragon Point if the northmen took the strand. "Hagen, blow your horn and make the forest shake. Tris, don some mail, it's time you tried out that sweet sword of yours." When she saw how pale he was, she pinched his cheek. "Splash some blood upon the moon with me, and I promise you a kiss for every kill."

"My queen," said Tristifer, "here we have the walls, but if we reach the sea and find that the wolves have taken our ships or driven them away . . ."

". . . we die," she finished cheerfully, "but at least we'll die with our feet wet. Ironborn fight better with salt spray in their nostrils and the sound of the waves at their backs."

Hagen blew three short blasts in quick succession, the signal that would send the ironborn back to their ships. From below came shouting, the clatter of spear and sword, the whinnying of horses. *Too few horses and too few riders.* Asha headed for the stair. In the bailey, she found Qarl the Maid waiting with her chestnut mare, her warhelm, and her throwing axes. Ironmen were leading horses from Galbart Glover's stables.

"A ram!" a voice shouted down from the walls. "*They have a battering ram!*"

"Which gate?" asked Asha, mounting up.

"The north!" From beyond Deepwood's mossy wooden walls came the sudden sound of trumpets.

Trumpets? Wolves with trumpets? That was wrong, but Asha had no time to ponder it. "Open the south gate," she commanded, even as the north gate shook to the impact of the ram. She pulled a short-hafted throwing axe from the belt across her shoulder. "The hour of the owl has fled, my brothers. Now comes the hour of the spear, the sword, the axe. Form up. We're going home."

From a hundred throats came roars of "*Home!*" and "*Asha!*" Tris Botley galloped up beside her on a tall roan stallion. In the bailey, her men closed about each other, hefting shields and spears. Qarl the Maid, no horse rider, took his place between Grimtongue and Lorren Longaxe. As Hagen came scrambling down the watchtower steps, a wolfling's arrow caught him in the belly and sent him plunging headfirst to the ground. His daughter ran to him, wailing. "Bring her," Asha commanded. This was no time for mourning. Rolfe the Dwarf pulled the girl onto his horse, her red hair flying. Asha could hear the north gate groaning as the ram slammed into it again. *We may need to cut our way through them,* she thought, as the south gate swung wide before them. The way was clear. *For how long?*

"Move out!" Asha drove her heels into her horse's flanks.

Men and mounts alike were trotting by the time they reached the trees on the far side of the sodden field, where dead shoots of winter wheat rotted beneath the moon. Asha held her horsemen back as a rear guard, to keep the stragglers moving and see that no one was left behind. Tall soldier pines and gnarled old oaks closed in around them. Deepwood was aptly named. The trees were huge and dark, somehow threatening. Their limbs wove through one another and creaked with every breath of wind, and their higher branches scratched at the face of the moon. *The sooner we are shut of here, the better I will like it,* Asha thought. *The trees hate us all, deep in their wooden hearts.*

They pressed on south and southwest, until the wooden towers of Deepwood Motte were lost to sight and the sounds of trumpets had been swallowed by the woods. *The wolves have their castle back,* she thought, *perhaps they will be content to let us go.*

Tris Botley trotted up beside her. "We are going the wrong way," he said, gesturing at the moon as it peered down through the canopy of branches. "We need to turn north, for the ships."

"West first," Asha insisted. "West until the sun comes up. Then north." She turned to Rolfe the Dwarf and Roggon Rustbeard, her best riders. "Scout ahead and make sure our way is clear. I want no surprises when we reach the shore. If you come on wolves, ride back to me with word."

"If we must," promised Roggon through his huge red beard.

After the scouts had vanished into the trees, the rest of the iron-born resumed their march, but the going was slow. The trees hid the moon and stars from them, and the forest floor beneath their feet was black and treacherous. Before they had gone half a mile, her cousin Quenton's mare stumbled into a pit and shattered her foreleg. Quenton had to slit her throat to stop her screaming. "We should make torches," urged Tris.

"Fire will bring the northmen down on us." Asha cursed beneath her breath, wondering if it had been a mistake to leave the castle. *No. If we had stayed and fought, we might all be dead by now.* But it was no good blundering on through the dark either. *These trees will kill us if they can.* She took off her helm and pushed back her sweat-soaked hair. "The sun will be up in a few hours. We'll stop here and rest till break of day."

Stopping proved simple; rest came hard. No one slept, not even Droopeye Dale, an oarsman who had been known to nap between strokes. Some of the men shared a skin of Galbart Glover's apple wine, passing it from hand to hand. Those who had brought food shared it with those who had not. The riders fed and watered their horses. Her cousin Quenton Greyjoy sent three men up trees, to watch for any sign of torches in the woods. Cromm honed his axe, and Qarl the Maid his sword. The horses cropped dead brown grass and weeds. Hagen's red-haired daughter seized Tris Botley by the hand to draw him off into the trees. When he refused her, she went off with Six-Toed Harl instead.

Would that I could do the same. It would be sweet to lose herself in Qarl's arms one last time. Asha had a bad feeling in her belly.

Would she ever feel *Black Wind*'s deck beneath her feet again? And if she did, where would she sail her? *The isles are closed to me, unless I mean to bend my knees and spread my legs and suffer Eric Ironmaker's embraces, and no port in Westeros is like to welcome the kraken's daughter.* She could turn merchanter, as Tris seemed to want, or else make for the Stepstones and join the pirates there. *Or . . .*

"I send you each a piece of prince," she muttered.

Qarl grinned. "I would sooner have a piece of you," he whispered, "the sweet piece that's—"

Something flew from the brush to land with a soft *thump* in their midst, bumping and bouncing. It was round and dark and wet, with long hair that whipped about it as it rolled. When it came to rest amongst the roots of an oak, Grimtongue said, "Rolfe the Dwarf's not so tall as he once was." Half her men were on their feet by then, reaching for shields and spears and axes. *They lit no torches either,* Asha had time enough to think, *and they know these woods better than we ever could.* Then the trees erupted all around them, and the northmen poured in howling. *Wolves,* she thought, *they howl like bloody wolves. The war cry of the north.* Her ironborn screamed back at them, and the fight began.

No singer would ever make a song about that battle. No maester would ever write down an account for one of the Reader's beloved books. No banners flew, no warhorns moaned, no great lord called his men about him to hear his final ringing words. They fought in the predawn gloom, shadow against shadow, stumbling over roots and rocks, with mud and rotting leaves beneath their feet. The ironborn were clad in mail and salt-stained leather, the northmen in furs and hides and piney branches. The moon and stars looked down upon their struggle, their pale light filtered through the tangle of bare limbs that twisted overhead.

The first man to come at Asha Greyjoy died at her feet with her throwing axe between his eyes. That gave her respite enough to slip her shield onto her arm. "*To me!*" she called, but whether she was calling to her own men or the foes even Asha could not have said for certain. A northman with an axe loomed up before her, swinging with both hands as he howled in wordless fury. Asha raised her shield to block his blow, then shoved in close to gut him with her dirk. His howling took on a different tone as he fell. She spun and found another wolf behind her, and slashed him across the brow beneath his helm. His own cut caught her below the breast, but her mail turned it, so she drove the point of her dirk into his throat and left him to drown in his own blood. A hand seized her hair, but short as it was he could not get a good enough grip to wrench her head back. Asha slammed her boot heel down onto his instep and wrenched loose when he cried out in pain. By the time she turned the man was down and dying, still clutching a handful of her hair. Qarl stood over him, with his longsword dripping and moonlight shining in his eyes.

Grimtongue was counting the northmen as he killed them, calling out, "Four," as one went down and, "Five," a heartbeat later. The horses screamed and kicked and rolled their eyes in terror, maddened by the butchery and blood . . . all but Tris Botley's big roan stallion. Tris had gained the saddle, and his mount was rearing and wheeling as he laid about with his sword. *I may owe him a kiss or three before the night is done,* thought Asha.

"Seven," shouted Grimtongue, but beside him Lorren Longaxe sprawled with one leg twisted under him, and the shadows kept on coming, shouting and rustling. *We are fighting shrubbery,* Asha thought as she slew a man who had more leaves on him than most of the surrounding trees. That made her laugh. Her laughter drew more wolves to her, and she killed them too, wondering if she should start a count of her own. *I am a woman wed, and here's my suckling babe.* She pushed her dirk into a northman's chest through fur and wool and boiled leather. His face was so close to hers that she could smell the sour stench of his breath, and his hand was at her throat. Asha felt iron scraping against bone as her point slid over a rib. Then the man shuddered and died. When she let go of him, she was so weak she almost fell on top of him.

Later, she stood back-to-back with Qarl, listening to the grunts and curses all around them, to brave men crawling through the shadows weeping for their mothers. A bush drove at her with a spear long enough to punch through her belly and Qarl's back as well, pinning them together as they died. *Better that than die alone,* she thought, but her cousin Quenton killed the spearman before he reached her. A heartbeat later another bush killed Quenton, driving an axe into the base of his skull.

Behind her Grimtongue shouted, "*Nine,* and damn you all." Hagen's daughter burst naked from beneath the trees with two wolves at her heels. Asha wrenched loose a throwing axe and sent it flying end over end to take one of them in the back. When he fell, Hagen's daughter stumbled to her knees, snatched up his sword, stabbed the second man, then rose again, smeared with blood and mud, her long red hair unbound, and plunged into the fight.

Somewhere in the ebb and flow of battle, Asha lost Qarl, lost Tris, lost all of them. Her dirk was gone as well, and all her throwing axes; instead she had a sword in hand, a short sword with a broad thick blade, almost like a butcher's cleaver. For her life she could not have said where she had gotten it. Her arm ached, her mouth tasted of blood, her legs were trembling, and shafts of pale dawn light were slanting through the trees. *Has it been so long? How long have we been fighting?*

Her last foe was a northman with an axe, a big man bald and bearded, clad in a byrnie of patched and rusted mail that could only mean he was a chief or champion. He was not pleased to find himself fighting a woman. "*Cunt!*" he roared each time he struck at her, his spittle dampening her cheeks. "*Cunt! Cunt!*"

Asha wanted to shout back at him, but her throat was so dry she could do no more than grunt. His axe was shivering her shield, cracking the wood on the downswing, tearing off long pale splinters when he wrenched it back. Soon she would have only a tangle of kindling on her arm. She backed away and shook free of the ruined shield, then backed away some more and danced left and right and left again to avoid the downrushing axe.

And then her back came up hard against a tree, and she could dance no more. The wolf raised the axe above his head to split her head in two. Asha tried to slip to her right, but her feet were tangled in some roots, trapping her. She twisted, lost her footing, and the axehead crunched against her temple with a scream of steel on steel. The world went red and black and red again. Pain crackled up her leg like lightning, and far away she heard her northman say, "You bloody cunt," as he lifted up his axe for the blow that would finish her.

A trumpet blew.

That's wrong, she thought. *There are no trumpets in the Drowned God's watery halls. Below the waves the merlings hail their lord by blowing into seashells.*

She dreamt of red hearts burning, and a black stag in a golden wood with flame streaming from his antlers.

TYRION

By the time they reached Volantis, the sky was purple to the west and black to the east, and the stars were coming out. *The same stars as in Westeros,* Tyrion Lannister reflected.

He might have taken some comfort in that if he had not been trussed up like a goose and lashed to a saddle. He had given up squirming. The knots that bound him were too tight. Instead he'd gone as limp as a sack of meal. *Saving my strength,* he told himself, though for what he could not have said.

Volantis closed its gates at dark, and the guardsmen on its northern gate were grumbling impatiently at the stragglers. They joined the queue behind a wagon laden with limes and oranges. The guards motioned the wagon through with their torches but took a harder look at the big Andal on his warhorse, with his longsword and his mail. A captain was summoned. Whilst he and the knight exchanged some words in Volantene, one of the guardsmen pulled off his clawed gauntlet and gave Tyrion's head a rub. "I'm full of good fortune," the dwarf told him. "Cut me loose, friend, and I'll see you're well rewarded."

His captor overheard. "Save your lies for those who speak your tongue, Imp," he said, when the Volantenes waved them on.

They were moving again, through the gate and beneath the city's massive walls. "*You* speak my tongue. Can I sway you with promises, or are you determined to buy a lordship with my head?"

"I *was* a lord, by right of birth. I want no hollow titles."

"That's all you're like to get from my sweet sister."

"And here I'd heard a Lannister always pays his debts."

"Oh, every penny . . . but never a groat more, my lord. You'll get the meal you bargained for, but it won't be sauced with gratitude, and in the end it will not nourish you."

"Might be all I want is to see you pay for crimes. The kinslayer is accursed in the eyes of gods and men."

"The gods are blind. And men see only what they wish."

"I see you plain enough, Imp." Something dark had crept into the knight's tone. "I have done things I am not proud of, things that brought shame onto my House and my father's name . . . but to kill your own sire? How could any man do that?"

"Give me a crossbow and pull down your breeches, and I'll show you." *Gladly.*

"You think this is a jape?"

"I think life is a jape. Yours, mine, everyone's."

Inside the city walls, they rode past guildhalls, markets, and bathhouses. Fountains splashed and sang in the centers of wide squares, where men sat at stone tables, moving *cyvasse* pieces and sipping wine from glass flutes as slaves lit ornate lanterns to hold the dark at bay. Palms and cedars grew along the cobbled road, and monuments stood at every junction. Many of the statues lacked heads, the dwarf noted, yet even headless they still managed to look imposing in the purple dusk.

As the warhorse plodded south along the river, the shops grew smaller and meaner, the trees along the street became a row of stumps. Cobblestones gave way to devilgrass beneath their horse's hooves, then to soft wet mud the color of a baby's nightsoil. The little bridges that spanned the small streams that fed the Rhoyne creaked alarmingly beneath their weight. Where a fort had once overlooked the river now stood a broken gate, gaping open like an old man's toothless mouth. Goats could be glimpsed peering over the parapets.

Old Volantis, first daughter of Valyria, the dwarf mused. *Proud Volantis, queen of the Rhoyne and mistress of the Summer Sea, home to noble lords and lovely ladies of the most ancient blood.* Never mind the packs of naked children that roamed the alleys screaming in shrill voices, or the bravos standing in the doors of wineshops fingering their sword hilts, or the slaves with their bent backs and tattooed faces who scurried everywhere like cockroaches. *Mighty Volantis, grandest and most populous of the Nine Free Cities.* Ancient wars had depopulated much of the city, however, and large areas of Volantis had begun to sink back into the mud on which it stood. *Beautiful Volantis, city of fountains and flowers.* But half the fountains were dry, half the pools cracked and stagnant. Flowering vines sent up creepers from every crack in the wall or pavement, and young trees had taken root in the walls of abandoned shops and roofless temples.

And then there was the smell. It hung in the hot, humid air, rich, rank, pervasive. *There's fish in it, and flowers, and some elephant dung as well. Something sweet and something earthy and something dead and rotten.* "This city smells like an old whore," Tyrion announced. "Like some sagging slattern who has drenched her privy parts in perfume to drown the stench between her legs. Not that I am complaining. With whores, the young ones smell much better, but the old ones know more tricks."

"You would know more of that than I do."

"Ah, of course. That brothel where we met, did you take it for a sept? Was that your virgin sister squirming in your lap?"

That made him scowl. "Give that tongue of yours a rest unless you'd rather I tied it in a knot."

Tyrion swallowed his retort. His lip was still fat and swollen from the last time he had pushed the big knight too far. *Hard hands and no sense of humor makes for a bad marriage.* That much he'd learned on the road from Selhorys. His thoughts went to his boot, to the mushrooms in the toe. His captor had not searched him quite as thoroughly as he might have. *There is always that escape. Cersei will not have me alive, at least.*

Farther south, signs of prosperity began to reappear. Abandoned buildings were seen less often, the naked children vanished, the bravos in the doorways seemed more sumptuously dressed. A few of the inns they passed actually looked like places where a man might sleep without fear of having his throat slit. Lanterns swung from iron stanchions along the river road, swaying when the wind blew. The streets grew broader, the buildings more imposing. Some were topped with great domes of colored glass. In the gathering dusk, with fires lit beneath them, the domes glowed blue and red and green and purple.

Even so, there was something in the air that made Tyrion uneasy. West of the Rhoyne, he knew, the wharves of Volantis teemed with sailors, slaves, and traders, and the wineshops, inns, and brothels all catered to them. East of the river, strangers from across the seas were seen less seldom. *We are not wanted here,* the dwarf realized.

The first time they passed an elephant, Tyrion could not help but stare. There had been an elephant in the menagerie at Lannisport when he had been a boy, but she had died when he was seven . . . and this great grey behemoth looked to be twice her size.

Farther on, they fell in behind a smaller elephant, white as old bone and pulling an ornate cart. "Is an oxcart an oxcart without an ox?" Tyrion asked his captor. When that sally got no response, he lapsed back into silence, contemplating the rolling rump of the white dwarf elephant ahead of them.

Volantis was overrun with white dwarf elephants. As they drew closer to the Black Wall and the crowded districts near the Long Bridge, they saw a dozen of them. Big grey elephants were not uncommon either—huge beasts with castles on their backs. And in the half-light of evening the dung carts had come out, attended by half-naked slaves whose task it was to shovel up the steaming piles left by elephants both great and small. Swarms of flies followed the carts, so the dung slaves had flies tattooed upon their cheeks, to mark them for what they were. *There's a trade for my sweet sister,* Tyrion mused. *She'd look so pretty with a little shovel and flies tattooed on those sweet pink cheeks.*

By then they had slowed to a crawl. The river road was thick with traffic, almost all of it flowing south. The knight went with it, a log caught in a current. Tyrion eyed the passing throngs. Nine men of every ten bore slave marks on their cheeks. "So many slaves . . . where are they all going?"

"The red priests light their nightfires at sunset. The High Priest will be speaking. I would avoid it if I could, but to reach the Long Bridge we must pass the red temple."

Three blocks later the street opened up before them onto a huge torchlit plaza, and there it stood. *Seven save me, that's got to be three times the size of the Great Sept of Baelor.* An enormity of pillars, steps, buttresses, bridges, domes, and towers flowing into one another as if they had all been chiseled from one collassal rock, the Temple of the Lord of Light loomed like Aegon's High Hill. A hundred hues of red, yellow, gold, and orange met and melded in the temple walls, dissolving one into the other like clouds at sunset. Its slender towers twisted ever upward, frozen flames dancing as they reached for the sky. *Fire turned to stone.* Huge nightfires burned beside the temple steps, and between them the High Priest had begun to speak.

Benerro. The priest stood atop a red stone pillar, joined by a slender stone bridge to a lofty terrace where the lesser priests and acolytes stood. The acolytes were clad in robes of pale yellow and bright orange, priests and priestesses in red.

The great plaza before them was packed almost solid. Many and more of the worshipers were wearing some scrap of red cloth pinned to their sleeves or tied around their brows. Every eye was on the high priest, save theirs. "Make way," the knight growled as his horse pushed through the throng. "Clear a path." The Volantenes gave way resentfully, with mutters and angry looks.

Benerro's high voice carried well. Tall and thin, he had a drawn face and skin white as milk. Flames had been tattooed across his cheeks and chin and shaven head to make a bright red mask that crackled about his eyes and coiled down and around his lipless mouth. "Is that a slave tattoo?" asked Tyrion.

The knight nodded. "The red temple buys them as children and makes them priests or temple prostitutes or warriors. Look there." He pointed at the steps, where a line of men in ornate armor and orange cloaks stood before the temple's doors, clasping spears with points like writhing flames. "The Fiery Hand. The Lord of Light's sacred soldiers, defenders of the temple."

Fire knights. "And how many fingers does this hand have, pray?"

"One thousand. Never more, and never less. A new flame is kindled for every one that gutters out."

Benerro jabbed a finger at the moon, made a fist, spread his hands wide. When his voice rose in a crescendo, flames leapt from his fingers with a sudden *whoosh* and made the crowd gasp. The priest could trace fiery letters in the air as well. *Valyrian glyphs.* Tyrion recognized perhaps two in ten; one was *Doom,* the other *Darkness.*

Shouts erupted from the crowd. Women were weeping and men were shaking their fists. *I have a bad feeling about this.* The dwarf was reminded of the day Myrcella sailed for Dorne and the riot that boiled up as they made their way back to the Red Keep.

Haldon Halfmaester had spoken of using the red priest to Young Griff's advantage, Tyrion recalled. Now that he had seen and heard the man himself, that struck him as a very bad idea. He hoped that Griff had better sense. *Some allies are more dangerous than enemies. But Lord Connington will need to puzzle that one out for himself. I am like to be a head on a spike.*

The priest was pointing at the Black Wall behind the temple, gesturing up at its parapets, where a handful of armored guardsmen stood gazing down. "What is he saying?" Tyrion asked the knight.

"That Daenerys stands in peril. The dark eye has fallen upon her, and the minions of night are plotting her destruction, praying to their false gods in temples of deceit . . . conspiring at betrayal with godless outlanders . . ."

The hairs on the back of Tyrion's neck began to prickle. *Prince Aegon will find no friend here.* The red priest spoke of ancient prophecy, a prophecy that foretold the coming of a hero to deliver the world from darkness. *One hero. Not two. Daenerys has dragons, Aegon does not.* The dwarf did not need to be a prophet himself to foresee how Benerro and his followers might react to a second Targaryen. *Griff will see that too, surely,* he thought, surprised to find how much he cared.

The knight had forced their way through most of the press at the back of the plaza, ignoring the curses that were flung at them as they passed. One man stepped in front of them, but his captor gripped the hilt of his longsword and drew it just far enough to show a foot of naked steel. The man melted away, and all at once an alley opened up before them. The knight urged his mount to a trot, and they left the crowd behind them. For a while Tyrion could still hear Benerro's voice growing fainter at their back and the roars his words provoked, sudden as thunder.

They came upon a stable. The knight dismounted, then hammered on the door until a haggard slave with a horsehead on his cheek came running. The dwarf was pulled down roughly from the saddle and lashed to a post whilst his captor woke the stable's owner and haggled with him over the price of his horse and saddle. *Cheaper to sell a horse than to ship one half across the world.* Tyrion sensed a ship in his immediate future. Perhaps he was a prophet after all.

When the dickering was done, the knight slung his weapons, shield, and saddlebag over his shoulder and asked for directions to the nearest smithy. That proved shuttered too, but opened quick enough at the knight's shout. The smith gave Tyrion a squint, then nodded and accepted a fistful of coins. "Come here," the knight told his prisoner. He drew his dagger and slit Tyrion's bonds apart. "My thanks," said the dwarf as he rubbed his wrists, but the knight only laughed and said, "Save your gratitude for someone who deserves it, Imp. You will not like this next bit."

He was not wrong.

The manacles were black iron, thick and heavy, each weighing a good two pounds, if the dwarf was any judge. The chains added even more weight. "I must be more fearsome than I knew," Tyrion confessed as the last links were hammered closed. Each blow sent a shock up his arm almost to the shoulder. "Or were you afraid that I would dash away on these stunted little legs of mine?"

The ironsmith did not so much as look up from his work, but the knight chuckled darkly. "It's your mouth that concerns me, not your legs. In fetters, you're a slave. No one will listen to a word you say, not even those who speak the tongue of Westeros."

"There's no need for this," Tyrion protested. "I will be a good little prisoner, I will, I will."

"Prove it, then, and shut your mouth."

So he bowed his head and bit his tongue as the chains were fixed, wrist to wrist, wrist to ankle, ankle to ankle. *These bloody things weigh more than I do.* Still, at least he drew breath. His captor could just as easily have cut his head off. That was all Cersei required, after all. Not striking it off straightaway had been his captor's first mistake. *There is half a world between Volantis and King's Landing, and much and more can happen along the way, ser.*

The rest of the way they went by foot, Tyrion clanking and clattering as he struggled to keep up with his captor's long, impatient strides. Whenever he threatened to fall behind, the knight would seize his fetters and yank them roughly, sending the dwarf stumbling and hopping along beside him. *It could be worse. He could be urging me along with a whip.*

Volantis straddled one mouth of the Rhoyne where the river kissed the sea, its two halves joined by the Long Bridge. The oldest, richest part of the city was east of the river, but sellswords, barbarians, and other uncouth outlanders were not welcome there, so they must needs cross over to the west.

The gateway to the Long Bridge was a black stone arch carved with sphinxes, manticores, dragons, and creatures stranger still. Beyond the arch stretched the great span that the Valyrians had built at the height of their glory, its fused stone roadway supported by massive piers. The road was just wide enough for two carts to pass abreast, so whenever a wagon headed west passed one going east, both had to slow to a crawl.

It was well they were afoot. A third of the way out, a wagon laden with melons had gotten its wheels tangled with one piled high with silken carpets and brought all wheeled traffic to a halt. Much of the foot traffic had stopped as well, to watch the drivers curse and scream at one another, but the knight grabbed hold of Tyrion's chain and bulled a path through the throng for both of them. In the middle of the press, a boy tried to reach into his purse, but a hard elbow put an end to that and spread the thief's bloody nose across half his face.

Buildings rose to either side of them: shops and temples, taverns and inns, *cyvasse* parlors and brothels. Most were three or four stories tall, each floor overhanging the one beneath it. Their top floors almost kissed. Crossing the bridge felt like passing through a torchlit tunnel.

Along the span were shops and stalls of every sort; weavers and lace-makers displayed their wares cheek by jowl with glassblowers, candle-makers, and fishwives selling eels and oysters. Each goldsmith had a guard at his door, and every spicer had two, for their goods were twice as valuable. Here and there, between the shops, a traveler might catch a glimpse of the river he was crossing. To the north the Rhoyne was a broad black ribbon bright with stars, five times as wide as the Blackwater Rush at King's Landing. South of the bridge the river opened up to embrace the briny sea.

At the bridge's center span, the severed hands of thieves and cutpurses hung like strings of onions from iron stanchions along the roadway. Three heads were on display as well—two men and a woman, their crimes scrawled on tablets underneath them. A pair of spearmen attended them, clad in polished helms and shirts of silver mail. Across their cheeks were tiger stripes as green as jade. From time to time the guards waved their spears to chase away the kestrels, gulls, and carrion crows paying court to the deceased. The birds returned to the heads within moments.

"What did they do?" Tyrion inquired innocently.

The knight glanced at the inscriptions. "The woman was a slave who raised her hand to her mistress. The older man was accused of fomenting rebellion and spying for the dragon queen."

"And the young one?"

"Killed his father."

Tyrion gave the rotting head a second look. *Why, it almost looks as if those lips are smiling.*

Farther on, the knight paused briefly to consider a jeweled tiara displayed upon a bed of purple velvet. He passed that by, but a few steps on he stopped again to haggle over a pair of gloves at a leather-worker's stall. Tyrion was grateful for the respites. The headlong pace had left him puffing, and his wrists were chafed raw from the manacles.

From the far end of the Long Bridge, it was only a short walk through the teeming waterfront districts of the west bank, down torchlit streets crowded with sailors, slaves, and drunken merrymakers. Once an elephant lumbered past with a dozen half-naked slave girls waving from the castle on its back, teasing passersby with glimpses of their breasts and crying, "Malaquo, Malaquo." They made such an entrancing sight that Tyrion almost waddled right into the steaming pile of dung the elephant had left to mark its passage. He was saved at the last instant when the knight snatched him aside, yanking on his chain so hard it made him reel and stumble.

"How much farther?" the dwarf asked.

"Just there. Fishmonger's Square."

Their destination proved to be the Merchant's House, a four-story monstrosity that squatted amongst the warehouses, brothels, and taverns of the waterside like some enormous fat man surrounded by children. Its common room was larger than the great halls of half the castles in Westeros, a dim-lit maze of a place with a hundred private alcoves and hidden nooks whose blackened beams and cracked ceilings echoed to the din of sailors, traders, captains, money changers, shippers, and slavers, lying, cursing, and cheating each other in half a hundred different tongues.

Tyrion approved the choice of hostelry. Soon or late the *Shy Maid* must reach Volantis. This was the city's biggest inn, first choice for shippers, captains, and merchantmen. A lot of business was done in that cavernous warren of a common room. He knew enough of Volantis to know that. Let Griff turn up here with Duck and Haldon, and he would be free again soon enough.

Meanwhile, he would be patient. His chance would come.

The rooms upstairs proved rather less than grand, however, particularly the cheap ones up on the fourth floor. Wedged into a corner of the building beneath a sloping roof, the bedchamber his captor had engaged featured a low ceiling, a sagging feather bed with an unpleasant odor, and a slanting wood-plank floor that reminded Tyrion of his sojourn at the Eyrie. *At least this room has walls.* It had windows too; those were its chief amenity, along with the iron ring set in the wall, so useful for chaining up one's slaves. His captor paused only long enough to light a tallow candle before securing Tyrion's chains to the ring.

"Must you?" the dwarf protested, rattling feebly. "Where am I going to go, out the window?"

"You might."

"We are four floors up, and I cannot fly."

"You can fall. I want you alive."

Aye, but why? Cersei is not like to care. Tyrion rattled his chains. "I know who you are, ser." It had not been hard to puzzle out. The bear on his surcoat, the arms on his shield, the lost lordship he had mentioned. "I know *what* you are. And if you know who I am, you also know that I was the King's Hand and sat in council with the Spider. Would it interest you to know that it was the eunuch who dispatched me on this journey?" *Him and Jaime, but I'll leave my brother out of it.* "I am as much his creature as you are. We ought not be at odds."

That did not please the knight. "I took the Spider's coin, I'll not deny it, but I was never his creature. And my loyalties lie elsewhere now."

"With Cersei? More fool you. All my sister requires is my head, and you have a fine sharp sword. Why not end this farce now and spare us both?"

The knight laughed. "Is this some dwarf's trick? Beg for death in hopes I'll let you live?" He went to the door. "I'll bring you something from the kitchens."

"How kind of you. I'll wait here."

"I know you will." Yet when the knight left, he locked the door behind him with a heavy iron key. The Merchant's House was famous for its locks. *As secure as a gaol,* the dwarf thought bitterly, *but at least there are those windows.*

Tyrion knew that the chances of his escaping his chains were little and less, but even so, he felt obliged to try. His efforts to slip a hand through the manacle served only to scrap off more skin and leave his wrist slick with blood, and all his tugging or twisting could not pull the iron ring from the wall. *Bugger this,* he thought, slumping back as far as his chains would allow. His legs had begun to cramp. This was going to be a hellishly uncomfortable night. *The first of many, I do not doubt.*

The room was stifling, so the knight had opened the shutters to let in a cross breeze. Cramped into a corner of the building under the eaves, the chamber was fortunate in having two windows. One looked toward the Long Bridge and the black-walled heart of Old Volantis across the river. The other opened on the square below. Fishermonger's Square, Mormont called it. As tight as the chains were, Tyrion found he could see out the latter by leaning sideways and letting the iron ring support his weight. *Not as long a fall as the one from Lysa Arryn's sky cells, but it would leave me just as dead. Perhaps if I were drunk . . .*

Even at this hour the square was crowded, with sailors roistering, whores prowling for custom, and merchants going about their business. A red priestess scurried past, attended by a dozen acolytes with torches, their robes whisking about their ankles. Elsewhere a pair of *cyvasse* players waged war outside a tavern. A slave stood beside their table, holding a lantern over the board. Tyrion could hear a woman singing. The words were strange, the tune was soft and sad. *If I knew what she was singing, I might cry.* Closer to hand, a crowd was gathering around a pair of jugglers throwing flaming torches at each other.

His captor returned shortly, carrying two tankards and a roasted duck. He kicked the door shut, ripped the duck in two, and tossed half of it to Tyrion. He would have snatched it from the air, but his chains brought him up short when he tried to lift his arms. Instead the bird struck his temple and slid hot and greasy down his face, and he had to hunker down and stretch for it with fetters clanking. He got it on the third try and tore into it happily with his teeth. "Some ale to wash this down?"

Mormont handed him a tankard. "Most of Volantis is getting drunk, why not you?"

The ale was sweet as well. It tasted of fruit. Tyrion drank a healthy swallow and belched happily. The tankard was pewter, very heavy. *Empty it and fling it at his head,* he thought. *If I am lucky, it might crack his skull. If I'm very lucky, it will miss, and he'll beat me to death with his fists.* He took another gulp. "Is this some holy day?"

"Third day of their elections. They last for ten. Ten days of madness. Torchlight marches, speeches, mummers and minstrels and dancers, bravos fighting death duels for the honor of their candidates, elephants with the names of would-be triarchs painted on their sides. Those jugglers are performing for Methyso."

"Remind me to vote for someone else." Tyrion licked grease from his fingers. Below, the crowd was flinging coins at the jugglers. "Do all these would-be triarchs provide mummer shows?"

"They do whatever they think will win them votes," said Mormont. "Food, drink, spectacle . . . Alios has sent a hundred pretty slave girls out into the streets to lie with voters."

"I'm for him," Tyrion decided. "Bring me a slave girl."

"They're for freeborn Volantenes with enough property to vote. Precious few voters west of the river."

"And this goes on for ten days?" Tyrion laughed. "I might enjoy that, though three kings is two too many. I am trying to imagine ruling the Seven Kingdoms with my sweet sister and brave brother beside me. One of us would kill the other two inside a year. I am surprised these triarchs don't do the same."

"A few have tried. Might be the Volantenes are the clever ones and us Westerosi the fools. Volantis has known her share of follies, but she's never suffered a boy triarch. Whenever a madman's been elected, his colleagues restrain him until his year has run its course. Think of the dead who might still live if Mad Aerys only had two fellow kings to share the rule."

Instead he had my father, Tyrion thought.

"Some in the Free Cities think that we're all savages on our side of the narrow sea," the knight went on. "The ones who don't think that we're children, crying out for a father's strong hand."

"Or a mother's?" *Cersei will love that. Especially when he presents her with my head.* "You seem to know this city well."

"I spent the best part of a year here." The knight sloshed the dregs at the bottom of his tankard. "When Stark drove me into exile, I fled to Lys with my second wife. Braavos would have suited me better, but Lynesse wanted someplace warm. Instead of serving the Braavosi I fought them on the Rhoyne, but for every silver I earned my wife spent ten. By the time I got back to Lys, she had taken a lover, who told me cheerfully that I would be enslaved for debt unless I gave her up and left the city. That was how I came to Volantis . . . one step ahead of slavery, owning nothing but my sword and the clothes upon my back."

"And now you want to run home."

The knight drained the last of his ale. "On the morrow I'll find us a ship. The bed is mine. You can have whatever piece of floor your chains will let you reach. Sleep if you can. If not, count your crimes. That should see you through till the morning."

You have your crimes to answer for, Jorah Mormont, the dwarf thought, but it seemed wiser to keep that thought to himself.

Ser Jorah hung his sword belt on a bedpost, kicked off his boots, pulled his chain mail over his head, and stripped out of his wool and leather and sweat-stained undertunic to reveal a scarred, brawny torso covered with dark hair. *If I could skin him, I could sell that pelt for a fur cloak,* Tyrion thought as Mormont tumbled into the slightly smelly comfort of his sagging feather bed.

In no time at all the knight was snoring, leaving his prize alone with his chains. With both windows open wide, the light of the waning moon spilled across the bedchamber. Sounds drifted up from the square below: snatches of drunken song, the yowling of a cat in heat, the far-off ring of steel on steel. *Someone's about to die,* thought Tyrion.

His wrist was throbbing where he'd torn the skin, and his fetters made it impossible for him to sit, let alone stretch out. The best he could do was twist sideways to lean against the wall, and before long he began to lose all feeling in his hands. When he moved to relieve the strain, sensation came flooding back as pain. He had to grind his teeth to keep from screaming. He wondered how much his father had hurt when the quarrel punched through his groin, what Shae had felt as he twisted the chain around her lying throat, what Tysha had been feeling as they raped her. His sufferings were nothing compared to their own, but that did not make him hurt any less. *Just make it stop.*

Ser Jorah had rolled onto one side, so all that Tyrion could see of him was a broad, hairy, muscular back. *Even if I could slip these chains, I'd need to climb over him to reach his sword belt. Perhaps if I could ease the dagger loose . . .* Or else he could try for the key, unlock the door, creep down the stairs and through the common room . . . *and go where? I have no friends, no coin, I do not even speak the local tongue.*

Exhaustion finally overwhelmed his pains, and Tyrion drifted off into a fitful sleep. But every time another cramp took root inside his calf and twisted, the dwarf would cry out in his sleep, trembling in his chains. He woke with every muscle aching, to find morning streaming through the windows bright and golden as the lion of Lannister. Below he could hear the cries of fishmongers and the rumble of iron-rimmed wheels on cobblestones.

Jorah Mormont was standing over him. "If I take you off the ring, will you do as you're told?"

"Will it involve dancing? I might find dancing difficult. I cannot feel my legs. They may have fallen off. Elsewise, I am your creature. On my honor as a Lannister."

"The Lannisters have no honor." Ser Jorah loosed his chains anyway. Tyrion took two wobbly steps and fell. The blood rushing back into his hands brought tears to his eyes. He bit his lip and said, "Wherever we're going, you will need to roll me there."

Instead the big knight carried him, hoisting him by the chain between his wrists.

The common room of the Merchant's House was a dim labyrinth of alcoves and grottoes built around a central courtyard where a trellis of flowering vines threw intricate patterns across the flagstone floor and green and purple moss grew between the stones. Slave girls scurried through light and shadow, bearing flagons of ale and wine and some iced green drink that smelled of mint. One table in twenty was occupied at this hour of the morning.

One of those was occupied by a dwarf. Clean-shaved and pink-cheeked, with a mop of chestnut hair, a heavy brow, and a squashed nose, he perched on a high stool with a wooden spoon in hand, contemplating a bowl of purplish gruel with red-rimmed eyes. *Ugly little bastard,* Tyrion thought.

The other dwarf felt his stare. When he raised his head and saw Tyrion, the spoon slipped from his hand.

"He saw me," Tyrion warned Mormont.

"What of it?"

"He *knows* me. Who I am."

"Should I stuff you in a sack, so no one will see you?" The knight touched the hilt of his longsword. "If he means to try and take you, he is welcome to try."

Welcome to die, you mean, thought Tyrion. *What threat could he pose to a big man like you? He is only a dwarf.*

Ser Jorah claimed a table in a quiet corner and ordered food and drink. They broke their fast with warm soft flatbread, pink fish roe, honey sausage, and fried locusts, washed down with a bittersweet black ale. Tyrion ate like a man half-starved. "You have a healthy appetite this morning," the knight observed.

"I've heard the food in hell is wretched." Tyrion glanced at the door, where a man had just come in: tall and stooped, his pointed beard dyed a splotchy purple. *Some Tyroshi trader.* A gust of sound came with him from outside; the cries of gulls, a woman's laughter, the voices of the fishmongers. For half a heartbeat he thought he glimpsed Illyrio Mopatis, but it was only one of those white dwarf elephants passing the front door.

Mormont spread some fish roe across a slice of flatbread and took a bite. "Are you expecting someone?"

Tyrion shrugged. "You never know who the wind might blow in. My one true love, my father's ghost, a duck." He popped a locust into his mouth and crunched it. "Not bad. For a bug."

"Last night the talk here was all of Westeros. Some exiled lord has hired the Golden Company to win back his lands for him. Half the captains in Volantis are racing upriver to Volon Therys to offer him their ships."

Tyrion had just swallowed another locust. He almost choked on it. *Is he mocking me? How much could he know of Griff and Aegon?* "Bugger," he said. "I meant to hire the Golden Company myself, to win me Casterly Rock." *Could this be some ploy of Griff's, false reports deliberately spread? Unless . . .* Could the pretty princeling have swallowed the bait? Turned them west instead of east, abandoning his hopes of wedding Queen Daenerys? *Abandoning the dragons . . . would Griff allow that?* "I'll gladly hire you as well, ser. My father's seat is mine by rights. Swear me your sword, and once I win it back I'll drown you in gold."

"I saw a man drowned in gold once. It was not a pretty sight. If you ever get my sword, it will be through your bowels."

"A sure cure for constipation," said Tyrion. "Just ask my father." He reached for his tankard and took a slow swallow, to help conceal whatever might be showing on his face. It had to be a stratagem, designed to lull Volantene suspicions. *Get the men aboard with this false pretext and seize the ships when the fleet is out to sea. Is that Griff's plan?* It might work. The Golden Company was ten thousand strong, seasoned and disciplined. *None of them seamen, though. Griff will need to keep a sword at every throat, and should they come on Slaver's Bay and need to fight . . .*

The serving girl returned. "The widow will see you next, noble ser. Have you brought a gift for her?"

"Yes. Thank you." Ser Jorah slipped a coin into the girl's palm and sent her on her way.

Tyrion frowned. "Whose widow is this?"

"The widow of the waterfront. East of the Rhoyne they still call her Vogarro's whore, though never to her face."

The dwarf was not enlightened. "And Vogarro was . . . ?"

"An elephant, seven times a triarch, very rich, a power on the docks. Whilst other men built the ships and sailed them, he built piers and storehouses, brokered cargoes, changed money, insured shipowners against the hazards of the sea. He dealt in slaves as well. When he grew besotted with one of them, a bedslave trained at Yunkai in the way of seven sighs, it was a great scandal . . . and a greater scandal when he freed her and took her for his wife. After he died, she carried on his ventures. No freedman may dwell within the Black Wall, so she was compelled to sell Vogarro's manse. She took up residence at the Merchant's House. That was thirty-two years ago, and she remains here to this day. That's her behind you, back by the courtyard, holding court at her customary table. No, don't look. There's someone with her now. When he's done, it will be our turn."

"And this old harridan will help you how?"

Ser Jorah stood. "Watch and see. He's leaving."

Tyrion hopped down off his chair with a rattle of iron. *This should be enlightening.*

There was something vulpine about the way the woman sat in her corner by the courtyard, something reptilian about her eyes. Her white hair was so thin that the pink of her scalp showed through. Under one eye she still bore faint scars where a knife had cut away her tears. The remnants of her morning meal littered the table—sardine heads, olive pits, chunks of flatbread. Tyrion did not fail to note how well chosen her "customary table" was; solid stone at her back, a leafy alcove to one side for entrances and exits, a perfect view of the inn's front door, yet so steeped in shadow that she herself was nigh invisible.

The sight of him made the old woman smile. "A dwarf," she purred, in a voice as sinister as it was soft. She spoke the Common Tongue with only a trace of accent. "Volantis has been overrun with dwarfs of late, it seems. Does this one do tricks?"

Yes, Tyrion wanted to say. *Give me a crossbow, and I'll show you my favorite.* "No," Ser Jorah answered.

"A pity. I once had a monkey who could perform all sorts of clever tricks. Your dwarf reminds me of him. Is he a gift?"

"No. I brought you these." Ser Jorah produced his pair of gloves, and slapped them down on the table beside the other gifts the widow had received this morning: a silver goblet, an ornate fan carved of jade leaves so thin they were translucent, and an ancient bronze dagger marked with runes. Beside such treasures the gloves looked cheap and tawdry.

"Gloves for my poor old wrinkled hands. How nice." The widow made no move to touch them.

"I bought them on the Long Bridge."

"A man can buy most anything on the Long Bridge. Gloves, slaves, monkeys." The years had bent her spine and put a crone's hump upon her back, but the widow's eyes were bright and black. "Now tell this old widow how she may be of service to you."

"We need swift passage to Meereen."

One word. Tyrion Lannister's world turned upside down.

One word. *Meereen.* Or had he misheard?

One word. *Meereen, he said Meereen, he's taking me to Meereen.* Meereen meant life. Or hope for life, at least.

"Why come to me?" the widow said. "I own no ships."

"You have many captains in your debt."

Deliver me to the queen, he says. Aye, but which queen? He isn't selling me to Cersei. He's giving me to Daenerys Targaryen. That's why he hasn't hacked my head off. We're going east, and Griff and his prince are going west, the bloody fools.

Oh, it was all too much. *Plots within plots, but all roads lead down the dragon's gullet.* A guffaw burst from his lips, and suddenly Tyrion could not stop laughing.

"Your dwarf is having a fit," the widow observed.

"My dwarf will be quiet, or I'll see him gagged."

Tyrion covered his mouth with his hands. *Meereen!*

The widow of the waterfront decided to ignore him. "Shall we have a drink?" she asked. Dust motes floated in the air as a serving girl filled two green glass cups for Ser Jorah and the widow. Tyrion's throat was dry, but no cup was poured for him. The widow took a sip, rolled the wine round her mouth, swallowed. "All the other exiles are sailing west, or so these old ears have heard. And all those captains in my debt are falling over one another to take them there and leach a little gold from the coffers of the Golden Company. Our noble triarchs have pledged a dozen warships to the cause, to see the fleet safely as far as the Stepstones. Even old Doniphos has given his assent. Such a glorious adventure. And yet you would go the other way, ser."

"My business is in the east."

"And what business is that, I wonder? Not slaves, the silver queen has put an end to that. She has closed the fighting pits as well, so it cannot be a taste for blood. What else could Meereen offer to a Westerosi knight? Bricks? Olives? *Dragons?* Ah, there it is." The old woman's smile turned feral. "I have heard it said that the silver queen feeds them with the flesh of infants while she herself bathes in the blood of virgin girls and takes a different lover every night."

Ser Jorah's mouth had hardened. "The Yunkai'i are pouring poison in your ears. My lady should not believe such filth."

"I am no lady, but even Vogarro's whore knows the taste of

falsehood. This much is true, though . . . the dragon queen has enemies . . . Yunkai, New Ghis, Tolos, Qarth . . . aye, and Volantis, soon enough. You would travel to Meereen? Just wait a while, ser. Swords will be wanted soon enough, when the warships bend their oars eastward to bring down the silver queen. Tigers love to bare their claws, and even elephants will kill if threatened. Malaquo hungers for a taste of glory, and Nyessos owes much of his wealth to the slave trade. Let Alios or Parquello or Belicho gain the triarchy, and the fleets will sail."

Ser Jorah scowled. "If Doniphos is returned . . ."

"Vogarro will be returned first, and my sweet lord has been dead these thirty years."

Behind them, some sailor was bellowing loudly. "They call this ale? *Fuck.* A monkey could piss better ale."

"And you would drink it," another voice replied.

Tyrion twisted around for a look, hoping against hope that it was Duck and Haldon he was hearing. Instead he saw two strangers . . . and the dwarf, who was standing a few feet away staring at him intently. He seemed somehow familiar.

The widow sipped daintily at her wine. "Some of the first elephants were women," she said, "the ones who brought the tigers down and ended the old wars. Trianna was returned four times. That was three hundred years ago, alas. Volantis has had no female triarch since, though some women have the vote. Women of good birth who dwell in ancient palaces behind the Black Walls, not creatures such as me. The Old Blood will have their dogs and children voting before any freedman. No, it will be Belicho, or perhaps Alios, but either way it will be war. Or so they think."

"And what do you think?" Ser Jorah asked.

Good, thought Tyrion. *The right question.*

"Oh, I think it will be war as well, but not the war they want." The old woman leaned forward, her black eyes gleaming. "I think that red R'hllor has more worshipers in this city than all the other gods together. Have you heard Benerro preach?"

"Last night."

"Benerro can see the morrow in his flames," the widow said.

"Triarch Malaquo tried to hire the Golden Company, did you know? He meant to clean out the red temple and put Benerro to the sword. He dare not use tiger cloaks. Half of them worship the Lord of Light as well. Oh, these are dire days in Old Volantis, even for wrinkled old widows. But not half so dire as in Meereen, I think. So tell me, ser . . . why do you seek the silver queen?"

"That is my concern. I can pay for our passage and pay well. I have the silver."

Fool, thought Tyrion. *It's not coin she wants, it's respect. Haven't you heard a word she's said?* He glanced back over his shoulder again. The dwarf had moved closer to their table. And he seemed to have a knife in his hand. The hairs on the back of Tyrion's neck began to prickle.

"Keep your silver. I have gold. And spare me your black looks, ser. I am too old to be frightened of a scowl. You are a hard man, I see, and no doubt skilled with that long sword at your side, but this is my realm. Let me crook a finger and you may find yourself traveling to Meereen chained to an oar in the belly of a galley." She lifted her jade fan and opened it. There was a rustle of leaves, and a man slid from the overgrown archway to her left. His face was a mass of scars, and in one hand he held a sword, short and heavy as a cleaver. "*Seek the widow of the waterfront*, someone told you, but they should have also warned you, *beware the widow's sons*. It is such a sweet morning, though, I shall ask again. Why would you seek Daenerys Targaryen, whom half the world wants dead?"

Jorah Mormont's face was dark with anger, but he answered. "To serve her. Defend her. Die for her, if need be."

That made the widow laugh. "You want to *rescue* her, is that the way of it? From more enemies than I can name, with swords beyond count . . . *this* is what you'd have the poor widow believe? That you are a true and chivalrous Westerosi knight crossing half the world to come to the aid of this . . . well, she is no maiden, though she may still be fair." She laughed again. "Do you think your dwarf will please her? Will she bathe in his blood, do you think, or content herself with striking off his head?"

Ser Jorah hesitated. "The dwarf is—"

"—I know who the dwarf is, and what he is." Her black eyes turned to Tyrion, hard as stone. "Kinslayer, kingslayer, murderer, turncloak. *Lannister.*" She made the last a curse. "What do *you* plan to offer the dragon queen, little man?"

My hate, Tyrion wanted to say. Instead he spread his hands as far as the fetters would allow. "Whatever she would have of me. Sage counsel, savage wit, a bit of tumbling. My cock, if she desires it. My tongue, if she does not. I will lead her armies or rub her feet, as she desires. And the only reward I ask is I might be allowed to rape and kill my sister."

That brought the smile back to the old woman's face. "This one at least is honest," she announced, "but you, ser . . . I have known a dozen Westerosi knights and a thousand adventurers of the same ilk, but none so pure as you would paint yourself. Men are beasts, selfish and brutal. However gentle the words, there are always darker motives underneath. I do not trust you, ser." She flicked them off with her fan, as if they were no more than flies buzzing about her head. "If you want to get to Meereen, swim. I have no help to give you."

Then seven hells broke out at once.

Ser Jorah started to rise, the widow snapped her fan closed, her scarred man slid out of the shadows . . . and behind them a girl screamed. Tyrion spun just in time to see the dwarf rushing toward him. *She's a girl,* he realized all at once, *a girl dressed up in man's clothes. And she means to gut me with that knife.*

For half a heartbeat Ser Jorah, the widow, and the scarred man stood still as stone. Idlers watched from nearby tables, sipping ale and wine, but no one moved to interfere. Tyrion had to move both hands at once, but his chains had just enough give for him to reach the flagon on the table. He closed his fist around it, spun, dashed its contents into the face of the charging dwarf girl, then threw himself to one side to avoid her knife. The flagon shattered underneath him as the floor came up to smack him in the head. Then the girl was on him once again. Tyrion rolled on one side as she buried the knife blade in the floorboards, yanked it free, raised it again . . .

. . . and suddenly she was rising off the floor, legs kicking wildly as she struggled in Ser Jorah's grasp. "No!" she wailed, in the Common

Tongue of Westeros. "Let *go*!" Tyrion heard her tunic rip as she fought to free herself.

Mormont had her by the collar with one hand. With the other he wrenched the dagger from her grasp. "Enough."

The landlord made his appearance then, a cudgel in his hand. When he saw the broken flagon, he uttered a blistering curse and demanded to know what had happened here. "Dwarf fight," replied the Tyroshi with the purple beard, chuckling.

Tyrion blinked up at the dripping girl twisting in the air. "Why?" he demanded. "What did I ever do to you?"

"They killed him." All the fight went out of her at that. She hung limply in Mormont's grasp as her eyes filled with tears. "My brother. They took him and they killed him."

"Who killed him?" asked Mormont.

"Sailors. Sailors from the Seven Kingdoms. There were five of them, drunk. They saw us jousting in the square and followed us. When they realized I was a girl they let me go, but they took my brother and killed him. *They cut his head off.*"

Tyrion felt a sudden shock of recognition. *They saw us jousting in the square.* He knew who the girl was then. "Did you ride the pig?" he asked her. "Or the dog?"

"The dog," she sobbed. "Oppo always rode the pig."

The dwarfs from Joffrey's wedding. It was their show that had started all the trouble that night. *How strange, to encounter them again half a world away.* Though perhaps not so strange as that. *If they had half the wits of their pig, they would have fled King's Landing the night Joff died, before Cersei could assign them some share of blame in her son's death.* "Let her down, ser," he told Ser Jorah Mormont. "She won't do us any harm."

Ser Jorah dumped the dwarf girl on the floor. "I am sorry for your brother . . . but we had no part in his murder."

"He did." The girl pushed herself to her knees, clutching her torn, wine-drenched tunic to small, pale breasts. "It was him they wanted. They thought Oppo was *him.*" The girl was weeping, begging for help from anyone who would listen. "He should die, the way my poor brother died. Please. Someone help me. Someone kill him." The landlord seized her roughly by one arm and wrenched her back to her feet, shouting in Volantene, demanding to know who was going to pay for this damage.

The widow of the waterfront gave Mormont a cool look. "Knights defend the weak and protect the innocent, they say. And I am the fairest maid in all Volantis." Her laugh was full of scorn. "What do they call you, child?"

"Penny."

The old woman called out to the landlord in the tongue of Old Volantis. Tyrion knew enough to understand that she was telling him to take the dwarf girl up to her rooms, give her wine, and find some clothes for her to wear.

When they were gone, the widow studied Tyrion, her black eyes shining. "Monsters should be larger, it seems to me. You are worth a lordship back in Westeros, little man. Here, I fear, your worth is somewhat less. But I think I had best help you after all. Volantis is no safe place for dwarfs, it seems."

"You are too kind." Tyrion gave her his sweetest smile. "Perhaps you would remove these charming iron bracelets as well? This monster has but half a nose, and it itches most abominably. The chains are too short for me to scratch it. I'll make you a gift of them, and gladly."

"How generous. But I have worn iron in my time, and now I find that I prefer gold and silver. And sad to say, this is Volantis, where fetters and chains are cheaper than day-old bread and it is forbidden to help a slave escape."

"I'm no slave."

"Every man ever taken by slavers sings that same sad song. I dare not help you ... here." She leaned forward again. "Two days from now, the cog *Selaesori Qhoran* will set sail for Qarth by way of New Ghis, carrying tin and iron, bales of wool and lace, fifty Myrish carpets, a corpse pickled in brine, twenty jars of dragon peppers, and a red priest. Be on her when she sails."

"We will," said Tyrion, "and thank you."

Ser Jorah frowned. "Qarth is not our destination."

"She will never reach Qarth. Benerro has seen it in his fires." The crone smiled a vulpine smile.

"As you say." Tyrion grinned. "If I were Volantene, and free, and had the blood, you'd have my vote for triarch, my lady."

"I am no lady," the widow replied, "just Vogarro's whore. You want to be gone from here before the tigers come. Should you reach your queen, give her a message from the slaves of Old Volantis." She touched the faded scar upon her wrinkled cheek, where her tears had been cut away. "Tell her we are waiting. Tell her to come soon."

JON

When he heard the order, Ser Alliser's mouth twisted into a semblance of a smile, but his eyes remained as cold and hard as flint. "So the bastard boy sends me out to die."

"*Die,*" cried Mormont's raven. "*Die, die, die.*"

You are not helping. Jon swatted the bird away. "The bastard boy is sending you out to range. To find our foes and kill them if need be. You are skilled with a blade. You were master-at-arms, here and at Eastwatch."

Thorne touched the hilt of his longsword. "Aye. I have squandered a third of my life trying to teach the rudiments of swordplay to churls, muttonheads, and knaves. Small good that will do me in those woods."

"Dywen will be with you, and another seasoned ranger."

"We'll learn you what you need t' know, ser," Dywen told Thorne, cackling. "Teach you how t' wipe your highborn arse with leaves, just like a proper ranger."

Kedge Whiteye laughed at that, and Black Jack Bulwer spat. Ser Alliser only said, "You would like me to refuse. Then you could hack off my head, same as you did for Slynt. I'll not give you that pleasure, bastard. You'd best pray that it's a wildling blade that kills me, though. The ones the Others kill don't stay dead . . . and they *remember*. I'm coming back, Lord Snow."

"I pray you do." Jon would never count Ser Alliser Thorne amongst his friends, but he was still a brother. *No one ever said you had to like your brothers.*

It was no easy thing to send men into the wild, knowing that the chances were good that they might never return. *They are all seasoned men,* Jon told himself . . . but his uncle Benjen and his rangers had been seasoned men as well, and the haunted forest had swallowed them up without a trace. When two of them finally came straggling back to the Wall, it had been as wights. Not for the first time, or the last, Jon Snow found himself wondering what had become of Benjen Stark. *Perhaps the rangers will come upon some sign of them,* he told himself, never truly believing it.

Dywen would lead one ranging, Black Jack Bulwer and Kedge Whiteye the other two. They at least were eager for the duty. "Feels good to have a horse under me again," Dywen said at the gate, sucking on his wooden teeth. "Begging your pardon, m'lord, but we were all o' us getting splinters up our arses from sitting about." No man in Castle Black knew the woods as well as Dywen did, the trees and streams, the plants that could be eaten, the ways of predator and prey. *Thorne is in better hands than he deserves.*

Jon watched the riders go from atop the Wall—three parties, each of three men, each carrying a pair of ravens. From on high their garrons looked no larger than ants, and Jon could not tell one ranger from another. He knew them, though. Every name was graven on his heart. *Eight good men,* he thought, *and one . . . well, we shall see.*

When the last of the riders had disappeared into the trees, Jon Snow rode the winch cage down with Dolorous Edd. A few scattered snowflakes were falling as they made their slow descent, dancing on the gusty wind. One followed the cage down, drifting just beyond the bars. It was falling faster than they were descending and from time to time would vanish beneath them. Then a gust of wind would catch it and push it upward once again. Jon could have reached through the bars and caught it if he had wished.

"I had a frightening dream last night, m'lord," Dolorous Edd confessed. "You were my steward, fetching my food and cleaning up my leavings. I was lord commander, with never a moment's peace."

Jon did not smile. "Your nightmare, my life."

Cotter Pyke's galleys were reporting ever-increasing numbers of free folk along the wooded shores to the north and east of the Wall. Camps had been seen, half-built rafts, even the hull of a broken cog that someone had begun repairing. The wildlings always vanished into the woods when seen, no doubt to reemerge as soon as Pyke's ships had passed. Meanwhile, Ser Denys Mallister was still seeing fires in the night north of the Gorge. Both commanders were asking for more men.

And where am I to get more men? Jon had sent ten of the Mole's Town wildlings to each of them: green boys, old men, some wounded and infirm, but all capable of doing work of one sort or another. Far from being pleased, Pyke and Mallister had both written back to complain. "When I asked for men, I had in mind men of the Night's Watch, trained and disciplined, whose loyalty I should never have reason to doubt," wrote Ser Denys. Cotter Pyke was blunter. "I could hang them from the Wall as a warning to other wildlings to stay away, but I don't see any other use for them," Maester Harmune wrote for him. "I wouldn't trust such to clean my chamber pot, and *ten is not enough.*"

The iron cage moved downward at the end of its long chain, creaking and rattling, until it finally jerked to a halt a foot above the ground at the base of the Wall. Dolorous Edd pushed open the door and hopped down, his boots breaking the crust of the last snow. Jon followed.

Outside the armory, Iron Emmett was still urging on his charges in the yard. The song of steel on steel woke a hunger in Jon. It reminded him of warmer, simpler days, when he had been a boy at Winterfell matching blades with Robb under the watchful eye of Ser Rodrik Cassel. Ser Rodrik too had fallen, slain by Theon Turncloak and his ironmen as he'd tried to retake Winterfell. The great stronghold of House Stark was a scorched desolation. *All my memories are poisoned.*

When Iron Emmett spied him, he raised a hand and combat ceased. "Lord Commander. How may we serve you?"

"With your three best."

Emmett grinned. "Arron. Emrick. Jace."

Horse and Hop-Robin fetched padding for the lord commander, along with a ringmail hauberk to go over it, and greaves, gorget, and halfhelm. A black shield rimmed with iron for his left arm, a blunted longsword for his right hand. The sword gleamed silvery grey in the dawn light, almost new. *One of the last to come from Donal's forge. A pity he did not live long enough to put an edge on it.* The blade was shorter than Longclaw but made of common steel, which made it heavier. His blows would be a little slower. "It will serve." Jon turned to face his foes. "Come."

"Which one do you want first?" asked Arron.

"All three of you. At once."

"Three on one?" Jace was incredulous. "That wouldn't be fair." He was one of Conwy's latest bunch, a cobbler's son from Fair Isle. Maybe that explained it.

"True. Come here."

When he did, Jon's blade slammed him alongside his head, knocking him off his feet. In the blink of an eye the boy had a boot on his chest and a swordpoint at his throat. "War is never fair," Jon told him. "It's two on one now, and you're dead."

When he heard gravel crunch, he knew the twins were coming. *Those two will make rangers yet.* He spun, blocking Arron's cut with the edge of his shield and meeting Emrick's with his sword. "Those aren't spears," he shouted. "Get in close." He went to the attack to show them how it was done. Emrick first. He slashed at his head and shoulders, right and left and right again. The boy got his shield up and tried a clumsy countercut. Jon slammed his own shield into Emrick's, and brought him down with a blow to the lower leg . . . none too soon, because Arron was on him, with a crunching cut to the back of his thigh that sent him to one knee. *That will leave a bruise.* He caught the next cut on his shield, then lurched back to his feet and drove Arron across the yard. *He's quick,* he thought, as the long-swords kissed once and twice and thrice, *but he needs to get stronger.* When he saw relief in Arron's eyes, he knew Emrick was behind him. He came around and dealt him a cut to the back of the shoulders that sent him crashing into his brother. By that time Jace had found his feet, so Jon put him down again. "I hate it when dead men get up. You'll feel the same the day you meet a wight." Stepping back, he lowered his sword.

"The big crow can peck the little crows," growled a voice behind him, "but has he belly enough to fight a man?"

Rattleshirt was leaning against a wall. A coarse stubble covered his sunken cheeks, and thin brown hair was blowing across his little yellow eyes.

"You flatter yourself," Jon said.

"Aye, but I'd flatten you."

"Stannis burned the wrong man."

"No." The wildling grinned at him through a mouth of brown and broken teeth. "He burned the man he had to burn, for all the world to see. We all do what we have to do, Snow. Even kings."

"Emmett, find some armor for him. I want him in steel, not old bones."

Once clad in mail and plate, the Lord of Bones seemed to stand a little straighter. He seemed taller too, his shoulders thicker and more powerful than Jon would have thought. *It's the armor, not the man,* he told himself. *Even Sam could appear almost formidable, clad head to heel in Donal Noye's steel.* The wildling waved away the shield Horse offered him. Instead he asked for a two-handed sword. "There's a sweet sound," he said, slashing at the air. "Flap closer, Snow. I mean to make your feathers fly."

Jon rushed him hard.

Rattleshirt took a step backwards and met the charge with a two-handed slash. If Jon had not interposed his shield, it might have staved his breastplate in and broken half his ribs. The force of the blow staggered him for a moment and sent a solid jolt up his arm. *He hits harder than I would have thought.* His quickness was another unpleasant surprise. They circled round each other, trading blow for blow. The Lord of Bones gave as good as he was getting. By rights the two-handed greatsword should have been a deal more cumbersome than Jon's longsword, but the wildling wielded it with blinding speed.

Iron Emmett's fledglings cheered their lord commander at the start, but the relentless speed of Rattleshirt's attack soon beat them down to silence. *He cannot keep this up for long,* Jon told himself as he stopped another blow. The impact made him grunt. Even dulled, the greatsword cracked his pinewood shield and bent the iron rim. *He will tire soon. He must.* Jon slashed at the wildling's face, and Rattleshirt pulled back his head. He hacked down at Rattleshirt's calf, only to have him deftly leap the blade. The greatsword crashed down onto Jon's shoulder, hard enough to ding his pouldron and numb the arm beneath. Jon backed away. The Lord of Bones came after, chortling. *He has no shield,* Jon reminded himself, *and that monster sword's too cumbersome for parries. I should be landing two blows for every one of his.*

Somehow he wasn't, though, and the blows he did land were having no effect. The wildling always seemed to be moving away or sliding sideways, so Jon's longsword glanced off a shoulder or an arm. Before long he found himself giving more ground, trying to avoid the other's crashing cuts and failing half the time. His shield had been reduced to kindling. He shook it off his arm. Sweat was running down his face and stinging his eyes beneath his helm. *He is too strong and too quick,* he realized, *and with that greatsword he has weight and reach on me.* It would have been a different fight if Jon had been armed with Longclaw, but . . .

His chance came on Rattleshirt's next backswing. Jon threw himself forward, bulling into the other man, and they went down together, legs entangled. Steel slammed on steel. Both men lost their swords as they rolled on the hard ground. The wildling drove a knee between Jon's legs. Jon lashed out with a mailed fist. Somehow Rattleshirt ended up on top, with Jon's head in his hands. He smashed it against the ground, then wrenched his visor open. "If I had me a dagger, you'd be less an eye by now," he snarled, before Horse and Iron Emmett dragged him off the lord commander's chest. "Let *go* o' me, you bloody crows," he roared.

Jon struggled to one knee. His head was ringing, and his mouth was full of blood. He spat it out and said, "Well fought."

"You flatter yourself, crow. I never broke a sweat."

"Next time you will," said Jon. Dolorous Edd helped him to his feet and unbuckled his helm. It had acquired several deep dents that had not been there when he'd donned it. "Release him." Jon tossed the helm to Hop-Robin, who dropped it.

"My lord," said Iron Emmett, "he threatened your life, we all heard. He said that if he had a dagger—"

"He does have a dagger. Right there on his belt." *There is always someone quicker and stronger,* Ser Rodrik had once told Jon and Robb. *He's the man you want to face in the yard before you need to face his like upon a battlefield.*

"Lord Snow?" a soft voice said.

He turned to find Clydas standing beneath the broken archway, a parchment in his hand. "From Stannis?" Jon had been hoping for some word from the king. The Night's Watch took no part, he knew, and it should not matter to him which king emerged triumphant. Somehow it did. "Is it Deepwood?"

"No, my lord." Clydas thrust the parchment forward. It was tightly rolled and sealed, with a button of hard pink wax. *Only the Dreadfort uses pink sealing wax.* Jon ripped off his gauntlet, took the letter, cracked the seal. When he saw the signature, he forgot the battering Rattleshirt had given him.

Ramsay Bolton, Lord of the Hornwood, it read, in a huge, spiky hand. The brown ink came away in flakes when Jon brushed it with his thumb. Beneath Bolton's signature, Lord Dustin, Lady Cerwyn, and four Ryswells had appended their own marks and seals. A cruder hand had drawn the giant of House Umber. "Might we know what it says, my lord?" asked Iron Emmett.

Jon saw no reason not to tell him. "Moat Cailin is taken. The flayed corpses of the ironmen have been nailed to posts along the kingsroad. Roose Bolton summons all leal lords to Barrowton, to affirm their loyalty to the Iron Throne and celebrate his son's wedding to . . ." His heart seemed to stop for a moment. *No, that is not possible. She died in King's Landing, with Father.*

"Lord Snow?" Clydas peered at him closely with his dim pink eyes. "Are you . . . unwell? You seem . . ."

"He's to marry Arya Stark. My little sister." Jon could almost see her in that moment, long-faced and gawky, all knobby knees and sharp elbows, with her dirty face and tangled hair. They would wash the one and comb the other, he did not doubt, but he could not imagine Arya in a wedding gown, nor Ramsay Bolton's bed. *No matter how afraid she is, she will not show it. If he tries to lay a hand on her, she'll fight him.*

"Your sister," Iron Emmett said, "how old is . . ."

By now she'd be eleven, Jon thought. *Still a child.* "I have no sister. Only brothers. Only you." Lady Catelyn would have rejoiced to hear those words, he knew. That did not make them easier to say. His fingers closed around the parchment. *Would that they could crush Ramsay Bolton's throat as easily.*

Clydas cleared his throat. "Will there be an answer?"

Jon shook his head and walked away.

By nightfall the bruises that Rattleshirt had given him had turned purple. "They'll go yellow before they fade away," he told Mormont's raven. "I'll look as sallow as the Lord of Bones."

"*Bones,*" the bird agreed. "*Bones, bones.*"

He could hear the faint murmur of voices coming from outside, although the sound was too weak to make out words. *They sound a thousand leagues away.* It was Lady Melisandre and her followers at their nightfire. Every night at dusk the red woman led her followers in their twilight prayer, asking her red god to see them through the dark. *For the night is dark and full of terrors.* With Stannis and most of the queen's men gone, her flock was much diminished; half a hundred of the free folk up from Mole's Town, the handful of guards the king had left her, perhaps a dozen black brothers who had taken her red god for their own.

Jon felt as stiff as a man of sixty years. *Dark dreams,* he thought, *and guilt.* His thoughts kept returning to Arya. *There is no way I can help her. I put all kin aside when I said my words. If one of my men told me his sister was in peril, I would tell him that was no concern of his.* Once a man had said the words his blood was black. *Black as a bastard's heart.* He'd had Mikken make a sword for Arya once, a bravo's blade, made small to fit her hand. *Needle.* He wondered if she still had it. *Stick them with the pointy end,* he'd told her, but if she tried to stick the Bastard, it could mean her life.

"*Snow*," muttered Lord Mormont's raven. "*Snow, snow.*"

Suddenly he could not suffer it a moment longer.

He found Ghost outside his door, gnawing on the bone of an ox to get at the marrow. "When did you get back?" The direwolf got to his feet, abandoning the bone to come padding after Jon.

Mully and Kegs stood inside the doors, leaning on their spears. "A cruel cold out there, m'lord," warned Mully through his tangled orange beard. "Will you be out long?"

"No. I just need a breath of air." Jon stepped out into the night. The sky was full of stars, and the wind was gusting along the Wall. Even the moon looked cold; there were goosebumps all across its face. Then the first gust caught him, slicing through his layers of wool and leather to set his teeth to chattering. He stalked across the yard, into the teeth of that wind. His cloak flapped loudly from his shoulders. Ghost came after. *Where am I going? What am I doing?* Castle Black was still and silent, its halls and towers dark. *My seat,* Jon Snow reflected. *My hall, my home, my command. A ruin.*

In the shadow of the Wall, the direwolf brushed up against his fingers. For half a heartbeat the night came alive with a thousand smells, and Jon Snow heard the crackle of the crust breaking on a patch of old snow. Someone was behind him, he realized suddenly. Someone who smelled warm as a summer day.

When he turned he saw Ygritte.

She stood beneath the scorched stones of the Lord Commander's Tower, cloaked in darkness and in memory. The light of the moon was in her hair, her red hair kissed by fire. When he saw that, Jon's heart leapt into his mouth. "Ygritte," he said.

"Lord Snow." The voice was Melisandre's.

Surprise made him recoil from her. "Lady Melisandre." He took a step backwards. "I mistook you for someone else." *At night all robes are grey.* Yet suddenly hers were red. He did not understand how he could have taken her for Ygritte. She was taller, thinner, older, though the moonlight washed years from her face. Mist rose from her nostrils, and from pale hands naked to the night. "You will freeze your fingers off," Jon warned.

"If that is the will of R'hllor. Night's powers cannot touch one whose heart is bathed in god's holy fire."

"You heart does not concern me. Just your hands."

"The heart is all that matters. Do not despair, Lord Snow. Despair is a weapon of the enemy, whose name may not be spoken. Your sister is not lost to you."

"I have no sister." The words were knives. *What do you know of my heart, priestess? What do you know of my sister?*

Melisandre seemed amused. "What is her name, this little sister that you do not have?"

"Arya." His voice was hoarse. "My half-sister, truly . . ."

". . . for you are bastard born. I had not forgotten. I have seen your sister in my fires, fleeing from this marriage they have made for her. Coming here, to you. A girl in grey on a dying horse, I have seen it plain as day. It has not happened yet, but it will." She gazed at Ghost. "May I touch your . . . wolf?"

The thought made Jon uneasy. "Best not."

"He will not harm me. You call him Ghost, yes?"

"Yes, but . . ."

"*Ghost.*" Melisandre made the word a song.

The direwolf padded toward her. Wary, he stalked about her in a circle, sniffing. When she held out her hand he smelled that too, then shoved his nose against her fingers.

Jon let out a white breath. "He is not always so . . ."

". . . warm? Warmth calls to warmth, Jon Snow." Her eyes were two red stars, shining in the dark. At her throat, her ruby gleamed, a third eye glowing brighter than the others. Jon had seen Ghost's eyes blazing red the same way, when they caught the light just right. "*Ghost,*" he called. "To me."

The direwolf looked at him as if he were a stranger.

Jon frowned in disbelief. "That's . . . queer."

"You think so?" She knelt and scratched Ghost behind his ear. "Your Wall is a queer place, but there is power here, if you will use it. Power in you, and in this beast. You resist it, and that is your mistake. Embrace it. Use it."

I am not a wolf, he thought. "And how would I do that?"

"I can show you." Melisandre draped one slender arm over Ghost, and the direwolf licked her face. "The Lord of Light in his wisdom made us male and female, two parts of a greater whole. In our joining there is power. Power to make life. Power to make light. Power to cast shadows."

"Shadows." The world seemed darker when he said it.

"Every man who walks the earth casts a shadow on the world. Some are thin and weak, others long and dark. You should look behind you, Lord Snow. The moon has kissed you and etched your shadow upon the ice twenty feet tall."

Jon glanced over his shoulder. The shadow was there, just as she had said, etched in moonlight against the Wall. *A girl in grey on a dying horse,* he thought. *Coming here, to you. Arya.* He turned back to the red priestess. Jon could feel her warmth. *She has power.* The thought came unbidden, seizing him with iron teeth, but this was not a woman he cared to be indebted to, not even for his little sister. "Dalla told me something once. Val's sister, Mance Rayder's wife. She said that sorcery was a sword without a hilt. There is no safe way to grasp it."

"A wise woman." Melisandre rose, her red robes stirring in the wind. "A sword without a hilt is still a sword, though, and a sword is a fine thing to have when foes are all about. Hear me now, Jon Snow. Nine crows flew into the white wood to find your foes for you. Three of them are dead. They have not died yet, but their death is out there waiting for them, and they ride to meet it. You sent them forth to be your eyes in the darkness, but they will be eyeless when they return to you. I have seen their pale dead faces in my flames. Empty sockets, weeping blood." She pushed her red hair back, and her red eyes shone. "You do not believe me. You will. The cost of that belief will be three lives. A small price to pay for wisdom, some might say . . . but not one you had to pay. Remember that when you behold the blind and ravaged faces of your dead. And come that day, take my hand." The mist rose from her pale flesh, and for a moment it seemed as if pale, sorcerous flames were playing about her fingers. "Take my hand," she said again, "and let me save your sister."

DAVOS

E ven in the gloom of the Wolf's Den, Davos Seaworth could sense that something was awry this morning.

He woke to the sound of voices and crept to the door of his cell, but the wood was too thick and he could not make out the words. Dawn had come, but not the porridge Garth brought him every morn to break his fast. That made him anxious. All the days were much the same inside the Wolf's Den, and any change was usually for the worse. *This may be the day I die. Garth may be sitting with a whetstone even now, to put an edge on Lady Lu.*

The onion knight had not forgotten Wyman Manderly's last words to him. *Take this creature to the Wolf's Den and cut off head and hands,* the fat lord had commanded. *I shall not be able to eat a bite until I see this smuggler's head upon a spike, with an onion shoved between his lying teeth.* Every night Davos went to sleep with those words in his head, and every morn he woke to them. And should he forget, Garth was always pleased to remind him. Dead man was his name for Davos. When he came by in the morning, it was always, "Here, porridge for the dead man." At night it was, "Blow out the candle, dead man."

Once Garth brought his ladies by to introduce them to the dead man. "The Whore don't look like much," he said, fondling a rod of cold black iron, "but when I heat her up red-hot and let her touch your cock, you'll cry for mother. And this here's my Lady Lu. It's her who'll take your head and hands, when Lord Wyman sends down word." Davos had never seen a bigger axe than Lady Lu, nor one with a sharper edge. Garth spent his days honing her, the other keepers said. *I will not plead for mercy,* Davos resolved. He would go to his death a knight, asking only that they take his head before his hands. Even Garth would not be so cruel as to deny him that, he hoped.

The sounds coming through the door were faint and muffled. Davos rose and paced his cell. As cells went, it was large and queerly comfortable. He suspected it might once have been some lordling's bedchamber. It was thrice the size of his captain's cabin on *Black Bessa,* and even larger than the cabin Salladhor Saan enjoyed on his *Valyrian.* Though its only window had been bricked in years before, one wall still boasted a hearth big enough to hold a kettle, and there was an actual privy built into a corner nook. The floor was made of warped planks full of splinters, and his sleeping pallet smelled of mildew, but those discomforts were mild compared to what Davos had expected.

The food had come as a surprise as well. In place of gruel and stale bread and rotten meat, the usual dungeon fare, his keepers brought him fresh-caught fish, bread still warm from the oven, spiced mutton, turnips, carrots, even crabs. Garth was none too pleased by that. "The dead should not eat better than the living," he complained, more than once. Davos had furs to keep him warm by night, wood to feed his fire, clean clothing, a greasy tallow candle. When he asked for paper, quill, and ink, Therry brought them the next day. When he asked for a book, so he might keep at his reading, Therry turned up with *The Seven-Pointed Star.*

For all its comforts, though, his cell remained a cell. Its walls were solid stone, so thick that he could hear nothing of the outside world. The door was oak and iron, and his keepers kept it barred. Four sets of heavy iron fetters dangled from the ceiling, waiting for the day Lord Manderly decided to chain him up and give him over to the Whore. *Today may be that day. The next time Garth opens my door, it may not be to bring me porridge.*

His belly was rumbling, a sure sign that the morning was creeping past, and still no sign of food. *The worst part is not the dying, it's not knowing when or how.* He had seen the inside of a few gaols and dungeons in his smuggling days, but those he'd shared with other prisoners, so there was always someone to talk with, to share your fears and hopes. Not here. Aside from his keepers, Davos Seaworth had the Wolf's Den to himself.

He knew there were true dungeons down in the castle cellars— oubliettes and torture chambers and dank pits where huge black rats scrabbled in the darkness. His gaolers claimed all of them were un- occupied at present. "Only us here, Onion," Ser Bartimus had told him. He was the chief gaoler, a cadaverous one-legged knight, with a scarred face and a blind eye. When Ser Bartimus was in his cups (and Ser Bartimus was in his cups most every day), he liked to boast of how he had saved Lord Wyman's life at the Battle of the Trident. The Wolf's Den was his reward.

The rest of "us" consisted of a cook Davos never saw, six guardsmen in the ground-floor barracks, a pair of washerwomen, and the two turnkeys who looked after the prisoner. Therry was the young one, the son of one of the washerwomen, a boy of ten-and-four. The old one was Garth, huge and bald and taciturn, who wore the same greasy leather jerkin every day and always seemed to have a glower on his face.

His years as a smuggler had given Davos Seaworth a sense of when a man was wrong, and Garth was wrong. The onion knight took care to hold his tongue in Garth's presence. With Therry and Ser Bartimus he was less reticent. He thanked them for his food, encouraged them to talk about their hopes and histories, answered their questions politely, and never pressed too hard with queries of his own. When he made requests, they were small ones: a basin of water and a bit of soap, a book to read, more candles. Most such favors were granted, and Davos was duly grateful.

Neither man would speak about Lord Manderly or King Stannis or the Freys, but they would talk of other things. Therry wanted to go off to war when he was old enough, to fight in battles and become a knight. He liked to complain about his mother too. She was bedding two of the guardsmen, he confided. The men were on different watches and neither knew about the other, but one day one man or t'other would puzzle it out, and then there would be blood. Some nights the boy would even bring a skin of wine to the cell and ask Davos about the smuggler's life as they drank.

Ser Bartimus had no interest in the world outside, or indeed anything that had happened since he lost his leg to a riderless horse and a maester's saw. He had come to love the Wolf's Den, however, and liked nothing more than to talk about its long and bloody history. The Den was much older than White Harbor, the knight told Davos. It had been raised by King Jon Stark to defend the mouth of the White Knife against raiders from the sea. Many a younger son of the King in the North had made his seat there, many a brother, many an uncle, many a cousin. Some passed the castle to their own sons and grandsons, and offshoot branches of House Stark had arisen; the Greystarks had lasted the longest, holding the Wolf's Den for five centuries, until they presumed to join the Dreadfort in rebellion against the Starks of Winterfell.

After their fall, the castle had passed through many other hands. House Flint held it for a century, House Locke for almost two. Slates, Longs, Holts, and Ashwoods had held sway here, charged by Winterfell to keep the river safe. Reavers from the Three Sisters took the castle once, making it their toehold in the north. During the wars between Winterfell and the Vale, it was besieged by Osgood Arryn, the Old Falcon, and burned by his son, the one remembered as the Talon. When old King Edrick Stark had grown too feeble to defend his realm, the Wolf's Den was captured by slavers from the Stepstones. They would brand their captives with hot irons and break them to the whip before shipping them off across the sea, and these same black stone walls bore witness.

"Then a long cruel winter fell," said Ser Bartimus. "The White Knife froze hard, and even the firth was icing up. The winds came howling from the north and drove them slavers inside to huddle round their fires, and whilst they warmed themselves the new king come down on them. *Brandon* Stark this was, Edrick Snowbeard's great-grandson, him that men called Ice Eyes. He took the Wolf's Den back, stripped the slavers naked, and gave them to the slaves he'd found chained up in the dungeons. It's said they hung their entrails in the branches of the heart tree, as an offering to the gods. The *old* gods, not these new ones from the south. Your Seven don't know winter, and winter don't know them."

Davos could not argue with the truth of that. From what he had seen at Eastwatch-by-the-Sea, he did not care to know winter either. "What gods do you keep?" he asked the one-legged knight.

"The old ones." When Ser Bartimus grinned, he looked just like a skull. "Me and mine were here before the Manderlys. Like as not, my own forebears strung those entrails through the tree."

"I never knew that northmen made blood sacrifice to their heart trees."

"There's much and more you southrons do not know about the north," Ser Bartimus replied.

He was not wrong. Davos sat beside his candle and looked at the letters he had scratched out word by word during the days of his confinement. *I was a better smuggler than a knight,* he had written to his wife, *a better knight than a King's Hand, a better King's Hand than a husband. I am so sorry. Marya, I have loved you. Please forgive the wrongs I did you. Should Stannis lose his war, our lands will be lost as well. Take the boys across the narrow sea to Braavos and teach them to think kindly of me, if you would. Should Stannis gain the Iron Throne, House Seaworth will survive and Devan will remain at court. He will help you place the other boys with noble lords, where they can serve as pages and squires and win their knighthoods.* It was the best counsel he had for her, though he wished it sounded wiser.

He had written to each of his three surviving sons as well, to help them remember the father who had bought them names with his fingertips. His notes to Steffon and young Stannis were short and stiff and awkward; if truth be told, he did not know them half as well as he had his older boys, the ones who'd burned or drowned upon the Blackwater. To Devan he wrote more, telling him how proud he was to see his own son as a king's squire and reminding him that as the eldest it was his duty to protect his lady mother and his younger brothers. *Tell His Grace I did my best,* he ended. *I am sorry that I failed him. I lost my luck when I lost my fingerbones, the day the river burned below King's Landing.*

Davos shuffled through the letters slowly, reading each one over several times, wondering whether he should change a word here or add one there. A man should have more to say when staring at the end of his life, he thought, but the words came hard. *I did not do so ill,* he tried to tell himself. *I rose up from Flea Bottom to be a King's Hand, and I learned to read and write.*

He was still hunched over the letters when he heard the sound of iron keys rattling on a ring. Half a heartbeat later, the door to his cell came swinging open.

The man who stepped through the door was not one of his gaolers. He was tall and haggard, with a deeply lined face and a shock of grey-brown hair. A longsword hung from his hip, and his deep-dyed scarlet cloak was fastened at the shoulder with a heavy silver brooch in the shape of a mailed fist. "Lord Seaworth," he said, "we do not have much time. Please, come with me."

Davos eyed the stranger warily. The "please" confused him. Men about to lose their heads and hands were not oft accorded such courtesies. "Who are you?"

"Robett Glover, if it please, my lord."

"Glover. Your seat was Deepwood Motte."

"My brother Galbart's seat. It was and is, thanks to your King Stannis. He has taken Deepwood back from the iron bitch who stole it and offers to restore it to its rightful owners. Much and more has happened whilst you have been confined within these walls, Lord Davos. Moat Cailin has fallen, and Roose Bolton has returned to the north with Ned Stark's younger daughter. A host of Freys came with him. Bolton has sent forth ravens, summoning all the lords of the north to Barrowton. He demands homage and hostages . . . and witnesses to the wedding of Arya Stark and his bastard Ramsay Snow, by which match the Boltons mean to lay claim to Winterfell. Now, will you come with me, or no?"

"What choice do I have, my lord? Come with you, or remain with Garth and Lady Lu?"

"Who is Lady Lu? One of the washerwomen?" Glover was growing impatient. "All will be explained if you will come."

Davos rose to his feet. "If I should die, I beseech my lord to see that my letters are delivered."

"You have my word on that . . . though if you die, it will not be at Glover's hands, nor Lord Wyman's. Quickly now, with me."

Glover led him along a darkened hall and down a flight of worn steps. They crossed the castle's godswood, where the heart tree had grown so huge and tangled that it had choked out all the oaks and elms and birch and sent its thick, pale limbs crashing through the walls and windows that looked down on it. Its roots were as thick around as a man's waist, its trunk so wide that the face carved into it looked fat and angry. Beyond the weirwood, Glover opened a rusted iron gate and paused to light a torch. When it was blazing red and hot, he took Davos down more steps into a barrel-vaulted cellar where the weeping walls were crusted white with salt, and seawater sloshed beneath their feet with every step. They passed through several cellars, and rows of small, damp, foul-smelling cells very different from the room where Davos had been confined. Then there was a blank stone wall that turned when Glover pushed on it. Beyond was a long narrow tunnel and still more steps. These led up.

"Where are we?" asked Davos as they climbed. His words echoed faintly though the darkness.

"The steps beneath the steps. The passage runs beneath the Castle Stair up to the New Castle. A secret way. It would not do for you to be seen, my lord. You are supposed to be dead."

Porridge for the dead man. Davos climbed.

They emerged through another wall, but this one was lath and plaster on the far side. The room beyond was snug and warm and comfortably furnished, with a Myrish carpet on the floor and beeswax candles burning on a table. Davos could hear pipes and fiddles playing, not far away. On the wall hung a sheepskin with a map of the north painted across it in faded colors. Beneath the map sat Wyman Manderly, the colossal Lord of White Harbor.

"Please sit." Lord Manderly was richly garbed. His velvet doublet was a soft blue-green, embroidered with golden thread at hem and sleeves and collar. His mantle was ermine, pinned at the shoulder with a golden trident. "Are you hungry?"

"No, my lord. Your gaolers have fed me well."

"There is wine, if you have a thirst."

"I will treat with you, my lord. My king commanded that of me. I do not have to drink with you."

Lord Wyman sighed. "I have treated you most shamefully, I know. I had my reasons, but . . . please, sit and drink, I beg you. Drink to my boy's safe return. Wylis, my eldest son and heir. He is home. That is the welcoming feast you hear. In the Merman's Court they are eating lamprey pie and venison with roasted chestnuts. Wynafryd is dancing with the Frey she is to marry. The other Freys are raising cups of wine to toast our friendship."

Beneath the music, Davos could hear the murmur of many voices, the clatter of cups and platters. He said nothing.

"I have just come from the high table," Lord Wyman went on. "I have eaten too much, as ever, and all White Harbor knows my bowels are bad. My friends of Frey will not question a lengthy visit to the privy, we hope." He turned his cup over. "There. You will drink and I will not. Sit. Time is short, and there is much we need to say. Robett, wine for the Hand, if you will be so good. Lord Davos, you will not know, but you are dead."

Robett Glover filled a wine cup and offered it to Davos. He took it, sniffed it, drank. "How did I die, if I may ask?"

"By the axe. Your head and hands were mounted above the Seal Gate, with your face turned so your eyes looked out across the harbor. By now you are well rotted, though we dipped your head in tar before we set it upon the spike. Carrion crows and seabirds squabbled over your eyes, they say."

Davos shifted uncomfortably. It was a queer feeling, being dead. "If it please my lord, who died in my place?"

"Does it matter? You have a common face, Lord Davos. I hope my saying so does not offend you. The man had your coloring, a nose of the same shape, two ears that were not dissimilar, a long beard that could be trimmed and shaped like yours. You can be sure we tarred him well, and the onion shoved between his teeth served to twist the features. Ser Bartimus saw that the fingers of his left hand were shortened, the same as yours. The man was a criminal, if that gives you any solace. His dying may accomplish more good than anything he ever did whilst living. My lord, I bear you no ill will. The rancor I showed you in the Merman's Court was a mummer's farce put on to please our friends of Frey."

"My lord should take up a life of mummery," said Davos. "You and yours were most convincing. Your good-daughter seemed to want me dead most earnestly, and the little girl . . ."

"Wylla." Lord Wyman smiled. "Did you see how brave she was? Even when I threatened to have her tongue out, she reminded me of the debt White Harbor owes to the Starks of Winterfell, a debt that can never be repaid. Wylla spoke from the heart, as did Lady Leona. Forgive her if you can, my lord. She is a foolish, frightened woman, and Wylis is her life. Not every man has it in him to be Prince Aemon the Dragonknight or Symeon Star-Eyes, and not every woman can be as brave as my Wylla and her sister Wynafryd . . . who *did* know, yet played her own part fearlessly.

"When treating with liars, even an honest man must lie. I did not dare defy King's Landing so long as my last living son remained a captive. Lord Tywin Lannister wrote me himself to say that he had Wylis. If I would have him freed unharmed, he told me, I must repent my treason, yield my city, declare my loyalty to the boy king on the Iron Throne . . . and bend my knee to Roose Bolton, his Warden of the North. Should I refuse, Wylis would die a traitor's death, White Harbor would be stormed and sacked, and my people would suffer the same fate as the Reynes of Castamere.

"I am fat, and many think that makes me weak and foolish. Mayhaps Tywin Lannister was one such. I sent him back a raven to say that I would bend my knee and open my gates *after* my son was returned, but not before. There the matter stood when Tywin died. Afterward the Freys turned up with Wendel's bones . . . to make a peace and seal it with a marriage pact, they claimed, but I was not about to give them what they wanted until I had Wylis, safe and whole, and they were not about to give me Wylis until I proved my loyalty. Your arrival gave me the means to do that. That was the reason for the discourtesy I showed you in the Merman's Court, and for the head and hands rotting above the Seal Gate."

"You took a great risk, my lord," Davos said. "If the Freys had seen through your deception . . ."

"I took no risk at all. If any of the Freys had taken it upon themselves to climb my gate for a close look at the man with the onion in his mouth, I would have blamed my gaolers for the error and produced you to appease them."

Davos felt a shiver up his spine. "I see."

"I hope so. You have sons of your own, you said."

Three, thought Davos, *though I fathered seven.*

"Soon I must return to the feast to toast my friends of Frey," Manderly continued. "They watch me, ser. Day and night their eyes are on me, noses sniffing for some whiff of treachery. You saw them, the arrogant Ser Jared and his nephew Rhaegar, that smirking worm who wears a dragon's name. Behind them both stands Symond, clinking coins. That one has bought and paid for several of my servants and two of my knights. One of his wife's handmaids has found her way into the bed of my own fool. If Stannis wonders that my letters say so little, it is because I dare not even trust my maester. Theomore is all head and no heart. You heard him in my hall. Maesters are supposed to put aside old loyalties when they don their chains, but I cannot forget that Theomore was born a Lannister of Lannisport and claims some distant kinship to the Lannisters of Casterly Rock. Foes and false friends are all around me, Lord Davos. They infest my city like roaches, and at night I feel them crawling over me." The fat man's fingers coiled into a fist, and all his chins trembled. "My son Wendel came to the Twins a guest. He ate Lord Walder's bread and salt, and hung his sword upon the wall to feast with friends. And they murdered him. *Murdered,* I say, and may the Freys choke upon their fables. I drink with Jared, jape with Symond, promise Rhaegar the hand of my own beloved granddaughter . . . but never think that means I have forgotten. The north remembers, Lord Davos. The north remembers, and the mummer's farce is almost done. My son is home."

Something about the way Lord Wyman said that chilled Davos to the bone. "If it is justice that you want, my lord, look to King Stannis. No man is more just."

Robert Glover broke in to add, "Your loyalty does you honor, my lord, but Stannis Baratheon remains your king, not our own."

"Your own king is dead," Davos reminded them, "murdered at the Red Wedding beside Lord Wyman's son."

"The Young Wolf is dead," Manderly allowed, "but that brave boy was not Lord Eddard's only son. Robett, bring the lad."

"At once, my lord." Glover slipped out the door.

The lad? Was it possible that one of Robb Stark's brothers had survived the ruin of Winterfell? Did Manderly have a Stark heir hidden away in his castle? *A found boy or a feigned boy?* The north would rise for either, he suspected . . . but Stannis Baratheon would never make common cause with an imposter.

The lad who followed Robett Glover through the door was not a Stark, nor could he ever hope to pass for one. He was older than the Young Wolf's murdered brothers, fourteen or fifteen by the look of him, and his eyes were older still. Beneath a tangle of dark brown hair his face was almost feral, with a wide mouth, sharp nose, and pointed chin. "Who are you?" Davos asked.

The boy looked to Robett Glover.

"He is a mute, but we have been teaching him his letters. He learns quickly." Glover drew a dagger from his belt and gave it to the boy. "Write your name for Lord Seaworth."

There was no parchment in the chamber. The boy carved the letters into a wooden beam in the wall. *W . . . E . . . X.* He leaned hard into the *X.* When he was done he flipped the dagger in the air, caught it, and stood admiring his handiwork.

"Wex is ironborn. He was Theon Greyjoy's squire. Wex was at Winterfell." Glover sat. "How much does Lord Stannis know of what transpired at Winterfell?"

Davos thought back on the tales they'd heard. "Winterfell was captured by Theon Greyjoy, who had once been Lord Stark's ward. He had Stark's two young sons put to death and mounted their heads above the castle walls. When the northmen came to oust him, he put the entire castle to sword, down to the last child, before he himself was slain by Lord Bolton's bastard."

"Not slain," said Glover. "Captured, and carried back to the Dreadfort. The Bastard has been flaying him."

Lord Wyman nodded. "The tale you tell is one we all have heard, as full of lies as a pudding's full of raisins. It was the Bastard of Bolton who put Winterfell to the sword . . . Ramsay Snow, he was called then, before the boy king made him a Bolton. Snow did not kill them all. He spared the women, roped them together, and marched them to the Dreadfort for his sport."

"His sport?"

"He is a great hunter," said Wyman Manderly, "and women are his favorite prey. He strips them naked and sets them loose in the woods. They have a half day's start before he sets out after them with hounds and horns. From time to time some wench escapes and lives to tell the tale. Most are less fortunate. When Ramsay catches them he rapes them, flays them, feeds their corpses to his dogs, and brings their skins back to the Dreadfort as trophies. If they have given him good sport, he slits their throats before he skins them. Elsewise, t'other way around."

Davos paled. "Gods be good. How could any man—"

"The evil is in his blood," said Robett Glover. "He is a bastard born of rape. A *Snow*, no matter what the boy king says."

"Was ever snow so black?" asked Lord Wyman. "Ramsay took Lord Hornwood's lands by forcibly wedding his widow, then locked her in a tower and forgot her. It is said she ate her own fingers in her extremity . . . and the Lannister notion of king's justice is to reward her killer with Ned Stark's little girl."

"The Boltons have always been as cruel as they were cunning, but this one seems a beast in human skin," said Glover.

The Lord of White Harbor leaned forward. "The Freys are no better. They speak of wargs and skinchangers and assert that it was Robb Stark who slew my Wendel. The arrogance of it! They do not expect the north to believe their lies, not truly, but they think we must pretend to believe or die. Roose Bolton lies about his part in the Red Wedding, and his bastard lies about the fall of Winterfell. And yet so long as they held Wylis I had no choice but to eat all this excrement and praise the taste."

"And now, my lord?" asked Davos.

He had hoped to hear Lord Wyman say, *And now I shall declare for King Stannis,* but instead the fat man smiled an odd, twinkling smile and said, "And now I have a wedding to attend. I am too fat to sit a horse, as any man with eyes can plainly see. As a boy I loved to ride, and as a young man I handled a mount well enough to win some small acclaim in the lists, but those days are done. My body has become a prison more dire than the Wolf's Den. Even so, I must go to Winterfell. Roose Bolton wants me on my knees, and beneath the velvet courtesy he shows the iron mail. I shall go by barge and litter, attended by a hundred knights and my good friends from the Twins. The Freys came here by sea. They have no horses with them, so I shall present each of them with a palfrey as a guest gift. Do hosts still give guest gifts in the south?"

"Some do, my lord. On the day their guest departs."

"Perhaps you understand, then." Wyman Manderly lurched ponderously to his feet. "I have been building warships for more than a year. Some you saw, but there are as many more hidden up the White Knife. Even with the losses I have suffered, I still command more heavy horse than any other lord north of the Neck. My walls are strong, and my vaults are full of silver. Oldcastle and Widow's Watch will take their lead from me. My bannermen include a dozen petty lords and a hundred landed knights. I can deliver King Stannis the allegiance of all the lands east of the White Knife, from Widow's Watch and Ramsgate to the Sheepshead Hills and the headwaters of the Broken Branch. All this I pledge to do if you will meet my price."

"I can bring your terms to the king, but—"

Lord Wyman cut him off. "If *you* will meet my price, I said. Not Stannis. It's not a king I need but a smuggler."

Robert Glover took up the tale. "We may never know all that happened at Winterfell, when Ser Rodrik Cassel tried to take the castle back from Theon Greyjoy's ironmen. The Bastard of Bolton claims that Greyjoy murdered Ser Rodrik during a parley. Wex says no. Until he learns more letters we will never know half the truth . . . but he came to us knowing *yes* and *no*, and those can go a long way once you find the right questions."

"It was the Bastard who murdered Ser Rodrik and the men of Winterfell," said Lord Wyman. "He slew Greyjoy's ironmen as well.

Wex saw men cut down trying to yield. When we asked how he escaped, he took a chunk of chalk and drew a tree with a face."

Davos thought about that. "The old gods saved him?"

"After a fashion. He climbed the heart tree and hid himself amongst the leaves. Bolton's men searched the godswood twice and killed the men they found there, but none thought to clamber up into the trees. Is that how it happened, Wex?"

The boy flipped up Glover's dagger, caught it, nodded.

Glover said, "He stayed up in the tree a long time. He slept amongst the branches, not daring to descend. Finally he heard voices down beneath him."

"The voices of the dead," said Wyman Manderly.

Wex held up five fingers, tapped each one with the dagger, then folded four away and tapped the last again.

"Six of them," asked Davos. "There were six."

"Two of them Ned Stark's murdered sons."

"How could a mute tell you that?"

"With chalk. He drew two boys . . . and two wolves."

"The lad is ironborn, so he thought it best not to show himself," said Glover. "He listened. The six did not linger long amongst the ruins of Winterfell. Four went one way, two another. Wex stole after the two, a woman and a boy. He must have stayed downwind, so the wolf would not catch his scent."

"He knows where they went," Lord Wyman said.

Davos understood. "You want the boy."

"Roose Bolton has Lord Eddard's daughter. To thwart him White Harbor must have Ned's son . . . and the direwolf. The wolf will prove the boy is who we say he is, should the Dreadfort attempt to deny him. That is my price, Lord Davos. Smuggle me back my liege lord, and I will take Stannis Baratheon as my king."

Old instinct made Davos Seaworth reach for his throat. His finger-bones had been his luck, and somehow he felt he would have need of luck to do what Wyman Manderly was asking of him. The bones were gone, though, so he said, "You have better men than me in your service. Knights and lords and maesters. Why would you need a smuggler? You have ships."

"Ships," Lord Wyman agreed, "but my crews are rivermen, or fisherfolk who have never sailed beyond the Bite. For this I must have a man who's sailed in darker waters and knows how to slip past dangers, unseen and unmolested."

"Where is the boy?" Somehow Davos knew he would not like the answer. "Where is it you want me to go, my lord?"

Robett Glover said, "Wex. Show him."

The mute flipped the dagger, caught it, then flung it end over end at the sheepskin map that adorned Lord Wyman's wall. It struck quivering. Then he grinned.

For half a heartbeat Davos considered asking Wyman Manderly to send him back to the Wolf's Den, to Ser Bartimus with his tales and Garth with his lethal ladies. In the Den even prisoners ate porridge in the morning. But there were other places in this world where men were known to break their fast on human flesh.

DAENERYS

Each morning, from her western ramparts, the queen would count the sails on Slaver's Bay.

Today she counted five-and-twenty, though some were far away and moving, so it was hard to be certain. Sometimes she missed one, or counted one twice. *What does it matter? A strangler only needs ten fingers.* All trade had stopped, and her fisherfolk did not dare put out into the bay. The boldest still dropped a few lines into the river, though even that was hazardous; more remained tied up beneath Meereen's walls of many-colored brick.

There were ships from Meereen out in the bay too, warships and trading galleys whose captains had taken them to sea when Dany's host first laid siege to the city, now returned to augment the fleets from Qarth, Tolos, and New Ghis.

Her admiral's counsel had proved worse than useless. "Let them see your dragons," Groleo said. "Let the Yunkishmen have a taste of fire, and the trade will flow again."

"Those ships are strangling us, and all my admiral can do is talk of dragons," Dany said. "You *are* my admiral, are you not?"

"An admiral without ships."

"*Build* ships."

"Warships cannot be made from brick. The slavers burned every stand of timber within twenty leagues of here."

"Then ride out two-and-twenty leagues. I will give you wagons, workers, mules, whatever you require."

"I am a sailor, not a shipwright. I was sent to fetch Your Grace back to Pentos. Instead you brought us here and tore my *Saduleon* to pieces for some nails and scraps of wood. I will never see her like again. I may never see my home again, nor my old wife. It was not me who refused the ships this Daxos offered. I cannot fight the Qartheen with fishing boats."

His bitterness dismayed her, so much so that Dany found herself wondering if the grizzled Pentoshi could be one of her three betrayers. *No, he is only an old man, far from home and sick at heart.* "There must be *something* we can do."

"Aye, and I've told you what. These ships are made of rope and pitch and canvas, of Qohorik pine and teak from Sothoros, old oak from Great Norvos, yew and ash and spruce. Wood, Your Grace. Wood burns. The dragons—"

"I will hear no more about my dragons. Leave me. Go pray to your Pentoshi gods for a storm to sink our foes."

"No sailor prays for storms, Your Grace."

"I am tired of hearing what you will not do. Go."

Ser Barristan remained. "Our stores are ample for the moment," he reminded her, "and Your Grace has planted beans and grapes and wheat. Your Dothraki have harried the slavers from the hills and struck the shackles from their slaves. They are planting too, and will be bringing their crops to Meereen to market. And you will have the friendship of Lhazar."

Daario won that for me, for all that it is worth. "The Lamb Men. Would that lambs had teeth."

"That would make the wolves more cautious, no doubt."

That made her laugh. "How fare your orphans, ser?"

The old knight smiled. "Well, Your Grace. It is good of you to ask." The boys were his pride. "Four or five have the makings of knights. Perhaps as many as a dozen."

"One would be enough if he were as true as you." The day might come soon when she would have need of every knight. "Will they joust for me? I should like that." Viserys had told her stories of the tourneys he had witnessed in the Seven Kingdoms, but Dany had never seen a joust herself.

"They are not ready, Your Grace. When they are, they will be pleased to demonstrate their prowess."

"I hope that day comes quickly." She would have kissed her good knight on the cheek, but just then Missandei appeared beneath the arched doorway. "Missandei?"

"Your Grace. Skahaz awaits your pleasure."

"Send him up."

The Shavepate was accompanied by two of his Brazen Beasts. One wore a hawk mask, the other the likeness of a jackal. Only their eyes could be seen behind the brass. "Your Radiance, Hizdahr was seen to enter the pyramid of Zhak last evening. He did not depart until well after dark."

"How many pyramids has he visited?" asked Dany.

"Eleven."

"And how long since the last murder?"

"Six-and-twenty days." The Shavepate's eyes brimmed with fury. It had been his notion to have the Brazen Beasts follow her betrothed and take note of all his actions.

"So far Hizdahr has made good on his promises."

"*How?* The Sons of the Harpy have put down their knives, but why? Because the noble Hizdahr asked sweetly? He is one of them, I tell you. That's why they obey him. He may well be the Harpy."

"If there is a Harpy." Skahaz was convinced that somewhere in Meereen the Sons of the Harpy had a highborn overlord, a secret general commanding an army of shadows. Dany did not share his belief. The Brazen Beasts had taken dozens of the Harpy's Sons, and those who had survived their capture had yielded names when questioned sharply . . . too many names, it seemed to her. It would have been pleasant to think that all the deaths were the work of a single enemy who might be caught and killed, but Dany suspected that the truth was otherwise. *My enemies are legion.* "Hizdahr zo Loraq is a persuasive man with many friends. And he is wealthy. Perhaps he has bought this peace for us with gold, or convinced the other highborn that our marriage is in their best interests."

"If he is not the Harpy, he knows him. I can find the truth of that easy enough. Give me your leave to put Hizdahr to the question, and I will bring you a confession."

"No," she said. "I do not trust these confessions. You've brought me too many of them, all of them worthless."

"Your Radiance—"

"*No*, I said."

The Shavepate's scowl turned his ugly face even uglier. "A mistake. The Great Master Hizdahr plays Your Worship for a fool. Do you want a serpent in your bed?"

I want Daario in my bed, but I sent him away for the sake of you and yours. "You may continue to watch Hizdahr zo Loraq, but no harm is to come to him. Is that understood?"

"I am not deaf, Magnificence. I will obey." Skahaz drew a parchment scroll from his sleeve. "Your Worship should have a look at this. A list of all the Meereenese ships in the blockade, with their captains. Great Masters all."

Dany studied the scroll. All the ruling families of Meereen were named: Hazkar, Merreq, Quazzar, Zhak, Rhazdar, Ghazeen, Pahl, even Reznak and Loraq. "What am I to do with a list of names?"

"Every man on that list has kin within the city. Sons and brothers, wives and daughters, mothers and fathers. Let my Brazen Beasts seize them. Their lives will win you back those ships."

"If I send the Brazen Beasts into the pyramids, it will mean open war inside the city. I have to trust in Hizdahr. I have to hope for peace." Dany held the parchment above a candle and watched the names go up in flame, while Skahaz glowered at her.

Afterward, Ser Barristan told her that her brother Rhaegar would have been proud of her. Dany remembered the words Ser Jorah had spoken at Astapor: *Rhaegar fought valiantly, Rhaegar fought nobly, Rhaegar fought honorably. And Rhaegar* died.

When she descended to the purple marble hall, she found it almost empty. "Are there no petitioners today?" Dany asked Reznak mo Reznak. "No one who craves justice or silver for a sheep?"

"No, Your Worship. The city is afraid."

"There is nothing to fear."

But there was much and more to fear as she learned that evening. As her young hostages Miklaz and Kezmya were laying out a simple supper of autumn greens and ginger soup for her, Irri came to tell her that Galazza Galare had returned, with three Blue Graces from the temple. "Grey Worm is come as well, *Khaleesi*. They beg words with you, most urgently."

"Bring them to my hall. And summon Reznak and Skahaz. Did the Green Grace say what this was about?"

"Astapor," said Irri.

Grey Worm began the tale. "He came out of the morning mists, a rider on a pale horse, dying. His mare was staggering as she approached the city gates, her sides pink with blood and lather, her eyes rolling with terror. Her rider called out, '*She is burning, she is burning,*' and fell from the saddle. This one was sent for, and gave orders that the rider be brought to the Blue Graces. When your servants carried him inside the gates, he cried out again, '*She is burning.*' Under his *tokar* he was a skeleton, all bones and fevered flesh."

One of the Blue Graces took up the tale from there. "The Unsullied brought this man to the temple, where we stripped him and bathed him in cool water. His clothes were soiled, and my sisters found half an arrow in his thigh. Though he had broken off the shaft, the head remained inside him, and the wound had mortified, filling him with poisons. He died within the hour, still crying out that she was burning."

" 'She is burning,' " Daenerys repeated. "Who is *she*?"

"Astapor, Your Radiance," said another of the Blue Graces. "He said it, once. He said '*Astapor* is burning.' "

"It might have been his fever talking."

"Your Radiance speaks wisely," said Galazza Galare, "but Ezzara saw something else."

The Blue Grace called Ezzara folded her hands. "My queen," she murmured, "his fever was not brought on by the arrow. He had soiled himself, not once but many times. The stains reached to his knees, and there was dried blood amongst his excrement."

"His horse was bleeding, Grey Worm said."

"This thing is true, Your Grace," the eunuch confirmed. "The pale mare was bloody from his spur."

"That may be so, Your Radiance," said Ezzara, "but this blood was mingled with his stool. It stained his smallclothes."

"He was bleeding from the bowels," said Galazza Galare.

"We cannot be certain," said Ezzara, "but it may be that Meereen has more to fear than the spears of the Yunkai'i."

"We must pray," said the Green Grace. "The gods sent this man to us. He comes as a harbinger. He comes as a sign."

"A sign of what?" asked Dany.

"A sign of wroth and ruin."

She did not want to believe that. "He was one man. One sick man with an arrow in his leg. A horse brought him here, not a god." *A pale mare.* Dany rose abruptly. "I thank you for your counsel and for all that you did for this poor man."

The Green Grace kissed Dany's fingers before she took her leave. "We shall pray for Astapor."

And for me. Oh, pray for me, my lady. If Astapor had fallen, nothing remained to prevent Yunkai from turning north.

She turned to Ser Barristan. "Send riders into the hills to find my bloodriders. Recall Brown Ben and the Second Sons as well."

"And the Stormcrows, Your Grace?"

Daario. "Yes. Yes." Just three nights ago she had dreamed of Daario lying dead beside the road, staring sightlessly into the sky as crows quarreled above his corpse. Other nights she tossed in her bed, imagining that he'd betrayed her, as he had once betrayed his fellow captains in the Stormcrows. *He brought me their heads.* What if he had taken his company back to Yunkai, to sell her for a pot of gold? *He would not do that. Would he?* "The Stormcrows too. Send riders after them at once."

The Second Sons were the first to return, eight days after the queen sent forth her summons. When Ser Barristan told her that her captain desired words with her, she thought for a moment that it was Daario, and her heart leapt. But the captain that he spoke of was Brown Ben Plumm.

Brown Ben had a seamed and weathered face, skin the color of old teak, white hair, and wrinkles at the corners of his eyes. Dany was so pleased to see his leathery brown face that she hugged him. His eyes crinkled in amusement. "I heard talk Your Grace was going to take a husband," he said, "but no one told me it was me." They laughed together as Reznak sputtered, but the laughter ceased when Brown Ben said, "We caught three Astapori. Your Worship had best hear what they say."

"Bring them."

Daenerys received them in the grandeur of her hall as tall candles burned amongst the marble pillars. When she saw that the Astapori were half-starved, she sent for food at once. These three were all that remained of a dozen who had set out together from the Red City: a bricklayer, a weaver, and a cobbler. "What befell the rest of your party?" the queen asked.

"Slain," said the cobbler. "Yunkai's sellswords roam the hills north of Astapor, hunting down those who flee the flames."

"Has the city fallen, then? Its walls were thick."

"This is so," said the bricklayer, a stoop-backed man with rheumy eyes, "but they were old and crumbling as well."

The weaver raised her head. "Every day we told each other that the dragon queen was coming back." The woman had thin lips and dull dead eyes, set in a pinched and narrow face. "Cleon had sent for you, it was said, and you were coming."

He sent for me, thought Dany. *That much is true, at least.*

"Outside our walls, the Yunkai'i devoured our crops and slaughtered our herds," the cobbler went on. "Inside we starved. We ate cats and rats and leather. A horsehide was a feast. King Cutthroat and Queen Whore accused each other of feasting on the flesh of the slain. Men and women gathered in secret to draw lots and gorge upon the flesh of him who drew the black stone. The pyramid of Nakloz was despoiled and set aflame by those who claimed that Kraznys mo Nakloz was to blame for all our woes."

"Others blamed Daenerys," said the weaver, "but more of us still loved you. 'She is on her way,' we said to one another. 'She is coming at the head of a great host, with food for all.'"

I can scarce feed my own folk. If I had marched to Astapor, I would have lost Meereen.

The cobbler told them how the body of the Butcher King had been disinterred and clad in copper armor, after the Green Grace of Astapor had a vision that he would deliver them from the Yunkai'i. Armored and stinking, the corpse of Cleon the Great was strapped onto the back of a starving horse to lead the remnants of his new Unsullied on a sortie, but they rode right into the iron teeth of a legion from New Ghis and were cut down to a man.

"Afterward the Green Grace was impaled upon a stake in the Plaza of Punishment and left until she died. In the pyramid of Ullhor, the survivors had a great feast that lasted half the night, and washed the last of their food down with poison wine so none need wake again come morning. Soon after came the sickness, a bloody flux that killed three men of every four, until a mob of dying men went mad and slew the guards on the main gate."

The old brickmaker broke in to say, "No. That was the work of healthy men, running to escape the flux."

"Does it matter?" asked the cobbler. "The guards were torn apart and the gates thrown open. The legions of New Ghis came pouring into Astapor, followed by the Yunkai'i and the sellswords on their horses. Queen Whore died fighting them with a curse upon her lips. King Cutthroat yielded and was thrown into a fighting pit, to be torn apart by a pack of starving dogs."

"Even then some said that you were coming," said the weaver. "They swore they had seen you mounted on a dragon, flying high above the camps of the Yunkai'i. Every day we looked for you."

I could not come, the queen thought. *I dare not.*

"And when the city fell?" demanded Skahaz. "What then?"

"The butchery began. The Temple of the Graces was full of the sick who had come to ask the gods to heal them. The legions sealed the doors and set the temple ablaze with torches. Within the hour fires were burning in every corner of the city. As they spread they joined with one another. The streets were full of mobs, running this way and that to escape the flames, but there was no way out. The Yunkai'i held the gates."

"Yet *you* escaped," the Shavepate said. "How is that?"

The old man answered. "I am by trade a brickmaker, as my father and his father were before me. My grandfather built our house up against the city walls. It was an easy thing to work loose a few bricks every night. When I told my friends, they helped me shore up the tunnel so it would not collapse. We all agreed that it might be good to have our own way out."

I left you with a council to rule over you, Dany thought, *a healer, a scholar, and a priest.* She could still recall the Red City as she had first seen it, dry and dusty behind its red brick walls, dreaming cruel dreams, yet full of life. *There were islands in the Worm where lovers kissed, but in the Plaza of Punishment they peeled the skin off men in strips and left them hanging naked for the flies.* "It is good that you have come," she told the Astapori. "You will be safe in Meereen."

The cobbler thanked her for that, and the old brickmaker kissed her foot, but the weaver looked at her with eyes as hard as slate. *She knows I lie,* the queen thought. *She knows I cannot keep them safe. Astapor is burning, and Meereen is next.*

"There's more coming," Brown Ben announced when the Astapori had been led away. "These three had horses. Most are afoot."

"How many are they?" asked Reznak.

Brown Ben shrugged. "Hundreds. Thousands. Some sick, some burned, some wounded. The Cats and the Windblown are swarming through the hills with lance and lash, driving them north and cutting down the laggards."

"Mouths on feet. And *sick,* you say?" Reznak wrung his hands. "Your Worship must not allow them in the city."

"I wouldn't," said Brown Ben Plumm. "I'm no maester, mind you, but I know you got to keep the bad apples from the good."

"These are not apples, Ben," said Dany. "These are men and women, sick and hungry and afraid." *My children.* "I should have gone to Astapor."

"Your Grace could not have saved them," said Ser Barristan. "You warned King Cleon against this war with Yunkai. The man was a fool, and his hands were red with blood."

And are my hands any cleaner? She remembered what Daario had said—that all kings must be butchers, or meat. "Cleon was the enemy of our enemy. If I had joined him at the Horns of Hazzat, we might have crushed the Yunkai'i between us."

The Shavepate disagreed. "If you had taken the Unsullied south to Hazzat, the Sons of the Harpy—"

"I know. I *know.* It is Eroeh all over again."

Brown Ben Plumm was puzzled. "Who is Eroeh?"

"A girl I thought I'd saved from rape and torment. All I did was make it worse for her in the end. And all I did in Astapor was make ten thousand Eroehs."

"Your Grace could not have known—"

"I am the queen. It was my place to know."

"What is done is done," said Reznak mo Reznak. "Your Worship, I beg you, take the noble Hizdahr for your king at once. He can speak with the Wise Masters, make a peace for us."

"On what terms?" *Beware the perfumed seneschal,* Quaithe had said. The masked woman had foretold the coming of the pale mare, was she right about the noble Reznak too? "I may be a young girl innocent of war, but I am not a lamb to walk bleating into the harpy's den. I still have my Unsullied. I have the Stormcrows and the Second Sons. I have three companies of freedmen."

"Them, and dragons," said Brown Ben Plumm, with a grin.

"In the pit, in chains," wailed Reznak mo Reznak. "What good are dragons that cannot be controlled? Even the Unsullied grow fearful when they must open the doors to feed them."

"What, o' the queen's little pets?" Brown Ben's eyes crinkled in amusement. The grizzled captain of the Second Sons was a creature of the free companies, a mongrel with the blood of a dozen different peoples flowing through his veins, but he had always been fond of the dragons, and them of him.

"Pets?" screeched Reznak. "Monsters, rather. Monsters that feed on children. We cannot—"

"*Silence,*" said Daenerys. "We will not speak of that."

Reznak shrank away from her, flinching from the fury in her tone. "Forgive me, Magnificence, I did not . . ."

Brown Ben Plumm bulled over him. "Your Grace, the Yunkish got three free companies against our two, and there's talk the Yunkishmen sent to Volantis to fetch back the Golden Company. Those bastards field ten thousand. Yunkai's got four Ghiscari legions too, maybe more, and I heard it said they sent riders across the Dothraki sea to maybe bring some big *khalasar* down on us. We *need* them dragons, the way I see it."

Dany sighed. "I am sorry, Ben. I dare not loose the dragons." She could see that was not the answer that he wanted.

Plumm scratched at his speckled whiskers. "If there's no dragons in the balance, well . . . we should leave before them Yunkish bastards close the trap . . . only first, make the slavers pay to see our backs. They pay the khals to leave their cities be, why not us? Sell Meereen back to them and start west with wagons full o' gold and gems and such."

"You want me to loot Meereen and flee? No, I will not do that. Grey Worm, are my freedmen ready for battle?"

The eunuch crossed his arms against his chest. "They are not Unsullied, but they will not shame you. This one will swear to that by spear and sword, Your Worship."

"Good. That's good." Daenerys looked at the faces of the men around her. The Shavepate, scowling. Ser Barristan, with his lined face and sad blue eyes. Reznak mo Reznak, pale, sweating. Brown Ben, white-haired, grizzled, tough as old leather. Grey Worm, smooth-cheeked, stolid, expressionless. *Daario should be here, and my bloodriders,* she thought. *If there is to be a battle, the blood of my blood should be with me.* She missed Ser Jorah Mormont too. *He lied to me, informed on me, but he loved me too, and he always gave good counsel.* "I defeated the Yunkai'i before. I will defeat them again. Where, though? How?"

"You mean to take the field?" The Shavepate's voice was thick with disbelief. "That would be folly. Our walls are taller and thicker than the walls of Astapor, and our defenders are more valiant. The Yunkai'i will not take this city easily."

Ser Barristan disagreed. "I do not think we should allow them to invest us. Theirs is a patchwork host at best. These slavers are no soldiers. If we take them unawares . . ."

"Small chance of that," the Shavepate said. "The Yunkai'i have many friends inside the city. They will know."

"How large an army can we muster?" Dany asked.

"Not large enough, begging your royal pardon," said Brown Ben Plumm. "What does Naharis have to say? If we're going to make a fight o' this, we need his Stormcrows."

"Daario is still in the field." *Oh, gods, what have I done? Have I sent him to his death?* "Ben, I will need your Second Sons to scout our enemies. Where they are, how fast they are advancing, how many men they have, and how they are disposed."

"We'll need provisions. Fresh horses too."

"Of course. Ser Barristan will see to it."

Brown Ben scratched his chin. "Might be we could get some o' them to come over. If Your Grace could spare a few bags o' gold and gems . . . just to give their captains a good taste, as it were . . . well, who knows?"

"Buy them, why not?" Dany said. That sort of thing went on all the time amongst the free companies of the Disputed Lands, she knew. "Yes, very good. Reznak, see to it. Once the Second Sons ride out, close the gates and double the watch upon the walls."

"It shall be done, Magnificence," said Reznak mo Reznak. "What of these Astapori?"

My children. "They are coming here for help. For succor and protection. We cannot turn our backs on them."

Ser Barristan frowned. "Your Grace, I have known the bloody flux to destroy whole armies when left to spread unchecked. The seneschal is right. We cannot have the Astapori in Meereen."

Dany looked at him helplessly. It was good that dragons did not cry. "As you say, then. We will keep them outside the walls until this . . . this curse has run its course. Set up a camp for them beside the river, west of the city. We will send them what food we can. Perhaps we can separate the healthy from the sick." All of them were looking at her. "Will you make me say it twice? Go and do as I've commanded you." Dany rose, brushed past Brown Ben, and climbed the steps to the sweet solitude of her terrace.

Two hundred leagues divided Meereen from Astapor, yet it seemed to her that the sky was darker to the southwest, smudged and hazy with the smoke of the Red City's passing. *Brick and blood built Astapor, and brick and blood its people.* The old rhyme rang in her head. *Ash and bone is Astapor, and ash and bone its people.* She tried to recall Eroeh's face, but the dead girl's features kept turning into smoke.

When Daenerys finally turned away, Ser Barristan stood near her, wrapped in his white cloak against the chill of evening. "Can we make a fight of this?" she asked him.

"Men can always fight, Your Grace. Ask rather if we can win. Dying is easy, but victory comes hard. Your freedmen are half-trained and unblooded. Your sellswords once served your foes, and once a man turns his cloak he will not scruple to turn it again. You have two dragons who cannot be controlled, and a third that may be lost to you. Beyond these walls your only friends are the Lhazarene, who have no taste for war."

"My walls are strong, though."

"No stronger than when we sat outside them. And the Sons of the Harpy are inside the walls with us. So are the Great Masters, both those you did not kill and the sons of those you did."

"I know." The queen sighed. "What do you counsel, ser?"

"Battle," said Ser Barristan. "Meereen is overcrowded and full of hungry mouths, and you have too many enemies within. We cannot long withstand a siege, I fear. Let me meet the foe as he comes north, on ground of my own choosing."

"Meet the foe," she echoed, "with the freedmen you've called half-trained and unblooded."

"We were all unblooded once, Your Grace. The Unsullied will help stiffen them. If I had five hundred knights . . ."

"Or five. And if I give you the Unsullied, I will have no one but the Brazen Beasts to hold Meereen." When Ser Barristan did not dispute her, Dany closed her eyes. *Gods,* she prayed, *you took Khal Drogo, who was my sun-and-stars. You took our valiant son before he drew a breath. You have had your blood of me. Help me now, I pray you. Give me the wisdom to see the path ahead and the strength to do what I must to keep my children safe.*

The gods did not respond.

When she opened her eyes again, Daenerys said, "I cannot fight two enemies, one within and one without. If I am to hold Meereen,

I must have the city behind me. The *whole* city. I need . . . I need . . ."
She could not say it.

"Your Grace?" Ser Barristan prompted, gently.

A queen belongs not to herself but to her people.

"I need Hizdahr zo Loraq."

MELISANDRE

It was never truly dark in Melisandre's chambers.

Three tallow candles burned upon her windowsill to keep the terrors of the night at bay. Four more flickered beside her bed, two to either side. In the hearth a fire was kept burning day and night. The first lesson those who would serve her had to learn was that the fire must never, ever be allowed to go out.

The red priestess closed her eyes and said a prayer, then opened them once more to face the hearthfire. *One more time.* She had to be certain. Many a priest and priestess before her had been brought down by false visions, by seeing what they wished to see instead of what the Lord of Light had sent. Stannis was marching south into peril, the king who carried the fate of the world upon his shoulders, Azor Ahai reborn. Surely R'hllor would vouchsafe her a glimpse of what awaited him. *Show me Stannis, Lord,* she prayed. *Show me your king, your instrument.*

Visions danced before her, gold and scarlet, flickering, forming and melting and dissolving into one another, shapes strange and terrifying and seductive. She saw the eyeless faces again, staring out at her from sockets weeping blood. Then the towers by the sea, crumbling as the dark tide came sweeping over them, rising from the depths. Shadows in the shape of skulls, skulls that turned to mist, bodies locked together in lust, writhing and rolling and clawing.

Through curtains of fire great winged shadows wheeled against a hard blue sky.

The girl. I must find the girl again, the grey girl on the dying horse. Jon Snow would expect that of her, and soon. It would not be enough to say the girl was fleeing. He would want more, he would want the when and where, and she did not have that for him. She had seen the girl only once. *A girl as grey as ash, and even as I watched she crumbled and blew away.*

A face took shape within the hearth. *Stannis?* she thought, for just a moment . . . but no, these were not his features. *A wooden face, corpse white.* Was this the enemy? A thousand red eyes floated in the rising flames. *He sees me.* Beside him, a boy with a wolf's face threw back his head and howled.

The red priestess shuddered. Blood trickled down her thigh, black and smoking. The fire was inside her, an agony, an ecstasy, filling her, searing her, transforming her. Shimmers of heat traced patterns on her skin, insistent as a lover's hand. Strange voices called to her from days long past. "Melony," she heard a woman cry. A man's voice called, "Lot Seven." She was weeping, and her tears were flame. And still she drank it in.

Snowflakes swirled from a dark sky and ashes rose to meet them, the grey and the white whirling around each other as flaming arrows arced above a wooden wall and dead things shambled silent through the cold, beneath a great grey cliff where fires burned inside a hundred caves. Then the wind rose and the white mist came sweeping in, impossibly cold, and one by one the fires went out. Afterward only the skulls remained.

Death, thought Melisandre. *The skulls are death.*

The flames crackled softly, and in their crackling she heard the whispered name *Jon Snow.* His long face floated before her, limned in tongues of red and orange, appearing and disappearing again, a shadow half-seen behind a fluttering curtain. Now he was a man, now a wolf, now a man again. But the skulls were here as well, the skulls were all around him. Melisandre had seen his danger before, had tried to warn the boy of it. *Enemies all around him, daggers in the dark.* He would not listen.

Unbelievers never listened until it was too late.

"What do you see, my lady?" the boy asked, softly.

Skulls. A thousand skulls, and the bastard boy again. Jon Snow. Whenever she was asked what she saw within her fires, Melisandre would answer, "Much and more," but seeing was never as simple as those words suggested. It was an art, and like all arts it demanded mastery, discipline, study. *Pain. That too.* R'hllor spoke to his chosen ones through blessed fire, in a language of ash and cinder and twisting flame that only a god could truly grasp. Melisandre had practiced her art for years beyond count, and she had paid the price. There was no one, even in her order, who had her skill at seeing the secrets half-revealed and half-concealed within the sacred flames.

Yet now she could not even seem to find her king. *I pray for a glimpse of Azor Ahai, and R'hllor shows me only Snow.* "Devan," she called, "a drink." Her throat was raw and parched.

"Yes, my lady." The boy poured her a cup of water from the stone jug by the window and brought it to her.

"Thank you." Melisandre took a sip, swallowed, and gave the boy a smile. That made him blush. The boy was half in love with her, she knew. *He fears me, he wants me, and he worships me.*

All the same, Devan was not pleased to be here. The lad had taken great pride in serving as a king's squire, and it had wounded him when Stannis commanded him to remain at Castle Black. Like any boy his age, his head was full of dreams of glory; no doubt he had been picturing the prowess he would display at Deepwood Motte. Other boys his age had gone south, to serve as squires to the king's knights and ride into battle at their side. Devan's exclusion must have seemed a rebuke, a punishment for some failure on his part, or perhaps for some failure of his father.

In truth, he was here because Melisandre had asked for him. The four eldest sons of Davos Seaworth had perished in the battle on the Blackwater, when the king's fleet had been consumed by green fire. Devan was the fifthborn and safer here with her than at the king's side. Lord Davos would not thank her for it, no more than the boy himself, but it seemed to her that Seaworth had suffered enough grief. Misguided as he was, his loyalty to Stannis could not be doubted. She had seen that in her flames.

Devan was quick and smart and able too, which was more than could be said about most of her attendants. Stannis had left a dozen of his men behind to serve her when he marched south, but most of them were useless. His Grace had need of every sword, so all he could spare were greybeards and cripples. One man had been blinded by a blow to his head in the battle by the Wall, another lamed when his falling horse crushed his legs. Her serjeant lost an arm to a giant's club. Three of her guard were geldings that Stannis had castrated for raping wildling women. She had two drunkards and a craven too. The last should have been hanged, as the king himself admitted, but he came from a noble family, and his father and brothers had been stalwart from the first.

Having guards about her would no doubt help keep the black brothers properly respectful, the red priestess knew, but none of the men that Stannis had given her were like to be much help should she find herself in peril. It made no matter. Melisandre of Asshai did not fear for herself. R'hllor would protect her.

She took another sip of water, laid her cup aside, blinked and stretched and rose from her chair, her muscles sore and stiff. After gazing into the flames so long, it took her a few moments to adjust to the dimness. Her eyes were dry and tired, but if she rubbed them, it would only make them worse.

Her fire had burned low, she saw. "Devan, more wood. What hour is it?"

"Almost dawn, my lady."

Dawn. Another day is given us, R'hllor be praised. The terrors of the night recede. Melisandre had spent the night in her chair by the fire, as she often did. With Stannis gone, her bed saw little use. She had no time for sleep, with the weight of the world upon her shoulders. And she feared to dream. *Sleep is a little death, dreams the whisperings of the Other, who would drag us all into his eternal night.* She would sooner sit bathed in the ruddy glow of her red lord's blessed flames, her cheeks flushed by the wash of heat as if by a lover's kisses. Some nights she drowsed, but never for more than an hour. One day, Melisandre prayed, she would not sleep at all. One day she would be free of dreams. *Melony,* she thought. *Lot Seven.*

Devan fed fresh logs to the fire until the flames leapt up again, fierce and furious, driving the shadows back into the corners of the room, devouring all her unwanted dreams. *The dark recedes again . . . for a little while. But beyond the Wall, the enemy grows stronger, and should he win the dawn will never come again.* She wondered if it had been his face that she had seen, staring out at her from the flames. *No. Surely not. His visage would be more frightening than that, cold and black and too terrible for any man to gaze upon and live.* The wooden man she had glimpsed, though, and the boy with the wolf's face . . . they were his servants, surely . . . his champions, as Stannis was hers.

Melisandre went to her window, pushed open the shutters. Outside the east had just begun to lighten, and the stars of morning still hung in a pitch-black sky. Castle Black was already beginning to stir as men in black cloaks made their way across the yard to break their fast with bowls of porridge before they relieved their brothers atop the Wall. A few snowflakes drifted by the open window, floating on the wind.

"Does my lady wish to break her fast?" asked Devan.

Food. Yes, I should eat. Some days she forgot. R'hllor provided her with all the nourishment her body needed, but that was something best concealed from mortal men.

It was Jon Snow she needed, not fried bread and bacon, but it was no use sending Devan to the lord commander. He would not come to her summons. Snow still chose to dwell behind the armory, in a pair of modest rooms previously occupied by the Watch's late blacksmith. Perhaps he did not think himself worthy of the King's Tower, or perhaps he did not care. That was his mistake, the false humility of youth that is itself a sort of pride. It was never wise for a ruler to eschew the trappings of power, for power itself flows in no small measure from such trappings.

The boy was not entirely naive, however. He knew better than to come to Melisandre's chambers like a supplicant, insisting she come to him instead should she have need of words with him. And oft as not, when she did come, he would keep her waiting or refuse to see her. That much, at least, was shrewd.

"I will have nettle tea, a boiled egg, and bread with butter. Fresh bread, if you please, not fried. You may find the wildling as well. Tell him that I must speak with him."

"Rattleshirt, my lady?"

"And quickly."

While the boy was gone, Melisandre washed herself and changed her robes. Her sleeves were full of hidden pockets, and she checked them carefully as she did every morning to make certain all her powders were in place. Powders to turn fire green or blue or silver, powders to make a flame roar and hiss and leap up higher than a man is tall, powders to make smoke. A smoke for truth, a smoke for lust, a smoke for fear, and the thick black smoke that could kill a man outright. The red priestess armed herself with a pinch of each of them.

The carved chest that she had brought across the narrow sea was more than three-quarters empty now. And while Melisandre had the knowledge to make more powders, she lacked many rare ingredients. *My spells should suffice.* She was stronger at the Wall, stronger even than in Asshai. Her every word and gesture was more potent, and she could do things that she had never done before. *Such shadows as I bring forth here will be terrible, and no creature of the dark will stand before them.* With such sorceries at her command, she should soon have no more need of the feeble tricks of alchemists and pyromancers.

She shut the chest, turned the lock, and hid the key inside her skirts in another secret pocket. Then came a rapping at her door. Her one-armed serjeant, from the tremulous sound of his knock. "Lady Melisandre, the Lord o' Bones is come."

"Send him in." Melisandre settled herself back into the chair beside the hearth.

The wildling wore a sleeveless jerkin of boiled leather dotted with bronze studs beneath a worn cloak mottled in shades of green and brown. *No bones.* He was cloaked in shadows too, in wisps of ragged grey mist, half-seen, sliding across his face and form with every step he took. *Ugly things. As ugly as his bones.* A widow's peak, close-set dark eyes, pinched cheeks, a mustache wriggling like a worm above a mouthful of broken brown teeth.

Melisandre felt the warmth in the hollow of her throat as her ruby stirred at the closeness of its slave. "You have put aside your suit of bones," she observed.

"The clacking was like to drive me mad."

"The bones protect you," she reminded him. "The black brothers do not love you. Devan tells me that only yesterday you had words with some of them over supper."

"A few. I was eating bean-and-bacon soup whilst Bowen Marsh was going on about the high ground. The Old Pomegranate thought that I was spying on him and announced that he would not suffer murderers listening to their councils. I told him that if that was true, maybe they shouldn't have them by the fire. Bowen turned red and made some choking sounds, but that was as far as it went." The wildling sat on the edge of the window, slid his dagger from its sheath. "If some crow wants to slip a knife between my ribs whilst I'm spooning up some supper, he's welcome to try. Hobb's gruel would taste better with a drop of blood to spice it."

Melisandre paid the naked steel no mind. If the wildling had meant her harm, she would have seen it in her flames. Danger to her own person was the first thing she had learned to see, back when she was still half a child, a slave girl bound for life to the great red temple. It was still the first thing she looked for whenever she gazed into a fire. "It is their eyes that should concern you, not their knives," she warned him.

"The glamor, aye." In the black iron fetter about his wrist, the ruby seemed to pulse. He tapped it with the edge of his blade. The steel made a faint *click* against the stone. "I feel it when I sleep. Warm against my skin, even through the iron. Soft as a woman's kiss. *Your* kiss. But sometimes in my dreams it starts to burn, and your lips turn into teeth. Every day I think how easy it would be to pry it out, and every day I don't. Must I wear the bloody bones as well?"

"The spell is made of shadow and suggestion. Men see what they expect to see. The bones are part of that." *Was I wrong to spare this one?* "If the glamor fails, they will kill you."

The wildling began to scrape the dirt out from beneath his nails with the point of his dagger. "I've sung my songs, fought my battles, drunk summer wine, tasted the Dornishman's wife. A man should die the way he's lived. For me that's steel in hand."

Does he dream of death? Could the enemy have touched him? Death is his domain, the dead his soldiers. "You shall have work for your steel soon enough. The enemy is moving, the true enemy. And Lord Snow's rangers will return before the day is done, with their blind and bloody eyes."

The wildling's own eyes narrowed. Grey eyes, brown eyes; Melisandre could see the color change with each pulse of the ruby. "Cutting out the eyes, that's the Weeper's work. The best crow's a blind crow, he likes to say. Sometimes I think he'd like to cut out his own eyes, the way they're always watering and itching. Snow's been assuming the free folk would turn to Tormund to lead them, because that's what he would do. He liked Tormund, and the old fraud liked him too. If it's the Weeper, though . . . that's not good. Not for him, and not for us."

Melisandre nodded solemnly, as if she had taken his words to heart, but this Weeper did not matter. None of his free folk mattered. They were a lost people, a doomed people, destined to vanish from the earth, as the children of the forest had vanished. Those were not words he would wish to hear, though, and she could not risk losing him, not now. "How well do you know the north?"

He slipped his blade away. "As well as any raider. Some parts more than others. There's a lot of north. Why?"

"The girl," she said. "A girl in grey on a dying horse. Jon Snow's sister." Who else could it be? She was racing to him for protection, that much Melisandre had seen clearly. "I have seen her in my flames, but only once. We must win the lord commander's trust, and the only way to do that is to save her."

"Me save her, you mean? The Lord o' Bones?" He laughed. "No one ever trusted Rattleshirt but fools. Snow's not that. If his sister needs saving, he'll send his crows. I would."

"He is not you. He made his vows and means to live by them. The Night's Watch takes no part. But you are not Night's Watch. You can do what he cannot."

"If your stiff-necked lord commander will allow it. Did your fires show you where to find this girl?"

"I saw water. Deep and blue and still, with a thin coat of ice just forming on it. It seemed to go on and on forever."

"Long Lake. What else did you see around this girl?"

"Hills. Fields. Trees. A deer, once. Stones. She is staying well away from villages. When she can she rides along the bed of little streams, to throw hunters off her trail."

He frowned. "That will make it difficult. She was coming north, you said. Was the lake to her east or to her west?"

Melisandre closed her eyes, remembering. "West."

"She is not coming up the kingsroad, then. Clever girl. There are fewer watchers on the other side, and more cover. And some hidey-holes I have used myself from time—" He broke off at the sound of a warhorn and rose swiftly to his feet. All over Castle Black, Melisandre knew, the same sudden hush had fallen, and every man and boy turned toward the Wall, listening, waiting. One long blast of the horn meant rangers returning, but two . . .

The day has come, the red priestess thought. *Lord Snow will have to listen to me now.*

After the long mournful cry of the horn had faded away, the silence seemed to stretch out to an hour. The wildling finally broke the spell. "Only one, then. Rangers."

"Dead rangers." Melisandre rose to her feet as well. "Go put on your bones and wait. I will return."

"I should go with you."

"Do not be foolish. Once they find what they will find, the sight of any wildling will inflame them. Stay here until their blood has time to cool."

Devan was coming up the steps of the King's Tower as Melisandre made her descent, flanked by two of the guards Stannis had left her. The boy was carrying her half-forgotten breakfast on a tray. "I waited for Hobb to pull the fresh loaves from the ovens, my lady. The bread's still hot."

"Leave it in my chambers." The wildling would eat it, like as not. "Lord Snow has need of me, beyond the Wall." *He does not know it yet, but soon . . .*

Outside, a light snow had begun to fall. A crowd of crows had gathered around the gate by the time Melisandre and her escort arrived, but they made way for the red priestess. The lord commander had preceded her through the ice, accompanied by Bowen Marsh and twenty spearmen. Snow had also sent a dozen archers to the top of the Wall, should any foes be hidden in the nearby woods. The guards on the gate were not queen's men, but they passed her all the same.

It was cold and dark beneath the ice, in the narrow tunnel that crooked and slithered through the Wall. Morgan went before her with a torch and Merrel came behind her with an axe. Both men were hopeless drunkards, but they were sober at this hour of the morning. Queen's men, at least in name, both had a healthy fear of her, and Merrel could be formidable when he was not drunk. She would have no need of them today, but Melisandre made it a point to keep a pair of guards about her everywhere she went. It sent a certain message. *The trappings of power.*

By the time the three of them emerged north of the Wall the snow was falling steadily. A ragged blanket of white covered the torn and tortured earth that stretched from the Wall to the edge of the haunted forest. Jon Snow and his black brothers were gathered around three spears, some twenty yards away.

The spears were eight feet long and made of ash. The one on the left had a slight crook, but the other two were smooth and straight. At the top of each was impaled a severed head. Their beards were full of ice, and the falling snow had given them white hoods. Where their eyes had been, only empty sockets remained, black and bloody holes that stared down in silent accusation.

"Who were they?" Melisandre asked the crows.

"Black Jack Bulwer, Hairy Hal, and Garth Greyfeather," Bowen Marsh said solemnly. "The ground is half-frozen. It must have taken the wildlings half the night to drive the spears so deep. They could still be close. Watching us." The Lord Steward squinted at the line of trees.

"Could be a hundred of them out there," said the black brother with the dour face. "Could be a thousand."

"No," said Jon Snow. "They left their gifts in the black of night, then ran." His huge white direwolf prowled around the shafts, sniffing, then lifted his leg and pissed on the spear that held the head of Black Jack Bulwer. "Ghost would have their scent if they were still out there."

"I hope the Weeper burned the bodies," said the dour man, the one called Dolorous Edd. "Elsewise they might come looking for their heads."

Jon Snow grasped the spear that bore Garth Greyfeather's head and wrenched it violently from the ground. "Pull down the other two," he commanded, and four of the crows hurried to obey.

Bowen Marsh's cheeks were red with cold. "We should never have sent out rangers."

"This is not the time and place to pick at that wound. Not here, my lord. Not now." To the men struggling with the spears Snow said, "Take the heads and burn them. Leave nothing but bare bone." Only then did he seem to notice Melisandre. "My lady. Walk with me, if you would."

At last. "If it please the lord commander."

As they walked beneath the Wall, she slipped her arm through his. Morgan and Merrel went before them, Ghost came prowling at their heels. The priestess did not speak, but she slowed her pace deliberately, and where she walked the ice began to drip. *He will not fail to notice that.*

Beneath the iron grating of a murder hole Snow broke the silence, as she had known he would. "What of the other six?"

"I have not seen them," Melisandre said.

"Will you look?"

"Of course, my lord."

"We've had a raven from Ser Denys Mallister at the Shadow Tower," Jon Snow told her. "His men have seen fires in the mountains on the far side of the Gorge. Wildlings massing, Ser Denys believes. He thinks they are going to try to force the Bridge of Skulls again."

"Some may." Could the skulls in her vision have signified this bridge? Somehow Melisandre did not think so. "If it comes, that attack will be no more than a diversion. I saw towers by the sea, submerged beneath a black and bloody tide. That is where the heaviest blow will fall."

"Eastwatch?"

Was it? Melisandre had seen Eastwatch-by-the-Sea with King Stannis. That was where His Grace left Queen Selyse and their daughter Shireen when he assembled his knights for the march to Castle Black. The towers in her fire had been different, but that was oft the way with visions. "Yes. Eastwatch, my lord."

"When?"

She spread her hands. "On the morrow. In a moon's turn. In a year. And it may be that if you act, you may avert what I have seen entirely." *Else what would be the point of visions?*

"Good," said Snow.

The crowd of crows beyond the gate had swollen to two score by the time they emerged from beneath the Wall. The men pressed close about them. Melisandre knew a few by name: the cook Three-Finger Hobb, Mully with his greasy orange hair, the dim-witted boy called Owen the Oaf, the drunkard Septon Celladar.

"Is it true, m'lord?" said Three-Finger Hobb.

"Who is it?" asked Owen the Oaf. "Not Dywen, is it?"

"Nor Garth," said the queen's man she knew as Alf of Runnymudd, one of the first to exchange his seven false gods for the truth of R'hllor. "Garth's too clever for them wildlings."

"How many?" Mully asked.

"Three," Jon told them. "Black Jack, Hairy Hal, and Garth."

Alf of Runnymudd let out a howl loud enough to wake sleepers in the Shadow Tower. "Put him to bed and get some mulled wine into him," Jon told Three-Finger Hobb.

"Lord Snow," Melisandre said quietly. "Will you come with me to the King's Tower? I have more to share with you."

He looked at her face for a long moment with those cold grey eyes of his. His right hand closed, opened, closed again. "As you wish. Edd, take Ghost back to my chambers."

Melisandre took that as a sign and dismissed her own guard as well. They crossed the yard together, just the two of them. The snow fell all around them. She walked as close to Jon Snow as she dared, close enough to feel the mistrust pouring off him like a black fog. *He does not love me, will never love me, but he will make use of me. Well and good.* Melisandre had danced the same dance with Stannis

Baratheon, back in the beginning. In truth, the young lord commander and her king had more in common than either one would ever be willing to admit. Stannis had been a younger son living in the shadow of his elder brother, just as Jon Snow, bastard-born, had always been eclipsed by his trueborn sibling, the fallen hero men had called the Young Wolf. Both men were unbelievers by nature, mistrustful, suspicious. The only gods they truly worshiped were honor and duty.

"You have not asked about your sister," Melisandre said, as they climbed the spiral steps of the King's Tower.

"I told you. I have no sister. We put aside our kin when we say our words. I cannot help Arya, much as I—"

He broke off as they stepped inside her chambers. The wildling was within, seated at her board, spreading butter on a ragged chunk of warm brown bread with his dagger. He had donned the bone armor, she was pleased to see. The broken giant's skull that was his helm rested on the window seat behind him.

Jon Snow tensed. "You."

"Lord Snow." The wildling grinned at them through a mouth of brown and broken teeth. The ruby on his wrist glimmered in the morning light like a dim red star.

"What are you doing here?"

"Breaking my fast. You're welcome to share."

"I'll not break bread with you."

"Your loss. The loaf's still warm. Hobb can do that much, at least." The wildling ripped off a bite. "I could visit you as easily, my lord. Those guards at your door are a bad jape. A man who has climbed the Wall half a hundred times can climb in a window easy enough. But what good would come of killing you? The crows would only choose someone worse." He chewed, swallowed. "I heard about your rangers. You should have sent me with them."

"So you could betray them to the Weeper?"

"Are we talking about betrayals? What was the name of that wildling wife of yours, Snow? Ygritte, wasn't it?" The wildling turned to Melisandre. "I will need horses. Half a dozen good ones. And this is nothing I can do alone. Some of the spearwives penned up at Mole's

Town should serve. Women would be best for this. The girl's more like to trust them, and they will help me carry off a certain ploy I have in mind."

"What is he talking about?" Lord Snow asked her.

"Your sister." Melisandre put her hand on his arm. "You cannot help her, but he can."

Snow wrenched his arm away. "I think not. You do not know this creature. Rattleshirt could wash his hands a hundred times a day and he'd still have blood beneath his nails. He'd be more like to rape and murder Arya than to save her. No. If this was what you have seen in your fires, my lady, you must have ashes in your eyes. If he tries to leave Castle Black without my leave, I'll take his head off myself."

He leaves me no choice. So be it. "Devan, leave us," she said, and the squire slipped away and closed the door behind him.

Melisandre touched the ruby at her neck and spoke a word.

The sound echoed queerly from the corners of the room and twisted like a worm inside their ears. The wildling heard one word, the crow another. Neither was the word that left her lips. The ruby on the wildling's wrist darkened, and the wisps of light and shadow around him writhed and faded.

The bones remained—the rattling ribs, the claws and teeth along his arms and shoulders, the great yellowed collarbone across his shoulders. The broken giant's skull remained a broken giant's skull, yellowed and cracked, grinning its stained and savage grin.

But the widow's peak dissolved. The brown mustache, the knobby chin, the sallow yellowed flesh and small dark eyes, all melted. Grey fingers crept through long brown hair. Laugh lines appeared at the corners of his mouth. All at once he was bigger than before, broader in the chest and shoulders, long-legged and lean, his face clean-shaved and windburnt.

Jon Snow's grey eyes grew wider. "Mance?"

"Lord Snow." Mance Rayder did not smile.

"*She burned you.*"

"She burned the Lord of Bones."

Jon Snow turned to Melisandre. "What sorcery is this?"

"Call it what you will. Glamor, seeming, illusion. R'hllor is Lord of Light, Jon Snow, and it is given to his servants to weave with it, as others weave with thread."

Mance Rayder chuckled. "I had my doubts as well, Snow, but why not let her try? It was that, or let Stannis roast me."

"The bones help," said Melisandre. "The bones remember. The strongest glamors are built of such things. A dead man's boots, a hank of hair, a bag of fingerbones. With whispered words and prayer, a man's shadow can be drawn forth from such and draped about another like a cloak. The wearer's essence does not change, only his seeming."

She made it sound a simple thing, and easy. They need never know how difficult it had been, or how much it had cost her. That was a lesson Melisandre had learned long before Asshai; the more effortless the sorcery appears, the more men fear the sorcerer. When the flames had licked at Rattleshirt, the ruby at her throat had grown so hot that she had feared her own flesh might start to smoke and blacken. Thankfully Lord Snow had delivered her from that agony with his arrows. Whilst Stannis had seethed at the defiance, she had shuddered with relief.

"Our false king has a prickly manner," Melisandre told Jon Snow, "but he will not betray you. We hold his son, remember. And he owes you his very life."

"Me?" Snow sounded startled.

"Who else, my lord? Only his life's blood could pay for his crimes, your laws said, and Stannis Baratheon is not a man to go against the law . . . but as you said so sagely, the laws of men end at the Wall. I told you that the Lord of Light would hear your prayers. You wanted a way to save your little sister and still hold fast to the honor that means so much to you, to the vows you swore before your wooden god." She pointed with a pale finger. "There he stands, Lord Snow. Arya's deliverance. A gift from the Lord of Light . . . and me."

REEK

He heard the girls first, barking as they raced for home. The drum of hoofbeats echoing off flagstone jerked him to his feet, chains rattling. The one between his ankles was no more than a foot long, shortening his stride to a shuffle. It was hard to move quickly that way, but he tried as best he could, hopping and clanking from his pallet. Ramsay Bolton had returned and would want his Reek on hand to serve him.

Outside, beneath a cold autumnal sky, the hunters were pouring through the gates. Ben Bones led the way, with the girls baying and barking all around him. Behind came Skinner, Sour Alyn, and Damon Dance-for-Me with his long greased whip, then the Walders riding the grey colts Lady Dustin had given them. His lordship himself rode Blood, a red stallion with a temper to match his own. He was laughing. That could be very good or very bad, Reek knew.

The dogs were on him before he could puzzle out which, drawn to his scent. The dogs were fond of Reek; he slept with them oft as not, and sometimes Ben Bones let him share their supper. The pack raced across the flagstones barking, circling him, jumping up to lick his filthy face, nipping at his legs. Helicent caught his left hand between her teeth and worried it so fiercely Reek feared he might lose two more fingers. Red Jeyne slammed into his chest and knocked him off his feet. She was lean, hard muscle, where

Reek was loose, grey skin and brittle bones, a white-haired starveling.

The riders were dismounting by the time he pushed Red Jeyne off and struggled to his knees. Two dozen horsemen had gone out and two dozen had returned, which meant the search had been a failure. That was bad. Ramsay did not like the taste of failure. *He will want to hurt someone.*

Of late, his lord had been forced to restrain himself, for Barrowton was full of men House Bolton needed, and Ramsay knew to be careful around the Dustins and Ryswells and his fellow lordlings. With them he was always courteous and smiling. What he was behind closed doors was something else.

Ramsay Bolton was attired as befit the lord of the Hornwood and heir to the Dreadfort. His mantle was stitched together from wolfskins and clasped against the autumn chill by the yellowed teeth of the wolf's head on his right shoulder. On one hip he wore a falchion, its blade as thick and heavy as a cleaver; on the other a long dagger and a small curved flaying knife with a hooked point and a razor-sharp edge. All three blades had matched hilts of yellow bone. "Reek," his lordship called down from Blood's high saddle, "you stink. I can smell you clear across the yard."

"I know, my lord," Reek had to say. "I beg your pardon."

"I brought you a gift." Ramsay twisted, reached behind him, pulled something from his saddle, and flung it. "Catch!"

Between the chain, the fetters, and his missing fingers, Reek was clumsier than he had been before he learned his name. The head struck his maimed hands, bounced away from the stumps of his fingers, and landed at his feet, raining maggots. It was so crusted with dried blood as to be unrecognizable.

"I told you to catch it," said Ramsay. "Pick it up."

Reek tried to lift the head up by the ear. It was no good. The flesh was green and rotting, and the ear tore off between his fingers. Little Walder laughed, and a moment later all the other men were laughing too. "Oh, leave him be," said Ramsay. "Just see to Blood. I rode the bastard hard."

"Yes, my lord. I will." Reek hurried to the horse, leaving the severed head for the dogs.

"You smell like pigshit today, Reek," said Ramsay.

"On him, that's an improvement," said Damon Dance-for-Me, smiling as he coiled his whip.

Little Walder swung down from the saddle. "You can see to my horse too, Reek. And to my little cousin's."

"I can see to my own horse," said Big Walder. Little Walder had become Lord Ramsay's best boy and grew more like him every day, but the smaller Frey was made of different stuff and seldom took part in his cousin's games and cruelties.

Reek paid the squires no mind. He led Blood off toward the stables, hopping aside when the stallion tried to kick him. The hunters strode into the hall, all but Ben Bones, who was cursing at the dogs to stop them fighting over the severed head.

Big Walder followed him into the stables, leading his own mount. Reek stole a look at him as he removed Blood's bit. "Who was he?" he said softly, so the other stablehands would not hear.

"No one." Big Walder pulled the saddle off his grey. "An old man we met on the road, is all. He was driving an old nanny goat and four kids."

"His lordship slew him for his goats?"

"His lordship slew him for calling him Lord Snow. The goats were good, though. We milked the mother and roasted up the kids."

Lord Snow. Reek nodded, his chains clinking as he wrestled with Blood's saddle straps. *By any name, Ramsay's no man to be around when he is in a rage. Or when he's not.* "Did you find your cousins, my lord?"

"No. I never thought we would. They're dead. Lord Wyman had them killed. That's what I would have done if I was him."

Reek said nothing. Some things were not safe to say, not even in the stables with his lordship in the hall. One wrong word could cost him another toe, even a finger. *Not my tongue, though. He will never take my tongue. He likes to hear me plead with him to spare me from the pain. He likes to make me say it.*

The riders had been sixteen days on the hunt, with only hard bread and salt beef to eat, aside from the occasional stolen kid, so that night Lord Ramsay commanded that a feast be laid to celebrate his return to Barrowton. Their host, a grizzled one-armed petty lord by the name of Harwood Stout, knew better than to refuse him, though by now his larders must be well nigh exhausted. Reek had heard Stout's servants muttering at how the Bastard and his men were eating through the winter stores. "He'll bed Lord Eddard's little girl, they say," Stout's cook complained when she did not know that Reek was listening, "but we're the ones who'll be fucked when the snows come, you mark my words."

Yet Lord Ramsay had decreed a feast, so feast they must. Trestle tables were set up in Stout's hall, an ox was slaughtered, and that night as the sun went down the empty-handed hunters ate roasts and ribs, barley bread, a mash of carrots and pease, washing it all down with prodigious quantities of ale.

It fell to Little Walder to keep Lord Ramsay's cup filled, whilst Big Walder poured for the others at the high table. Reek was chained up beside the doors lest his odor put the feasters off their appetites. He would eat later, off whatever scraps Lord Ramsay thought to send him. The dogs enjoyed the run of the hall, however, and provided the night's best entertainment, when Maude and Grey Jeyne tore into one of Lord Stout's hounds over an especially meaty bone that Will Short had tossed them. Reek was the only man in the hall who did not watch the three dogs fight. He kept his eyes on Ramsay Bolton.

The fight did not end until their host's dog was dead. Stout's old hound never stood a mummer's chance. He had been one against two, and Ramsay's bitches were young, strong, and savage. Ben Bones, who liked the dogs better than their master, had told Reek they were all named after peasant girls Ramsay had hunted, raped, and killed back when he'd still been a bastard, running with the first Reek. "The ones who give him good sport, anywise. The ones who weep and beg and won't run don't get to come back as bitches." The next litter to come out of the Dreadfort's kennels would include a Kyra, Reek did not doubt. "He's trained 'em to kill wolves as well," Ben Bones had confided. Reek said nothing. He knew which wolves the girls were meant to kill, but he had no wish to watch the girls fighting over his severed toe.

Two serving men were carrying off the dead dog's carcass and an old woman had fetched out a mop and rake and bucket to deal with the blood-soaked rushes when the doors to the hall flew open in a wash of wind, and a dozen men in grey mail and iron halfhelms stalked through, shouldering past Stout's pasty-faced young guards in their leather brigandines and cloaks of gold and russet. A sudden silence seized the feasters . . . all but Lord Ramsay, who tossed aside the bone he had been gnawing, wiped his mouth on his sleeve, smiled a greasy, wet-lipped smile, and said, "Father."

The Lord of the Dreadfort glanced idly at the remnants of the feast, at the dead dog, at the hangings on the walls, at Reek in his chains and fetters. "Out," he told the feasters, in a voice as soft as a murmur. "Now. The lot of you."

Lord Ramsay's men pushed back from the tables, abandoning cups and trenchers. Ben Bones shouted at the girls, and they trotted after him, some with bones still in their jaws. Harwood Stout bowed stiffly and relinquished his hall without a word. "Unchain Reek and take him with you," Ramsay growled at Sour Alyn, but his father waved a pale hand and said, "No, leave him."

Even Lord Roose's own guards retreated, pulling the doors shut behind them. When the echo died away, Reek found himself alone in the hall with the two Boltons, father and son.

"You did not find our missing Freys." The way Roose Bolton said it, it was more a statement than a question.

"We rode back to where Lord Lamprey claims they parted ways, but the girls could not find a trail."

"You asked after them in villages and holdfasts."

"A waste of words. The peasants might as well be blind for all they ever see." Ramsay shrugged. "Does it matter? The world won't miss a few Freys. There's plenty more down at the Twins should we ever have need of one."

Lord Roose tore a small piece off a heel of bread and ate it. "Hosteen and Aenys are distressed."

"Let them go looking, if they like."

"Lord Wyman blames himself. To hear him tell it, he had become especially fond of Rhaegar."

Lord Ramsay was turning wroth. Reek could see it in his mouth, the curl of those thick lips, the way the cords stood up in his neck. "The fools should have stayed with Manderly."

Roose Bolton shrugged. "Lord Wyman's litter moves at a snail's pace . . . and of course his lordship's health and girth do not permit him to travel more than a few hours a day, with frequent stops for meals. The Freys were anxious to reach Barrowton and be reunited with their kin. Can you blame them for riding on ahead?"

"If that's what they did. Do you believe Manderly?"

His father's pale eyes glittered. "Did I give you that impression? Still. His lordship is most distraught."

"Not so distraught that he can't eat. Lord Pig must have brought half the food in White Harbor with him."

"Forty wayns full of foodstuffs. Casks of wine and hippocras, barrels of fresh-caught lampreys, a herd of goats, a hundred pigs, crates of crabs and oysters, a monstrous codfish . . . Lord Wyman likes to eat. You may have noticed."

"What I noticed was that he brought no hostages."

"I noticed that as well."

"What do you mean to do about it?"

"It is a quandary." Lord Roose found an empty cup, wiped it out on the tablecloth, and filled it from a flagon. "Manderly is not alone in throwing feasts, it would seem."

"It should have been you who threw the feast, to welcome me back," Ramsay complained, "and it should have been in Barrow Hall, not this pisspot of a castle."

"Barrow Hall and its kitchens are not mine to dispose of," his father said mildly. "I am only a guest there. The castle and the town belong to Lady Dustin, and she cannot abide you."

Ramsay's face darkened. "If I cut off her teats and feed them to my girls, will she abide me then? Will she abide me if I strip off her skin to make myself a pair of boots?"

"Unlikely. And those boots would come dear. They would cost us Barrowton, House Dustin, and the Ryswells." Roose Bolton seated himself across the table from his son. "Barbrey Dustin is my second wife's younger sister, Rodrik Ryswell's daughter, sister to Roger, Rickard, and mine own namesake, Roose, cousin to the other

Ryswells. She was fond of my late son and suspects you of having some part in his demise. Lady Barbrey is a woman who knows how to nurse a grievance. Be grateful for that. Barrowton is staunch for Bolton largely because she still holds Ned Stark to blame for her husband's death."

"*Staunch?*" Ramsay seethed. "All she does is spit on me. The day will come when I'll set her precious wooden town afire. Let her spit on that, see if it puts out the flames."

Roose made a face, as if the ale he was sipping had suddenly gone sour. "There are times you make me wonder if you truly are my seed. My forebears were many things, but never fools. No, be quiet now, I have heard enough. We appear strong for the moment, yes. We have powerful friends in the Lannisters and Freys, and the grudging support of much of the north . . . but what do you imagine is going to happen when one of Ned Stark's sons turns up?"

Ned Stark's sons are all dead, Reek thought. *Robb was murdered at the Twins, and Bran and Rickon . . . we dipped the heads in tar . . .* His own head was pounding. He did not want to think about anything that had happened before he knew his name. There were things too hurtful to remember, thoughts almost as painful as Ramsay's flaying knife . . .

"Stark's little wolflings are dead," said Ramsay, sloshing some more ale into his cup, "and they'll stay dead. Let them show their ugly faces, and my girls will rip those wolves of theirs to pieces. The sooner they turn up, the sooner I kill them again."

The elder Bolton sighed. "*Again?* Surely you misspeak. You never slew Lord Eddard's sons, those two sweet boys we loved so well. That was Theon Turncloak's work, remember? How many of our grudging friends do you imagine we'd retain if the truth were known? Only Lady Barbrey, whom you would turn into a pair of boots . . . *inferior* boots. Human skin is not as tough as cowhide and will not wear as well. By the king's decree you are now a Bolton. Try and act like one. Tales are told of you, Ramsay. I hear them everywhere. People fear you."

"Good."

"You are mistaken. It is not good. No tales were ever told of me. Do you think I would be sitting here if it were otherwise? Your amusements are your own, I will not chide you on that count, but you must be more discreet. A peaceful land, a quiet people. That has always been my rule. Make it yours."

"Is this why you left Lady Dustin and your fat pig wife? So you could come down here and tell me to be *quiet*?"

"Not at all. There are tidings that you need to hear. Lord Stannis has finally left the Wall."

That got Ramsay halfway to his feet, a smile glistening on his wide, wet lips. "Is he marching on the Dreadfort?"

"He is not, alas. Arnolf does not understand it. He swears that he did all he could to bait the trap."

"I wonder. Scratch a Karstark and you'll find a Stark."

"After the scratch the Young Wolf gave Lord Rickard, that may be somewhat less true than formerly. Be that as it may. Lord Stannis has taken Deepwood Motte from the ironmen and restored it to House Glover. Worse, the mountain clans have joined him, Wull and Norrey and Liddle and the rest. His strength is growing."

"Ours is greater."

"Now it is."

"Now is the time to smash him. Let me march on Deepwood."

"After you are wed."

Ramsay slammed down his cup, and the dregs of his ale erupted across the tablecloth. "I'm sick of waiting. We have a girl, we have a tree, and we have lords enough to witness. I'll wed her on the morrow, plant a son between her legs, and march before her maiden's blood has dried."

She'll pray for you to march, Reek thought, *and she'll pray that you never come back to her bed.*

"You will plant a son in her," Roose Bolton said, "but not here. I've decided you shall wed the girl at Winterfell."

That prospect did not appear to please Lord Ramsay. "I laid waste to Winterfell, or had you forgotten?"

"No, but it appears you have . . . the *ironmen* laid waste to Winterfell, and butchered all its people. Theon Turncloak."

Ramsay gave Reek a suspicious glance. "Aye, so he did, but still . . . a wedding in that ruin?"

"Even ruined and broken, Winterfell remains Lady Arya's home. What better place to wed her, bed her, and stake your claim? That is only half of it, however. We would be fools to march on Stannis. Let Stannis march on us. He is too cautious to come to Barrowton . . . but he *must* come to Winterfell. His clansmen will not abandon the daughter of their precious Ned to such as you. Stannis must march or lose them . . . and being the careful commander that he is, he will summon all his friends and allies when he marches. He will summon Arnolf Karstark."

Ramsay licked his chapped lips. "And we'll have him."

"If the gods will it." Roose rose to his feet. "You'll wed at Winterfell. I shall inform the lords that we march in three days and invite them to accompany us."

"You are the Warden of the North. Command them."

"An invitation will accomplish the same thing. Power tastes best when sweetened by courtesy. You had best learn that if you ever hope to rule." The Lord of the Dreadfort glanced at Reek. "Oh, and unchain your pet. I am taking him."

"Taking him? Where? He's mine. You cannot have him."

Roose seemed amused by that. "All you have I gave you. You would do well to remember that, bastard. As for this . . . Reek . . . if you have not ruined him beyond redemption, he may yet be of some use to us. Get the keys and remove those chains from him, before you make me rue the day I raped your mother."

Reek saw the way Ramsay's mouth twisted, the spittle glistening between his lips. He feared he might leap the table with his dagger in his hand. Instead he flushed red, turned his pale eyes from his father's paler ones, and went to find the keys. But as he knelt to unlock the fetters around Reek's wrists and ankles, he leaned close and whispered, "Tell him nothing and remember every word he says. I'll have you back, no matter what that Dustin bitch may tell you. Who are you?"

"Reek, my lord. Your man. I'm Reek, it rhymes with sneak."

"It does. When my father brings you back, I'm going to take another finger. I'll let you choose which one."

Unbidden, tears began to trickle down his cheeks. "*Why?*" he cried, his voice breaking. "I never asked for him to take me from you. I'll do whatever you want, serve, obey, I . . . please, no . . ."

Ramsay slapped his face. "Take him," he told his father. "He's not even a man. The way he smells disgusts me."

The moon was rising over the wooden walls of Barrowton when they stepped outside. Reek could hear the wind sweeping across the rolling plains beyond the town. It was less than a mile from Barrow Hall to Harwood Stout's modest keep beside the eastern gates. Lord Bolton offered him a horse. "Can you ride?"

"I . . . my lord, I . . . I think so."

"Walton, help him mount."

Even with the fetters gone, Reek moved like an old man. His flesh hung loosely on his bones, and Sour Alyn and Ben Bones said he twitched. And his smell . . . even the mare they'd brought for him shied away when he tried to mount.

She was a gentle horse, though, and she knew the way to Barrow Hall. Lord Bolton fell in beside him as they rode out the gate. The guards fell back to a discreet distance. "What would you have me call you?" the lord asked, as they trotted down the broad straight streets of Barrowton.

Reek, I'm Reek, it rhymes with wreak. "Reek," he said, "if it please my lord."

"*M'lord.*" Bolton's lips parted just enough to show a quarter inch of teeth. It might have been a smile.

He did not understand. "My lord? I said—"

"—*my lord,* when you should have said *m'lord.* Your tongue betrays your birth with every word you say. If you want to sound a proper peasant, say it as if you had mud in your mouth, or were too stupid to realize it was two words, not just one."

"If it please my—m'lord."

"Better. Your stench *is* quite appalling."

"Yes, m'lord. I beg your pardon, m'lord."

"Why? The way you smell is my son's doing, not your own. I am well aware of that." They rode past a stable and a shuttered inn with a wheat sheaf painted on its sign. Reek heard music coming through its windows. "I knew the first Reek. He stank, though not for want of washing. I have never known a cleaner creature, truth be told. He bathed thrice a day and wore flowers in his hair as if he were a maiden. Once, when my second wife was still alive, he was caught stealing scent from her bedchamber. I had him whipped for that, a dozen lashes. Even his blood smelled wrong. The next year he tried it again. This time he drank the perfume and almost died of it. It made no matter. The smell was something he was born with. A curse, the smallfolk said. The gods had made him stink so that men would know his soul was rotting. My old maester insisted it was a sign of sickness, yet the boy was otherwise as strong as a young bull. No one could stand to be near him, so he slept with the pigs . . . until the day that Ramsay's mother appeared at my gates to demand that I provide a servant for my bastard, who was growing up wild and unruly. I gave her Reek. It was meant to be amusing, but he and Ramsay became inseparable. I do wonder, though . . . was it Ramsay who corrupted Reek, or Reek Ramsay?" His lordship glanced at the new Reek with eyes as pale and strange as two white moons. "What was he whispering whilst he unchained you?"

"He . . . he said . . ." *He said to tell you nothing.* The words caught in his throat, and he began to cough and choke.

"Breathe deep. I know what he said. You're to spy on me and keep his secrets." Bolton chuckled. "As if he had secrets. Sour Alyn, Luton, Skinner, and the rest, where does he think they came from? Can he truly believe they are *his* men?"

"His men," Reek echoed. Some comment seemed to be expected of him, but he did not know what to say.

"Has my bastard ever told you how I got him?"

That he *did* know, to his relief. "Yes, my . . . m'lord. You met his mother whilst out riding and were smitten by her beauty."

"Smitten?" Bolton laughed. "Did he use that word? Why, the boy has a singer's soul . . . though if you believe that song, you may well be dimmer than the first Reek. Even the riding part is wrong. I was hunting a fox along the Weeping Water when I chanced upon a mill and saw a young woman washing clothes in the stream. The old miller had gotten himself a new young wife, a girl not half his age. She was a tall, willowy creature, very *healthy*-looking. Long legs and small firm breasts, like two ripe plums. Pretty, in a common sort of way. The moment that I set eyes on her I wanted her. Such was my due. The maesters will tell you that King Jaehaerys abolished the lord's right to the first night to appease his shrewish queen, but where the old gods rule, old customs linger. The Umbers keep the first night too, deny it as they may. Certain of the mountain clans as well, and on Skagos . . . well, only heart trees ever see half of what they do on Skagos.

"This miller's marriage had been performed without my leave or knowledge. The man had cheated me. So I had him hanged, and claimed my rights beneath the tree where he was swaying. If truth be told, the wench was hardly worth the rope. The fox escaped as well, and on our way back to the Dreadfort my favorite courser came up lame, so all in all it was a dismal day.

"A year later this same wench had the impudence to turn up at the Dreadfort with a squalling, red-faced monster that she claimed was my own get. I should've had the mother whipped and thrown her child down a well . . . but the babe *did* have my eyes. She told me that when her dead husband's brother saw those eyes, he beat her bloody and drove her from the mill. That annoyed me, so I gave her the mill and had the brother's tongue cut out, to make certain he did not go running to Winterfell with tales that might disturb Lord Rickard. Each year I sent the woman some piglets and chickens and a bag of stars, on the understanding that she was never to tell the boy who had fathered him. A peaceful land, a quiet people, that has always been my rule."

"A fine rule, m'lord."

"The woman disobeyed me, though. You see what Ramsay is. She made him, her and Reek, always whispering in his ear about his rights. He should have been content to grind corn. Does he truly think that he can ever rule the north?"

"He fights for you," Reek blurted out. "He's strong."

"Bulls are strong. Bears. I have seen my bastard fight. He is not entirely to blame. Reek was his tutor, the first Reek, and Reek was never trained at arms. Ramsay is ferocious, I will grant you, but he swings that sword like a butcher hacking meat."

"He's not afraid of anyone, m'lord."

"He should be. Fear is what keeps a man alive in this world of treachery and deceit. Even here in Barrowton the crows are circling, waiting to feast upon our flesh. The Cerwyns and the Tallharts are not to be relied on, my fat friend Lord Wyman plots betrayal, and Whoresbane . . . the Umbers may seem simple, but they are not without a certain low cunning. Ramsay should fear them all, as I do. The next time you see him, tell him that."

"Tell him . . . tell him to be afraid?" Reek felt ill at the very thought of it. "M'lord, I . . . if I did that, he'd . . ."

"I know." Lord Bolton sighed. "His blood is bad. He needs to be leeched. The leeches suck away the bad blood, all the rage and pain. No man can think so full of anger. Ramsay, though . . . his tainted blood would poison even leeches, I fear."

"He is your only son."

"For the moment. I had another, once. Domeric. A quiet boy, but most accomplished. He served four years as Lady Dustin's page, and three in the Vale as a squire to Lord Redfort. He played the high harp, read histories, and rode like the wind. Horses . . . the boy was mad for horses, Lady Dustin will tell you. Not even Lord Rickard's daughter could outrace him, and that one was half a horse herself. Redfort said he showed great promise in the lists. A great jouster must be a great horseman first."

"Yes, m'lord. Domeric. I . . . I have heard his name . . ."

"Ramsay killed him. A sickness of the bowels, Maester Uthor says, but I say poison. In the Vale, Domeric had enjoyed the company of Redfort's sons. He wanted a brother by his side, so he rode up the Weeping Water to seek my bastard out. I forbade it, but Domeric was a man grown and thought that he knew better than his father. Now his bones lie beneath the Dreadfort with the bones of his brothers, who died still in the cradle, and I am left with Ramsay. Tell me, my lord . . . if the kinslayer is accursed, what is a father to do when one son slays another?"

The question frightened him. Once he had heard Skinner say that the Bastard had killed his trueborn brother, but he had never dared to believe it. *He could be wrong. Brothers die sometimes, it does not*

mean that they were killed. My brothers died, and I never killed them.
"My lord has a new wife to give him sons."

"And won't my bastard love that? Lady Walda *is* a Frey, and she
has a fertile feel to her. I have become oddly fond of my fat little
wife. The two before her never made a sound in bed, but this one
squeals and shudders. I find that quite endearing. If she pops out
sons the way she pops in tarts, the Dreadfort will soon be overrun
with Boltons. Ramsay will kill them all, of course. That's for the
best. I will not live long enough to see new sons to manhood, and
boy lords are the bane of any House. Walda will grieve to see them
die, though."

Reek's throat was dry. He could hear the wind rattling the bare
branches of the elms that lined the street. "My lord, I—"

"*M'lord,* remember?"

"M'lord. If I might ask . . . why did you want me? I'm no use to
anyone, I'm not even a man, I'm broken, and . . . the smell . . ."

"A bath and change of clothes will make you smell sweeter."

"A bath?" Reek felt a clenching in his guts. "I . . . I would sooner
not, m'lord. Please. I have . . . wounds, I . . . and these clothes, Lord
Ramsay gave them to me, he . . . he said that I was never to take them
off, save at his command . . ."

"You are wearing rags," Lord Bolton said, quite patiently. "Filthy
things, torn and stained and stinking of blood and urine. And thin.
You must be cold. We'll put you in lambswool, soft and warm. Perhaps
a fur-lined cloak. Would you like that?"

"No." He could not let them take the clothes Lord Ramsay gave
him. He could not let them *see* him.

"Would you prefer to dress in silk and velvet? There was a time
when you were fond of such, I do recall."

"*No,*" he insisted, shrilly. "No, I only want these clothes. Reek's
clothes. I'm Reek, it rhymes with peek." His heart was beating like a
drum, and his voice rose to a frightened squeak. "I don't want a bath.
Please, m'lord, don't take my clothes."

"Will you let us wash them, at least?"

"No. No, m'lord. *Please.*" He clutched his tunic to his chest with
both hands and hunched down in the saddle, half-afraid that Roose

Bolton might command his guardsmen to tear the clothes off him right there in the street.

"As you wish." Bolton's pale eyes looked empty in the moonlight, as if there were no one behind them at all. "I mean you no harm, you know. I owe you much and more."

"You do?" Some part of him was screaming, *This is a trap, he is playing with you, the son is just the shadow of the father.* Lord Ramsay played with his hopes all the time. "What . . . what do you owe me, m'lord?"

"The north. The Starks were done and doomed the night that you took Winterfell." He waved a pale hand, dismissive. "All this is only squabbling over spoils."

Their short journey reached its end at the wooden walls of Barrow Hall. Banners flew from its square towers, flapping in the wind: the flayed man of the Dreadfort, the battle-axe of Cerwyn, Tallhart's pines, the merman of Manderly, old Lord Locke's crossed keys, the Umber giant and the stony hand of Flint, the Hornwood moose. For the Stouts, chevrony russet and gold, for Slate, a grey field within a double tressure white. Four horseheads proclaimed the four Ryswells of the Rills—one grey, one black, one gold, one brown. The jape was that the Ryswells could not even agree upon the color of their arms. Above them streamed the stag-and-lion of the boy who sat upon the Iron Throne a thousand leagues away.

Reek listened to the vanes turning on the old windmill as they rode beneath the gatehouse into a grassy courtyard where stableboys ran out to take their horses. "This way, if you please." Lord Bolton led him toward the keep, where the banners were those of the late Lord Dustin and his widowed wife. His showed a spiked crown above crossed longaxes; hers quartered those same arms with Rodrik Ryswell's golden horsehead.

As he climbed a wide flight of wooden steps to the hall, Reek's legs began to shake. He had to stop to steady them, staring up at the grassy slopes of the Great Barrow. Some claimed it was the grave of the First King, who had led the First Men to Westeros. Others argued that it must be some King of the Giants who was buried there, to account for its size. A few had even been known to say it was no barrow, just a hill, but if so it was a lonely hill, for most of the barrowlands were flat and windswept.

Inside the hall, a woman stood beside the hearth, warming thin hands above the embers of a dying fire. She was clad all in black, from head to heel, and wore no gold nor gems, but she was highborn, that was plain to see. Though there were wrinkles at the corners of her mouth and more around her eyes, she still stood tall, unbent, and handsome. Her hair was brown and grey in equal parts and she wore it tied behind her head in a widow's knot.

"Who is this?" she said. "Where is the boy? Did your bastard refuse to give him up? Is this old man his . . . oh, gods be good, what is that *smell*? Has this creature soiled himself?"

"He has been with Ramsay. Lady Barbrey, allow me to present the rightful Lord of the Iron Islands, Theon of House Greyjoy."

No, he thought, *no, don't say that name, Ramsay will hear you, he'll know, he'll know, he'll hurt me.*

Her mouth pursed. "He is not what I expected."

"He is what we have."

"What did your bastard do to him?"

"Removed some skin, I would imagine. A few small parts. Nothing too essential."

"Is he mad?"

"He may be. Does it matter?"

Reek could hear no more. "Please, m'lord, m'lady, there's been some mistake." He fell to his knees, trembling like a leaf in a winter storm, tears streaming down his ravaged cheeks. "I'm not him, I'm not the turncloak, he died at Winterfell. My name is Reek." He had to remember his *name*. "It rhymes with freak."

TYRION

The *Selaesori Qhoran* was seven days from Volantis when Penny finally emerged from her cabin, creeping up on deck like some timid woodland creature emerging from a long winter's sleep. It was dusk and the red priest had lit his nightfire in the great iron brazier amidships as the crew gathered round to pray. Moqorro's voice was a bass drum that seemed to boom from somewhere deep within his massive torso. "*We thank you for your sun that keeps us warm,*" he prayed. "*We thank you for your stars that watch over us as we sail this cold black sea.*" A huge man, taller than Ser Jorah and wide enough to make two of him, the priest wore scarlet robes embroidered at sleeve and hem and collar with orange satin flames. His skin was black as pitch, his hair as white as snow; the flames tattooed across his cheeks and brow yellow and orange. His iron staff was as tall as he was and crowned with a dragon's head; when he stamped its butt upon the deck, the dragon's maw spat crackling green flame.

His guardsmen, five slave warriors of the Fiery Hand, led the responses. They chanted in the tongue of Old Volantis, but Tyrion had heard the prayers enough to grasp the essence. *Light our fire and protect us from the dark, blah blah, light our way and keep us toasty warm, the night is dark and full of terrors, save us from the scary things, and blah blah blah some more.*

He knew better than to voice such thoughts aloud. Tyrion Lannister had no use for any god, but on this ship it was wise to show a certain respect for red R'hllor. Jorah Mormont had removed Tyron's chains and fetters once they were safely under way, and the dwarf did not wish to give him cause to clap them on again.

The *Selaesori Qhoran* was a wallowing tub of five hundred tons, with a deep hold, high castles fore and aft, and a single mast between. At her forecastle stood a grotesque figurehead, some worm-eaten wooden eminence with a constipated look and a scroll tucked up under one arm. Tyrion had never seen an uglier ship. Her crew was no prettier. Her captain, a mean-mouthed, flinty, kettle-bellied man with close-set, greedy eyes, was a bad *cyvasse* player and a worse loser. Under him served four mates, freedmen all, and fifty slaves bound to the ship, each with a crude version of the cog's figurehead tattooed upon one cheek. *No-Nose,* the sailors liked to call Tyrion, no matter how many times he told them his name was Hugor Hill.

Three of the mates and more than three-quarters of the crew were fervent worshipers of the Lord of Light. Tyrion was less certain about the captain, who always emerged for the evening prayers but took no other part in them. But Moqorro was the true master of the *Selaesori Qhoran,* at least for this voyage.

"*Lord of Light, bless your slave Moqorro, and light his way in the dark places of the world,*" the red priest boomed. "*And defend your righteous slave Benerro. Grant him courage. Grant him wisdom. Fill his heart with fire.*"

That was when Tyrion noticed Penny, watching the mummery from the steep wooden stair that led down beneath the sterncastle. She stood on one of the lower steps, so only the top of her head was visible. Beneath her hood her eyes shone big and white in the light of the nightfire. She had her dog with her, the big grey hound she rode in the mock jousts.

"My lady," Tyrion called softly. In truth, she was no lady, but he could not bring himself to mouth that silly name of hers, and he was not about to call her *girl* or *dwarf.*

She cringed back. "I . . . I did not see you."

"Well, I am small."

"I . . . I was unwell . . ." Her dog barked.

Sick with grief, you mean. "If I can be of help . . ."

"No." And quick as that she was gone again, retreating back below to the cabin she shared with her dog and sow. Tyrion could not fault her. The crew of the *Selaesori Qhoran* had been pleased enough when he first came on board; a dwarf was good luck, after all. His head had been rubbed so often and so vigorously that it was a wonder he wasn't bald. But Penny had met with a more mixed reaction. She might be a dwarf, but she was also a woman, and women were bad luck aboard ship. For every man who tried to rub her head, there were three who muttered maledictions under their breath when she went by.

And the sight of me can only be salt in her wound. They hacked off her brother's head in the hope that it was mine, yet here I sit like some bloody gargoyle, offering empty consolations. If I were her, I'd want nothing more than to shove me into the sea.

He felt nothing but pity for the girl. She did not deserve the horror visited on her in Volantis, any more than her brother had. The last time he had seen her, just before they left port, her eyes had been raw from crying, two ghastly red holes in a wan, pale face. By the time they raised sail she had locked herself in her cabin with her dog and her pig, but at night they could hear her weeping. Only yesterday he had heard one of the mates say that they ought to throw her overboard before her tears could swamp the ship. Tyrion was not entirely sure he had been japing.

When the evening prayers had ended and the ship's crew had once again dispersed, some to their watch and others to food and rum and hammocks, Moqorro remained beside his nightfire, as he did every night. The red priest rested by day but kept vigil through the dark hours, to tend his sacred flames so that the sun might return to them at dawn.

Tyrion squatted across from him and warmed his hands against the night's chill. Moqorro took no notice of him for several moments. He was staring into the flickering flames, lost in some vision. *Does he see days yet to come, as he claims?* If so, that was a fearsome gift. After a time the priest raised his eyes to meet the dwarf's. "Hugor Hill," he said, inclining his head in a solemn nod. "Have you come to pray with me?"

"Someone told me that the night is dark and full of terrors. What do you see in those flames?"

"Dragons," Moqorro said in the Common Tongue of Westeros. He spoke it very well, with hardly a trace of accent. No doubt that was one reason the high priest Benerro had chosen him to bring the faith of R'hllor to Daenerys Targaryen. "Dragons old and young, true and false, bright and dark. And you. A small man with a big shadow, snarling in the midst of all."

"Snarling? An amiable fellow like me?" Tyrion was almost flattered. *And no doubt that is just what he intends. Every fool loves to hear that he's important.* "Perhaps it was Penny you saw. We're almost of a size."

"No, my friend."

My friend? When did that happen, I wonder? "Did you see how long it will take us to reach Meereen?"

"You are eager to behold the world's deliverer?"

Yes and no. The world's deliverer may snick off my head or give me to her dragons as a savory. "Not me," said Tyrion. "For me, it is all about the olives. Though I fear I may grow old and die before I taste one. I could dog-paddle faster than we're sailing. Tell me, was *Selaesori Qhoran* a triarch or a turtle?"

The red priest chuckled. "Neither. *Qhoran* is . . . not a ruler, but one who serves and counsels such, and helps conduct his business. You of Westeros might say *steward* or *magister.*"

King's Hand? That amused him. "And *selaesori*?"

Moqorro touched his nose. "Imbued with a pleasant aroma. Fragrant, would you say? Flowery?"

"So *Selaesori Qhoran* means *Stinky Steward,* more or less?"

"*Fragrant Steward,* rather."

Tyrion gave a crooked grin. "I believe I will stay with *Stinky.* But I do thank you for the lesson."

"I am pleased to have enlightened you. Perhaps someday you will let me teach you the truth of R'hllor as well."

"Someday." *When I am a head on a spike.*

The quarters he shared with Ser Jorah were a cabin only by courtesy; the dank, dark, foul-smelling closet had barely enough space to hang a pair of sleeping hammocks, one above the other. He found

Mormont stretched out in the lower one, swaying slowly with the motion of the ship. "The girl finally poked her nose abovedecks," Tyrion told him. "One look at me and she scurried right back down below."

"You're not a pretty sight."

"Not all of us can be as comely as you. The girl is lost. It would not surprise me if the poor creature wasn't sneaking up to jump over the side and drown herself."

"The poor creature's name is Penny."

"I know her name." He hated her name. Her brother had gone by the name of Groat, though his true name had been Oppo. *Groat and Penny. The smallest coins, worth the least, and what's worse, they chose the names themselves.* It left a bad taste in Tyrion's mouth. "By any name, she needs a friend."

Ser Jorah sat up in his hammock. "Befriend her, then. Marry her, for all I care."

That left a bad taste in his mouth as well. "Like with like, is that your notion? Do you mean to find a she-bear for yourself, ser?"

"You were the one who insisted that we bring her."

"I said we could not abandon her in Volantis. That does not mean I want to fuck her. She wants me dead, have you forgotten? I'm the last person she's like to want as a friend."

"You're both dwarfs."

"Yes, and so was her brother, who was killed because some drunken fools took him for me."

"Feeling guilty, are you?"

"No." Tyrion bristled. "I have sins enough to answer for; I'll have no part of this one. I might have nurtured some ill will toward her and her brother for the part they played the night of Joffrey's wedding, but I never wished them harm."

"You are a harmless creature, to be sure. Innocent as a lamb." Ser Jorah got to his feet. "The dwarf girl is your burden. Kiss her, kill her, or avoid her, as you like. It's naught to me." He shouldered past Tyrion and out of the cabin.

Twice exiled, and small wonder, Tyrion thought. *I'd exile him too if I could. The man is cold, brooding, sullen, deaf to humor. And those are his good points.* Ser Jorah spent most of his waking hours pacing the forecastle or leaning on the rail, gazing out to sea. *Looking for his silver queen. Looking for Daenerys, willing the ship to sail faster. Well, I might do the same if Tysha waited in Meereen.*

Could Slaver's Bay be where whores went? It seemed unlikely. From what he'd read, the slaver cities were the place where whores were made. *Mormont should have bought one for himself.* A pretty slave girl might have done wonders to improve his temper . . . particularly one with silvery hair, like the whore who had been sitting on his cock back in Selhorys.

On the river Tyrion had to endure Griff, but there had at least been the mystery of the captain's true identity to divert him and the more congenial companionship of the rest of the poleboat's little company. On the cog, alas, everyone was just who they appeared to be, no one was particularly congenial, and only the red priest was interesting. *Him, and maybe Penny. But the girl hates me, and she should.*

Life aboard the *Selaesori Qhoran* was nothing if not tedious, Tyrion had found. The most exciting part of his day was pricking his toes and fingers with a knife. On the river there had been wonders to behold: giant turtles, ruined cities, stone men, naked septas. One never knew what might be lurking around the next bend. The days and nights at sea were all the same. Leaving Volantis, the cog had sailed within sight of land at first, so Tyrion could gaze at passing headlands, watch clouds of seabirds rise from stony cliffs and crumbling watchtowers, count bare brown islands as they slipped past. He saw many other ships as well: fishing boats, lumbering merchantmen, proud galleys with their oars lashing the waves into white foam. But once they struck out into deeper waters, there was only sea and sky, air and water. The water looked like water. The sky looked like sky. Sometimes there was a cloud. *Too much blue.*

And the nights were worse. Tyrion slept badly at the best of times, and this was far from that. Sleep meant dreams as like as not, and in his dreams the Sorrows waited, and a stony king with his father's face. That left him with the beggar's choice of climbing up into his hammock and listening to Jorah Mormont snore beneath him, or remaining abovedecks to contemplate the sea. On moonless nights the water was as black as maester's ink, from horizon to horizon. Dark and deep and forbidding, beautiful in a chilly sort of way, but when he looked at it too long Tyrion found himself musing on how easy it would be to slip over the gunwale and drop down into that darkness. One very small splash, and the pathetic little tale that was his life would soon be done. *But what if there is a hell and my father's waiting for me?*

The best part of each evening was supper. The food was not especially good, but it was plentiful, so that was where the dwarf went next. The galley where he took his meals was a cramped and uncomfortable space, with a ceiling so low that the taller passengers were always in danger of cracking their heads, a hazard the strapping slave soldiers of the Fiery Hand seemed particularly prone to. As much as Tyrion enjoyed sniggering at that, he had come to prefer taking his meals alone. Sitting at a crowded table with men who did not share a common language with you, listening to them talk and jape whilst understanding none of it, had quickly grown wearisome. Particularly since he always found himself wondering if the japes and laughter were directed at him.

The galley was also where the ship's books were kept. Her captain being an especially bookish man, she carried three—a collection of nautical poetry that went from bad to worse, a well-thumbed tome about the erotic adventures of a young slave girl in a Lysene pillow house, and the fourth and final volume of *The Life of the Triarch Belicho,* a famous Volantene patriot whose unbroken succession of conquests and triumphs ended rather abruptly when he was eaten by giants. Tyrion had finished them all by their third day at sea. Then, for lack of any other books, he started reading them again. The slave girl's story was the worst written but the most engrossing, and that was the one he took down this evening to see him through a supper of buttered beets, cold fish stew, and biscuits that could have been used to drive nails.

He was reading the girl's account of the day she and her sister were taken by slavers when Penny entered the galley. "Oh," she said, "I thought . . . I did not mean to disturb m'lord, I . . ."

"You are not disturbing me. You're not going to try to kill me again, I hope."

"No." She looked away, her face reddening.

"In that case, I would welcome some company. There's little enough aboard this ship." Tyrion closed the book. "Come. Sit. Eat." The girl had left most of her meals untouched outside her cabin door. By now she must be starving. "The stew is almost edible. The fish is fresh, at least."

"No, I . . . I choked on a fish bone once, I can't eat fish."

"Have some wine, then." He filled a cup and slid it toward her. "Compliments of our captain. Closer to piss than Arbor gold, if truth be told, but even piss tastes better than the black tar rum the sailors drink. It might help you sleep."

The girl made no move to touch the cup. "Thank you, m'lord, but no." She backed away. "I should not be bothering you."

"Do you mean to spend your whole life running away?" Tyrion asked before she could slip back out the door.

That stopped her. Her cheeks turned a bright pink, and he was afraid she was about to start weeping again. Instead she thrust out her lip defiantly and said, "You're running too."

"I am," he confessed, "but I am running *to* and you are running *from,* and there's a world of difference there."

"We would never have had to run at all but for you."

It took some courage to say that to my face. "Are you speaking of King's Landing or Volantis?"

"Both." Tears glistened in her eyes. "Everything. Why couldn't you just come joust with us, the way the king wanted? You wouldn't have gotten hurt. What would that have cost m'lord, to climb up on our dog and ride a tilt to please the boy? It was just a bit of fun. They would have laughed at you, that's all."

"They would have laughed at me," said Tyrion. *I made them laugh at Joff instead. And wasn't that a clever ploy?*

"My brother says that is a good thing, making people laugh. A *noble* thing, and honorable. My brother says . . . he . . ." The tears fell then, rolling down her face.

"I am sorry about your brother." Tyrion had said the same words to her before, back in Volantis, but she was so far gone in grief back there that he doubted she had heard them.

She heard them now. "Sorry. You are sorry." Her lip was trembling, her cheeks were wet, her eyes were red-rimmed holes. "We left King's Landing that very night. My brother said it was for the best, before someone wondered if we'd had some part in the king's death and decided to torture us to find out. We went to Tyrosh first. My brother thought that would be far enough, but it wasn't. We knew a juggler there. For years and years he would juggle every day by the Fountain of the Drunken God. He was old, so his hands were not as deft as they had been, and sometimes he would drop his balls and chase them across the square, but the Tyroshi would laugh and throw him coins all the same. Then one morning we heard that his body had been found at the Temple of Trios. Trios has three heads, and there's a big statue of him beside the temple doors. The old man had been cut into three parts and pushed inside the threefold mouths of Trios. Only when the parts were sewn back together, his head was gone."

"A gift for my sweet sister. He was another dwarf."

"A little man, aye. Like you, and Oppo. Groat. Are you sorry about the juggler too?"

"I never knew your juggler existed until this very moment . . . but yes, I am sorry he is dead."

"He died for you. His blood is on your hands."

The accusation stung, coming so hard on the heels of Jorah Mormont's words. "His blood is on my sister's hands, and the hands of the brutes who killed him. My hands . . ." Tyrion turned them over, inspected them, coiled them into fists. ". . . my hands are crusted with old blood, aye. Call me kinslayer, and you won't be wrong. Kingslayer, I'll answer to that one as well. I have killed mothers, fathers, nephews, lovers, men and women, kings and whores. A singer once annoyed me, so I had the bastard stewed. But I have never killed a juggler, nor a dwarf, and I am not to blame for what happened to your bloody brother."

Penny picked the cup of wine he'd poured for her and threw it in his face. *Just like my sweet sister.* He heard the galley door slam but never saw her leave. His eyes were stinging, and the world was a blur. *So much for befriending her.*

Tyrion Lannister had scant experience with other dwarfs. His lord father had not welcomed any reminders of his son's deformities, and such mummers as featured little folk in their troupes soon learned to stay away from Lannisport and Casterly Rock, at the risk of his displeasure. Growing up, Tyrion heard reports of a dwarf jester at the seat of the Dornish Lord Fowler, a dwarf maester in service on the Fingers, and a female dwarf amongst the silent sisters, but he never felt the least need to seek them out. Less reliable tales also reached his ears, of a dwarf witch who haunted a hill in the riverlands, and a dwarf whore in King's Landing renowned for coupling with dogs. His own sweet sister had told him of the last, even offering to find him a bitch in heat if he cared to try it out. When he asked politely if she were referring to herself, Cersei had thrown a cup of wine in his face. *That was red, as I recall, and this is gold.* Tyrion mopped at his face with a sleeve. His eyes still stung.

He did not see Penny again until the day of the storm.

The salt air lay still and heavy that morning, but the western sky was a fiery red, streaked with lowering clouds that glowed as bright as Lannister crimson. Sailors were dashing about battening hatches, running lines, clearing the decks, lashing down everything that was not already lashed down. "Bad wind coming," one warned him. "No-Nose should get below."

Tyrion remembered the storm he'd suffered crossing the narrow sea, the way the deck had jumped beneath his feet, the hideous creaking sounds the ship had made, the taste of wine and vomit. "No-Nose will stay up here." If the gods wanted him, he would sooner die by drowning than choking on his own vomit. And overhead the cog's canvas sail rippled slowly, like the fur of some great beast stirring from a long sleep, then filled with a sudden *crack* that turned every head on the ship.

The winds drove the cog before them, far off her chosen course. Behind them black clouds piled one atop another against a blood-red sky. By midmorning they could see lightning flickering to the west, followed by the distant crash of thunder. The sea grew rougher, and dark waves rose up to smash against the hull of the *Stinky Steward*. It was about then that the crew started hauling down the canvas. Tyrion was underfoot amidships, so he climbed the forecastle and hunkered down, savoring the lash of cold rain on his cheeks. The cog went up and down, bucking more wildly than any horse he'd ever ridden, lifting with each wave before sliding down into the troughs between, jarring him to the bones. Even so, it was better here where he could see than down below locked in some airless cabin.

By the time the storm broke, evening was upon them and Tyrion Lannister was soaked through to the smallclothes, yet somehow he felt elated . . . and even more so later, when he found a drunken Jorah Mormont in a pool of vomit in their cabin.

The dwarf lingered in the galley after supper, celebrating his survival by sharing a few tots of black tar rum with the ship's cook, a great greasy loutish Volantene who spoke only one word of the Common Tongue (*fuck*), but played a ferocious game of *cyvasse*, particularly when drunk. They played three games that night. Tyrion won the first, then lost the other two. After that he decided that he'd had enough and stumbled back up on deck to clear his head of rum and elephants alike.

He found Penny on the forecastle, where he had so often found Ser Jorah, standing by the rail beside the cog's hideous half-rotted figurehead and gazing out across the inky sea. From behind, she looked as small and vulnerable as a child.

Tyrion thought it best to leave her undisturbed, but it was too late. She had heard him. "Hugor Hill."

"If you like." *We both know better.* "I am sorry to intrude on you. I will retire."

"No." Her face was pale and sad, but she did not look to have been crying. "I'm sorry too. About the wine. It wasn't you who killed my brother or that poor old man in Tyrosh."

"I played a part, though not by choice."

"I miss him so much. My brother. I . . ."

"I understand." He found himself thinking of Jaime. *Count yourself lucky. Your brother died before he could betray you.*

"I thought I wanted to die," she said, "but today when the storm came and I thought the ship would sink, I . . . I . . ."

"You realized that you wanted to live after all." *I have been there too. Something else we have in common.*

Her teeth were crooked, which made her shy with her smiles, but she smiled now. "Did you truly cook a singer in a stew?"

"Who, me? No. I do not cook."

When Penny giggled, she sounded like the sweet young girl she was . . . seventeen, eighteen, no more than nineteen. "What did he do, this singer?"

"He wrote a song about me." *For she was his secret treasure, she was his shame and his bliss. And a chain and a keep are nothing, compared to a woman's kiss.* It was queer how quick the words came back to him. Perhaps they had never left him. *Hands of gold are always cold, but a woman's hands are warm.*

"It must have been a very bad song."

"Not really. It was no 'Rains of Castamere,' mind you, but some parts were . . . well . . ."

"How did it go?"

He laughed. "No. You do *not* want to hear me sing."

"My mother used to sing to us when we were children. My brother and me. She always said that it didn't matter what your voice was like so long as you loved the song."

"Was she . . . ?"

". . . a little person? No, but our father was. His own father sold him to a slaver when he was three, but he grew up to be such a famous mummer that he bought his freedom. He traveled to all the Free Cities, and Westeros as well. In Oldtown they used to call him Hop-Bean."

Of course they did. Tyrion tried not to wince.

"He's dead now," Penny went on. "My mother too. Oppo . . . he was my last family, and now he's gone too." She turned her head away and gazed out across the sea. "What will I do? Where will I go? I have no trade, just the jousting show, and that needs two."

No, thought Tyrion. *That is not a place you want to go, girl. Do not ask that of me. Do not even think it.* "Find yourself some likely orphan boy," he suggested.

Penny did not seem to hear that. "It was Father's idea to do the tilts. He even trained the first pig, but by then he was too sick to ride her, so Oppo took his place. I always rode the dog. We performed for the Sealord of Braavos once, and he laughed so hard that afterward he gave each of us a . . . a grand gift."

"Is that where my sister found you? In Braavos?"

"Your sister?" The girl looked lost.

"Queen Cersei."

Penny shook her head. "She never . . . it was a man who came to us, in Pentos. Osmund. No, Oswald. Something like that. Oppo met with him, not me. Oppo made all of our arrangements. My brother always knew what to do, where we should go next."

"Meereen is where we're going next."

She gave him a puzzled look. "Qarth, you mean. We're bound for Qarth, by way of New Ghis."

"Meereen. You'll ride your dog for the dragon queen and come away with your weight in gold. Best start eating more, so you'll be nice and plump when you joust before Her Grace."

Penny did not return the smile. "By myself, all I can do is ride around in circles. And even if the queen should laugh, where will I go afterward? We never stay in one place long. The first time they see us they laugh and laugh, but by the fourth or fifth time, they know what we're going to do before we do it. Then they stop laughing, so we have to go somewhere new. We make the most coin in the big cities, but I always liked the little towns the best. Places like that, the people have no silver, but they feed us at their own tables, and the children follow us everywhere."

That's because they have never seen a dwarf before, in their wretched pisspot towns, Tyrion thought. *The bloody brats would follow around a two-headed goat if one turned up. Until they got bored with its bleating and slaughtered it for supper.* But he had no wish to make her weep again, so instead he said, "Daenerys has a kind heart and a generous nature." It was what she needed to hear. "She will find a place for you at her court, I don't doubt. A safe place, beyond my sister's reach."

Penny turned back to him. "And you will be there too."

Unless Daenerys decides she needs some Lannister blood, to pay for the Targaryen blood my brother shed. "I will."

After that, the dwarf girl was seen more frequently above deck.

The next day Tyrion encountered her and her spotted sow amidships in mid-afternoon, when the air was warm and the sea calm. "Her name is Pretty," the girl told him, shyly.

Pretty the pig and Penny the girl, he thought. *Someone has a deal to answer for.* Penny gave Tyrion some acorns, and he let Pretty eat them from his hand. *Do not think I don't see what you are doing, girl,* he thought, as the big sow snuffled and squealed.

Soon they began to take their meals together. Some nights it was just the two of them; at other meals they crowded in with Moqorro's guards. *The fingers,* Tyrion called them; they were men of the Fiery Hand, after all, and there were five of them. Penny laughed at that, a sweet sound, though not one that he heard often. Her wound was too fresh, her grief too deep.

He soon had her calling the ship the *Stinky Steward,* though she got somewhat wroth with him whenever he called Pretty *Bacon.* To atone for that Tyrion made an attempt to teach her *cyvasse,* though he soon realized that was a lost cause. "No," he said, a dozen times, "the dragon flies, not the elephants."

That same night, she came right out and asked him if he would like to tilt with her. "No," he answered. Only later did it occur to him that perhaps *tilt* did not mean tilt. His answer would still have been no, but he might not have been so brusque.

Back in the cabin he shared with Jorah Mormont, Tyrion twisted in his hammock for hours, slipping in and out of sleep. His dreams were full of grey, stony hands reaching for him from out of the fog, and a stair that led up to his father.

Finally he gave it up and made his way up top for a breath of night air. The *Selaesori Qhoran* had furled her big striped sail for the night, and her decks were all but deserted. One of the mates was on the sterncastle, and amidships Moqorro sat by his brazier, where a few small flames still danced amongst the embers.

Only the brightest stars were visible, all to the west. A dull red glow lit the sky to the northeast, the color of a blood bruise. Tyrion had never seen a bigger moon. Monstrous, swollen, it looked as if it had swallowed the sun and woken with a fever. Its twin, floating on the sea beyond the ship, shimmered red with every wave. "What hour is this?" he asked Moqorro. "That cannot be sunrise unless the east has moved. Why is the sky red?"

"The sky is always red above Valyria, Hugor Hill."

A cold chill went down his back. "Are we close?"

"Closer than the crew would like," Moqorro said in his deep voice. "Do you know the stories, in your Sunset Kingdoms?"

"I know some sailors say that any man who lays eyes upon that coast is doomed." He did not believe such tales himself, no more than his uncle had. Gerion Lannister had set sail for Valyria when Tyrion was eighteen, intent on recovering the lost ancestral blade of House Lannister and any other treasures that might have survived the Doom. Tyrion had wanted desperately to go with them, but his lord father had dubbed the voyage a "fool's quest," and forbidden him to take part.

And perhaps he was not so wrong. Almost a decade had passed since the *Laughing Lion* headed out from Lannisport, and Gerion had never returned. The men Lord Tywin sent to seek after him had traced his course as far as Volantis, where half his crew had deserted him and he had bought slaves to replace them. No free man would willingly sign aboard a ship whose captain spoke openly of his intent to sail into the Smoking Sea. "So those are fires of the Fourteen Flames we're seeing, reflected on the clouds?"

"Fourteen or fourteen thousand. What man dares count them? It is not wise for mortals to look too deeply at those fires, my friend. Those are the fires of god's own wrath, and no human flame can match them. We are small creatures, men."

"Some smaller than others." *Valyria.* It was written that on the day of Doom every hill for five hundred miles had split asunder to fill the air with ash and smoke and fire, blazes so hot and hungry that even the dragons in the sky were engulfed and consumed. Great rents had opened in the earth, swallowing palaces, temples, entire towns. Lakes boiled or turned to acid, mountains burst, fiery fountains spewed molten rock a thousand feet into the air, red clouds rained down dragonglass and the black blood of demons, and to the north the ground splintered and collapsed and fell in on itself and an angry sea came rushing in. The proudest city in all the world was gone in an instant, its fabled empire vanished in a day, the Lands of the Long Summer scorched and drowned and blighted.

An empire built on blood and fire. The Valyrians reaped the seed they had sown. "Does our captain mean to test the curse?"

"Our captain would prefer to be fifty leagues farther out to sea, well away from that accursed shore, but I have commanded him to steer the shortest course. Others seek Daenerys too."

Griff, with his young prince. Could all that talk of the Golden Company sailing west have been a feint? Tyrion considered saying something, then thought better. It seemed to him that the prophecy that drove the red priests had room for just one hero. A second Targaryen would only serve to confuse them. "Have you seen these others in your fires?" he asked, warily.

"Only their shadows," Moqorro said. "One most of all. A tall and twisted thing with one black eye and ten long arms, sailing on a sea of blood."

BRAN

The moon was a crescent, thin and sharp as the blade of a knife. A pale sun rose and set and rose again. Red leaves whispered in the wind. Dark clouds filled the skies and turned to storms. Lightning flashed and thunder rumbled, and dead men with black hands and bright blue eyes shuffled round a cleft in the hillside but could not enter. Under the hill, the broken boy sat upon a weirwood throne, listening to whispers in the dark as ravens walked up and down his arms.

"You will never walk again," the three-eyed crow had promised, "but you will fly." Sometimes the sound of song would drift up from someplace far below. *The children of the forest,* Old Nan would have called the singers, but *those who sing the song of earth* was their own name for themselves, in the True Tongue that no human man could speak. The ravens could speak it, though. Their small black eyes were full of secrets, and they would *caw* at him and peck his skin when they heard the songs.

The moon was fat and full. Stars wheeled across a black sky. Rain fell and froze, and tree limbs snapped from the weight of the ice. Bran and Meera made up names for those who sang the song of earth: Ash and Leaf and Scales, Black Knife and Snowylocks and Coals. Their true names were too long for human tongues, said Leaf. Only she could speak the Common Tongue, so what the others thought of their new names Bran never learned.

After the bone-grinding cold of the lands beyond the Wall, the caves were blessedly warm, and when the chill crept out of the rock the singers would light fires to drive it off again. Down here there was no wind, no snow, no ice, no dead things reaching out to grab you, only dreams and rushlight and the kisses of the ravens. And the whisperer in darkness.

The last greenseer, the singers called him, but in Bran's dreams he was still a three-eyed crow. When Meera Reed had asked him his true name, he made a ghastly sound that might have been a chuckle. "I wore many names when I was quick, but even I once had a mother, and the name she gave me at her breast was Brynden."

"I have an uncle Brynden," Bran said. "He's my mother's uncle, really. Brynden Blackfish, he's called."

"Your uncle may have been named for me. Some are, still. Not so many as before. Men forget. Only the trees remember." His voice was so soft that Bran had to strain to hear.

"Most of him has gone into the tree," explained the singer Meera called Leaf. "He has lived beyond his mortal span, and yet he lingers. For us, for you, for the realms of men. Only a little strength remains in his flesh. He has a thousand eyes and one, but there is much to watch. One day you will know."

"What will I know?" Bran asked the Reeds afterward, when they came with torches burning brightly in their hand, to carry him back to a small chamber off the big cavern where the singers had made beds for them to sleep. "What do the trees remember?"

"The secrets of the old gods," said Jojen Reed. Food and fire and rest had helped restore him after the ordeals of their journey, but he seemed sadder now, sullen, with a weary, haunted look about the eyes. "Truths the First Men knew, forgotten now in Winterfell . . . but not in the wet wild. We live closer to the green in our bogs and crannogs, and we remember. Earth and water, soil and stone, oaks and elms and willows, they were here before us all and will still remain when we are gone."

"So will you," said Meera. That made Bran sad. *What if I don't want to remain when you are gone?* he almost asked, but he swallowed the words unspoken. He was almost a man grown, and he did not want Meera to think he was some weepy babe. "Maybe you could be greenseers too," he said instead.

"No, Bran." Now Meera sounded sad.

"It is given to a few to drink of that green fountain whilst still in mortal flesh, to hear the whisperings of the leaves and see as the trees see, as the gods see," said Jojen. "Most are not so blessed. The gods gave me only greendreams. My task was to get you here. My part in this is done."

The moon was a black hole in the sky. Wolves howled in the wood, sniffing through the snowdrifts after dead things. A murder of ravens erupted from the hillside, screaming their sharp cries, black wings beating above a white world. A red sun rose and set and rose again, painting the snows in shades of rose and pink. Under the hill, Jojen brooded, Meera fretted, and Hodor wandered through dark tunnels with a sword in his right hand and a torch in his left. Or was it Bran wandering?

No one must ever know.

The great cavern that opened on the abyss was as black as pitch, black as tar, blacker than the feathers of a crow. Light entered as a trespasser, unwanted and unwelcome, and soon was gone again; cook-fires, candles, and rushes burned for a little while, then guttered out again, their brief lives at an end.

The singers made Bran a throne of his own, like the one Lord Brynden sat, white weirwood flecked with red, dead branches woven through living roots. They placed it in the great cavern by the abyss, where the black air echoed to the sound of running water far below. Of soft grey moss they made his seat. Once he had been lowered into place, they covered him with warm furs.

There he sat, listening to the hoarse whispers of his teacher. "Never fear the darkness, Bran." The lord's words were accompanied by a faint rustling of wood and leaf, a slight twisting of his head. "The strongest trees are rooted in the dark places of the earth. Darkness will be your cloak, your shield, your mother's milk. Darkness will make you strong."

The moon was a crescent, thin and sharp as the blade of a knife.

Snowflakes drifted down soundlessly to cloak the soldier pines and sentinels in white. The drifts grew so deep that they covered the entrance to the caves, leaving a white wall that Summer had to dig through whenever he went outside to join his pack and hunt. Bran did not oft range with them in those days, but some nights he watched them from above.

Flying was even better than climbing.

Slipping into Summer's skin had become as easy for him as slipping on a pair of breeches once had been, before his back was broken. Changing his own skin for a raven's night-black feathers had been harder, but not as hard as he had feared, not with *these* ravens. "A wild stallion will buck and kick when a man tries to mount him, and try to bite the hand that slips the bit between his teeth," Lord Brynden said, "but a horse that has known one rider will accept another. Young or old, these birds have all been ridden. Choose one now, and fly."

He chose one bird, and then another, without success, but the third raven looked at him with shrewd black eyes, tilted its head, and gave a *quork,* and quick as that he was not a boy looking at a raven but a raven looking at a boy. The song of the river suddenly grew louder, the torches burned a little brighter than before, and the air was full of strange smells. When he tried to speak it came out in a scream, and his first flight ended when he crashed into a wall and ended back inside his own broken body. The raven was unhurt. It flew to him and landed on his arm, and Bran stroked its feathers and slipped inside of it again. Before long he was flying around the cavern, weaving through the long stone teeth that hung down from the ceiling, even flapping out over the abyss and swooping down into its cold black depths.

Then he realized he was not alone.

"Someone else was in the raven," he told Lord Brynden, once he had returned to his own skin. "Some girl. I felt her."

"A woman, of those who sing the song of earth," his teacher said. "Long dead, yet a part of her remains, just as a part of you would remain in Summer if your boy's flesh were to die upon the morrow. A shadow on the soul. She will not harm you."

"Do all the birds have singers in them?"

"All," Lord Brynden said. "It was the singers who taught the First Men to send messages by raven . . . but in those days, the birds would speak the words. The trees remember, but men forget, and so now they write the messages on parchment and tie them round the feet of birds who have never shared their skin."

Old Nan had told him the same story once, Bran remembered, but when he asked Robb if it was true, his brother laughed and asked him if he believed in grumkins too. He wished Robb were with them now. *I'd tell him I could fly, but he wouldn't believe, so I'd have to show him. I bet that he could learn to fly too, him and Arya and Sansa, even baby Rickon and Jon Snow. We could all be ravens and live in Maester Luwin's rookery.*

That was just another silly dream, though. Some days Bran wondered if all of this wasn't just some dream. Maybe he had fallen asleep out in the snows and dreamed himself a safe, warm place. *You have to wake,* he would tell himself, *you have to wake right now, or you'll go dreaming into death.* Once or twice he pinched his arm with his fingers, really hard, but the only thing that did was make his arm hurt. In the beginning he had tried to count the days by making note of when he woke and slept, but down here sleeping and waking had a way of melting into one another. Dreams became lessons, lessons became dreams, things happened all at once or not at all. Had he done that or only dreamed it?

"Only one man in a thousand is born a skinchanger," Lord Brynden said one day, after Bran had learned to fly, "and only one skinchanger in a thousand can be a greenseer."

"I thought the greenseers were the wizards of the children," Bran said. "The singers, I mean."

"In a sense. Those you call the children of the forest have eyes as golden as the sun, but once in a great while one is born amongst them with eyes as red as blood, or green as the moss on a tree in the heart of the forest. By these signs do the gods mark those they have chosen to receive the gift. The chosen ones are not robust, and their quick years upon the earth are few, for every song must have its balance. But once inside the wood they linger long indeed. A thousand eyes, a hundred skins, wisdom deep as the roots of ancient trees. *Greenseers.*"

Bran did not understand, so he asked the Reeds. "Do you like to read books, Bran?" Jojen asked him.

"Some books. I like the fighting stories. My sister Sansa likes the kissing stories, but those are stupid."

"A reader lives a thousand lives before he dies," said Jojen. "The man who never reads lives only one. The singers of the forest had no books. No ink, no parchment, no written language. Instead they had the trees, and the weirwoods above all. When they died, they went into the wood, into leaf and limb and root, and the trees remembered. All their songs and spells, their histories and prayers, everything they knew about this world. Maesters will tell you that the weirwoods are sacred to the old gods. The singers believe they *are* the old gods. When singers die they become part of that godhood."

Bran's eyes widened. "They're going to *kill* me?"

"No," Meera said. "Jojen, you're scaring him."

"He is not the one who needs to be afraid."

The moon was fat and full. Summer prowled through the silent woods, a long grey shadow that grew more gaunt with every hunt, for living game could not be found. The ward upon the cave mouth still held; the dead men could not enter. The snows had buried most of them again, but they were still there, hidden, frozen, waiting. Other dead things came to join them, things that had once been men and women, even children. Dead ravens sat on bare brown branches, wings crusted with ice. A snow bear crashed through the brush, huge and skeletal, half its head sloughed away to reveal the skull beneath. Summer and his pack fell upon it and tore it into pieces. Afterward they gorged, though the meat was rotted and half-frozen, and moved even as they ate it.

Under the hill they still had food to eat. A hundred kinds of mushrooms grew down here. Blind white fish swam in the black river, but they tasted just as good as fish with eyes once you cooked them up. They had cheese and milk from the goats that shared the caves with the singers, even some oats and barleycorn and dried fruit laid by during the long summer. And almost every day they ate blood stew, thickened with barley and onions and chunks of meat. Jojen thought it might be squirrel meat, and Meera said that it was rat. Bran did not care. It was meat and it was good. The stewing made it tender.

The caves were timeless, vast, silent. They were home to more than three score living singers and the bones of thousands dead, and extended far below the hollow hill. "Men should not go wandering in this place," Leaf warned them. "The river you hear is swift and black, and flows down and down to a sunless sea. And there are passages that go even deeper, bottomless pits and sudden shafts, forgotten ways that lead to the very center of the earth. Even my people have not explored them all, and we have lived here for a thousand thousand of your man-years."

Though the men of the Seven Kingdoms might call them the *children of the forest,* Leaf and her people were far from childlike. *Little wise men of the forest* would have been closer. They were small compared to men, as a wolf is smaller than a direwolf. That does not mean it is a pup. They had nut-brown skin, dappled like a deer's with paler spots, and large ears that could hear things that no man could hear. Their eyes were big too, great golden cat's eyes that could see down passages where a boy's eyes saw only blackness. Their hands had only three fingers and a thumb, with sharp black claws instead of nails.

And they *did* sing. They sang in True Tongue, so Bran could not understand the words, but their voices were as pure as winter air. "Where are the rest of you?" Bran asked Leaf, once.

"Gone down into the earth," she answered. "Into the stones, into the trees. Before the First Men came all this land that you call Westeros was home to us, yet even in those days we were few. The gods gave us long lives but not great numbers, lest we overrun the world as deer will overrun a wood where there are no wolves to hunt them. That was in the dawn of days, when our sun was rising. Now it sinks, and this is our long dwindling. The giants are almost gone as well, they who were our bane and our brothers. The great lions of the western hills have been slain, the unicorns are all but gone, the mammoths down to a few hundred. The direwolves will outlast us all, but their time will come as well. In the world that men have made, there is no room for them, or us."

She seemed sad when she said it, and that made Bran sad as well. It was only later that he thought, *Men would not be sad. Men would be wroth. Men would hate and swear a bloody vengeance. The singers sing sad songs, where men would fight and kill.*

One day Meera and Jojen decided to go see the river, despite Leaf's cautions. "I want to come too," Bran said.

Meera gave him a mournful look. The river was six hundred feet below, down steep slopes and twisty passages, she explained, and the last part required climbing down a rope. "Hodor could never make the climb with you on his back. I'm sorry, Bran."

Bran remembered a time when no one could climb as good as him, not even Robb or Jon. Part of him wanted to shout at them for leaving him, and another part wanted to cry. He was almost a man grown, though, so he said nothing. But after they were gone, he slipped inside Hodor's skin and followed them.

The big stableboy no longer fought him as he had the first time, back in the lake tower during the storm. Like a dog who has had all the fight whipped out of him, Hodor would curl up and hide whenever Bran reached out for him. His hiding place was somewhere deep within him, a pit where not even Bran could touch him. *No one wants to hurt you, Hodor,* he said silently, to the child-man whose flesh he'd taken. *I just want to be strong again for a while. I'll give it back, the way I always do.*

No one ever knew when he was wearing Hodor's skin. Bran only had to smile, do as he was told, and mutter "Hodor" from time to time, and he could follow Meera and Jojen, grinning happily, without anyone suspecting it was really him. He often tagged along, whether he was wanted or not. In the end, the Reeds were glad he came. Jojen made it down the rope easily enough, but after Meera caught a blind white fish with her frog spear and it was time to climb back up, his arms began to tremble and he could not make it to the top, so they had to tie the rope around him and let Hodor haul him up. "Hodor," he grunted every time he gave a pull. "Hodor, hodor, hodor."

The moon was a crescent, thin and sharp as the blade of a knife. Summer dug up a severed arm, black and covered with hoarfrost, its fingers opening and closing as it pulled itself across the frozen snow. There was still enough meat on it to fill his empty belly, and after that was done he cracked the arm bones for the marrow. Only then did the arm remember it was dead.

Bran ate with Summer and his pack, as a wolf. As a raven he flew with the murder, circling the hill at sunset, watching for foes, feeling the icy touch of the air. As Hodor he explored the caves. He found chambers full of bones, shafts that plunged deep into the earth, a place where the skeletons of gigantic bats hung upside down from the ceiling. He even crossed the slender stone bridge that arched over the abyss and discovered more passages and chambers on the far side. One was full of singers, enthroned like Brynden in nests of weirwood roots that wove under and through and around their bodies. Most of them looked dead to him, but as he crossed in front of them their eyes would open and follow the light of his torch, and one of them opened and closed a wrinkled mouth as if he were trying to speak. "Hodor," Bran said to him, and he felt the real Hodor stir down in his pit.

Seated on his throne of roots in the great cavern, half-corpse and half-tree, Lord Brynden seemed less a man than some ghastly statue made of twisted wood, old bone, and rotted wool. The only thing that looked alive in the pale ruin that was his face was his one red eye, burning like the last coal in a dead fire, surrounded by twisted roots and tatters of leathery white skin hanging off a yellowed skull.

The sight of him still frightened Bran—the weirwood roots snaking in and out of his withered flesh, the mushrooms sprouting from his cheeks, the white wooden worm that grew from the socket where one eye had been. He liked it better when the torches were put out. In the dark he could pretend that it was the three-eyed crow who whispered to him and not some grisly talking corpse.

One day I will be like him. The thought filled Bran with dread. Bad enough that he was broken, with his useless legs. Was he doomed to lose the rest too, to spend all of his years with a weirwood growing in him and through him? Lord Brynden drew his life from the tree,

Leaf told them. He did not eat, he did not drink. He slept, he dreamed, he watched. *I was going to be a knight,* Bran remembered. *I used to run and climb and fight.* It seemed a thousand years ago.

What was he now? Only Bran the broken boy, Brandon of House Stark, prince of a lost kingdom, lord of a burned castle, heir to ruins. He had thought the three-eyed crow would be a sorcerer, a wise old wizard who could fix his legs, but that was some stupid child's dream, he realized now. *I am too old for such fancies,* he told himself. *A thousand eyes, a hundred skins, wisdom deep as the roots of ancient trees.* That was as good as being a knight. *Almost as good, anyway.*

The moon was a black hole in the sky. Outside the cave the world went on. Outside the cave the sun rose and set, the moon turned, the cold winds howled. Under the hill, Jojen Reed grew ever more sullen and solitary, to his sister's distress. She would often sit with Bran beside their little fire, talking of everything and nothing, petting Summer where he slept between them, whilst her brother wandered the caverns by himself. Jojen had even taken to climbing up to the cave's mouth when the day was bright. He would stand there for hours, looking out over the forest, wrapped in furs yet shivering all the same.

"He wants to go home," Meera told Bran. "He will not even try and fight his fate. He says the greendreams do not lie."

"He's being brave," said Bran. *The only time a man can be brave is when he is afraid,* his father had told him once, long ago, on the day they found the direwolf pups in the summer snows. He still remembered.

"He's being stupid," Meera said. "I'd hoped that when we found your three-eyed crow . . . now I wonder why we ever came."

For me, Bran thought. "His greendreams," he said.

"His greendreams." Meera's voice was bitter.

"Hodor," said Hodor.

Meera began to cry.

Bran hated being crippled then. "Don't cry," he said. He wanted to put his arms around her, hold her tight the way his mother used to hold him back at Winterfell when he'd hurt himself. She was right there, only a few feet from him, but so far out of reach it might have been a hundred leagues. To touch her he would need to pull himself along the ground with his hands, dragging his legs behind him. The floor was rough and uneven, and it would be slow going, full of scrapes and bumps. *I could put on Hodor's skin,* he thought. *Hodor could hold her and pat her on the back.* The thought made Bran feel strange, but he was still thinking it when Meera bolted from the fire, back out into the darkness of the tunnels. He heard her steps recede until there was nothing but the voices of the singers.

The moon was a crescent, thin and sharp as the blade of a knife. The days marched past, one after the other, each shorter than the one before. The nights grew longer. No sunlight ever reached the caves beneath the hill. No moonlight ever touched those stony halls. Even the stars were strangers there. Those things belonged to the world above, where time ran in its iron circles, day to night to day to night to day.

"It is time," Lord Brynden said.

Something in his voice sent icy fingers running up Bran's back. "Time for what?"

"For the next step. For you to go beyond skinchanging and learn what it means to be a greenseer."

"The trees will teach him," said Leaf. She beckoned, and another of the singers padded forward, the white-haired one that Meera had named Snowylocks. She had a weirwood bowl in her hands, carved with a dozen faces, like the ones the heart trees wore. Inside was a white paste, thick and heavy, with dark red veins running through it. "You must eat of this," said Leaf. She handed Bran a wooden spoon.

The boy looked at the bowl uncertainly. "What is it?"

"A paste of weirwood seeds."

Something about the look of it made Bran feel ill. The red veins were only weirwood sap, he supposed, but in the torchlight they looked remarkably like blood. He dipped the spoon into the paste, then hesitated. "Will this make me a greenseer?"

"Your blood makes you a greenseer," said Lord Brynden. "This will help awaken your gifts and wed you to the trees."

Bran did not want to be married to a tree . . . but who else would wed a broken boy like him? *A thousand eyes, a hundred skins, wisdom deep as the roots of ancient trees. A greenseer.*

He ate.

It had a bitter taste, though not so bitter as acorn paste. The first spoonful was the hardest to get down. He almost retched it right back up. The second tasted better. The third was almost sweet. The rest he spooned up eagerly. Why had he thought that it was bitter? It tasted of honey, of new-fallen snow, of pepper and cinnamon and the last kiss his mother ever gave him. The empty bowl slipped from his fingers and clattered on the cavern floor. "I don't feel any different. What happens next?"

Leaf touched his hand. "The trees will teach you. The trees remember." He raised a hand, and the other singers began to move about the cavern, extinguishing the torches one by one. The darkness thickened and crept toward them.

"Close your eyes," said the three-eyed crow. "Slip your skin, as you do when you join with Summer. But this time, go into the roots instead. Follow them up through the earth, to the trees upon the hill, and tell me what you see."

Bran closed his eyes and slipped free of his skin. *Into the roots,* he thought. *Into the weirwood. Become the tree.* For an instant he could see the cavern in its black mantle, could hear the river rushing by below.

Then all at once he was back home again.

Lord Eddard Stark sat upon a rock beside the deep black pool in the godswood, the pale roots of the heart tree twisting around him like an old man's gnarled arms. The greatsword Ice lay across Lord Eddard's lap, and he was cleaning the blade with an oilcloth.

"*Winterfell,*" Bran whispered.

His father looked up. "Who's there?" he asked, turning . . .

. . . and Bran, frightened, pulled away. His father and the black pool and the godswood faded and were gone and he was back in the cavern, the pale thick roots of his weirwood throne cradling his limbs as a mother does a child. A torch flared to life before him.

"Tell us what you saw." From far away Leaf looked almost a girl, no older than Bran or one of his sisters, but close at hand she seemed far older. She claimed to have seen two hundred years.

Bran's throat was very dry. He swallowed. "Winterfell. I was back in Winterfell. I saw my father. He's not dead, he's *not*, I saw him, he's back at Winterfell, he's still alive."

"No," said Leaf. "He is gone, boy. Do not seek to call him back from death."

"I *saw* him." Bran could feel rough wood pressing against one cheek. "He was cleaning Ice."

"You saw what you wished to see. Your heart yearns for your father and your home, so that is what you saw."

"A man must know how to look before he can hope to see," said Lord Brynden. "Those were shadows of days past that you saw, Bran. You were looking through the eyes of the heart tree in your godswood. Time is different for a tree than for a man. Sun and soil and water, these are the things a weirwood understands, not days and years and centuries. For men, time is a river. We are trapped in its flow, hurtling from past to present, always in the same direction. The lives of trees are different. They root and grow and die in one place, and that river does not move them. The oak is the acorn, the acorn is the oak. And the weirwood . . . a thousand human years are a moment to a weirwood, and through such gates you and I may gaze into the past."

"But," said Bran, "he *heard* me."

"He heard a whisper on the wind, a rustling amongst the leaves. You cannot speak to him, try as you might. I know. I have my own ghosts, Bran. A brother that I loved, a brother that I hated, a woman I desired. Through the trees, I see them still, but no word of mine has ever reached them. The past remains the past. We can learn from it, but we cannot change it."

"Will I see my father again?"

"Once you have mastered your gifts, you may look where you will and see what the trees have seen, be it yesterday or last year or a thousand ages past. Men live their lives trapped in an eternal present, between the mists of memory and the sea of shadow that is all we know of the days to come. Certain moths live their whole lives in a day, yet to them that little span of time must seem as long as years and decades do to us. An oak may live three hundred years, a redwood tree three thousand. A weirwood will live forever if left undisturbed. To them seasons pass in the flutter of a moth's wing, and past, present, and future are one. Nor will your sight be limited to your godswood. The singers carved eyes into their heart trees to awaken them, and those are the first eyes a new greenseer learns to use . . . but in time you will see well beyond the trees themselves."

"When?" Bran wanted to know.

"In a year, or three, or ten. That I have not glimpsed. It will come in time, I promise you. But I am tired now, and the trees are calling me. We will resume on the morrow."

Hodor carried Bran back to his chamber, muttering "Hodor" in a low voice as Leaf went before them with a torch. He had hoped that Meera and Jojen would be there, so he could tell them what he had seen, but their snug alcove in the rock was cold and empty. Hodor eased Bran down onto his bed, covered him with furs, and made a fire for them. *A thousand eyes, a hundred skins, wisdom deep as the roots of ancient trees.*

Watching the flames, Bran decided he would stay awake till Meera came back. Jojen would be unhappy, he knew, but Meera would be glad for him, He did not remember closing his eyes.

. . . but then somehow he was back at Winterfell again, in the godswood looking down upon his father. Lord Eddard seemed much younger this time. His hair was brown, with no hint of grey in it, his head bowed. ". . . let them grow up close as brothers, with only love between them," he prayed, "and let my lady wife find it in her heart to forgive . . ."

"Father." Bran's voice was a whisper in the wind, a rustle in the leaves. "Father, it's me. It's Bran. Brandon."

Eddard Stark lifted his head and looked long at the weirwood, frowning, but he did not speak. *He cannot see me,* Bran realized, despairing. He wanted to reach out and touch him, but all that he could do was watch and listen. *I am in the tree. I am inside the heart tree, looking out of its red eyes, but the weirwood cannot talk, so I can't.*

Eddard Stark resumed his prayer. Bran felt his eyes fill up with tears. But were they his own tears, or the weirwood's? *If I cry, will the tree begin to weep?*

The rest of his father's words were drowned out by a sudden clatter of wood on wood. Eddard Stark dissolved, like mist in a morning sun. Now two children danced across the godswood, hooting at one another as they dueled with broken branches. The girl was the older and taller of the two. *Arya!* Bran thought eagerly, as he watched her leap up onto a rock and cut at the boy. But that couldn't be right. If the girl was Arya, the boy was Bran himself, and he had never worn his hair so long. *And Arya never beat me playing swords, the way that girl is beating him.* She slashed the boy across his thigh, so hard that his leg went out from under him and he fell into the pool and began to splash and shout. "You be quiet, stupid," the girl said, tossing her own branch aside. "It's just *water*. Do you want Old Nan to hear and run tell Father?" She knelt and pulled her brother from the pool, but before she got him out again, the two of them were gone.

After that the glimpses came faster and faster, till Bran was feeling lost and dizzy. He saw no more of his father, nor the girl who looked like Arya, but a woman heavy with child emerged naked and dripping from the black pool, knelt before the tree, and begged the old gods for a son who would avenge her. Then there came a brown-haired girl slender as a spear who stood on the tips of her toes to kiss the lips of a young knight as tall as Hodor. A dark-eyed youth, pale and fierce, sliced three branches off the weirwood and shaped them into arrows. The tree itself was shrinking, growing smaller with each vision, whilst the lesser trees dwindled into saplings and vanished, only to be replaced by other trees that would dwindle and vanish in their turn. And now the lords Bran glimpsed were tall and hard, stern men in fur and chain mail. Some wore faces he remembered from the statues in the crypts, but they were gone before he could put a name to them.

Then, as he watched, a bearded man forced a captive down onto his knees before the heart tree. A white-haired woman stepped toward them through a drift of dark red leaves, a bronze sickle in her hand.

"No," said Bran, "*no, don't*," but they could not hear him, no more than his father had. The woman grabbed the captive by the hair, hooked the sickle round his throat, and slashed. And through the mist of centuries the broken boy could only watch as the man's feet drummed against the earth . . . but as his life flowed out of him in a red tide, Brandon Stark could taste the blood.

JON

The sun had broken through near midday, after seven days of dark skies and snow flurries. Some of the drifts were higher than a man, but the stewards had been shoveling all day and the paths were as clean as they were like to get. Reflections glimmered off the Wall, every crack and crevice glittering pale blue.

Seven hundred feet up, Jon Snow stood looking down upon the haunted forest. A north wind swirled through the trees below, sending thin white plumes of snow crystals flying from the highest branches, like icy banners. Elsewise nothing moved. *Not a sign of life.* That was not entirely reassuring. It was not the living that he feared. Even so . . .

The sun is out. The snow has stopped. It may be a moon's turn before we have another chance as good. It may be a season. "Have Emmett assemble his recruits," he told Dolorous Edd. "We'll want an escort. Ten rangers, armed with dragonglass. I want them ready to leave within the hour."

"Aye, m'lord. And to command?"

"That would be me."

Edd's mouth turned down even more than usual. "Some might think it better if the lord commander stayed safe and warm south of the Wall. Not that I'd say such myself, but some might."

Jon smiled. "Some had best not say so in my presence."

A sudden gust of wind set Edd's cloak to flapping noisily. "Best go down, m'lord. This wind's like to push us off the Wall, and I never did learn the knack of flying."

They rode the winch lift back to the ground. The wind was gusting, cold as the breath of the ice dragon in the tales Old Nan had told when Jon was a boy. The heavy cage was swaying. From time to time it scraped against the Wall, starting small crystalline showers of ice that sparkled in the sunlight as they fell, like shards of broken glass.

Glass, Jon mused, *might be of use here. Castle Black needs its own glass gardens, like the ones at Winterfell. We could grow vegetables even in the deep of winter.* The best glass came from Myr, but a good clear pane was worth its weight in spice, and green and yellow glass would not work as well. *What we need is gold. With enough coin, we could buy 'prentice glassblowers and glaziers in Myr, bring them north, offer them their freedom for teaching their art to some of our recruits. That would be the way to go about it. If we had the gold. Which we do not.*

At the base of the Wall he found Ghost rolling in a snowbank. The big white direwolf seemed to love fresh snow. When he saw Jon he bounded back onto his feet and shook himself off. Dolorous Edd said, "He's going with you?"

"He is."

"A clever wolf, him. And me?"

"You're not."

"A clever lord, you. Ghost's the better choice. I don't have the teeth for biting wildlings anymore."

"If the gods are good, we won't encounter any wildlings. I'll want the grey gelding."

Word spread fast at Castle Black. Edd was still saddling the grey when Bowen Marsh stomped across the yard to confront Jon at the stables. "My lord, I wish you would reconsider. The new men can take their vows in the sept as easily."

"The sept is home to the new gods. The old gods live in the wood, and those who honor them say their words amongst the weirwoods. You know that as well as I."

"Satin comes from Oldtown, and Arron and Emrick from the westerlands. The old gods are not their gods."

"I do not tell men which god to worship. They were free to choose the Seven or the red woman's Lord of Light. They chose the trees instead, with all the peril that entails."

"The Weeping Man may still be out there, watching."

"The grove is no more than two hours' ride, even with the snow. We should be back by midnight."

"Too long. This is not wise."

"Unwise," said Jon, "but necessary. These men are about to pledge their lives to the Night's Watch, joining a brotherhood that stretches back in an unbroken line for thousands of years. The words matter, and so do these traditions. They bind us all together, highborn and low, young and old, base and noble. They make us brothers." He clapped Marsh on his shoulder. "I promise you, we shall return."

"Aye, my lord," said the Lord Steward, "but will it be as living men or heads on spears with your eyes scooped out? You will be returning through the black of night. The snowdrifts are waist deep in places. I see that you are taking seasoned men with you, that is good, but Black Jack Bulwer knew these woods as well. Even Benjen Stark, your own uncle, he—"

"I have something they did not." Jon turned his head and whistled. "*Ghost.* To me." The direwolf shook the snow from his back and trotted to Jon's side. The rangers parted to let him through, though one mare whinnied and shied away till Rory gave her reins a sharp tug. "The Wall is yours, Lord Bowen." He took his horse by the bridle and walked him to the gate and the icy tunnel that snaked beneath the Wall.

Beyond the ice, the trees stood tall and silent, huddled in the thick white cloaks. Ghost stalked beside Jon's horse as the rangers and recruits formed up, then stopped and sniffed, his breath frosting in the air. "What is it?" Jon asked. "Is someone there?" The woods were empty as far as he could see, but that was not very far.

Ghost bounded toward the trees, slipped between two white-cloaked pines, and vanished in a cloud of snow. *He wants to hunt, but what?*

Jon did not fear for the direwolf so much as for any wildlings he might encounter. *A white wolf in a white wood, silent as a shadow. They will never know he's coming.* He knew better than to go chasing him. Ghost would return when he wanted to and not before. Jon put his heels into his horse. His men fell in around them, the hooves of their garrons breaking through the icy crust to the softer snow beneath. Into the woods they went, at a steady walking pace, as the Wall dwindled behind them.

The soldier pines and sentinels wore thick white coats, and icicles draped the bare brown limbs of the broadleafs. Jon sent Tom Barleycorn ahead to scout for them, though the way to the white grove was oft trod and familiar. Big Liddle and Luke of Longtown slipped into the brush to east and west. They would flank the column to give warning of any approach. All were seasoned rangers, armed with obsidian as well as steel, warhorns slung across their saddles should they need to summon help.

The others were good men too. *Good men in a fight, at least, and loyal to their brothers.* Jon could not speak for what they might have been before they reached the Wall, but he did not doubt that most had pasts as black as their cloaks. Up here, they were the sort of men he wanted at his back. Their hoods were raised against the biting wind, and some had scarves wrapped about their faces, hiding their features. Jon knew them, though. Every name was graven on his heart. They were his men, his brothers.

Six more rode with them—a mix of young and old, large and small, seasoned and raw. *Six to say the words.* Horse had been born and raised in Mole's Town, Arron and Emrick came from Fair Isle, Satin from the brothels of Oldtown at the other end of Westeros. All of them were boys. Leathers and Jax were older men, well past forty, sons of the haunted forest, with sons and grandsons of their own. They had been two of the sixty-three wildlings who had followed Jon Snow back to the Wall the day he made his appeal, so far the only two to decide they wanted a black cloak. Iron Emmett said they all were ready, or as ready as they were ever going to be. He and Jon and Bowen Marsh had weighed each man in turn and assigned him to an order: Leathers, Jax, and Emrick to the rangers, Horse to the builders, Arron and Satin to the stewards. The time had come for them to take their vows.

Iron Emmett rode at the head of the column, mounted on the ugliest horse Jon had ever seen, a shaggy beast that looked to be all hair and hooves. "Talk is there was some trouble at Harlot's Tower last night," the master-at-arms said.

"Hardin's Tower." Of the sixty-three who had come back with him from Mole's Town, nineteen had been women and girls. Jon had housed them in the same abandoned tower where he had once slept when he had been new to the Wall. Twelve were spearwives, more than capable of defending both themselves and the younger girls from the unwanted attentions of black brothers. It was some of the men they'd turned away who'd given Hardin's Tower its new, inflammatory name. Jon was not about to condone the mockery. "Three drunken fools mistook Hardin's for a brothel, that's all. They are in the ice cells now, contemplating their mistake."

Iron Emmett grimaced. "Men are men, vows are words, and words are wind. You should put guards around the women."

"And who will guard the guards?" *You know nothing, Jon Snow.* He had learned, though, and Ygritte had been his teacher. If he could not hold to his own vows, how could he expect more of his brothers? But there were dangers in trifling with wildling women. *A man can own a woman, and a man can own a knife,* Ygritte had told him once, *but no man can own both.* Bowen Marsh had not been all wrong. Hardin's Tower was tinder waiting for a spark. "I mean to open three more castles," Jon said. "Deep Lake, Sable Hall, and the Long Barrow. All garrisoned with free folk, under the command of our own officers. The Long Barrow will be all women, aside from the commander and chief steward." There would be some mingling, he did not doubt, but the distances were great enough to make that difficult, at least.

"And what poor fool will get that choice command?"

"I am riding beside him."

The look of mingled horror and delight that passed across Iron Emmett's face was worth more than a sack of gold. "What have I done to make you hate me so, my lord?"

Jon laughed. "Have no fear, you won't be alone. I mean to give you Dolorous Edd as your second and your steward."

"The spearwives will be so happy. You might do well to bestow a castle on the Magnar."

Jon's smile died. "I might if I could trust him. Sigorn blames me for his father's death, I fear. Worse, he was bred and trained to give orders, not to take them. Do not confuse the Thenns with free folk. *Magnar* means *lord* in the Old Tongue, I am told, but Styr was closer to a god to his people, and his son is cut from the same skin. I do not require men to kneel, but they do need to obey."

"Aye, m'lord, but you had best do something with the Magnar. You'll have trouble with the Thenns if you ignore them."

Trouble is the lord commander's lot, Jon might have said. His visit to Mole's Town was giving him plenty, as it happened, and the women were the least of it. Halleck was proving to be just as truculent as he had feared, and there were some amongst the black brothers whose hatred of the free folk was bone deep. One of Halleck's followers had already cut off a builder's ear in the yard, and like as not that was just a taste of the bloodshed to come. He had to get the old forts open soon, so Harma's brother could be sent off to garrison Deep Lake or Sable Hall. Just now, though, neither of those was fit for human habitation, and Othell Yarwyck and his builders were still off trying to restore the Nightfort. There were nights when Jon Snow wondered if he had not made a grievous mistake by preventing Stannis from marching all the wildlings off to be slaughtered. *I know nothing, Ygritte,* he thought, *and perhaps I never will.*

Half a mile from the grove, long red shafts of autumn sunlight were slanting down between the branches of the leafless trees, staining the snowdrifts pink. The riders crossed a frozen stream, between two jagged rocks armored in ice, then followed a twisting game trail to the north-east. Whenever the wind kicked up, sprays of loose snow filled the air and stung their eyes. Jon pulled his scarf up over his mouth and nose and raised the hood on his cloak. "Not far now," he told the men. No one replied.

Jon smelled Tom Barleycorn before he saw him. Or was it Ghost who smelled him? Of late, Jon Snow sometimes felt as if he and the direwolf were one, even awake. The great white wolf appeared first, shaking off the snow. A few moments later Tom was there. "Wildlings," he told Jon, softly. "In the grove."

Jon brought the riders to a halt. "How many?"

"I counted nine. No guards. Some dead, might be, or sleeping. Most look to be women. One child, but there's a giant too. Just the one that I saw. They got a fire burning, smoke drifting through the trees. Fools."

Nine, and I have seven-and-ten. Four of his were green boys, though, and none were giants.

Jon was not of a mind to fall back to the Wall, however. *If the wildlings are still alive, it may be we can bring them in. And if they are dead, well . . . a corpse or two could be of use.* "We'll continue on foot," he said, dropping lightly to the frozen ground. The snow was ankle deep. "Rory, Pate, stay with the horses." He might have given that duty to the recruits, but they would need to be blooded soon enough. This was as good a time as any. "Spread out and form a crescent. I want to close in on the grove from three sides. Keep the men to your right and left in sight, so the gaps do not widen. The snow should muffle our steps. Less chance of blood if we take them unawares."

Night was falling fast. The shafts of sunlight had vanished when the last thin slice of the sun was swallowed beneath the western woods. The pink snow drifts were going white again, the color leaching out of them as the world darkened. The evening sky had turned the faded grey of an old cloak that had been washed too many times, and the first shy stars were coming out.

Ahead he glimpsed a pale white trunk that could only be a weirwood, crowned with a head of dark red leaves. Jon Snow reached back and pulled Longclaw from his sheath. He looked to right and left, gave Satin and Horse a nod, watched them pass it on to the men beyond. They rushed the grove together, kicking through drifts of old snow with no sound but their breathing. Ghost ran with them, a white shadow at Jon's side.

The weirwoods rose in a circle around the edges of the clearing. There were nine, all roughly of the same age and size. Each one had a face carved into it, and no two faces were alike. Some were smiling, some were screaming, some were shouting at him. In the deepening glow their eyes looked black, but in daylight they would be blood-red, Jon knew. *Eyes like Ghost's.*

The fire in the center of the grove was a small sad thing, ashes and embers and a few broken branches burning slow and smoky. Even then, it had more life than the wildlings huddled near it. Only one of them reacted when Jon stepped from the brush. That was the child, who began to wail, clutching at his mother's ragged cloak. The woman raised her eyes and gasped. By then the grove was ringed by rangers, sliding past the bone-white trees, steel glinting in black-gloved hands, poised for slaughter.

The giant was the last to notice them. He had been asleep, curled up by the fire, but something woke him—the child's cry, the sound of snow crunching beneath black boots, a sudden indrawn breath. When he stirred it was as if a boulder had come to life. He heaved himself into a sitting position with a snort, pawing at his eyes with hands as big as hams to rub the sleep away ... until he saw Iron Emmett, his sword shining in his hand. Roaring, he came leaping to his feet, and one of those huge hands closed around a maul and jerked it up.

Ghost showed his teeth in answer. Jon grabbed the wolf by the scruff of the neck. "We want no battle here." His men could bring the giant down, he knew, but not without cost. Once blood was shed, the wildlings would join the fray. Most or all would die here, and some of his own brothers too. "This is a holy place. Yield, and we—"

The giant bellowed again, a sound that shook the leaves in the trees, and slammed his maul against the ground. The shaft of it was six feet of gnarled oak, the head a stone as big as a loaf of bread. The impact made the ground shake. Some of the other wildlings went scrambling for their own weapons.

Jon Snow was about to reach for Longclaw when Leathers spoke, from the far side of the grove. His words sounded gruff and guttural, but Jon heard the music in it and recognized the Old Tongue. Leathers spoke for a long while. When he was done, the giant answered. It sounded like growling, interspersed with grunts, and Jon could not understand a word of it. But Leathers pointed at the trees and said something else, and the giant pointed at the trees, ground his teeth, and dropped his maul.

"It's done," said Leathers. "They want no fight."

"Well done. What did you tell him?"

"That they were our gods too. That we came to pray."

"We shall. Put away your steel, all of you. We will have no blood shed here tonight."

Nine, Tom Barleycorn had said, and nine there were, but two were dead and one so weak he might have died by morning. The six who remained included a mother and child, two old men, a wounded Thenn in battered bronze, and one of the Hornfoot folk, his bare feet so badly frostbitten that Jon knew at a glance he would never walk again. Most had been strangers to one another when they came to the grove, he learned subsequently; when Stannis broke Mance Rayder's host, they had fled into the woods to escape the carnage, wandered for a time, lost friends and kin to cold and starvation, and finally washed up here, too weak and weary to go on. "The gods are here," one of the old men said. "This was as good a place to die as any."

"The Wall is only a few hours south of here," said Jon. "Why not seek shelter there? Others yielded. Even Mance."

The wildlings exchanged looks. Finally one said, "We heard stories. The crows burned all them that yielded."

"Even Mance hisself," the woman added.

Melisandre, Jon thought, *you and your red god have much and more to answer for.* "All those who wish are welcome to return with us. There is food and shelter at Castle Black, and the Wall to keep you safe from the things that haunt these woods. You have my word, no one will burn."

"A crow's word," the woman said, hugging her child close, "but who's to say that you can keep it? Who are you?"

"Lord Commander of the Night's Watch, and a son of Eddard Stark of Winterfell." Jon turned to Tom Barleycorn. "Have Rory and Pate bring up the horses. I do not mean to stay here one moment longer than we must."

"As you say, m'lord."

One last thing remained before they could depart: the thing that they had come for. Iron Emmett called forth his charges, and as the rest of the company watched from a respectful distance, they knelt before the weirwoods. The last light of day was gone by then; the only light came from the stars above and the faint red glow of the dying fire in the center of the grove.

With their black hoods and thick black cowls, the six might have been carved from shadow. Their voices rose together, small against the vastness of the night. "Night gathers, and now my watch begins," they said, as thousands had said before them. Satin's voice was sweet as song, Horse's hoarse and halting, Arron's a nervous squeak. "It shall not end until my death."

May those deaths be long in coming. Jon Snow sank to one knee in the snow. *Gods of my fathers, protect these men. And Arya too, my little sister, wherever she might be. I pray you, let Mance find her and bring her safe to me.*

"I shall take no wife, hold no lands, father no children," the recruits promised, in voices that echoed back through years and centuries. "I shall wear no crowns and win no glory. I shall live and die at my post."

Gods of the wood, grant me the strength to do the same, Jon Snow prayed silently. *Give me the wisdom to know what must be done and the courage to do it.*

"I am the sword in the darkness," said the six, and it seemed to Jon as though their voices were changing, growing stronger, more certain. "I am the watcher on the walls. I am the fire that burns against the cold, the light that brings the dawn, the horn that wakes the sleepers, the shield that guards the realms of men."

The shield that guards the realms of men. Ghost nuzzled up against his shoulder, and Jon draped an arm around him. He could smell Horse's unwashed breeches, the sweet scent Satin combed into his beard, the rank sharp smell of fear, the giant's overpowering musk. He could hear the beating of his own heart. When he looked across the grove at the woman with her child, the two greybeards, the Hornfoot man with his maimed feet, all he saw was men.

"I pledge my life and honor to the Night's Watch, for this night and all the nights to come."

Jon Snow was the first onto his feet. "Rise now as men of the Night's Watch." He gave Horse a hand to pull him up.

The wind was rising. It was time to go.

The journey back took much longer than the journey to the grove. The giant's pace was a ponderous one, despite the length and girth of those legs, and he was forever stopping to knock snow off low-hanging limbs with his maul. The woman rode double with Rory, her son with Tom Barleycorn, the old men with Horse and Satin. The Thenn was frightened of the horses, however, and preferred to limp along despite his wounds. The Hornfoot man could not sit a saddle and had to be tied over the back of a garron like a sack of grain; so too the pale-faced crone with the stick-thin limbs, whom they had not been able to rouse.

They did the same with the two corpses, to the puzzlement of Iron Emmett. "They will only slow us, my lord," he said to Jon. "We should chop them up and burn them."

"No," said Jon. "Bring them. I have a use for them."

They had no moon to guide them home, and only now and then a patch of stars. The world was black and white and still. It was a long, slow, endless trek. The snow clung to their boots and breeches, and the wind rattled the pines and made their cloaks snap and swirl. Jon glimpsed the red wanderer above, watching them through the leafless branches of great trees as they made their way beneath. *The Thief,* the free folk called it. The best time to steal a woman was when the Thief was in the Moonmaid, Ygritte had always claimed. She never mentioned the best time to steal a giant. *Or two dead men.*

It was almost dawn before they saw the Wall again.

A sentry's horn greeted them as they approached, sounding from on high like the cry of some huge, deep-throated bird, a single long blast that meant *rangers returning.* Big Liddle unslung his own warhorn and gave answer. At the gate, they had to wait a few moments before Dolorous Edd Tollett appeared to slide back the bolts and swing open the iron bars. When Edd caught sight of the ragged band of wildlings, he pursed his lips and gave the giant a long look. "Might need some butter to slide that one through the tunnel, m'lord. Shall I send someone to the larder?"

"Oh, I think he'll fit. Unbuttered."

So he did . . . on hands and knees, crawling. *A big boy, this one. Fourteen feet, at least. Even bigger than Mag the Mighty.* Mag had died beneath this very ice, locked in mortal struggle with Donal Noye. *A good man. The Watch has lost too many good men.* Jon took Leathers aside. "Take charge of him. You speak his tongue. See that he is fed and find him a warm place by the fire. Stay with him. See that no one provokes him."

"Aye." Leathers hesitated. "M'lord."

The living wildlings Jon sent off to have their wounds and frostbites tended. Some hot food and warm clothes would restore most of them, he hoped, though the Hornfoot man was like to lose both feet. The corpses he consigned to the ice cells.

Clydas had come and gone, Jon noted as he was hanging his cloak on the peg beside the door. A letter had been left on the table in his solar. *Eastwatch or the Shadow Tower,* he assumed at first glance. But the wax was gold, not black. The seal showed a stag's head within a flaming heart. *Stannis.* Jon cracked the hardened wax, flattened the roll of parchment, read. *A maester's hand, but the king's words.*

Stannis had taken Deepwood Motte, and the mountain clans had joined him. Flint, Norrey, Wull, Liddle, all.

> *And we had other help, unexpected but most welcome, from a daughter of Bear Island. Alysane Mormont, whose men name her the She-Bear, hid fighters inside a gaggle of fishing sloops and took the ironmen unawares where they lay off the strand. Greyjoy's longships are burned or taken, her crews slain or surrendered. The captains, knights, notable warriors, and others of high birth we shall ransom or make other use of, the rest I mean to hang . . .*

The Night's Watch was sworn to take no side in the quarrels and conflicts of the realm. Nonetheless, Jon Snow could not help but feel a certain satisfaction. He read on.

... more northmen coming in as word spreads of our victory. Fisherfolk, freeriders, hillmen, crofters from the deep of the wolfswood and villagers who fled their homes along the stony shore to escape the ironmen, survivors from the battle outside the gates of Winterfell, men once sworn to the Hornwoods, the Cerwyns, and the Tallharts. We are five thousand strong as I write, our numbers swelling every day. And word has come to us that Roose Bolton moves toward Winterfell with all his power, there to wed his bastard to your half sister. He must not be allowed to restore the castle to its former strength. We march against him. Arnolf Karstark and Mors Umber will join us. I will save your sister if I can, and find a better match for her than Ramsay Snow. You and your brothers must hold the Wall until I can return.

It was signed, in a different hand,

> *Done in the Light of the Lord, under the sign and seal of Stannis of House Baratheon, the First of His Name, King of the Andals, the Rhoynar, and the First Men, Lord of the Seven Kingdoms, and Protector of the Realm.*

The moment Jon set the letter aside, the parchment curled up again, as if eager to protect its secrets. He was not at all sure how he felt about what he had just read. Battles had been fought at Winterfell before, but never one without a Stark on one side or the other. "The castle is a shell," he said, "not Winterfell, but the ghost of Winterfell." It was painful just to think of it, much less say the words aloud. And still ...

He wondered how many men old Crowfood would bring to the fray, and how many swords Arnolf Karstark would be able to conjure up. Half the Umbers would be across the field with Whoresbane, fighting beneath the flayed man of the Dreadfort, and the greater part of the strength of both houses had gone south with Robb, never to return. Even ruined, Winterfell itself would confer a considerable advantage on whoever held it. Robert Baratheon would have seen that at once and moved swiftly to secure the castle, with the forced marches and midnight rides for which he had been famous. Would his brother be as bold?

Not likely. Stannis was a deliberate commander, and his host was a half-digested stew of clansmen, southron knights, king's men and queen's men, salted with a few northern lords. *He should move on Winterfell swiftly, or not at all,* Jon thought. It was not his place to advise the king, but . . .

He glanced at the letter again. *I will save your sister if I can.* A surprisingly tender sentiment from Stannis, though undercut by that final, brutal *if I can* and the addendum *and find a better match for her than Ramsay Snow.* But what if Arya was not there to be saved? What if Lady Melisandre's flames had told it true? Could his sister truly have escaped such captors? *How would she do that? Arya was always quick and clever, but in the end she's just a little girl, and Roose Bolton is not the sort who would be careless with a prize of such great worth.*

What if Bolton never had his sister? This wedding could well be just some ruse to lure Stannis into a trap. Eddard Stark had never had any reason to complain of the Lord of the Dreadfort, so far as Jon knew, but even so he had never trusted him, with his whispery voice and his pale, pale eyes.

A grey girl on a dying horse, fleeing from her marriage. On the strength of those words he had loosed Mance Rayder and six spearwives on the north. "Young ones, and pretty," Mance had said. The unburnt king supplied some names, and Dolorous Edd had done the rest, smuggling them from Mole's Town. It seemed like madness now. He might have done better to strike down Mance the moment he revealed himself. Jon had a certain grudging admiration for the late King-Beyond-the-Wall, but the man was an oathbreaker and a turncloak. He had even less trust in Melisandre. Yet somehow here he was, pinning his hopes on them. *All to save my sister. But the men of the Night's Watch have no sisters.*

When Jon had been a boy at Winterfell, his hero had been the Young Dragon, the boy king who had conquered Dorne at the age of fourteen. Despite his bastard birth, or perhaps because of it, Jon Snow had dreamed of leading men to glory just as King Daeron had, of growing up to be a conqueror. Now he was a man grown and the Wall was his, yet all he had were doubts. He could not even seem to conquer those.

DAENERYS

The stench of the camp was so appalling it was all that Dany could do not to gag.

Ser Barristan wrinkled up his nose, and said, "Your Grace should not be here, breathing these black humors."

"I am the blood of the dragon," Dany reminded him. "Have you ever seen a dragon with the flux?" Viserys had oft claimed that Targaryens were untroubled by the pestilences that afflicted common men, and so far as she could tell, it was true. She could remember being cold and hungry and afraid, but never sick.

"Even so," the old knight said, "I would feel better if Your Grace would return to the city." The many-colored brick walls of Meereen were half a mile back. "The bloody flux has been the bane of every army since the Dawn Age. Let us distribute the food, Your Grace."

"On the morrow. I am here now. I want to see." She put her heels into her silver. The others trotted after her. Jhogo rode before her, Aggo and Rakharo just behind, long Dothraki whips in hand to keep away the sick and dying. Ser Barristan was at her right, mounted on a dapple grey. To her left was Symon Stripeback of the Free Brothers and Marselen of the Mother's Men. Three score soldiers followed close behind the captains, to protect the food wagons. Mounted men all, Dothraki and Brazen Beasts and freedmen, they were united only by their distaste for this duty.

The Astapori stumbled after them in a ghastly procession that grew longer with every yard they crossed. Some spoke tongues she did not understand. Others were beyond speaking. Many lifted their hands to Dany, or knelt as her silver went by. "Mother," they called to her, in the dialects of Astapor, Lys, and Old Volantis, in guttural Dothraki and the liquid syllables of Qarth, even in the Common Tongue of Westeros. "Mother, please . . . mother, help my sister, she is sick . . . give me food for my little ones . . . please, my old father . . . help him . . . help her . . . help me . . ."

I have no more help to give, Dany thought, despairing. The Astapori had no place to go. Thousands remained outside Meereen's thick walls—men and women and children, old men and little girls and newborn babes. Many were sick, most were starved, and all were doomed to die. Daenerys dare not open her gates to let them in. She had tried to do what she could for them. She had sent them healers, Blue Graces and spell-singers and barber-surgeons, but some of those had sickened as well, and none of their arts had slowed the galloping progression of the flux that had come on the pale mare. Separating the healthy from the sick had proved impractical as well. Her Stalwart Shields had tried, pulling husbands away from wives and children from their mothers, even as the Astapori wept and kicked and pelted them with stones. A few days later, the sick were dead and the healthy ones were sick. Dividing the one from the other had accomplished nothing.

Even feeding them had grown difficult. Every day she sent them what she could, but every day there were more of them and less food to give them. It was growing harder to find drivers willing to deliver the food as well. Too many of the men they had sent into the camp had been stricken by the flux themselves. Others had been attacked on the way back to the city. Yesterday a wagon had been overturned and two of her soldiers killed, so today the queen had determined that she would bring the food herself. Every one of her advisors had argued fervently against it, from Reznak and the Shavepate to Ser Barristan, but Daenerys would not be moved. "I will not turn away from them," she said stubbornly. "A queen must know the sufferings of her people."

Suffering was the only thing they did not lack. "There is scarcely a horse or mule left, though many rode from Astapor," Marselen reported to her. "They've eaten every one, Your Grace, along with every rat and scavenger dog that they could catch. Now some have begun to eat their own dead."

"Man must not eat the flesh of man," said Aggo.

"It is known," agreed Rahkaro. "They will be cursed."

"They're past cursing," said Symon Stripeback.

Little children with swollen stomachs trailed after them, too weak or scared to beg. Gaunt men with sunken eyes squatted amidst sand and stones, shitting out their lives in stinking streams of brown and red. Many shat where they slept now, too feeble to crawl to the ditches she'd commanded them to dig. Two women fought over a charred bone. Nearby a boy of ten stood eating a rat. He ate one-handed, the other clutching a sharpened stick lest anyone try to wrest away his prize. Unburied dead lay everywhere. Dany saw one man sprawled in the dirt under a black cloak, but as she rode past his cloak dissolved into a thousand flies. Skeletal women sat upon the ground clutching dying infants. Their eyes followed her. Those who had the strength called out. "Mother . . . please, Mother . . . bless you, Mother . . ."

Bless me, Dany thought bitterly. *Your city is gone to ash and bone, your people are dying all around you. I have no shelter for you, no medicine, no hope. Only stale bread and wormy meat, hard cheese, a little milk. Bless me, bless me.*

What kind of mother has no milk to feed her children?

"Too many dead," Aggo said. "They should be burned."

"Who will burn them?" asked Ser Barristan. "The bloody flux is everywhere. A hundred die each night."

"It is not good to touch the dead," said Jhogo.

"This is known," Aggo and Rakharo said, together.

"That may be so," said Dany, "but this thing must be done, all the same." She thought a moment. "The Unsullied have no fear of corpses. I shall speak to Grey Worm."

"Your Grace," said Ser Barristan, "the Unsullied are your best fighters. We dare not loose this plague amongst them. Let the Astapori bury their own dead."

"They are too feeble," said Symon Stripeback.

Dany said, "More food might make them stronger."

Symon shook his head. "Food should not be wasted on the dying, Your Worship. We do not have enough to feed the living."

He was not wrong, she knew, but that did not make the words any easier to hear. "This is far enough," the queen decided. "We'll feed them here." She raised a hand. Behind her the wagons bumped to a halt, and her riders spread out around them, to keep the Astapori from rushing at the food. No sooner had they stopped than the press began to thicken around them, as more and more of the afflicted came limping and shambling toward the wagons. The riders cut them off. "Wait your turn," they shouted. "No pushing. Back. Stay back. Bread for everyone. Wait your turn."

Dany could only sit and watch. "Ser," she said to Barristan Selmy, "is there no more we can do? You have provisions."

"Provisions for Your Grace's soldiers. We may well need to withstand a long siege. The Stormcrows and the Second Sons can harry the Yunkishmen, but they cannot hope to turn them. If Your Grace would allow me to assemble an army . . ."

"If there must be a battle, I would sooner fight it from behind the walls of Meereen. Let the Yunkai'i try and storm my battlements." The queen surveyed the scene around her. "If we were to share our food equally . . ."

". . . the Astapori would eat through their portion in days, and we would have that much less for the siege."

Dany gazed across the camp, to the many-colored brick walls of Meereen. The air was thick with flies and cries. "The gods have sent this pestilence to humble me. So many dead . . . I will *not* have them eating corpses." She beckoned Aggo closer. "Ride to the gates and bring me Grey Worm and fifty of his Unsullied."

"*Khaleesi.* The blood of your blood obeys." Aggo touched his horse with his heels and galloped off.

Ser Barristan watched with ill-concealed apprehension. "You should not linger here overlong, Your Grace. The Astapori are being fed, as you commanded. There's no more we can do for the poor wretches. We should repair back to the city."

"Go if you wish, ser. I will not detain you. I will not detain any of you." Dany vaulted down from the horse. "I cannot heal them, but I can show them that their Mother cares."

Jhogo sucked in his breath. "*Khaleesi,* no." The bell in his braid rang softly as he dismounted. "You must not get any closer. Do not let them touch you! Do not!"

Dany walked right past him. There was an old man on the ground a few feet away, moaning and staring up at the grey belly of the clouds. She knelt beside him, wrinkling her nose at the smell, and pushed back his dirty grey hair to feel his brow. "His flesh is on fire. I need water to bathe him. Seawater will serve. Marselen, will you fetch some for me? I need oil as well, for the pyre. Who will help me burn the dead?"

By the time Aggo returned with Grey Worm and fifty of the Unsullied loping behind his horse, Dany had shamed all of them into helping her. Symon Stripeback and his men were pulling the living from the dead and stacking up the corpses, while Jhogo and Rakharo and their Dothraki helped those who could still walk toward the shore to bathe and wash their clothes. Aggo stared at them as if they had all gone mad, but Grey Worm knelt beside the queen and said, "This one would be of help."

Before midday a dozen fires were burning. Columns of greasy black smoke rose up to stain a merciless blue sky. Dany's riding clothes were stained and sooty as she stepped back from the pyres. "Worship," Grey Worm said, "this one and his brothers beg your leave to bathe in the salt sea when our work here is done, that we might be purified according to the laws of our great goddess."

The queen had not known that the eunuchs had a goddess of their own. "Who is this goddess? One of the gods of Ghis?"

Grey Worm looked troubled. "The goddess is called by many names. She is the Lady of Spears, the Bride of Battle, the Mother of Hosts, but her true name belongs only to these poor ones who have burned their manhoods upon her altar. We may not speak of her to others. This one begs your forgiveness."

"As you wish. Yes, you may bathe if that is your desire. Thank you for your help."

"These ones live to serve you."

When Daenerys returned to her pyramid, sore of limb and sick of heart, she found Missandei reading some old scroll whilst Irri and Jhiqui argued about Rakharo. "You are too skinny for him," Jhiqui was saying. "You are almost a boy. Rakharo does not bed with boys. This is known." Irri bristled back. "It is known that you are almost a cow. Rakharo does not bed with cows."

"Rakharo is blood of my blood. His life belongs to me, not you," Dany told the two of them. Rakharo had grown almost half a foot during his time away from Meereen and returned with arms and legs thick with muscle and four bells in his hair. He towered over Aggo and Jhogo now, as her handmaids had both noticed. "Now be quiet. I need to bathe." She had never felt more soiled. "Jhiqui, help me from these clothes, then take them away and burn them. Irri, tell Qezza to find me something light and cool to wear. The day was very hot."

A cool wind was blowing on her terrace. Dany sighed with pleasure as she slipped into the waters of her pool. At her command, Missandei stripped off her clothes and climbed in after her. "This one heard the Astapori scratching at the walls last night," the little scribe said as she was washing Dany's back.

Irri and Jhiqui exchanged a look. "No one was scratching," said Jhiqui. "Scratching . . . how could they scratch?"

"With their hands," said Missandei. "The bricks are old and crumbling. They are trying to claw their way into the city."

"This would take them many years," said Irri. "The walls are very thick. This is known."

"It is known," agreed Jhiqui.

"I dream of them as well." Dany took Missandei's hand. "The camp is a good half-mile from the city, my sweetling. No one was scratching at the walls."

"Your Grace knows best," said Missandei. "Shall I wash your hair? It is almost time. Reznak mo Reznak and the Green Grace are coming to discuss—"

"—the wedding preparations." Dany sat up with a splash. "I had almost forgotten." *Perhaps I wanted to forget.* "And after them, I am to dine with Hizdahr." She sighed. "Irri, bring the green *tokar,* the silk one fringed with Myrish lace."

"That one is being repaired, *Khaleesi.* The lace was torn. The blue *tokar* has been cleaned."

"Blue, then. They will be just as pleased."

She was only half-wrong. The priestess and the seneschal were happy to see her garbed in a *tokar,* a proper Meereenese lady for once, but what they really wanted was to strip her bare. Daenerys heard them out, incredulous. When they were done, she said, "I have no wish to give offense, but I will *not* present myself naked to Hizdahr's mother and sisters."

"But," said Reznak mo Reznak, blinking, "but you must, Your Worship. Before a marriage it is traditional for the women of the man's house to examine the bride's womb and, ah . . . her female parts. To ascertain that they are well formed and, ah . . ."

". . . fertile," finished Galazza Galare. "An ancient ritual, Your Radiance. Three Graces shall be present to witness the examination and say the proper prayers."

"Yes," said Reznak, "and afterward there is a special cake. A women's cake, baked only for betrothals. Men are not allowed to taste it. I am told it is delicious. Magical."

And if my womb is withered and my female parts accursed, is there a special cake for that as well? "Hizdahr zo Loraq may inspect my women's parts after we are wed." *Khal Drogo found no fault with them, why should he?* "Let his mother and his sisters examine one another and share the special cake. I shall not be eating it. Nor shall I wash the noble Hizdahr's noble feet."

"Magnificence, you do not understand," protested Reznak. "The washing of the feet is hallowed by tradition. It signifies that you shall be your husband's handmaid. The wedding garb is fraught with meaning too. The bride is dressed in dark red veils above a *tokar* of white silk, fringed with baby pearls."

The queen of the rabbits must not be wed without her floppy ears. "All those pearls will make me rattle when I walk."

"The pearls symbolize fertility. The more pearls Your Worship wears, the more healthy children she will bear."

"Why would I want a hundred children?" Dany turned to the Green Grace. "If we should wed by Westerosi rites . . ."

"The gods of Ghis would deem it no true union." Galazza Galare's face was hidden behind a veil of green silk. Only her eyes showed, green and wise and sad. "In the eyes of the city you would be the noble Hizdahr's concubine, not his lawful wedded wife. Your children would be bastards. Your Worship must marry Hizdahr in the Temple of the Graces, with all the nobility of Meereen on hand to bear witness to your union."

Get the heads of all the noble houses out of their pyramids on some pretext, Daario had said. *The dragon's words are fire and blood.* Dany pushed the thought aside. It was not worthy of her. "As you wish," she sighed. "I shall marry Hizdahr in the Temple of the Graces wrapped in a white *tokar* fringed with baby pearls. Is there anything else?"

"One more small matter, Your Worship," said Reznak. "To celebrate your nuptials, it would be most fitting if you would allow the fighting pits to open once again. It would be your wedding gift to Hizdahr and to your loving people, a sign that you had embraced the ancient ways and customs of Meereen."

"And most pleasing to the gods as well," the Green Grace added in her soft and kindly voice.

A bride price paid in blood. Daenerys was weary of fighting this battle. Even Ser Barristan did not think she could win. "No ruler can make a people good," Selmy had told her. "Baelor the Blessed prayed and fasted and built the Seven as splendid a temple as any gods could wish for, yet he could not put an end to war and want." *A queen must listen to her people,* Dany reminded herself. "After the wedding Hizdahr will be king. Let him reopen the fighting pits if he wishes. I want no part of it." *Let the blood be on his hands, not mine.* She rose. "If my husband wishes me to wash his feet, he must first wash mine. I will tell him so this evening." She wondered how her betrothed would take that.

She need not have been concerned. Hizdahr zo Loraq arrived an hour after the sun had set. His own *tokar* was burgundy, with a golden stripe and a fringe of golden beads. Dany told him of her meeting with Reznak and the Green Grace as she was pouring wine for him.

"These rituals are empty," Hizdahr declared, "just the sort of thing we must sweep aside. Meereen has been steeped in these foolish old traditions for too long." He kissed her hand and said, "Daenerys, my queen, I will gladly wash you from head to heel if that is what I must do to be your king and consort."

"To be my king and consort, you need only bring me peace. Skahaz tells me you have had messages of late."

"I have." Hizdahr crossed his long legs. He looked pleased with himself. "Yunkai will give us peace, but for a price. The disruption of the slave trade has caused great injury throughout the civilized world. Yunkai and her allies will require an indemnity of us, to be paid in gold and gemstones."

Gold and gems were easy. "What else?"

"The Yunkai'i will resume slaving, as before. Astapor will be rebuilt, as a slave city. You will not interfere."

"The Yunkai'i resumed their slaving before I was two leagues from their city. Did I turn back? King Cleon begged me to join with him against them, and I turned a deaf ear to his pleas. *I want no war with Yunkai.* How many times must I say it? What promises do they require?"

"Ah, there is the thorn in the bower, my queen," said Hizdahr zo Loraq. "Sad to say, Yunkai has no faith in your promises. They keep plucking the same string on the harp, about some envoy that your dragons set on fire."

"Only his *tokar* was burned," said Dany scornfully.

"Be that as it may, they do not trust you. The men of New Ghis feel the same. Words are wind, as you yourself have so oft said. No words of yours will secure this peace for Meereen. Your foes require deeds. They would see us wed, and they would see me crowned as king, to rule beside you."

Dany filled his wine cup again, wanting nothing so much as to pour the flagon over his head and drown his complacent smile. "Marriage or carnage. A wedding or a war. Are those my choices?"

"I see only one choice, Your Radiance. Let us say our vows before the gods of Ghis and make a new Meereen together."

The queen was framing her response when she heard a step behind her. *The food,* she thought. Her cooks had promised her to serve the noble Hizdahr's favorite meal, dog in honey, stuffed with prunes and peppers. But when she turned to look, it was Ser Barristan standing there, freshly bathed and clad in white, his longsword at his side. "Your Grace," he said, bowing, "I am sorry to disturb you, but I thought that you would want to know at once. The Stormcrows have returned to the city, with word of the foe. The Yunkishmen are on the march, just as we had feared."

A flicker of annoyance crossed the noble face of Hizdahr zo Loraq. "The queen is at her supper. These sellswords can wait."

Ser Barristan ignored him. "I asked Lord Daario to make his report to me, as Your Grace had commanded. He laughed and said that he would write it out in his own blood if Your Grace would send your little scribe to show him how to make the letters."

"Blood?" said Dany, horrified. "Is that a jape? No. No, don't tell me, I must see him for myself." She was a young girl, and alone, and young girls can change their minds. "Convene my captains and commanders. Hizdahr, I know you will forgive me."

"Meereen must come first." Hizdahr smiled genially. "We will have other nights. A thousand nights."

"Ser Barristan will show you out." Dany hurried off, calling for her handmaids. She would not welcome her captain home in a *tokar*. In the end she tried a dozen gowns before she found one she liked, but she refused the crown that Jhiqui offered her.

As Daario Naharis took a knee before her, Dany's heart gave a lurch. His hair was matted with dried blood, and on his temple a deep cut glistened red and raw. His right sleeve was bloody almost to the elbow. "You're hurt," she gasped.

"This?" Daario touched his temple. "A crossbowman tried to put a quarrel through my eye, but I outrode it. I was hurrying home to my queen, to bask in the warmth of her smile." He shook his sleeve, spattering red droplets. "This blood is not mine. One of my serjeants said we should go over to the Yunkai'i, so I reached down his throat and pulled his heart out. I meant to bring it to you as a gift for my silver queen, but four of the Cats cut me off and came snarling and spitting after me. One almost caught me, so I threw the heart into his face."

"Very gallant," said Ser Barristan, in a tone that suggested it was anything but, "but do you have tidings for Her Grace?"

"Hard tidings, Ser Grandfather. Astapor is gone, and the slavers are coming north in strength."

"This is old news, and stale," growled the Shavepate.

"Your mother said the same of your father's kisses," Daario replied. "Sweet queen, I would have been here sooner, but the hills are aswarm with Yunkish sellswords. Four free companies. Your Stormcrows had to cut their way through all of them. There is more, and worse. The Yunkai'i are marching their host up the coast road, joined by four legions out of New Ghis. They have elephants, a hundred, armored and towered. Tolosi slingers too, and a corps of Qartheen camelry. Two more Ghiscari legions took ship at Astapor. If our captives told it true, they will be landed beyond the Skahazadhan to cut us off from the Dothraki sea."

As he told his tale, from time to time a drop of bright red blood would patter against the marble floor, and Dany would wince. "How many men were killed?" she asked when he was done.

"Of ours? I did not stop to count. We gained more than we lost, though."

"More turncloaks?"

"More brave men drawn to your noble cause. My queen will like them. One is an axeman from the Basilisk Isles, a brute, bigger than Belwas. You should see him. Some Westerosi too, a score or more. Deserters from the Windblown, unhappy with the Yunkai'i. They'll make good Stormcrows."

"If you say." Dany would not quibble. Meereen might soon have need of every sword.

Ser Barristan frowned at Daario. "Captain, you made mention of *four* free companies. We know of only three. The Windblown, the Long Lances, and the Company of the Cat."

"Ser Grandfather knows how to count. The Second Sons have gone over to the Yunkai'i." Daario turned his head and spat. "That's for Brown Ben Plumm. When next I see his ugly face I will open him from throat to groin and rip out his black heart."

Dany tried to speak and found no words. She remembered Ben's face the last time she had seen it. *It was a warm face, a face I trusted.* Dark skin and white hair, the broken nose, the wrinkles at the corners of his eyes. Even the dragons had been fond of old Brown Ben, who liked to boast that he had a drop of dragon blood himself. *Three treasons will you know. Once for gold and once for blood and once for love.* Was Plumm the third treason, or the second? And what did that make Ser Jorah, her gruff old bear? Would she never have a friend that she could trust? *What good are prophecies if you cannot make sense of them? If I marry Hizdahr before the sun comes up, will all these armies melt away like morning dew and let me rule in peace?*

Daario's announcement had sparked an uproar. Reznak was wailing, the Shavepate was muttering darkly, her bloodriders were swearing vengeance. Strong Belwas thumped his scarred belly with his fist and swore to eat Brown Ben's heart with plums and onions. "Please," Dany said, but only Missandei seemed to hear. The queen got to her feet. "*Be quiet!* I have heard enough."

"Your Grace." Ser Barristan went to one knee. "We are yours to command. What would you have us do?"

"Continue as we planned. Gather food, as much as you can." *If I look back I am lost.* "We must close the gates and put every fighting man upon the walls. No one enters, no one leaves."

The hall was quiet for a moment. The men looked at one another. Then Reznak said, "What of the Astapori?"

She wanted to scream, to gnash her teeth and tear her clothes and beat upon the floor. Instead she said, "*Close the gates.* Will you make me say it thrice?" They were her children, but she could not help them now. "Leave me. Daario, remain. That cut should be washed, and I have more questions for you."

The others bowed and went. Dany took Daario Naharis up the steps to her bedchamber, where Irri washed his cut with vinegar and Jhiqui wrapped it in white linen. When that was done she sent her handmaids off as well. "Your clothes are stained with blood," she told Daario. "Take them off."

"Only if you do the same." He kissed her.

His hair smelled of blood and smoke and horse, and his mouth was hard and hot on hers. Dany trembled in his arms. When they broke apart, she said, "I thought you would be the one to betray me. Once for blood and once for gold and once for love, the warlocks said. I thought . . . I never thought Brown Ben. Even my dragons seemed to trust him." She clutched her captain by the shoulders. "Promise me that you will never turn against me. I could not bear that. Promise me."

"Never, my love."

She believed him. "I swore that I should wed Hizdahr zo Loraq if he gave me ninety days of peace, but now . . . I wanted you from the first time that I saw you, but you were a sellsword, fickle, *treacherous.* You boasted that you'd had a hundred women."

"A hundred?" Daario chuckled through his purple beard. "I lied, sweet queen. It was a thousand. But never once a dragon."

She raised her lips to his. "What are you waiting for?"

THE PRINCE OF WINTERFELL

The hearth was caked with cold black ash, the room unheated but for candles. Every time a door opened their flames would sway and shiver. The bride was shivering too. They had dressed her in white lambswool trimmed with lace. Her sleeves and bodice were sewn with freshwater pearls, and on her feet were white doeskin slippers—pretty, but not warm. Her face was pale, bloodless.

A face carved of ice, Theon Greyjoy thought as he draped a fur-trimmed cloak about her shoulders. *A corpse buried in the snow.* "My lady. It is time." Beyond the door, the music called them, lute and pipes and drum.

The bride raised her eyes. Brown eyes, shining in the candlelight. "I will be a good wife to him, and t-true. I . . . I will please him and give him sons. I will be a better wife than the real Arya could have been, he'll see."

Talk like that will get you killed, or worse. That lesson he had learned as Reek. "You are the real Arya, my lady. Arya of House Stark, Lord Eddard's daughter, heir to Winterfell." Her name, she had to know her *name.* "Arya Underfoot. Your sister used to call you Arya Horseface."

"It was me made up that name. Her face was long and horsey. Mine isn't. I was pretty." Tears spilled from her eyes at last. "I was never beautiful like Sansa, but they all said I was pretty. Does Lord Ramsay think I am pretty?"

"Yes," he lied. "He's told me so."

"He knows who I am, though. Who I really am. I see it when he looks at me. He looks so angry, even when he smiles, but it's not my fault. They say he likes to hurt people."

"My lady should not listen to such . . . lies."

"They say that he hurt you. Your hands, and . . ."

His mouth was dry. "I . . . I deserved it. I made him angry. You must not make him angry. Lord Ramsay is a . . . a sweet man, and kindly. Please him, and he will be good to you. Be a good wife."

"Help me." She clutched at him. "Please. I used to watch you in the yard, playing with your swords. You were so handsome." She squeezed his arm. "If we ran away, I could be your wife, or your . . . your whore . . . whatever you wanted. You could be my man."

Theon wrenched his arm away from her. "I'm no . . . I'm no one's man." *A man would help her.* "Just . . . just be Arya, be his wife. Please him, or . . . just please him, and stop this talk about being someone else." *Jeyne, her name is Jeyne, it rhymes with pain.* The music was growing more insistent. "It is time. Wipe those tears from your eyes." *Brown eyes. They should be grey. Someone will see. Someone will remember.* "Good. Now smile."

The girl tried. Her lips, trembling, twitched up and froze, and he could see her teeth. *Pretty white teeth,* he thought, *but if she angers him, they will not be pretty long.* When he pushed the door open, three of the four candles fluttered out. He led the bride into the mist, where the wedding guests were waiting.

"Why me?" he had asked when Lady Dustin told him he must give the bride away.

"Her father is dead and all her brothers. Her mother perished at the Twins. Her uncles are lost or dead or captive."

"She has a brother still." *She has three brothers still,* he might have said. "Jon Snow is with the Night's Watch."

"A half-brother, bastard-born, and bound to the Wall. You were her father's ward, the nearest thing she has to living kin. It is only fitting that you give her hand in marriage."

The nearest thing she has to living kin. Theon Greyjoy had grown up with Arya Stark. Theon would have known an imposter. If he was seen to accept Bolton's feigned girl as Arya, the northern lords who had gathered to bear witness to the match would have no grounds to question her legitimacy. Stout and Slate, Whoresbane Umber, the quarrelsome Ryswells, Hornwood men and Cerywn cousins, fat Lord Wyman Manderly . . . not one of them had known Ned Stark's daughters half so well as he. And if a few entertained private doubts, surely they would be wise enough to keep those misgivings to themselves.

They are using me to cloak their deception, putting mine own face on their lie. That was why Roose Bolton had clothed him as a lord again, to play his part in this mummer's farce. Once that was done, once their false Arya had been wedded and bedded, Bolton would have no more use for Theon Turncloak. "Serve us in this, and when Stannis is defeated we will discuss how best to restore you to your father's seat," his lordship had said in that soft voice of his, a voice made for lies and whispers. Theon never believed a word of it. He would dance this dance for them because he had no choice, but afterward . . . *He will give me back to Ramsay then,* he thought, *and Ramsay will take a few more fingers and turn me into Reek once more.* Unless the gods were good, and Stannis Baratheon descended on Winterfell and put all of them to the sword, himself included. That was the best he could hope for.

It was warmer in the godswood, strange to say. Beyond its confines, a hard white frost gripped Winterfell. The paths were treacherous with black ice, and hoarfrost sparkled in the moonlight on the broken panes of the Glass Gardens. Drifts of dirty snow had piled up against the walls, filling every nook and corner. Some were so high they hid the doors behind them. Under the snow lay grey ash and cinders, and here and there a blackened beam or a pile of bones adorned with scraps of skin and hair. Icicles long as lances hung from the battlements and fringed the towers like an old man's stiff white whiskers. But inside the godswood, the ground remained unfrozen, and steam rose off the hot pools, as warm as baby's breath.

The bride was garbed in white and grey, the colors the true Arya would have worn had she lived long enough to wed. Theon wore black and gold, his cloak pinned to his shoulder by a crude iron kraken that a smith in Barrowton had hammered together for him. But under the hood, his hair was white and thin, and his flesh had an old man's greyish undertone. *A Stark at last,* he thought. Arm in arm, the bride and he passed through an arched stone door, as wisps of fog stirred round their legs. The drum was as tremulous as a maiden's heart, the pipes high and sweet and beckoning. Up above the treetops, a crescent moon was floating in a dark sky, half-obscured by mist, like an eye peering through a veil of silk.

Theon Greyjoy was no stranger to this godswood. He had played here as a boy, skipping stones across the cold black pool beneath the weirwood, hiding his treasures in the bole of an ancient oak, stalking squirrels with a bow he made himself. Later, older, he had soaked his bruises in the hot springs after many a session in the yard with Robb and Jory and Jon Snow. In amongst these chestnuts and elms and soldier pines he had found secret places where he could hide when he wanted to be alone. The first time he had ever kissed a girl had been here. Later, a different girl had made a man of him upon a ragged quilt in the shade of that tall grey-green sentinel.

He had never seen the godswood like this, though—grey and ghostly, filled with warm mists and floating lights and whispered voices that seemed to come from everywhere and nowhere. Beneath the trees, the hot springs steamed. Warm vapors rose from the earth, shrouding the trees in their moist breath, creeping up the walls to draw grey curtains across the watching windows.

There was a path of sorts, a meandering footpath of cracked stones overgrown with moss, half-buried beneath blown dirt and fallen leaves and made treacherous by thick brown roots pushing up from underneath. He led the bride along it. *Jeyne, her name is Jeyne, it rhymes with pain.* He must not think that, though. Should that name pass his lips, it might cost him a finger or an ear. He walked slowly, watching every step. His missing toes made him hobble when he hurried, and it would not do to stumble. Mar Lord Ramsay's wedding with a misstep, and Lord Ramsay might rectify such clumsiness by flaying the offending foot.

The mists were so thick that only the nearest trees were visible; beyond them stood tall shadows and faint lights. Candles flickered beside the wandering path and back amongst the trees, pale fireflies floating in a warm grey soup. It felt like some strange underworld, some timeless place between the worlds, where the damned wandered mournfully for a time before finding their way down to whatever hell their sins had earned them. *Are we all dead, then? Did Stannis come and kill us in our sleep? Is the battle yet to come, or has it been fought and lost?*

Here and there a torch burned hungrily, casting its ruddy glow over the faces of the wedding guests. The way the mists threw back the shifting light made their features seem bestial, half-human, twisted. Lord Stout became a mastiff, old Lord Locke a vulture, Whoresbane Umber a gargoyle, Big Walder Frey a fox, Little Walder a red bull, lacking only a ring for his nose. Roose Bolton's own face was a pale grey mask, with two chips of dirty ice where his eyes should be.

Above their heads the trees were full of ravens, their feathers fluffed as they hunched on bare brown branches, staring down at the pageantry below. *Maester Luwin's birds.* Luwin was dead, and his maester's tower had been put to the torch, yet the ravens lingered. *This is their home.* Theon wondered what that would be like, to have a home.

Then the mists parted, like the curtain opening at a mummer show to reveal some new tableau. The heart tree appeared in front of them, its bony limbs spread wide. Fallen leaves lay about the wide white trunk in drifts of red and brown. The ravens were the thickest here, muttering to one another in the murderers' secret tongue. Ramsay Bolton stood beneath them, clad in high boots of soft grey leather and a black velvet doublet slashed with pink silk and glittering with garnet teardrops. A smile danced across his face. "Who comes?" His lips were moist, his neck red above his collar. "Who comes before the god?"

Theon answered. "Arya of House Stark comes here to be wed. A woman grown and flowered, trueborn and noble, she comes to beg the blessings of the gods. Who comes to claim her?"

"Me," said Ramsay. "Ramsay of House Bolton, Lord of the Hornwood, heir to the Dreadfort. I claim her. Who gives her?"

"Theon of House Greyjoy, who was her father's ward." He turned to the bride. "Lady Arya, will you take this man?"

She raised her eyes to his. *Brown eyes, not grey. Are all of them so blind?* For a long moment she did not speak, but those eyes were begging. *This is your chance,* he thought. *Tell them. Tell them now. Shout out your name before them all, tell them that you are not Arya Stark, let all the north hear how you were made to play this part.* It would mean her death, of course, and his own as well, but Ramsay in his wroth might kill them quickly. The old gods of the north might grant them that small boon.

"I take this man," the bride said in a whisper.

All around them lights glimmered through the mists, a hundred candles pale as shrouded stars. Theon stepped back, and Ramsay and his bride joined hands and knelt before the heart tree, bowing their heads in token of submission. The weirwood's carved red eyes stared down at them, its great red mouth open as if to laugh. In the branches overhead a raven *quork*ed.

After a moment of silent prayer, the man and woman rose again. Ramsay undid the cloak that Theon had slipped about his bride's shoulders moments before, the heavy white wool cloak bordered in grey fur, emblazoned with the direwolf of House Stark. In its place he fastened a pink cloak, spattered with red garnets like those upon his doublet. On its back was the flayed man of the Dreadfort done in stiff red leather, grim and grisly.

Quick as that, it was done. Weddings went more quickly in the north. It came of not having priests, Theon supposed, but whatever the reason it seemed to him a mercy. Ramsay Bolton scooped his wife up in his arms and strode through the mists with her. Lord Bolton and his Lady Walda followed, then the rest. The musicians began to play again, and the bard Abel began to sing "Two Hearts That Beat as One." Two of his women joined their voices to his own to make a sweet harmony.

Theon found himself wondering if he should say a prayer. *Will the old gods hear me if I do?* They were not his gods, had never been his gods. He was ironborn, a son of Pyke, his god was the Drowned God of the islands . . . but Winterfell was long leagues from the sea. It had been a lifetime since any god had heard him. He did not know who he was, or what he was, why he was still alive, why he had ever been born.

"Theon," a voice seemed to whisper.

His head snapped up. "Who said that?" All he could see were the trees and the fog that covered them. The voice had been as faint as rustling leaves, as cold as hate. *A god's voice, or a ghost's.* How many died the day that he took Winterfell? How many more the day he lost it? *The day that Theon Greyjoy died, to be reborn as Reek. Reek, Reek, it rhymes with shriek.*

Suddenly he did not want to be here.

Once outside the godswood the cold descended on him like a ravening wolf and caught him in its teeth. He lowered his head into the wind and made for the Great Hall, hastening after the long line of candles and torches. Ice crunched beneath his boots, and a sudden gust pushed back his hood, as if a ghost had plucked at him with frozen fingers, hungry to gaze upon his face.

Winterfell was full of ghosts for Theon Greyjoy.

This was not the castle he remembered from the summer of his youth. This place was scarred and broken, more ruin than redoubt, a haunt of crows and corpses. The great double curtain wall still stood, for granite does not yield easily to fire, but most of the towers and keeps within were roofless. A few had collapsed. The thatch and timber had been consumed by fire, in whole or in part, and under the shattered panes of the Glass Garden the fruits and vegetables that would have fed the castle during the winter were dead and black and frozen. Tents filled the yard, half-buried in the snow. Roose Bolton had brought his host inside the walls, along with his friends the Freys; thousands huddled amongst the ruins, crowding every court, sleeping in cellar vaults and under topless towers, and in buildings abandoned for centuries.

Plumes of grey smoke snaked up from the rebuilt kitchens and reroofed barracks keep. The battlements and crenellations were crowned with snow and hung with icicles. All the color had been leached from Winterfell until only grey and white remained. *The Stark colors.* Theon did not know whether he ought to find that ominous or reassuring. Even the sky was grey. *Grey and grey and greyer. The whole world grey, everywhere you look, everything grey except the eyes of the bride.* The eyes of the bride were brown. *Big and brown and full of fear.* It was not right that she should look to him for rescue. What had she been thinking, that he would whistle up a winged horse and fly her out of here, like some hero in the stories she and Sansa used to love? He could not even help himself. *Reek, Reek, it rhymes with meek.*

All about the yard, dead men hung half-frozen at the end of hempen ropes, swollen faces white with hoarfrost. Winterfell had been crawling with squatters when Bolton's van had reached the castle. More than two dozen had been driven at spearpoint from the nests they had made amongst the castle's half-ruined keeps and towers. The boldest and most truculent had been hanged, the rest put to work. Serve well, Lord Bolton told them, and he would be merciful. Stone and timber were plentiful with the wolfswood so close at hand. Stout new gates had gone up first, to replace those that had been burned. Then the collapsed roof of the Great Hall had been cleared away and a new one raised hurriedly in its stead. When the work was done, Lord Bolton hanged the workers. True to his word, he showed them mercy and did not flay a one.

By that time, the rest of Bolton's army had arrived. They raised King Tommen's stag and lion above the walls of Winterfell as the wind came howling from the north, and below it the flayed man of the Dreadfort. Theon arrived in Barbrey Dustin's train, with her ladyship herself, her Barrowton levies, and the bride-to-be. Lady Dustin had insisted that she should have custody of Lady Arya until such time as she was wed, but now that time was done. *She belongs to Ramsay now. She said the words.* By this marriage Ramsay would be Lord of Winterfell. So long as Jeyne took care not to anger him, he should have no cause to harm her. *Arya. Her name is Arya.*

Even inside fur-lined gloves, Theon's hands had begun to throb with pain. It was often his hands that hurt the worst, especially his missing fingers. Had there truly been a time when women yearned for his touch? *I made myself the Prince of Winterfell,* he thought, *and from that came all of this.* He had thought that men would sing of him for a hundred years and tell tales of his daring. But if anyone spoke of him now, it was as Theon Turncloak, and the tales they told were of his treachery. *This was never my home. I was a hostage here.* Lord Stark had not treated him cruelly, but the long steel shadow of his greatsword had always been between them. *He was kind to me, but never warm. He knew that one day he might need to put me to death.*

Theon kept his eyes downcast as he crossed the yard, weaving between the tents. *I learned to fight in this yard,* he thought, remembering warm summer days spent sparring with Robb and Jon Snow under the watchful eyes of old Ser Rodrik. That was back when he was whole, when he could grasp a sword hilt as well as any man. But the yard held darker memories as well. This was where he had assembled Stark's people the night Bran and Rickon fled the castle. Ramsay was Reek then, standing at his side, whispering that he should flay a few of his captives to make them tell him where the boys had gone. *There will be no flaying here whilst I am Prince of Winterfell,* Theon had responded, little dreaming how short his rule would prove. *None of them would help me. I had known them all for half my life, and not one of them would help me.* Even so, he had done his best to protect them, but once Ramsay put Reek's face aside he'd slain all the men, and Theon's ironborn as well. *He set my horse afire.* That was the last sight he had seen the day the castle fell: Smiler burning, the flames leaping from his mane as he reared up, kicking, screaming, his eyes white with terror. *Here in this very yard.*

The doors of the Great Hall loomed up in front of him; new-made, to replace the doors that burned, they seemed crude and ugly to him, raw planks hastily joined. A pair of spearmen guarded them, hunched and shivering under thick fur cloaks, their beards crusty with ice. They eyed Theon resentfully as he hobbled up the steps, pushed against the right-hand door, and slipped inside.

The hall was blessedly warm and bright with torchlight, as crowded as he had ever seen it. Theon let the heat wash over him, then made his way toward the front of the hall. Men sat crammed knee to knee along the benches, so tightly packed that the servers had to squirm between them. Even the knights and lords above the salt enjoyed less space than usual.

Up near the dais, Abel was plucking at his lute and singing "Fair

Maids of Summer." *He calls himself a bard. In truth he's more a pander.*
Lord Manderly had brought musicians from White Harbor, but none
were singers, so when Abel turned up at the gates with a lute and six
women, he had been made welcome. "Two sisters, two daughters, one
wife, and my old mother," the singer claimed, though not one looked
like him. "Some dance, some sing, one plays the pipe and one the
drums. Good washerwomen too."

Bard or pander, Abel's voice was passable, his playing fair. Here
amongst the ruins, that was as much as anyone might expect.

Along the walls the banners hung: the horseheads of the Ryswells
in gold, brown, grey, and black; the roaring giant of House Umber;
the stone hand of House Flint of Flint's Finger; the moose of
Hornwood and the merman of Manderly; Cerwyn's black battle-axe
and the Tallhart pines. Yet their bright colors could not entirely cover
the blackened walls behind them, nor the boards that closed the
holes where windows once had been. Even the roof was wrong, its
raw new timbers light and bright, where the old rafters had been
stained almost black by centuries of smoke.

The largest banners were behind the dais, where the direwolf of
Winterfell and the flayed man of the Dreadfort hung back of the
bride and groom. The sight of the Stark banner hit Theon harder
than he had expected. *Wrong, it's wrong, as wrong as her eyes.* The
arms of House Poole were a blue plate on white, framed by a grey
tressure. Those were the arms they should have hung.

"Theon Turncloak," someone said as he passed. Other men turned
away at the sight of him. One spat. *And why not?* He was the traitor
who had taken Winterfell by treachery, slain his foster brothers,
delivered his own people to be flayed at Moat Cailin, and given his
foster sister to Lord Ramsay's bed. Roose Bolton might make use of
him, but true northmen must despise him.

The missing toes on his left foot had left him with a crabbed,
awkward gait, comical to look upon. Back behind him, he heard a
woman laugh. Even here in this half-frozen lichyard of a castle,
surrounded by snow and ice and death, there were women.
Washerwomen. That was the polite way of saying *camp follower,* which
was the polite way of saying *whore.*

Where they came from Theon could not say. They just seemed to appear, like maggots on a corpse or ravens after a battle. Every army drew them. Some were hardened whores who could fuck twenty men in a night and drink them all blind. Others looked as innocent as maids, but that was just a trick of their trade. Some were camp brides, bound to the soldiers they followed with words whispered to one god or another but doomed to be forgotten once the war was done. They would warm a man's bed by night, patch the holes in his boots at morning, cook his supper come dusk, and loot his corpse after the battle. Some even did a bit of washing. With them, oft as not, came bastard children, wretched, filthy creatures born in one camp or the other. And even such as these made mock of Theon Turncloak. *Let them laugh.* His pride had perished here in Winterfell; there was no place for such in the dungeons of the Dreadfort. When you have known the kiss of a flaying knife, a laugh loses all its power to hurt you.

Birth and blood accorded him a seat upon the dais at the end of the high table, beside a wall. To his left sat Lady Dustin, clad as ever in black wool, severe in cut and unadorned. To his right sat no one. *They are all afraid the dishonor might rub off on them.* If he had dared, he would have laughed.

The bride had the place of highest honor, between Ramsay and his father. She sat with eyes downcast as Roose Bolton bid them drink to Lady Arya. "In her children our two ancient houses will become as one," he said, "and the long enmity between Stark and Bolton will be ended." His voice was so soft that the hall grew hushed as men strained to hear. "I am sorry that our good friend Stannis has not seen fit to join us yet," he went on, to a ripple of laughter, "as I know Ramsay had hoped to present his head to Lady Arya as a wedding gift." The laughs grew louder. "We shall give him a splendid welcome when he arrives, a welcome worthy of true northmen. Until that day, let us eat and drink and make merry . . . for winter is almost upon us, my friends, and many of us here shall not live to see the spring."

The Lord of White Harbor had furnished the food and drink, black stout and yellow beer and wines red and gold and purple, brought up from the warm south on fat-bottomed ships and aged in his deep cellars. The wedding guests gorged on cod cakes and winter squash, hills of neeps and great round wheels of cheese, on smoking slabs of mutton and beef ribs charred almost black, and lastly on three great wedding pies, as wide across as wagon wheels, their flaky crusts stuffed to bursting with carrots, onions, turnips, parsnips, mushrooms, and chunks of seasoned pork swimming in a savory brown gravy. Ramsay hacked off slices with his falchion and Wyman Manderly himself served, presenting the first steaming portions to Roose Bolton and his fat Frey wife, the next to Ser Hosteen and Ser Aenys, the sons of Walder Frey. "The best pie you have ever tasted, my lords," the fat lord declared. "Wash it down with Arbor gold and savor every bite. I know I shall."

True to his word, Manderly devoured six portions, two from each of the three pies, smacking his lips and slapping his belly and stuffing himself until the front of his tunic was half-brown with gravy stains and his beard was flecked with crumbs of crust. Even Fat Walda Frey could not match his gluttony, though she did manage three slices herself. Ramsay ate heartily as well, though his pale bride did no more than stare at the portion set before her. When she raised her head and looked at Theon, he could see the fear behind her big brown eyes.

No longswords had been allowed within the hall, but every man there wore a dagger, even Theon Greyjoy. How else to cut his meat? Every time he looked at the girl who had been Jeyne Poole, he felt the presence of that steel at his side. *I have no way to save her,* he thought, *but I could kill her easy enough. No one would expect it. I could beg her for the honor of a dance and cut her throat. That would be a kindness, wouldn't it? And if the old gods hear my prayer, Ramsay in his wroth might strike me dead as well.* Theon was not afraid to die. Underneath the Dreadfort, he had learned there were far worse things than death. Ramsay had taught him that lesson, finger by finger and toe by toe, and it was not one that he was ever like to forget.

"You do not eat," observed Lady Dustin.

"No." Eating was hard for him. Ramsay had left him with so many broken teeth that chewing was an agony. Drinking was easier, though he had to grasp the wine cup with both hands to keep from dropping it.

"No taste for pork pie, my lord? The best pork pie we ever tasted, our fat friend would have us believe." She gestured toward Lord Manderly with her wine cup. "Have you ever seen a fat man so happy? He is almost dancing. Serving with his own hands."

It was true. The Lord of White Harbor was the very picture of the jolly fat man, laughing and smiling, japing with the other lords and slapping them on the back, calling out to the musicians for this tune or that tune. "Give us 'The Night That Ended,' singer," he bellowed. "The bride will like that one, I know. Or sing to us of brave young Danny Flint and make us weep." To look at him, you would have thought that he was the one newly wed.

"He's drunk," said Theon.

"Drowning his fears. He is craven to the bone, that one."

Was he? Theon was not certain. His sons had been fat as well, but they had not shamed themselves in battle. "Ironborn will feast before a battle too. A last taste of life, should death await. If Stannis comes . . ."

"He will. He must." Lady Dustin chuckled. "And when he does, the fat man will piss himself. His son died at the Red Wedding, yet he's shared his bread and salt with Freys, welcomed them beneath his roof, promised one his granddaughter. He even serves them pie. The Manderlys ran from the south once, hounded from their lands and keeps by enemies. Blood runs true. The fat man would like to kill us all, I do not doubt, but he does not have the belly for it, for all his girth. Under that sweaty flesh beats a heart as craven and cringing as . . . well . . . yours."

Her last word was a lash, but Theon dared not answer back in kind. Any insolence would cost him skin. "If my lady believes Lord Manderly wants to betray us, Lord Bolton is the one to tell."

"You think Roose does not know? Silly boy. Watch him. Watch how he watches Manderly. No dish so much as touches Roose's lips until he sees Lord Wyman eat of it first. No cup of wine is sipped until he sees Manderly drink of the same cask. I think he would be pleased if the fat man attempted some betrayal. It would amuse him. Roose has no feelings, you see. Those leeches that he loves so well sucked all the passions out of him years ago. He does not love, he does not hate, he does not grieve. This is a game to him, mildly diverting. Some men hunt, some hawk, some tumble dice. Roose plays with men. You and me, these Freys, Lord Manderly, his plump new wife, even his bastard, we are but his playthings." A serving man was passing by. Lady Dustin held out her wine cup and let him fill it, then gestured for him to do the same for Theon. "Truth be told," she said, "Lord Bolton aspires to more than mere lordship. Why not King of the North? Tywin Lannister is dead, the Kingslayer is maimed, the Imp is fled. The Lannisters are a spent force, and you were kind enough to rid him of the Starks. Old Walder Frey will not object to his fat little Walda becoming a queen. White Harbor might prove troublesome should Lord Wyman survive this coming battle . . . but I am quite sure that he will not. No more than Stannis. Roose will remove both of them, as he removed the Young Wolf. Who else is there?"

"You," said Theon. "There is you. The Lady of Barrowton, a Dustin by marriage, a Ryswell by birth."

That pleased her. She took a sip of wine, her dark eyes sparkling, and said, "The *widow* of Barrowton . . . and yes, if I so choose, I could be an inconvenience. Of course, Roose sees that too, so he takes care to keep me sweet."

She might have said more, but then she saw the maesters. Three of them had entered together by the lord's door behind the dais—one tall, one plump, one very young, but in their robes and chains they were three grey peas from a black pod. Before the war, Medrick had served Lord Hornwood, Rhodry Lord Cerwyn, and young Henly Lord Slate. Roose Bolton had brought them all to Winterfell to take charge of Luwin's ravens, so messages might be sent and received from here again.

As Maester Medrick went to one knee to whisper in Bolton's ear, Lady Dustin's mouth twisted in distaste. "If I were queen, the first thing I would do would be to kill all those grey rats. They scurry everywhere, living on the leavings of the lords, chittering to one another, whispering in the ears of their masters. But who are the masters and who are the servants, truly? Every great lord has his maester, every lesser lord aspires to one. If you do not have a maester, it is taken to mean that you are of little consequence. The grey rats read and write our letters, even for such lords as cannot read themselves, and who can say for a certainty that they are not twisting the words for their own ends? What good are they, I ask you?"

"They heal," said Theon. It seemed to be expected of him.

"They heal, yes. I never said they were not subtle. They tend to us when we are sick and injured, or distraught over the illness of a parent or a child. Whenever we are weakest and most vulnerable, there they are. Sometimes they heal us, and we are duly grateful. When they fail, they console us in our grief, and we are grateful for that as well. Out of gratitude we give them a place beneath our roof and make them privy to all our shames and secrets, a part of every council. And before too long, the ruler has become the ruled.

"That was how it was with Lord Rickard Stark. Maester Walys was his grey rat's name. And isn't it clever how the maesters go by only one name, even those who had two when they first arrived at the Citadel? That way we cannot know who they truly are or where they come from . . . but if you are dogged enough, you can still find out. Before he forged his chain, Maester Walys had been known as Walys Flowers. Flowers, Hill, Rivers, Snow . . . we give such names to base-born children to mark them for what they are, but they are always quick to shed them. Walys Flowers had a Hightower girl for a mother . . . and an archmaester of the Citadel for a father, it was rumored. The grey rats are not as chaste as they would have us believe. Oldtown maesters are the worst of all. Once he forged his chain, his secret father and his friends wasted no time dispatching him to Winterfell to fill Lord Rickard's ears with poisoned words as sweet as honey. The Tully marriage was his notion, never doubt it, he—"

She broke off as Roose Bolton rose to his feet, pale eyes shining in the torchlight. "My friends," he began, and a hush swept through the hall, so profound that Theon could hear the wind plucking at the boards over the windows. "Stannis and his knights have left Deepwood Motte, flying the banner of his new red god. The clans of the northern hills come with him on their shaggy runtish horses. If the weather holds, they could be on us in a fortnight. And Crowfood Umber marches down the kingsroad, whilst the Karstarks approach from the east. They mean to join with Lord Stannis here and take this castle from us."

Ser Hosteen Frey pushed to his feet. "We should ride forth to meet them. Why allow them to combine their strength?"

Because Arnolf Karstark awaits only a sign from Lord Bolton before he turns his cloak, thought Theon, as other lords began to shout out counsel. Lord Bolton raised his hands for silence. "The hall is not the place for such discussions, my lords. Let us adjourn to the solar whilst my son consummates his marriage. The rest of you, remain and enjoy the food and drink."

As the Lord of the Dreadfort slipped out, attended by the three maesters, other lords and captains rose to follow. Hother Umber, the gaunt old man called Whoresbane, went grim-faced and scowling. Lord Manderly was so drunk he required four strong men to help him from the hall. "We should have a song about the Rat Cook," he was muttering, as he staggered past Theon, leaning on his knights. "Singer, give us a song about the Rat Cook."

Lady Dustin was amongst the last to bestir herself. When she had gone, all at once the hall seemed stifling. It was not until Theon pushed himself to his feet that he realized how much he'd drunk. When he stumbled from the table, he knocked a flagon from the hands of a serving girl. Wine splashed across his boots and breeches, a dark red tide.

A hand grabbed his shoulder, five fingers hard as iron digging deep into his flesh. "You're wanted, Reek," said Sour Alyn, his breath foul with the smell from his rotten teeth. Yellow Dick and Damon Dance-for-Me were with him. "Ramsay says you're to bring his bride to his bed."

A shiver of fear went through him. *I played my part,* he thought. *Why me?* He knew better than to object, though.

Lord Ramsay had already left the hall. His bride, forlorn and seem-ingly forgotten, sat hunched and silent beneath the banner of House Stark, clutching a silver goblet in both hands. Judging from the way she looked at him when he approached, she had emptied that goblet more than once. Perhaps she hoped that if she drank enough, the ordeal would pass her by. Theon knew better. "Lady Arya," he said. "Come. It is time you did your duty."

Six of the Bastard's boys accompanied them as Theon led the girl out the back of the hall and across the frigid yard to the Great Keep. It was up three flights of stone steps to Lord Ramsay's bedchamber, one of the rooms the fires had touched but lightly. As they climbed, Damon Dance-for-Me whistled, whilst Skinner boasted that Lord Ramsay had promised him a piece of the bloody sheet as a mark of special favor.

The bedchamber had been well prepared for the consummation. All the furnishings were new, brought up from Barrowton in the baggage train. The canopy bed had a feather mattress and drapes of blood-red velvet. The stone floor was covered with wolfskins. A fire was burning in the hearth, a candle on the bedside table. On the sideboard was a flagon of wine, two cups, and a half wheel of veined white cheese.

There was a chair as well, carved of black oak with a red leather seat. Lord Ramsay was seated in it when they entered. Spittle glistened on his lips. "There's my sweet maid. Good lads. You may leave us now. Not you, Reek. You stay."

Reek, Reek, it rhymes with peek. He could feel his missing fingers cramping: two on his left hand, one on his right. And on his hip his dagger rested, sleeping in its leather sheath, but heavy, oh so heavy. *It is only my pinky gone on my right hand,* Theon reminded himself. *I can still grip a knife.* "My lord. How may I serve you?"

"You gave the wench to me. Who better to unwrap the gift? Let's have a look at Ned Stark's little daughter."

She is no kin to Lord Eddard, Theon almost said. *Ramsay knows, he has to know. What new cruel game is this?* The girl was standing by a bedpost, trembling like a doe. "Lady Arya, if you will turn your back, I must needs unlace your gown."

"No." Lord Ramsay poured himself a cup of wine. "Laces take too long. Cut it off her."

Theon drew the dagger. *All I need do is turn and stab him. The knife is in my hand.* He knew the game by then. *Another trap,* he told himself, remembering Kyra with her keys. *He wants me to try to kill him. And when I fail, he'll flay the skin from the hand I used to hold the blade.* He grabbed a handful of the bride's skirt. "Stand still, my lady." The gown was loose below the waist, so that was where he slid the blade in, slicing upward slowly, so as not to cut her. Steel whispered through wool and silk with a faint, soft sound. The girl was shaking. Theon had to grab her arm to hold her still. *Jeyne, Jeyne, it rhymes with pain.* He tightened his grip, as much as his maimed left hand would allow. "Stay still."

Finally the gown fell away, a pale tangle round her feet. "Her smallclothes too," Ramsay commanded. Reek obeyed.

When it was done the bride stood naked, her bridal finery a heap of white and grey rags about her feet. Her breasts were small and pointed, her hips narrow and girlish, her legs as skinny as a bird's. *A child.* Theon had forgotten how young she was. *Sansa's age. Arya would be even younger.* Despite the fire in the hearth, the bedchamber was chilly. Jeyne's pale skin was pebbled with gooseprickles. There was a moment when her hands rose, as if to cover her breasts, but Theon mouthed a silent *no* and she saw and stopped at once.

"What do you think of her, Reek?" asked Lord Ramsay.

"She . . ." *What answer does he want?* What was it the girl had said, before the godswood? *They all said that I was pretty.* She was not pretty now. He could see a spiderweb of faint thin lines across her back where someone had whipped her. ". . . she is beautiful, so . . . so beautiful."

Ramsay smiled his wet smile. "Does she make your cock hard, Reek? Is it straining against your laces? Would you like to fuck her first?" He laughed. "The Prince of Winterfell should have that right, as all lords did in days of old. The first night. But you're no lord, are you? Only Reek. Not even a man, truth be told." He took another gulp of wine, then threw the cup across the room to shatter off a wall. Red rivers ran down across the stone. "Lady Arya. Get on the bed. Yes, against the pillows, that's a good wife. Now spread your legs. Let us see your cunt."

The girl obeyed, wordless. Theon took a step back toward the door. Lord Ramsay sat beside his bride, slid his hand along her inner thigh, then jammed two fingers up inside her. The girl let out a gasp of pain. "You're dry as an old bone." Ramsay pulled his hand free and slapped her face. "I was told that you'd know how to please a man. Was that a lie?"

"N-no, my lord. I was t-trained."

Ramsay rose, the firelight shining on his face. "Reek, get over here. Get her ready for me."

For a moment he did not understand. "I . . . do you mean . . . m'lord, I have no . . . I . . ."

"With your mouth," Lord Ramsay said. "And be quick about it. If she's not wet by the time I'm done disrobing, I will cut off that tongue of yours and nail it to the wall."

Somewhere in the godswood, a raven screamed. The dagger was still in his hand.

He sheathed it.

Reek, my name is Reek, it rhymes with weak.

Reek bent to his task.

THE WATCHER

"Let us look upon this head," his prince commanded.

Areo Hotah ran his hand along the smooth shaft of his longaxe, his ash-and-iron wife, all the while watching. He watched the white knight, Ser Balon Swann, and the others who had come with him. He watched the Sand Snakes, each at a different table. He watched the lords and ladies, the serving men, the old blind seneschal, and the young maester Myles, with his silky beard and servile smile. Standing half in light and half in shadow, he saw all of them. *Serve. Protect. Obey.* That was his task.

All the rest had eyes only for the chest. It was carved of ebony, with silver clasps and hinges. A fine-looking box, no doubt, but many of those assembled here in the Old Palace of Sunspear might soon be dead, depending on what was in that chest.

His slippers whispering against the floor, Maester Caleotte crossed the hall to Ser Balon Swann. The round little man looked splendid in his new robes, with their broad bands of dun and butternut and narrow stripes of red. Bowing, he took the chest from the hands of the white knight and carried it to the dais, where Doran Martell sat in his rolling chair between his daughter Arianne and his dead brother's beloved paramour, Ellaria. A hundred scented candles perfumed the air. Gemstones glittered on the fingers of the lords and the girdles and hairnets of the ladies. Areo Hotah had polished his shirt of copper scales mirror-bright so he would blaze in the candle-light as well.

A hush had fallen across the hall. *Dorne holds its breath.* Maester Caleotte set the box on the floor beside Prince Doran's chair. The maester's fingers, normally so sure and deft, turned clumsy as he worked the latch and opened the lid, to reveal the skull within. Hotah heard someone clear his throat. One of the Fowler twins whispered something to the other. Ellaria Sand had closed her eyes and was murmuring a prayer.

Ser Balon Swann was taut as a drawn bow, the captain of guards observed. This new white knight was not so tall nor comely as the old one, but he was bigger across the chest, burlier, his arms thick with muscle. His snowy cloak was clasped at the throat by two swans on a silver brooch. One was ivory, the other onyx, and it seemed to Areo Hotah as if the two of them were fighting. The man who wore them looked a fighter too. *This one will not die so easy as the other. He will not charge into my axe the way Ser Arys did. He will stand behind his shield and make me come at him.* If it came to that, Hotah would be ready. His longaxe was sharp enough to shave with.

He allowed himself a brief glance at the chest. The skull rested on a bed of black felt, grinning. All skulls grinned, but this one seemed happier than most. *And bigger.* The captain of guards had never seen a larger skull. Its brow shelf was thick and heavy, its jaw massive. The bone shone in the candlelight, white as Ser Balon's cloak. "Place it on the pedestal," the prince commanded. He had tears glistening in his eyes.

The pedestal was a column of black marble three feet taller than Maester Caleotte. The fat little maester hopped up on his toes but still could not quite reach. Areo Hotah was about to go and help him, but Obara Sand moved first. Even without her whip and shield, she had an angry mannish look to her. In place of a gown, she wore men's breeches and a calf-length linen tunic, cinched at the waist with a belt of copper suns. Her brown hair was tied back in a knot. Snatching the skull from the maester's soft pink hands, she placed it up atop the marble column.

"The Mountain rides no more," the prince said, gravely.

"Was his dying long and hard, Ser Balon?" asked Tyene Sand, in the tone a maiden might use to ask if her gown was pretty.

"He screamed for days, my lady," the white knight replied, though it was plain that it pleased him little to say so. "We could hear him all over the Red Keep."

"Does that trouble you, ser?" asked the Lady Nym. She wore a gown of yellow silk so sheer and fine that the candles shone right through it to reveal the spun gold and jewels beneath. So immodest was her garb that the white knight seemed uncomfortable looking at her, but Hotah approved. Nymeria was least dangerous when nearly naked. Elsewise she was sure to have a dozen blades concealed about her person. "Ser Gregor was a bloody brute, all men agree. If ever a man deserved to suffer, it was him."

"That is as it may be, my lady," said Balon Swann, "but Ser Gregor was a knight, and a knight should die with sword in hand. Poison is a foul and filthy way to kill."

Lady Tyene smiled at that. Her gown was cream and green, with long lace sleeves, so modest and so innocent that any man who looked at her might think her the most chaste of maids. Areo Hotah knew better. Her soft, pale hands were as deadly as Obara's callused ones, if not more so. He watched her carefully, alert to every little flutter of her fingers.

Prince Doran frowned. "That is so, Ser Balon, but the Lady Nym is right. If ever a man deserved to die screaming, it was Gregor Clegane. He butchered my good sister, smashed her babe's head against a wall. I only pray that now he is burning in some hell, and that Elia and her children are at peace. This is the justice that Dorne has hungered for. I am glad that I lived long enough to taste it. At long last the Lannisters have proved the truth of their boast and paid this old blood debt."

The prince left it to Ricasso, his blind seneschal, to rise and propose the toast. "Lords and ladies, let us all now drink to Tommen, the First of His Name, King of the Andals, the Rhoynar, and the First Men, and Lord of the Seven Kingdoms."

Serving men had begun to move amongst the guests as the seneschal was speaking, filling cups from the flagons that they bore. The wine was Dornish strongwine, dark as blood and sweet as vengeance. The captain did not drink of it. He never drank at feasts. Nor did the prince himself partake. He had his own wine, prepared by Maester Myles and well laced with poppy juice to ease the agony in his swollen joints.

The white knight did drink, as was only courteous. His companions likewise. So did the Princess Arianne, Lady Jordayne, the Lord of Godsgrace, the Knight of Lemonwood, the Lady of Ghost Hill . . . even Ellaria Sand, Prince Oberyn's beloved paramour, who had been with him in King's Landing when he died. Hotah paid more note to those who did not drink: Ser Daemon Sand, Lord Tremond Gargalen, the Fowler twins, Dagos Manwoody, the Ullers of the Hellholt, the Wyls of the Boneway. *If there is trouble, it could start with one of them.* Dorne was an angry and divided land, and Prince Doran's hold on it was not as firm as it might be. Many of his own lords thought him weak and would have welcomed open war with the Lannisters and the boy king on the Iron Throne.

Chief amongst those were the Sand Snakes, the bastard daughters of the prince's late brother Oberyn, the Red Viper, three of whom were at the feast. Doran Martell was the wisest of princes, and it was not the place of his captain of guards to question his decisions, but Areo Hotah did wonder why he had chosen to release the ladies Obara, Nymeria, and Tyene from their lonely cells in the Spear Tower.

Tyene declined Ricasso's toast with a murmur and Lady Nym with a flick of a hand. Obara let them fill her cup to the brim, then upended it to spill the red wine on the floor. When a serving girl knelt to wipe up the spilled wine, Obara left the hall. After a moment Princess Arianne excused herself and went after her. *Obara would never turn her rage on the little princess,* Hotah knew. *They are cousins, and she loves her well.*

The feast continued late into the night, presided over by the grinning skull on its pillar of black marble. Seven courses were served, in honor of the seven gods and the seven brothers of the Kingsguard. The soup was made with eggs and lemons, the long green peppers stuffed with cheese and onions. There were lamprey pies, capons glazed with honey, a whiskerfish from the bottom of the Greenblood that was so big it took four serving men to carry it to table. After that came a savory snake stew, chunks of seven different sorts of snake slow-simmered with dragon peppers and blood oranges and a dash of venom to give it a good bite. The stew was fiery hot, Hotah knew, though he tasted none of it. Sherbet followed, to cool the tongue. For the sweet, each guest was served a skull of spun sugar. When the crust was broken, they found sweet custard inside and bits of plum and cherry.

Princess Arianne returned in time for the stuffed peppers. *My little princess,* Hotah thought, but Arianne was a woman now. The scarlet silks she wore left no doubt of that. Of late she had changed in other ways as well. Her plot to crown Myrcella had been betrayed and smashed, her white knight had perished bloodily at Hotah's hand, and she herself had been confined to the Spear Tower, condemned to solitude and silence. All of that had chastened her. There was something else as well, though, some secret her father had confided in her before releasing her from her confinement. What that was, the captain did not know.

The prince had placed his daughter between himself and the white knight, a place of high honor. Arianne smiled as she slipped into her seat again, and murmured something in Ser Balon's ear. The knight did not choose to respond. He ate little, Hotah observed: a spoon of soup, a bite of the pepper, the leg off a capon, some fish. He shunned the lamprey pie and tried only one small spoonful of the stew. Even that made his brow break out in sweat. Hotah could sympathize. When first he came to Dorne, the fiery food would tie his bowels in knots and burn his tongue. That was years ago, however; now his hair was white, and he could eat anything a Dornishman could eat.

When the spun-sugar skulls were served, Ser Balon's mouth grew tight, and he gave the prince a lingering look to see if he was being mocked. Doran Martell took no notice, but his daughter did. "It is the cook's little jape, Ser Balon," said Arianne. "Even death is not sacred to a Dornishmen. You won't be cross with us, I pray?" She brushed the back of the white knight's hand with her fingers. "I hope you have enjoyed your time in Dorne."

"Everyone has been most hospitable, my lady."

Arianne touched the pin that clasped his cloak, with its quarreling swans. "I have always been fond of swans. No other bird is half so beautiful, this side of the Summer Isles."

"Your peacocks might dispute that," said Ser Balon.

"They might," said Arianne, "but peacocks are vain, proud creatures, strutting about in all those gaudy colors. Give me a swan serene in white or beautiful in black."

Ser Balon gave a nod and sipped his wine. *This one is not so easily seduced as was his Sworn Brother,* Hotah thought. *Ser Arys was a boy, despite his years. This one is a man, and wary.* The captain had only to look at him to see that the white knight was ill at ease. *This place is strange to him, and little to his liking.* Hotah could understand that. Dorne had seemed a queer place to him as well when first he came here with his own princess, many years ago. The bearded priests had drilled him on the Common Speech of Westeros before they sent him forth, but the Dornishmen all spoke too quickly for him to understand. Dornish women were lewd, Dornish wine was sour, and Dornish food was full of queer hot spices. And the Dornish sun was hotter than the pale, wan sun of Norvos, glaring down from a blue sky day after day.

Ser Balon's journey had been shorter but troubling in its own way, the captain knew. Three knights, eight squires, twenty men-at-arms, and sundry grooms and servants had accompanied him from King's Landing, but once they crossed the mountains into Dorne their progress had been slowed by a round of feasts, hunts, and celebrations at every castle that they chanced to pass. And now that they had reached Sunspear, neither Princess Myrcella nor Ser Arys Oakheart was on hand to greet them. *The white knight knows that something is amiss,* Hotah could tell, *but it is more than that.* Perhaps the presence of the Sand Snakes unnerved him. If so, Obara's return to the hall must have been vinegar in the wound. She slipped back into her place without a word, and sat there sullen and scowling, neither smiling nor speaking.

Midnight was close at hand when Prince Doran turned to the white knight and said, "Ser Balon, I have read the letter that you brought me from our gracious queen. Might I assume that you are familiar with its contents, ser?"

Hotah saw the knight tense. "I am, my lord. Her Grace informed me that I might be called upon to escort her daughter back to King's Landing. King Tommen has been pining for his sister and would like Princess Myrcella to return to court for a short visit."

Princess Arianne made a sad face. "Oh, but we have all grown so fond of Myrcella, ser. She and my brother Trystane have become inseparable."

"Prince Trystane would be welcome in King's Landing as well," said Balon Swann. "King Tommen would wish to meet him, I am sure. His Grace has so few companions near his own age."

"The bonds formed in boyhood can last a man for life," said Prince Doran. "When Trystane and Myrcella wed, he and Tommen will be as brothers. Queen Cersei has the right of it. The boys should meet, become friends. Dorne will miss him, to be sure, but it is past time Trystane saw something of the world beyond the walls of Sunspear."

"I know King's Landing will welcome him most warmly."

Why is he sweating now? the captain wondered, watching. *The hall is cool enough, and he never touched the stew.*

"As for the other matter that Queen Cersei raises," Prince Doran was saying, "it is true, Dorne's seat upon the small council has been vacant since my brother's death, and it is past time that it was filled again. I am flattered that Her Grace feels my counsel might be of use to her, though I wonder if I have the strength for such a journey. Perhaps if we went by sea?"

"By ship?" Ser Balon seemed taken aback. "That ... would that be safe, my prince? Autumn is a bad season for storms, or so I've heard, and ... the pirates in the Stepstones, they ..."

"The pirates. To be sure. You may be right, ser. Safer to return the way you came." Prince Doran smiled pleasantly. "Let us talk again on the morrow. When we reach the Water Gardens, we can tell Myrcella. I know how excited she will be. She misses her brother too, I do not doubt."

"I am eager to see her once again," said Ser Balon. "And to visit your Water Gardens. I've heard they are very beautiful."

"Beautiful and peaceful," the prince said. "Cool breezes, sparkling water, and the laughter of children. The Water Gardens are my favorite place in this world, ser. One of my ancestors had them built to please his Targaryen bride and free her from the dust and heat of Sunspear. *Daenerys* was her name. She was sister to King Daeron the Good, and it was her marriage that made Dorne part of the Seven Kingdoms. The whole realm knew that the girl loved Daeron's bastard brother Daemon Blackfyre, and was loved by him in turn, but the king was wise enough to see that the good of thousands must come before the desires of two, even if those two were dear to him. It was Daenerys who filled the gardens with laughing children. Her own children at the start, but later the sons and daughters of lords and landed knights were brought in to be companions to the boys and girls of princely blood. And one summer's day when it was scorching hot, she took pity on the children of her grooms and cooks and serving men and invited them to use the pools and fountains too, a tradition that has endured till this day." The prince grasped the wheels of his chair and pushed himself from the table. "But now you must excuse me, ser. All this talk has wearied me, and we should leave at break of day. Obara, would you be so kind as to help me to my bed? Nymeria, Tyene, come as well, and bid your old uncle a fond good night."

So it fell to Obara Sand to roll the prince's chair from Sunspear's feast hall and down a long gallery to his solar. Areo Hotah followed with her sisters, along with Princess Arianne and Ellaria Sand. Maester Caleotte hurried behind on slippered feet, cradling the Mountain's skull as if it were a child.

"You cannot seriously intend to send Trystane and Myrcella to King's Landing," Obara said as she was pushing. Her strides were long and angry, much too fast, and the chair's big wooden wheels *clack*ed noisily across rough-cut stone floors. "Do that, and we will never see the girl again, and your son will spend his life a hostage to the Iron Throne."

"Do you take me for a fool, Obara?" The prince sighed. "There is much you do not know. Things best not discussed here, where anyone can hear. If you hold your tongue, I may enlighten you." He winced. "*Slower,* for the love you bear me. That last jolt sent a knife right through my knee."

Obara slowed her pace by half. "What will you do, then?"

Her sister Tyene gave answer. "What he always does," she purred. "Delay, obscure, prevaricate. Oh, no one does that half so well as our brave uncle."

"You do him wrong," said Princess Arianne.

"Be quiet, all of you," the prince commanded.

Not until the doors of his solar were safely closed behind them did he wheel his chair about to face the women. Even that effort left him breathless, and the Myrish blanket that covered his legs caught between two spokes as he rolled, so he had to clutch it to keep it from being torn away. Beneath the coverlet, his legs were pale, soft, ghastly. Both of his knees were red and swollen, and his toes were almost purple, twice the size they should have been. Areo Hotah had seen them a thousand times and still found them hard to look upon.

Princess Arianne came forward. "Let me help you, Father."

The prince pulled the blanket free. "I can still master mine own blanket. That much at least." It was little enough. His legs had been useless for three years, but there was still some strength in his hands and shoulders.

"Shall I fetch my prince a thimble cup of milk of the poppy?" Maester Caleotte asked.

"I would need a bucket, with this pain. Thank you, but no. I want my wits about me. I'll have no more need of you tonight."

"Very good, my prince." Maester Caleotte bowed, Ser Gregor's head still clutched in his soft pink hands.

"I'll take that." Obara Sand plucked the skull from him and held it at arm's length. "What did the Mountain look like? How do we know that this is him? They could have dipped the head in tar. Why strip it to the bone?"

"Tar would have ruined the box," suggested Lady Nym, as Maester Caleotte scurried off. "No one *saw* the Mountain die, and no one saw his head removed. That troubles me, I confess, but what could the bitch queen hope to accomplish by deceiving us? If Gregor Clegane is alive, soon or late the truth will out. The man was eight feet tall, there is not another like him in all of Westeros. If any such appears again, Cersei Lannister will be exposed as a liar before all the Seven

Kingdoms. She would be an utter fool to risk that. What could she hope to gain?"

"The skull is large enough, no doubt," said the prince. "And we know that Oberyn wounded Gregor grievously. Every report we have had since claims that Clegane died slowly, in great pain."

"Just as Father intended," said Tyene. "Sisters, truly, I know the poison Father used. If his spear so much as broke the Mountain's skin, Clegane is dead, I do not care how big he was. Doubt your little sister if you like, but never doubt our sire."

Obara bristled. "I never did and never shall." She gave the skull a mocking kiss. "This is a start, I'll grant."

"A *start*?" said Ellaria Sand, incredulous. "Gods forbid. I would it were a finish. Tywin Lannister is dead. So are Robert Baratheon, Amory Lorch, and now Gregor Clegane, all those who had a hand in murdering Elia and her children. Even Joffrey, who was not yet born when Elia died. I saw the boy perish with mine own eyes, clawing at his throat as he tried to draw a breath. Who else is there to kill? Do Myrcella and Tommen need to die so the shades of Rhaenys and Aegon can be at rest? Where does it end?"

"It ends in blood, as it began," said Lady Nym. "It ends when Casterly Rock is cracked open, so the sun can shine on the maggots and the worms within. It ends with the utter ruin of Tywin Lannister and all his works."

"The man died at the hand of his own son," Ellaria snapped back. "What more could you wish?"

"I could wish that he died at *my* hand." Lady Nym settled in a chair, her long black braid falling across one shoulder to her lap. She had her father's widow's peak. Beneath it her eyes were large and lustrous. Her wine-red lips curled in a silken smile. "If he had, his dying would not have been so easy."

"Ser Gregor does look lonely," said Tyene, in her sweet septa's voice. "He would like some company, I'm certain."

Ellaria's cheeks were wet with tears, her dark eyes shining. *Even weeping, she has a strength in her,* the captain thought.

"Oberyn wanted vengeance for Elia. Now the three of you want vengeance for him. I have four daughters, I remind you. Your sisters.

My Elia is fourteen, almost a woman. Obella is twelve, on the brink of maidenhood. They worship you, as Dorea and Loreza worship them. If you should die, must El and Obella seek vengeance for you, then Dorea and Loree for them? Is that how it goes, round and round forever? I ask again, *where does it end*?" Ellaria Sand laid her hand on the Mountain's head. "I saw your father die. Here is his killer. Can I take a skull to bed with me, to give me comfort in the night? Will it make me laugh, write me songs, care for me when I am old and sick?"

"What would you have us do, my lady?" asked the Lady Nym. "Shall we lay down our spears and smile, and forget all the wrongs that have been done to us?"

"War will come, whether we wish it or not," said Obara. "A boy king sits the Iron Throne. Lord Stannis holds the Wall and is gathering northmen to his cause. The two queens are squabbling over Tommen like bitches with a juicy bone. The ironmen have taken the Shields and are raiding up the Mander, deep into the heart of the Reach, which means Highgarden will be preoccupied as well. Our enemies are in disarray. The time is ripe."

"Ripe for what? To make more skulls?" Ellaria Sand turned to the prince. "They will not see. I can hear no more of this."

"Go back to your girls, Ellaria," the prince told her. "I swear to you, no harm will come to them."

"My prince." Ellaria kissed him on the brow and took her leave. Areo Hotah was sad to see her go. *She is a good woman.*

When she had gone, Lady Nym said, "I know she loved our father well, but it is plain she never understood him."

The prince gave her a curious look. "She understood more than you ever will, Nymeria. And she made your father happy. In the end a gentle heart may be worth more than pride or valor. Be that as it may, there are things Ellaria does not know and should not know. This war has already begun."

Obara laughed. "Aye, our sweet Arianne has seen to that."

The princess flushed, and Hotah saw a spasm of anger pass across her father's face. "What she did, she did as much for you as for herself. I would not be so quick to mock."

"That was praise," Obara Sand insisted. "Procrastinate, obscure, prevaricate, dissemble, and delay all you like, Uncle, Ser Balon must still come face-to-face with Myrcella at the Water Gardens, and when he does he's like to see she's short an ear. And when the girl tells him how your captain cut Arys Oakheart from neck to groin with that steel wife of his, well . . ."

"No." Princess Arianne unfolded from the cushion where she sat and put a hand on Hotah's arm. "That wasn't how it happened, Cousin. Ser Arys was slain by Gerold Dayne."

The Sand Snakes looked at one another. "Darkstar?"

"Darkstar did it," his little princess said. "He tried to kill Princess Myrcella too. As she will tell Ser Balon."

Nym smiled. "That part at least is true."

"It is all true," said the prince, with a wince of pain. *Is it his gout that hurts him, or the lie?* "And now Ser Gerold has fled back to High Hermitage, beyond our reach."

"Darkstar," Tyene murmured, with a giggle. "Why not? It is all his doing. But will Ser Balon believe it?"

"He will if he hears it from Myrcella," Arianne insisted.

Obara snorted in disbelief. "She may lie today and lie tomorrow, but soon or late she'll tell the truth. If Ser Balon is allowed to carry tales back to King's Landing, drums will sound and blood will flow. He should not be allowed to leave."

"We could kill him, to be sure," said Tyene, "but then we would need to kill the rest of his party too, even those sweet young squires. That would be . . . oh, so *messy.*"

Prince Doran shut his eyes and opened them again. Hotah could see his leg trembling underneath the blanket. "If you were not my brother's daughters, I would send the three of you back to your cells and keep you there until your bones were grey. Instead I mean to take you with us to the Water Gardens. There are lessons there if you have the wit to see them."

"Lessons?" said Obara. "All I've seen are naked children."

"Aye," the prince said. "I told the story to Ser Balon, but not all of it. As the children splashed in the pools, Daenerys watched from amongst the orange trees, and a realization came to her. She could not tell the highborn from the low. Naked, they were only children.

All innocent, all vulnerable, all deserving of long life, love, protection. *'There is your realm,'* she told her son and heir, *'remember them, in everything you do.'* My own mother said those same words to me when I was old enough to leave the pools. It is an easy thing for a prince to call the spears, but in the end the children pay the price. For their sake, the wise prince will wage no war without good cause, nor any war he cannot hope to win.

"I am not blind, nor deaf. I know that you all believe me weak, frightened, feeble. Your father knew me better. Oberyn was ever the viper. Deadly, dangerous, unpredictable. No man dared tread on him. I was the grass. Pleasant, complaisant, sweet-smelling, swaying with every breeze. Who fears to walk upon the grass? But it is the grass that hides the viper from his enemies and shelters him until he strikes. Your father and I worked more closely than you know . . . but now he is gone. The question is, can I trust his daughters to serve me in his place?"

Hotah studied each of them in turn. Obara, rusted nails and boiled leather, with her angry, close-set eyes and rat-brown hair. Nymeria, languid, elegant, olive-skinned, her long black braid bound up in red-gold wire. Tyene, blue-eyed and blond, a child-woman with her soft hands and little giggles.

Tyene answered for the three of them. "It is doing nothing that is hard, Uncle. Set a task for us, any task, and you shall find us as leal and obedient as any prince could hope for."

"That is good to hear," the prince said, "but words are wind. You are my brother's daughters and I love you, but I have learned I cannot trust you. I want your oath. Will you swear to serve me, to do as I command?"

"If we must," said Lady Nym.

"Then swear it now, upon your father's grave."

Obara's face darkened. "If you were not my uncle—"

"I *am* your uncle. And your prince. Swear, or go."

"I swear," said Tyene. "On my father's grave."

"I swear," said Lady Nym. "By Oberyn Martell, the Red Viper of Dorne, and a better man than you."

"Aye," said Obara. "Me as well. By Father. I swear."

Some of the tension went out of the prince. Hotah saw him sag back into his chair. He held out his hand, and Princess Arianne moved to his side to hold it. "Tell them, Father."

Prince Doran took a jagged breath. "Dorne still has friends at court. Friends who tell us things we were not meant to know. This invitation Cersei sent us is a ruse. Trystane is never meant to reach King's Landing. On the road back, somewhere in the kingswood, Ser Balon's party will be attacked by outlaws, and my son will die. I am asked to court only so that I may witness this attack with my own eyes and thereby absolve the queen of any blame. Oh, and these outlaws? They will be shouting, 'Halfman, Halfman,' as they attack. Ser Balon may even catch a quick glimpse of the Imp, though no one else will."

Areo Hotah would not have believed it possible to shock the Sand Snakes. He would have been wrong.

"Seven save us," whispered Tyene. "*Trystane?* Why?"

"The woman must be mad," Obara said. "He's just a boy."

"This is monstrous," said Lady Nym. "I would not have believed it, not of a Kingsguard knight."

"They are sworn to obey, just as my captain is," the prince said. "I had my doubts as well, but you all saw how Ser Balon balked when I suggested that we go by sea. A ship would have disturbed all the queen's arrangements."

Obara's face was flushed. "Give me back my spear, Uncle. Cersei sent us a head. We should send her back a bag of them."

Prince Doran raised a hand. His knuckles were as dark as cherries and near as big. "Ser Balon is a guest beneath my roof. He has eaten of my bread and salt. I will not do him harm. No. We will travel to the Water Gardens, where he will hear Myrcella's story and send a raven to his queen. The girl will ask him to hunt down the man who hurt her. If he is the man I judge, Swann will not be able to refuse. Obara, you will lead him to High Hermitage to beard Darkstar in his den. The time is not yet come for Dorne to openly defy the Iron Throne, so we must needs return Myrcella to her mother, but I will not be accompanying her. That task will be yours, Nymeria. The Lannisters will not like it, no more than they liked it when I sent them Oberyn, but they dare not refuse. We need a voice in council, an ear at court. Be careful, though. King's Landing is a pit of snakes."

Lady Nym smiled. "Why, Uncle, I love snakes."

"And what of me?" asked Tyene.

"Your mother was a septa. Oberyn once told me that she read to you in the cradle from the *Seven-Pointed Star.* I want you in King's Landing too, but on the other hill. The Swords and the Stars have been re-formed, and this new High Septon is not the puppet that the others were. Try and get close to him."

"Why not? White suits my coloring. I look so . . . pure."

"Good," the prince said, "good." He hesitated. "If . . . if certain things should come to pass, I will send word to each of you. Things can change quickly in the game of thrones."

"I know you will not fail us, cousins." Arianne went to each of them in turn, took their hands, kissed them lightly on the lips. "Obara, so fierce. Nymeria, my sister. Tyene, sweetling. I love you all. The sun of Dorne goes with you."

"*Unbowed, unbent, unbroken,*" the Sand Snakes said, together.

Princess Arianne lingered when her cousins had departed. Areo Hotah remained as well, as was his place.

"They are their father's daughters," the prince said.

The little princess smiled. "Three Oberyns, with teats."

Prince Doran laughed. It had been so long since Hotah last heard him laugh, he had almost forgotten what it sounded like.

"I still say it should be me who goes to King's Landing, not Lady Nym," Arianne said.

"It is too dangerous. You are my heir, the future of Dorne. Your place is by my side. Soon enough, you'll have another task."

"That last part, about the message. Have you had tidings?"

Prince Doran shared his secret smile with her. "From Lys. A great fleet has put in there to take on water. Volantene ships chiefly, carrying an army. No word as to who they are, or where they might be bound. There was talk of elephants."

"No dragons?"

"Elephants. Easy enough to hide a young dragon in a big cog's hold, though. Daenerys is most vulnerable at sea. If I were her, I would keep myself and my intentions hidden as long as I could, so I might take King's Landing unawares."

"Do you think that Quentyn will be with them?"

"He could be. Or not. We will know by where they land if Westeros is indeed their destination. Quentyn will bring her up the Greenblood if he can. But it does no good to speak of it. Kiss me. We leave for the Water Gardens at first light."

We may depart by midday, then, Hotah thought.

Later, when Arianne had gone, he put down his longaxe and lifted Prince Doran into his bed. "Until the Mountain crushed my brother's skull, no Dornishmen had died in this War of the Five Kings," the prince murmured softly, as Hotah pulled a blanket over him. "Tell me, Captain, is that my shame or my glory?"

"That is not for me to say, my prince." *Serve. Protect. Obey. Simple vows for simple men.* That was all he knew.

JON

Val waited by the gate in the predawn cold, wrapped up in a bearskin cloak so large it might well have fit Sam. Beside her was a garron, saddled and bridled, a shaggy grey with one white eye. Mully and Dolorous Edd stood with her, a pair of unlikely guards. Their breath frosted in the cold black air.

"You gave her a blind horse?" Jon said, incredulous.

"He's only half-blind, m'lord," offered Mully. "Elsewise he's sound enough." He patted the garron on the neck.

"The horse may be half-blind, but I am not," said Val. "I know where I must go."

"My lady, you do not have to do this. The risk—"

"—is mine, Lord Snow. And I am no southron lady but a woman of the free folk. I know the forest better than all your black-cloaked rangers. It holds no ghosts for me."

I hope not. Jon was counting on that, trusting that Val could succeed where Black Jack Bulwer and his companions had failed. She need fear no harm from the free folk, he hoped . . . but both of them knew too well that wildlings were not the only ones waiting in the woods. "You have sufficient food?"

"Hard bread, hard cheese, oat cakes, salt cod, salt beef, salt mutton, and a skin of sweet wine to rinse all that salt out of my mouth. I will not die of hunger."

"Then it's time you were away."

"You have my word, Lord Snow. I will return, with Tormund or without him." Val glanced at the sky. The moon was but half-full. "Look for me on the first day of the full moon."

"I will." *Do not fail me,* he thought, *or Stannis will have my head.* "Do I have your word that you will keep our princess closely?" the king had said, and Jon had promised that he would. *Val is no princess, though. I told him that half a hundred times.* It was a feeble sort of evasion, a sad rag wrapped around his wounded word. His father would never have approved. *I am the sword that guards the realm of men,* Jon reminded himself, *and in the end, that must be worth more than one man's honor.*

The road beneath the Wall was as dark and cold as the belly of an ice dragon and as twisty as a serpent. Dolorous Edd led them through with a torch in hand. Mully had the keys for the three gates, where bars of black iron as thick as a man's arm closed off the passage. Spearmen at each gate knuckled their foreheads at Jon Snow but stared openly at Val and her garron.

When they emerged north of the Wall, through a thick door made of freshly hewn green wood, the wildling princess paused for a moment to gaze out across the snow-covered field where King Stannis had won his battle. Beyond, the haunted forest waited, dark and silent. The light of the half-moon turned Val's honey-blonde hair a pale silver and left her cheeks as white as snow. She took a deep breath. "The air tastes sweet."

"My tongue is too numb to tell. All I can taste is cold."

"Cold?" Val laughed lightly. "No. When it is cold it will hurt to breathe. When the Others come . . ."

The thought was a disquieting one. Six of the rangers Jon had sent out were still missing. *It is too soon. They may yet be back.* But another part of him insisted, *They are dead, every man of them. You sent them out to die, and you are doing the same to Val.* "Tell Tormund what I've said."

"He may not heed your words, but he will hear them." Val kissed him lightly on the cheek. "You have my thanks, Lord Snow. For the half-blind horse, the salt cod, the free air. For hope."

Their breath mingled, a white mist in the air. Jon Snow drew back and said, "The only thanks I want is—"

"—Tormund Giantsbane. Aye." Val pulled up the hood of her bearskin. The brown pelt was well salted with grey. "Before I go, one question. Did you kill Jarl, my lord?"

"The Wall killed Jarl."

"So I'd heard. But I had to be sure."

"You have my word. I did not kill him." *Though I might have if things had gone otherwise.*

"This is farewell, then," she said, almost playfully.

Jon Snow was in no mood for it. *It is too cold and dark to play, and the hour is too late.* "Only for a time. You will return. For the boy, if for no other reason."

"Craster's son?" Val shrugged. "He is no kin to me."

"I have heard you singing to him."

"I was singing to myself. Am I to blame if he listens?" A faint smile brushed her lips. "It makes him laugh. Oh, very well. He is a sweet little monster."

"Monster?"

"His milk name. I had to call him something. See that he stays safe and warm. For his mother's sake, and mine. And keep him away from the red woman. She knows who he is. She sees things in her fires."

Arya, he thought, hoping it was so. "Ashes and cinders."

"Kings and dragons."

Dragons again. For a moment Jon could almost see them too, coiling in the night, their dark wings outlined against a sea of flame. "If she knew, she would have taken the boy away from us. Dalla's boy, not your monster. A word in the king's ear would have been the end of it." *And of me. Stannis would have taken it for treason.* "Why let it happen if she knew?"

"Because it suited her. Fire is a fickle thing. No one knows which way a flame will go." Val put a foot into a stirrup, swung her leg over her horse's back, and looked down from the saddle. "Do you remember what my sister told you?"

"Yes." *A sword without a hilt, with no safe way to hold it.* But

Melisandre had the right of it. Even a sword without a hilt is better than an empty hand when foes are all around you.

"Good." Val wheeled the garron toward the north. "The first night of the full moon, then." Jon watched her ride away wondering if he would ever see her face again. *I am no southron lady,* he could hear her say, *but a woman of the free folk.*

"I don't care what she says," muttered Dolorous Edd, as Val vanished behind a stand of soldier pines. "The air *is* so cold it hurts to breathe. I would stop, but that would hurt worse." He rubbed his hands together. "This is going to end badly."

"You say that of everything."

"Aye, m'lord. Usually I'm right."

Mully cleared his throat. "M'lord? The wildling princess, letting her go, the men may say—"

"—that I am half a wildling myself, a turncloak who means to sell the realm to our raiders, cannibals, and giants." Jon did not need to stare into a fire to know what was being said of him. The worst part was, they were not wrong, not wholly. "Words are wind, and the wind is always blowing at the Wall. Come."

It was still dark when Jon returned to his chambers behind the armory. Ghost was not yet back, he saw. *Still hunting.* The big white direwolf was gone more oft than not of late, ranging farther and farther in search of prey. Between the men of the Watch and the wildlings down in Mole's Town, the hills and fields near Castle Black had been hunted clean, and there had been little enough game to begin with. *Winter is coming,* Jon reflected. *And soon, too soon.* He wondered if they would ever see a spring.

Dolorous Edd made the trek to the kitchens and soon was back with a tankard of brown ale and a covered platter. Under the lid Jon discovered three duck's eggs fried in drippings, a strip of bacon, two sausages, a blood pudding, and half a loaf of bread still warm from the oven. He ate the bread and half an egg. He would have eaten the bacon too, but the raven made off with it before he had the chance. "Thief," Jon said, as the bird flapped up to the lintel above the door to devour its prize.

"*Thief,*" the raven agreed.

Jon tried a bite of sausage. He was washing the taste from his mouth with a sip of ale when Edd returned to tell him Bowen Marsh was without. "Othell's with him, and Septon Cellador."

That was quick. He wondered who was telling tales and if there was more than one. "Send them in."

"Aye, m'lord. You'll want to watch your sausages with this lot, though. They have a hungry look about them."

Hungry was not the word Jon would have used. Septon Cellador appeared confused and groggy and in dire need of some scales from the dragon that had flamed him, whilst First Builder Othell Yarwyck looked as if he had swallowed something he could not quite digest. Bowen Marsh was angry. Jon could see it in his eyes, the tightness around his mouth, the flush to those round cheeks. *That red is not from cold.* "Please sit," he said. "May I offer you food or drink?"

"We broke our fast in the commons," said Marsh.

"I could do with more." Yarwyck eased himself down onto a chair. "Good of you to offer."

"Perhaps some wine?" said Septon Cellador.

"*Corn*," screamed the raven from the lintel. "*Corn, corn.*"

"Wine for the septon and a plate for our First Builder," Jon told Dolorous Edd. "Nothing for the bird." He turned back to his visitors. "You're here about Val."

"And other matters," said Bowen Marsh. "The men have concerns, my lord."

And who is it who appointed you to speak for them? "As do I. Othell, how goes the work at the Nightfort? I have had a letter from Ser Axell Florent, who styles himself the Queen's Hand. He tells me that Queen Selyse is not pleased with her quarters at Eastwatch-by-the-Sea and wishes to move into her husband's new seat at once. Will that be possible?"

Yarwyck shrugged. "We've got most of the keep restored and put a roof back on the kitchens. She'd need food and furnishings and firewood, mind you, but it might serve. Not so many comforts as Eastwatch, to be sure. And a long way from the ships, should Her Grace wish to leave us, but ... aye, she could live there, though it will be years before the place looks a proper castle. Sooner if I had more builders."

"I could offer you a giant."

That gave Othell a start. "The monster in the yard?"

"His name is Wun Weg Wun Dar Wun, Leathers tells me. A lot to wrap a tongue around, I know. Leathers calls him Wun Wun, and that seems to serve." Wun Wun was very little like the giants in Old Nan's tales, those huge savage creatures who mixed blood into their morning porridge and devoured whole bulls, hair and hide and horns. This giant ate no meat at all, though he was a holy terror when served a basket of roots, crunching onions and turnips and even raw hard neeps between his big square teeth. "He's a willing worker, though getting him to understand what you want is not always easy. He speaks the Old Tongue after a fashion, but nothing of the Common. Tireless, though, and his strength is prodigious. He could do the work of a dozen men."

"I . . . my lord, the men would never . . . giants eat human flesh, I think . . . no, my lord, I thank you, but I do not have the men to watch over such a creature, he . . ."

Jon Snow was unsurprised. "As you wish. We will keep the giant here." Truth be told, he would have been loath to part with Wun Wun. *You know nothing, Jon Snow,* Ygritte might say, but Jon spoke with the giant whenever he could, through Leathers or one of the free folk they had brought back from the grove, and was learning much and more about his people and their history. He only wished that Sam were here to write the stories down.

That was not to say that he was blind to the danger Wun Wun represented. The giant would lash out violently when threatened, and those huge hands were strong enough to rip a man apart. He reminded Jon of Hodor. *Hodor twice as big, twice as strong, and half as clever. There's a thought to sober even Septon Cellador. But if Tormund has giants with him, Wun Weg Wun Dar Wun may help us treat with them.*

Mormont's raven muttered his annoyance as the door opened beneath him, heralding the return of Dolorous Edd with a flagon of wine and a plate of eggs and sausages. Bowen Marsh waited with obvious impatience as Edd poured, resuming only when he left again. "Tollett is a good man, and well liked, and Iron Emmett has been a fine master-at-arms," he said then. "Yet the talk is that you mean to send them away."

"We need good men at Long Barrow."

"Whore's Hole, the men have started calling it," said Marsh, "but be that as it may. Is it true that you mean to replace Emmett with this savage Leathers as our master-at-arms? That is an office most oft reserved for knights, or rangers at the least."

"Leathers *is* savage," Jon agreed mildly. "I can attest to that. I've tried him in the practice yard. He's as dangerous with a stone axe as most knights are with castle-forged steel. I grant you, he is not as patient as I'd like, and some of the boys are terrified of him . . . but that's not all for the bad. One day they'll find themselves in a real fight, and a certain familiarity with terror will serve them well."

"He's a *wildling*."

"He was, until he said the words. Now he is our brother. One who can teach the boys more than swordcraft. It would not hurt them to learn a few words of the Old Tongue and something of the ways of the free folk."

"*Free*," the raven muttered. "*Corn. King.*"

"The men do not trust him."

Which men? Jon might have asked. *How many?* But that would lead him down a road he did not mean to ride. "I am sorry to hear that. Is there more?"

Septon Cellador spoke up. "This boy Satin. It's said you mean to make him your steward and squire, in Tollett's place. My lord, the boy's a whore . . . a . . . dare I say . . . a painted *catamite* from the brothels of Oldtown."

And you are a drunk. "What he was in Oldtown is none of our concern. He's quick to learn and very clever. The other recruits started out despising him, but he won them over and made friends of them all. He's fearless in a fight and can even read and write after a fashion. He should be capable of fetching me my meals and saddling my horse, don't you think?"

"Most like," said Bowen Marsh, stony-faced, "but the men do not like it. Traditionally the lord commander's squires are lads of good birth being groomed for command. Does my lord believe the men of the Night's Watch would ever follow a whore into battle?"

Jon's temper flashed. "They have followed worse. The Old Bear left a few cautionary notes about certain of the men, for his successor. We have a cook at the Shadow Tower who was fond of raping septas. He burned a seven-pointed star into his flesh for every one he claimed. His left arm is stars from wrist to elbow, and stars mark his calves as well. At Eastwatch we have a man who set his father's house afire and barred the door. His entire family burned to death, all nine. Whatever Satin may have done in Oldtown, he is our brother now, and he *will* be my squire."

Septon Cellador drank some wine. Othell Yarwyck stabbed a sausage with his dagger. Bower Marsh sat red-faced. The raven flapped its wings and said, "*Corn, corn, kill.*" Finally the Lord Steward cleared his throat. "Your lordship knows best, I am sure. Might I ask about these corpses in the ice cells? They make the men uneasy. And to keep them *under guard*? Surely that is a waste of two good men, unless you fear that they . . ."

". . . will rise? I pray they do."

Septon Cellador paled. "Seven save us." Wine dribbled down his chin in a red line. "Lord Commander, wights are monstrous, unnatural creatures. Abominations before the eyes of the gods. You . . . you cannot mean to try to *talk* with them?"

"*Can* they talk?" asked Jon Snow. "I think not, but I cannot claim to know. Monsters they may be, but they were men before they died. How much remains? The one I slew was intent on killing Lord Commander Mormont. Plainly it remembered who he was and where to find him." Maester Aemon would have grasped his purpose, Jon did not doubt; Sam Tarly would have been terrified, but he would have understood as well. "My lord father used to tell me that a man must know his enemies. We understand little of the wights and less about the Others. We need to learn."

That answer did not please them. Septon Cellador fingered the crystal that hung about his neck and said, "I think this most unwise, Lord Snow. I shall pray to the Crone to lift her shining lamp and lead you down the path of wisdom."

Jon Snow's patience was exhausted. "We could all do with a bit more wisdom, I am sure." *You know nothing, Jon Snow.* "Now, shall we speak of Val?"

"It is true, then?" said Marsh. "You have released her."

"Beyond the Wall."

Septon Cellador sucked in his breath. "The king's prize. His Grace will be most wroth to find her gone."

"Val will return." *Before Stannis, if the gods are good.*

"How can you know that?" demanded Bowen Marsh.

"She said she would."

"And if she lied? If she meets with misadventure?"

"Why, then, you may have a chance to choose a lord commander more to your liking. Until such time, I fear you'll still need to suffer me." Jon took a swallow of ale. "I sent her to find Tormund Giantsbane and bring him my offer."

"If we may know, what offer is this?"

"The same offer I made at Mole's Town. Food and shelter and peace, if he will join his strength to ours, fight our common enemy, help us hold the Wall."

Bowen Marsh did not appear surprised. "You mean to let him pass." His voice suggested he had known all along. "To open the gates for him and his followers. Hundreds, thousands."

"If he has that many left."

Septon Cellador made the sign of the star. Othell Yarwyck grunted. Bowen Marsh said, "Some might call this treason. These are wildlings. Savages, raiders, rapers, more beast than man."

"Tormund is none of those things," said Jon, "no more than Mance Rayder. But even if every word you said was true, they are still men, Bowen. Living men, human as you and me. Winter is coming, my lords, and when it does, we living men will need to stand together against the dead."

"*Snow,*" screamed Lord Mormont's raven. "*Snow, Snow.*"

Jon ignored him. "We have been questioning the wildlings we brought back from the grove. Several of them told an interesting tale, of a woods witch called Mother Mole."

"Mother *Mole*?" said Bowen Marsh. "An unlikely name."

"Supposedly she made her home in a burrow beneath a hollow tree. Whatever the truth of that, she had a vision of a fleet of ships arriving to carry the free folk to safety across the narrow sea. Thousands of those who fled the battle were desperate enough to believe her. Mother Mole has led them all to Hardhome, there to pray and await salvation from across the sea."

Othell Yarwyck scowled. "I'm no ranger, but . . . Hardhome is an unholy place, it's said. Cursed. Even your uncle used to say as much, Lord Snow. Why would they go *there*?"

Jon had a map before him on the table. He turned it so they could see. "Hardhome sits on a sheltered bay and has a natural harbor deep enough for the biggest ships afloat. Wood and stone are plentiful near there. The waters teem with fish, and there are colonies of seals and sea cows close at hand."

"All that's true, I don't doubt," said Yarwyck, "but it's not a place I'd want to spend a night. You know the tale."

He did. Hardhome had been halfway toward becoming a town, the only true town north of the Wall, until the night six hundred years ago when hell had swallowed it. Its people had been carried off into slavery or slaughtered for meat, depending on which version of the tale you believed, their homes and halls consumed in a conflagration that burned so hot that watchers on the Wall far to the south had thought the sun was rising in the north. Afterward ashes rained down on haunted forest and Shivering Sea alike for almost half a year. Traders reported finding only nightmarish devastation where Hardhome had stood, a landscape of charred trees and burned bones, waters choked with swollen corpses, blood-chilling shrieks echoing from the cave mouths that pocked the great cliff that loomed above the settlement.

Six centuries had come and gone since that night, but Hardhome was still shunned. The wild had reclaimed the site, Jon had been told, but rangers claimed that the overgrown ruins were haunted by ghouls and demons and burning ghosts with an unhealthy taste for blood. "It is not the sort of refuge I'd chose either," Jon said, "but Mother Mole was heard to preach that the free folk would find salvation where once they found damnation."

Septon Cellador pursed his lips. "Salvation can be found only through the Seven. This witch has doomed them all."

"And saved the Wall, mayhaps," said Bowen Marsh. "These are enemies we speak of. Let them pray amongst the ruins, and if their gods send ships to carry them off to a better world, well and good. In this world I have no food to feed them."

Jon flexed the fingers of his sword hand. "Cotter Pyke's galleys sail past Hardhome from time to time. He tells me there is no shelter there but the caves. *The screaming caves,* his men call them. Mother Mole and those who followed her will perish there, of cold and starvation. Hundreds of them. Thousands."

"Thousands of enemies. Thousands of *wildlings.*"

Thousands of people, Jon thought. *Men, women, children.* Anger rose inside him, but when he spoke his voice was quiet and cold. "Are you so blind, or is it that you do not wish to see? What do you think will happen when all these enemies are dead?"

Above the door the raven muttered, "*Dead, dead, dead.*"

"Let me tell you what will happen," Jon said. "The dead will rise again, in their hundreds and their thousands. They will rise as wights, with black hands and pale blue eyes, and *they will come for us.*" He pushed himself to his feet, the fingers of his sword hand opening and closing. "You have my leave to go."

Septon Cellador rose grey-faced and sweating, Othell Yarwyck stiffly, Bowen Marsh tight-lipped and pale. "Thank you for your time, Lord Snow." They left without another word.

TYRION

The sow had a sweeter temper than some horses he had ridden. Patient and sure-footed, she accepted Tyrion with hardly a squeal when he clambered onto her back, and remained motionless as he reached for shield and lance. Yet when he gathered up her reins and pressed his feet into her side, she moved at once. Her name was Pretty, short for Pretty Pig, and she had been trained to saddle and bridle since she was a piglet.

The painted wooden armor clattered as Pretty trotted across the deck. Tyrion's armpits were prickly with perspiration, and a bead of sweat was trickling down his scar beneath the oversized, ill-fitting helm, yet for one absurd moment he felt almost like Jaime, riding out onto a tourney field with lance in hand, his golden armor flashing in the sun.

When the laughter began, the dream dissolved. He was no champion, just a dwarf on a pig clutching a stick, capering for the amusement of some restless rum-soaked sailors in hopes of sweetening their mood. Somewhere down in hell his father was seething and Joffrey was chuckling. Tyrion could feel their cold dead eyes watching this mummer's farce, as avid as the crew of the *Selaesori Qhoran*.

And now here came his foe. Penny rode her big grey dog, her striped lance waving drunkenly as the beast bounded across the deck.

Her shield and armor had been painted red, though the paint was chipped and fading; his own armor was blue. *Not mine. Groat's. Never mine, I pray.*

Tyrion kicked at Pretty's haunches to speed her to a charge as the sailors urged him on with hoots and shouts. Whether they were shouting encouragement or mocking him he could not have said for certain, though he had a fair notion. *Why did I ever allow myself to be talked into this farce?*

He knew the answer, though. For twelve days now the ship had floated becalmed in the Gulf of Grief. The mood of the crew was ugly, and like to turn uglier when their daily rum ration went dry. There were only so many hours a man could devote to mending sails, caulking leaks, and fishing. Jorah Mormont had heard the muttering about how dwarf luck had failed them. Whilst the ship's cook still gave Tyrion's head a rub from time to time, in hopes that it might stir a wind, the rest had taken to giving him venomous looks whenever he crossed their paths. Penny's lot was even worse, since the cook had put about the notion that squeezing a dwarf girl's breast might be just the thing to win their luck back. He had also started referring to Pretty Pig as *Bacon,* a jape that had seemed much funnier when Tyrion had made it.

"We have to make them laugh," Penny had said, pleading. "We have to make them like us. If we give them a show, it will help them forget. *Please,* m'lord." And somehow, somewise, someway he had consented. *It must have been the rum.* The captain's wine had been the first thing to run out. You could get drunk much quicker on rum than on wine, Tyrion Lannister had discovered.

So he found himself clad in Groat's painted wooden armor, astride Groat's sow, whilst Groat's sister instructed him in the finer points of the mummer's joust that had been their bread and salt. It had a certain delicious irony to it, considering that Tyrion had almost lost his head once by refusing to mount the dog for his nephew's twisted amusement. Yet somehow he found it difficult to appreciate the humor of it all from sowback.

Penny's lance descended just in time for its blunted point to brush his shoulder; his own lance wobbled as he brought it down and banged it noisily off a corner of her shield. She kept her seat. He lost his. But then, he was supposed to.

Easy as falling off a pig . . . though falling off this particular pig was harder than it looked. Tyrion curled into a ball as he dropped, remembering his lesson, but even so, he hit the deck with a solid *thump* and bit his tongue so hard he tasted blood. He felt as if he were twelve again, cartwheeling across the supper table in Casterly Rock's great hall. Back then his uncle Gerion had been on hand to praise his efforts, in place of surly sailors. Their laughter seemed sparse and strained compared to the great gales that had greeted Groat's and Penny's antics at Joffrey's wedding feast, and some hissed at him in anger. "No-Nose, you ride same way you look, ugly," one man shouted from the sterncastle. "Must have no balls, let girl beat you." *He wagered coin on me,* Tyrion decided. He let the insult wash right over him. He had heard worse in his time.

The wooden armor made rising awkward. He found himself flailing like a turtle on its back. That, at least, set a few of the sailors to laughing. *A shame I did not break my leg, that would have left them howling. And if they had been in that privy when I shot my father through the bowels, they might have laughed hard enough to shit their breeches right along with him. But anything to keep the bloody bastards sweet.*

Jorah Mormont finally took pity on Tyrion's struggles and pulled him to his feet. "You looked a fool."

That was the intent. "It is hard to look a hero when mounted on a pig."

"That must be why I stay off pigs."

Tyrion unbuckled his helm, twisted it off, and spat a gobbet of bloody pink phlegm over the side. "It feels as though I bit through half my tongue."

"Next time bite harder." Ser Jorah shrugged. "Truth be told, I've seen worse jousters."

Was that praise? "I fell off the bloody pig and bit my tongue. What could possibly be worse than that?"

"Getting a splinter through your eye and dying."

Penny had vaulted off her dog, a big grey brute called Crunch.

"The thing is not to joust well, Hugor." She was always careful to call him Hugor where anyone might hear. "The thing is to make them laugh and throw coins."

Poor payment for the blood and bruises, Tyrion thought, but he kept that to himself as well. "We failed at that as well. No one threw coins." *Not a penny, not a groat.*

"They will when we get better." Penny pulled off her helm. Mouse-brown hair spilled down to her ears. Her eyes were brown too, beneath a heavy shelf of brow, her cheeks smooth and flushed. She pulled some acorns from a leather bag for Pretty Pig. The sow ate them from her hand, squealing happily. "When we perform for Queen Daenerys the silver will rain down, you'll see."

Some of the sailors were shouting at them and slamming their heels against the deck, demanding another tilt. The ship's cook was the loudest, as always. Tyrion had learned to despise that man, even if he was the only half-decent *cyvasse* player on the cog. "You see, they liked us," Penny said, with a hopeful little smile. "Shall we go again, Hugor?"

He was on the point of refusing when a shout from one of the mates spared him the necessity. It was midmorning, and the captain wanted the boats out again. The cog's huge striped sail hung limply from her mast, as it had for days, but he was hopeful that they could find a wind somewhere to the north. That meant rowing. The boats were small, however, and the cog was large; towing it was hot, sweaty, exhausting work that left the hands blistered and the back aching, and accomplished nothing. The crew hated it. Tyrion could not blame them. "The widow should have put us on a galley," he muttered sourly. "If someone could help me out of these bloody planks, I would be grateful. I think I may have a splinter through my crotch."

Mormont did the duty, albeit with poor grace. Penny collected her dog and pig and led them both below. "You might want to tell your lady to keep her door closed and barred when she's inside," Ser Jorah said as he was undoing the buckles on the straps that joined the wooden breastplate to the backplate. "I'm hearing too much talk about ribs and hams and bacon."

"That pig is half her livelihood."

"A Ghiscari crew would eat the dog as well." Mormont pulled the breastplate and backplate apart. "Just tell her."

"As you wish." His tunic was soaked with sweat and clinging to his chest. Tyrion plucked at it, wishing for a bit of breeze. The wooden armor was as hot and heavy as it was uncomfortable. Half of it looked to be old paint, layer on layer on layer of it, from a hundred past repaintings. At Joffrey's wedding feast, he recalled, one rider had displayed the direwolf of Robb Stark, the other the arms and colors of Stannis Baratheon. "We will need both animals if we're to tilt for Queen Daenerys," he said. If the sailors took it in their heads to butcher Pretty Pig, neither he nor Penny could hope to stop them . . . but Ser Jorah's longsword might give them pause, at least.

"Is that how you hope to keep your head, Imp?"

"Ser Imp, if you please. And yes. Once Her Grace knows my true worth, she'll cherish me. I am a lovable little fellow, after all, and I know many useful things about my kin. But until such time I had best keep her amused."

"Caper as you like, it won't wash out your crimes. Daenerys Targaryen is no silly child to be diverted by japes and tumbles. She will deal with you justly."

Oh, I hope not. Tyrion studied Mormont with his mismatched eyes. "And how will she welcome you, this just queen? A warm embrace, a girlish titter, a headsman's axe?" He grinned at the knight's obvious discomfit. "Did you truly expect me to believe you were about the queen's business in that whorehouse? Defending her from half a world away? Or could it be that you were running, that your dragon queen sent you from her side? But why would she . . . oh, wait, you were *spying* on her." Tyrion made a clucking sound. "You hope to buy your way back into her favor by presenting her with me. An ill-considered scheme, I'd say. One might even say an act of drunken desperation. Perhaps if I were Jaime . . . but Jaime killed her father, I only killed my own. You think Daenerys will execute me and pardon you, but the reverse is just as likely. Maybe you *should* hop up on that pig, Ser Jorah. Put on a suit of iron motley, like Florian the—"

The blow the big knight gave him cracked his head around and knocked him sideways, so hard that his head bounced off the deck.

Blood filled his mouth as he staggered back onto one knee. He spat out a broken tooth. *Growing prettier every day, but I do believe I poked a wound.* "Did the dwarf say something to offend you, ser?" Tyrion asked innocently, wiping bubbles of blood off his broken lip with the back of his hand.

"I am sick of your mouth, dwarf," said Mormont. "You still have a few teeth left. If you want to keep them, stay away from me for the rest of this voyage."

"That could be difficult. We share a cabin."

"You can find somewhere else to sleep. Down in the hold, up on deck, it makes no matter. Just keep out of my sight."

Tyrion pulled himself back to his feet. "As you wish," he answered, through a mouthful of blood, but the big knight was already gone, his boots pounding on the deckboards.

Below, in the galley, Tyrion was rinsing out his mouth with rum and water and wincing at the sting when Penny found him. "I heard what happened. Oh, are you hurt?"

He shrugged. "A bit of blood and a broken tooth." *But I believe I hurt him more.* "And him a knight. Sad to say, I would not count on Ser Jorah should we need protection."

"What did you do? Oh, your lip is bleeding." She slipped a square from her sleeve and dabbed at it. "What did you say?"

"A few truths Ser Bezoar did not care to hear."

"You mustn't mock him. Don't you know *anything*? You can't talk that way to a big person. They can *hurt* you. Ser Jorah could have tossed you in the sea. The sailors would have laughed to see you drown. You have to be careful around big people. Be jolly and playful with them, keep them smiling, make them laugh, that's what my father always said. Didn't your father ever tell you how to act with big people?"

"My father called them smallfolk," said Tyrion, "and he was not what you'd call a jolly man." He took another sip of watered rum, sloshed it around his mouth, spat it out. "Still, I take your point. I have a deal to learn about being a dwarf. Perhaps you will be good enough to teach me, in between the jousting and the pig-riding."

"I will, m'lord. Gladly. But . . . what were these truths? Why did Ser Jorah hit you so hard?"

"Why, for love. The same reason that I stewed that singer." He thought of Shae and the look in her eyes as he tightened the chain about her throat, twisting it in his fist. A chain of golden hands. *For hands of gold are always cold, but a woman's hands are warm.* "Are you a maid, Penny?"

She blushed. "Yes. Of course. Who would have—"

"Stay that way. Love is madness, and lust is poison. Keep your maidenhead. You'll be happier for it, and you're less like to find yourself in some dingy brothel on the Rhoyne with a whore who looks a bit like your lost love." *Or chasing across half the world, hoping to find wherever whores go.* "Ser Jorah dreams of rescuing his dragon queen and basking in her gratitude, but I know a thing or two about the gratitude of kings, and I'd sooner have a palace in Valyria." He broke off suddenly. "Did you feel that? The ship moved."

"It did." Penny's face lit up with joy. "We're moving again. The wind . . ." She rushed to the door. "I want to see. Come, I'll race you up." Off she went.

She is young, Tyrion had to remind himself, as Penny scrambled from the galley and up the steep wooden steps as fast as her short legs would allow. *Almost a child.* Still, it tickled him to see her excitement. He followed her topside.

The sail had come to life again, billowing, emptying, then billowing again, the red stripes on the canvas wriggling like snakes. Sailors dashed across the decks and hauled on lines as the mates bellowed orders in the tongue of Old Volantis. The rowers in the ship's boats had loosed their tow ropes and turned back toward the cog, stroking hard. The wind was blowing from the west, swirling and gusting, clutching at ropes and cloaks like a mischievous child. The *Selaesori Qhoran* was under way.

Might be we'll make Meereen after all, Tyrion thought.

But when he clambered up the ladder to the sterncastle and looked off from the stern, his smile faltered. *Blue sky and blue sea here, but off west . . . I have never seen a sky that color.* A thick band of clouds ran along the horizon. "A bar sinister," he said to Penny, pointing.

"What does that mean?" she asked.

"It means some big bastard is creeping up behind us."

He was surprised to find that Moqorro and two of his fiery fingers had joined them on the sterncastle. It was only midday, and the red priest and his men did not normally emerge till dusk. The priest gave him a solemn nod. "There you see it, Hugor Hill. God's wroth. The Lord of Light will not be mocked."

Tyrion had a bad feeling about this. "The widow said this ship would never reach her destination. I took that to mean that once we were out to sea beyond the reach of triarchs, the captain would change course for Meereen. Or perhaps that you would seize the ship with your Fiery Hand and take us to Daenerys. But that isn't what your high priest saw at all, is it?"

"No." Moqorro's deep voice tolled as solemnly as a funeral bell. "This is what he saw." The red priest lifted his staff, and inclined its head toward the west.

Penny was lost. "I don't understand. What does it mean?"

"It means we had best get below. Ser Jorah has exiled me from our cabin. Might I hide in yours when the time comes?"

"Yes," she said. "You would be . . . oh . . ."

For the better part of three hours they ran before the wind, as the storm grew closer. The western sky went green, then grey, then black. A wall of dark clouds loomed up behind them, churning like a kettle of milk left on the fire too long. Tyrion and Penny watched from the forecastle, huddled by the figurehead and holding hands, careful to stay out of the way of captain and crew.

The last storm had been thrilling, intoxicating, a sudden squall that had left him feeling cleansed and refreshed. This one felt different right from the first. The captain sensed it too. He changed their course to north by northeast to try and get out of the storm's path.

It was a futile effort. This storm was too big. The seas around them grew rougher. The wind began to howl. The *Stinky Steward* rose and fell as waves smashed against her hull. Behind them lightning stabbed down from the sky, blinding purple bolts that danced across the sea in webs of light. Thunder followed. "The time has come to hide." Tyrion took Penny by the arm and led her belowdecks.

Pretty and Crunch were were both half-mad with fear. The dog was barking, barking, barking. He knocked Tyrion right off his feet as they entered. The sow had been shitting everywhere. Tyrion cleaned that up as best he could whilst Penny tried to calm the animals. Then they tied down or put away anything that was still loose. "I'm frightened," Penny confessed. The cabin had begun to tilt and jump, going this way and that as the waves hammered at the hull of the ship.

There are worse ways to die than drowning. Your brother learned that, and so did my lord father. And Shae, that lying cunt. Hands of gold are always cold, but a woman's hands are warm. "We should play a game," Tyrion suggested. "That might help take our thoughts off the storm."

"Not *cyvasse*," she said at once.

"Not *cyvasse*," Tyrion agreed, as the deck rose under him. That would only lead to pieces flying violently across the cabin and raining down on sow and dog. "When you were a little girl, did you ever play come-into-my-castle?"

"No. Can you teach me?"

Could he? Tyrion hesitated. *Fool of a dwarf. Of course she's never played come-into-my-castle. She never had a castle.* Come-into-my-castle was a game for highborn children, one meant to teach them courtesy, heraldry, and a thing or two about their lord father's friends and foes. "That won't . . ." he started. The deck gave another violent heave, slamming the two of them together. Penny gave a squeak of fright. "That game won't do," Tyrion told her, gritting his teeth. "Sorry. I don't know what game—"

"I do." Penny kissed him.

It was an awkward kiss, rushed, clumsy. But it took him utterly by surprise. His hands jerked up and grabbed hold of her shoulders to shove her away. Instead he hesitated, then pulled her closer, gave her a squeeze. Her lips were dry, hard, closed up tighter than a miser's purse. *A small mercy,* thought Tyrion. This was nothing he had wanted. He liked Penny, he pitied Penny, he even admired Penny in a way, but he did not desire her. He had no wish to hurt her, though; the gods and his sweet sister had given her enough pain. So he let the kiss go on, holding her gently by the shoulders. His own lips stayed firmly shut. The *Selaesori Qhoran* rolled and shuddered around them.

Finally she pulled back an inch or two. Tyrion could see his own reflection shining in her eyes. *Pretty eyes,* he thought, but he saw other things as well. *A lot of fear, a little hope . . . but not a bit of lust. She does not want me, no more than I want her.*

When she lowered her head, he took her under the chin and raised it up again. "We cannot play that game, my lady." Above the thunder boomed, close at hand now.

"I never meant . . . I never kissed a boy before, but . . . I only thought, what if we drown, and I . . . I . . ."

"It was sweet," lied Tyrion, "but I am married. She was with me at the feast, you may remember her. Lady Sansa."

"Was she your wife? She . . . she was very beautiful . . ."

And false. Sansa, Shae, all my women . . . Tysha was the only one who ever loved me. Where do whores go? "A lovely girl," said Tyrion, "and we were joined beneath the eyes of gods and men. It may be that she is lost to me, but until I know that for a certainty I must be true to her."

"I understand." Penny turned her face away from his.

My perfect woman, Tyrion thought bitterly. *One still young enough to believe such blatant lies.*

The hull was creaking, the deck moving, and Pretty was squealing in distress. Penny crawled across the cabin floor on her hands and knees, wrapped her arms around the sow's head, and murmured reassurance to her. Looking at the two of them, it was hard to know who was comforting whom. The sight was so grotesque it should have been hilarious, but Tyrion could not even find a smile. *The girl deserves better than a pig,* he thought. *An honest kiss, a little kindness, everyone deserves that much, however big or small.* He looked about for his wine cup, but when he found it all the rum had spilled. *Drowning is bad enough,* he reflected sourly, *but drowning sad and sober, that's too cruel.*

In the end, they did not drown . . . though there were times when the prospect of a nice, peaceful drowning had a certain appeal. The storm raged for the rest of that day and well into the night. Wet winds howled around them and waves rose like the fists of drowned giants to smash down on their decks. Above, they learned later, a mate and two sailors were swept overboard, the ship's cook was blinded when a kettle of hot grease flew up into his face, and the captain was thrown from the sterncastle to the main deck so violently he broke both legs. Below, Crunch howled and barked and snapped at Penny, and Pretty Pig began to shit again, turning the cramped, damp cabin into a sty. Tyrion managed to avoid retching his way through all of this, chiefly thanks to the lack of wine. Penny was not so fortunate, but he held her anyway as the ship's hull creaked and groaned alarmingly around them, like a cask about to burst.

Nearby midnight the winds finally died away, and the sea grew calm enough for Tyrion to make his way back up onto deck. What he saw there did not reassure him. The cog was drifting on a sea of dragonglass beneath a bowl of stars, but all around the storm raged on. East, west, north, south, everywhere he looked, the clouds rose up like black mountains, their tumbled slopes and collossal cliffs alive with blue and purple lightning. No rain was falling, but the decks were slick and wet underfoot.

Tyrion could hear someone screaming from below, a thin, high voice hysterical with fear. He could hear Moqorro too. The red priest stood on the forecastle facing the storm, his staff raised above his head as he boomed a prayer. Amidships, a dozen sailors and two of the fiery fingers were struggling with tangled lines and sodden canvas, but whether they were trying to raise the sail again or pull it down he never knew. Whatever they were doing, it seemed to him a very bad idea. And so it was.

The wind returned as a whispered threat, cold and damp, brushing over his cheek, flapping the wet sail, swirling and tugging at Moqorro's scarlet robes. Some instinct made Tyrion grab hold of the nearest rail, just in time. In the space of three heartbeats the little breeze became a howling gale. Moqorro shouted something, and green flames leapt from the dragon's maw atop his staff to vanish in the night. Then the rains came, black and blinding, and forecastle and sterncastle both vanished behind a wall of water. Something huge flapped overhead, and Tyrion glanced up in time to see the sail taking wing, with two men still dangling from the lines. Then he heard a *crack*. *Oh, bloody hell,* he had time to think, *that had to be the mast.*

He found a line and pulled on it, fighting toward the hatch to get himself below out of the storm, but a gust of wind knocked his feet from under him and a second slammed him into the rail and there he clung. Rain lashed at his face, blinding him. His mouth was full of blood again. The ship groaned and growled beneath him like a constipated fat man straining to shit.

Then the mast burst.

Tyrion never saw it, but he heard it. That *crack*ing sound again and then a scream of tortured wood, and suddenly the air was full of shards and splinters. One missed his eye by half an inch, a second found his neck, a third went through his calf, boots and breeches and all. He screamed. But he held on to the line, held on with a desperate strength he did not know he had. *The widow said this ship would never reach her destination,* he remembered. Then he laughed and laughed, wild and hysterical, as thunder boomed and timbers moaned and waves crashed all around him.

By the time the storm abated and the surviving passengers and crew came crawling back on deck, like pale pink worms wriggling to the surface after a rain, the *Selaesori Qhoran* was a broken thing, floating low in the water and listing ten degrees to port, her hull sprung in half a hundred places, her hold awash in seawater, her mast a splintered ruin no taller than a dwarf. Even her figurehead had not escaped; one of his arms had broken off, the one with all his scrolls. Nine men had been lost, including a mate, two of the fiery fingers, and Moqorro himself.

Did Benerro see this in his fires? Tyrion wondered, when he realized the huge red priest was gone. *Did Moqorro?*

"Prophecy is like a half-trained mule," he complained to Jorah Mormont. "It looks as though it might be useful, but the moment you trust in it, it kicks you in the head. That bloody widow knew the ship would never reach her destination, she warned us of that, said Benerro saw it in his fires, only I took that to mean . . . well, what does it matter?" His mouth twisted. "What it really meant was that some bloody big storm would turn our mast to kindling so we could drift aimlessly across the Gulf of Grief until our food ran out and we started eating one another. Who do you suppose they'll carve up first . . . the pig, the dog, or me?"

"The noisiest, I'd say."

The captain died the following day, the ship's cook three nights later. It was all that the remaining crew could do to keep the wreck afloat. The mate who had assumed command reckoned that they were somewhere off the southern end of the Isle of Cedars. When he lowered the ship's boats to tow them toward the nearest land, one sank and the men in the other cut the line and rowed off north, abandoning the cog and all their shipmates.

"Slaves," said Jorah Mormont, contemptuous.

The big knight had slept through the storm, to hear him tell it. Tyrion had his doubts, but he kept them to himself. One day he might want to bite someone in the leg, and for that you needed teeth. Mormont seemed content to ignore their disagreement, so Tyrion decided to pretend it had not happened.

For nineteen days they drifted, as food and water dwindled. The sun beat down on them, relentless. Penny huddled in her cabin with her dog and her pig, and Tyrion brought her food, limping on his bandaged calf and sniffing at the wound by night. When he had nothing else to do, he pricked his toes and fingers too. Ser Jorah made a point of sharpening his sword each day, honing the point until it gleamed. The three remaining fiery fingers lit the nightfire as the sun went down, but they wore their ornate armor as they led the crew in prayer, and their spears were close at hand. And not a single sailor tried to rub the head of either dwarf.

"Should we joust for them again?" Penny asked one night.

"Best not," said Tyrion. "That would only serve to remind them we have a nice plump pig." Though Pretty was growing less plump with every passing day, and Crunch was fur and bones.

That night he dreamed that he was back in King's Landing again, a crossbow in his hand. "Wherever whores go," Lord Tywin said, but when Tyrion's finger clenched and the bowstring *thrumm*ed, it was Penny with the quarrel buried in her belly.

He woke to the sound of shouting.

The deck was moving under him, and for half a heartbeat he was so confused he thought he was back on the *Shy Maid*. A whiff of pigshit brought him to his senses. The Sorrows were behind him, half a world away, and the joys of that time as well. He remembered how sweet Lemore had looked after her morning swims, with beads of water glistening on her naked skin, but the only maiden here was his poor Penny, the stunted little dwarf girl.

Something was afoot, though. Tyrion slipped from the hammock, yawning, and looked about for his boots. And mad though it was, he looked for the crossbow as well, but of course there was none such to be found. *A pity,* he mused, *it might have been some use when the big folk come to eat me.* He pulled his boots on and climbed on deck to see what the shouting was about. Penny was there before him, her eyes wide with wonder. "A sail," she shouted, "there, there, do you see? A sail, and they've seen us, they have. A *sail.*"

This time he kissed her . . . once on each cheek, once on the brow, and one last one on the mouth. She was flushed and laughing by the last kiss, suddenly shy again, but it made no matter. The other ship was closing. A big galley, he saw. Her oars left a long white wake behind her. "What ship is that?" he asked Ser Jorah Mormont. "Can you read her name?"

"I don't need to read her name. We're downwind. I can smell her." Mormont drew his sword. "That's a slaver."

APPENDIX

THE KINGS AND THEIR COURTS

THE BOY KING

TOMMEN BARATHEON, the First of His Name, King of the Andals, the Rhoynar, and the First Men, Lord of the Seven Kingdoms, a boy of eight years,

—his wife, QUEEN MARGAERY of House Tyrell, thrice wed, twice widowed, accused of high treason, held captive in the Great Sept of Baelor,
—her lady companions and cousins, MEGGA, ALLA, and ELINOR TYRELL, accused of fornications,
—Elinor's betrothed, ALYN AMBROSE, squire,
—his mother, CERSEI of House Lannister, Queen Dowager, Lady of Casterly Rock, accused of high treason, captive in the Great Sept of Baelor,
—his siblings:
—his elder brother, {KING JOFFREY I BARATHEON}, poisoned during his wedding feast,
—his elder sister, PRINCESS MYRCELLA BARATHEON, a girl of nine, a ward of Prince Doran Martell at Sunspear, betrothed to his son Trystane,
—his kittens, SER POUNCE, LADY WHISKERS, BOOTS,
—his uncles:
—SER JAIME LANNISTER, called THE KINGSLAYER, twin to Queen Cersei, Lord Commander of the Kingsguard,
—TYRION LANNISTER, called THE IMP, a dwarf, accused and condemned for regicide and kinslaying,

—his other kin:
  —his grandfather, {TYWIN LANNISTER}, Lord of
    Casterly Rock, Warden of the West, and Hand of the
    King, murdered in the privy by his son Tyrion,
—his great-uncle, SER KEVAN LANNISTER, Lord Regent
    and Protector of the Realm, m. Dorna Swyft,
    —their children:
    —SER LANCEL LANNISTER, a knight of the Holy Order
      of the Warrior's Sons,
    —{WILLEM}, twin to Martyn, murdered at Riverrun,
    —MARTYN, twin to Willem, a squire,
    —JANEI, a girl of three,
—his great-aunt, GENNA LANNISTER, m. Ser Emmon Frey,
    —their children:
    —{SER CLEOS FREY}, killed by outlaws,
      —his son, SER TYWIN FREY, called TY,
      —his son, WILLEM FREY, a squire,
    —SER LYONEL FREY, Lady Genna's second son,
    —{TION FREY}, a squire, murdered at Riverrun,
    —WALDER FREY, called RED WALDER, a page at
      Casterly Rock,
—his great-uncle, {SER TYGETT LANNISTER}, m. Darlessa
    Marbrand
    —their children:
    —TYREK LANNISTER, a squire, vanished during the
      food riots in King's Landing,
      —LADY ERMESANDE HAYFORD, Tyrek's child wife,
—his great uncle, GERION LANNISTER, lost at sea,
    —JOY HILL, his bastard daughter,

—King Tommen's small council:
  —SER KEVAN LANNISTER, Lord Regent,
  —LORD MACE TYRELL, Hand of the King,
  —GRAND MAESTER PYCELLE, counselor and healer,
  —SER JAIME LANNISTER, Lord Commander of the
    Kingsguard,

—LORD PAXTER REDWYNE, grand admiral and master of ships,

—QYBURN, a disgraced maester and reputed necromancer, master of whisperers,

—Queen Cersei's former small council,
  —{LORD GYLES ROSBY}, lord treasurer and master of coin, dead of a cough,
  —LORD ORTON MERRYWEATHER, justiciar and master of laws, fled to Longtable upon Queen Cersei's arrest,
  —AURANE WATERS, the Bastard of Driftmark, grand admiral and master of ships, fled to sea with the royal fleet upon Queen Cersei's arrest,

—King Tommen's Kingsguard:
  —SER JAIME LANNISTER, Lord Commander,
  —SER MERYN TRANT,
  —SER BOROS BLOUNT, removed and thence restored,
  —SER BALON SWANN, in Dorne with Princess Myrcella,
  —SER OSMUND KETTLEBLACK,
  —SER LORAS TYRELL, the Knight of Flowers,
  —{SER ARYS OAKHEART}, dead in Dorne,

—Tommen's court at King's Landing:
  —MOON BOY, the royal jester and fool,
  —PATE, a lad of eight, King Tommen's whipping boy,
  —ORMOND OF OLDTOWN, the royal harper and bard,
  —SER OSFRYD KETTLEBLACK, brother to Ser Osmund and Ser Osney, a captain in the City Watch,
  —NOHO DIMITTIS, envoy from the Iron Bank of Braavos,
  —{SER GREGOR CLEGANE}, called THE MOUNTAIN THAT RIDES, dead of a poisoned wound,
  —RENNIFER LONGWATERS, chief undergaoler of the Red Keep's dungeons,

—Queen Margaery's alleged lovers:
  —WAT, a singer styling himself THE BLUE BARD, a captive driven mad by torment,
  —{HAMISH THE HARPER}, an aged singer, died a captive,
  —SER MARK MULLENDORE, who lost a monkey and half an arm in the Battle of the Blackwater,
  —SER TALLAD called THE TALL, SER LAMBERT TURNBERRY, SER BAYARD NORCROSS, SER HUGH CLIFTON,
  —JALABHAR XHO, Prince of the Red Flower Vale, an exile from the Summer Isles,
  —SER HORAS REDWYNE, found innocent and freed,
  —SER HOBBER REDWYNE, found innocent and freed,

—Queen Cersei's chief accuser,
  —SER OSNEY KETTLEBLACK, brother to Ser Osmund and Ser Osfryd, held captive by the Faith,

—the people of the Faith:
  —THE HIGH SEPTON, Father of the Faithful, Voice of the Seven on Earth, an old man and frail,
    —SEPTA UNELLA, SEPTA MOELLE, SEPTA SCOLERA, the queen's gaolers,
    —SEPTON TORBERT, SEPTON RAYNARD, SEPTON LUCEON, SEPTON OLLIDOR, of the Most Devout,
    —SEPTA AGLANTINE, SEPTA HELICENT, serving the Seven at the Great Sept of Baelor,
    —SER THEODAN WELLS, called THEODAN THE TRUE, pious commander of the Warrior's Sons,
    —the "sparrows," the humblest of men, fierce in their piety,

—people of King's Landing:
  —CHATAYA, proprietor of an expensive brothel,
    —ALAYAYA, her daughter,
    —DANCY, MAREI, two of Chataya's girls,
  —TOBHO MOTT, a master armorer,

—lords of the crownlands, sworn to the Iron Throne:
   —RENFRED RYKKER, Lord of Duskendale,
      —SER RUFUS LEEK, a one-legged knight in his service, castellan of the Dun Fort at Duskendale,
   —{TANDA STOKEWORTH}, Lady of Stokeworth, died of a broken hip,
      —her eldest daughter, {FALYSE}, died screaming in the black cells,
         —{SER BALMAN BYRCH}, Lady Falyse's husband, killed in a joust,
      —her younger daughter, LOLLYS, weak of wit, Lady of Stokeworth,
         —her newborn son, TYRION TANNER, of the hundred fathers,
         —her husband, SER BRONN OF THE BLACKWATER, sellsword turned knight,
   —MAESTER FRENKEN, in service at Stokeworth,

King Tommen's banner shows the crowned stag of Baratheon, black on gold, and the lion of Lannister, gold on crimson, combatant.

THE KING AT THE WALL

STANNIS BARATHEON, the First of His Name, second son of Lord Steffon Baratheon and Lady Cassana of House Estermont, Lord of Dragonstone, styling himself King of Westeros,

  —with King Stannis at Castle Black:
    —LADY MELISANDRE OF ASSHAI, called THE RED WOMAN, a priestess of R'hllor, the Lord of Light,
    —his knights and sworn swords:
      —SER RICHARD HORPE, his second-in-command,
      —SER GODRY FARRING, called GIANTSLAYER,
      —SER JUSTIN MASSEY,
      —LORD ROBIN PEASEBURY,
      —LORD HARWOOD FELL,
      —SER CLAYTON SUGGS, SER CORLISS PENNY, queen's men and fervent followers of the Lord of Light,
      —SER WILLAM FOXGLOVE, SER HUMFREY CLIFTON, SER ORMUND WYLDE, SER HARYS COBB, knights
    —his squires, DEVAN SEAWORTH and BRYEN FARRING
    —his captive, MANCE RAYDER, King-Beyond-the-Wall,
      —Rayder's infant son, "the wildling prince,"
        —the boy's wet nurse, GILLY, a wildling girl,
          —Gilly's infant son, "the abomination," fathered by her father {CRASTER},

—at Eastwatch-by-the-Sea:

—QUEEN SELYSE of House Florent, his wife,

—PRINCESS SHIREEN, their daughter, a girl of eleven,

—PATCHFACE, Shireen's tattooed fool,

—her uncle, SER AXELL FLORENT, foremost of the queen's men, styling himself the Queen's Hand,

—her knights and sworn swords, SER NARBERT GRANDISON, SER BENETHON SCALES, SER PATREK OF KING'S MOUNTAIN, SER DORDEN THE DOUR, SER MALEGORN OF REDPOOL, SER LAMBERT WHITEWATER, SER PERKIN FOLLARD, SER BRUS BUCKLER

—SER DAVOS SEAWORTH, Lord of the Rainwood, Admiral of the Narrow Sea, and Hand of the King, called THE ONION KNIGHT,

—SALLADHAR SAAN of Lys, a pirate and sellsail, master of the *Valyrian* and a fleet of galleys,

—TYCHO NESTORIS, emissary from the Iron Bank of Braavos.

Stannis has taken for his banner the fiery heart of the Lord of Light—a red heart surrounded by orange flames upon a yellow field. Within the heart is the crowned stag of House Baratheon, in black.

KING OF THE ISLES AND THE NORTH

The Greyjoys of Pyke claim descent from the Grey King of the Age of Heroes. Legend says the Grey King ruled the sea itself and took a mermaid to wife. Aegon the Dragon ended the line of the last King of the Iron Islands, but allowed the ironborn to revive their ancient custom and choose who should have primacy among them. They chose Lord Vickon Greyjoy of Pyke. The Greyjoy sigil is a golden kraken upon a black field. Their words are *We Do Not Sow*.

> EURON GREYJOY, the Third of His Name Since the Grey King, King of the Iron Islands and the North, King of Salt and Rock, Son of the Sea Wind, and Lord Reaper of Pyke, captain of the *Silence*, called CROW'S EYE,
> —his elder brother, {BALON}, King of the Iron Islands and the North, the Ninth of His Name Since the Grey King, killed in a fall,
> > —LADY ALANNYS, of House Harlaw, Balon's widow,
> > —their children:
> > > —{RODRIK}, slain during Balon's first rebellion,
> > > —{MARON}, slain during Balon's first rebellion,
> > > —ASHA, captain of the *Black Wind* and conqueror of Deepwood Motte, m. Erik Ironmaker,
> > > —THEON, called by northmen THEON TURN-CLOAK, a captive at the Dreadfort,
> —his younger brother, VICTARION, Lord Captain of the Iron Fleet, master of the *Iron Victory*,

—his youngest brother, AERON, called DAMPHAIR, a priest
   of the Drowned God,
—his captains and sworn swords:
—TORWOLD BROWNTOOTH, PINCHFACE JON MYRE,
   RODRIK FREEBORN, THE RED OARSMAN,
   LEFT-HAND LUCAS CODD, QUELLON HUMBLE,
   HARREN HALF-HOARE, KEMMETT PYKE THE
   BASTARD, QARL THE THRALL, STONEHAND, RALF
   THE SHEPHERD, RALF OF LORDSPORT
—his crewmen:
—{CRAGORN}, who blew the hellhorn and died,
—his lords bannermen:
—ERIK IRONMAKER, called ERIK ANVIL-BREAKER and
   ERIK THE JUST, Lord Steward of the Iron Islands,
   castellan of Pyke, an old man once renowned, m. Asha
   Greyjoy,
—lords of Pyke:
   —GERMUND BOTLEY, Lord of Lordsport,
   —WALDON WYNCH, Lord of Iron Holt,
—lords of Old Wyk:
   —DUNSTAN DRUMM, The Drumm, Lord of Old
      Wyk,
   —NORNE GOODBROTHER, of Shatterstone,
   —THE STONEHOUSE,
—lords of Great Wyk:
   —GOROLD GOODBROTHER, Lord of the Hammer
      horn,
   —TRISTON FARWYND, Lord of Sealskin Point,
   —THE SPARR,
   —MELDRED MERLYN, Lord of Pebbleton,
—lords of Orkmont:
   —ALYN ORKWOOD, called ORKWOOD OF
      ORKMONT,
   —LORD BALON TAWNEY,
—lords of Saltcliffe:
   —LORD DONNOR SALTCLIFFE,

—LORD SUNDERLY
—lords of Harlaw:
  —RODRIK HARLAW, called THE READER, Lord of
  Harlaw, Lord of Ten Towers, Harlaw of Harlaw,
  —SIGFRYD HARLAW, called SIGFRYD SILVERHAIR,
  his great uncle, master of Harlaw Hall,
  —HOTHO HARLAW, called HOTHO HUMPBACK, of
  the Tower of Glimmering, a cousin,
  —BOREMUND HARLAW, called BOREMUND THE
  BLUE, master of Harridan Hill, a cousin,
—lords of the lesser isles and rocks:
  —GYLBERT FARWYND, Lord of the Lonely Light,

—the ironborn conquerors:
—on the Shield Islands
  —ANDRIK THE UNSMILING, Lord of Southshield,
  —NUTE THE BARBER, Lord of Oakenshield,
  —MARON VOLMARK, Lord of Greenshield,
  —SER HARRAS HARLAW, Lord of Greyshield, the
  Knight of Grey Gardens,
—at Moat Cailin
  —RALF KENNING, castellan and commander,
    —ADRACK HUMBLE, short half an arm,
    —DAGON CODD, who yields to no man,
—at Torrhen's Square
  —DAGMER, called CLEFTJAW, captain of *Foamdrinker,*
—at Deepwood Motte
  —ASHA GREYJOY, the kraken's daughter, captain of the
  Black Wind,
    —her lover, QARL THE MAID, a swordsman,
    —her former lover, TRISTIFER BOTLEY, heir to
    Lordsport, dispossessed of his lands,
    —her crewmen, ROGGON RUSTBEARD,
    GRIMTONGUE, ROLFE THE DWARF, LORREN
    LONGAXE, ROOK, FINGERS, SIX-TOED HARL,
    DROOPEYE DALE, EARL HARLAW, CROMM,

HAGEN THE HORN and his beautiful red-haired daughter,
—her cousin, QUENTON GREYJOY,
—her cousin, DAGON GREYJOY, called DAGON THE DRUNKARD.

OTHER HOUSES GREAT AND SMALL

HOUSE ARRYN

The Arryns are descended from the Kings of Mountain and Vale. Their sigil is a white moon-and-falcon upon a sky blue field. House Arryn has taken no part in the War of the Five Kings.

ROBERT ARRYN, Lord of the Eyrie, Defender of the Vale, a sickly boy of eight years, called SWEETROBIN,
—his mother, {LADY LYSA of House Tully}, widow of Lord Jon Arryn, pushed from the Moon Door to her death,
—his guardian, PETYR BAELISH, called LITTLEFINGER, Lord of Harrenhal, Lord Paramount of the Trident, and Lord Protector of the Vale,
  —ALAYNE STONE, Lord Petyr's natural daughter, a maid of three-and-ten, actually Sansa Stark,
  —SER LOTHOR BRUNE, a sellsword in Lord Petyr's service, captain of guards at the Eyrie,
  —OSWELL, a grizzled man-at-arms in Lord Petyr's service, sometimes called KETTLEBLACK,
  —SER SHADRICK OF THE SHADY GLEN, called THE MAD MOUSE, a hedge knight in Lord Petyr's service,
  —SER BYRON THE BEAUTIFUL, SER MORGARTH THE MERRY, hedge knights in Lord Petyr's service,
—his household and retainers:
  —MAESTER COLEMON, counselor, healer, and tutor,
  —MORD, a brutal gaoler with teeth of gold,
  —GRETCHEL, MADDY, and MELA, servingwomen,
—his bannermen, the Lords of Mountain and Vale:

—YOHN ROYCE, called BRONZE YOHN, Lord of Runestone,
  —his son, SER ANDAR, heir to Runestone,
—LORD NESTOR ROYCE, High Steward of the Vale and castellan of the Gates of the Moon,
  —his son and heir, SER ALBAR,
  —his daughter, MYRANDA, called RANDA, a widow, but scarce used,
  —MYA STONE, bastard daughter of King Robert,
—LYONEL CORBRAY, Lord of Heart's Home,
  —SER LYN COBRAY, his brother, who wields the famed blade Lady Forlorn,
  —SER LUCAS CORBRAY, his younger brother,
—TRISTON SUNDERLAND, Lord of the Three Sisters,
  —GODRIC BORRELL, Lord of Sweetsister,
  —ROLLAND LONGTHORPE, Lord of Longsister,
  —ALESANDOR TORRENT, Lord of Littlesister,
—ANYA WAYNWOOD, Lady of Ironoaks Castle,
  —SER MORTON, her eldest son and heir,
  —SER DONNEL, the Knight of the Bloody Gate,
  —WALLACE, her youngest son,
  —HARROLD HARDYNG, her ward, a squire oft called HARRY THE HEIR,
—SER SYMOND TEMPLETON, the Knight of Ninestars,
—JON LYNDERLY, Lord of the Snakewood,
—EDMUND WAXLEY, the Knight of Wickenden,
—GEROLD GRAFTON, the Lord of Gulltown,
—{EON HUNTER}, Lord of Longbow Hall, recently deceased,
  —SER GILWOOD, Lord Eon's eldest son and heir, now called YOUNG LORD HUNTER,
  —SER EUSTACE, Lord Eon's second son,
  —SER HARLAN, Lord Eon's youngest son,
  —Young Lord Hunter's household:
    —MAESTER WILLAMEN, counselor, healer, tutor,
—HORTON REDFORT, Lord of Redfort, thrice wed,

—SER JASPER, SER CREIGHTON, SER JON, his sons,
—SER MYCHEL, his youngest son, a new-made knight,
  m. Ysilla Royce of Runestone,
—BENEDAR BELMORE, Lord of Strongsong,

—clan chiefs from the Mountains of the Moon,
  —SHAGGA SON OF DOLF, OF THE STONE CROWS, presently leading a band in the kingswood,
    —TIMETT SON OF TIMETT, OF THE BURNED MEN,
    —CHELLA DAUGHTER OF CHEYK, OF THE BLACK EARS,
    —CRAWN SON OF CALOR, OF THE MOON BROTHERS.

The Arryn words are *As High as Honor*.

HOUSE BARATHEON

The youngest of the Great Houses, House Baratheon was born during the Wars of Conquest when Orys Baratheon, rumored to be a bastard brother of Aegon the Conqueror, defeated and slew Argilac the Arrogant, the last Storm King. Aegon rewarded him with Argilac's castle, lands, and daughter. Orys took the girl to bride and adopted the banner, honors, and words of her line.

In the 283rd year after Aegon's Conquest, Robert of House Baratheon, Lord of Storm's End, overthrew the Mad King, Aenys II Targaryen, to win the Iron Throne. His claim to the crown derived from his grandmother, a daughter of King Aegon V Targaryen, though Robert preferred to say his warhammer was his claim.

{ROBERT BARATHEON}, the First of His Name, King of the Andals, the Rhoynar, and the First Men, Lord of the Seven Kingdoms and Protector of the Realm, killed by a boar,
—his wife, QUEEN CERSEI of House Lannister,
—their children:
  —{KING JOFFREY BARATHEON}, the First of His Name, murdered at his wedding feast,
  —PRINCESS MYRCELLA, a ward in Sunspear, betrothed to Prince Trystane Martell,
  —KING TOMMEN BARATHEON, the First of His Name,
—his brothers:
  —STANNIS BARATHEON, rebel Lord of Dragonstone

and pretender to the Iron Throne,
  —his daughter, SHIREEN, a girl of eleven,
—{RENLY BARATHEON}, rebel Lord of Storm's End and
pretender to the Iron Throne, murdered at Storm's End
in the midst of his army,
—his bastard children:
  —MYA STONE, a maid of nineteen, in the service of Lord
  Nestor Royce, of the Gates of the Moon,
  —GENDRY, an outlaw in the riverlands, ignorant of his
  heritage,
  —EDRIC STORM, his acknowledged bastard son by Lady
  Delena of House Florent, hiding in Lys,
    —SER ANDREW ESTERMONT, his cousin and
    guardian,
    —his guards and protectors:
      —SER GERALD GOWER, LEWYS called THE
      FISHWIFE, SER TRISTON OF TALLY HILL,
      OMER BLACKBERRY,
  —{BARRA}, his bastard daughter by a whore of King's
  Landing, killed by the command of his widow,
—his other kin:
  —his great-uncle, SER ELDON ESTERMONT, Lord of
  Greenstone,
    —his cousin, SER AEMON ESTERMONT, Eldon's son,
      —his cousin, SER ALYN ESTERMONT, Aemon's
      son,
    —his cousin, SER LOMAS ESTERMONT, Eldon's son,
      —his cousin, SER ANDREW ESTERMONT, Lomas's
      son,

—bannermen sworn to Storm's End, the storm lords:
  —DAVOS SEAWORTH, Lord of the Rainwood, Admiral of
  the Narrow Sea, and Hand of the King,
    —his wife, MARYA, a carpenter's daughter,
      —their sons, {DALE, ALLARD, MATTHOS, MARIC},
      killed in the Battle of the Blackwater,

—their son DEVAN, squire to King Stannis,

—their sons, STANNIS and STEFFON,

—SER GILBERT FARRING, castellan of Storm's End,

—his son, BRYEN, squire to King Stannis,

—his cousin, SER GODRY FARRING, called GIANT-SLAYER,

—ELWOOD MEADOWS, Lord of Grassfield Keep, seneschal at Storm's End,

—SELWYN TARTH, called THE EVENSTAR, Lord of Tarth,

—his daughter, BRIENNE, THE MAID OF TARTH, also called BRIENNE THE BEAUTY,

—her squire, PODRICK PAYNE, a boy of ten,

—SER RONNET CONNINGTON, called RED RONNET, the Knight of Griffin's Roost,

—his younger siblings, RAYMUND and ALYNNE,

—his bastard son, RONALD STORM,

—his cousin, JON CONNINGTON, once Lord of Storm's End and Hand of the King, exiled by Aerys II Targaryen, believed dead of drink,

—LESTER MORRIGEN, Lord of Crows Nest,

—his brother and heir, SER RICHARD MORRIGEN,

—his brother, {SER GUYARD MORRIGEN, called GUYARD THE GREEN}, slain in the Battle of the Blackwater,

—ARSTAN SELMY, Lord of Harvest Hall,

—his great-uncle, SER BARRISTAN SELMY,

—CASPER WYLDE, Lord of the Rain House,

—his uncle, SER ORMUND WYLDE, an aged knight,

—HARWOOD FELL, Lord of Felwood,

—HUGH GRANDISON, called GREYBEARD, Lord of Grandview,

—SEBASTION ERROL, Lord of Haystack Hall,

—CLIFFORD SWANN, Lord of Stonehelm,

—BERIC DONDARRION, Lord of Blackwater, called THE LIGHTNING LORD, an outlaw in the riverlands, oft slain and now thought dead,

—{BRYCE CARON}, Lord of Nightsong, slain by Ser Philip Foote on the Blackwater,

—his slayer, SER PHILIP FOOTE, a one-eyed knight, Lord of Nightsong,

—his baseborn half-brother, SER ROLLAND STORM, called THE BASTARD OF NIGHTSONG, pretender Lord of Nightsong,

—ROBIN PEASEBURY, Lord of Poddingfield,

—MARY MERTYNS, Lady of Mistwood,

—RALPH BUCKLER, Lord of Bronzegate,

—his cousin, SER BRUS BUCKLER.

The Baratheon sigil is a crowned stag, black, on a golden field. Their words are *Ours Is the Fury*.

HOUSE FREY

The Freys are bannermen to House Tully, but have not always been diligent in their duty. At the outset of the War of the Five Kings, Robb Stark won Lord Walder's allegiance by pledging to marry one of his daughters or granddaughters. When he wed Lady Jeyne Westerling instead, the Freys conspired with Roose Bolton and murdered the Young Wolf and his followers at what became known as the Red Wedding.

WALDER FREY, Lord of the Crossing,
—by his first wife, {LADY PERRA, of House Royce}:
 —{SER STEVRON FREY}, died after the Battle of Oxcross,
 —SER EMMON FREY, his second son,
 —SER AENYS FREY, leading the Frey forces in the north,
  —Aenys's son, AEGON BLOODBORN, an outlaw,
  —Aenys's son, RHAEGAR, an envoy to White Harbor,
 —PERRIANE, his eldest daughter, m. Ser Leslyn Haigh,
—by his second wife, {LADY CYRENNA, of House Swann}:
 —SER JARED FREY, an envoy to White Harbor,
 —SEPTON LUCEON, his fifth son,
—by his third wife, {LADY AMAREI of House Crakehall}:
 —SER HOSTEEN FREY, a knight of great repute,
 —LYENTHE, his second daughter, m. Lord Lucias Vypren,
 —SYMOND FREY, his seventh son, a counter of coins,
  an envoy to White Harbor,
 —SER DANWELL FREY, his eighth son,

—{MERRETT FREY}, his ninth son, hanged at Oldstones,
  —Merrett's daughter, WALDA, called FAT WALDA, m.
  Roose Bolton, Lord of the Dreadfort,
  —Merrett's son, WALDER, called LITTLE WALDER,
  eight, a squire in service to Ramsay Bolton,
—{SER GEREMY FREY}, his tenth son, drowned,
—SER RAYMUND FREY, his eleventh son,
—by his fourth wife, {LADY ALYSSA, of House Blackwood}:
  —LOTHAR FREY, his twelfth son, called LAME LOTHAR,
  —SER JAMMOS FREY, his thirteenth son,
    —Jammos's son, WALDER, called BIG WALDER,
    eight, a squire in service to Ramsey Bolton,
  —SER WHALEN FREY, his fourteenth son,
  —MORYA, his third daughter, m. Ser Flement Brax,
  —TYTA, his fourth daughter, called TYTA THE MAID,
—by his fifth wife, {LADY SARYA of House Whent}:
  —no progeny,
—by his sixth wife, {LADY BETHANY of House Rosby}:
  —SER PERWYN FREY, his Walder's fifteenth son,
  —{SER BENFREY FREY}, his Walder's sixteenth son, died
  of a wound received at the Red Wedding,
  —MAESTER WILLAMEN, his seventeenth son, in service
  at Longbow Hall,
  —OLYVAR FREY, his eighteenth son, once a squire to
  Robb Stark,
  —ROSLIN, his fifth daughter, m. Lord Edmure Tully at
  the Red Wedding, pregnant with his child,

—by his seventh wife, {LADY ANNARA of House Farring}:
  —ARWYN, his sixth daughter, a maid of fourteen,
  —WENDEL, his nineteenth son, a page at Seagard,
  —COLMAR, his twentieth son, eleven and promised to
  the Faith,
  —WALTYR, called TYR, his twenty-first son, ten,
  —ELMAR, his twenty-second and lastborn son, a boy of

nine briefly betrothed to Arya Stark,
—SHIREI, his seventh daughter and youngest child, a girl of seven,
—his eighth wife, LADY JOYEUSE of House Erenford,
—presently with child,
—Lord Walder's natural children, by sundry mothers,
—WALDER RIVERS, called BASTARD WALDER,
—MAESTER MELWYS, in service at Rosby,
—JEYNE RIVERS, MARTYN RIVERS, RYGER RIVERS, RONEL RIVERS, MELLARA RIVERS, others

HOUSE LANNISTER

The Lannisters of Casterly Rock remain the principal support of King Tommen's claim to the Iron Throne. They boast of descent from Lann the Clever, the legendary trickster of the Age of Heroes. The gold of Casterly Rock and the Golden Tooth has made them the wealthiest of the Great Houses. The Lannister sigil is a golden lion upon a crimson field. Their words are *Hear Me Roar!*

{TYWIN LANNISTER}, Lord of Casterly Rock, Shield of Lannisport, Warden of the West, and Hand of the King, murdered by his dwarf son in his privy,
—Lord Tywin's children:
   —CERSEI, twin to Jaime, widow of King Robert I Baratheon, a prisoner at the Great Sept of Baelor,
   —SER JAIME, twin to Cersei, called THE KINGSLAYER, Lord Commander of the Kingsguard,
      —his squires, JOSMYN PECKLEDON, GARRETT PAEGE, LEW PIPER,
      —SER ILYN PAYNE, a tongueless knight, lately the King's Justice and headsman,
      —SER RONNET CONNINGTON, called RED RONNET, the Knight of Griffin's Roost, sent to Maidenpool with a prisoner,
      —SER ADDAM MARBRAND, SER FLEMENT BRAX, SER ALYN STACKSPEAR, SER STEFFON SWYFT, SER HUMFREY SWYFT, SER LYLE CRAKEHALL called STRONGBOAR, SER JON BETTLEY called

BEARDLESS JON, knights serving with Ser Jaime's host at Riverrun,
—TYRION, called THE IMP, dwarf and kinslayer, a fugitive in exile across the narrow sea,

—the household at Casterly Rock:
—MAESTER CREYLEN, healer, tutor, and counselor,
—VYLARR, captain of guards,
—SER BENEDICT BROOM, master-at-arms,
—WHITESMILE WAT, a singer,

—Lord Tywin's siblings and their offspring:
—SER KEVAN LANNISTER, m. Dorna of House Swyft,
—LADY GENNA, m. Ser Emmon Frey, now Lord of Riverrun,
    —Genna's eldest son, {SER CLEOS FREY}, m. Jeyne of House Darry, killed by outlaws,
        —Cleos's eldest son, SER TYWIN FREY, called TY, now heir to Riverrun,
        —Cleos's second son, WILLEM FREY, a squire,
    —Genna's younger sons, SER LYONEL FREY, {TION FREY}, WALDER FREY called RED WALDER,
—{SER TYGETT LANNISTER}, died of a pox,
    —TYREK, Tygett's son, missing and feared dead,
        —LADY ERMESANDE HAYFORD, Tyrek's child wife,
—{GERION LANNISTER}, lost at sea,
    —JOY HILL, Gerion's bastard daughter, eleven,

—Lord Tywin's other close kin:
—{SER STAFFORD LANNISTER}, a cousin and brother to Lord Tywin's wife, slain in battle at Oxcross,
    —CERENNA and MYRIELLE, Stafford's daughters,
    —SER DAVEN LANNISTER, Stafford's son,
—SER DAMION LANNISTER, a cousin, m. Lady Shiera Crakehall,

—their son, SER LUCION,
—their daughter, LANNA, m. Lord Antario Jast,
—LADY MARGOT, a cousin, m. Lord Titus Peake,

—bannermen and sworn swords, Lords of the West:
  —DAMON MARBRAND, Lord of Ashemark,
  —ROLAND CRAKEHALL, Lord of Crakehall,
  —SEBASTON FARMAN, Lord of Fair Isle,
  —TYTOS BRAX, Lord of Hornvale,
  —QUENTEN BANEFORT, Lord of Banefort,
  —SER HARYS SWYFT, goodfather to Ser Kevan Lannister,
  —REGENARD ESTREN, Lord of Wyndhall,
  —GAWEN WESTERLING, Lord of the Crag,
  —LORD SELMOND STACKSPEAR,
  —TERRENCE KENNING, Lord of Kayce,
  —LORD ANTARIO JAST,
  —LORD ROBIN MORELAND,
  —LADY ALYSANNE LEFFORD,
  —LEWYS LYDDEN, Lord of the Deep Den,
  —LORD PHILIP PLUMM,
  —LORD GARRISON PRESTER,
  —SER LORENT LORCH, a landed knight,
  —SER GARTH GREENFIELD, a landed knight,
  —SER LYMOND VIKARY, a landed knight,
  —SER RAYNARD RUTTIGER, a landed knight
  —SER MANFRYD YEW, a landed knight,
  —SER TYBOLT HETHERSPOON, a landed knight.

HOUSE MARTELL

Dorne was the last of the Seven Kingdoms to swear fealty to the Iron Throne. Blood, custom, geography, and history all helped to set the Dornishmen apart from the other kingdoms. At the outbreak of the War of the Five Kings, Dorne took no part but when Myrcella Baratheon was betrothed to Prince Trystane, Sunspear declared its support for King Joffrey. The Martell banner is a red sun pierced by a golden spear. Their words are *Unbowed, Unbent, Unbroken*.

DORAN NYMEROS MARTELL, Lord of Sunspear, Prince of Dorne,
—his wife, MELLARIO, of the Free City of Norvos,
—their children:
  —PRINCESS ARIANNE, heir to Sunspear,
  —PRINCE QUENTYN, a new-made knight, fostered at Yronwood,
  —PRINCE TRYSTANE, betrothed to Myrcella Baratheon,
    —SER GASCOYNE OF THE GREENBLOOD, his sworn shield,
—his siblings:
  —{PRINCESS ELIA}, raped and murdered during the Sack of King's Landing,
    —her daughter {RHAENYS TARGARYEN}, murdered during the Sack of King's Landing,
    —her son, {AEGON TARGARYEN}, a babe at the breast, murdered during the Sack of King's Landing,

—{PRINCE OBERYN, called THE RED VIPER}, slain by
Ser Gregor Clegane during a trial by combat,
—his paramour, ELLARIA SAND, natural daughter of
Lord Harmen Uller,
—his bastard daughters, THE SAND SNAKES:
—OBARA, his daughter by an Oldtown whore,
—NYMERIA, called LADY NYM, his daughter by
a noblewoman of Old Volantis,
—TYENE, his daughter by a septa,
—SARELLA, his daughter by a trader captain from
the Summer Isles,
—ELIA, his daughter by Ellaria Sand,
—OBELLA, his daughter by Ellaria Sand,
—DOREA, his daughter by Ellaria Sand,
—LOREZA, his daughter by Ellaria Sand,

—Prince Doran's court
—at the Water Gardens:
—AREO HOTAH, of Norvos, captain of guards,
—MAESTER CALEOTTE, counselor, healer, and tutor,
—at Sunspear:
—MAESTER MYLES, counselor, healer, and tutor,
—RICASSO, seneschal, old and blind,
—SER MANFREY MARTELL, castellan at Sunspear
—LADY ALYSE LADYBRIGHT, lord treasurer,

—his ward, PRINCESS MYRCELLA BARATHEON, betrothed
to Prince Trystane,
—her sworn shield, {SER ARYS OAKHEART}, slain by
Areo Hotah,
—her bedmaid and companion, ROSAMUND
LANNISTER, a distant cousin,

—his bannermen, the Lords of Dorne:
—ANDERS YRONWOOD, Lord of Yronwood, Warden
of the Stone Way, the Bloodroyal,

—YNYS, his eldest daughter, m. Ryon Allyrion,

—SER CLETUS, his son and heir,

—GWYNETH, his youngest daughter, a girl of twelve,

—HARMEN ULLER, Lord of Hellholt,

—DELONNE ALLYRION, Lady of Godsgrace,

—RYON ALLYRION, her son and heir,

—DAGOS MANWOODY, Lord of Kingsgrave,

—LARRA BLACKMONT, Lady of Blackmont,

—NYMELLA TOLAND, Lady of Ghost Hill,

—QUENTYN QORGYLE, Lord of Sandstone,

—SER DEZIEL DALT, the Knight of Lemonwood,

—FRANKLYN FOWLER, Lord of Skyreach, called THE OLD HAWK, the Warden of the Prince's Pass,

—SER SYMON SANTAGAR, the Knight of Spottswood,

—EDRIC DAYNE, Lord of Starfall, a squire,

—TREBOR JORDAYNE, Lord of the Tor,

—TREMOND GARGALEN, Lord of Salt Shore,

—DAERON VAITH, Lord of the Red Dunes.

HOUSE STARK

The Starks trace their descent from Brandon the Builder and the Kings of Winter. For thousands of years, they ruled from Winterfell as Kings in the North, until Torrhen Stark, the King Who Knelt, chose to swear fealty to Aegon the Dragon rather than give battle. When Lord Eddard Stark of Winterfell was executed by King Joffrey, the northmen foreswore their loyalty to the Iron Throne and proclaimed Lord Eddard's son Robb as King in the North. During the War of the Five Kings, he won every battle, but was betrayed and murdered by the Freys and Boltons at the Twins during his uncle's wedding.

{ROBB STARK}, King in the North, King of the Trident, Lord of Winterfell, called THE YOUNG WOLF, murdered at the Red Wedding,
—{GREY WIND}, his direwolf, killed at the Red Wedding,
—his trueborn siblings:
    —SANSA, his sister, m. Tyrion of House Lannister,
        —{LADY}, her direwolf, killed at Castle Darry,
    —ARYA, a girl of eleven, missing and thought dead,
        —NYMERIA, her direwolf, prowling the riverlands,
    —BRANDON, called BRAN, a crippled boy of nine, heir to Winterfell, believed dead,
        —SUMMER, his direwolf,
    —RICKON, a boy of four, believed dead,
        —SHAGGYDOG, his direwolf, black and savage,
        —OSHA, a wildling woman once captive at Winterfell,
—his bastard half-brother, JON SNOW, of the Night's Watch,

—GHOST, Jon's direwolf, white and silent,
—his other kin:
—his uncle, BENJEN STARK, First Ranger of the Night's Watch, lost beyond the Wall, presumed dead,
—his aunt, {LYSA ARRYN}, Lady of the Eyrie,
—her son, ROBERT ARRYN, Lord of the Eyrie and Defender of the Vale, a sickly boy,
—his uncle, EDMURE TULLY, Lord of Riverrun, taken captive at the Red Wedding,
—LADY ROSLIN, of House Frey, Edmure's bride, great with child,
—his great-uncle, SER BRYNDEN TULLY, called THE BLACKFISH, lately castellan of Riverrun, now a hunted man,

—bannermen of Winterfell, the Lords of the North:
—JON UMBER, called THE GREATJON, Lord of the Last Hearth, a captive at the Twins,
—{JON, called THE SMALLJON}, the Greatjon's eldest son and heir, slain at the Red Wedding,
—MORS called CROWFOOD, uncle to the Greatjon, castellan at the Last Hearth,
—HOTHER called WHORESBANE, uncle to the Greatjon, likewise castellan at the Last Hearth,
—{CLEY CERWYN}, Lord of Cerwyn, killed at Winterfell,
—JONELLE, his sister, a maid of two-and-thirty,
—ROOSE BOLTON, Lord of the Dreadfort,
—{DOMERIC}, his heir, died of a bad belly,
—WALTON called STEELSHANKS, his captain,
—RAMSAY BOLTON, his natural son, called THE BASTARD OF BOLTON, Lord of the Hornwood,
—WALDER FREY and WALDER FREY, called BIG WALDER and LITTLE WALDER, Ramsay's squires,
—BEN BONES, kennelmaster at the Dreadfort,
—{REEK}, a man-at-arms infamous for his stench,

slain while posing as Ramsay,
—the Bastard's Boys, Ramsay's men-at-arms:
—YELLOW DICK, DAMON DANCE-FOR-ME, LUTON, SOUR ALYN, SKINNER, GRUNT,
—{RICKARD KARSTARK}, Lord of Karhold, beheaded by the Young Wolf for murdering prisoners,
—{EDDARD}, his son, slain in the Whispering Wood,
—{TORRHEN}, his son, slain in the Whispering Wood,
—HARRION, his son, a captive at Maidenpool,
—ALYS, his daughter, a maid of fifteen,
—his uncle ARNOLF, castellan of Karhold,
—CREGAN, Arnolf's elder son,
—ARTHOR, Arnolf's younger son,
—WYMAN MANDERLY, Lord of White Harbor, vastly fat,
—SER WYLIS MANDERLY, his eldest son and heir, very fat, a captive at Harrenhal,
—Wylis's wife, LEONA of House Woolfield,
—WYNAFRYD, their eldest daughter,
—WYLLA, their younger daughter,
—{SER WENDEL MANDERLY}, his second son, slain at the Red Wedding,
—SER MARLON MANDERLY, his cousin, commander of the garrison at White Harbor,
—MAESTER THEOMORE, counselor, tutor, healer,
—WEX, a boy of twelve, once squire to Theon Greyjoy, mute,
—SER BARTIMUS, an old knight, one-legged, one-eyed, and oft drunk, castellan of the Wolf's Den,
—GARTH, a gaoler and headsman,
—his axe, LADY LU,
—THERRY, a young turnkey,
—MAEGE MORMONT, Lady of Bear Island, the She-Bear,
—{DACEY}, her eldest daughter, slain at the Red Wedding,

—ALYSANE, her daughter, the young She-Bear
—LYRA, JORELLE, LYANNA, her younger daughters,
—{JEOR MORMONT}, her brother, Lord Commander of the Night's Watch, slain by his own men,
—SER JORAH MORMONT, his son, an exile,
—HOWLAND REED, Lord of Greywater Watch, a crannogman,
　—his wife, JYANA, of the crannogmen,
　—their children:
　　—MEERA, a young huntress,
　　—JOJEN, a boy blessed with green sight,
—GALBART GLOVER, Master of Deepwood Motte, unwed,
　—ROBETT GLOVER, his brother and heir,
　　—Robert's wife, SYBELLE of House Locke,
　—BENJICOT BRANCH, NOSELESS NED WOODS, men of the wolfswood sworn to Deepwood Motte,
—{SER HELMAN TALLHART}, Master of Torrhen's Square, slain at Duskendale,
　—{BENFRED}, his son and heir, slain by ironmen on the Stony Shore,
　—EDDARA, his daughter, captive at Torrhen's Square,
　—{LEOBALD}, his brother, killed at Winterfell,
　　—Leobald's wife, BERENA of House Hornwood, captive at Torrhen's Square,
　　—their sons, BRANDON and BEREN, likewise captives at Torrhen's Square,
—RODRIK RYSWELL, Lord of the Rills,
　—BARBREY DUSTIN, his daughter, Lady of Barrowton, widow of Lord Willam Dustin,
　　—HARWOOD STOUT, her liege man, a petty lord at Barrowton,
　—{BETHANY BOLTON}, his daughter, second wife of Lord Roose Bolton, died of a fever,

—ROGER RYSWELL, RICKARD RYSWELL, ROOSE
   RYSWELL, his quarrelsome cousins and bannermen,
—LYESSA FLINT, Lady of Widow's Watch,
—ONDREW LOCKE, Lord of Oldcastle, an old man,

—the chiefs of the mountain clans:
   —HUGO WULL, called BIG BUCKET, or THE WULL,
   —BRANDON NORREY, called THE NORREY,
      —BRANDON NORREY, the Younger, his son,
   —TORREN LIDDLE, called THE LIDDLE,
      —DUNCAN LIDDLE, his eldest son, called BIG
      LIDDLE, a man of the Night's Watch,
      —MORGAN LIDDLE, his second son, called
      MIDDLE LIDDLE,
      —RICKARD LIDDLE, his third son, called LITTLE
      LIDDLE,
   —TORGHEN FLINT, of the First Flints, called THE
   FLINT, or OLD FLINT,
      —BLACK DONNEL FLINT, his son and heir,
      —ARTOS FLINT, his second son, half-brother to
      Black Donnel.

The Stark arms show a grey direwolf racing across an ice-white field.
The Stark words are *Winter Is Coming*.

HOUSE TULLY

Lord Edmyn Tully of Riverrun was one of the first of the river lords to swear fealty to Aegon the Conqueror. King Aegon rewarded him by raising House Tully to dominion over all the lands of the Trident. The Tully sigil is a leaping trout, silver, on a field of rippling blue and red. The Tully words are *Family, Duty, Honor*.

EDMURE TULLY, Lord of Riverrun, taken captive at his wedding and held prisoner by the Freys,
—his bride, LADY ROSLIN of House Frey, now with child,
—his sister, {LADY CATELYN STARK}, widow of Lord Eddard Stark of Winterfell, slain at the Red Wedding,
—his sister, {LADY LYSA ARRYN}, widow of Lord Jon Arryn of the Vale, pushed to her death from the Eyrie,
—his uncle, SER BRYNDEN TULLY, called THE BLACKFISH, lately castellan of Riverrun, now an outlaw
—his household at Riverrun:
    —MAESTER VYMAN, counselor, healer, and tutor,
    —SER DESMOND GRELL, master-at-arms,
    —SER ROBIN RYGER, captain of the guard,
        —LONG LEW, ELWOOD, DELP, guardsmen,
    —UTHERYDES WAYN, steward of Riverrun,

—his bannermen, the Lords of the Trident:
    —TYTOS BLACKWOOD, Lord of Raventree Hall,
        —BRYNDEN, his eldest son and heir,
        —{LUCAS}, his second son, slain at the Red Wedding,

—HOSTER, his third son, a bookish boy,
—EDMUND and ALYN, his younger sons,
—BETHANY, his daughter, a girl of eight,
—{ROBERT}, his youngest son, died of loose bowels,
—JONOS BRACKEN, Lord of the Stone Hedge,
  —BARBARA, JAYNE, CATELYN, BESS, ALYSANNE, his five daughters,
  —HILDY, a camp follower,
—JASON MALLISTER, Lord of Seagard, a prisoner in his own castle,
  —PATREK, his son, imprisoned with his father,
  —SER DENYS MALLISTER, Lord Jason's uncle, a man of the Night's Watch,
—CLEMENT PIPER, Lord of Pinkmaiden Castle,
  —his son and heir, SER MARQ PIPER, taken captive at the Red Wedding,
—KARYL VANCE, Lord of Wayfarer's Rest,
—NORBERT VANCE, the blind Lord of Atranta,
—THEOMAR SMALLWOOD, Lord of Acorn Hall,
—WILLIAM MOOTON, Lord of Maidenpool,
  —ELEANOR, his daughter and heir, thirteen, m. Dickon Tarly of Horn Hill,
—SHELLA WHENT, dispossessed Lady of Harrenhal,
—SER HALMON PAEGE,
—LORD LYMOND GOODBROOK.

HOUSE TYRELL

The Tyrells rose to power as stewards to the Kings of the Reach, though they claim descent from Garth Greenhand, gardener king of the First Men. When the last king of House Gardener was slain on the Field of Fire, his steward, Harlen Tyrell, surrendered Highgarden to Aegon the Conqueror. Aegon granted him the castle and dominion over the Reach. Mace Tyrell declared his support for Renly Baratheon at the onset of the War of the Five Kings, and gave him the hand of his daughter Margaery. Upon Renly's death, Highgarden made alliance with House Lannister, and Margaery was betrothed to King Joffrey.

> MACE TYRELL, Lord of Highgarden, Warden of the South, Defender of the Marches, and High Marshal of the Reach,
> —his wife, LADY ALERIE, of House Hightower of Oldtown,
> —their children:
>> —WILLAS, their eldest son, heir to Highgarden,
>> —SER GARLAN, called THE GALLANT, their second son, newly raised to Lord of Brightwater,
>>> —Garlan's wife, LADY LEONETTE of House Fossoway,
>> —SER LORAS, the Knight of Flowers, their youngest son, a Sworn Brother of the Kingsguard, wounded on Dragonstone
>> —MARGAERY, their daughter, twice wed and twice widowed,
>>> —Margaery's companions and ladies-in-waiting:
>>> —her cousins, MEGGA, ALLA, and ELINOR TYRELL,
>>>> —Elinor's betrothed, ALYN AMBROSE, squire,

—LADY ALYSANNE BULWER, LADY ALYCE GRACEFORD, LADY TAENA MERRYWEATHER, MEREDYTH CRANE called MERRY, SEPTA NYSTERICA, her companions,
—his widowed mother, LADY OLENNA of House Redwyne, called THE QUEEN OF THORNS,
—his sisters:
  —LADY MINA, m. Paxter Redwyne, Lord of the Arbor,
    —her son, SER HORAS REDWYNE, called HORROR,
    —her son, SER HOBBER REDWYNE, called SLOBBER,
    —her daughter, DESMERA REDWYNE, sixteen,
  —LADY JANNA, wed to Ser Jon Fossoway,
—his uncles:
  —his uncle, GARTH TYRELL, called THE GROSS, Lord Seneschal of Highgarden,
    —Garth's bastard sons, GARSE and GARRETT FLOWERS,
  —his uncle, SER MORYN TYRELL, Lord Commander of the City Watch of Oldtown,
  —his uncle, MAESTER GORMON, serving at the Citadel,

—Mace's household at Highgarden:
  —MAESTER LOMYS, counselor, healer, and tutor,
  —IGON VYRWEL, captain of the guard,
  —SER VORTIMER CRANE, master-at-arms,
  —BUTTERBUMPS, fool and jester, hugely fat,

—his bannermen, the Lords of the Reach:
  —RANDYLL TARLY, Lord of Horn Hill, commanding King Tommen's army on the Trident,
  —PAXTER REDWYNE, Lord of the Arbor,
    —SER HORAS and SER HOBBER, his twin sons,
    —Lord Paxter's healer, MAESTER BALLABAR,
  —ARWYN OAKHEART, Lady of Old Oak,
  —MATHIS ROWAN, Lord of Goldengrove

—LEYTON HIGHTOWER, Voice of Oldtown, Lord of
the Port,
—HUMFREY HEWETT, Lord of Oakenshield,
  —FALIA FLOWERS, his bastard daughter,
—OSBERT SERRY, Lord of Southshield,
—GUTHOR GRIMM, Lord of Greyshield,
—MORIBALD CHESTER, Lord of Greenshield,
—ORTON MERRYWEATHER, Lord of Longtable,
  —LADY TAENA, his wife, a woman of Myr,
    —RUSSELL, her son, a boy of six,
—LORD ARTHUR AMBROSE,
—LORENT CASWELL, Lord of Bitterbridge,

—his knights and sworn swords:
  —SER JON FOSSOWAY, of the green-apple Fossoways,
  —SER TANTON FOSSOWAY, of the red-apple Fossoways.

The Tyrell sigil is a golden rose on a grass-green field. Their words
are *Growing Strong*.

THE SWORN BROTHERS OF THE NIGHT'S WATCH

JON SNOW, the Bastard of Winterfell, nine-hundred-and-ninety-eighth Lord Commander of the Night's Watch,
—GHOST, his white direwolf,
—his steward, EDDISON TOLLETT, called DOLOROUS EDD,

—at Castle Black
  —MAESTER AEMON (TARGARYEN), healer and coun-selor, a blind man, one hundred and two years old,
    —Aemon's steward, CLYDAS,
    —Aemon's steward, SAMWELL TARLY, fat and bookish,
  —BOWEN MARSH, Lord Steward,
    —THREE-FINGER HOBB, steward and chief cook,
    —{DONAL NOYE}, one-armed armorer and smith, slain at the gate by Mag the Mighty
    —OWEN called THE OAF, TIM TANGLETONGUE, MULLY, CUGEN, DONNEL HILL called SWEET DONNEL, LEFT HAND LEW, JEREN, TY, DANNEL, WICK WHITTLESTICK, stewards,
  —OTHELL YARWYCK, First Builder,
    —SPARE BOOT, HALDER, ALBETT, KEGS, ALF OF RUNNYMUDD, builders,
  —SEPTON CELLADOR, a drunken devout,

—BLACK JACK BULWER, First Ranger,
  —DYWEN, KEDGE WHITEYE, BEDWYCK called GIANT, MATTHAR, GARTH GREYFEATHER, ULMER OF THE KINGSWOOD, ELRON, GARRETT GREENSPEAR, FULK THE FLEA, PYPAR called PYP, GRENN called AUROCHS, BERNARR called BLACK BERNARR, TIM STONE, RORY, BEARDED BEN, TOM BARLEYCORN, GOADY BIG LIDDLE, LUKE OF LONGTOWN, HAIRY HAL, rangers
—LEATHERS, a wildling turned crow,
—SER ALLISER THORNE, former master-at-arms,
—LORD JANOS SLYNT, former commander of the City Watch of King's Landing, briefly Lord of Harrenhal,
—IRON EMMETT, formerly of Eastwatch, master-at-arms,
  —HARETH called HORSE, the twins ARRON and EMRICK, SATIN, HOP-ROBIN, recruits in training,

—at the Shadow Tower
  —SER DENYS MALLISTER, commander,
    —his steward and squire, WALLACE MASSEY,
    —MAESTER MULLIN, healer and counselor,
    —{QHORIN HALFHAND, SQUIRE DALBRIDGE, EGGEN}, rangers, slain beyond the Wall,
    —STONESNAKE, a ranger, lost afoot in Skirling Pass,

—at Eastwatch-by-the-Sea
  —COTTER PYKE, a bastard of the Iron Islands, commander,
    —MAESTER HARMUNE, healer and counselor,
    —OLD TATTERSALT, captain of the *Blackbird*,
    —SER GLENDON HEWETT, master-at-arms,
    —SER MAYNARD HOLT, captain of the *Talon*,
    —RUSS BARLEYCORN, captain of the *Storm Crow*.

the WILDLINGS, or THE FREE FOLK

MANCE RAYDER, King-Beyond-the-Wall, a captive at Castle Black,
—his wife, {DALLA}, died in childbirth,
—their newborn son, born in battle, as yet unnamed,
——VAL, Dalla's younger sister, "the wildling princess," a captive at Castle Black,
———{JARL}, Val's lover, killed in a fall,
—his captains, chiefs, and raiders:
——THE LORD OF BONES, mocked as RATTLESHIRT, a raider and leader of a war band, captive at Castle Black,
———{YGRITTE}, a young spearwife, Jon Snow's lover, killed during the attack on Castle Black,
———RYK, called LONGSPEAR, a member of his band,
———RAGWYLE, LENYL, members of his band,
——TORMUND, Mead-King of Ruddy Hall, called GIANTSBANE, TALL-TALKER, HORN-BLOWER, and BREAKER OF ICE, also THUNDERFIST, HUSBAND TO BEARS, SPEAKER TO GODS, and FATHER OF HOSTS,
———Tormund's sons, TOREGG THE TALL, TORWYRD THE TAME, DORMUND, and DRYN, his daughter MUNDA,
——THE WEEPER, called THE WEEPING MAN, a notorious raider and leader of a war band,

—{HARMA, called DOGSHEAD}, slain beneath the Wall,
  —HALLECK, her brother,
—{STYR}, Magnar of Thenn, slain attacking Castle Black,
  —SIGORN, Styr's son, new Magnar of Thenn,
—VARAMYR called SIXSKINS, a skinchanger and warg,
  called LUMP as a boy,
  —ONE EYE, SLY, STALKER, his wolves,
  —his brother, {BUMP}, killed by a dog,
  —his foster father, {HAGGON}, a warg and hunter,
—THISTLE, a spearwife, hard and homely,
—{BRIAR, GRISELLA}, skinchangers, long dead,
—BORROQ, called THE BOAR, a skinchanger, much
  feared,
—GERRICK KINGSBLOOD, of the blood of Raymun
  Redbeard,
  —his three daughters,
—SOREN SHIELDBREAKER, a famed warrior,
—MORNA WHITE MASK, the warrior witch, a raider,
—YGON OLDFATHER, a clan chief with eighteen wives,
—THE GREAT WALRUS, leader on the Frozen Shore,
—MOTHER MOLE, a woods witch, given to prophecy,
—BROGG, GAVIN THE TRADER, HARLE THE
  HUNTSMAN, HARLE THE HANDSOME, HOWD
  WANDERER, BLIND DOSS, KYLEG OF THE
  WOODEN EAR, DEVYN SEALSKINNER, chiefs and
  leaders amongst the free folk,
—{ORELL, called ORELL THE EAGLE}, a skinchanger
  slain by Jon Snow in the Skirling Pass,
—{MAG MAR TUN DOH WEG, called MAG THE
  MIGHTY}, a giant, slain by Donal Noye at the gate of
  Castle Black,
—WUN WEG WUN DAR WUN, called WUN WUN, a
  giant,
—ROWAN, HOLLY, SQUIRREL, WILLOW WITCH-EYE,
  FRENYA, MYRTLE, spearwives, captive at the Wall.

BEYOND THE WALL

—in the Haunted Forest
—BRANDON STARK, called BRAN, Prince of Winterfell
and heir to the North, a crippled boy of nine,
  —his companions and protectors:
    —MEERA REED, a maid of sixteen, daughter of Lord
    Howland Reed of Greywater Watch,
    —JOJEN REED, her brother, thirteen, cursed with
    greensight,
    —HODOR, a simple lad, seven feet tall,
  —his guide, COLDHANDS, clad in black, once perhaps
  a man of the Night's Watch, now a mystery,

—at Craster's Keep
  —the betrayers, once men of the Night's Watch:
    —DIRK, who murdered Craster,
    —OLLO LOPHAND, who slew the Old Bear, Jeor
    Mormont,
    —GARTH OF GREENAWAY, MAWNEY, GRUBBS,
    ALAN OF ROSBY, former rangers
    —CLUBFOOT KARL, ORPHAN OSS, MUTTERING
    BILL, former stewards,

—in the caverns beneath a hollow hill
  —THE THREE-EYED CROW, also called THE LAST
  GREENSEER, sorcerer and dreamwalker, once a man
  of the Night's Watch named BRYNDEN, now more

tree than man,
—the children of the forest, those who sing the song of
earth, last of their dying race:
—LEAF,   ASH,   SCALES,   BLACK   KNIFE,
SNOWYLOCKS, COALS.

ESSOS
BEYOND THE NARROW SEA

IN BRAAVOS

FERREGO ANTARYON, Sealord of Braavos, sickly and failing,
—QARRO VOLENTIN, First Sword of Braavos, his protector,
—BELLEGERE OTHERYS called THE BLACK PEARL, a courtesan descended from the pirate queen of the same name,
—THE VEILED LADY, THE MERLING QUEEN, THE MOONSHADOW, THE DAUGHTER OF THE DUSK, THE NIGHTINGALE, THE POETESS, famous courtesans,
—THE KINDLY MAN and THE WAIF, servants of the Many-Faced God at the House of Black and White,
  —UMMA, the temple cook,
  —THE HANDSOME MAN, THE FAT FELLOW, THE LORDLING, THE STERN FACE, THE SQUINTER, and THE STARVED MAN, secret servants of Him of Many Faces,
—ARYA of House Stark, a novice in service at the House of Black and White, also known as ARRY, NAN, WEASEL, SQUAB, SALTY, and CAT OF THE CANALS,
—BRUSCO, a fishmonger,
  —his daughters, TALEA and BREA,
—MERALYN, called MERRY, proprietor of the Happy Port, a brothel near the Ragman's Harbor,
  —THE SAILOR'S WIFE, a whore at the Happy Port,
    —LANNA, her daughter, a young whore,

—RED ROGGO, GYLORO DOTHARE, GYLENO DOTHARE, a scribbler called QUILL, COSSOMO THE CONJURER, patrons of the Happy Port,

—TAGGANARO, a dockside cutpurse and thief,

—CASSO, KING OF THE SEALS, his trained seal,

—S'VRONE, a dockside whore of a murderous bent,

—THE DRUNKEN DAUGHTER, a whore of uncertain temper.

IN OLD VOLANTIS

the reigning triarchs:
—MALAQUO MAEGYR, Triarch of Volantis, a tiger,
—DONIPHOS PAENYMION, Triarch of Volantis, an elephant,
—NYESSOS VHASSAR, Triarch of Volantis, an elephant,

people of Volantis:
—BENERRO, High Priest of R'hllor, the Lord of Light,
  —his right hand, MOQORRO, a priest of R'hllor,
—THE WIDOW OF THE WATERFRONT, a wealthy freed-woman of the city, also called VOGARRO'S WHORE,
  —her fierce protectors, THE WIDOW'S SONS,
—PENNY, a dwarf girl and mummer,
  —her pig, PRETTY PIG,
  —her dog, CRUNCH,
—{GROAT}, brother to Penny, a dwarf mummer, murdered and beheaded,
—ALIOS QHAEDAR, a candidate for triarch,
—PARQUELLO VAELAROS, a candidate for triarch,
—BELICHO STAEGONE, a candidate for triarch,
—GRAZDAN MO ERAZ, an envoy from Yunkai.

ON SLAVER'S BAY

—in Yunkai, the Yellow City:
  —YURKHAZ ZO YUNZAK, Supreme Commander of the Armies and Allies of Yunkai, a slaver and aged noble of impeccable birth,
  —YEZZAN ZO QAGGAZ, mocked as the YELLOW WHALE, monstrously obese, sickly, hugely rich,
    —NURSE, his slave overseer,
    —SWEETS, a hermaphrodite slave, his treasure,
    —SCAR, a serjeant and slave soldier,
    —MORGO, a slave soldier,
  —MORGHAZ ZO ZHERZYN, a nobleman oft in his cups, mocked as THE DRUNKEN CONQUEROR,
  —GORZHAK ZO ERAZ, a nobleman and slaver, mocked as PUDDING FACE,
  —FAEZHAR ZO FAEZ, a nobleman and slaver, known as THE RABBIT,
  —GHAZDOR ZO AHLAQ, a nobleman and slaver, mocked as LORD WOBBLECHEEKS,
  —PAEZHAR ZO MYRAQ, a nobleman of small stature, mocked as THE LITTLE PIGEON,
  —CHEZDHAR ZO RHAEZN, MAEZON ZO RHAEZN, GRAZDHAN ZO RHAEZN, noblemen and brothers, mocked as THE CLANKER LORDS,
  —THE CHARIOTEER, THE BEASTMASTER, THE PERFUMED HERO, noblemen and slavers,

—in Astapor, the Red City:
  —CLEON THE GREAT, called THE BUTCHER KING,
  —CLEON II, his successor, king for eight days,
  —KING CUTTHROAT, a barber, slit the throat of Cleon II to steal his crown,
  —QUEEN WHORE, concubine to King Cleon II, claimed the throne after his murder.

THE QUEEN ACROSS THE WATER

DAENERYS TARGARYEN, the First of Her Name, Queen of Meereen, Queen of the Andals and the Rhoynar and the First Men, Lord of the Seven Kingdoms, Protector of the Realm, *Khaleesi* of the Great Grass Sea, called DAENERYS STORMBORN, the UNBURNT, MOTHER OF DRAGONS,
—her dragons, DROGON, VISERION, RHAEGAL,
—her brother, {RHAEGAR}, Prince of Dragonstone, slain by Robert Baratheon on the Trident,
  —Rhaegar's daughter, {RHAENYS}, murdered during the Sack of King's Landing,
  —Rhaegar's son, {AEGON}, a babe in arms, murdered during the Sack of King's Landing,
—her brother {VISERYS}, the Third of His Name, called THE BEGGAR KING, crowned with molten gold,
—her lord husband, {DROGO}, a *khal* of the Dothraki, died of a wound gone bad,
  —her stillborn son by Drogo, {RHAEGO}, slain in the womb by the *maegi* Mirri Maz Duur,

—her protectors:
—SER BARRISTAN SELMY, called BARRISTAN THE BOLD, Lord Commander of the Queensguard,
  —his lads, squires training for knighthood:
    —TUMCO LHO, of the Basilisk Isles,
    —LARRAQ, called THE LASH, of Meereen,

—THE RED LAMB, a Lhazarene freedman,
—the BOYS, three Ghiscari brothers,
—STRONG BELWAS, eunuch and former fighting slave,
—her Dothraki bloodriders:
  —JHOGO, the whip, blood of her blood,
  —AGGO, the bow, blood of her blood,
  —RAKHARO, the *arakh*, blood of her blood,

—her captains and commanders:
  —DAARIO NAHARIS, a flamboyant Tyroshi sellsword, captain of the Stormcrows, a free company,
  —BEN PLUMM, called BROWN BEN, a mongrel sellsword, captain of the Second Sons, a free company.
  —GREY WORM, a eunuch, commander of the Unsullied, a company of eunuch infantry,
    —HERO, an Unsullied captain, second-in-command,
    —STALWART SHIELD, an Unsullied spearman,
  —MOLLONO YOS DOB, commander of the Stalwart Shields, a company of freedmen,
  —SYMON STRIPEBACK, commander of FREE BROTHERS, a company of freedmen,
  —MARSELEN, commander of the MOTHER'S MEN, a company of freedman, a eunuch, brother to Missandei,
  —GROLEO of Pentos, formerly captain of the great cog *Saduleon*, now an admiral without a fleet,
  —ROMMO, a *jaqqa rhan* of the Dothraki,

—her Meereenese court:
  —REZNAK MO REZNAK, her seneschal, bald and unctuous,
  —SKAHAZ MO KANDAQ, called THE SHAVEPATE, shaven-headed commander of the Brazen Beasts, her city watch,

—her handmaids and servants:
—IRRI and JHIQUI, young women of the Dothraki,
—MISSANDEI, a Naathi scribe and translator,
—GRAZDAR, QEZZA, MEZZARA, KEZMYA, AZZAK, BHAKAZ, MIKLAZ, DHAZZAR, DRAQAZ, JHEZANE, children of the pyramids of Meereens, her cupbearers and pages,

—people of Meereen, highborn and common:
—GALAZZA GALARE, the Green Grace, high priestess at the Temple of the Graces,
—GRAZDAM ZO GALARE, her cousin, a nobleman,
—HIZDAHR ZO LORAQ, a wealthy Meereenese nobleman, of ancient lineage,
—MARGHAZ ZO LORAQ, his cousin,
—RYLONA RHEE, freedwoman and harpist,
—{HAZZEA}, a farmer's daughter, four years of age,
—GOGHOR THE GIANT, KHRAZZ, BELAQUO BONEBREAKER, CAMARRON OF THE COUNT, FEARLESS ITHOKE, THE SPOTTED CAT, BARSENA BLACKHAIR, STEELSKIN, pit fighters and freed slaves,

—her uncertain allies, false friends, and known enemies:
—SER JORAH MORMONT, formerly Lord of Bear Island,
—{MIRRI MAZ DUUR}, godswife and *maegi*, a servant of the Great Shepherd of Lhazar,
—XARO XHOAN DAXOS, a merchant prince of Qarth,
—QUAITHE, a masked shadowbinder from Asshai,
—ILLYRIO MOPATIS, a magister of the Free City of Pentos, who brokered her marriage to Khal Drogo,
—CLEON THE GREAT, butcher king of Astapor,

—the Queen's Suitors
—on Slaver's Bay:
—DAARIO NAHARIS, late of Tyrosh, a sellsword and captain of the Stormcrows,

—HIZDAHR ZO LORAQ, a wealthy Meereenese nobleman,
—SKAHAZ MO KANDAQ, called THE SHAVEPATE, a lesser nobleman of Meereen,
—CLEON THE GREAT, Butcher King of Astapor,

—in Volantis:
—PRINCE QUENTYN MARTELL, eldest son of Doran Martell, Lord of Sunspear and Prince of Dorne,
—his sworn shields and companions:
—{SER CLETUS YRONWOOD}, heir to Yronwood, slain by corsairs,
—SER ARCHIBALD YRONWOOD, cousin to Cletus, called THE BIG MAN,
—SER GERRIS DRINKWATER,
—{SER WILLAM WELLS}, slain by corsairs
—{MAESTER KEDRY}, slain by corsairs,

—on the Rhoyne:
—YOUNG GRIFF, a blue-haired lad of eighteen years,
—his foster father, GRIFF, a sellsword late of the Golden Company,
—his companion, teachers, and protectors:
—SER ROLLY DUCKFIELD, called DUCK, a knight,
—SEPTA LEMORE, a woman of the Faith,
—HALDON, called THE HALFMAESTER, his tutor,
—YANDRY, master and captain of the *Shy Maid*,
—YSILLA, his wife,

—at sea:
—VICTARION GREYJOY, Lord Captain of the Iron Fleet, called THE IRON CAPTAIN,
—his bedwarmer, a dusky woman without a tongue, a gift from Euron Crow's Eye,
—his healer, MAESTER KERWIN, late of Greenshield, a gift from Euron Crow's Eye,
—his crew on the *Iron Victory*:

> —WULFE ONE-EAR, RAGNOR PYKE, LONGWATER
> PYKE, TOM TIDEWOOD, BURTON HUMBLE,
> QUELLON HUMBLE, STEFFAR STAMMERER
> —his captains:
> > —RODRIK SPARR, called THE VOLE, captain of
> > *Grief*,
> > —RED RALF STONEHOUSE, captain of *Red Jester*,
> > —MANFRYD MERLYN, captain of *Kite*,
> > —RALF THE LIMPER, captain of *Lord Quellon*,
> > —TOM CODD, called BLOODLESS TOM, captain of
> > the *Lamentation*,
> > —DAEGON SHEPHERD, called THE BLACK
> > SHEPHERD, captain of the *Dagger*.

The Targaryens are the blood of the dragon, descended from the high lords of the ancient Freehold of Valyria, their heritage marked by lilac, indigo, and violet eyes and hair of silver-gold. To preserve their blood and keep it pure, House Targaryen has oft wed brother to sister, cousin to cousin, uncle to niece. The founder of the dynasty, Aegon the Conqueror, took both his sisters to wife and fathered sons on each. The Targaryen banner is a three-headed dragon, red on black, the three heads representing Aegon and his sisters. The Targaryen words are *Fire and Blood*.

THE SELLSWORDS
MEN AND WOMEN OF
THE FREE COMPANIES

THE GOLDEN COMPANY, ten thousand strong, of uncertain loyalty:
—HOMELESS HARRY STRICKLAND, captain-general,
  —WATKYN, his squire and cupbearer,
—{SER MYLES TOYNE, called BLACKHEART}, four years dead, the previous captain-general,
—BLACK BALAQ, a white-haired Summer Islander, commander of the company archers,
—LYSONO MAAR, a sellsword late of the Free City of Lys, company spymaster,
—GORYS EDORYEN, a sellsword late of the Free City of Volantis, company paymaster,
—SER FRANKLYN FLOWERS, the Bastard of Cider Hall, a sellsword from the Reach,
—SER MARQ MANDRAKE, an exile escaped from slavery, scarred by pox,
—SER LASWELL PEAKE, an exile lord,
  —his brothers, TORMAN and PYKEWOOD,
—SER TRISTAN RIVERS, bastard, outlaw, exile,
—CASPOR HILL, HUMFREY STONE, MALO JAYN, DICK COLE, WILL COLE, LORIMAS MUDD, JON LOTHSTON, LYMOND PEASE, SER BRENDEL BYRNE, DUNCAN STRONG, DENYS STRONG, CHAINS, YOUNG JOHN MUDD, serjeants of the company,

—{SER AEGOR RIVERS, called BITTERSTEEL}, a bastard son of King Aegon IV Targaryen, founder of the company},

—{MAELYS I BLACKFYRE, called MAELYS THE MONSTROUS}, captain-general of the company, pretender to the Iron Throne of Westeros, member of the Band of Nine, slain during the War of the Ninepenny Kings,

THE WINDBLOWN, two thousand horse and foot, sworn to Yunkai,

—THE TATTERED PRINCE, a former nobleman of the Free City of Pentos, captain and founder,

  —CAGGO, called CORPSEKILLER, his right hand,

  —DENZO D'HAN, the warrior bard, his left hand,

  —HUGH HUNGERFORD, serjeant, former company paymaster, fined three fingers for stealing,

  —SER ORSON STONE, SER LUCIFER LONG, WILL OF THE WOODS, DICK STRAW, GINJER JACK, Westerosi sellswords,

  —PRETTY MERIS, the company torturer,

  —BOOKS, a Volantene swordsman and notorious reader,

  —BEANS, a crossbowman, late of Myr,

  —OLD BILL BONE, a weathered Summer Islander,

  —MYRIO MYRAKIS, a sellsword late of Pentos,

THE COMPANY OF THE CAT, three thousand strong, sworn to Yunkai,

—BLOODBEARD, captain and commander,

THE LONG LANCES, eight hundred horse-riders, sworn to Yunkai,

—GYLO RHEGAN, captain and commander,

THE SECOND SONS, five hundred horse-riders, sworn to Queen Daenerys,

—BROWN BEN PLUMM, captain and commander,

—KASPORIO, called KASPORIO THE CUNNING, a bravo,

second-in-command,
—TYBERO ISTARION, called INKPOTS, company paymaster,
—HAMMER, a drunken blacksmith and armorer,
 —his apprentice, called NAIL,
—SNATCH, a serjeant, one-handed,
—KEM, a young sellsword, from Flea Bottom,
—BOKKOKO, an axeman of formidable repute,
—UHLAN, a serjeant of the company,

THE STORMCROWS, five hundred horse-riders, sworn to Queen Daenerys,
—DAAERIO NAHARIS, captain and commander,
 —THE WIDOWER, his second-in-command,
 —JOKIN, commander of the company archers.